THE TECHNIC CIVILIZATION SAGA
FLANDRY'S LEGACY

W9-AIB-953

Baen Books by Poul Anderson

✦

The Technic Civilization Saga
The Van Rijn Method
David Falkayn: Star Trader
Rise of the Terran Empire
Young Flandry
Captain Flandry: Defender of the Terran Empire
Sir Dominic Flandry: The Last Knight of Terra
Flandry's Legacy

The High Crusade

To Outlive Eternity and Other Stories

Time Patrol

Hoka! Hoka! Hoka! (with Gordon R. Dickson)
Hokas Pokas! (with Gordon R. Dickson)

THE TECHNIC CIVILIZATION SAGA
FLANDRY'S LEGACY

POUL ANDERSON

Compiled by
Hank Davis

BAEN

FLANDRY'S LEGACY

This is a work of fiction. All the characters and events portrayed in this book are fictional, and any resemblance to real people or incidents is purely coincidental.

"Introduction" copyright © 2011 by Hank Davis. "A Chronology of Technic Civilization" by Sandra Miesel copyright © 2008 by Sandra Miesel.

Acknowledgements
A Stone in Heaven, copyright © 1979 by Poul Anderson, original publication by Ace Books, October 1979.
The Game of Empire, copyright © 1985 by Poul Anderson, original publication by Baen Books, May 1985.
"A Tragedy of Errors,"copyright © 1967 by Galaxy Publishing Corp., original publication in *Galaxy*, February 1968.
"The Night Face," copyright © 1963 by Ace Books, Inc., original publication under the title of Let the Spacemen Beware by Ace Books, 1963. Reprinted as *The Night Face* by Ace Books, February 1978. A shorter version was published in *Fantastic Universe*, January 1960, as "A Twelvemonth and a Day."
"The Sharing of Flesh," copyright © 1968 by Galaxy Publishing Corp., original appearance in *Galaxy*, December 1968.
"Starfog," copyright © 1967 by Condé Nast Publications, Inc., original publication in *Analog*, August 1967.

All rights reserved, including the right to reproduce this book or portions thereof in any form.

A Baen Books Original

Baen Publishing Enterprises
P.O. Box 1403
Riverdale, NY 10471
www.baen.com

ISBN: 978-1-4391-3427-6

Cover art by David Seeley
Maps by Karen Anderson

First Baen printing, April 2011

Distributed by Simon & Schuster
1230 Avenue of the Americas
New York, NY 10020

Library of Congress Cataloging-in-Publication Data

Anderson, Poul, 1926-2001.
  Flandry's legacy / by Poul Anderson.
    p. cm.
  ISBN 978-1-4391-3427-6 (trade pbk.)
  I. Title.
  PS3551.N378F55 2011
  813'.54--dc22
                                    2011000592

Printed in the United States of America

10 9 8 7 6 5 4 3 2 1

CONTENTS

———————————— ✴ ————————————

THE WHEEL TURNS

Whether the wheel (or mandala) of time or the ceaselessly rotating wheel of the galaxy—time passes. The captains and the kings depart. And the admirals and the emperors as well . . .

This seventh volume of Poul Anderson's monumental Technic Civilization future history completes the series as it was published in bits and pieces over four decades, now assembled, for the first time, complete and in internal chronological order. The saga, spanning future centuries, is an impressive achievement, and yet (there's no pleasing some people), one might wish for a few more stories set during the "little night" (between the sacking of Earth by space-voyaging barbarians and the rise of the Terran Empire) and the Long Night (between the simultaneous collapse of the Terran Empire and the Merseian Roidhunate, and the rebirth, millennia later, of interstellar civilization).

Perhaps Poul Anderson found such bleak times uninteresting and didn't wish to chronicle them. Or maybe he thought he had already explored enough of the darker aspects of humans and their universe in the stories which he did write, (not all of them in the Technic Civilization series). Two stories included herein are unabashed tragedies, and one of those two is a hundred-megaton heartbreaker.

After all, one might wish for more stories, but considering the bounty that a prolific and inventive author provided, greed is not called for. And gratitude for what we do have *is* most certainly called for.

These include the novel, *A Stone in Heaven*, wherein Dominic Flandry is now a Vice Admiral who isn't quite in the good graces of the present Emperor, who's not the man his father was. Miriam Abrams, daughter of Imperial Intelligence spymaster Max Abrams, who recruited and mentored young Dominic Flandry long ago, is another character. Unlike the present Emperor, she *is* the human her father was . . . so to speak. . . . A xenologist, she's trying to get help for the Ramnuans, who cannot survive on their rapidly cooling homeworld without Terran help. But such help is not forthcoming. Worse, when she travels to Earth, she finds that people who might be able to grease the bureaucratic wheels refuse to talk to her.

But Flandry lends a sympathetic ear, of course, and finds something more sinister than monolithic bureaucratic inertia is at work. The present emperor may be a disappointment, but at least he isn't the tyrant another character will become if his scheme to seize the throne succeeds. Bracing action ensues and, at the end, this time Flandry actually walks off into the sunset (or, "into the autumn") *with* the girl. Before that happens, there're plenty of droll quips from Flandry, such as when he meets Cairncross, the villain of the piece:

> "Well, well," [Cairncross] said. "So this is the legendary Admiral Flandry."
>
> "No, the objectively real Admiral Flandry, I hope. Some would say the objectionably real."

One might also note that the dying planet Ramnu is an echo of the dying Terran Empire. And there's that password that Flandry imparts to Miriam: the name of a town in England. Does the town still exist in the 31st century? Could Flandry, who repeatedly claims no interest in music, be making a reference to Gilbert and Sullivan's *Ruddigore*? I have no trouble believing that pair's operettas could survive for another millennium, and if the music didn't appeal to him, the witty dialogue might.

Next comes the last novel in the saga, *The Game of Empire*. There's a new Merseian maneuver to be countered. Flandry is a player therein, and we learn that he and Miriam are now married, but the novel belongs to Diana Crowfeather, Flandry's daughter, along with her client, Axor, a visiting Wodenite, and her friend Targovi, a felinesque Tigery. Those who have read earlier installments of the saga will recall another of the reptilian centauroid Wodenites, Adzel, valuable member of Nicholas van Rijn's trader team. As for the Tigeries, not only did they play a crucial role in young Ensign Flandry's first extravagant adventure, but a Tigery who knew Flandry back then makes a brief appearance here.

That is the last we see of Dominic Flandry. Possibly, he had other adventures, but the bard named Anderson did not record them. Even with life-extending drugs, Flandry likely didn't live to see the Terran Empire's fall. (Did his daughter? One wonders . . .) At some point, he, Miriam, and Chives must have set course for Valhalla in *Hooligan*, where they may have joined up with Nick van Rijn, David Falkayn, Adzel, Chee Lan, and maybe even Muddlehead.

The remaining chapters of the Technic Civilization saga are set centuries, even millennia apart, with no recurring characters. Only one is set during the Long Night itself, over half a century after *The Game of Empire*: "A Tragedy of Errors," which features a flamboyant rogue reminiscent of C.L. Moore's immortal Northwest Smith. (He might remind others of Han Solo, though the Anderson novella appeared almost a decade before *Star Wars*.) Interstellar communications have broken down, and the characters have no idea what's going in elsewhere in the sphere of galactic space which once was the dominion of Terra. Consequently, neither do we readers. The falling apart of the Empire is underlined by the way that languages are beginning to change, leading to an unfortunate misunderstanding that sets the story in motion.

But far more than languages were mutating. In the novella "The Night Face," some star colonies are slowly rebuilding human civilization and sending expeditions to other star systems. However, the humans of one long-isolated colony have changed from the original human blueprint, and when the nature of the change becomes apparent, stark tragedy ensues. At the same time, quiet heroism takes center stage: no blazing blasters, no battling starships, just a fatal choice and a personal sacrifice. Poul Anderson well understood both the tragic and the heroic aspects of living in a universe that does not *care*.

A century later, humans on a planet who have lost all but the simplest technology are discovered by other humans who have regained interstellar travel, and once again the passage of time in isolation has wrought a deadly change in the former. "The Sharing of Flesh" has aspects of a mystery story—though the question is not "whodunit" but "whydunnit"—as well as being a inquiry into the nature of justice. It won both the Hugo and Nebula Awards for the year it was published.

The end of the saga comes over three millennia later. In "Starfog," human civilization has rebounded, surpassing the technology of the days of Dominic Flandry, and possibly surpassing the freedom and lack of regimentation of the earlier days of Nicholas van Rijn as well. This far future tale hearkens back to the past, as descendants of the rebels who fled into unexplored space in the Dominic Flandry novel, *The Rebel Worlds*, make contact with the new civilization, but cannot find their way home again. The solution to that problem is ingenious— but this story's ending is also bittersweet.

Will the new, looser interstellar civilization have a longer life than the long-fallen Terran Empire? Perhaps, since no competing nonhuman sentients are mentioned in "Starfog." That doesn't mean that some might not be waiting elsewhere in the galaxy. The Terran Empire, it should be remembered, only occupied a small part of one arm of our spiral galaxy, and almost certainly other intelligences exist elsewhere, waiting to be discovered. And not all of them could be expected to be friendly or even nonbelligerent. Even without competition, water runs downhill, entropy increases, and as long as humans are still human, the social structures they erect will likely have a limited sell-by date. One should remember that galaxies and even the protons making up matter are thought to have limited lifetimes. But while the stars still burn, human will find new opportunities for adventures, possibly villainous, hopefully noble, certainly heroic, as humans and other sentients continue to attempt (if I may borrow a phrase from E. E. "Doc" Smith) to unscrew the inscrutable.

And, as the saga ends, I'll borrow another phrase, overused but very true, and say that it has been an honor and a privilege to have been entrusted with assembling these seven volumes which comprise a major landmark of science fiction.

✿   ✿   ✿

As with some of the earlier installments, two essays by Sandra Miesel, noted authority on the works of Poul Anderson, are included with the e-book version of *Flandry's Legacy*: "The Price of Buying Time" (originally written as an afterword to *A Stone in Heaven*) and an afterword to "The Night Face." They are far more intelligent and illuminating than this introduction. Go to www.baen.com for details.

—Hank Davis, 2011

A STONE IN HEAVEN

DEDICATION

—————— ✴ ——————

To John K. Hord

A STONE IN HEAVEN

✷ ❚ ✷

Through time beyond knowing, the Kulembarach clan had ranged those lands which reach south of Lake Roah and east of the Kiiong River. The Forebear was said to have brought her family up from the Ringdales while the Ice was still withdrawing beyond the Guardian Mountains. Her descendants were there on the territory she took when traders from West-Oversea brought in the arts of ironworking and writing. They were old in possession when the first Seekers of Wisdom arose, and no few of them joined the College as generations passed. They were many and powerful when the long-slumbering fires in Mount Gungnor awoke again, and the Golden Tide flowed forth to enrich this whole country, and the clans together established the Lords of the Volcano. They were foremost in welcoming and dealing with the strangers from the stars.

But about that time, the Ice began returning, and now the folk of Kulembarach were in as ill a plight as any of their neighbors.

Yewwl had gone on a long hunt with her husband Robreng and their three youngest children, Ngao, Ych, and little Ungn. That was only partly to get food, when the ranchlands could no more support enough livestock. It was also to get away, move about, unleash some of their rage against the fates upon game animals. Besides, her oath-sister Banner was eager to learn how regions distant from

3

Wainwright Station were changed by cold and snow, and Yewwl was glad to oblige.

The family rode east for an afternoon and most of the following night. Though they did not hurry, and often stopped to give chase or to rest, that much travel took them a great ways, to one of the horn-topped menhirs which marked the territorial border of the Arrohdzaroch clan. Scarcity of meat would have made trespass dangerous as well as wrong. Yewwl turned off in a northwesterly direction.

"We will go home by way of the Shrine," she explained to the others—and to Banner, who saw and heard and even felt what she did, through the collar around her neck. Had she wished to address the human unheard by anybody else, she would have formed the words voicelessly, down in her throat.

The alien tone never came to any hearing but Yewwl's; Banner had said the sound went in through her skull. Eighteen years had taught Yewwl to recognize trouble in it: "I've seen pictures lately, taken from moon-height. You would not like what you found there, dear."

Fur bristled, vanes spread and rippled, in sign of defiance. "I understand that. Shall the Ice keep me from my Forebear?" Anger died out. For Banner alone, Yewwl added softly, "And those with me hope for a token from her—an oracular dream, perhaps. And . . . I may be an unbeliever in such things, because of you, but I myself can nonetheless draw strength from them."

Her band rode on. Night faded into hours of slowly brightening twilight. The storminess common around dawn and sunset did not come. Instead was eerie quiet under a moon and a half. The nullfire hereabouts did not grow tall, as out on the veldt, but formed a thick turf, hoarfrost-white, that muffled the hoofbeats of the onsars. Small crepuscular creatures were abroad, darters, scuttlers, light-flashers, and the chill was softened by a fragrance of nightwort, but life had grown scant since Yewwl and Robreng were young. They felt how silence starkened the desolation, and welcomed a wind that sprang up near morning, though it bit them to the bone and made stands of spearcane rattle like skeletons.

The sun rose at last. For a while it was a red step pyramid, far and far on the blurry horizon. The sky was opalescent. Below, land rolled steeply upward, cresting in a thousand-meter peak where snow and ice flushed in the early light. That burden spilled down the slopes and across the hills, broken here and there by a crag, a boulder, a tawny patch of uncovered nullfire, a tree—brightcrown or saw-frond—which the cold had slain. A flyer hovered aloft, wings dark against a squat mass of clouds. Yewwl didn't recognize its kind. Strange things from beyond the Guardian Range were moving in with the freeze.

Ungn, her infant, stirred and mewed in her pouch. Her belly muscles seemed to glow with it. She might have stopped and dismounted to feed him, but a ruddy canyon and a tarn gone steel-hard told her through memory how near she was to her goal. She jabbed foot-claws at her onsar's extensors and the beast stepped up its pace from a walk to a shamble, as if realizing, weary though it was and rapidly though the air was thinning, that it could soon rest. Yewwl reached into a saddlebag, took forth a strip of dried meat, swallowed a part for herself and chewed the remainder into pulp. Meanwhile she had lifted Ungn into her arms and cuddled him. Her vanes she folded around her front to give the beloved mite shelter from the whining, seeking wind.

Ych rode ahead. The sun entered heaven fully, became round and dazzling, gilded his pelt and sent light aflow over the vanes that he spread in sheer eagerness. He was nearly grown, lithe, handsome; no ruinous weather could dim the pride of his youth. His sister Ngao, his junior by three years, rode behind, leading several pack animals which bore camp gear and the smoked spoils of the hunt. She was slightly built and quiet, but Yewwl knew she was going to become a real beauty. Let fate be kind to her!

Having well masticated the food, the mother brought her lips around her baby's and, with the help of her tongue, fed him. He gurgled and went back to sleep. She imagined him doing it happily, but knew that was mere imagination. Just six days old—or fourteen, if you counted from his begetting—he was as yet tiny and unshapen. His eyes wouldn't open for another four or five days, and he wouldn't be crawling around on his own till almost half a year after that.

Robreng drew alongside. "Here," Yewwl said. "You take him a while." She handed Ungn over for her husband to tuck in his pouch. With a close look: "What's wrong?"

The tautness of his vane-ribs, the quivering along their surfaces, the backward slant of his ears, everything about him cried unease. He need but say: "I sense grief before us."

Yewwl lifted her right thigh to bring within reach the knife sheathed there. (Strapped to the left was a purse for flint, steel, tinderbox, and other such objects.) "Beasts?" Veldt lopers seldom attacked folk, but a pack of them—or some different kind of carnivore—might have been driven desperate by hunger. "Invaders?" The nightmare which never ended was of being overrun by foreigners whom starvation had forced out of their proper territory.

His muzzle wrinkled, baring fangs, in a negative. "Not those, as far as I can tell. But things feel wrong here."

In twenty years of marriage, she had learned to trust his judgment nearly as much as her own. While a bachelor, he had fared widely around, even spending two seasons north of the Guardians to hunt in the untenanted barrens there. He it was who had argued, when last the clan leaders met before the Lord of the Volcano, that this country need not be abandoned. Orchards and grazing would wither, ranching come to an end, but creatures native to the cold lands would move in; the Golden Tide would make them abundant; folk could live entirely off the chase, without falling back into savagery. Of course, the transition would take lifetimes, and those would be grim, but surely the star-beings would help. . . .

Thus it was daunting to see him shaken. "What do you mark, then?" Yewwl asked.

"I am not sure," Robreng confessed. "It's been too long since I was in snow-decked uplands. Once my partner went down in a deep drift and was stuck, but we got him out. Our guide took us well clear of high hillsides, but I can't recall why. He had few words of our language."

"Banner," Yewwl said aloud, each word a fog-puff, "do you know of any danger we might be in?"

Across hundreds of kilometers, the secret voice replied, "No. That doesn't mean there is none, you realize. Your world is so different from mine—and so few humans have visited it, really, in all these centuries—and now everything is changing so fast—How I wish I could warn you."

"Well, thank you, my oath-sister." Yewwl told Robreng what she had heard. Decision came. "I think I grasp what the matter is. It's within us—in me too. I remember how these parts were fair and alive when we were children; we remember caretakers, pilgrims, offerings and feasts and Oneness. Today we come back and find all gone dead and hollow. No wonder if dread arises." She straightened in her saddle. "Strike it down! Onward!"

Ych crossed a root of the mountain and dropped out of sight. In a moment, his shout rang over ice and rock. He had spied the Shrine.

His kin urged their onsars to speed, from shamble to swing. Four massive legs went to and fro; sparks flew where hoofs smote rock. Between, the thick extensors did more than help support the body; they gripped, pulled, shoved, let go, seized hold afresh on the ground. Aft of the hump where saddles or packs were, dorsal fins wagged, black triangles as high as a rider's head. Sweat gleamed on gray skin, sparse brown hair, big ears. Breath went loud, harsh, in and out of muzzles. Thews pulsed to the rocking motion.

Yewwl topped the ridge and glanced aloft. Sharply through the thin, clear air of the heights, she saw her goal.

The tomb of Kulembarach stood on a ledge a third of the way up the mountainside. It was a dolmen, rough granite slabs chiseled out of some quarry, somehow brought here and fitted together, in an age before iron. But around it, generation after generation had built terraces, raised houses and statues, nurtured exquisite gardens where fountains played and flutes replied. Here had been gathered the finest works of the clan and the best that traders abroad could bring home: pictures, jewelry, weavings, books, such awesome memorabilia as the Sword Which Held the Bridge, Amarao's cup, the skulls of the Seven Heroes, the quern of Gro the Healer.

Today—

Nearing, Yewwl could barely make out the balustrades of the terraces, overflowed by snow. Frost had shattered several, and brought low a number of the sculptures which elsewhere stood forlorn as the stricken trees. When the last caretakers must depart or die, cold had numbed them into carelessness, fire had escaped a hearth, nothing but blackened stonework was left of the delicately carpentered buildings. Bereft of its wooden gate, the arch before the tomb gaped with horrible emptiness.

The onsars turned onto the road which led thither. It ascended too abruptly to be much drifted over, and the paving blocks were not yet sundered and tumbled and split, except in a few places. They rang under hoofs, answering the wind that wailed and bit and scattered a haze of dry ice crystals to shatter what sunlight came over the eastern shoulder into this darkling passage. Beyond the Shrine grounds the mountain rose steeper yet for a space, in a talus slope which clingplant had once made colorful but which was now only jagged and bleak. Above it, where the slope was easier, the snowpack began, that went on over the peak. It formed a white cliff, kilometers tall, mysteriously blue-shadowed.

Nonetheless . . . amidst the ruins, rearing over banks, upbearing what had fallen upon it during the night, the dolmen remained, foursquare. Kulembarach abided, at watch over her people. To those who sought her, she would still give dreams and luck . . . or, at least, the strength that came from remembering that she had prevailed in her day, and her blood endured. . . . Yewwl's pulse thuttered.

Ych was already there. When no keepers were left, that had earned him the right to greet the Forebear on behalf of his party. He unslung the bugle at his saddlebow and put it to his lips. Riding around and around the tomb, he challenged desolation with the hunting call of his mother.

The snowcliff stirred.

A mighty wind rushed downward from it, smote like hammers, roared like thunder. Statues and tree boles toppled before the blow.

Earth shuddered. Hill-huge masses broke from the sliding precipice, flew, struck, smashed and buried what they hit. Behind them came the doom-fall itself.

Yewwl never remembered what happened. Surely she vaulted to a stance on her saddle and sprang from it, spreading her vanes, as if she were about to attack game on an open plain. Surely she went gliding, and she did not come down soon enough to be engulfed. Therefore surely she caught updrafts, rode the buffeting airs that the slide hurled before it, crashed bruised and bleeding but not truly wounded in her body, down onto a ridge above the path of destruction.

What she knew, at first, was nothing but a noise that should break the world apart, blindness, choked throat, tumbling well-nigh helpless—being tossed against raw rock and clawing herself fast while chaos raged—finally, silence, but for the ringing in her ears; and pain; and dazedly rising to stare.

Where the Shrine had been, the road, the onsars, her companions: snow filled the vale, nearly as high as she was. A mist of crystals swallowed vision within fifty meters; it would be hours in settling. Suddenly there was no wind, as if that also had been seized and overwhelmed.

"Robreng!" Yewwl screamed. "Ungn! Ych! Ngao!"

It took her hours of crawling about and shouting to become certain that none of them had escaped. By then she was at the bottom of the slide, in the foothills under the mountain.

She staggered away. She would not rest before she must, before flesh and bones fell down in a heap. And then she would not be long aswoon; she would rise again, again she would howl and snarl her sorrow, she would hunt and kill whatever stirred in the waste, because she could not kill the thing that had slain her darlings.

In Wainwright Station, Miriam Abrams slapped the switch of her multitransceiver, tore herself free of every connection to it, and surged from her chair. A calculator happened to be lying on the console shelf. She dashed it to the floor. It didn't break as she wanted, but it skittered. "God damn them!" she yelled. "God damn them to the deepest hole in hell!"

The single person in the room with her was Ivan Polevoy, electronician, who had had some tinkering to do on a different piece of equipment. He had seen Abrams rapt in her rapport with the native, but not what was happening, for side panels effectively blocked his view of the video screen. The woman maintained that her relationship was sufficient invasion of privacy—though she admitted "privacy" was a notion hard to apply between unlike species. She herself spent incredible lengths of time following the life of her subject. The Ramnuan obviously didn't mind, no matter how intimate events became. Possibly she'd not mind if other humans observed too. However, Abrams had made it plain from the start, a couple of decades ago, that she alone would receive the raw data. The reports she prepared on that basis were detailed, insightful contributions to Xenology; but nobody else knew how much she chose to leave out.

The former chief of planetside operations had supported her in that policy. It was doubtless prudent, when little was known about Ramnuan psychology. Nowadays Abrams was the chief, so the staff didn't object either. Besides, their own jobs or projects kept them amply busy, undermanned as the place was.

Hence Polevoy had to ask in surprise: "Damn who? What's wrong, Banner?"

It was as if her nickname calmed her a little. Yet she had borne it for many years. Translated from the local language—wherein it derived from the flag which identified Wainwright Station at a distance to travelers—it had practically supplanted "Miriam," even in her mind. At this hour, it seemed to tell her that dear ones died, but the race lived on.

Regardless, tears glistened on her lashes. The hand shook that fished a cigarette from a tunic pocket, struck it, and brought it to her mouth. Cheeks caved in with the violence of her smoking. Her voice was hoarse rather than husky, and wavered.

"Avalanche. Wiped out Yewwl's whole family . . . and, oh, God, the Shrine, the heart of her clan's history—like wiping out Jerusalem—" A fist beat itself unmercifully against the console. "I should have guessed. But . . . no experience. . . . I'm from Dayan, you know, warm, dry, no snow anywhere, and I've just been a visitor on worlds like Terra—" Her lips drew wide, her eyes squinched nearly shut. "If I'd thought! That much snowpack, and seven Terrestrial gravities to accelerate it—Yewwl, Yewwl, I'm sorry."

"Why, that's terrible," Polevoy said. After a pause: "Your subject, she's alive?"

Abrams jerked a nod. "Yes. With nothing to ride, no tent or supplies or tools or anything but what she's got on her person, and doubtless not a soul for a hundred kilometers around."

"Well, we'd better send a gravsled for her. It can home on her transceiver, can't it?" Polevoy was fairly new here.

"Sure, sure. Not right away, though. Don't you know what grief usually does to a Ramnuan? It's apt to drive him or her berserk." Abrams spoke in rough chunks of phrase. "Coping with that is a problem which every society on this planet has had to solve, one way or another. Maybe that's a main reason why they've never had wars—plenty of individual fights, but no wars, no armies, therefore no states—A soldier who lost his buddy would run amok." Laughter rattled from her. "Too bad we humans don't have the same trait. We wouldn't be cobwebbed into our Terran Empire then, would we?"

She stubbed out the cigarette, viciously, and started the next. "We'll go fetch Yewwl when she's worked off the worst of what's in her, if she lives through it. Sometime this afternoon." That would be several standard days hence. "Meanwhile, I can be preparing to take on the wretched Empire."

Shocked, Polevoy could merely say, "I beg your pardon?"

Abrams slumped. She turned from him and stared out a viewscreen. It gave a broad overlook across the locality. On her right, the Kiiong River flowed seaward, more rapidly than any stream on Terra or Dayan would have gone through a bed as level as was here. Spray off rocks dashed brilliant above water made gray-green by glacial flour. Sonic receptors brought in a booming of great slow airs under more than thirty bars of pressure. Beyond the river was forest: low, thick trunks from which slender branches swayed, upheld by big leaves shaped like parachutes, surrounded by yellowish shrubs.

To her left, eastward, chanced to be rare clarity. Dun pyrasphale rippled across twelve kilometers to Ramnu's horizon. Trees and canebrakes broke the sameness of that veldt; a kopje reared distance-blued; clouds cruised above, curiously flattened. A small herd of grazers wandered about, under guard of a mounted native. A score of flying creatures were aloft. When Abrams first arrived, this country had swarmed with life.

Overhead, the sky was milky. Niku, the sun, appearing two-thirds as wide as Sol seen from Terra, cast amber light; a frost halo circled it. Diris, the innermost moon, glimmered pale toward the west. It would not set until Ramnu's long day had become darkness.

"Another ice age on its way," Abrams mumbled. "The curse of this world. And we could stop it and all its kind. Whatever becomes of us and our Empire, we could be remembered as saviors, redeemers, for the next million years. But the Duke will not listen. And now Yewwl's people are dead."

"Uh," Polevoy ventured, "uh, doesn't she have a couple of children who're adult, married?"

"Yes. And *they* have children, who may well not survive what's coming down from the north," Abrams said. "Meanwhile she's lost her husband, her two youngsters, the last baby she'll ever bear; her clan has lost its Jerusalem; and none of that needed to happen."

Tendons stood forth in her neck. "None of it! But the Grand Duke of Hermes would never listen to me!"

After more silence, she straightened, turned around, said quite calmly: "Well, I'm done with him. This has been the last thing necessary to decide me. I'm going to leave pretty soon, Ivan. Leave for Terra itself, and appeal for help to the very top."

Polevoy choked. "The Emperor?"

Abrams grinned in gallows mirth. "No, hardly him. Not at the start, anyhow. But . . . have you ever perchance heard of Admiral Flandry?"

✧ ▌▌ ✧

First she must go to the Maian System, nineteen light-years off, a journey of four standard days in the poky little starcraft belonging to the Ramnu Research Foundation. The pilot bade her farewell at Williams Field on Hermes and went into Starfall to see what fleshpots he could find before returning. Banner also sought the planet's chief city, but with less frivolous intentions. Mainly she wanted shelter, and not from the mild climate.

She had cut her schedule as close as feasible. The liner *Queen of Apollo* would depart for Sol in fifty hours. Through Sten Runeberg, to whom she had sent a letter, she had a ticket. However, coming as she did from a primitive world of basically terrestroid biochemistry, she must get a checkup at a clinic licensed to renew her medical certificate. That was a ridiculous formality—even had she been exposed in shirtsleeves to Ramnu, no germ there could have lived a minute in her bloodstream—but the bureaucrats of Terra were adamant unless you held rank or title. Equally absurd, she thought, was the quasi-necessity of updating her wardrobe. She didn't think Flandry would care if she looked provincial. Yet others would, and her mission was difficult enough without her being at a psychological disadvantage.

Therefore she sallied forth on the morning after she arrived at the Runebergs' town house, and didn't come back, her tasks completed, till sundown. "You must be exhausted, fairling," said her host. "How about a drink before dinner?"

Fairling—The mild Hermetian endearment had taken on a special meaning for the two of them, when he was in charge of industrial operations at Ramnu and they had been lovers whenever they could steal time together. The three-year relationship had ended five years ago, with his inexplicable replacement by taciturn Nigel Broderick; it had never been deeply passionate; now he was married, and they had exchanged no more than smiles and glances during her stay, nor would they. Nonetheless, memory stabbed.

Runeberg's wife was belated at her office. He, who had become a consulting engineer, had quit work early for his guest and put his child in charge of the governess. He mixed two martinis himself and led the way onto a balcony. "Pick a seat," he invited, gesturing at a couple of loungers.

Banner stayed by the rail. "I'd forgotten how beautiful this is," she whispered.

Dusk flowed across the quicksilver gleam of Daybreak Bay. The mansion stood on the southern slope of Pilgrim Hill, near the Palomino River. It commanded a view of the keeps above; of its own garden, fragrant with daleflower and roses, where a tilirra flew trilling and glowflies were blinking alight; of Riverside Common, stately with millionleaf and rainroof trees; of multitudinous old spires beyond and windows that had begun to shine; of domes and towers across the stream, arrogantly radiant as if this were still that heyday of their world in which they had been raised. The air was barely cooled by a breeze and murmured only slightly of traffic. Heaven ranged from blue in the west to violet in the east. Antares was already visible, rising Venus-bright and ruby-red out of the Auroral Ocean.

"You should have come here more often," Runeberg said.

"You know I could hardly drag myself away from my work, ever, and then mostly to visit my parents," Banner replied. "Since Dad's death—" She broke off.

The big blond man regarded her carefully. She stood profile to, so that he saw the curve of her nose below the high forehead, the set of her wide mouth and the jut of her chin and the long sweep of her throat down to the small bosom. Clad in a shimmerlyn gown—for practice at being a lady, she had said—she stood tall and slim, athletic despite the scattered silver in a shoulder-length light-brown mane.

Then she turned around, briefly silhouetting a cheekbone ivory against the sky, and her eyes confronted his. They were perhaps her best feature, large and luminous green under dark brows.

"Yes," he blurted, "you've let yourself get crazily wrapped up in those beings. Sometimes I'd find you slipping into styles of thought, emotion, that, well, that weren't human. It must have gotten worse since I left. Come back, Miri."

He disliked calling me Banner, she remembered. "You imply that involvement with an intelligent, feeling race was bad in the first place," she said. "Why? On the whole, I've had a wonderful, fascinating, exciting life. And how else can we get to understand them? A different psychology, explored in depth. . . . What can we not learn, also about ourselves?"

Runeberg sighed. "Who is really paying attention? Be honest. You're studying one clutch of sophonts among countless thousands; and they're barbarians, impoverished, insignificant. Their planet was always more interesting to science than they were, and it was investigated centuries back, in plenty of detail. Xenology is a dying discipline anyway. Every pure science is; we live in that kind of era. Why do you think your foundation is marginally funded? Hai-ah, it'd have been closed down before you were born, if Ramnu didn't happen to have some value to Hermetian industry. You've sacrificed every heritage that was yours—for what, Miri?"

"We've wasted time on that battleground in the past," she snapped. Her tone softened. "I don't want to quarrel, Sten. You mean well, I know. From your viewpoint, I suppose you're right."

"I care about you, my very dear friend," he said.

And it hurt you from the start to learn what I'd lost, she did not answer aloud. *My marriage*—Already established in the profession when he took a fresh graduate from the Galactic Academy for his bride, Feodor Sumarokov had seen their appointments to Ramnu as a stepping stone to higher positions; when he left after three years, she would not. *My true love*—She had never wedded Jason Kamunya, because they wanted to do that back on Dayan where her parents were, and somehow they never found a time when so long an absence wouldn't harmfully interrupt their research, and meanwhile they could live and work together . . . until that day in their fourth year when a stone falling from a height under seven gravities shattered his air helmet and head . . . *My chance for children*—Well, perhaps not yet. She was only forty-four. But not all the gero treatment known to man could stave off menopause for more than a decade, or add more than two or three to a lifespan; and where she was, she had had access to nothing but routine cell therapy. *My home, my kindred, my whole civilization*—

Ramnu is my home! Yewwl and her folk are my kin in everything but flesh. And what is Technic civilization worth any longer? Unless I can make it save my oath-sister's world.

Banner smiled and reached out to stroke the man's cheek. "Thank you for that," she murmured. "And for a lot else." Raising her glass: "*Shalom.*"

Rims clinked together. The liquor was cold and pungent on her tongue. She and he reclined facing each other. Twilight deepened.

"You completed your business today?" he inquired.

"Yes. Inconspicuously, I hope."

He frowned. "You really are obsessive about secrecy, aren't you?"

"Or forethoughtful." Her voice wavered the least bit. "Sten, you did do your best to handle my reservation and such confidentially, didn't you?"

"Of course, since you asked. I'm not sure why you did."

"I explained. If the Duke knew, he might well decide to stop me. And he could, in a dozen different ways."

"Why would he, though?"

Banner took a protracted sip. Her free hand fumbled in her sash pocket for a cigarette case. "He's neutronium-solid set against any project to reverse the glaciation on Ramnu."

"Hoy? . . . True, true, you complained to me, in person and afterward in those rare letters you sent, that he won't consider Hermes making the effort." Runeberg drew breath for an argument. "Maybe he is being ungenerous. We could afford it. But he may well deem—in fact, you've quoted him to me to that effect—that our duty to ourselves is overriding. Hermes isn't poor, but it's not the rich, powerful world it used to be, either, and we're developing plenty of problems, both domestic and *vis-á-vis* the Imperium. I can understand how Duke Edwin may think an expensive undertaking for the sake of aliens who can never pay us back—how that might strain us dangerously, rouse protest, maybe even provoke an attempt at revolution."

Banner started her smoke before she said bitterly, "Yes, he must feel insecure, yes, indeed. It's not as if he belonged to the House of Tamarin, or as if constitutional government still existed here. His grandfather was the latest in a string of caudillos, and he himself eased his elder brother off the throne."

"Now, wait," Runeberg protested. "You realize I'm not too happy with him either. But he is doing heroic things for Hermes, and he does have ample popular support. If he has no Tamarin genes in him, he does carry a few Argolid ones, distantly, but from the Founder of the Empire just the same. It's the Imperium that's jeopardized its own right to rule—Hans Molitor seizing the crown by force—later robbing us of Mirkheim, to buy the goodwill of the money lords on Terra—" He checked himself. It was talk heard often nowadays, in private. But he didn't want to speak anger this evening. Moreover, she was leaving tomorrow in hopes of getting help there.

"The point is," he said, "why should the Duke mind having your project financed and organized from outside? He ought to welcome that. Most of the resources and labor could come from our economic sphere. We'd get nice jobs, profits, contacts, every sort of benefit."

"I don't know why he should object," Banner admitted. "I do know he will, if he finds out. I've exchanged enough letters and tapes with his immediate staff. I've come in person, twice, to plead, and got private audiences both times. Oh, the responses were more or less courteous, but always absolutely negative; and meeting with him, I could sense outright hostility."

Runeberg gulped from his drink before he ventured to say: "Are you sure you weren't reading that into his manner? No offense, fairling, but you are not too well acquainted with humankind."

"I've objective facts in addition, in full measure," she retorted. "My last request was that he ask the Emperor to aid Ramnu. His answer, through an undersecretary, was that this would be politically inadvisable. I'm not too naïve to recognize when I'm being fobbed off. Especially when the message closed by stating that they were tired of this business, and if I persisted in it I could be replaced. Edwin Cairncross is quite willing to use his influence on Terra to crush one obscure scientist!"

She drew hard on her cigarette, leaned forward, and continued: "That's not the only clue. For instance, why were you discharged from General Enterprises? Everybody I talked to was astounded. You'd been doing outstanding work."

"I was simply told 'reorganization,'" he reminded her. "I did get handsome severance pay and testimonials. As near as I've been able to find out, somebody in a high position wanted Nigel Broderick to have my post. Bribery? Blackmail? Nepotism? Who knows?"

"Broderick's been less and less cooperative with the Foundation," she said. "And that in spite of his expanding operations on Ramnu as well as its moons. Though it's impossible to learn exactly what the expansion amounts to. The time is past when my people or I could freely visit any of those installations."

"Um-m, security precautions—There's been a lot of restriction in the Protectorate, too, lately. These are uneasy years. If the Imperium breaks down again—which could give the Merseians a chance to strike—"

"What threat to security is a xenological research establishment? But we're being denied adequate supplies, that we used to get as a matter of course from Dukeston and Elaveli. The pretexts are mighty thin, stuff like unspecified 'technical difficulties.' Sten, we're being slowly strangled. The Duke wants us severely restricted in our activities on both Ramnu and Diris, if not out of there altogether. Why?"

Banner finished her cigarette and reopened the case. "You smoke too much, Miri," Runeberg said.

"And drink too little?" Her laugh clanked. "Very well, let's assume my troubles have made me paranoid. What harm in keeping alert? If I return in force, maybe my questions will get answered."

He raised his brows. "In force?"

"Oh, not literally. But with backing too powerful for a mere lord of a few planetary systems."

"Whose backing?"

"Haven't you heard me mention Admiral Flandry?"

"Ye-es, occasionally in conversation, I believe. I got the impression he is—was a friend of your father's."

"Dad was his first superior in action, during the Starkad affair," she said proudly. "He got him started in Naval Intelligence. They kept in touch afterward. I met Flandry myself, as a girl, when he paid a visit to a base where Dad was stationed. I liked him, and he wouldn't have stayed Dad's friend if he weren't a decent man at heart, no matter what he may have had to do in his career. He'll receive a daughter of Max Abrams. And . . . he has the Emperor's ear."

She tossed down her cigarette case, raised her glass, and said almost cheerfully, "Come, let's drink to my success, and then let's hear more about what's been happening to you, Sten, old dear."

Night rolled westward across Greatland. Four hours after it had covered Starfall it reached Lythe, in the middle of the continent.

That estate of Edwin Cairncross, Grand Duke of Hermes, was among his most cherished achievements. Reclamation of the interior for human settlement had faltered a century ago, as the wealth and importance of the planet declined. Civil war had stopped it entirely, and it had not resumed at once after Hans Molitor battered the Empire back together. He, Cairncross, had seen an extinct shield volcano rising mightily above an arid steppe, and desired an eyrie on the heights. He had decreed that canals be driven, land be resculptured and planted, lovely ornithoids and big game be introduced, a town be founded down below and commerce make it prosper. The undertaking was minor compared to other works of his, but somehow, to him, Lythe symbolized the will to prevail, to conquer.

It was no sanctuary for fantasy, but a nucleus for renewed growth. From it he did considerable of his governing, through an electronic web that reached across the globe and beyond. An invitation to spend some days here could be portentous. This evening he had passed hours alone in his innermost office, hunched above the screen whose sealed circuits brought him information gathered by a bare dozen secret agents. They were the elite of their corps; they reported directly to him, and he decided if their nominal superiors would be told.

Now he must make a heavier choice than that. With a blind urge to draw strength from his land, he strode out of the room and through the antechambers.

Beyond, a sentry snapped a salute. Cairncross returned it as precisely. His years in the Imperial Navy had taught him that a leader is wise to give his underlings every courtesy due them. An aide sprang from a chair and inquired, "Sir?"

"I don't want to be disturbed, Wyatt," Cairncross said.

"Sir!"

Cairncross nodded and went on down the hall. Until new orders came, the lieutenant would make sure that nobody, not the Duchess herself, got near the Grand Duke.

A gravshaft brought Cairncross up onto a tower. He crossed its deck and halted at the battlement. That was pure ornamentation, but not useless; he had ordered it built because he wanted to feel affirmed in his kinship to Shi Huang Ti, Charlemagne, Suleiman the Magnificent, Pyotr the Great, every man who had ever been dominant on Terra.

Silence dwelt enormous. The fog of his breath caught the light of a crescent Sandalion; he savored the bracing chill that he inhaled. Vision winged across roofs, walls, hoar treetops, cliffs and crags, a misty shimmer of plains, finally the horizon. He raised his eyes and beheld stars in their thousands.

Antares burned brightest. Mogul was sufficiently near to rival it, an orange spark: Mogul, sun of Babur, the Protectorate. His gaze did not seek Olga, for in that constellation, invisible to him, was the black sun of Mirkheim; and he had no time on hand to think about regaining the treasure planet for Hermes. Sol was hidden too, by distance. But Sol—Terra—was ruler of the rest. . . . He turned his glance from the Milky Way. Its iciness declared that the Empire was an incident upon certain attendants of a hundred thousand stars, lost in the outskirts of a galaxy which held more than a hundred billion. A man must ignore mockery.

Wryness: *A man must also buckle down to practical details.* What Cairncross had learned today demanded instant action.

The trouble was, he could not do the quick and simple thing. Abrams had been too wary. His fists knotted.

Thank God for giving him the foresight to have Sten Runeberg's house bugged, after he'd gotten the man fired from Ramnu. Not that Runeberg had made trouble. He might have, though. The family was extensive and influential; Duchess Iva was a second cousin of Sten. And he had been at Ramnu, he had been close to Abrams, he had surely acquired ideas from her . . . and maybe worse ones afterward, since they did irregularly correspond and meet.

Nothing worth reporting had happened until today. But what finally came was a blow to the guts.

The witch outmaneuvered me, Cairncross thought. *I have the self-confidence to realize that.* She'd written to Runeberg in care of the spaceship he used in his business; no bug could escape the safety inspections there. She'd arrived unannounced and gone straight to his place. The ducal government lacked facilities to monitor every slightly distrusted site continuously; tapes were scanned at intervals. Given reasonable luck, Abrams would have been in and out of Hermes well before Cairncross knew.

She did chance to pick the wrong time slot. (That was partly because surveillance was programmed to intensify whenever a passenger liner was due in, until it had departed.) But she had anticipated the possibility. Runeberg and a couple of his spacemen were going to escort her tomorrow, not just onto the shuttle but to the Queen in orbit, and see her off. He had objected that that was needless, but to soothe her he had agreed. Meanwhile, his wife and several others knew about it all. There was no way, under these conditions, to arrange an abduction or assassination. Anything untoward would be too damnably suspicious, in a period when a degree of suspicion was already aimed at Cairncross.

Well, I've made my own contingency plans. I didn't foresee this turn of events exactly, but—

Decision crystallized. *Yes, I'll go to Terra myself. My speedster can outrun her by days.*

Cairncross made a fighting grin. Whatever came next should at least be interesting!

✧ **III** ✧

Vice Admiral Sir Dominic Flandry, Intelligence Corps, Imperial Terran Navy, maintained three retreats in different areas that he liked. None was as sybaritic as his home base in Archopolis, a part of which served him for an office. A part of that, in turn, was austere, for times when he found it helpful to give such an impression of himself. Which room he used seldom mattered; ordinarily he did his business through computers, infotrieves, and eidophone, with the latter set to show no background. Some people, though, must be received in person. A governing noble who wanted to see him privately was an obvious example.

This meant rising at an unsanctified hour—after a visitor had kept him awake past midnight—to review available data in advance of the appointment. The visitor had been warned she must go before breakfast, since he couldn't afford the time for gallantries. Flandry left her drowsy warmth and a contrail of muttered curses behind him, groped his way to the gymnasium, and plunged. A dozen laps around the pool brought him to alertness. They failed to make the exercises which followed any fun. He had loathed calisthenics more in every successive year of his sixty-one. But they had given him a quickly responsive body in his youth, and it was still trim and tough beyond anything due to gero treatments.

At last he could shower. When he emerged, Chives proffered a Turkish towel and coffee royal. "Good morning, sir," he greeted.

Flandry took the cup. "That phrase is a contradiction in terms," he said. "How are you doing?"

"Quite well, thank you, sir." Chives began to rub his master dry. He wasn't as deft as erstwhile. He didn't notice that he nearly caused the coffee to spill. Flandry kept silence. Had he, in this place, let anyone but Chives attend him, the Shalmuan's heart would have cracked open.

Flandry regarded the short green form—something like a hairless human with a long tail, if you ignored countless differences in shapes and proportions of features—through eyes that veiled concern. This early, Chives wore merely a kilt. Wrinkles, skinniness, stiff movements were far too plain to sight. No research institution had ever considered developing the means to slow down aging in the folk of his backward world.

Well, if that were done, how many other sophont races would clamor for the same work on each of their wildly separate biochemistries? the man thought, for perhaps the thousandth sad time. *I may have my valet-majordomo-cook-bodyguard-pilot-factotum-arbiter for a decade yet, if I'm lucky,*

Chives finished and gave the towel a reassuringly vigorous snap. "I have laid out your formal uniform and decorations, sir," he announced.

"Formal—one cut below court? And decorations? He'll take me for a popinjay."

"My impression of the Duke is otherwise, sir."

"When did you get at his dossier? . . . Never mind. No use arguing."

"I suggest you be ready for breakfast in twenty minutes, sir. There will be a soufflé."

"Twenty minutes on the dot. Very good, Chives." Flandry left.

As usual when it was unoccupied, the clothes were in a guestroom. Flandry draped them over his tall frame with the skill of a foppish lifetime. These days, he didn't really care—had not since a lady died on Dennitza, fourteen years ago—but remained a fashion plate out of habit, and because it was expected of him. Deep-blue tunic, gold on collar and sleeves, nebula and star on either shoulder; scarlet sash; white iridon trousers bagged into half-boots of lustrous black beefleather; and the assorted ribbons, of course, each a brag about an exploit though most of the citations were recorded only in the secret files; and the Imperial sunburst, jewel-encrusted, hung from his neck, to proclaim him a member of the Order of Manuel, silliest boast of the lot—

Brushing his sleek iron-gray hair, he checked to make sure his last dash of beard inhibitor wasn't wearing off. It wasn't, but he decided to trim the mustache that had, thus far, stayed brown. The face behind hadn't changed much either: high in the cheekbones, straight in the nose, cleft in the chin, relic of a period when everybody who could afford it got biosculped into comeliness. (The present generation scorned that; in many ways, these were puritanical times.) The eyes of changeable gray were more clear than they deserved to be after last night. The skin, lightly tanned, stayed firm, though lines ran over the brow, crow's-feet beneath, deep furrows from nostrils to lips.

Yes, he thought a trifle smugly, *we're holding our own against the Old Man.* A sudden, unexpected thrust brought a gasp. *Why not? What's his hurry? He's hauled in Kossara and young Dominic and Hans and—how many more? I can be left to wait his convenience.*

He rallied. *Self-pity! First sign of senility? Squash it, fellow. You've got health, money, power, friends, women, interesting work that you can even claim is of some importance if you want to. Your breakfast is being prepared by none less than Chives—*

He glanced at his watch, whistled, and made haste to the dining room.

The Shalmuan met him at the entrance. "Excuse me, sir," he said, and reached up to adjust the sunburst on its ribbon before he seated his master and went to bring the food.

The weather bureau had decreed a fine spring day. Chives had therefore retracted the outer wall. Flowers, Terran and exotic, made the roof garden beyond into an explosion of colors and perfumes. A Cynthian yaoti perched bright-plumed on a bough of a blossoming orange tree and harped out of its throat. Everywhere around, towers soared heavenward in fluid grace; this quarter of the city went back two centuries, to when an inspired school of architecture had flourished. White clouds wandered through blue clarity; aircars sparkled in sunlight. A breeze brought coolness and a muted pulse of machines in the service of man. And here came the soufflé.

Later was the first, the truly delicious cigarette, out in the garden beside a dancing fountain. What followed was less pleasant, namely, spadework. But all this had to be paid for somehow. Flandry could retire whenever he chose: to a modest income from pension and investments, and an early death from boredom. He preferred to stay in the second oldest profession. In between adventures and enjoyments, an Intelligence officer—a spy—must needs do a vast amount of grubby foundation-laying.

He sought the fancier office and keyed for information on Edwin Cairncross, Grand Duke of Hermes. That meant a historical and social review of the planet itself.

The sun, Maia (not to be confused with giant 20 Tauri), was in Sector Antares. Its attendants included a terrestroid globe which had been colonized early on, largely by northern Europeans. Basic conditions, including biology, were homelike enough that the settlement did well. The inevitable drawbacks included the concentration of most land in a single huge continent whose interior needed modification—for instance, entire systems of rivers and lakes to relieve its aridity—before it was fit for humans to live in. Meanwhile they prospered along the coasts. Originally their polity was a rather curious development out of private corporations, with a head of state elected from a particular family to serve for life or good behavior. Society got stratified in the course of time, and reaction against that was fuelled by the crisis that the Babur War brought. Reforms turned Hermes into an ordinary type of crowned republic.

The war had also resulted in making it an interstellar power. It assumed protectorship over the defeated Baburites; they were too alien for close relations, but what there were, political and commercial, appeared to have been pretty amicable through the centuries. Hermetians started colonies and enterprises in several nearby systems. Most significantly, they had stewardship of Mirkheim, the sole known source of supermetals.

They needed their wealth and strength, for the Troubles were upon Technic civilization. Wars, revolutions, plundering raids raged throughout its space. Hermes must often fight. This led to a military-oriented state and a concentration of authority in the executive. When at last Manuel had established the Terran Empire and its Pax was spreading afar, that state was able to join on highly favorable terms.

Afterward . . . well, naturally the files couldn't say so, but as the Empire decayed, Hermes did too. Again and again, lordship went to the man with the armed force to take it. The economy declined, the sphere of influence shrank. Hans Molitor finally reasserted the supremacy of Terra. Generally he was welcomed by folk weary of chaos. But he had political debts to pay, and one payment involved putting lucrative Mirkheim directly under the Imperium. It was then a reasonable precaution to reduce sharply the autonomy of the Grand Duchy, disband its fighting services, require its businesses to mesh with some elsewhere—which worsened resentment. Riots erupted and Imperial agents were murdered, before the Marines restored order.

Today's Duke, Edwin Cairncross, appeared properly submissive; but appearances were not very reliable across a couple of hundred light-years, and certainly he had several odd items in his record. Now fifty-five, he had been the youngest son by a second marriage of a predecessor who gave Hans much trouble before yielding. Thus he had no obvious prospect of becoming more than a member of the gentry. Reviving an old Hermetian tradition, he enlisted in the Imperial Navy for a five-year hitch and left it bearing the rank of lieutenant commander. That was only partly due to family; he had served well, earning promotions during the suppression of the Nyanzan revolt and in the Syrax confrontation.

Returning home, he embarked energetically on a number of

projects. Among these, he enlarged what had been a petty industrial operation on the strange planet Ramnu and its moons. Meanwhile he held a succession of political posts and built up support for himself. Ten years ago, he became ready to compel the abdication of his older half-brother and his own election to the throne. Since then, he had put various measures into effect and undertaken various public works that were popular.

Hence on the surface, he seemed a desirable man in his position. The staff of the Imperial legate on Hermes were less sure of that. Their reports over the past decade showed increasing worry. Cairncross' image, writings, recorded speeches were everywhere. Half the adolescents on the home globe joined an organization which was devoted to outdoorsmanship and sports, but which was called the Cairncross Pioneers; its counselors preached a patriotism that was integral with adoration of him. Scholars were prodded into putting on symposia about his achievements and his prospects for restoring the greatness of his people. News media trumpeted his glories.

None of this was actually subversive. Many local lords exhibited egomania but were otherwise harmless. However, it was a possible danger signal. The impression was reinforced by the legate's getting no more exact information than law required—on space traffic, demography, production and distribution of specified goods, etc.— and his agents being unable to gather more for themselves or even ascertain whether what they were given was accurate. "We respect the right of individual choice here" was the usual bland response to an inquiry. The Babur Protectorate had been virtually sealed off: ostensibly at the desire of the natives, who were not Imperial subjects and therefore were free to demand it; but how could an outsider tell? Anything might be in preparation, anywhere throughout a volume of space that included scores of suns. Recent messages from the legate urged that Terra mount a full investigation.

The recommendation has drowned, Flandry thought, in the data, pleas, alarms that come here from a hundred thousand worlds. It has never gotten anywhere near the attention of the Policy Board. No lower-echelon official has flagged it. Why should he? Hermes is far off, close to that march of the Empire. By no possibility could it muster the power to make itself independent again, let alone pose any serious threat to Terra. The clearly dangerous cases are too many, too many.

Is there a danger, anyway . . . when the Duke has arrived of his free will and wants to see me, of all unlikely candidates?

Flandry searched for personal items. They were surprisingly few, considering what a cult the chap had built around himself. Cairncross was long married, but childlessly; indications were that that was due to a flaw in him, not his wife. Yet he had never cloned, which seemed odd for an egotist unless you supposed that his vainglory was too much for him to make such an admission. He was a mighty womanizer, but usually picked his bedmates from the lower classes and took care to keep them humble. Men found him genial when he was in the right mood, though always somewhat overawing, and terrifying when he grew angry. He had no close friends, but was generally considered to be trustworthy and a just master. He was an ardent sportsman, hunter, crack shot; he piloted his own spacecraft and had explored lethally unterrestroid environments; he was an excellent amateur cabinetmaker; his tastes were fairly simple, except that he enjoyed and understood wine; distilled beverages he consumed a bit heavily, without showing any effects; he was not known to use more drugs than alcohol—

Flandry decided to receive him in this office.

"Welcome, your Grace."

"Thank you." A firm handshake ended. Cairncross was putting on no airs.

"Please be seated. May I offer your Grace refreshments? I'm well stocked."

"M-m-m . . . Scotch and soda, then. And let's drop the titles while we're the two of us. I aim to talk frankly."

Chives shimmered in and took orders. Cairncross stared curiously after the Shalmuan—probably he'd never met any before—and swung attention back to his host. "Well, well," he said. "So this is the legendary Admiral Flandry."

"No, the objectively real Admiral Flandry, I hope. Some would say objectionably real."

Cairncross formed a smile and a chuckle, both short-lived. "The objectors have ample cause," he said. "Thank God for that."

"Indeed?"

"They've been our enemies, haven't they? I know why you got

that medallion you're wearing. The business wasn't publicized—would've been awkward for diplomacy, right?—but a man in my kind of position has ways of learning things if he's interested. You pulled the fangs of the Merseians at Chereion, and we no longer have to worry about them."

Flandry quelled a wince, for that episode had cost him heavily. "Oh, but I'm afraid we do," he said. "Their Intelligence apparatus suffered severe damage, true. However, nothing else did, and they're hard at work rebuilding it. They'll be giving us fun and games again."

"Not if we stay strong." Cairncross' gaze probed and probed. "Which is basically what I'm here about."

Flandry returned the look. Cairncross was tall and broad, with a tigerish suppleness to his movements. His face was wide on a wedge-shaped cranium, Roman-nosed, thin-lipped, fully de-bearded. The hair was red and starting to get scant, the eyes pale blue, the complexion fair and slightly freckled. His voice was deep and sonorous, crisply accented. He was wearing ordinary civilian garb, blouse and trousers in subdued hues, but a massive ring of gold and emerald sparkled on a furry finger.

Flandry lighted a cigarette. "Pray proceed," he invited.

"Strength demands unity," Cairncross replied. "Out my way, unity is threatened. I believe you can save it."

Chives brought the whisky, a glass of white Burgundy, and canapés. When he had gone, the Duke resumed in a rush:

"You'll have checked my dossier. You're aware that I'm some-what under suspicion. I've listened to your legate often enough; he makes no direct accusations, but he complains. Word that he sends here gets back to me through channels you can easily guess at. And I doubt if I'll shock you by saying that, in self-defense, I've sicced agents of mine onto agents of the Imperium on Hermes, to learn what they're doing and conjecturing. Am I secretly preparing for a revolt, a coup, or what? They wonder, yes, they wonder very hard."

"Being suspected of dreadful things is an occupational hazard of high office, isn't it?" Flandry murmured.

"But I'm innocent!" Cairncross protested. "I'm loyal! The fact of my presence on Terra—"

His tone eased: "I've grown more and more troubled about this.

Finally I've decided to take steps. I'm taking them myself, rather than sending a representative, because, frankly, I'm not sure who I can trust anymore.

"You know how impossible it is for a single man, no matter what power he supposedly has, to control everything, or know most of what's going on. Underlings can evade, falsify, conceal, drag their feet; your most useful officials can be conspirators against you, biding their time—Well, you understand, Admiral.

"I've begun to think there actually is a conspiracy on Hermes. In that case, I am its sacrificial goat."

Flandry trickled smoke ticklingly through his nostrils. "What do you mean, please?" he asked, though he thought he knew.

He was right. "Take an example," Cairncross said. "The legate wants figures on our production of palladium and where it is consumed. My government isn't technically required to provide that information, but it is required to cooperate with the representative of the Imperium, and his request for those figures is reasonable under the circumstances. After all, palladium is essential to protonic control systems, which are essential to any military machine. Now can I, personally, supply the data? Of course not. But when his agents try to collect them, and fail, I get blamed."

"No offense," Flandry said, "but you realize that, theoretically, the guilt could trace back to you. If you'd issued the right orders to the right individuals—"

Cairncross nodded. "Yes. Yes. That's the pure hell of it.

"I don't know if the plotters mean to discredit me so that somebody else can take my title, or if something worse is intended. I can't prove there is a plot. Maybe not; maybe it's an unfortunate set of coincidences. But I do know my good name is being gnawed away. I also know this kind of thing—disunity—can only harm the Empire. I've come for help."

Flandry savored his wine. "I sympathize," he said. "What can I do?"

"You're known to the Emperor."

Flandry sighed. "That impression dies hard, doesn't it? I was moderately close to Hans. After he died, Dietrich consulted me now and then, but not frequently. And I'm afraid Gerhart doesn't like me a whole lot."

"Well, still, you have influence, authority, reputation."

"These days, I have what amounts to a roving commission, and I can call on resources of the Corps. That's all."

"That's plenty!" Cairncross exclaimed. "See here. What I want is an investigation that will exonerate me and turn up whatever traitors are nested in Hermes. It would look peculiar if I suddenly appeared before the Policy Board and demanded this; it would damage me politically at home, as you can well imagine. But a discreet investigation, conducted by a person of unimpeachable loyalty and ability—Do you see?"

Loyalty? passed through Flandry. *To what? Scarcely to faithless Gerhart; scarcely even to this walking corpse of an Empire. Well, to the Pax, I suppose; to some generations of relative security that people can use to live in, before the Long Night falls; to my corps and my job, which have given me quite a bit of satisfaction; to a certain tomb on Dennitza, and to various memories.*

"I can't issue several planets a clean bill of health just by myself," he said.

"Oh, no," Cairncross answered. "Gather what staff you need. Take as much time as you like. You'll get every kind of cooperation I'm able to give. If you don't get it from elsewhere, well, isn't that what your mission will be about?"

"Hm." *I have been idle for awhile. It is beginning to pall. Besides, I've never been on Hermes; and from what little I know about them, planets like Babur and Ramnu may prove fascinating.* "It definitely interests; and, as you say, it could affect a few billion beings more than you. What have you in mind, exactly?"

"I want you and your immediate aides to come back with me at once," Cairncross said. "I've brought my yacht; she's fast. I realize that'll be too few personnel, but you can reconnoiter and decide what else to send for."

"Isn't this rather sudden?"

"Damn it," Cairncross exploded, "I've been strangling in the net for years! We may not have much time left." Calmer: "Your presence would help by itself. We'd not make a spectacle of it, of course, but the right parties—starting with his Majesty's legate—would know you'd come, and feel reassured."

"A moment, please, milord." Flandry stretched out an arm

and keyed his infotrieve. What he wanted flashed onto the screen.

"The idea tempts," he said, "assuming that one can be tempted to do a good deed. You'll understand that I'd have arrangements to make first. Also, I've grown a smidgin old for traveling on a doubtless comfortless speedster; and I might want assistants from the start who themselves cannot leave on short notice." He waved a hand. "This is assuming I undertake the assignment. I'll have to think further about that. But as for a preliminary look-see, well, I note that the *Queen of Apollo* arrives next week. She starts back to Hermes three days later, and first class accommodations are not filled. We can talk *en route.* Your crew can take your boat home."

Cairncross flushed. He smote the arm of his seat. "Admiral, this is an Imperial matter. It cannot wait."

"It has waited, by your account," Flandry drawled. Instinct, whetted throughout a long career, made him add: "Besides, I need answers to a hundred questions before I can know whether I ought to do this."

"You will do it!" Cairncross declared. Catching his breath: "If need be—the Emperor is having a reception for me, the normal thing. I'll speak to him about this if you force me to. I would prefer, for your sake, that you don't get a direct order from the throne; but I can arrange it if I must."

"Sir," Flandry purred, while his inwardness uncoiled itself for action, "my apologies. I meant no disrespect. You've simply taken me by surprise. Please think. I've commitments of my own. In fact, considering them, I realize they require my absence for about two weeks. After that, I can probably make for Hermes in my personal craft. When I've conducted enough interviews and studies there, I should know who else to bring."

He lifted his glass. "Shall we discuss details, milord?"

Hours later, when Cairncross had left, Flandry thought: *Oh, yes, something weird is afoot in Sector Antares.*

Perhaps the most suggestive thing was his reaction to my mention of the Queen of Apollo. *He tried to hide it, but. . . . Now who or what might be aboard her?*

✣ IV ✣

Banner had not seen Terra since she graduated at the age of twenty-one, to marry Sumarokov and depart for Ramnu. Moreover, the Academy had been an intense, largely self-contained little world, from which cadets seldom found chances to venture during their four years. She had not hankered to, either. Childhood on Dayan, among the red-gold Tammuz Mountains, followed by girlhood as a Navy brat in the strange outposts where her father got stationed, had not prepared her for any gigapolis. Nor had her infrequent later visits to provincial communities. Starfall, the biggest, now seemed like a village, nearly as intimate and unterrifying as Bethyaakov her birthplace.

She had made acquaintances in the ship. A man among them had told her a number of helpful facts, such as the names of hotels she could afford in the capital. He offered to escort her around as well, but his kindnesses were too obviously in aid of getting her into bed, and she resented that. Only one of her few affairs had been a matter of real love, but none had been casual.

Thus she found herself more alone, more daunted among a million people and a thousand towers, than ever in a wildwood or the barrenness of a moon. Maybe those numbers, million, thousand, were wrong. It felt as if she could see that many from the groundside terminal, but she was dazed. She did know that they went on beyond sight, multiplied over and over around the curve of the planet. Archopolis was merely a nexus; no matter if the globe had blue oceans and green open spaces—some huge, being property of nobility—it was a single city.

She collected her modest baggage, hailed a cab, blurted her destination to the autopilot, and fled. In nightmare beauty, the city gleamed, surged, droned around her.

At first the Fatima Caravanserai seemed a refuge. It occupied the upper third of an unpretentious old building, and had itself gone dowdy; yet it was quiet, reasonably clean, adequately equipped, and the registry desk held a live clerk, not a machine, who gave her cordial greeting and warned against the fish in the restaurant; the meat was good, he said.

But when she entered her room and the door slid shut, suddenly it was as though the walls drew close.

Nonsense! she told herself. *I'm tired and tense. I need to relax, and this evening have a proper dinner, with wine and the works.*

And who for company?

That question chilled. Solitude had never before oppressed her. If anything, she tended to be too independent of her fellow humans. But it was horrible to find herself an absolute stranger in an entire world.

Nonsense! she repeated. *I do know Admiral Flandry . . . slightly. . . . Will he remember me? No doubt several of my old instructors are still around. . . . Are they? The Xenological Society maintains a clubhouse, and my name may strike a chord in somebody if I drop in. . . . Can it?*

A cigarette between her lips, she began a whirl of unpacking. Thereafter a hot shower and a soft robe gave comfort. She blanked the viewer wall and keyed for a succession of natural scenes and historic monuments which the infotrieve told her was available, plus an excellent rendition of the pipa music she particularly enjoyed. The conveyor delivered a stiff cognac as ordered. Local time was 1830; in a couple of hours she might feel like eating. Now she settled down in a lounger to ease off.

No. She remained too restless. Rising, prowling, she reached the phone. There she halted. For a moment her fingers wrestled each other. It would likely be pointless to try calling Flandry before tomorrow. And then she could perhaps spend days getting her message through. A prominent man on Terra must have to live behind a shield-burg of subordinates.

Well, what harm in finding out the number?

That kept the system busy for minutes, since she did not know how to program its search through the bureaucratic structure. No private listing turned up, nor had she expected any. Two strings of digits finally flashed onto the screen. The first was coded for "Office," the second for "Special."

Was the latter an answering service? In that case, she could record her appeal immediately.

To her surprise, a live face appeared, above a uniform that sported twin silver comets on the shoulders. To her amazement, though the Anglic she heard was unmistakably Terran, the person was an alert-looking young woman. Banner had had the idea that Terran women these days were mostly ornaments, drudges, or whores. "Lieutenant Okuma," she heard. "May I help you?"

"I—well, I—" Banner collected herself. "Yes, please. I'm anxious to get in touch with Admiral Flandry. It's important. If you'll tell him my name, Miriam Abrams, and remind him I'm the daughter of Max Abrams, I'm sure he—"

"Hold on!" Okuma rapped. "Have you newly arrived?"

"Yes, a few hours ago."

"On the *Queen of Apollo?*"

"Why, yes, but—"

"Have you contacted anybody else?"

"Only customs and immigration officers, and the hotel staff, and—" Banner bridled. "What does this mean?"

"Excuse me," Okuma said. "I believe it means a great deal. I've been manning this line all day. Don't ask me why; I've not been told." She leaned forward. Her manner intensified. "Would you tell me where you are and what you want?"

"Fatima Caravanserai, Room 776," Banner blurted, "and I'm hoping he'll use his influence on behalf of a sophont species that desperately needs help. The Grand Duke of Hermes has refused it, so—" Her words faltered, her heart stammered.

"Grand Duke, eh? . . . Enough," Okuma said. "Please pay attention. Admiral Flandry has been called away on business. Where, has not been given out, and he isn't expected back until next week."

"Oh, I can wait."

"Listen! I have a message for whoever might debark from the Queen and try calling him. That seems to be you, Donna Abrams. Stay where you are. Keep the door double-secured. Do not leave on any account. Do not admit anyone whatsoever, no matter what that person may claim, unless he gives you a password. When you hear it, be prepared to leave immediately. Do what you are told, and save your questions till later, when you're safe. Do you understand?"

"What? No, I don't. What's wrong?"

"I have not been informed." The lieutenant's mouth twisted into a smile. "But Sir Dominic is usually right about such things."

Banner had met danger more than once. She had always found it exhilarating. Her back straightened, her pulse slowed. Having repeated the instructions, she asked, "What's the password?"

"'Basingstoke.'" Okuma smiled again, wryly. "I don't know what it signifies. He has an odd sense of humor. Stand by. I've a call to make. Good luck." The screen darkened.

Banner started repacking.

The phone chimed.

The face she saw when she accepted was round and rubicund under yellow curls. "Dr. Abrams?" the man said. "Welcome to Terra. My name is Leighton, Tom Leighton, and I'm in the lobby. May I come up, or would you like to come down and join me?"

Again she sensed her aloneness. "Why?" she whispered.

"Well, I'm a colleague of yours. I've admired your work tremendously; those are classic presentations. By sheer chance, I was meeting a friend off the *Queen of Apollo* today, and he mentioned you'd been aboard. Believe me, it took detective work to track you down! Apparently you threw yourself into a cab and disappeared. I've had a data scan checking every hotel and airline and—Well, anyway, Dr. Abrams, I was hoping we could go out to dinner. My treat. I'd be honored."

She stared into the bland blue eyes. "Tell me," she said, "what do you think of the cater-cousin relationship among the Greech on Ramnu?"

"Huh?"

"Do you agree with me it's religious in origin, or do you think Brunamonti is right and it's a relic of the former military organization?"

"Oh, that! I agree with you absolutely."

"How interesting," Banner said, "in view of the fact that no such people as the Greech exist, that Ramnuans don't have religions of human type and most definitely have never had armies, and nobody named Brunamonti has ever done Xenology on their planet. Have you any further word for me, Citizen Leighton?"

"Ai, wait, wait a minute—"

She cut him off.

Presently her door was pealing. She punched the callbox and his voice came through: "Dr. Abrams, please, this is a terrible misunderstanding. Let me in and I'll explain."

"Go away." Despite the steadiness in her voice, her flesh crawled. She was concerned.

"Dr. Abrams, I must insist. The matter involves a very high-ranking person. If you don't open the door, we'll have to take measures."

"Or I will. Like calling the police."

"I tell you, it's a top-grade noble who wants to see you. He can have the police break you out of there. He'd rather not, because what he wants is for your benefit too, but—Uh, who are you?" Leighton asked somebody else. "What do you want?"

"*Basingstoke*," rippled a baritone voice. A moment later, Banner heard a thud. "You can open up now," the newcomer continued.

She did. Leighton lay in a huddle on the hall floor. Above him stood a figure in a hooded cloak. He drew the cowl back and she knew Flandry.

He gestured at the fallen shape. "A stun gun shot," he said. "I'll drag him in here to sleep it off. He's not worth killing, just a petty predator hired through an agency that provides reputable people with disreputable services. He's probably got a companion or two down below, on the *qui vive*. We'll spirit you upward. Chives—do you remember Chives?—has an aircar on the roof for us." He bowed and quickly, deftly kissed her hand. "I'm sorry about this informal reintroduction, my dear. I'll try to make amends at dinner. We have a reservation a couple of hours hence at Deirdre's. You wouldn't believe what they do with seafood there."

✧ V ✧

His Imperial Majesty, High Emperor Gerhart Siegmund Molitor, graciously agreed to withdraw from the reception for a private talk with its guest of honor. They passed in stateliness through the swirl of molten rainbows which several hundred costumes made of the grand ballroom. Folk bowed, curtsied, or saluted, depending on status, and hoped for a word from the august mouth. A few got one, and promptly became centers of eager attention. There were exceptions to this, of course, mostly older men of reserved demeanor, admirals, ministers of state, members of the Policy Board, the power brokers. Their stares followed the Duke of Hermes. He would be invited later to meet with various of them.

A gravshaft took Gerhart and Cairncross to a suite in the top of the loftiest tower that the Coral Palace boasted. The guards outside were not gorgeously uniformed like those on ground level; they were hard of face and hands, and their weapons had seen use. Gerhart motioned them not to follow, and let the door close behind himself and his companion.

A clear dome overlooked lower roofs, lesser spires, gardens, trianons, pools, bowers, finally beach, sand, surf, nearby residential rafts, and the Pacific Ocean. Sheening and billowing under a full Luna, those waters gave a sense of ancient forces still within this planet that man had so oedipally made his own, still biding their time. That feeling was strengthened by the sparsely furnished chamber. On the floor lay a rug made from the skin of a Germanian dolchzahn, on a desk stood a model of a corvette, things which had belonged to Hans. His picture hung on the wall. It had been taken seven years ago, shortly before his death, and Cairncross saw how wasted the big ugly countenance had become by then; but in caverns of bone, the gaze burned.

"Sit down," Gerhart said. "Smoke if you wish."

"I don't, but your Majesty is most kind."

Gerhart sighed. "Spare me the unction till we have to go back. When the lord of a fairly significant province arrives unannounced on Terra, I naturally look at whatever file we have on him. You don't strike me as the sort who would come here for a vacation."

"No, that was my cover story . . . sir." The Emperor having taken a chair, the Duke did likewise.

"Ye-es," Gerhart murmured, "it is interesting that you put your head in the lion's mouth. Why?"

Cairncross regarded him closely. He didn't seem leonine, being of medium height, with blunt, jowly features and graying sandy hair. The iridescent, carefully draped robe he wore could not quite hide the fact that, in middle age, he was getting pudgy. But he had his father's eyes, small, dark, searching, the eyes of a wild boar.

He smiled as he opened a box and took out a cigar for himself. "Interesting enough," he went on, "that I've agreed to receive you like this. Ordinarily, you know, any special audiences you got would be with persons such as Intelligence officers."

"Frankly, sir," Cairncross answered, emboldened, "I started out that way, but got no satisfaction. Or so it appears. Maybe I'm doing the man an injustice. You can probably tell me—though Admiral Flandry is a devious devil, isn't he?"

"Flandry, eh? Hm-m." Gerhart kindled the cigar. Smoke curled blue and pungent. "Proceed."

"Sir," Cairncross began, "having seen my file, you know about the accusations and innuendos against me. I'm here partly to declare them false, to offer my body as a token of my loyalty. But you'll agree that more is needed, solid proof . . . not only to exonerate me, but to expose any actual plot."

"This is certainly an age of plots," Gerhart observed, through the same cold smile as before.

And murders, revolutions, betrayals, upheavals, Cairncross replied silently. *Brother against brother—When that spacecraft crashed, Gerhart, and killed Dietrich, was it really an accident? Incredible that safety routines could have slipped so far awry, for a ship which would carry the Emperor. Never mind what the board of inquiry reported afterward; the new Emperor kept tight control of its proceedings.*

You are widely believed to be a fratricide, Gerhart. (And a parricide? No; old Hans was too shrewd.) If you are nevertheless tolerated on the throne, it is because you are admittedly more able than dullard Dietrich was. The Empire needs a strong, skilled hand upon it, lest it splinter again in civil war and the Merseians or the barbarians return.

Yet that is your only claim to rulership, Gerhart. It was Hans' only claim, too. He, however, was coping as best he could, after the Wang dynasty fell apart. There was no truly legitimate heir. When most of the Navy rallied to him, he could offer domestic order and external security, at the cost of establishing a military dictatorship.

But . . . no blood of the Founder ever ran in his veins. His coronation was a solemn farce, played out under the watch of his Storm Corps, whose oath was not to the Imperium but to him alone. He broke aristocrats and made new ones at his pleasure. He kept no ancient pacts between Terra and her daughter worlds, unless they happened to suit his purposes. Law became nothing more than his solitary will.

He is of honored memory here, because of the peace he restored. That is not the case everywhere else. . . .

"You are suddenly very quiet," Gerhart said.

Cairncross started. "I beg your pardon, sir. I was thinking how to put my case with the least strain on your time and patience."

He cleared his throat and embarked on much the same discourse as he had given Flandry. The Emperor listened, watching him from behind a cloud of smoke.

Finally Gerhart nodded and said, "Yes, you are right. An investigation is definitely required. And it had better be discreet, or it would embarrass you politically—and therefore, indirectly, the Imperium." *If you are indeed loyal to us,* he left understood. "You ought to have instigated it earlier, in fact." *But a single planet is too huge, too diverse and mysterious, for anybody, to rule wisely. As for an empire of planets—*"Now why do you insist that Vice Admiral Flandry take charge?"

"His reputation, sir," Cairncross declared. "He's accomplished fabulous things in the past when he had inadequate support or none. Who could better handle our problem at Hermes, which includes the need not to bring in an army-sized team?"

Gerhart scowled. "You may have an exaggerated view of his abilities."

Yes, you don't like him, do you? Cairncross retorted inwardly. *He was your father's indispensable fox, he delivered a masterstroke at Chereion, and Dietrich relied on him too, occasionally. Rivalry; a living reminder of what you may prefer to forget; and, to be sure, I've learned in conversations with noblefolk, these last few days, that Flandry is apt to get flippant. He is not altogether reverent toward a crown that does not rest absolutely securely on a brow where it doesn't belong.*

"If so," he murmured, "then wouldn't a little demythologizing of him be welcome, sir?"

Gerhart stiffened in his chair. "By God—!"

"I don't imagine he would botch the assignment," Cairncross pursued. "He might perform brilliantly. He would at least be competent. But if he proved to be merely that—if, perhaps, a younger man had to come and take over—well, sir, it would be natural for you to do him the honor of relieving him of his duties yourself, with public thanks for past services."

Gerhart nodded hard. "Yes. Yes. High officers who've outlived their usefulness but can't be dismissed are always a nuisance. They've built their personal organizations, you see, and blocs of associates and admirers. . . . Well, Flandry. Since the middle of my father's reign, he has in effect been dreaming up his own assignments, and ruling over a tight-knit staff who report to nobody else. His conduct hasn't been insubordinate, but sometimes it has come close."

"I take your meaning, sir, after having dealt with him."

"What's happened?"

"Sir, I don't want to get above myself in the Imperial presence. Nevertheless, I am a ranking, governing noble of the Empire. Its welfare requires that its leaders get the respect they're entitled to. He didn't exactly refuse my commission, but he told me he'd have to think about whether or not he would condescend to accept it. After which he promptly disappeared on unspecified business, and is not expected back till next week. Meanwhile, I cool my heels."

Gerhart stroked his chin. "A direct order—putting him under your command—"

"Your Majesty is foresighted as well as generous." Look met look in what Cairncross hoped Gerhart would assume was mutual understanding.

The guestroom door fluted. Banner jerked her head around. She had almost succeeded in losing herself in a starball game beamcast from Luna. At first she was attracted because she was a fan of several sports, and played when she could; but soon the ballet-like, dreamlike beauty of the motion took her. Now abruptly it was unreal, against the leap in her pulse and the dryness in her mouth.

Angered by that, she told herself to calm down and act like an adult. Aloud, she asked, "Who is it, please?"

There should be no danger. Flandry had decided his place right in Archopolis was probably her safest hideaway. He could smuggle her in; Chives, in constant electronic touch with his immediate juniors, could fend off any visitors while the admiral was away.

He had been gone for two achingly idle days. She felt more relief than was rational to hear his voice: "The gentleman from Basingstoke. Come on out, if you will. I bear tidings."

"A, a minute, please." She'd been basking under a sunlamp, after a lengthy swim, while she watched the contest. He had not so much as hinted at a pass. Mostly, in what little conversation they'd held on personal topics, he reminisced about her father and drew forth her own memories of his old mentor. Besides, mores were casual on Terra. Nevertheless, she didn't want to meet him unclad. She scrambled into slacks, blouse, sandals. Only after she was through the door did she remember that she hadn't stopped to brush her hair and it must look like two comets colliding.

He didn't appear to notice, though she suspected he did. He himself wore inconspicuous civilian garb. His expression was grim. "How've you been?" he asked.

"In suspense," she admitted. "And you?"

"Skulking, but busy. I had to keep out of sight, you see, to maintain the pretense that I'd never returned here. At the same time, I had to learn what's been going on; and my people are as wary as anyone could want, but I dared not simply ring them up and inquire." He shrugged. "Details. I managed. Let's have a drink while I bring you *au courant.*"

She didn't recognize that expression. Her knowledge of non-Anglic human languages was limited, and fresh only as regarded terms in the Oriental classics that, translated, she enjoyed. She understood him in context, however, and followed him eagerly. As a rule she was a light drinker, her vice was tobacco, but in this hour she desired a large cognac.

Rain washed silvery down the outer side of the living room, which had been left transparent. Often lightning flashed. She heard no thunder through the soundproofing, and that made the whole scene feel eerily unreal. They settled into loungers opposite each other, amidst soft-colored drapes whose textures were meant to be touched, art from a dozen worlds, a drift of incense. Chives heard their wishes and departed. They lit cigarettes.

"Well?" Banner demanded. "Speak up. . . . I'm sorry, I didn't mean to bark at you."

"Would you care for some nerve soother?"

She shook her head. "Just the drink. I—In my line of work, we dare not use much chemical calming. The temptation could get too great—no addiction, of course, but the temptation."

He nodded and said low, "Yes, you've suffered a lot of tension and pain, as well as excitement, vicariously, haven't you?"

"Vicariously? No! It's as real for me as it's been for Yewwl!" Banner was surprised at her vehemence. She quenched it. "I'll try to explain later, if we have a chance."

"Oh, we ought to have that," Flandry said. "We're off together for Ramnu."

"What?" She stared.

Chives brought the drinks. Flandry's was beer. He savored a long swallow. "Aaah." He smiled. "You know, that's among the things I miss the most on an extended job. Hard liquor can be carried along in ample supply, or can usually be found if a person isn't fussy, but dear old beer doesn't tolerate concentration and reconstitution as certain people who lack taste buds believe, and it has too much volume for more than a few cases to go aboard *Hooligan*." He inhaled above the goblet. "Gather ye bubbles while ye may."

"Do you always joke?" she wondered.

He shrugged again. "Might as well. The grief will take care of itself, never fear." His mouth fell into harsh curves, his gray eyes locked onto hers. "All right, I'll get serious. To begin, what understanding of the situation do you have?"

"Hardly any, for certain," she reminded him. "I've made my guesses, and told you them, but you were, oh, noncommittal."

"I'd too few facts," he explained, "and empty speculation is worse than a waste of time, it's apt to mislead. Actually, for a person who's been sheltered from the nastier facts of political life, you made a pretty canny surmise or two. But maybe I'd best retrace everything from my viewpoint."

He wet his throat afresh, filled his lungs, and proceeded: "It appeared plausible, from your account, that Cairncross is conducting business that he doesn't care to reveal before he's ready. If it doesn't center at Ramnu, at least Ramnu is critical to it. Several years ago, he replaced the management of the commercial Hermetian enterprise there. Since, it's expanded operations, but at the same time grown remarkably tight-lipped. It also gives your scientific outfit less and less cooperation. The pretexts are not convincing. This hampers your work, restricts its scope, and may at last choke it off altogether.

"Meanwhile, Cairncross has declined to consider rehabilitating Ramnu. He might reasonably maintain it's too expensive for his budget. But why wouldn't he pass your appeal on to Terra? His rank is sufficient that he'd have a fair chance of getting approval; nowadays the Policy Board likes to start worthy projects, if they don't cost a lot, to help build goodwill for an Imperium that badly needs it. The influx of technicians and money, the stimulus given local industries, would benefit a Hermetian economy that is not in ideal shape at present.

"Well, you decided to invoke my influence, for old times' sake. Your idea of its magnitude was unrealistic, but you couldn't know that. You could at least have persuaded me to go look the place over, and see if I couldn't invent a lever that would pry authorization loose from the Board.

"Before your liner could reach Terra, Cairncross arrived personally in a speedster. He wanted me to flit home with him immediately. Coincidence? He is in fact getting a bad name in some limited Imperial circles. Not bad enough to provoke action by our lumbering, creaky, half-programmed Empire, but still—Nevertheless, why insist on me handling his chestnuts, and no one else? Why so stiffly opposed to traveling in leisure and comfort on the Queen? Could it be that somebody was bound here aboard her, somebody he'd prefer I not meet?

"You may remember how I inquired at tedious length about what went on at your host's place in Starfall, including the layout of the house. You'd taken precautions. But neither you nor yonder Citizen Runeberg is a professional in that field. I can think of a thousand ways to eavesdrop on you."

Flandry stopped and drained his beer. "Chives!" he bawled. "More!" To Banner: "I require a pitcher of this whenever I lecture on my trade, which is twice a year at the Corps Academy. Excuse me if I've droned on. Professoring is a habit that gets hard to break."

She comforted her body with cognac. "No, you've done right," she whispered. "That is, most of it had become fairly clear to me, but you've put it in perspective."

"The rest is more briefly told. For small blessings, give thanks," he said. Chives brought a fresh goblet, glanced at how Banner was doing, and withdrew.

"You made an excuse to delay matters," she said, to demonstrate that she was not lost. "This required you drop out of sight till after the Queen had left Terra, as if you gave her no more thought. But you alerted your staff."

"On a basis of guesswork. I had scant notion of who, or what, if anything, would arrive, or even if that arrival would concern me. It was merely a contingency that needed to be covered. If nothing had come of it, I'd have used the time to think of more contingencies and try to provide against them. As was, I played by ear. It seems likely that Cairncross engaged agents to head you off, but I can't prove it. No use carting away the one I clobbered, for a quiz. He wouldn't have known. His bosses are professionals too."

"What have you done since?"

"Research, and assorted preparation-making, and—Yesterday, checking with this office, I found it had received a direct Imperial order placing me under the Duke's command, to report to him without delay and be prepared to depart for Hermes pronto if not sooner." Flandry's grin was' vulpine. "Since it's clear that I would not break contact with my staff, I couldn't stay away on plea of ignorance. As an experiment, I requested an audience with his Majesty, and was quite unsurprised to be told that no time will be available for me until next month."

He sipped. "Therefore I've returned like a nice boy," he said. "His Grace was equally nice. If he thinks I may have had a part in the sudden sleepiness of that agent and in your disappearance, he didn't let on. And perhaps he doesn't. A heavy stun gun blast has an amnesiac effect on the preceding few hours, you know. For all that chap can tell, you admitted him and shot him yourself before you fled. The Duke knows how leery of him you are, and that you've spent many years partaking in a violent milieu. One thing I have ascertained is that he's put the rent-a-thug organization on a full-scale hunt for you. But in any event, he was glad to learn I can leave tomorrow early." He winced. "Exceedingly early."

Dismay smote. "But what shall *I* do?" Banner asked.

"The plan, such as it is, is this," Flandry told her. "I've explained that it's best I go in my own speedster. She's equipped for field work, you see. I can commence in a preliminary way as soon as I reach Hermes. She doesn't have room for him and his entourage—polite word for bodyguards, plus an aide or two and perhaps a mistress—but his craft is nearly as fast.

"Once there . . . well, he'll suppose, maybe I can be won over. Surely I can be stalled, bogged down, put on false scents, possibly hoodwinked altogether. If not, I can be made to die. My distinct impression is that his Grace doesn't need much longer to launch his scheme. Else he wouldn't be acting this boldly; he's too committed by now to dare be timid."

"Can't you tell anyone?" she breathed.

"Oh, yes, if I want to endanger those persons needlessly," he answered. "For what could an underling do? I've left a record of what I think, keyed into a computer, which will release it to selected individuals upon my death or prolonged vanishment. A gesture, mostly, I'm afraid. After all, thus far it amounts to scarcely more than conjecture; no firm evidence. Besides, my insubordination will gravely discredit it."

"In . . . insubordination?" Her scalp tingled.

He nodded. "Yes. I won't be steering for Hermes but for Ramnu. That is, if you'll come along as my absolutely necessary guide. Ramnu's apparently a vulnerable flank that he may or may not have covered well enough—probably not, since he's so anxious to keep me from it. We might discover what we need to discover, though time will be damnably short. If we fail, or if it turns out there really is nothing amiss—then we're liable to charges of treason, having disobeyed an order of the very Emperor, and they will certainly be brought."

His smooth manner was gone; he looked miserable. "I've committed my share of evil, in line of work," he said. "Inviting a daughter of Max Abrams to accompany me may be the worst of the lot. I hope you'll have the sense to refuse."

It blazed in her. She sprang to her feet. "Of course I don't!" she cried, and lifted her glass on high.

Lightning glared. The rainstorm grew more wild.

✳ **VI** ✳

Hooligan raised her lean form off the spacefield and hit the sky as fast as regulations allowed. Thunder trailed. Beyond atmosphere, she curved away as per flight plan, accelerating harder all the time. Presently she was far enough distant from regular traffic trajectories that she could unbind the full power of her gravs. Before long, Terra was visibly dwindling in eyesight, more quickly for each second that passed.

None of this was felt inboard, where fields maintained a steady one gee of weight. Only the faintest susurrus resounded, and most of that was from the ventilators which kept vernal breezes moving. *Hooligan* was a deceptive craft: small, but overpowered, with armament to match a corvette's, equipment and data banks to match an explorer's (and an Intelligence laboratory's), luxury to match—but here Banner's experience failed her.

In her stateroom, which gave on a private bath cubicle, she removed her disguise. It came off easier than she had expected, not just the dress and wig but the items which had altered her looks and prints to fit the passport Flandry had given her.

Sarah Pipelini—"Is this anybody real?" she had asked.

"Well, several real persons have found it convenient to be her for a while," he replied. "She's got the standard entries in official records, birth, education, residence, employment, et cetera, plus occasional changes to stay plausible. I've a number of identities available. Sarah's is the easiest to suit you to. Besides, creating her was fun."

"I'm no good at playacting," Banner said nervously. "It's too short notice even to learn what her past life is supposed to have been."

"No need. Simply memorize what's in the passport. Stay close to me and don't speak unless spoken to. No harm if you register excitement; that's natural, when you're off on a trip to far-off, exotic Hermes. It'll also be natural for you to clutch my arm and give me intermittent adoring glances, if you can bring yourself to that."

"You mean—?"

"Why, I thought it was obvious. We have to get you aboard.

Besides the regular Naval clearance procedures, Cairncross will doubtless have agents unobtrusively watching. No surprise if I bring a lady along to help pass the time of voyage. In fact, that will reinforce the impression—together with just Chives coming otherwise—that I am indeed going where I'm supposed to. If I brought any of my staff, then his Grace might well demand that men of his be included. As is, I've already filed our list, the three of us, you described as a 'friend.' Cairncross may snigger when he reads it, but he should believe." Flandry's tone grew serious. "Of course, this is strictly a ruse. Have no fears."

When he applied the deceptive materials, her face had burned beneath his fingers.

Now she showered the sweat of tension off her. For a moment she regarded her rangy form in the mirror and considered putting the glamorous gown on again. But once more she flushed, and chose the plainest coverall she had packed. She did brush her hair till it shone and let it flow free under a headband of lovely weave.

Emerging, she found the saloon where Flandry had said they would meet, and drew a quick breath. She had often seen open space, through a faceplate as well as a viewscreen. Yet somehow, at this instant, those star-fires crowding yonder clear blackness, that icy sweep of the galaxy, and Terra already a blue jewel falling away into depths beyond depths—reached in and seized her.

Music drew her back. A lilt of horns, flutes, violins . . . Mozart? Flandry entered. He too had changed clothes, his uniform for an open-necked bouffalon shirt, bell-bottomed slacks, curly-toed slippers. *Is he being casual on my account?* she wondered. *If so, he still can't help being elegant. The way he bears his head, and the light makes its gray come alive—*

"How're you doing?" he greeted. "Relaxed, I trust? You may as well be. We've a good two weeks' travel before us." He grinned. "At least, I hope we can make them good."

"Won't we have work to do?" she inquired hastily.

"Oh, the ship conns herself *en route,* and handles other routines like housekeeping. Chives handles the meals, which, believe me, will not be routine. He promises lunch in an hour." Flandry gestured at a table of dark-red wood—actual mahogany? Banner had seen literary references to mahogany. "Let's have an apéritif meanwhile."

"But, but you admitted you know almost nothing about Ramnu. I'm sure you've loaded the data banks with information on it, but won't you need a lot of that in your mind, also?"

He guided her by the elbow to a padded bench that curved around three sides of the table. Above it, on a bulkhead that shimmered slightly iridescent, was screened a picture she recognized: snowscape, three trudging peasants, a row of primitive houses, winter-bare trees, a mountain, all matching the grace of the music. Hiroshige had wrought it, twelve hundred years ago.

"Please sit," he urged. They did. "My dear," he continued, "of course I'll have to work. We both will. But I'm a quick study; and what's the use of laying elaborate plans when most of the facts are unknown? We'll do best to enjoy yourselves while we can. For openers, you need a day off to learn, down in your bones, that for the nonce you're *safe.*" Chives appeared. "What will you drink? Since I understand a seafood salad is in preparation, I'd recommend a dry white wine."

"Specifically, sir, the Chateau Huon '58," said the Shalmuan.

Flandry raised his brows. "A pinot noir blanc?"

"The salad will be based upon Unan Besarian skimmerfish, sir."

Flandry stroked his mustache. "I see. Then when we eat, we'll probably want—oh, never mind, you'll pick the bottle anyway. Very good, Chives."

The servant left, waving his tail. Banner sighed. "Where can you possibly find time for gourmandizing, Admiral?" she asked.

"Why, isn't that the purpose of self-abnegation, to gain the means of self-indulgence?" Flandry chuckled. "I'd prefer to be a decadent aristocrat, but wasn't born to it; I've had to earn my decadence."

"I can't believe that," she challenged.

"Well, at any rate, frankly, you strike me as being too earnest. Your father knew how to savor the cosmos, in his gutsy fashion. So did your mother, in her quieter way, and I daresay she does yet. Why not you?"

"Oh, I do. It's simply that—" Banner stared past him, into brilliance and darkness. She wasn't given to revealing herself, especially on acquaintance as brief as this. However, Flandry was an old family friend, and they'd be together in running between the claws of death, and—and—

"I never had a chance to learn much about conventional pleasures," she explained with difficulty. "Navy brat, you know, shunted from planet to planet, educated mostly by machines. Then the Academy; I had an idea of enlisting in Dad's corps—yours—and a xenological background would help. But I got into the science entirely, instead, and left for Ramnu, and that's where I've been ever since." She met his eyes. They were kindly. "I wouldn't want it any different, either," she said. "I have the great good fortune to love what I do . . . and those I do it with, the Ramnuans themselves."

He nodded. "I can see how it would make you its own. Nothing less than total dedication will serve, will it? On a world so strange." His vision likewise sought the deeps outside. "Gods of mystery," he whispered, "it wasn't supposed to be possible, was it? A planet like that. Yes, I do have a brain-scorching lot of homework ahead of me. To start off, I don't even know how Ramnu is supposed to have happened."

Originally a dwarf sun had a superjovian attendant, a globe of some 3000 Terrestrial masses. Such a monster was, inevitably, of starlike composition, mainly hydrogen, with a small percentage of helium, other elements a mere dash of impurities.

Indeed, it must have been more nearly comparable to a star than to, say, Jupiter. The latter is primarily liquid, beneath a vast atmosphere; a slag of light metal compounds does float about in continent-sized pieces, but most solid material is at the core (if it can be called solid, under that pressure). The slow downdrift of matter, drawn by the gravity of the stupendous mass, releases energy; Jupiter radiates about twice what it receives from Sol, making the surface warm.

Increase the size by a factor of 10, and everything changes. The body glows red; it is liquid, or fiercely compressed gas, throughout, save that the heavy elements which have sunken to the center are squeezed into quantum degeneracy, rigid beyond any stuff we will ever hold in our hands. At the same time, because its gravitational grip upon itself is immense, a globe like this can form, and can survive, rather close to an ordinary sun. Energy input from light and solar wind is insufficient to blow molecules away from it.

Unless—

Close by, as astronomical distances go, was a giant star. It went supernova. This may have occurred by chance, when it was passing precisely far enough away. Likelier, giant and dwarf were companions, with precisely the right orbits around each other. In the second case, the catastrophe tore them apart, for mass was lost at such a rate that conservation of momentum whirled the pair off at greater than escape velocity.

A violence that briefly rivalled the combined output of billions of suns did more than this. It filled surrounding space with gas that, for millennia afterward, made a nebula visible across light-years, till at last expansion thinned it away into the abyss. The dwarf star may well have captured a little of that cloud, and moved up the main sequence.

The huge planet was too small for that; parameters were wrong for producing another Mirkheim. Bombardment and sheer incandescence blew away more than 90 percent of it, the hydrogen and helium. They volatilized mainly as a plasma, which interacted with the core of heavier elements through magnetic fields. Thus the rotation of that core was drastically slowed. It exploded too, out of super-compaction into a state we might call normal. This outburst was insufficient to shatter the remnant, though perhaps a fraction was lost. But the ball of silicon, nickel, iron, carbon, oxygen, nitrogen, uranium . . . was molten for eons afterward.

Meanwhile, its lesser satellites, like its lesser sister planets, had been vaporized. A part of three big ones survived. The shrinkage of their primary sent them spiraling outward to new orbits. Movement was hindered by friction with the nebula, which was substantial for thousands of years. That may have caused an inner moon or two to crash on the planet. Certainly it moved the globe itself sunward.

When finally things had stabilized, there was Niku, a late G-type star of 0.48 Solar luminosity, unusual only in having a higher percentage of metals than is common for bodies its age (and this only if we have estimated that age correctly). There were four small, virtually airless planets. And there was Ramnu, circling Niku at a mean distance, which varied little, of 1.10 astronomical unit, in a period of 1.28 standard year. Its mass was 310 times the Terrestrial, its mean density 1.1 times—but the density was due to self-compression under 7.2 standard gees, for the overall compositions were similar. The axial tilt of Ramnu was about 4 degrees, its rotation period equal to 15.7 standard days.

As the stone cooled, it outgassed, forming oceans and a primordial atmosphere. Chemical evolution began. Eventually photosynthesizing life developed, and the pace of that evolution quickened. Today the atmosphere resembled Terra's, apart from slight differences in proportions of constituents. The most striking unlikeness was its concentration, 4.68 times the Terrestrial at sea level, which meant 33.7 times the pressure. Thus, although irradiation from the sun was 0.4 what Terra gets, greenhouse effect kept the surface reasonably warm . . . but this fluctuated.

The world was discovered not by humans but by Cynthians, early in the pioneering era. Intrigued, they established a scientific base on its innermost moon and bestowed names from a mythology of theirs. Politico-economic factors, which also fluctuate, soon caused them to depart. Later, humans arrived, intending to stay and operate on a larger scale. But the facilities made available to them were never adequate, and lessened across the centuries. For all its uniqueness, Ramnu remained obscure, even among planetologists.

There are so many, many worlds, in this tiny segment of space we have somewhat explored.

When safely high in Sol's potential well, *Hooligan* switched to secondary drive. Her oscillators gave her a pseudovelocity almost twice that of most vessels, better than half a light-year per hour. Yet she would take half a month to reach the region of Sol's near neighbor Antares. Had she been able to range that far, it would have taken her twenty years to cross the galaxy. Their compensators cancelling the optical effects of continuous spatial displacement, her screens showed heaven slowly changing, as old constellations became new; unless made to amplify, on the fourth day they no longer showed Sol.

"Which shows you how we rate in the scheme of things, doesn't it?" Flandry said apropos. He and Banner were relaxing over drinks after she had led him through a hard session of study. The drinks now totalled several.

She leaned elbows on the table and gave him a serious regard. "Depends on what you mean by that," she replied. "If God can care about the workmanship in an electron, He can care about us."

He looked back. It was worth doing, he thought. She wasn't beautiful by conventional measures, but her face had good bones and was more alive than most—like her springy body and those leaf-green, sea-green eyes. . . . "I didn't know you were religious," he said. "Well, Max was, though he made no production of it."

"I'm not sure if I'd call myself religious," she admitted. "I'm not observant in any faith. But Creation must have a purpose."

He sipped his Scotch and followed the smoke-bite with a little water. "The present moment could make me believe that," he said. "Unfortunately, I've seen too many moments which are not the least like it. I don't find much self-created purpose in our lives, either. And our public creations, like the Empire, are exercises in absurdity." He took forth his cigarette case. "Ah, well, we went through this argument at the age of eighteen or thereabouts, didn't we? Smoke?"

She accepted, and they kindled together. He had selected for music a concert by an ensemble of tuned Freyan ornithoids. They twittered, they trilled, they sang of treetops and twilit skies. He had given the air a greenwood odor and made it summer-mild. The lights were low.

Banner seemed abruptly to have forgotten her surroundings. She inhaled as sharply as her gaze focused on him. "Did you?" she asked. "At just about that age, weren't you serving the Empire . . . under my father? And afterward, everything you've done—No, don't bother playing your cynicism game with me."

He shrugged and laughed. "*Touché!* I confess I matured a trifle late. Max was a stout Imperial loyalist, of course, and I admired him more than any other man I've ever met, including the one alleged to have been my own father. So it took me a while to see what the Empire really is. Since then, if you must know, like everybody else who can think, I have indeed been playing games, for lack of better occupation. Mine happen to be useful to Terra—and, to be sure, to myself, since our pre-eminence is more fun than subjugation, barbarism, or death. But as for taking the Imperial farce seriously—"

He stopped, seeing appalled anger upon her. "Do you say my father was a fool?" cracked forth.

Am I drunk? flashed through him. *A bit, maybe, what with alcohol poured straight over weariness and, yes, loneliness. I ought to have been more careful.*

"I'm sorry, Banner," he apologized. "I spoke heedlessly. No, your father was right at the time. The Empire was worth something then, on balance. Afterward, well, from his standpoint it doubtless continued to be. If he grew disappointed, he would have felt obliged to keep silent. He was that kind of man. I like to imagine that he lived and died in the hope of a renascence—which I wish I could share."

Her countenance softened. "You don't?" she murmured. "But why? The Empire keeps the Pax, holds the trade lanes open, fends off the outside enemy, guards the heritage—*That's* what you've spent your life doing."

Aye, she remains her father's daughter, he saw. *It explains much about her.*

"Excuse me," he said. "I was being grumpy."

"No, you weren't," she declared. "I may not be a very skilled human-reader, but you meant your words. Unmistakably. Please tell me more."

Her spirit is bent to the search for truth.

"Oh, it's a long story and a longer thesis," he said. "The Empire had value once. It still does, to a degree. Nevertheless, what was it ever in the first place, but the quickest and crudest remedy for chaos? And what brought on the chaos, the Troubles, except the suicide of an earlier order, which couldn't muster the will to keep freedom alive? So again, as before, came Caesar.

"But a universal state is not a new beginning for a civilization, it's the start of the death, and it has to follow the same course over and over through history, like a kind of slow but terminal sickness."

He sipped, he smoked, feeling the slight burns of each. "I'd really rather not give you a lecture tonight," he said. "I've spent hundreds of hours when I'd nothing else to do, reading and meditating; and I've talked to historians, psychodynamicists, philosophers; yes, nonhuman observers of us have had cogent remarks to make—but the point is simply that you and I happen to be living in a critical stage of the Empire's decline, the interregnum between its principate and dominate phases."

"You *are* getting abstract," Banner said.

Flandry smiled. "Then let's drop the subject and watch it squash. Chives will clean up the mess."

She shook her head. Subtle shadows went over the curves around cheekbones and jawline. "No, please, not like that. Dominic— Admiral, I'm not entirely ignorant. I know about corruption and abuse of power, not to mention civil wars or plain stupidity. My father used to do some wonderful cursing, when a piece of particularly nauseous news came in. But he'd always tell me not to expect perfection of mortal beings; our duty was to keep on trying."

He didn't remark on her use of his first name, though his heart did. "I suppose that's forever true, but it's not forever possible," he responded gravely. "Once as a young fellow I found myself supporting the abominable Josip against McCormac—Remember McCormac's Rebellion? He was infinitely the better man. Anybody would have been. But Josip was the legitimate Emperor, and legitimacy is the root and branch of government. How else, in spite of the cruelties and extortions and ghastly mistakes it's bound to perpetrate—how else, by what right, can it command loyalty? If it is not the servant of Law, then it is nothing but a temporary convenience at best. At worst, it's raw force.

"And this is where we are today. Hans Molitor did his damnedest to restore the old institutions, which is why I did my damnedest for him. But we were too late. They'd been perverted too much for too long; too little faith in them remained. Now nobody can claim power by right—only by strength. Fear makes the rulers ever more oppressive, which provokes ever more unhappiness with them, which rouses dreams in the ambitious—"

He slapped the tabletop. "No, I do not like the tone of this conversation!" he exclaimed. "Can't we discuss something cheerful? Tell me about Ramnuan funeral customs."

She touched his hand. "Yes. Give me one word more, only one, and we'll see if we can't ease off. You're right, Dad never gave up hope. Have you, really?"

"Oh, no," he said with a smile and a dram of sincerity. "The sophont races will survive. In due course, they'll build fascinating new civilizations. Cultures of mixed species look especially promising. Consider Avalon already."

"I mean for us," she insisted. "Our children and grandchildren."

Do you still think of having children, Banner? "There too," Flandry told her. "That is, I'm not optimistic about this period we're in; but it can be made less terrible than it'd otherwise be. And that isn't so little, is it—buying years for billions of sentient beings, that they can live in? But it'll not be easy."

"Which is why you're bound where you are," she said low. Her eyes lingered upon him.

"And you, my dear. And good old Chives." He stubbed out his cigarette. "Now you've had your answer, such as it is, and I demand my turn. I want to discourse on anything else, preferably trivial. Or what say we play dance music and try a few steps? Else I'll grow downright eager to study onward about our destination."

Because of its gravity, which prevents the rise of very high lands, and because of the enormous outwelling of water from its interior, Ramnu has proportionately less dry surface than Terra. However, what it does have equals about 20 times the Terran, and some of the continents are Eurasia-sized. There are many islands.

Its surviving moons, what is left of them, are still of respectable mass: Diris, 1.69 Luna's; Tiglaia, 4.45; Elaveli, 6.86, comparable to Ganymede. But only the first is close enough to have a significant tidal effect, and that is small and moves creepingly. Niku's pull is slightly more. The oceans are less salty than Terra's, with far less in the way of currents.

The weakness of the tides is partially offset by the weight and speed of ocean waves. Winds, slow but ponderous, raise great rollers across those immensities, which reach shore with crushing power. Hence sea cliffs and fjords are rare. Coasts are usually jumbles of rock, or long beaches, or brackish marshes.

Mountains are farther apart on the average than on Terra, and the tallest stands a mere 1500 meters. (There the steep pressure gradient has reduced air pressure to one-fourth its sea-level value.) Elevated areas do tend to spread more widely than on Terra, because of heavier erosion carrying material down from the heights as well as because of stronger forces raising them. In the working of those forces, plumes are more important than plate movement. Thus much landscape consists of hills or of high plains, carved and scored by wind, water, frost, creep, and similar action of the planet. Volcanoes are abundant and, while uplands are rapidly worn away, elsewhere new ones are always being lifted.

Given the thick atmosphere, small Coriolis force, and comparatively low irradiation, cyclonic winds are weak and cyclonic storms very rare. The boiling point of water, about 241°C at sea level, also has a profound effect on meteorology. Moisture comes more commonly as mist than as rain or snow, making haziness normal. Once formed in the quickly thinning upper air, clouds tend to be long-lived and to make overcasts. Above them, the sky is often full of ice crystals. When precipitation does occur, it is apt to be violent, and to bring radical changes in the weather.

Atmospheric circulation is dominated by two basic motions. First is the flow of cold air from the poles toward the equator, forcing warmer air aloft and poleward—Hadley cells. Second is the horizontal flow engendered by the temperature differential between day and night sides. Consequently, tropical winds tend to blow against the sun; the winds of the temperate zones generally have an equatorward slant; and storms are everywhere frequent about dawn and sunset, this being when precipitation is likeliest. In higher latitudes, cold fronts often collide, with impressive results. As observed before, though winds are slow by Terran standards, *ceteris paribus*, they push hard.

Even during interglacial periods, the polar caps are extensive; having fallen there frozen, water does not readily rise again. Moreover, the circulation patterns of air and water combine with the slight axial tilt to make for much greater dependence of climate on latitude alone than is true of terrestroid worlds. Because of that same axial tilt, plus the nearly circular orbit, there are no real seasons on Ramnu. The basic cycle is not of the year but of the half-month-long day.

Across it strides another cycle, irregular, millennial, and vast— that of the glaciers. Given its overall chilliness, its extensive cloud decks, and its reluctance to let water evaporate, Ramnu is always close to the brink of an ice age, or else over it. No more is necessary than the upthrust of a new highland in a high latitude. Accompanied as it is by massive vulcanism, which fills the upper atmosphere with dust that will be decades in settling, this makes snow fall; and given the pressure gradient, the snow line is low. The ice spreads outward and outward, sometimes through a single hemisphere, sometimes through both. Nothing stops it but the subtropical belts. Nothing makes it retreat but the sinking of the upland that formed it.

For the past billion years or more, Ramnu had alternated between glacial and interglacial periods. The former usually prevailed longer. Humans arrived when the ice was again on the march. Now it was advancing at terrible speed, kilometers each year. Whole ecologies withered before it. Native cultures fled or crumbled—as how many times before in unrecorded ages?

Banner sought help for them. A starfaring civilization could readily provide that. Intensive studies would be needed at first, of course, followed by research and development, but the answer was simple in principle. Orbit giant solar mirrors in the right sizes and numbers and paths, equipped with sensors, computers, and regulators so that they would continuously adjust their orientations to the optimum for a given set of conditions. Have them send down the right amounts of extra warmth to properly chosen regions. That was all. The glaciers would crawl back to the poles where they belonged, and never return.

Banner sought help. The Grand Duke of Hermes placed himself squarely in her way. Flandry could guess why.

Hooligan contained a miniature gymnasium. Her captain and passenger took to using it daily after work, together. Then they would return to their cabins, wash, dress well, and meet for cocktails before dinner.

In a certain watch, about mid-passage, they were playing handball. The sphere sprang between them, caromed off bulkheads, whizzed through space, smacked against palms, flew opponentward followed and met by laughter. Bare feet knew the springiness of deck covering, the jubilation of upward flight. Sweat ran down skin and across lips with a rousing sting of salt. Lungs drew deep, hearts drummed, blood coursed.

She was ahead by a few points, but it hadn't been easy and she was not a bit sure it would last. Seventeen years made amazingly little difference. He was nearly as fast and enduring as a youth.

And nearly as slim and supple, she saw. Above and below his shorts, under smooth brown skin, muscles went surging, not heavy but long, lively, greyhound and race horse muscles. Wetness made him gleam. He grinned at her, flash after white flash in those features that time had not blurred, simply whetted. She realized he was enjoying the sight of her in turn, more than he was the game. The knowledge tingled.

He took the ball, whirled on his heel, and sped it aside. Before it had rebounded, he was running to intercept. She was too. They collided. In a ridiculous tangle of limbs, they fell.

He raised himself to his knees. "Banner, are you all right?" As she regained her breath, she heard anxiety in his tone. Looking up, she saw it in his face.

"Yes," she mumbled. "Just had the wind knocked out of me."

"Are you sure? I'm bloody sorry. Both my left feet must've been screwed on backwards this morning."

"Oh, not your fault, Dominic. Not any more than mine. I'm all right, really I am. Are you?" She sat up.

It brought them again in close contact, thighs, arms, a breast touching him. She felt his warmth and sweat through the halter. The clean man-smell enfolded her, entered her. Their lips were centimeters apart. *I'd better rise, fast,* she thought in a distant realm, but couldn't. Their eyes were holding too hard. As if of themselves, hers closed partway, while her mouth barely opened.

The kiss lasted for minutes of sweetness and lightning.

When he reached below the halter, alarm shrilled her awake. She disengaged her face and pushed at his chest. "No, Dominic," she heard herself say. It wavered. "No, please."

If he insists, she knew, *I won't.* And she did not know what she felt, or was supposed to feel, when he immediately let go.

He sprang to his feet and offered his assistance. They stood for a moment and looked. Finally he smiled in his wry fashion.

"I won't say I'm sorry, because I don't want to lie to you," he told her. "It was delightful. But I do beg your pardon."

She managed a shaken laugh. "I'm not sorry either, and no pardon is called for. We both did that."

"Then—" He half reached for her, before his arm dropped. "Have no fears," he said gently. "I can mind my manners. I've done it in the past . . . yes, right here."

How many women has he traveled with? How few have denied him?

If only I can make him understand. If only I do myself.

She knotted her fists, swallowed twice, and forced out: "Dominic, listen. You're a damned attractive man, and I'm no timid virgin. But I, I'm not wanton either."

"No," he said, with utmost gravity, "the daughter of Max and Marta wouldn't be. I forgot myself. It won't happen again."

"I told you, I forgot too!" she cried. "Or—well, I w-wish we knew each other better."

"I hope we will. As friends, whether or not you ever feel like more than that. Shake on it?"

Tears blurred the sight of him as they clasped hands. She blinked them off her lashes, vexedly. Too fast for her to stop it, her voice blurted, "Oh, hell, if I had a normal sex drive we'd be down on the deck yet!"

He cocked his head. "You mean you don't? I decline to believe that." In haste: "Not that it'd be any disgrace. Nobody is strong in every department, and no single department is at the core of life. But I think you're mistaken. The cause is easy to see."

She stared at her toes. "I've not had much to do . . . there . . . ever . . . nor missed it much."

"Same cause. You've been too thoroughly directed toward the nonhuman." He laid a hand on her shoulders. "That's not wrong. In many ways, it's wonderful. But it has given your emotions different expression from what's customary, and I think that in turn has made you a bit confused about them. Not to worry, dear."

All at once her face was buried against him, and he was holding her around the waist and stroking her hair and murmuring.

Presently she could stand back. "Would you like to talk about it?" he asked. With a disarming chuckle: "I'll bend a sympathetic ear, but it'll also be a fascinated one. What is it like, to share the life of an alien . . . to be an alien?"

"Oh, no, you exaggerate," she said. Relief billowed through her. *Yes, I do want to talk about what matters to me. I can't just go take a shower as if nothing had happened, I have to let out this fire. He's shown me I needn't be afraid to, because the talk needn't be about us.* "It's basically nothing but a wide-band communication link, you know."

(The collar that Yewwl wore was a piece of electronic sorcery. A television scanner saw in the same direction as her eyes. An audio pickup heard what she did. Thermocouples, vibrosensors, chemosensors analyzed their surroundings to get at least a clue to what she felt, smelled, tasted. The whole of the result became more than the sum of the parts, after it reached Banner.)

(It did that by radio, at the highest frequencies to which Ramnu's air was transparent. A well-shielded gram of radioisotope sufficed to power a signal that human-made comsats could detect and relay. A specialized computer in Wainwright Station received the signals and converted them back to sensory-like data. The ultimate translation, though, had to be by a human, brain and body alike, intellect, imagination, empathy developed through year after year. Seated beneath the helmet, before the video screen, hands flat on a pair of subtly vibrant plates, Banner could almost—almost—submerge herself in her oath-sister.)

(How she wished it could be a two-way joining. But save when they were together in the flesh, they could merely speak back and forth, via a bone-conduction unit. Nevertheless, they were oath-sisters in truth. They were!)

"It's not telepathy," she said. "The channel won't carry but a tiny fraction of the total information. Most of what I experience is actually my own intuition, filling in the gaps. I've spent my career training that intuition. I'm trying to discover how accurate it really is."

"I understand," Flandry replied. "And you aren't linked continuously, or even as much as half the day, as a rule, let alone your absences from the planet. Still, you've been very deeply involved with this being. Your chief purpose has been to learn how to feel and think like her, hasn't it? Without that, there can be no true comprehension. So of course you've been affected yourself, in the most profound way."

They sat down on the rubbery deck and leaned against the bulkhead, side by side. "And therefore I won't know you, Banner, before I know more about Yewwl," he said. "Will you tell me?"

"How?" she sighed. "There's too much. Where can I begin?"

"Wherever you like. I do have a fair stock of so-called objective facts to go on by now, remember. You've taken me well into the biology—"

Although the Ramnuan atmosphere resembles Terra's percentagewise, the proportions of the minor constituents vary. Notably, we find less water vapor most places, because of the pressure and temperatures; more nitrogen oxides, because of frequent and tremendous lightning flashes; more carbon dioxide, hydrogen sulfide, and sulfur oxides, because of vulcanism. These would not be what killed us, if we breathed the air directly; they would simply make it acrid and malodorous. What we would die of, pretty soon, would be oxygen and nitrogen. They are not present at concentrations which are intolerable for a limited span, but their pressure, under seven gravities, would force them into our lungs and bloodstreams faster than we can stand. Incidentally, that pull by itself forbids us to leave our home-conditioned base for any long while. Our cardiovascular system isn't built for it. Gravanol and tight skinsuits help, but the stress quickly becomes too much.

Just the same, Ramnuan life reminds us of our kind in many ways. It employs proteins in water solution, carbohydrates, lipids, and the rest. The chemical details vary enormously. For example, the amino acids are not all identical; since weather provides abundant nitrates, nitrogen-fixing microorganisms, while they do exist, are—like Terra's anaerobic bacteria—archaic forms of rather minor ecological significance; et cetera endlessly. In a broad sense, though, evolution has followed a similar course to ours. Here too it has founded a plant and an animal kingdom.

The critical secondary element is sulfur. It is so common in the environment, thanks to vulcanism, that biology has adopted it somewhat as Terran biology has adopted phosphorus. On Ramnu, sulfur is vital to several functions, including reproduction. It is usually taken up by plants as sulfate, or in the tissues which herbivores and carnivores eat. Where an area is deficient in it, life is sparse. Forest fires help, redistributing it in ash which the dense atmosphere disperses widely. Most important are certain microbes which can metabolize the pure element.

When it becomes freshly abundant, as around an active volcano, these organisms multiply until sheer numbers make them visible, a yellow smoke in air, a hue in water. Dying, they enrich the soil. This is the Golden Tide whose coming has brought fertility to land after land, whose dwindling has brought famine till populations died sufficiently back. The natives also transport sulfur, on a far smaller scale; their trade in it has conditioned their histories more than the salt trade has those of humans.

Given the oxygen concentration and the incidence of lightning, fires kindle easily and burn fiercely. Outside of wetlands, such a thing as a climax forest scarcely exists; woods burn down too often. Vegetation has made various adaptations to this, deep roots or bulbs, rapid reseeding, and the like. Most striking is that of the huge, diverse botanical family which we call pyrasphale. It synthesizes a silicon compound which makes it incombustible.

The pyrasphales have numerous analogies to the grasses of Terra or the yerbs of Hermes. They are comparative latecomers, that have taken over the larger part of most lands and proliferated into a bewildering variety of forms. Many do bear a superficial resemblance to this or that grass. Their appearance was doubtless responsible for a period of massive extinction about fifty million years ago; they crowded out older plants, and countless animals could not digest their fireproofing. Later herbivores have adjusted, either excreting it unchanged or breaking it down with the help of symbiotic microbes.

Pyrasphale has not displaced everything else. Where it reigns alone, that is apt to be by default. Ordinarily, a landscape covered by it has stands of trees, shrubs, thorn, or cane as well.

The animals of Ramnu exhibit their own abundant analogies to those of Terra, including two sexes, vertebrates and invertebrates, exothermic and endothermic metabolisms. The typical vertebrate has a head in front, with jaws, nose, two eyes, two ears; it bears four true limbs; commonly it sports a tail. But the differences exceed the likenesses.

Among the most obvious is the general smallness, under that gravity. Outside the seas, the very biggest creatures mass a couple of tonnes; and they inhabit regions of lake and swamp, where the water supports most of their weight as they browse around. A plain may teem with herds of assorted species, but nearly every one is dog-sized or less. An occasional horse-tall beast may loom majestic above them. It has a special feature, of which more later. Otherwise, at first it strikes a human odd to see a graviportal build on an animal no bigger than a collie. The gracile forms are tiny.

The long, cold nights set a premium on endothermy. Exotherms must find a place to sleep where they won't freeze (or, they hope, be dug up and eaten) or else start a new generation by sunset whose juvenile stage can survive. Plants have developed their own solutions to the same problem, including a family which secretes antifreeze and several families which make freezing a part of their life cycles.

An intermediate sort of animal has a high metabolism to keep warm at night but—outside the polar regions and highlands—must take shelter by day, lest it get too warm. Complete endothermy is harder to achieve than on Terra, since water evaporates reluctantly. The larger animals grow cooling surfaces such as big ears or dorsal fins.

Flyers face less difficulty in this regard, for their wings provide those surfaces; but it is worth noting that none have feathers. They are abundant on Ramnu, where the gravity is more or less offset by the thickness of the atmosphere. The swift drop of pressure with altitude does make most of them stay close to the ground. A few scavengers can soar high. Then there are the gliders; but of these, too, more later.

Among the land vertebrates, an order of viviparous endotherms exists which has no Terran parallel: the pleurochladoi. Between the fore- and hindlimbs, a pair of ribs has become the foundation, anchored to an elaborate scapular process, of two false limbs, which humans call extensors. It is thought that these lengths of muscle originated in a primitive, short-legged creature which thus found a way to hitch itself along a trifle faster. The development was so successful that descendants radiated into hundreds of kinds.

Extensors give added support; grasping, hauling, pushing, they give added locomotion. Hence they have enabled certain of their possessors to become as big as mustangs.

In quite a different direction, extensors produced the sub-order of gliding animals. These grew membranes from the forequarters to the tips of the extensors, and from the tips to the hindquarters. The membranes doubtless began as a cooling device, which they remain, but they have elaborated into airfoils—vanes. Such a beast can fold them and run around freely. Or it can stiffen the extensors, thereby spreading the vanes, and glide down from a height. Given favorable currents, it can go astonishingly far in the dense air, or perform extraordinary maneuvers. Thereby it gets fruit, prey, escape from enemies, easy transportation.

Most gliders are bat-sized, but a few have become larger, and a few of these have become bipedal. Among them are the sophonts.

Red-gold, Niku waxed bright among the stars. In less than a day, it would be the sun.

Flandry saw how Banner's glance kept straying to its image in the screen. This was to have been a happy evenwatch, the last peaceful span they would know for a time they did not know—perhaps an eternity. Garbed in the finest they had along, they sipped their drinks in between dances until Chives set forth the best dinner he was capable of. Afterward Flandry had him join them in a valedictory glass, but the batman said goodnight as soon as that was done. Now—

Cognac was mellow on the tongue, fragrant in the nostrils, ardent along the throat and in the blood. Flandry didn't smoke while he savored stuff as lordly as this. He did make it an obbligato to the sight and nearness of Banner. They were side by side; when she looked ahead, into the stars, he saw the proud profile. Tonight a silver circlet harnessed the tide of her mane. The hair flowed lustrous brown, touched by minute, endearing streaks of white. A bracelet Yewwl had given her, raw gemstones set in bronze, would have been barbarically massive on her left wrist, save that the casting was exquisite. She wore a deep-blue velvyl gown, long, low-cut, and though her bosom was small, the curve of it up toward her throat made him remember Botticelli.

He was not in love with her, nor—he supposed—she with him, except to the gentle degree that was only natural and that, in ordinary life, would only have added piquancy to friendship. He did find her attractive, and thought the cosmos of her as a person, in her own right, not merely because she was daughter to Max Abrams. So much had he come to respect her on this voyage that he no longer felt guilty about having brought her.

Soft in the background, music played as it had done for forty generations before theirs, the New World Symphony.

Abruptly she turned face and body about, toward him. The green eyes widened. "Dominic," she asked, "why are you here?"

"Huh?" he responded inelegantly. *Don't let her get too serious. Help her stay happy.* "Well, that depends on your exact meaning of the word 'why.' In an empirical sense, I am here because sixty-odd years ago, an operatic diva had an affair with a space captain. In the higher or philosophical sense—"

She interrupted by laying a hand over his. "Please don't clown. I want to understand." She sighed. "Though maybe you won't want to tell me. Then I won't insist; but I hope you will."

He surrendered. "What is it you'd like to know?"

"Why you are here—bound for Ramnu instead of Hermes." Quickly: "I know you had to investigate what Cairncross is hiding. If he really does plan a coup—"

Yes, I do believe that's his aim. What else? As Grand Duke, he's gone as far as he can, and he's known to be a man of vaulting ambition. He's popular among his people, and they are resentful of the Imperium; it'd be no trick to quietly collect personnel for the illicit preparation of war materiel, and he controls plenty of places where the work can go on in secret—Babur, Ramnu—When he's ready, when he announces his intention, men will flock to his standard. It won't take any enormous striking force if the operation is well organized. He can exploit surprise, punch through, kill Gerhart, and proclaim himself Emperor. When Terra lies hostage to his missiles, he won't be directly attacked.

Fighting will occur elsewhere, no doubt, but it will be between those who'll want to accept him and those who'll not. Many will. Gerhart is not beloved. Cairncross can set forth the claim that he is righting grievous wrongs and intends to right others; that in this dangerous era, the Empire needs the leader of greatest, proven ability; even that he has a dash of Argolid in his ancestry. A lot of Navy officers will feel they should go along with him simply to end the strife before it ruins too much, and because he is now the alternative to a throne back up for grabs. Others, as his cause gathers momentum, will deem it prudent to join. Yes, Edwin has a good chance of pulling it off, amply good for a warrior born.

"—though things you've said about the Emperor do make me wonder if you care what happens to him," Banner stumbled onward.

Flandry scowled. "I don't, *per se.* However, he isn't intolerably bad; in fact, he shows reasonable intelligence and restraint. Besides, well, he is a son of Hans, and I rather liked that old bastard. But mainly, we can't afford a new civil war, and anybody who'd start one is a monster."

Her fingers tightened across his. "You talked about buying years for people to live in."

He nodded. "I'm no sentimentalist, but I've witnessed wars. I don't relish the idea of sentient beings with their skins burnt off and their eyeballs melted, but not yet able to die." He stopped. "Sorry. That's not nice dinner table conversation."

She gave him a faint smile. "No, but I'm not a perfectly nice person myself. All right, agreed, this has to be prevented. Before it's too late, you have to find out if a coup is in the works, and in that case get proof that'll make the Navy act. You think probably there's evidence in the Nikuan System. But why are you going to collect it yourself? Wouldn't it be wiser to proceed to Hermes and potter around, being harmless? Meanwhile I could accompany men of yours to Ramnu and they'd do the job."

Flandry shook his head. "I considered that, obviously," he replied; "but I've told you before, I'm afraid Cairncross is almost ready to strike. I dare not be leisurely."

"Still, you could have covered your ass, couldn't you?"

He blinked, then laughed. "Perhaps. Though on Hermes I'd be at Cairncross' mercy, you realize."

"But you could have made an excuse to stay home, and dispatched a crew in secret," she persisted. "Feigned illness or whatnot. You're too clever for anybody to make you go where you don't want to."

"You're trying to flatter me," he said. "You're succeeding. As a matter of fact, with my usual humility I admit that you've pointed to the real reason. I've trained several excellent people, but none are quite as clever as me. None would have quite the probability of success that I do." He preened his mustache. "Also, to be honest, I confess I was getting bored. I was much overdue for raising a bit of hell."

Still her eyes would not release him. "Is that the whole truth, Dominic?"

He shrugged. "In a well-known phrase from an earlier empire, what is truth?"

Her tone shivered. "I think your underlying reason is this. The mission is dangerous. Failure means a terrible punishment for whoever went and got caught afterward. The fact that he went under your orders wouldn't save him from the wrath of a Grand Duke whose 'insulted honor' the Imperium would find it politic to avenge." She drew breath. "Dominic, you served under my father, and he was an officer of the old school. An officer does not send men to do anything he would not do himself. Isn't that it, dear?"

"Oh, I suppose a bit of it is," he grumbled.

Her glance dropped. How long the lashes lay, above those finely carven cheekbones. He saw the blood rise in face and bosom. "I felt sure, but I wanted to hear it from you," she whispered. "We've got plenty of noble titles around these days, but damn few noble spirits."

"Oh, hai, hai," he protested. "You know better. I lie, I steal, I cheat, I kill, I fornicate and commit adultery, I use shocking language, I covet, and once I had occasion to make a graven image. Now can we relax and enjoy our evening?"

She raised her countenance to his. Her smile brightened. "Oh, yes," she said. "Why, in your company I'd expect to enjoy exile."

They had talked about that, what to do if the mission failed but they survived. A court martial would find him guilty of worse than insubordination; defiance of a direct Imperial command was treason. She was an accomplice. The maximum penalty was death, but Flandry feared they would get the "lighter" sentence of life enslavement. He didn't propose to risk that. He'd steer for a remote planet where he could assume a new identity, unless he decided to seek asylum in the Domain of Ythri or collect a shipful of kindred souls and fare off into the altogether unknown.

Banner had agreed, in pain. She had far more to lose than he did, a mother, a brother and sister and their families, Yewwl and her lifework.

Has she found hope, now, beyond the wreckage of hope? His heart sprang for joy.

She leaned close. Her blush had faded to a glow, her look and voice were steady. "Dominic, dear," she said, "ever since that hour in the gym, you've been the perfect knight. It isn't necessary any longer."

✿ VII ✿

Ramnu swelled steadily in the forward screen, until it owned the sky and its dayside radiance drowned stars out of vision. The colors were mostly white upon azure, like Terra's, though a golden tinge lay across them in this weaker, mellower sunlight. Cloud patterns were not the same, but wider spread and more in the form of bands, spots, and sheets than of swirls; surface features were hidden from space, save as vague shadowiness here and there. The night side glimmered ghostly under moonlight and starlight. Brief, tiny fire-streaks near the terminator betokened monstrous lightning strokes. Brought into being by a magnetic field less than Jovian but stronger than Terran, auroras shook their flags for an incoming man to see above polar darkness.

Flandry sat at the pilot console. *Hooligan* continued doing the basic navigation and steering herself, but he wanted his hand and judgment upon her, that he might arrive in secret. Besides, he meant to use the instruments in the control section to study the moons and any possible traffic in the system.

He passed close enough by Diris, the innermost, that he could make out Port Lulang, the scientific base. It was a huddle of domes, hemicylinders, masts, dishes, beside a spacefield, in the middle of a large, symmetrical formation oddly like Sullivan's Hoofprint on Io; little that was Cynthian remained except the name. Otherwise the satellite was nearly featureless. Once it had exceeded his mother world in size; but the supernova whiffed away everything above its metallic core. Probably naught whatsoever would have survived, had not the shrunken bulk of Ramnu given some shielding. As the melted ball cooled to solidity, no asteroids or meteoroids smote to crater it. Those had been turned into gas, and dissipated with the rest of the nebula among the stars.

Tiglaia showed a measure of ruggedness; it had kept the mass to generate orogenic forces. Elaveli, outermost and largest, bore mountains, sharp-edged as when first they were uplifted.

Flandry probed toward the latter, but got no sight of Port Asmundsen, the industrial base there. He wasn't observing from the proper angle, and dared not accelerate into a different course lest he be noticed. If his idea about Cairncross was right, these days the expanded facilities included warcraft. Anyway, Banner had confirmed that nothing unusual was apparent from outside. Whatever evil was hatching did so under camouflage or in man-made caverns. Neutrino detectors spoke of substantial nuclear powerplants. *Yes, they impress me as being rather more than required by mining operations. Having an exposed planetary core makes the enterprise worthwhile for Hermes—but scarcely this profitable, when the same metals are available closer to home.*

As for Dukeston—his look strayed back to Ramnu. The commercial base on the planet had likewise been a minor thing, until lately. A sulfur-rich marshland produced certain biologicals, notably a finegrained hardwood and the antibiotic oricin, effective against the Hermetian disease cuprodermy. They were barely cheaper to obtain here and to ship back than to synthesize. They might not have been were not the nearby Chromatic Hills a well-endowed source of palladium and other minerals.

Why had Dukeston, too, seen considerable recent growth? And why had it, too, become hard to enter and to deal with? True, it and Wainwright Station were separated by five thousand kilometers of continent. A parameter in choosing the site for it had been the desire that its cultural influence reach only the natives in its vicinity, not those whom the xenologists made their principal subjects of study. Nevertheless, people used to flit freely back and forth, often just to visit. General Enterprises used to be generous in supplying the Ramnu Research Foundation with help, equipment, materials.

But under the present director, Nigel Broderick—Well, he explained the niggardliness and the infrequency of contact by declaring that the expansion itself, under adverse conditions, took virtually all the resources at his beck. The undertaking was a part of great Duke Edwin's far-sighted plan for restoring the glory and prosperity of Hermes. His Grace had ordered stringent security measures against the possibility of sabotage, in these uneasy times. No exceptions could be made, since a naive scientist might innocently pass information to the wrong persons. If this attitude seemed exaggerated, that was because you did not know the ramifications of the whole situation. His Grace alone did that, and ours was not to question him.

Which I aim to do, if time and chance allow, Flandry thought. *Oh, I am a bad, rebellious boy, I am. I actually nurture a few doubts about the wisdom and benevolence of statesmen.*

Hooligan set down with admirable smoothness, considering. For a few minutes Flandry was addressing the hastily summoned ground control officer. (He was a young fellow named Ivan Polevoy, whose primary job was electronician.) The station spacecraft occupied the sole proper connection to the interior which the minuscule field possessed. It would be necessary to send a car for the newcomers.

Having spoken his thanks and requested that no word of this go out— "Dr. Abrams will tell you why, in due course"—Flandry made his routine check of guardian devices: irrespective of the fact that Chives would stay aboard till it was certain that no backup would be needed. Meanwhile his glance roved around outside. Port Wainwright consisted of several conjoined buildings, whose low profiles and deep foundations were designed for this world. A pole displayed a flag of gaudy, fluorescent stripes. Beyond, the landscape reached tremendous.

Niku stood at early afternoon, ruddy-aureate in an opalescent heaven; its light suffused the hazy air in a way to remind of autumn on Terra. Nothing else was like home. Broad, gray-green, a river flowed past more swiftly than it should, casting spray that lingered shining above rocks and current-whirls. The woods on the opposite shore were not dense, though they stretched out of sight. Squat brown boles sprouted withy-like branches with outsize leaves of cupped form and hues of dark olive, amber, or russet. A slow, heavy breeze sent the stalks rippling about and stirred the underbrush.

On this bank and eastward was open country, a plain dominated by pyrasphale. Most of that resembled tall grass wherein the wind roused waves. Its dull tawniness was relieved in place by stands of trees or canes, by white plumes and vivid blossoms. He couldn't see through mistiness to the remote horizon, but he made out a kopje in that direction; and northward, a darkening must be mountains, for a volcano sent smoke aloft from there. The pillar of black widened quickly, to form a mushroom shape whose top drifted away like fog.

Leathery wings cruised low overhead, big in proportion to the bodies they upheld. He knew that herds of animals were out in the pyrasphale, but it hid their low shapes from him. A family of giants loomed above, not far off, grazing with the calm of creatures which had no natural enemies. Humans refrained from hunting near the station, and no native Ramnuans were around at the moment.

He watched the beasts interestedly, for he recognized them as wild onsars. Domesticated, the onsar was the foundation of sophont life over much of the world. It was more than a carrier of riders and burdens; it was a platform from which a hunter could see quarry afar, and then launch himself on a long glide. Before they had that help, the Ramnuans were mostly confined to the forests and the hilliest parts of this planet, whose land surface consisted largely of savannah, pampa, prairie, veldt, and steppe.

An onsar stood big enough for a man to mount, if he wouldn't mind his feet dangling close to the ground. Its build was vaguely suggestive of a rhinoceros, given a high hump at the forequarters and a high black triangle of dorsal fin on the after half of the back. The skin was gray, sparsely brown-haired save on the big-eared, curve-muzzled head, where it grew thicker. Most conspicuous to Flandry were the extensors. They seemed akin to a pair of elephants' trunks, sprouting from muscular masses behind the hump, but they terminated in pads and clawed, prehensile tendrils.

"Excuse me, sir," Chives reminded from the entrance.

Flandry realized that a sealed car was on its way toward *Hooligan.* Shaking himself, he hurried to join Banner. She waited at the main personnel airlock. "Welcome home," he said.

"Welcome to my home, Dominic," she answered softly. They exchanged a kiss.

The car halted alongside and extended a gang tube from its metal shell. When that had snugly fitted itself around the lock, Banner valved through. Flandry followed. He had done this kind of thing before, but each planet was a special case requiring special configurations of equipment, and he was glad to let her coach him. Safety harness—careful positioning on the conveyor belt—when inside the chassis, doubly careful crawling into a seat, and grateful relaxation as it reclined—the vehicle had no grav generators, and for this short a trip it carried no drugs or body supports. Seven-plus times his normal weight dragged at Flandry like a troll. Breath strained, heart slugged, every movement was leaden, he felt his cheeks sag downward and avoided looking at the woman; consciousness began to blur at the edges.

The robopilot disengaged, retracted the tube, drove rapidly over the ferrocrete. It cycled through into the garage pretty fast, too, and blessed lightness returned.

Banner scrambled forth. A gaunt, middle-aged man stood waiting. "How did your mission go?" he asked immediately, anxiously. Long-term personnel here were devoted folk.

"That's quite a story," she told him in a clipped voice. "Admiral Sir Dominic Flandry, I'd like you to meet Huang Shao-Yi, our deputy director and one blaze of a good linguist."

"An honor, sir."—"The honor is mine, Dr. Huang."

"What's been happening?" burst from Banner.

Huang shrugged. "Little out of the ordinary. Yewwl allowed us at last to bring her back. I believe she's presently in the Lake Roah neighborhood, and is recovering well from her loss."

Banner nodded. "She would. She doesn't surrender. I want to get in touch at once."

"But—" Huang said at her retreating form. "But you've just arrived, you must be tired, we want to receive you properly, and our distinguished guest—"

"Your distinguished guest is in an ant-bitten hurry himself," Flandry said, and followed Banner. Huang stayed behind. He had learned the ways of his chief.

Striding through rooms and passages, Flandry saw how the station had gone shabby-comfortable during centuries of use. Murals by amateurs brightened walls; planters held beds of flowers and fresh vegetables; playback simulated windows opening on a dozen distant worlds. The hour chanced to be late on human clocks, and most people were in the recreation facilities or their private apartments. What few were not and encountered Banner greeted her with pleasure. She might be on the austere and reticent side, Flandry thought, but she was well-liked, and that was well-deserved.

She entered her centrum. He saw how she trembled as she sat down amidst the instruments which bristled about her chair. He stroked her head. She gave him an absent-minded smile and set about lowering the helmet. He stepped back.

She grew busy making adjustments. Meters flickered, telltales blinked in the dimness of the chamber. It was quiet here; only a murmur of the thick breeze outside penetrated. At present, in its variant pattern, station air was cool, moist, bearing a smell of Terran seas.

The screen before Banner flickered to life. Flandry could see it over her shoulder if he leaned down and forward. She laid her palms on two plates in the arms of her chair. What sensations came to her from them, she would interpret as perceptions of the world beyond these walls. She had told him that by now they seemed almost like the real thing.

"Yewwl," she called low, and added words in a purring, ofttimes mewing or snarling language unknown to him. A vocalizer circuit transformed them into sounds that were clear to a Ramnuan, whose mouth and throat were not made like hers. "Ee-yah, Yewwl."

Flandry must content himself with what was in the screen. That was remarkably clear, given the handicaps under which the system labored. Colors, perspectives, contours did appear subtly strange, until he remembered that the apparatus tried to duplicate what alien eyes saw, as they did.

A hand lifted into sight—Yewwl's, perhaps raised in surprise when the message came. It was probably the most humanoid thing about her, the thumb and four fingers laid out very similarly to his. They were short, though, their nails were sharp and yellow, the entire hand was densely muscular, and tan fur covered it.

She was indoors, doubtless in a ranch house belonging to a family of her clan. Furnishing was simple but handsome. On a couch in view sat a pair of natives who must be kinfolk, male and female. No matter how many pictures he had studied while traveling, Flandry focused his whole attention on them.

They were both bipeds who would stand slightly over a meter. Extreme stockiness might have seemed grotesque, were it not clear that their build was what enabled them to move gracefully. The feet were four-toed, clawed, big even in proportion. The lower torso was nearly rigid for support, the high pelvic girdle making it impossible to bend over—not a good idea on Ramnu anyhow—and requiring them to squat instead. This also forced the young to be born tiny, after a short gestation; male and female both had pouches on the belly to protect an infant till it had developed further. These and the genitalia did not come to Flandry's vision, for the beings happened to be dressed in garments vaguely resembling hospital gowns, decking the front, the most convenient if you had vanes in back. Fur grew everywhere, save for footsoles and the insides of the hands.

The head was round. Its face could be called either blunt-muzzled or platyrrhine and prognathous; the jaw was heavy and had a chin, the brow swelled lofty. The mouth was wide, thin-lipped for the sucking of blood and juices and for the feeding of infants; yellow fangs bespoke a carnivore, though not an obligate one. The ears sat far up, pointed and mobile. The eyes were beautiful—big, golden, variable of pupils, adaptable to night. The whole countenance made Flandry recall, the least bit, a Terran lynx.

From the back, under the shoulders, sprang the extensors. The female had brought hers around in front, making a sort of cloak; perhaps she was cold, in this gathering ice age. The male had spread his when reacting to Banner, as if readying for a glide. From behind his neck, the membranes of the vanes stretched thinly furred, nearly a meter on either side, to the ends of the extensors: thence downward, semicircularly, to the buttocks. Flandry knew they were attached along the entire back, above the spine. They were no simple flaps of skin, they were muscular tissue, heavily vascularized, their nerve endings providing a great deal of sensory input, their complex ripplings and attitudes providing a body language that humans would never really be able to interpret.

As Flandry watched, the male relaxed, lowered his extensors till the vanes hung in folds behind him, and settled himself alertly. Belike Yewwl had told her companions what was occurring.

Flandry stole a look at Banner's face. It was intent with the desperation of this hour, but it was likewise rapt; she had gone beyond him. She barely whispered what she said. When she stopped to listen, she alone heard.

The view in the screen shifted jerkily, then changed, changed, changed. Yewwl had jumped to her feet, was pacing—might be cursing or yelling, for all he could tell. The message she got had carried a shock.

Flandry and Banner had planned it together, but today he must merely guess how matters went. What she was asking was fearsome.

In the end, when she had blanked the screen and disconnected herself, she slumped, eyes closed, breathing hard, shivering. Sweat stood forth on a pale visage.

Flandry cupped her cheeks between his hands. "How are you?" he asked, half afraid.

The green gaze opened as she tilted her head back. "Oh, I'm all right," she said faintly.

"She—will she—"

The woman nodded. "Yes. She doesn't understand much of what it's about. How could she? But if nothing else, out of loyalty, she'll believe her oath-sister, that this has to be done before her country can be saved." A sigh. "May that be true."

He would have tried to comfort her, but time lashed him. "Shall we have her flitted to Mount Gungnor?"

"No." Banner's self-possession returned fast. She straightened; her tone briskened. "No point in that. In fact, it'd be counterproductive. Best she proceed overland, sending messengers out on either side to ask other leaders if they'll meet her along the way. She has to persuade them to go along with the idea, you see, and with her in person. Else she'd be a single individual arriving at the Volcano, who could speak for her immediate family at best. Whereas, leading a delegation from what amounts to the whole of Kulembarach, and maybe a couple of neighbors' clans as well—do you see?"

Flandry frowned. "How long will this take?"

"M-m. . . . Three or four Terran days, I'd guess. She's fairly close to the mountain, and Ramnuans can travel fast when they want to."

Flandry clicked his tongue. "You're cutting it molecular fine. The Duke can't be much further behind us than that. Allowing a short while for him to decide on Hermes what to do, and getting an expedition here from there—"

"It can't be helped, dear." Banner rose. "I'll monitor Yewwl closely, of course, and urge her to keep moving. Furthermore, you know some of my younger colleagues have links like mine, to different individuals, through a wide territory. None are anything like as close as this relationship; but we can make contact, we can request them to pass the word on and to rendezvous with Yewwl if possible. We can scarcely explain why, either to those colleagues or their subjects. But I think several will oblige, out of curiosity and friendship. That should help."

"Well, you're the expert," he said reluctantly. "As for myself meanwhile, I'm a master of the science and art of heelcooling."

She chuckled. "You'll be busy aplenty if I know you, studying maps and data banks, talking to people, laying contingency plans. And . . . we do want some time in between for ourselves, don't we?"

He laughed and caught her to him. Last night-watch had not been spectacular, but in its manyfold ways it had been good, as liking deepened with intimacy. He was a little old for the spectacular, anyway.

✧ VIII ✧

Yewwl fared north from the house by Lake Roah in company, as befitted a ranking matron of the clan on her way to meet with her peers on the Volcano. She and certain of her retainers had been visiting her oldest son—he and his sister her last surviving children—and his family; they had discussed combining their ranches, now that her husband and youngsters were gone. He rode off at her side, followed by half a dozen of his own hands. His wife would manage the place in his absence . . . perhaps better than in his presence, Yewwl thought tartly, for Skogda was an over-impulsive sort.

Before leaving, they dispatched couriers to homesteads that were not too far off. These went afoot, or aglide when possible, faster than onsars. Yewwl's party was mounted, since there was no point in arriving ahead of a quorum. Besides, it suited her dignity and she would need that at her goal, antagonistic to her as many of the Seekers were. Her route she laid out to pass by some more households, where she requested the heads to come along. All did. These stops were brief, and otherwise they made none, so progress was rapid. Eventually folk and onsars would have to sleep, but they could keep moving without rest for most of a day or night, and often did.

Thus Yewwl came to the Volcano, in the ancient manner of her people. The Kulembarach *dzai'h'ü*—"clan," humans called it, for lack of a better word that they could pronounce—was showing by the number of its representatives present that most of it would support her, once news of her intent had spread throughout the territory. That was to be expected. Not only were its members her kin, in various degrees; she took a foremost role, her opinions carried weight, in the yearly moot, when leaders of households gathered to discuss matters of mutual concern (and to trade, gossip, arrange marriages and private ventures, play games, revel, make Oneness). Moreover, two from different territories, Arachan and Raava, had joined the group.

This was important. The Lord of the Volcano could not act on behalf of the clans together, when just a single one had speakers present. But if Zh of Arachan and Ngaru of Raava raised no objection, he could, if he saw fit, accede to the wish of Kulembarach—in a matter like this, which presumably would involve no major commitment of everybody else.

Hard though the band traveled, day was drawing to an end when they reached the mountain. From the trail which wound up its flank, Yewwl saw far across the plain beneath, aglow in long red sun-rays. Clouds, banked murky toward the northeast, told of a storm that would arrive with the early dusk . . . but by then, she remembered, or soon after, she would be on the distant side of it, in lands where full night would have fallen . . . if she could carry out this first part of Banner's enigmatic plan. . . .

Cold streamed downward from the snows which covered the upper half of Mount Gungnor, and which yearly lay thicker. Moltenness laired underneath; steam from fumaroles blew startlingly white against yellow evening overcast and black smoke from the crater. A stream flowed out of a place where melt water had formed a spring. It cascaded down the slopes in noise and spray. The Golden Tide colored it, and drifted in streamers on muttering breezes. Yewwl could smell and taste the pungency of the life-bestower on every breath; what weariness was in her dropped away.

Because of that potent substance, the lower sides of the mountain were not bare. Their darkness was crusted with color, tiny plants that etched a root-hold for themselves in the rock, and above them buzzed equally minute flying things, whose wings glittered. Yet those had become few, and Yewwl saw more brown patches, frost-killed, across the reaches than there had been when last she was here. Rounding a shoulder that had barred her view northward, she saw the Guardian range rearing over the horizon, and it shimmered blue with the Ice.

The same curve in the trail brought her out onto a plateau which jutted ledge-like from the steeps. This was her goal. A turf of low nullfire, lately gone sere, decked the top of it; hoofbeats, which had rung on the way up, now padded. Boldly near the precipice edge reared the hall that the clans had raised for the Lords of the Volcano to inhabit, in that wonderful age when the land suddenly redoubled its fertility and folk grew in number until they needed more than their kin-moots to maintain law. The building was of stone, long and broad, shale-roofed. Flanking the main door were six weather-worn statues, the Forebears of each clan. A seventh, spear in hand, faced outward at the end of the rows. It stood for the chosen family, bred out of all the clans, from which the successive Lords were elected. It stood armed, peering over the cliff, as though to keep ward against those little-known people, beyond the territories, whose ways were not the ways of the clans.

The Lord and his household lived by hunting, not ranching: for the country around the foot of the mountain was of course incredibly rich, or had been. However, just as had happened elsewhere, a small settlement of sedentary artisans had grown up. From one of the half-timbered cottages clustered nearby, Yewwl heard the clamor of iron being forged; from another came the hum of a loom-wheel; from a third drifted the acrid odors of tanning leather. These died out as persons grew aware of visitors and emerged to see.

Ere long someone also left a building which stood by itself at the far end of the plateau. It was oldest by centuries, much like the hall but the stone of it made smooth-edged, the carvings blurred, by untold rains, gritty winds, acid fumes—even in this thin air. Changeless, a great, faceted crystal caught the light where it was inset above the entrance. It proclaimed this a sanctuary of the College. Here, as in houses they owned elsewhere, the Seekers of Wisdom kept books, instruments, ceremonial gear, mysteries.

At first, those who stepped out, male and female, were those who lived there, together with their children. They numbered ten adults. Half were young, initiates studying for higher orders, meanwhile acting as caretakers, copyists, handlers of routine College business. The rest were aging; they lacked the gifts needed to attain an upper degree, and were resigned to that. Yewwl had no quarrel with any of these; in truth, she seldom encountered them.

But then a different figure trod from inside, male, clad throat to feet in a white apron, bearing a gilt harp under his left arm and a bronze chaplet on his brows. Across a kilometer, Yewwl knew him. Her vanes snapped wide. She bristled. A hiss went between her fangs.

Skogda brushed a vane of his across hers. The play beneath the skin said: *I am with you, Mother, whatever may happen. What alarms you?*

"Erannda," she told him, and pointed her ears at the senior Seeker. "Ill luck that he's not exacting hospitality from a homestead afar." She willed the tension out of her muscles. "I'll not let him check me. He'll try, but he can't sing away the truth."

Inwardly, she wondered: *Truth? I dare not speak truth myself, what little of it I grasp. To hear the real purpose of my mission would bewilder them utterly. The Lord would refuse to act, in a matter so weird and dangerous, without first holding a full assembly of clan-heads; and most of my own following would agree he was right.*

By law and custom he would be, too. (Maybe the most baffling and disturbing thing about the star-folk is the way they submit their wills, their fates, to the will of others, whom they may never even have met. That is, if I have discerned what Banner has tried over the years to explain to me. Sometimes I have hoped I am mistaken about this.)

But by the time a full assembly can be gathered, it would be too late. Banner said we likeliest have less than a day to do what must be done . . . whatever that is, beyond my part in it. Else a wrong will happen, and the star-folk will not be able to drive the Ice back.

I do not understand, really. I can only keep faith with my oath-sister, who has asked for my help.

But Banner, will you help me in turn? I'll need you to strengthen my wits against Erannda's. Banner, send your voice back into my head. Soon. Please.

Meanwhile, she would not quail. "Come!" she cried, and her body added: *Come in style!* She straightened to present her jeweled leather breastplate. She displayed her vanes at full. She drew her knife and held the blade on high. Her foot-claws pricked the extensors of her onsar, and the gait of the beast became a rapid swing. Behind her, drawing haughtiness from her, thundered two score of householders and retainers.

The cottage dwellers stood humbly aside. Useful though they were, their sort could not claim the respect due a hunter, herder, or Seeker; for they did not kill their own food, nor did they range freely about.

Yewwl's band drew rein outside the hall. Skogda winded the horn that announced their coming. Echoes flew shrill through the evening. It would have been improper for the Lord of the Volcano to come forth, as if out of curiosity, before he got such a call. Now he did. A scarlet cloth, wrapped around brow and neck, streamed down his front to the ground. He carried a spear, which he gravely dipped and left thrust in the turf, a sign of welcome.

His family and servants were at his back, less impressive. They were not numerous, either, for none but he, his wife, and their offspring dwelt here, together with servants. The rest of his kin were below the mountain, save for those who had chosen to join the College or to be adopted into a clan. They were the people from whom an assembly would choose his successor, after his death.

Yewwl thought the last election could well have gone differently. Wion was not the keenest-minded person alive. He did get good advice from his wife, better than from the College which was supposed to supply him with councillors. She was a female of Arrohdzaroch. But she could not sit beside him at the meeting. The ancestors had decided that the Lord of the Volcano must always be male, to counterbalance the preponderance of females who took the initiative in household and clan affairs.

Erannda was approaching. Yewwl dismounted. "May you ever be swift in the chase," she greeted Wion formally. "We are come on behalf of many more, to lay for them and ourselves a demand upon your stewardship."

Oil lamps brightened the meeting room in the hall, bringing frescos to vivid life. An iron stove at either end held outside chill at bay. Lamps, stoves, maps, medicines, windmills, printing, water-powered machinery . . . above all, knowledge of this world and its universe, and an eagerness to learn more . . . how much had the star-folk given!

Else the chamber was not changed from of old, nor were the procedures. Wion sat on a dais between carven beasts, confronting two rows of tiered benches for the visitors. Whoever would speak raised an arm, was recognized by the Lord of the Volcano, and stepped or glided down to stand before him. This being much less than a full assembly, everyone was close in and matters went faster than usual.

Yewwl addressed them: "I need not relate how cold, hunger, and suffering range across our country in advance of the Ice, and how these can but worsen, and most of us die, as it moves onward. We have talked of what we might do. Some would flee south, some would stay and become hunters entirely, some have still other ideas in pouch. But any such action will cost us heavily at best. Have we no better hope?

"You know what the star-folk have taught us. You know they have always held, in the House of the Banner, that they will not give us what we cannot learn to make for ourselves, lest we become dependent on it and then one day they must leave us. What we have gotten from them has led us to progress of our own, slower than we might like but firmly rooted and ever growing. Think of better steel than aforetime, or glassmaking, or painkillers and deep surgery, or postal couriers, or what else you will. Yet it is no longer enough, when the Ice is coming. Unaided, we will lose it all; our descendants will forget.

"You know, too, that I am intimate with the chieftain of the star-folk, Banner herself." *Oath-sister, where are you? You promised you would join me.* "You know I have asked her for their help, and she has told me this lies not within her power. But she has told me further, of late, that perhaps help may be gotten elsewhere."

Wion stiffened on his seat. The Seekers present remained impassive as was their wont, save for Erannda, who half spread his vanes and crooked his fingers as if to attack.

"You wonder how this may be," Yewwl continued. "It—" She broke off. The voice was in her.

"Yewwl, are you awake? Do you want me? Good. . . . Oh, has your meeting begun already? I'm sorry. I didn't think you'd arrive so fast, and—" a hesitation; a shyness?— "private matters engaged me more than they should have. How are you faring? What can I do?"

Wion leaned forward. "Is aught amiss, clan-head?" he asked. Eyes stared from the benches.

"No. I, I pause to gather words," Yewwl said. "I wish to put things as briefly as may be, lest we wrangle till nightfall."

—"Don't you want them to know I'm listening?" Banner asked.

—"No, best not, I believe," Yewwl replied in her hidden speech. "Erannda is here, by vile luck. You've seen how he hates your kind. Give him no arrows for his quiver."

There flashed through her: *Once the Seekers of Wisdom alone possessed the high knowledge, arcane mysteries, healing, poetry, music, history. Traveling from stead to stead, they were the carriers of news and of lore about distant places. They counselled, mediated, consoled, heartened, chastised, taught, set a lofty example. Yes, our ancestors did right to hold them in awe.*

That is gone. Respect remains, unless among the most impatient of the young. The Seekers still do good. They could do more. But for that, they must change, as the rest of us have changed, because of the star-folk. Some of the Seekers are willing. Others are not. Erannda leads that faction; and many in the clans still heed him.

She hastened to inform Banner of what had happened thus far: fortunately, very little. The unseen presence fell silent, and Yewwl resumed speaking:

"You may or may not be aware that the star-folk maintain a second outpost." *And outposts on two moons, but best not remind them of that. Erannda calls it a defilement.* "It is no secret; sometimes people have come here from there. However, yon settlement has had nothing to do with us, since it lies far off, beyond the territories and what we know of the wilderness. Thus we have had no cause to think about it.

"I have newly learned that it is not like the House of the Banner. It is larger, stronger, and its purpose is not simply to gather knowledge, but to maintain industries. Furthermore, its chiefs have more freedom of decision. As near as I have learned"—*which is not near at all, for I cannot understand; but my oath-sister would not lie to me*—"they can act even in weighty matters, without having first to get permission elsewhere.

"I, my following, and those for whom we speak propose this. Let me take a party there and ask for help. I cannot foresay if they will grant it; and if they will, I cannot foresay what form it may take. Perhaps they will give us firearms, that we may hunt more easily; perhaps they will let us have onsarless vehicles; perhaps they will supply us with fireless heat-makers; perhaps they will build huge, warm shelters for our herds—I know not, and I have not ventured to ask Banner."

No need. She has long since told me that such things are possible, yes, that it is possible to turn the Ice back, but she and her fellows do not command the means, nor has she been able to get the yea of those who do.

"For this, we would no doubt have to make return. What, I do not know either. Trade, maybe; we have furs, hides, minerals. Labor, maybe; they might need native hands. The cost may prove too much and the clans refuse to pay. Very well, then. But it may not. The bargain may actually leave us better off than we ever were before.

"I propose to go ask, and negotiate if I can, and bring back word for an assembly to consider. To do this, I must go for our whole folk.

"Therefore, Lord of the Volcano, I, my following, and those for whom we speak demand of you that you grant us the right to act on behalf of the clans, and give me a letter attesting that this is so."

Yewwl snapped her vanes open and shut, to show that she had finished, and waited for questions.

They seethed about her. Was it not a dangerous journey, and many days in length? "Yes, but I am willing, and have friends who are willing too. How else can I strike back at the Ice, that robbed me of my darlings?"

Why could the party not simply be flown there? "We cannot breathe air as thin as the star-folk do. Not for years has the House of the Banner possessed a large flying machine with a cabin that can be left open, since it was wrecked in a dusk-storm. They have lacked the wealth to replace it. Their lesser vehicles can carry but a single person besides the pilot, and he would fall ill of heaviness on so long a flight."

Why cannot Banner herself go speak for us, or talk across distance as we know they are able to? "She fears she would be refused. Remember, the rule that she is under forbids giving us things like that. She doubts if I am being wise. Also, her kind are not innocent of rivalries and jealousies. The other chiefs might not welcome a proposal that would put her in the lead, yet listen to us if she is out of it."

Several more; and then Erannda came down, and Yewwl whispered, unheard here—"Now the fight begins."

Tall in his white garb, the Seeker struck a shivery chord from his harp. Silence pounced and gripped. His bard's voice rolled forth:

"Lord of the Volcano, colleagues, clanfolk, hear me. Harken when I say that this is either the maddest thought that ever was flung out, or else the evillest.

"Slowly have the aliens wrought among us, oh, very slowly and cunningly. Centuries have passed since first they came, avowing they did but wish to learn of us and of our country. Be it confessed, the College of those days welcomed them, seeing in them kindred spirits, and hoping in turn to range through new realms of knowledge. Yes, we too trusted them . . . in those days. But the College has a long memory; and today we look back, against the wind of time, and what we see is not what we endure.

"Piece by piece, the new things, the new words slipped in among us; and we thought they were good, and never paused to reckon the cost. New skills, new arts and crafts seemed to make life richer; but it came to pass that those who practiced them could not be free rovers, nor could each household provide for every need of its own. So died the wholeness of the folk.

"Behold this chaplet. It has been given from old hand to young hand for five hundred years. It can never be replaced. The making of such beauty in bronze is lost to our craftspeople. This may seem little, when instead we have steel; but the ugly coppersmithing of today cannot uplift the soul, and this is but the smallest token of the emptiness within us. Who now sings the ancient epics, who now honors the ancient wisdom and righteousness? The links of kinship corrode, as youth mocks at age and wants its way in everything. And why not? Is not our whole world a mere dust-fleck adrift in limitless, meaningless hollowness? Are we ourselves anything save wind made flesh, chance-formed, impotent, and foredoomed? *This* is the teaching the strangers have sent seeping into us, a teaching of despair so deep that few of us even recognize it as despair."

The harp rang. "But you have heard me chant this lay before. What of the present gathering? What shall we say?

"I bid you think. Yewwl has never hidden that she is the creature of an alien. What she does keep hidden is what that alien may have bidden her do, for its cold purposes. Long have they declared, at the House of the Banner, that we must not become dependent for our lives on things of theirs. This is true; but has it been a truth uttered to lull our wariness? For at last Yewwl proposes that we do indeed make such things necessary to our survival. I tell you, if that happens, we will be helpless before the demands of their makers. And what might those demands be? Who can tell? Yewwl herself admits she does not understand the strangers.

"Perhaps"—sarcasm ran venomous—"she is honest in her intent, in what she thinks she has said. Perhaps. But then, how can she hope to deal for us? What miscomprehensions might result, and what disasters follow? Better the glacier grind down across this whole country, and we flee to impoverished exile. At least we will remain free.

"Deny yonder witch. Cast her hence!"

The harp snarled to a finish.

Skogda sprang onto his bench, vanes wide. "You slime-soul, you dare speak thus of my mother!" he yelled. Almost, he launched himself against the Seeker. Two friends barely pulled him down and quieted him.

Erannda gave Yewwl a triumphant look. "That," he murmured, "deserves I put a satire upon him, and upon you."

—"Banner, what shall I do? I haven't his word-skill. If he makes a poem against me, I will be unheeded in council for the rest of my world-faring."

—"Oh! . . . But hold, Yewwl, don't panic, stand fast. I thought about this, that you might someday run into just this danger, years ago. I didn't discuss it with you, because it was a nasty subject, for you much more than for me; but I did prepare—"

Wion stirred on the dais. "It is a terrible thing you would do, Erannda," he warned. "Worse than the outburst of a way-wearied young male calls for. Such excess could bring reproach on you and the whole College. Best let him humble himself to you."

"I will that," Erannda replied, "if his mother and her gang will abandon their crazy scheme."

Banner had been whispering, fast and fiercely. The sense of her nearness in spirit sufficed by itself to kindle the heart anew. Yewwl stood forth and said:

"No. Are we not yet gorged with senseless rantings? What does he preach but fear and subservience—fear of tomorrow, subservience first to him and later to doom? Yes, the star-folk have caused changes, and in those changes is loss. But would you call it wrong that as your child grows, you lose the warmth of his little body in your pouch? Do you not, instead, rejoice to watch him soar forth?

"What threat have the star-folk ever been, save to those who would fetter us down and require we honor them into the bargain? The threat is from *them*, I tell you. If they prevail, everything we have achieved will perish, and likewise countless of us and our children and children's children. Shall we not even have a chance to seek help?"

Her audience listened aghast. Nobody had ever defied a senior Seeker thus openly, and before the very Lord of the Volcano.

Yewwl's words had been her own, following the advice she received from Banner. Having uttered them, she stalked toward Erannda, her vanes open, fur a-bristle, fangs bare. She said, before she herself could be appalled at what it was:

"I will lay a satire on you instead, old one, that all may ken you for what you truly are."

He controlled his rage, made his harp laugh, and retorted, "You? And what poetics have you studied?"

"I begin," she answered, halting close to him. And she declaimed Banner's words, as they were given her:

> *"Wind, be the witness of this withering!*
> *Carry abroad, crying, calling,*
> *The name I shall name. Let nobody*
> *Forget who the fool was, or fail*
> *To know how never once the not-wise*
> *Had counsel worth keeping, in time of care—"*

"Stop!" he yelled. As he lurched back, his harp dropped to the clay floor.

He would have needed a night or longer to compose his satire. She threw hers at him, in perfect form, on the instant.

—"Don't be vengeful," Banner urged. "Leave him a way out."

—"Oh, yes," Yewwl agreed. Pity surprised her.

Erannda straightened, gathered around him what was left of his dignity, and said, almost too low to hear: "Lord of the Volcano, colleagues, clanfolk . . . I have opposed the proposal. I could possibly be mistaken. There is no mistaking that quarrels among us . . . like this . . . are worse than anything else that might happen. Better we be destroyed by outsiders than by each other. . . . I withdraw my opposition."

He turned and stumbled toward his bench. On impulse, Yewwl picked up his harp and gave it to him.

After a hush, Wion said, not quite steadily, "If none has further speech, let the thing be done."

The inscribed parchment felt stiff in her fingers, and somehow cold.

She tucked it carefully into her travel pack, which lay by her saddle. Not far off, her tethered onsar cropped, loud in the quietness round-about. Yewwl had wanted a while alone, to bring her whirling thoughts back groundward. Now she walked toward the camp, for they would be making Oneness.

They were out on the plain. The short, stiff nullfire that grew here glowed in the last light of the sun, a red step pyramid enormous amidst horizon mists. Lurid colors in the west gave way to blue-gray that, eastward, deepened to purple. In the north, Mount Gungnor was an uplooming of blackness; flames tinged the smoke of it, which blurred a moon. Northwestward the oncoming storm towered, flashed, and rumbled. The air was cold and getting colder. It slid sighing around Yewwl, stirring her fur.

Ahead, a fire ate scrubwood that the party had collected and waxed ever more high and more high. She heard it brawl, she began to feel its warmth. They were six who spread their vanes to soak up that radiance. The others were already homebound. Skogda, his retainer and companion Ych (oh, memory), Zh of Arachan were male; Yewwl's retainers Iyaai and Kuzhinn, and Ngaru of Raava, were female; Yewwl herself made the seventh. More were not needed. Maybe seven were too many. But they had wanted to go, from loyalty to her or from clan-honor, and she could not deny them.

Let them therefore make Oneness, and later rest a while; then she would call Banner, who would be standing by about the time that Fathermoon rose. And the ship would come—the new ship, whereof a part could hold breathable air—and carry them east at wizard speed.

Yewwl winced. She had not liked lying before the assembly. Yet she must. Else Wion would never have understood why she needed a credential which, undated as was usual, made no mention, either, of cooperation by the star-folk. After all, he would have asked, were they not star-folk too in—?—but he would have failed to remember what the place was called, Dukeston. Yewwl herself had trouble doing that, when the noise was practically impossible to utter.

She likewise had trouble comprehending that star-folk could be at strife, and in the deadly way Banner had intimated. Why? How? What did it portend? The idea was as bewildering as it was terrifying. But she must needs keep trust in her oath-sister.

Oneness would comfort, bring inner peace and the strength to go onward. Skogda had started to beat a tomtom, Kuzhinn to pipe forth a tune. Feet were beginning to move in the earliest rhythms of dance. Zh cast fragrant herbs onto the fire.

It would be an ordinary Oneness, for everybody was not perfectly familiar with everybody else. They would just lose themselves in dance, in music, in chanted words, in winds and distances, until they ceased to have names; finally the world would have no name. Afterward would be sleep, and awakening renewed. Was this remotely akin to what Banner called, in her language, "worship?" No, worship involved a supposed entity dwelling beyond the stars—

Yewwl put that question from her. It was too reminding of the strangeness she would soon enter, not as an emissary—whatever she pretended—but as a spy. She hastened toward her folk.

IX

Clouds made night out of dusk, save again and again when lightning coursed among them. Then it was as if every huge raindrop stood forth to sight, while thunder, in that thick air, was like being under bombardment. Though the wind thrust hard, it was slow, its voice more drumroll than shriek. The rain fell almost straight down, but struck in explosive violence. Through it winged those small devil shapes that humans called storm bats.

Hooligan descended. Even using her detectors, it had not been easy, in such weather, to home on Yewwl's communicator. It might have been impossible, had Banner not supplied landmarks for radars and infrascopes to pick out. Nor was it easy to land; Flandry and the vessel's systems must work together, and he felt how sweat ran pungent over his skin after he was down.

But time was likely too short for a sigh of relief and a cigarette. He swept a searchbeam about, and found the encampment. The

Ramnuans were busy striking a tent they had raised for shelter, a sturdy affair of hide stretched over poles. He swore at the delay. They'd have no use for the thing where they were bound—except, of course, to help make plausible their story that they had fared overland. He might as well have that smoke.

And talk to Banner. He keyed for her specially rigged extension. "Hello. Me. We're here," he said, hearing every word march by on little platitude feet.

"Yes, I see," came her voice from Wainwright Station. More remoteness blurred it than lay in the hundreds of kilometers between them. She was hooked into her co-experience circuit, she was with Yewwl and of Yewwl. The extension was audio only because there would have been no point in scanning her face; she never looked away from the screen. Yet Flandry would have given much for a glimpse of her.

"Anything happen since I left?" he asked, mainly against a silence that the racket of the gale deepened.

"In those few minutes?" Did she sound irritated. "Certainly not."

"Well, you did mean to give your people a halfway plausible explanation of this sudden scurry."

"I told Huang what we'd agreed on. He may have been a bit skeptical, but I'm not sure. Now do be quiet. I've got to help Yewwl lead the rest aboard; they know nothing about spacecraft. And we're afraid the onsars will balk."

The man broke the connection, fired up the promised cigarette, and punished his lungs with it. Huang, skeptical? That could spell trouble, if and when the second in command was interviewed by ducal agents. *Why shouldn't he doubt us, though? I would,* Flandry thought. *Granted, a nasty, suspicious mind is part of my stock in trade, while he's supposed to be an unworldly scientist. Nevertheless—*

He reviewed the situation. He had nothing else to do at the moment. It would have been folly, on the order of that committed by the famous young lady named Alice, to confide in the station personnel. A few might be inclined to support him, but most would be shocked, especially the majority of Hermetians. Everybody grumbled at the slow throttling of their work; most wanted climate modification and deplored how Cairncross had dragged his tail. But it was a quantum jump from that to acceptance of possible rebellion, and to defiance of both his authority and the Emperor's. Someone would be certain to call Dukeston or Port Asmundsen and warn. Ducal militia were (supposedly!) few in this system, more a rescue corps than a police force; but it wouldn't take many to abort Flandry's mission.

Overtly, therefore, he had simply come to Ramnu to see for himself. If he decided the climate project was worthy, he would use his good offices at court. On this trip tonight, the announced plan was for him to observe native life, employing Yewwl/Banner as guide.

Everything was quite reasonable in outline. The details were the problem, as commonly with lies. Why had he waited till sunset to depart? Why had Banner gotten her fellows who also practiced linkage to urge their Ramnuans to contact Yewwl on her way to the Volcano? Explanations—that he felt he must first absorb a lot of information from the data banks; that she hoped a formal appeal by the clans would exert moral pressure on the Imperium—were inevitably weak.

Flandry had relied on the basic human tendency to swallow any positive statement. After all, these people lived insulated from politics, except for what they played among themselves; besides, to them, he represented Authority. But the yarn would come unraveled at the first tug on it by a professional investigator. And if Huang, or whoever, called one in, even before Cairncross' troubleshooters arrived—

Well, that wouldn't be long in any event. Meanwhile Banner sat chained to her unit. It could not be shifted aboard the spacecraft, being integral with the station. What could happen to her if she was arrested was the stuff of nightmare, sleeping and waking, for whatever excess time Flandry survived.

I've sacrificed enough lives and dreams by now, haven't I? Not hers too! Max's daughter, facing the risk with his curt gallantry and planning against it with his remembered coolness. The cigarette stub scorched his fingers. He crushed it as he would a foeman. *And she's become the closest friend I've got, maybe the only real friend, for I am certainly not one to myself.* He shivered back from any thought of love. It had never been a lucky thing to be in love with Dominic Flandry.

"The Ramnuans are prepared to board, sir," Chives reported on the intercom.

"Eh?" The man adjusted a viewscreen. Yes, there they came, leading their animals through the rain-cataract. An extruded ramp awaited them, their route into a compartment of the hold. He'd seal it off during flight.

An onsar studied the metal shape before it and grew suspicious. It dug hoofs and extensors into the ground. Its brethren took their cue from that, milled about, stamped, butted snouts at their masters, heedless of reins and thorny whips. Might they stampede?

"Beasts of burdensome," Flandry muttered in frustrated anger. They couldn't be abandoned, they were essential to the deception.

"Excuse me, sir," Chives said. "I believe if I went out I might be of assistance."

"You? In that gravity?"

"I will fly on impellers, of course."

"What's your scheme? I think nature's better equipped me for any such job."

"No, sir. You are too important. Anticipating difficulties, I have taken the liberty of donning my spacesuit, and am about to close the faceplate and cycle through. Should an accident occur, I suggest that for dinner you heat the packet numbered 'three' in the freezer. The Eastmarch Camay Beaujolais '53 would complement it well. But I trust you will not be forced to such an extremity, sir."

"Carry on, Chives," Flandry said helplessly.

Wind made a steady roar about the hull, which trembled under its force. Rain smote like hammers. Lightning flew, thunder rattled teeth in jaws. No matter how well outfitted, a skinny old Shalmuan aflit in that fury, in the grasp of that gravity, could well lose control and be dashed to his death. *And still he plays his part. Well, it's the sole part he can play, alone among aliens; therefore I must play mine without ever faltering. We can never really communicate, but this dance we dance between us does say, "I care for you."*

Flandry need not have worried, though. It soon became a joy to watch how elegantly Chives darted through the air. He had set his blaster to lowest beam, and the onsars had thick hides. However, the flicks of energy sufficed to herd them, and then chastise them. They shuffled aboard as meek as taxpayers.

Flandry whooped laughter. "How about that, Banner?" he cried.

Her voice was strained. "The hull screens Yewwl's signal. We're cut off. Can you relay?"

"Nothing so complex, I'm afraid."

"Well, then, get to your destination fast!" she shrilled.

Chives came back inboard. Flandry prepared to lift.

Banner spoke in a subdued tone. "I'm sorry, Dominic. I shouldn't have yelled at you. Nerves overstrung."

"Sure, I understand, dear," he said. Inwardly: *Do I? How deep into her soul does that linkage go? She can break it for a while without pain, but what if it broke forever?*

Hooligan rose, leveled off, and lined out east-northeast. She had to fly low, lest by malevolent luck a ship going to or from Port Asmundsen should notice. Despite her ample capabilities, Flandry didn't like it. He felt boxed in.

Regardless, the journey was uneventful—for him and Chives; surely not for the Ramnuans, who must be terrified in their metal cave, weighing a seventh of what they ought to, under light they saw as harsh blue-white, while cloven air rumbled and screamed outside and that which they breathed grew foul. Banner could have reassured Yewwl, but Yewwl and her followers now had naught but courage to uphold them. A scanner showed them iron-steady. Flandry admired.

The storm fell behind. He passed fully into this planet's long, long night. Plains grew frost-silvery; snow whitened hillcrests, and not all that fell in the dark would melt when day returned. Had he lacked optical amplification, he would have been virtually blind. Diris was a crescent, half Luna size though brighter; Tiglaia showed tiny; Elaveli was not aloft, and would have seemed smaller yet. The visible stars were few and dim, save for the red spark of Antares, and the Milky Way was lost to sight.

Five thousand kilometers rolled beneath, and he approached a coast. Ahead glimmered the Chromatic Hills, where Dukeston stood amidst its mines and refineries and—what else was there. Beyond, the St. Carl River ran down into brackish marshlands, once rich with life and still, he had heard, worth harvesting. Beyond those, an ocean lay sluggish until winds raised monstrous billows upon it. In recent years, the waves had brought icebergs crashing ashore.

They mustn't detect *Hooligan* at the settlement. Flandry's navigational system identified a site he and Banner had chosen off maps, blocked from view by an outcrop which a few hours' riding would serve to get around. He made a gingerly descent onto roughness and told the woman, flat-voiced: "We're here."

"Good. Let them out." Her words quivered. "Send them on their way."

"A minute first, just a minute," he begged. "Listen, I can flange up an excuse for returning to Wainwright this soon. Then I'd be right there, for snatching you away if the Duke's boys come."

"No, Dominic." She spoke softer than before. "We agreed otherwise. How did you say? 'Let's not put all our eggs in one basket.'" Her chuckle was tender. "You have a marvelous gift for making phrases."

"Well, I—Look, I've been thinking further. Yes, you have to keep in touch with Yewwl till her task's accomplished, or till everything falls apart for us. And, yes, in the second case, *Hooligan* ought to remain at large, in the faint hope that something can be done some different way. But . . . you probably don't appreciate how powerfully armed she is. We can fight through anything Cairncross is likely to send, at least that he's likely to send at first. And we can outrun everything else."

Banner sighed. "Dominic, we discussed this before. You yourself admitted that that requires opening fire at the start, on little or no provocation. It gives us no flexibility, no chance to get more clues. It puts this station, its innocent staff, its work of centuries, in mortal danger. It alerts the Duke so thoroughly that his whole force will be mobilized to kill us or keep us at a distance. What can we do after that? Especially if we're wrong and he is not plotting a coup. Whereas, if he merely knows you've been skulking about—"

"He'll take what precautions he's able," Flandry interrupted, "and the precautions that involve you won't make your future worth reaching. . . . Well, I had to ask, but I knew you'd refuse. We'll stay by the original plan."

"We're wasting time right now."

"True. Very well, I'll let the Ramnuans off, and Chives and I will go wait at the place agreed on."

Incommunicado, for fear of detection. It will be a hard wait. In several ways, harder for me *than for her. She'll be in the worse peril, but she'll be with her oath-sister.*

"Goodbye, darling."

✧ **X** ✧

Things have the vices of their virtues. Today Edwin Cairncross had reason to curse the fact that there was no interstellar equivalent of radio. He actually caught himself trying to imagine means of getting past the unfeasibility. The "instantaneous" pulses emitted by a ship in hyperdrive are detectable at an extreme range of about a light-year. They can be modulated to carry information. Unfortunately, within a few million kilometers quantum effects degrade the signal beyond recovery; even the simplest binary code becomes unintelligible. The number of relay stations that would be required between two stars of average separation is absurdly enormous; multiply by the factor necessary for just several hundred interconnections, and you find it would take more resources than the entire Empire contains.

But couldn't something very small, simple, cheap be devised, that we can afford in such quantities? I'll organize a research team to look into it when I am Emperor. That will also help rouse enterprise again in the human race.

Cairncross checked the thought and barked laughter. He'd have plenty to do before his throne was that secure! Until then, he should be thankful. When messages took half a month or more to go straight from Hermes to Terra, and few ships per year made the entire crossing, his realm was satisfactorily isolated. Only ambiguous hints as to what might be amiss trickled back from an undermanned Imperial legation. With patience, intelligence, sophistication, a bold leader could mount a mighty effort in obscure parts of his domain. Lacking that advantage, he could never have given flesh and steel to his desire.

Therefore, let the Empire be thankful too.

Meanwhile, though, he had no way of tracing Admiral Flandry. Where was the old devil a-prowl? The single certainty was that he had not reported in at Hermes as he was supposed to. Well, it was also known that he had left Terra, and that the Abrams bitch had disappeared under the kind of queer circumstances you'd expect him to engineer.

Cairncross hunched forward in his pilot seat. The speedster had no need of his guidance, but he felt he drew strength from the power at work below his fingers. A touch, and he could release missiles capable of wiping out a city, or the sunlike flame of a blaster cannon. He sat alone here, but within this same hull were men who adored him. Niku stood before him in heaven, become the brightest of the stars, and yonder poised nearly half the force he would presently unleash, to make himself lord of a hundred thousand worlds.

Maybe that's why I'm going in person, when I decided I'd waited too long at home on Flandry. I could have dispatched a trusty officer, but it feels good to be in action again, myself. Cairncross scowled. *Besides, he might outwit anybody else. I know better than to under-estimate him.*

A waft of chill seemed to pass through the air that rustled from the ventilator. *If he went directly, he's been there for days.*

Cairncross squared his shoulders and summoned confidence. How could a solitary human creature evade his precautions in that scant a time? Nigel Broderick allowed no laxity. No stranger would get access to any place where he might see what was building. *After all, my original idea was to neutralize Flandry by bringing him to Hermes.*

Just the same—

We'll take no chances, we'll strike immediately and hard. In a few more hours, Cairncross would be on the moon Elaveli, issuing orders. Let Broderick lead a detachment to Port Lulang and occupy it, on the grounds that he was searching for a spy—true, as far as it went. But probably Flandry was on Ramnu. *I'll command the planetside operation. The stakes are too high for a lesser player. They are the destiny of civilization.*

Brief wistfulness tugged at Cairncross. He'd cherished a secondary hope of winning Flandry over to his cause. The man would be valuable. *And why shouldn't he join me? What does he owe Gerhart? He's been slighted, ignored, shunted aside. I'd have the brains to reward such a follower as he deserved, and listen to him. My aim is to give the Empire the strong, wise government it so desperately needs, to found a dynasty armored in legitimacy against usurpers . . . yes, then I'll clone myself. . . . Why, there'll no longer be any reason not to reverse the glaciation on Ramnu. In fact, it will be a suitably glorious*

*achievement for my reign. An entire race of beings will revere my name
for as long as their sun endures.*

*Though that will be the littlest part of what I shall do. I could be
remembered through the lifetime of the universe.*

Beneath the triumphant vision went a sigh. It is very lonely to be
an embodiment of fate. He had daydreamed of gaining a friend in
Flandry; their spirits were much alike, and the officer's derisive
humor would relieve the Emperor's austere seriousness. But as
matters had developed, the odds were that Cairncross would seize
the other, wring him dry of everything he knew with a deep hypnoprobing, and mercifully obliterate what was left.

Civilization was deathly ill; the rot had reached the heart.
Nothing could save it but radical surgery.

Yewwl's first encounter was with a couple of native workers. Her
party was riding toward Dukeston, which was as yet hidden from
sight by a ridge in between. Its lights made a glow that night-adapted
eyes saw as brilliant. Thence rolled a low rumbling, the sound of
machines at their toil. Here the land seemed untouched. Hills lifted
stark, white-mantled save where crags reared forth, above gorges full
of blackness. Frosty soil rang beneath hoofs; stones rattled; brush
cracked. The air hung still and bitterly cold, making the travelers
keep their vanes wrapped around them; breath formed frost crystals
that lingered in glittery streamers. Overhead twinkled more stars
than a human would have seen unaided, though fewer than Yewwl
had observed on pictures from Terra. Mothermoon was a crescent,
scarcely moved from its earlier place among them, while
Fathermoon was well down the sky. Child-moon rose tiny in the east.

The strangers appeared suddenly, around the corner of a bluff.
They halted, like Yewwl's group. Stares went back and forth. She saw
them quite clearly, except that she couldn't be sure of the precise
color of their fur. It was paler than hers, and the two were tall and
slender. In their hands and strapped to their thighs they carried
objects that must be made by star-folk.

After a moment, one of them spoke something that could be a
question. Yewwl opened and drooped her vanes, trying to show she
didn't understand. She emphasized it by saying aloud, "We share not
the same language."

To her surprise, the male of the pair addressed her in Anglic. He had less vocabulary and grammar than she had acquired from Banner, and neither of them had a vocalizer to turn the sounds into those that a human would have formed. Nevertheless, a degree of comprehensibility got through: "Do you know this talk?"

"Yes," she replied.

—"Don't admit to knowing much," Banner warned in her head. "They mustn't identify you."

"A little," Yewwl added, nervously fingering the scarf that hid her collar. "How did you guess?"

"You are from afar," the male answered shrewdly. "I have never seen your kind before, though my mate and I range widely in our work. But they say that off westward is another human settlement, and I thought you might well have come from there. None of the barbarians known to us do any business here."

Communication was not truly that easy. It was full of obscurities, false starts, requests for repetition, annoyed rephrasings. But persistence kept it limping along.

Like many local natives, in these hills and the marshes below, the couple were employed by the star-folk. Live timber cruisers, harvesters, and so forth—including operators of various machines—came cheaper than robots. They were paid in trade goods, by which this region had become prosperous but upon which it was now, after centuries, totally dependent. (—"Don't you think we have been kinder to your people at Wainwright?" Banner murmured.) These two were prospectors, searching out the ores for which Dukeston's appetite had become insatiable of late. The colony itself had grown at the same pace. Why? Who knew? The humans must have their reasons, but those were beyond the grasp of simple Ramnuans.

Yewwl bristled to hear that.

She gave a brief explanation of her ostensible errand, and the pair guided her band onward. This was an exciting development for them! *En route,* she cautioned her followers anew, "Forget not: say nothing about our having been flown here, should we meet somebody who knows our tongue. We are supposed to have spent days going overland. Nor ever let fall that I am in tie with a star-person. We are to spy out what may be a hostile territory, under guise of being envoys. Let me talk for everyone."

"I seize no sense," Ngaru of Raava complained.

In truth, the idea of organized enmity was vague and tricky as wind, and felt as icy. "Suppose a feud is between Banner and the clan-head at this place," Yewwl said. "Their retainers are naturally loyal to them, and thus likewise at odds."

"But we're asking for her/his help," Kuzhinn protested. "Why should we abide with the House of the Banner, which gives us naught?"

The time for explanation had been far too short—not that Yewwl had a great deal more to go on, herself, than faith in her oath-sister. "Banner would help us if she could, and in a mightier way," Yewwl said. "First she must overcome those who are holding her back from it. She believes the leaders here are among them. I don't expect they would ever really grant aid. Why should they? It is with the House of the Banner that the clans have ancient friendship."

"What is it, again, that we are to do?" Iyaai inquired.

Yewwl rumpled her vanes in sign of exasperation. "Whatever I tell you," she snapped. "Belike that will mainly be to stay cautious. I alone will know what to look for."

—"Will I indeed?" she asked her distant comrade.—"I will, seeing through your eyes," the woman reminded her. "Don't get reckless. I could hardly bear to have anything bad happen to you . . . on my account."

—"On account of us all, I think."

Skogda clapped hand to knife. "If luck turns ill," he said, "let me take the lead. I'll make sure they know they've been in a fight!" His retainer Yen growled agreement.

"You will do what you're told, as long as I remain a-glide," Yewwl responded angrily. Inside, she wondered if her son was capable of obedience. She wished she could confide her fears to Banner. But what good would it do? Her oath-sister had woe abundant already. She could not so much as stir her body while the mission lasted. That took a bleak bravery Yewwl knew she herself lacked.

The travelers topped the ridge, and Dukeston blazed ahead. Yewwl had sufficient knowledge of such places, from what Banner had shown and explained over the years, that she was not utterly stupefied. She recognized an old central complex of buildings, akin to those at Wainwright Station. Newer, larger units spread across several kilometers of hills. She discerned housing for native workers, foreign though the designs and materials were. Elsewhere, structures that droned or purred must hold industries of different kinds. The enigmatic shapes that moved along the streets were machines. Air intake towers bespoke extensive underground installations. (Banner identified those, adding that the air was altered for her race to breathe.) A paved field some ways off, surrounded by equipment, bore a couple of objects that the woman said were moonships. Overhead circled raindrop shapes that she said were aircraft, armed for battle.

Despite this, it was mostly a dream-jumble, hard to see; the mind could not take hold of forms so outlandish. Besides, the illuminating tubes above the streets were cruelly bright. They curtained off heaven. Had she not had Banner with her in spirit, Yewwl might well have turned and fled.

As was, she must encourage her companions. Their vanes held wide, their fur on end, they were close to panic—apart from Skogda, in whom it took the form of a snarl that meant rage. The onsars were worse, and must be left in care of folk who came out to meet the newcomers. Yewwl's party continued afoot. Between these high, blank walls, she could scarcely glide had she sought to, and felt trapped.

At the end, she stopped in a square whereon were tiers of benches. It faced a large screen set inside a clear dome. —"Yes, this is for assemblies," Banner declared in Yewwl's head. The magnified image of a man appeared. —"I've met him occasionally," Banner said. "The deputy chief, an appointee of Duke Edwin's. . . ." Yewwl did not follow the second part.

Talk scuttled back and forth until a female human was fetched to interpret. Using a vocalizer, she could somewhat speak the language of the clans; unaided Ramnuan pronunciation of Anglic seemed to baffle her. "What is your purpose?" she demanded.

Yewwl stepped forward. The blood was loud within her; both vanes throbbed to its beat. She saw in blade-edge clarity each single line, curve, hue on the face in the screen, the face that was so dreadfully like Banner's. If those lips released a particular word, she and her son and their companions would be dead.

—"Courage," came the whisper. "I know her too, Gillian Vincent, a fellow xenologist. I felt sure they'd call on her, and . . . I think we can handle her."

Yewwl took forth her parchment, which she had been holding, and unrolled it before the screen for inspection. Banner laughed dryly. —"She can't read your written language very well, but doesn't want to admit it. Quite likely she won't notice your name, if you don't say it yourself."

That had been a fang of trouble in the planning. The document was bound to specify its bearer, and her relationship to Wainwright Station was well-known. Since the name was common, and the scheme implausibly audacious, it could be hoped that no suspicions would rise. But—

"Declare your purpose," Gillian Vincent said.

Yewwl described her request for help against the Ice, the offer to exchange resources or labor for it. At first the woman said, "No, no, impossible." Prompted by Banner, Yewwl urged the case. At last the man was summoned back into view. Conference muttered.

—"I can hear them fairly well. They don't know what to make of this, and don't want to dismiss you out of hand," Banner exulted. "The bureaucratic mentality." That bit was in Anglic, and gibberish to Yewwl.

In the end, Gillian Vincent told her: "This requires further consideration. We doubt we can reach the kind of agreement you want; but we will discuss it among ourselves, and later with you again. In the meantime, we will direct our workers to provide you food and shelter."

Eagerness blazed high in Yewwl. Those folk would take for granted that newly arrived foreigners—primitives, in their viewpoint—would wander about gaping at the marvels of the town. And nobody would suppose that primitives would recognize the secret things Banner thought might be here.

Whatever those were.

❖ XI ❖

Hooligan flitted back westward until the broad dim sheet of Lake Roah glimmered below her. The terminator storm had moved on and the night was at peace.

There was no peace in Flandry. The lines were drawn harsh in his face and his fingers moved with controlled savagery as he piloted. The navigation system and a map found for him the bay on the south marge that Banner had picked. Instruments told him that everything was sealed; Chives pattered about to make certain. For a minute, gravity drive roiled water, then the little ship was under the surface. She sank fifty meters before coming to rest in ooze and murk.

Her topside was less far down. Flandry shut off or damped powered units as much as he could. The lake screened most emission, but not all; an intensive search could find him, and he lived by the principle of never giving an enemy a free ride. The largest demand on the generators while lying quiet was for the interior fields that maintained normal weight against Ramnu's pull. It helped to be oriented lengthwise, not needing a tensor component to keep feet drawn deckward as when the vessel was in vertical mode. Yet six out of seven standard gees were still being counteracted. He and Chives could endure being heavier than on Terra—say two gees—for as long as they must endure this wait.

First he activated one of the numerous gadgets he had had made for *Hooligan* over the years. A miniature hatch in the outer hull opened and a buoyant object emerged, trailing a wire. Its casing was of irregular shape; unless you came within centimeters, it looked like a chance bit of vegetable matter, on any of hundreds of planets, bobbing about. In reality, it was an antenna and a fish-eye video scanner. Transmitted, computer-refined, optically amplified, the image on the screen beneath was of less than homeview quality—"but 'tis enough, 'twill serve," Flandry judged. He set a monitor to sound an alarm if a member of certain classes of objects appeared. Thereafter he reduced the negagravity, and his mass laid hold of him and dragged.

"That was fun," he said to no one in particular. "Now what shall we play?"

Can't get drunk, or drugged any different way, he thought. *If and when I need to be alert, I'll receive no advance notice. Electrostim? No, the after-euphoria might fade too slowly. I need to be mean and keen. Besides, it wouldn't feel right to sit tickling my pleasure center while Banner's in peril of her life and hurting on account of her friend.*

Ha, getting moral, am I? Probably need a fresh course of antisenescents.

He rose and made his way aft, feeling every step, feeling how he must strain to hold his spine erect. In earlier days, he had shortened his hated exercises by turning up the weight before he did them; and under standard conditions, he seldom noticed himself walking—he floated. Nowadays—well, he wasn't yet elderly, he could still pace most men twenty or thirty years his junior, but a hundred variable cues kept him reminded that time was always gnawing, the snake at the root of Yggdrasil. Who was it had said once that youth is too precious to be wasted on the young?

Chives was in the saloon, stooped under the burden. "Sir," he reproached, "you did not warn me of this change in environment. May I ask how long it is to prevail?"

"Sure, you may, but don't expect an answer," Flandry said. "Hours, days? Sorry. You knew we'd have to lie doggo, so I assumed you'd realize this was included." With concern: "Is it too hard on you?"

"No, sir. I do fear it will adversely affect luncheon. I was planning an omelet. Under two gravities, it would get leathery. Will sandwiches be acceptable instead?"

Flandry sat down and laughed. Why not? The gods, if any, did. *I sometimes think we were created because the gods wanted to be entertained one evening by a farce—but no, that can't be. We are high comedy at least.*

The prospector who spoke some Anglic was called Ayon Oressa'ul. Folk hereabouts did not live in the large, shared territory of a clan, but on patches of land, each owned by a single family which bequeathed a common surname to its children. Ayon was evidently trusted by the chief (?) of Dukeston, for he was put in charge of the visitors. That involved a lengthy discussion on a farseer in his house, while they waited outside. He came back to them looking self-important.

"We will quarter you in my dwelling and its neighbors," he announced. His gestures included three round-walled, peak-roofed structures. Their sameness made them yet more peculiar than did their foreign style and artificial materials. Inhabitants stared at the strangers but made no advances. Their postures suggested they were used to regarding all outsiders as inferior, no matter whether one among those understood human language. "You are not to leave except under escort, and always together."

Yewwl sensed a catch of Banner's breath. It brought home anew to her how cut off her band was, how precarious its grip on events. Her natural reaction was anger, an impulse to strike out. She suppressed it. Not only would it compromise her venture, but that in turn would gust her and her companions down into mortal jeopardy. She was ready to die if that would help avenge Robreng and their young ones upon the Ice; but having worked off the worst grief, she was once more finding too many splendors in the world to wish to leave it.

She smoothed her stance and asked politely, "Why? We intend no harm, we who came in search of aid."

"You might well come to harm yourselves," Ayon said. "Or you might, through ignorance, cause damage. Things strange and powerful are at work here."

Yewwl seized the chance. "We are eager to see them. Besides being curious, perhaps we will get an idea of how our country can be rescued. Please!"

"Well . . . well, I suppose that would be safe enough."

"At once, I beg you."

"What, you do not want to rest and eat first?"

"We have no sharp need of either. Also, we fear that at any moment the humans may decide to deny our plea. Then we would be sent away, no? Unless, before, we have thought of a more exact proposal to make. Please, kind male."

(The conversation was not this straightforward. Yewwl and Ayon had gained a bit more mutual fluency, talking on the way to town, but it remained awkward. She saw advantages in that, such as not having to explain precisely—and falsely—what she had to do with Wainwright Station.)

Ayon relented. He was proud of the community he served and would enjoy showing it off. "I am required to take certain things along when conducting you," he said, and went back into his house. He re-emerged with a box strapped to his left wrist, which Banner identified as a radiophone, and a larger object sheathed on his right thigh, which Yewwl recognized as a blaster. "Stay close by me and touch nothing without permission," he ordered.

—"This is less than we hoped for," she told her oath-sister. "I meant to go about freely."

—"They're showing normal caution," the woman decided. "They can't suspect your real purpose, or you'd be prisoners. We may actually manage to turn the situation to our use. The guide may well answer key questions . . . if he continues to take you for an ignorant barbarian."

"What's going on, Mother?" Skogda asked. He radiated impatience. "What's he about?"

Yewwl explained. Her son spread vanes and showed teeth. "That's an insult," he rasped.

"Calm, calm," she urged. "We *must* put our pride away here. Later, homebound, we'll track down plenty of animals and kill them."

Ayon gave them both a hard stare. Banner saw and warned: — "Body language doesn't differ much from end to end of the continent. He senses tension. Never forget, he can call armed force to him from above."

"Skogda too is anxious to start off," Yewwl assured Ayon. "Overly anxious, maybe, but we've fared a long, gruelling way for this."

He eased. "If nothing else, you will carry back tales of wonder," he replied. "Come."

They left the native quarter and followed a street that descended into a hollow between two hills. The entire bottom was occupied by a single building, blank of walls and roof. Intake towers showed that still more was underground. Stacks vented steam and smoke. In the glare of lights, vehicles trundled back and forth.

—"That is, or was, the palladium refinery; but it's incredibly enlarged." Banner's voice shook. "Ask him about it. I'll give you the questions."

—"You'd best," Yewwl said sardonically, "for I've no wisp of an idea what you're talking about."

Discourse struggled. Ayon described the ore that went in and the metal that came out. (—"Yes, palladium.") He related how the ingots were taken to the field, loaded aboard the sky-ships, and carried off. He supposed it went to the distant home of the humans. (—"There's no reason for any planet but Hermes to import it from here, and I've never heard that Hermes is using an unusual amount. . . .")

"I will show you something more interesting," Ayon offered.

The street climbed to a crest whereon stood another big building, this one with many transparent sections—which Yewwl thought of as glass—in walls and roof. Within, beneath lights less clement than the sun, a luminance like that aboard the vessel she had ridden, were rows and tiers of tanks. Plants grew there, exotically formed, intensely green.

"Here the humans raise food they can eat," Ayon said. "It isn't vital, for the ships bring in supplies, but they like to add something fresh." Banner had already informed Yewwl of this; now the latter must translate for her followers. "In late years they have added far more rooms for the purpose, underground. Many of us worked in the construction, and no few of us now work at preparing and packing what is gathered, for shipment elsewhere." He strutted. "It must be uncommonly tasty, for the humans to want it at their home."

—"It doesn't go there," Banner observed. "Not anywhere . . . except to a military depot?"

At her prompting, Yewwl inquired, "What else do you—your folk—make for them?"

"Lumber and *iha* oil in the lowlands. Ores in the hills, though mainly those are dug by machines after persons like me have found veins. Lately we've been set searching for a different kind. And about the same time, a number of us were trained to handle machines that make clothes and armor."

"Clothes? Armor?" Yewwl and Banner exclaimed almost together.

"Yes, come and see." Ayon took a westbound street toward the outskirts of town.

"What is all this?" Skogda asked.

"Nothing," Yewwl said. She needed silence in which to think, to sort out everything that was bursting upon her.

"Oh, no, other than naught is in the air," Skogda retorted, close to fury. "See how your own vanes are stiffened. Am I an infant, that you pouch me away from truth?"

"Yes, we fared as your friends, not your onsars," Ych added.

"*You,* a friend, an equal?" Iyaai snapped, indignant on her mistress' behalf. "You're not even in her service."

"But Zh and I are your equals, Yewwl, and have our clans to

answer to," Ngaru reminded. "For them, we require you share what you learn with us, your way-siblings."

—"It may be for the best." Trouble was heavy in Banner's voice. "A fuller understanding of what's afoot may make them calmer, more cooperative. You must judge, dear."

Yewwl decided. She had thin choice, anyhow. "It begins to seem these star-folk are secretly readying for an outright attack on ours," she said. "I know not why; my oath-sister has tried to make the reason clear to me, and failed. If we see that they forge the stuff of battle here, the likelihood of it heightens."

"Attack—!" Kuzhinn gasped. "All of them together, like a pack of lopers?"

Ayon halted. His hand dropped to the blaster, his vanes and ears drew back, his pupils narrowed beyond what the glare brought about. "What are you saying among each other?" he demanded. "You do not bear yourselves like peaceful people."

Yewwl had taken a lead in moots at home and assemblies on the Volcano for well-nigh twenty years. She relaxed her whole frame, signalled graciousness with her vanes, and purred, "I was translating, of course, but I fear I alarmed them. Remember, we are completely new to this kind of place. The high walls, the narrownesses between, light, noise, smells, vehicles rushing by, everything sets us on edge. Mention of armor has raised a fear that you—the local Ramnuans— may plan to oust us from our lands, against the coming of the Ice. Or if you plot no direct attack on us, you may mount one on neighboring barbarians. That could start a wave of invasions off westward, which would finally crash over our country." She spread open palms. "Ai-ah, I know well it's ridiculous. Why should you, when you already have from the humans more than what we came seeking? But it would soothe them to see what you really do make."

—"Oh, good, good!" Banner cheered.

Ayon dropped his wariness, in a slightly contemptuous manner. "Come," he invited.

Clangor, lividness, a vast sooty hall where natives controlled engines that cut, hammered, annealed, transported . . . a warehouse where rack after rack held what appeared to be helmets, corselets, arm-and legpieces, and shapes more eldritch which Banner had names for. . . . It was as if Yewwl could feel the woman's horror.

"You see that none of this could fit any of us," Ayon fleered. "It is for humans. They take it elsewhere."

—"Combat space armor; auxiliary gear; small arms components." The Anglic words in Yewwl's head were a terrible litany. "I suppose he's established a score of factories on out-of-the-way worlds, none too big to be hidden or disguised—" Urgently, in the tongue of the clans: "Find out about those garments."

"Yes, we receive cloth and tailor it to pattern," was Ayon's reply to Yewwl's leading questions. "The finished clothes are alike, except in size and ornament; yes, also for humans to wear."

—"Uniforms," Banner nearly groaned. "Instead of making a substantial, traceable investment in automated plants, he uses native hand labor where he can, for this and the fighting equipment and—and how much else?"

Fear walked the length of Yewwl's spine. "Oath-sister," she asked, "have I seen enough for you?"

—"No. It's not conclusive. Learn all you can, brave dear." Anguish freighted the tone.

"Does this prove what you have fretted over?" Skogda breathed.

"Thus it seems," his mother answered low. "But we need our fangs deeper in the facts, for if the thing is true, it is frightful."

"We will take that bite," he vowed.

Ayon led them out. "We've walked far," he said. "I grow hungry, whether or not you do. We'll return home."

"Can we go forth again later?" Yewwl requested. "This is such a wonder."

He rippled his vanes. "If the humans haven't dismissed you. I've no hope for your errand. What under the sky can you offer them?"

"Well, could we go back by a different route?"

Ayon conceded that, and padded rapidly from the factory. Its metal clamor dwindled behind Yewwl. She looked around her with eyes that a sense of time blowing past had widened.

The tour had gone beyond the compact part of town. New structures stood well apart, surrounded by link fences and guarded by armed Ramnuans. The street was now a road, running along a high ridge from north to south, over stony, thinly snow-covered ground. Eastward, the hill was likewise bare of anything except brush, to its foot. There a frozen river gleamed. Across a bridge,

Dukeston reared and roared and glared. Westward lay only night, wild valleys, tors, canyons, cliffs, tarns. A cold wind crept out of the wastes and ruffled her pelt. The few stars she could see were as chill, and very small. Banner said they were suns, but how remote, then, how ghastly remote. . . .

Ahead, the road looped past another featureless building which air towers showed to be the cover of caverns beneath. "What is in that?" Yewwl queried, pointing.

"There they work the new ore I spoke of earlier," Ayon said.

—"Find out what it is!" Banner hissed. Yewwl tried. The clumsiness of conversation helped mask her directness, and the rest of her party, in their unmistakable hostility, trailed her and the guide. "*Ruad'a'a*," Ayon responded finally. "I have no other word for it. The humans use ours."

—"Oh, *shit!*" Banner exploded; and: "But why would they go to that trouble? Ordinarily they use Anglic names for such things. Get him to describe it."

Yewwl made the attempt. Ayon wanted to know why she cared. She thought fast and explained that, if the Dukeston humans valued the stuff, and her homeland chanced to be supplied with it, that would be a bargaining point for her.

"Well, it's black and often powdery," Ayon said. "They get a kind of metal from it."

—"Could be pitchblende," Banner muttered in Anglic. To Yewwl: "Find out more."

Ayon could relate little else. Native labor had done only the basic construction; after that, secrecy had clamped down. He did know that large, complex apparatus had been installed, and the interior was conditioned for humans, and machines regularly collected the residue that came out and hauled it off to dump at sea, and the end product left here in sealed boxes which must be thick, perhaps lead-lined, since they were heavy for their size.

—"Fissionable? Nobody uses fission for anything important . . . except in warheads—" The incomprehensible words from afar were a chant of desperation. In Yewwl's speech, Banner said out of lips that must be stretched tight across her teeth: "It would be the final proof. But I can't think how you could learn, my sister—"

"What is this?" Skogda growled.

"Nothing," Yewwl said hastily. "He's just been describing what they make there." If her son knew that Banner thought it might be the very house of destruction—if that *was* what Banner thought—he could go wild.

"No," he denied. "You may fool everybody else, Mother, but I can read you." His fangs glistened forth, hackles lifted, ears lay back, vanes extended and shivered. "You agreed we, your companions, have the right to know what's happening."

"Well, yes, it does seem that something weird goes on, but I don't understand what," she replied with mustered calm. "I would guess we've discovered as much as we're able to. Let's stay quiet, give no alarm, till we're safe—"

Ayon stepped backward. "The young fellow stands as if he's about to attack me," he said. His own voice and posture were charged with mistrust. "The rest of your following are fight-ready too."

"No, no, they are simply excited by this experience." Yewwl insisted. A sick feeling swept through her. Ayon didn't believe. And surely it must seem peculiar to him that a group of touring foreigners were so taut.

"Perhaps," he said. "But I've served the humans through my whole life—"

And grown loyal, as I am to Banner, Yewwl realized. *And observed that in these past few years they have been working on a thing vital to them. They have not told you what, but you sense that this is true, and for their sake you are wary. No doubt it is a reason why they put us in your charge.*

"You may be harmless," Ayon continued. "Or you may be spies for a horde plotting to sack the town, or—I know not. Let the humans investigate." His blaster came forth. "Tell your friends to hold where they are," he ordered. "I am going to call for assistance. If you behave yourselves, if you really have no evil intentions, you will not be hurt."

"What does he mean?" Skogda roared.

—"Yewwl, Yewwl." Banner's tone shuddered. "Do as he says. Don't resist. It would be hopeless. Dominic and I will free you somehow—"

"He's grown suspicious, thanks to the lot of you and the fuss you've made," Yewwl told her group. "He's sending for people to take us prisoner—"

She got no chance to explain that surrender was the single sensible course. Skogda howled and sprang.

Even as he did, his mother saw upon him his astonished regret, the instant knowledge that his nerves had betrayed him. Then the blaster shot.

Its blue-white flare would have left her blinded for a while, had she seen it full on. As was, her son's body shielded her eyes from most of it. After-images danced burning; they did not hide how Skogda crashed into Ayon and the two of them went down, but Skogda was now only a carcass which had had a great hole scorched through it.

"*Ee-hooa!*" shrieked Yewwl, and launched herself. Ayon was struggling out from under the corpse. His left wrist brought the caller to his mouth. "Help, help," he moaned. Yewwl was upon him. Her knife struck. She felt the heaviness of the blow, the flesh giving way beneath it. She twisted the blade and saw blood spurt.

Iyaai and Kuzhinn were shaking her. "We must flee," they were saying. "Come, please come." In her head, Banner stopped weeping and said almost levelly, —"Yes, get away fast. They have instruments which can track you by your body heat, but first they'll need to give those to people who can use them—"

Skogda is destroyed, Robreng's son and mine, Skogda whom I bore and pouched and sent off laughing for joy on his first glide and saw wedded, Skogda who gave me grandchildren to love. This thing was done in Dukeston. Aii, aii, I will give Dukeston to the wildfire, I will strew its dwellers for the carrion fowl, I am become the lightning against them. Here I am, slayers. Come and be slain!

"Yewwl, go," Banner pleaded. "If you stay, you'll die, and for nothing. *I* will punish them, Dominic and I. Your oath-sister swears it."

Almost, Yewwl obeyed. *They can take such a vengeance as the world has never seen. Let me abide until they are ready.* A few words more would have mastered the blind rage that was grief. But—

Huang flipped the main switch. The system went off line; the night at the far end of the continent blanked out; Banner stared into his face and the barren walls behind it.

"I'm sorry, Dr. Abrams," she heard, and knew in a dim way that his formality was meant to show his regret was genuine. "I know you aren't supposed to be disturbed when you're in rapport. But you did issue strict orders—"

"What?" She couldn't see him well through her tears.

"About newcomers. You were to be informed immediately, under any circumstances."

"Yes. . . ."

"Well, we've received a call. Three spacecraft of the militia will land in half an hour. The Duke himself is aboard, and requires your attendance." Anxiety: "I hope I didn't do wrong to tell him you're here, when he asked."

"I didn't tell you not to," Banner said mechanically. *How could I have?*

Huang scowled. "What's going on, anyhow? Something deucedly strange."

"You'll hear later—"

For a moment, nearly every part of Banner's being cried to be back with Yewwl. Nothing but the memory of Dominic stood between. But he had described, unsparingly, what could happen if she fell into Cairncross' hands—to her and afterward to several billion sentient beings. Yewwl, Yewwl, Yewwl was an atom among them.

Banner removed the helmet and lurched to her feet. Flandry's words against this contingency flowed of themselves. "Listen. We have an emergency situation. As you may have guessed, the admiral didn't come here just to oblige me; it was on his Grace's personal commission. I have to leave for a while—at once—alone—No, not a word! I haven't time. Tell them I'll be back shortly. His Grace will know what I mean."

All too well, he'll know. But I can be gone by then, a flying speck on a monster world.

She ran from the chamber and the bemused man. She ran from Yewwl. It was the hardest thing she had ever done. The news of her father's death had not hurt so much.

From somewhere far down inside herself, Yewwl found speech. "Go," she commanded her followers. "Scatter. Hide in the wilderness. Make your ways home." It was no fault of theirs that they had helped kill Skogda.

They saw that her fate was upon her, and departed. Air currents streamed over the hillside. They leaped from the ridge, their vanes took hold, they planed off into darkness.

It boomed around Yewwl. A flyer was descending. She took the blaster from Ayon's slack hand, the weapon that had slain her son. Her oath-sister had let her practice with such things in the past, for sport. She grinned at the oncoming machine, into the wickedness of its guns, and sprang.

Her own vanes thrilled. Each muscle in them rejoiced to stir, tense and flex, become one with the sky and steer her in a long swoop above the world. The chill brought blood alive in them; she felt it throb and glow. Overhead burned stars.

Had the pilot seen her? She'd make sure of that. She took aim and fired. By whatever trick, when she was shooting the beam was merely bright, it did not dazzle. It raised a sharp noise and a stormy odor. When it smote, brilliance fountained.

The flyer veered. Its wake thundered around Yewwl. She rode that surge, rising higher on it. Then she was above her foe, she could glide down as if upon prey.

A hailstorm struck. She tumbled under the blows. There was no pain, she wouldn't live long enough to feel any, but she knew she had been torn open. Somehow she recovered, kept her vanes proudly bearing her, went arching toward the frozen river. The aircraft slowed, drew near, sought to give its pilot a good look at his opponent. Yewwl saw it blurrily, through waves of blindness, but she saw it, and his head within the transparent canopy. She took aim again and held the beam fast on target.

The pilot died. His aircraft spun away, hit the ice below, broke through and sank. More machines hovered close. No matter them. Yewwl spent her last strength in swerving about and aiming herself at the opened water. She would lay her bones to rest above those of the man she had slain to her wounding. Oath-sister, farewell.

✣ XII ✣

The technician who reported at the garage, in response to Banner's intercom call, was shocked. "Donna, you can't do that!" he protested.

"Going out by yourself, at night, no preparation, not even a shot of gravanol—it's suicide."

"It's necessary, and I expect to survive," she clipped. "We've no time to squander, and gravanol spends hours reaching full effect. I've just a short ways to go, on an errand that can't wait, and I'll return immediately."

"Uh, let me accompany you, at least."

"No. You're on watch. Anyway, it'd take half an hour to rig both of us. Now help me. That's an order."

The sight of his concern softened her a mite. He was a pleasant young Hermetian who had shyly mentioned to her that a girl waited at home, and after his contract here was up they'd have the stake they needed to start a business. *But . . . quite likely he was in the Cairncross Pioneers.* She retained her martinet manner.

He set his jaw and obeyed. Armor against Ramnuan conditions was more complex than a spacesuit; you could not put it on single-handed. The minutes dragged past, clocked by her pulse. She smelled her sweat and felt it creep down her skin. Never before had she imagined that making ready—undergarb, bracings, harness, outer pieces, their assembly upon her, checkoff, tests, assistance to a gravsled, connection to life support units, strap-in, more checks and tests, closure of canopy—would be torture.

After a century of heartbeats, the vehicle did at last lift off the ferrocrete and slide silently forward. It passed among larger ones, both crawlers and flyers, most intended for remote-controlled, telemetered use. A sled was hardly more than a flexible means for a person or two to get about for brief periods, ordinarily operating out of a mother vessel. For instance, they might want to inspect something at close range, and perhaps send the collector robot forth from its bay aft of the cockpit, to gather specimens or take pictures.

When Dominic suggested this plan, he didn't know how risky the passage might become for me, Banner recalled, *and I didn't tell him.* She was no longer sure that that had been wise. Not that she feared for herself; no, exertion and hazard would be overwhelmingly welcome. But if she failed to convey the information to Flandry that Yewwl had bought for the price which has no end—

The inner gate of the sally port swung back. Banner steered into the lock. For a spell she was closed off, as if in a tomb; then a valve opened, she heard the air of Ramnu whistle inward, the outer gate turned, and she came forth.

The sled had no room for an interior-field generator. Seven Terran gravities laid hold on Banner. It was not as bad, at first, as a crossing from spaceship to dome with no special equipment. The suit in its manifold modules supported her, gave pressure that helped against downward pooling of body fluids, gently helped her draw breath; elastic bands ran from wrists and elbows to a framework above the well-cushioned seat; safety webs embraced; she had swallowed a couple of stimpills, which pumped strength and alertness up from her cellular reserves. Yet already she felt the brutal heaviness through and through her, even as she peered around.

The sled was not airtight; ambient pressure was safest in so lightly built a shell. She heard every sound loudened and tonally shifted: despite hull and helmet, louder than a Ramnuan would, whose ears were not meant for Terra's thin atmosphere. The night had become quiet, but she sensed the movement of scuttering animals, the trek of wings overhead—and high, faint, rapidly increasing, the noise of ships bound downward. She was barely in time.

With the deftness of experience, she turned the sled north and kicked in the power. The wind of her passage drowned out the booming from above, and the Sol-light on the spacefield fast receded to naught. Alone in the dark, she adjusted the helmet's optics for nocturnal vision.

There was scant light to amplify, though, and she couldn't see far with any clarity. Stars glistened scattered in blackness, moons looked shrunken and lost. The Kiiong River wound as a triple belt, ebon in the middle, gray-white on the edges where freezing advanced from either bank. The forest was a shapeless murk, the veldt hoar. Ponds and rivulets lay locked into ice. And still the cold deepened, as the week-long night wore on.

She could remember when it had only been this frigid in the last few hours before dawn. Now those were often lethal. The sun would rise on entire herds which had perished and on great reaches of land where many plants would not enter the daylight half of their cycles ever again. *Yewwl, your grandchildren will see death driven back to its polar home. This I swear by my own hope for life.* If sentience did not abate the accidents of a blind universe, what meaning had sentience itself?

And yet—Nothing seems to stand in the way of it but this secret struggle for the throne. I daresay if Cairncross became Emperor, he'd be quite willing to hear my petition—if I hadn't antagonized him—Is it too late to make amends?

She thrust the treachery from her with her whole force. The agony of a single world could not be weighed against the ruin of scores. *The possible ruin. Dominic said Cairncross must be planning a neat, quick, precise operation. Its aftermath may not be as bad as he fears. And those other planets are mostly abstractions to me, names, something read, something seen on a show, they do not hold* my *people.*

But Dominic is real! came to her. *I'm pledged to him, his cause . . . am I not? I owe him much . . . how much of it done for my father's sake, how much for the abstract people, how much for the sheer game he is always playing? I'll never know. Maybe he doesn't either. He gives away nothing of his inmost self, not to anybody.*

In a chamber of her spirit that was warm and softly lit, Max Abrams knocked out his pipe, leaned back in his worn old armchair, and said to his little girl with a solemnity that smiled, "Miri, a lot of qualities are known as virtues, but most of them don't do more than please or convenience folks. Real virtue wears different faces, of course, but it doesn't come in different kinds. One way or another, what it always amounts to is loyalty."

And if we are not loyal to our few friends, what else—in these years of the Empire—have we?

Being sure why she fled, she glanced at a clock. Cairncross would have entered Wainwright Station and learned. He'd scarcely wait passive for her to do whatever she intended. He didn't know which way she'd gone, and his means for search were limited, but he would order out a hunt regardless. Flying well above the river, she was conspicuous to several sorts of instruments. It behooved her to commence evasive tactics, ground-hugging zigzags over the veldt and between its kopjes. Those were dangerous. The sled had rudimentary automation; she was the pilot, growing more weary and mind-blunted every minute. A slight error, and seventy meters per second per second of acceleration would smash her into the planet.

A laugh fluttered in her throat. She'd enjoy her flight. Or at least, while it happened she wouldn't have time for remembering.

✵ ✵ ✵

Hour by hour, ice grew outward over the lake. Flandry contemplated a move to deeper, still-open water before his telltale on the surface was immobilized and perhaps incapacitated. Suddenly the alarm rang, and the grindstone of his vigil exploded into flying shards.

He had stayed in the pilot's seat as much as possible, and was there now. An image was transitting the watch-screen, unclear but recognizable. Blasphemy crackled from his lips. That was a spacecraft. Far aloft though it cruised, he identified it as a corvette: agile enough to operate in atmosphere, armed enough to kill a larger ship or lay a city waste.

Luck had broken down—not that it hadn't been flimsy all along. If it had lasted, then Banner would have fared here peacefully, he'd have taken her aboard, she'd have told him what Yewwl had or had not observed, and on that basis they would have decided their next action. As was, a ducal party had arrived first. Hearing of recent events, it was in quest of him; he could merely hope that it sought her also. Chances were, he was safe from immediate detection. She would not be. While her vehicle was small, the radiations of its systems weak, those were powerful and subtle instruments yonder. She'd have to do a masterly job of skulking. *I'd not be able to. Ramnu is too strange to me. Is it to her?*

The ship dropped slowly under the distance-veiled horizon. If it was tracing a standard search pattern, it would cross twice more, low and high but keeping this spot in its field of survey. He could make nothing but the roughest estimate of when it would be back, forty-five minutes, give or take half that.

Banner, where are you?

As if it had heard, a speaker brought her voice, likewise faint and indistinct but sufficient to make him cry out. "Dominic, I'm close by. I lay in a gully till I figured that ship must be gone, and I'm using minimum amplitude on the radio." Her words rushed. "Yewwl found clues, oh, yes. Production of combat gear, uniforms, possible military rations, certainly more palladium than a civilian economy can account for, and maybe—this isn't sure—maybe a plant for fissionable isotopes. A fight broke out and I, I'm afraid she's been killed. At the same moment, three spacecraft announced they were coming in on us, with the Duke aboard. I scrambled.

"That's the basic information, Dominic. Make what you can of it. Don't risk calling me back or picking me up. I'll be all right. You be careful, dear, and get home safe."

"Like hell," he barked into the transmitter. "Hell in truth. Stay put for five minutes, then come to the shore and hover at a hundred meters. We'll work close and open the forward cargo lock. Can you steer in through that?"

"Y-yes," she stammered, "but, oh, if it lets that ship spot you—"

"Then her captain will mightily regret it," Flandry said. "Chives," he added at the intercom, "stand by for reversion to normal weight and liftoff, followed by take-on of a gravsled in the Number One hold and whatever medical attention Donna Abrams may require."

Hardly above treetop level, *Hooligan* slunk north to the Guardian Mountains. Beyond these, she found herself over a vast whiteness, the glacier, where Cairncross' men would scarcely be. Her skipper stood her on her tail and speared skyward. Stratospherically high, he retrieved navigational data and told the autopilot to make for Dukeston at an aircraft rate. Thus he would be less liable to detection; besides, he needed time with Banner.

She reclined on the saloon bench, against cushions Chives had arranged. The hands shook with which she brought a cup of tea to her mouth. Framed in loosened brown hair, ivory pale, her countenance had thinned during the short while past; bones stood beautifully outlined and eyes smoldered copper-flame green. The view was of stars and a cloud-bright edge of Ramnu.

"How are you?" he asked.

"Better." He could barely hear. She quirked a slight smile. "I suffered no permanent damage. The stim's wearing off, I begin to feel how exhausted I am, but I can stay awake an hour or two yet."

He sat down beside her. "I'm afraid we need you for longer than that." He grimaced. "More stim, a tranquilizer, intravenous nutrients—rotten practice. You're tough, though. Later you can take a month off and recuperate. There shouldn't be any demands on you, homebound, and not too many after you've arrived."

Despite her tiredness, a quick intelligence seized on his words. "I? Just what does that mean, Dominic?"

"Nothing is predictable," he said hurriedly. "I want to minimize the stress on you, that's all. You've gotten an undue share of it, you know." He took forth his cigarette case and they both drank smoke. "But first we must have a complete account of what Yewwl found, for immediate reference and an eventual report." He laid a taper on the table. "I've already put in the background. You describe in detail what happened at Dukeston."

Her head drooped. "I don't know if I can without crying," she whispered.

He took her hand. "Cry if you want to." She did not see him wince as he remarked, "We're used to hearing that in the Corps."

At the end, he held her close, but not for long. They were too near their goal. He and Chives medicated her, and he gave her his arm to lean on while they made their way to the control cabin. Sometimes she gulped or hiccoughed, but she buckled firmly in beside him.

The strike was meteor swift. It had to be, for surely the place possessed ground defenses. *Hooligan* burst from the sky, trailing a thunderclap. Guided by Banner, who was guided by a ghost of Yewwl, Flandry aimed at the forbidden building on the hilltop. A torpedo flew ahead, set for low yield. Fire, smoke, debris erupted from the roof. Flandry brought his vessel about and employed energy beams like scalpels, widening the hole, baring the interior. Aircraft and missiles darted toward her where she hung. She cut them down with a few sword-slashes, swung her nose high, and climbed. Walls trembled to the noise of her speed. She was out of sight in seconds.

Flandry worked a minute or two with the autopilot. *Hooligan* curved around and departed from Ramnu. The planet became a shield, emblazoned azure, argent, and sable, against the stars.

"You can rest a piece," Flandry told Banner, and left her for the laboratory. He soon emerged, starkness on his face. "Yes," he said, "the readings and pictures are plenty good; they clinch the case. That plant was producing fissionables. I don't know where those were processed for warheads, but the outer moon is a logical guess."

She considered him, where he stood tall and, now, a trifle stooped before her. The surrounding luxury of the saloon seemed as remote as a constellation. She wasn't fatigued any more, the drugs in her would not permit that, but she felt removed somehow from her body, though it was as if she heard a chill singing go along its nerves. Her mind was passionlessly clear.

"So we have the evidence?" she asked. "We can bring it to Terra for the Navy to act on?"

He stared past her. "Matters aren't that simple, I'm afraid," he replied, flat-voiced. "Cairncross will shortly have an excellent idea of the situation. He knows Gerhart can't afford to bargain with him and won't show clemency if he surrenders. Maybe he'll flee. But you've heard my supposition that, as boldly as he's moved, he's almost ready to fight. Forewarning will rule out any immediate blow at Terra, but can't stop him from mobilizing and deploying his strength before a task force can get here. He could carry on a hit-and-run campaign for years—especially if he accepts the *sub rosa* help the Merseians will be delighted to offer. He'd hope for luck in battle; and his vanity would convince him that, one by one, the worlds will rally to his standard." He nodded. "Yes, Cairncross is a warrior born. My opinion is that if he sees himself as having any kind of chance, he'll fight."

Banner glanced back at Ramnu, already dwindled enough that the screen framed its entire image. Might such a war touch it, and forever end the dream she and Yewwl had dreamed against the Ice? She knew that then she would sorrow for as long as she lived.

"What can be done?" she inquired.

Flandry grinned like a death's head. "Well," he answered, "our friend can't have many major installations, and each must be cram-full of materiel. The unexpected loss of a single one should cripple him. I've set our course for Elaveli."

✳ XIII ✳

Dark, cold, silent, every system turned off or throttled down to bare minimum, *Hooligan* drifted swiftly outward in a hyperbolic orbit. It would take her close to the moon, past the hemisphere opposite Port Asmundsen. The chance of her being observed was therefore slim, no matter how many were the instruments standing sentry. If a radar beam did happen to flick her, she ought to register as a bit of cosmic scrap. No natural meteoroids attended Niku, but an occasional rock must go by on its way through interstellar space; also, during centuries of human occupation, considerable junk must have accumulated around the planet.

Weightless, Flandry entered the saloon where Banner poised in midair. He caught a doorjamb to check his flight. The flashbeam in his hand picked her features out of shadow, a sculpture of strong curves and jewel-bright eyes in a sheening coif of hair. Her light sought him in turn. For a moment they were mute.

She drew breath. "It's time for action, I'm sure." Her tone was calm, but he could guess what stirred behind it. "Now will you tell me your plan?"

"I'm sorry to have shunted you off like this," he said. "You deserved better. But Chives and I had a fiendish lot to do on short notice. Besides, knowing you, I decided it was best to present you with a *fait accompli*."

"A what?"

"Listen," he said, neither grimly nor jestingly—seriously. "We can't dive in and shoot up the place ahead as we could Dukeston. That's a naval base, intended for war." *Unless I've made a grisly mistake and am scheming to slaughter x many innocents.* "No single craft could get by its defenses. Moreover, you understand it's absolutely essential that we bring word to Terra. If we don't, a blow struck here won't make any final difference. Cairncross can rebuild, in the same secrecy as before. Even if we have the luck to scatter his atoms, the temptation would be very great for an officer of his to take over the dukedom and carry on the project. That could well be from idealism; they're surely dedicated men." Flandry shrugged. "Idealism has killed a lot of people throughout history."

Her gaze intensified. "What do you intend?"

"I've programmed this ship. In a few hours, she'll reactivate herself and accelerate like a scalded bat. Shortly thereafter, she'll go on hyperdrive; she can do it closer to a sun than most. She'll proceed to Sol, resume relativistic state, and beam a call for assistance, in a particular code. That'll fetch certain Corpsmen. You won't have had anything to do under way but fix your meals, rest, and recover. Nor will you have much to do at journey's end. Just tell the captain I've left a top secret record, triple-A priority. You needn't even tell him where it is in the data bank; he'll know. You'll be interrogated at length later on, but it'll be friendly, and you can expect substantial rewards." Flandry smiled. "No doubt you can get your Ramnu job included among them."

"But you won't be there," she pounced.

He nodded. "Chives and I are going to sneak our warheads in." Her lips parted. He raised a palm. "Not a word out of you, my dear. You're not qualified to do anything further hereabouts, either by training or by your current physical condition. You've done abundantly much; and you'll be needed—needed, I repeat—on Terra."

"Why can't *Hooligan* retrieve you?"

"Too risky. She's got to keep in free fall till the base is destroyed, if it is; and afterward, whatever craft were in space will still exist, revenge-hungry. Too many unforeseeables. A computer lacks the judgment to cope with them."

She started to say something, but curbed herself.

"We'll try to make Port Lulang, on Diris," he told her.

"Do you imagine—" Again she stopped.

I read your thought, passed through him. *Spacesuit impellers can't transport us across some twenty million kilometers—alive, anyway. The odds aren't much better if we ride a missile, especially considering the radiation belt we have to traverse. Anyhow, we'd doubtless be detected by a ducal ship. Or supposing, fantastically, we did make it, the militia will be ransacking every site where Foundation personnel are, and quizzing them under narco, to make lying impossible. How could we hide?*

"It's a tadge bit dangerous, I admit," he said lightly. "But come worst to worst, well, I've had a wine cask of fun in my life, and always did hope to depart in a hellratious blaze of fireworks."

She bit her lip. Blood broke forth and drifted away in droplets that, catching diffused light, gleamed like stars.

He thrust with a foot, arrowed across to her, hooked a leg in the rail on the outer edge of the table as she had done, and let his flashbeam bob free. His hands took her by the shoulders, his gaze came to rest on hers, and he smiled.

"I apologize for not confiding in you earlier," he said. "We simply lacked the time for arguments. But you have your mission to complete. Our mission. You're Max Abrams' daughter. You won't fail."

"You trust me too much," she whispered.

"No, I suspect I don't trust you enough," he replied. "I've learned that you're quite a girl, and can dimly see what a wonderful lot more there is to you. I'd like to continue the exploration, but—" His tongue had lost its wonted smoothness. "Banner, you're a completely decent human being. That kind has grown mighty rare. Thank you for everything." She could only answer him with a kiss that lingered and tasted of blood and tears.

An airlock opened. Flandry and Chives stepped forth into space.

Sharing the orbital velocity of the ship, they did not leave her at once. The hull seemed to lie unmoving, agleam in savage sunlight. Elsewhere were the stars in their myriads, argent sweep of the Milky Way, nebulae where new suns and worlds were being born, mysterious glimmer of sister galaxies. Elaveli filled much of the scene, its lighted three-quarters a jumble of peaks, ridges, scarps, clefts, blank plains, long shadows—airless, lifeless, a stone in heaven. Ramnu was a partial disc, gone tiny but shining lovely bright blue.

A sapphire, Flandry reflected. *Yes, another stone, where a molten ball of star-stuff should by rights have been; but this one is a precious jewel, because it holds beings who are aware. I'm glad my last expedition brought me to a thing so marvelous*—irresistibly, his mouth bent upward—*so oddball.*

Chives' voice came through his earplugs: "The weapons are emerging, sir." Bulky in his suit, but his withered green countenance visible through the helmet plate, the Shalmuan flitted ahead.

Hooligan had discharged a missile on minimum impetus. The five-meter-long cylinder moved slowly off, drive tubes quiescent. Chives caught up. Behind the blunt, deadly nose, he welded a cable which secured harness for two; near the tail he fastened a tow attachment with an electrically operated release; forward again, he installed a control box which would take over guidance. Not everything had had to be made from scratch; Flandry had had a few occasions in the past to use a torpedo for an auxiliary. Banner's sled was not adaptable to that, being underpowered and intended for planetary conditions.

The man himself was equally occupied. A cargo handler had cast forth half a dozen warheads which had been removed from their carriers. The rounded cones, a meter in height, were linked by steel cords; the ensemble tumbled leisurely as it moved, like some kind of multiple bola. But the gaucho who would cast it was after big game. Within each gray shell waited atoms that, fusing, could release up to a megaton. Flandry went among them, pushing, pulling, till he had them in the configuration he wanted. Chives steered the missile close. Together, he and the Terran prepared the warheads for towing.

The task was lengthy, complex, beset by the special perversity of objects in free fall. By the time it was done, Flandry's undergarment was wet and reeking. An ache in every muscle reminded him that he was no young man. Chives trembled till it showed on his suit.

"Squoo-hoo, what a chore!" Flandry panted. "Well, we get to rest a while, after a fashion. Come on, into the saddle, and do you know any ancient cowboy ballads?"

"No, sir, I regret I do not even know what a cowboy is," his companion replied. "However, I retain those arias from *Rigoletto* which you once desired me to learn."

"Never mind, never mind. Let's go."

Astraddle on the cylinder, held by a reinforced safety web, the control box under his hands, Chives at his back, Flandry cast a final glance at *Hooligan.* In the course of making ready, he had wandered from her; she looked minute and lost amidst the stars. He thought of calling a farewell to Banner. But no, she couldn't break radio silence to reply, it would be cruel to her. *Luck ride with you, you good lass,* he wished, and activated the drive.

Acceleration tugged him backward, but it was mild and he could relax into his harness. A look aft assured him that the warheads were trailing in orderly wise at the ends of their separate lines. From a clasp at his waist he took a sextant. That, a telescope, and a calculator were his instruments, unless you counted the seat of his pants. He got busy.

His intention was to round the moon and make for Port Asmundsen. This would require that he fall free during the last part of the trip; grav tubes radiated when at work. It must needs be a rather exact trajectory, for at the end he'd have seconds before the defenses knew him and lashed out. Well, he'd correct it once the base hove in view, and he'd done a fair amount of eyeball-directed space maneuvering in his time. The "broomstick" you rode when playing comet polo was not totally unlike this steed. . . .

Having taken his sights, run off his computations, and adjusted his vectors, he restowed the apparatus. Chives coughed. "I beg your pardon, sir," he said. "Would you like a spot of tea?"

"Eh?"

"I brought a thermos of nice, hot tea along, sir, and recommend it. In the vernacular phrase, it bucks you up."

"W-well . . . thanks." Flandry took the proffered flask, connected its tube to the feeder valve on his helmet, put his lips to the nipple inside, and sucked. The flavor was strong and tarry.

"Lapsang Soochong, sir," Chives explained. "I know that isn't your favorite, but feared a more delicate type would be insufficiently appreciated under these circumstances."

"I suppose you're right," Flandry said. "You generally are. When you aren't, I have to submit anyway."

He hesitated. "Chives, old fellow," he got awkwardly forth, "I'm sorry, truly sorry about dragging you into this."

"Sir, my task is to be of assistance to you."

"Yes, but—you could have returned aboard after we got our lashup completed. I thought of it. But with the uncertainties—you might conceivably make the difference."

"I shall endeavor to give satisfaction, sir."

"All right, for God's dubious sake, don't make me bawl! How about a duet to pass the time? 'Laurie From Centauri,' that's a fine, interminable ballad."

"I fear I do not know it, sir."

Flandry laughed. "You lie, chum. You've heard it at a hundred drunken parties, and you've got a memory like a neutron star's gravity well. You simply lack human filthiness."

"As you wish, sir," Chives sniffed. "Since you insist."

The hours went by.

Flandry spent much of them remembering. It was true what he'd told Banner, by and large he'd had a good life. His spirit had taken many terrible wounds, but had scarred them over and carried on. More hurtful, perhaps, had been its erosion, piece by piece, as he wrought evil, unleashed destruction, caused unmerited, bewildering pain, in the service of—of what? A civilization gone iniquitous in its senility, foredoomed not by divine justice but by the laws of a universe in which he could find no meaning. A Corps that was, as yet, less corrupt, but ruthless as a machine. A career that was, well, interesting, but for whose gold he had paid the Nibelung's price.

Still he declined to pity himself. He had met wild adventures, deep serenities, mystery, beauty, luxury, sport, mirth, admiration, comradeship, on world after world after world in an endlessly fascinating cosmos. He had drunk noble wines, bedded exquisite women, overcome enemies who were worth the trouble, conversed with beings who possessed wisdom—yes, except for hearth and home, he had enjoyed practically everything a man can. And . . . he had saved more lives than he ruined; he had helped win untold billions of man-years of peace; new, perhaps more hopeful civilizations would come to birth in the future, and he had been among those who guarded their womb.

Indeed, he thought, *I am grossly overprivileged. Which is how it should be.*

Port Asmundsen appeared on the limb of Elaveli. At this remove, the telescope picked out hardly more than a blur and a glitter, but Flandry got his sight and did his figuring. He made finicky adjustments on the controls. "Hang on to your bowels, Chives," he warned. "Here comes the big boost."

It was not the full acceleration of which the missile was capable. That would have killed the riders while it tore them out of their harness. But a force hauled them back for minutes, crushed ribs and flesh together, choked off all but a whistle of breath, blinded the eyes and darkened the awareness. After it ended, despite the gravanol in him, Flandry floated for a while conscious only of pain.

When he could look behind him, he saw the Shalmuan unrevived. The green head wobbled loosely in its helmet. Nothing save a dribble of blood-bubbles from nostrils showed Chives was not dead; the noise of his emergency pump, sucking away the fluid before he should choke, drowned shallow breathing.

With shaky hands, which often fumbled, Flandry took a new sight and ran a fresh computation. No further changes of trajectory seemed called for, praise fortune. To be sure, if later he found he'd been wrong about that, a burst of power at close range would give him away. But he allowed himself to hope otherwise.

There'd be little to do but hope, for the next hour or so. His velocity was high, and Elaveli would add several kilometers per second to it, which helped his chances of escaping notice. Yet he couldn't arrive too fast, for last-moment adjustments would certainly be needed and his reaction time was merely human.

"Chives," he mumbled, "wake up. Please."

Though would that be any mercy?

The death-horse plunged onward. Port Asmundsen took form in the telescope. Flandry's mind filled out the image from his recollection of pictures he had studied at Wainwright Station—none recent. A cluster of buildings occupied a flat valley floor surrounded by mountains. Most was underground, of course. Ships crowded a sizeable spacefield. Installations were visible on several peaks, and he felt pretty sure what their nature was.

No doubt the base had a negafield generator. If his missile was identified in time, it would suddenly be confronted by a shield of force it could not penetrate, except with radiation that would do negligible damage. If it did not detonate, it would fall prey to an energy beam or a countermissile, fired from beyond the screened area. Flandry was betting that it would not be noticed soon enough.

It and its tow were just a cluster of cold bodies, smaller than the smallest spacecraft, in swift motion. A radar might register a blip, an optical pickup a flick, but the computers should dismiss these as glitches. He had hypothesized that the defenses were served chiefly by computers. Cairncross' men, especially his experienced officers, must be spread thin; he couldn't raise a substantial body of reservists until he was ready to strike, without revealing his hand. Port Asmundsen held mostly workers. (Flandry had no compunctions about them; they knew what they were working for.) Of naval personnel there, few if any could have more than a theoretical knowledge of war.

Moreover, not even a commander with battle ribbons would likely have imagined this kind of attack. Missiles were launched from warcraft, and none which didn't serve the ducal cause were known to be anywhere near. The raid on Dukeston would have brought a general alert. But the assumption was natural that *Hooligan* was bound straight home to tattle. Cairncross would have ordered a search by such vessels as had the appropriate capabilities—which meant that those vessels were not on sentry-go around Elaveli.

We'll find out, rather soon, how right I am.

Flandry felt a stirring through his harness. A weak voice trickled into his earplugs: "Sir? How are you, sir?"

"Fine and dandy," he fibbed, while his pulse throbbed relief. "You?"

"Somewhat debilitated, sir. . . . Oh, dear. I am afraid the tea flask broke free of us during acceleration."

Flandry reached to his hip. "Well," he said, "would you care to substitute a nip of cognac?"

They couldn't afford the least intoxication, but it would be best if they could relax a bit. Time was ample for regaining spryness before the last move in the game.

Presently Flandry settled himself to recalling, sight by sight, touch by touch, a girl who lay buried on a distant planet.

His attack was from the direction of the sun, whose brilliance torrented out of blackness, over knife-sharp heights and crags, across ashen valley and crouching buildings and the gaunt forms of ships. They grew below him, they reached, they reeled in his vision.

"Ya-a-ah!" he screamed, and gave a final burst of power. His thumb pushed a button. The tow attachment opened and released the warheads. They swept on. Flandry spun a pair of dials. The missile surged, the leap went through his bones, it was as if he felt the metal strain against its own speed.

"Don't look down!" he yelled. Himself he peered ahead. His groundward vector was enormous. He was fighting it with as much thrust as he could stand while remaining wholly awake, but there was no telling if he would clear the mountain before him.

Hai, what a ride! Here comes the Wild Huntsman!

The mountain was twin-peaked. With all the skill that was in him, Flandry sought the gap between. Cliffs loomed dark and sheer. Suddenly they blazed. The warheads had begun to strike.

He saw the mountain shudder and crack. A landslide went across it. Another burst of reflected lividness left him dazzled. The first flung shards hurtled incandescent around, and the first night-like dust.

Somehow he got through. A precipice went by within centimeters, but somehow he did not crash. And he was beyond, falling toward barren hills underneath but more slowly for every furious instant. He might . . . he might yet . . . yes, by Satan, he *would* clear the horizon! He and Chives were returning starward.

When he knew that, he stared back. A pillar of murk rose and swelled, up, up, up above the shaken range. Lightnings lanced through it. That dust would quickly scatter and settle in airlessness, apart from what escaped to space. Radioactivity would poison the stone soil for years to come. The molten-bottomed craters in the valley floor would congeal around what twisted, charred fragments were left of Port Asmundsen—a terrible warning which no future powermonger would heed.

Well, but there was sufficient evidence for a properly equipped investigative team. No question survived as to what had been hatching here. Flying, Flandry had seen camouflaged portals torn open by quake and collapse; the glare of his bombs had bounced off torpedoes, artillery, armored vehicles, nothing that an honest provincial governor needed or would have concealed.

He felt incalculably glad. It would have been unbearable had his final great fireworks show destroyed harmless folk. Peace welled forth within him.

Elaveli fell behind. The residue of its former velocity, combined with the acceleration to escape, had put the missile in orbit—an eccentric orbit about Ramnu or Niku or the core of the galaxy, not yonder poor damned moon. No matter which. He'd try for Diris, but only from a sense of duty to Chives' sense of duty. With his primitive equipment, the chances of getting there before the tanked air gave out, or just of getting there, were less than slight. Besides, under drive they'd be easily detectable by any warcraft that hurried back to learn what catastrophe had happened. Whether or not the multiple blast was seen from afar, neutrino bursts had carried the news at light speed.

Flandry grinned. He kept a warhead. If an enemy tried to capture him, he'd produce one more pyrotechnic display—unless the captain was smart and opened fire immediately, which wouldn't be a bad way to go either.

He turned off the engine and let his bruised flesh savor its immemorial dream of flying weightless. Quiet laved him. The sun at his back, he saw the host of his old friends the stars.

"Sir," Chives said, "permit me to offer congratulations."

"Thank you," Flandry replied. "Permit me to offer cognac." They had no reason not to empty the flask. Rather, every reason prevailed for doing so.

"Are you hungry, sir? We have rations, albeit not up to your customary standard!"

"No, not yet, Chives. Help yourself if you are. I'm quite satisfied."

Soon, however, the Shalmuan asked, "Excuse me, sir, but would it not be advisable to begin course corrections?"

Flandry shrugged. "Why not?"

He took aim at Ramnu and set off at half a gee, about as much as he guessed his companion could take without pain. They would continue to draw farther away for—he wasn't sure how long—until their outward velocity had been shed. Then they would start approaching the planet; when they got close, he could pick out the inner moon and attempt rendezvous. The whole effort was ridiculous . . . except that, yes, it probably would attract a warship, and death in battle was better than death by asphyxiation.

It was bare minutes until Chives announced, "Sir, I believe I spy a spacecraft, at six o'clock and minus thirty degrees approximately. It seems to be nearing."

Flandry twisted about and extended his telescope. "Yes," he said. Inwardly: *If he's armed, we fight. If he's a peaceful merchantman—I have my blaster. Maybe when we've boarded, we can commandeer him. . . . No.* The hull grew fast in his sight. *That's no freighter, not with those lines.*

He choked on an oath.

"Sir," Chives said, audibly astounded, "I do think it is the *Hooligan.*"

"What the—the—" *I can but gibber.*

The spearhead shape glided close. Flandry halted acceleration, and his ship smoothly matched vectors. Across a few hundred meters he saw an outer airlock door swing wide. He and Chives unharnessed and flitted across.

Nobody waited to greet them when they had cycled through. Flandry heard the low throb of full power commence, felt its pulse almost subliminally. *Hooligan* was running home again. He shed his armor and shuffled forward along the corridor under a planet's weight of exhaustion. Chives trailed at a discreet distance.

Banner came from the pilot cabin. She halted amidst the metal, and he did, and for many heartbeats there was silence between them.

Finally he groaned: "How? And why, why? Compromising the mission—"

"No." Pride looked back at him. "Not really. No other vessel is in a position to intercept us. I made sure of that, and I also dispatched a written report in a message carrier, before turnabout. Did you suppose a daughter of Max Abrams would not have learned how to do such things?"

"But—Listen, the chances of our survival were so wretched, you were crazy to—"

She smiled. "I gave them a better rating. I've come to know you, Dominic. Now let's tuck you both in bed and start the therapy for radiation exposure."

But then her strength gave way. She leaned against the bulkhead, face buried in arms, and shuddered in sudden weeping. "Forgive me! I, I did wrong, I know, you must despise me, that c-c-couldn't follow orders, and me a Navy brat, but I n-n-never was any good at it—"

He gathered her to him. "Well," he said, with hardly more steadiness, "I never was either."

✧ XIV ✧

Fall comes early to the High Sierra. When Flandry was free of the Cairncross episode and its aftermath, that range in western North America was frosty by day and hard frozen by night. It was also at its fairest. He owned a cabin and a few hectares. Banner had stayed on Terra; first Naval Intelligence had questioned her in depth, and afterward civilian travel to planets of the Hermetian domain was suspended until security could be made certain. They had rarely communicated.

At last he could call and invite her to join him for a vacation. She accepted.

They left the cabin next morning on a hike. Chives took a fishing rod in another direction, promising trout meuniére for dinner. In the beginning, man and woman walked silent. The air was diamond clear; breath smoked, and blew away on a cold breeze that smelled of fir. Those darkling trees were intermingled with golden-leaved aspen, which trembled and rustled. On the right of the trail, forest stood thin and soon came to an end. Thus wayfarers could see between trunks and boughs, to a dropoff into a canyon. On its opposite side, a kilometer distant, bluish rock lifted too steep for more than a few shrubs to grow, toward heights where snow already lay. The sky was cloudless, the sun incredibly bright. A hawk hovered, wings aglow.

After a while Banner said, looking straight before her, "We didn't talk about politics, or much of anything, yesterday."

"No, we'd better things to do, hm?"

The earnestness that he remembered was back upon her. "What is the situation? Nothing worthwhile comes in the news, ever."

"Of course not. The Imperium isn't about to publicize an affair like that. Embarrassing. And dangerous; it might generate ideas elsewhere. The fact of a conspiracy to rebel and usurp can't be totally hidden away. But it can be underplayed in the extreme, it can be made downright boring to hear about, and more entertaining events can be manufactured to crowd it out of what passes for the public consciousness."

She clenched her fists. "You know the facts, don't you?"

He nodded. "Obviously. I'm not supposed to mention them, and I wouldn't to most people, but you can keep your mouth shut. Besides, you've earned the right to learn whatever you want to."

"Well, what has happened?"

"Oh, let's not drag through the details. The whole movement fell to pieces. Some crews surrendered voluntarily, gave help to the Imperialists—led them to the various installations, for example— and have been punished by no more than dishonorable discharges, fines, or perhaps a bit of nerve-lash. Others fled, whether disappearing into the Hermetian population or establishing new identities on different planets or leaving the Empire altogether."

"Cairncross?"

"Unknown." Flandry shrugged. "I apologize for lacking a tidy answer, but life is always festooned with loose ends. It's been ascertained that his speedster was in the hunt for us when we blew his moon base out from under him. Presumably he skipped. However, interrogations of associates lead me to think the men aboard wouldn't unanimously have felt like staying under the command of an outlaw, a failure. They could have mutinied, disposed of him and the vessel, and scattered.

"No large matter, really. At worst, the Merseians or a barbarian state will gain an able, energetic officer—who'll dwell for the rest of his years in a hell of frustration and loneliness. What counts is that he and his cause are overthrown, discredited, *kaput*. We've been spared a war."

She turned her head to regard him. "Your doing, Dominic," she said.

He kissed her briefly. "Yours, at least as much. You inherited your dad's talents, my dear." They went on, hand in hand.

"What about Hermes and the rest?" she asked.

Flandry sighed. "There's the messy part. Hermes did have legitimate grievances, and they still obtain. I talked the Emperor into leniency for the people—no purges or mass confiscations or anything like that. He and the Policy Board do want changes which'll take away what extra power Hermes had. Its authority everywhere outside the Maian System has been revoked, for instance, and it's under martial law itself, pending 'reconstruction.' But you can't blame Gerhart too much; and, as said, ordinary people are being allowed to continue their ordinary lives. They're good stock; they'll become important again in the Empire . . . and afterward."

Her gaze held wonder. "The Emperor heeds you?"

"Oh, my, yes. We maintain our mutual dislike, but he realizes how useful I can be. And for my part, well, my advice isn't the worst he could get; and his son and heir isn't such a bad young fellow. I'm afraid I'll end my days as a kind of gray eminence." He paused. "Though scarcely in holy orders."

"I'll get you to explain that later," she said. Her voice stumbled. "What about Ramnu?"

"Why, you do know that the climate modification project has been approved, don't you?"

"Yes." Barely to be heard: "Yewwl's memorial. Her name will be on it."

"Work can't start till things have gotten satisfactorily organized in that sector. A couple of years hence, I'd guess. Thereafter, maybe a decade till completion, and three or four more decades till the glaciated territory has been reclaimed, right? But the Ramnuans will get assistance meanwhile, I promise."

"Thank you," she breathed. Tiny brightnesses glinted on her lashes, around the big green eyes.

"The interdict on travel ought to be lifted soon. Are you eager to return?"

"I could be helpful."

Flandry stroked his mustache. "You haven't exactly answered my question. Tell me, if you will—You didn't need to hang around on Terra this entire while. You could have gone to your family on Dayan."

"Yes, I should have."

"But you didn't. Why?"

She stopped, and he did, and they stood facing in the nave made by trail and trees. A yellow leaf blew down and settled in her hair. He took both her hands. They were cool.

She spoke with a resolution she must have been long in gathering: "I had to think. To understand. Everything has changed, been shattered, could be rebuilt but never in the same shape. Half of me died when Yewwl did. I need new life, and came to see—it was slow, finding the truth, because the search hurt so much—I don't want to begin again with another Ramnuan. Our sisterhood, Yewwl's and mine, was wonderful, I'll always warm my soul by it, but it came to be when we were young, and that is gone."

The forest soughed. Wind boomed through the canyon. "I stayed on Terra, Dominic, because of hoping you and I would meet again."

"I spent the whole time hoping I'd hear those words," he replied.

When the kiss had ended, he said to her: "Let's be honest with each other, always. We're not a boy and girl in love. We're both a little old, more than a little sad, and friends. But we make one crackling hell of a team. A pity if we disbanded. Would you like to continue?"

"I think I would," she told him. "I certainly want to try. Thank you, dear friend."

They walked on into the autumn.

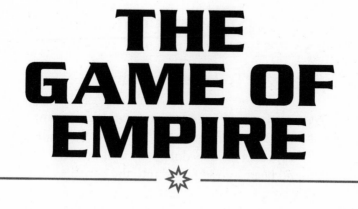
THE GAME OF EMPIRE

DEDICATION

※

To James P. Baen

Writers aren't supposed to say anything pleasant
about editors or publishers, but the fact is that in both
capacities Jim has done very well by me,
and been a good friend into the bargain.

INTRODUCTION

—— ✲ ——

This book is a sort of coda to the biography of Dominic Flandry, Intelligence agent for the Terran Empire. His chronicles had occupied five novels and two collections of shorter stories, written over a span of thirty-odd years. They were meant to be first and foremost science fiction adventures, entertainment. Yet I tried, as well, to convey some feeling of how endlessly varied and wonderful the universe is in which we live, and to provoke a little thought about real history and politics. At last the time came for a new generation to take over the saga—but I do not expect to continue it further than here. There is too much else to write about.

You may enjoy a bit of background. Under the pseudonym Daedalus, David E. H. Jones used to publish brilliant speculative essays in the magazine *New Scientist*. In one of them he pointed out that, were Earth slightly different in certain respects, we would see no horizon. I seized upon this fact to help me design an imaginary world, which it was only fair to name Daedalus. But why would its fictitious discoverers have done so? Well, suppose they called its sun Patricius, perhaps as a religious gesture. In the technical college where I studied, long and long ago, St. Patrick was alleged to be the patron of engineers, because when he expelled the snakes from Ireland he invented the worm drive. Logically, then, the planets of this star would receive the names of great engineers in legend and history. My wife and I had fun with that, although just two of them got into the story.

The book also, in a very small way, does homage to Rudyard Kipling. I hope that the first and the final sentence, especially, will raise a few smiles.

—Poul Anderson, 1994

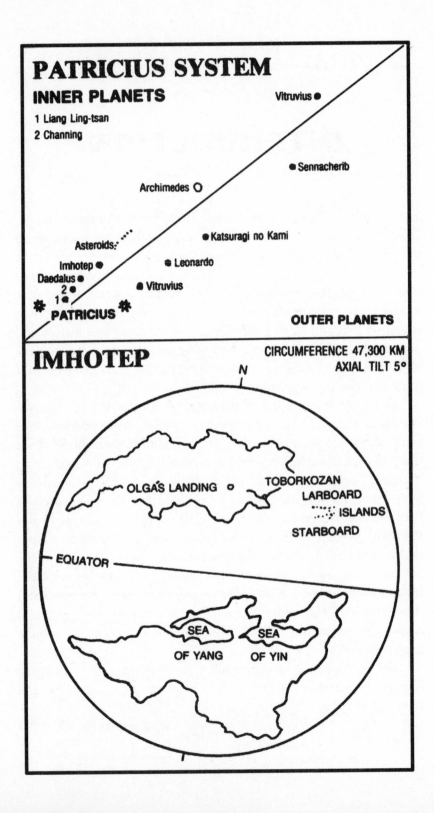

PATRICIUS SYSTEM
INNER PLANETS

1 Liang Ling-tsan
2 Channing

Vitruvius ●

● Sennacherib

Archimedes ○

Asteroids: ....

● Katsuragi no Kami

Imhotep ●

● Leonardo

Daedalus ●

2 ●

● Vitruvius

1 ●

✳ PATRICIUS ✳

OUTER PLANETS

IMHOTEP

CIRCUMFERENCE 47,300 KM
AXIAL TILT 5°

N

OLGA'S LANDING ▫

TOBORKOZAN
LARBOARD
···· ISLANDS
STARBOARD

— EQUATOR ——————

SEA
OF YANG

SEA
OF YIN

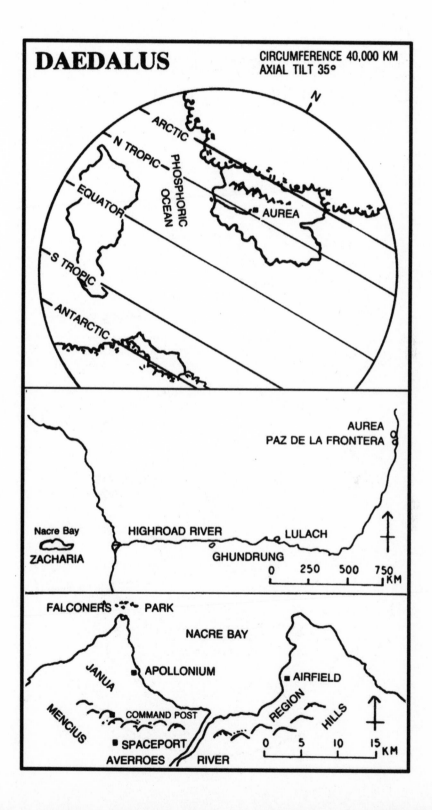

CHAPTER ONE

She sat on the tower of St. Barbara, kicking her heels from the parapet, and looked across immensity. Overhead, heaven was clear, deep blue save where the sun Patricius stood small and fierce at midmorning. Two moons were wanly aloft. The sky grew paler horizonward, until in the east it lost itself behind a white sea of cloud deck. A breeze blew cool. It would have been deadly cold before her people came to Imhotep; the peak of Mt. Horn lifts a full twelve kilometers above sea level.

Westward Diana could see no horizon, for the city had grown tall at its center during the past few decades. There the Pyramid, which housed Imperial offices and machinery, gleamed above the campus of the Institute, most of whose buildings were new. Industries, stores, hotels, apartments sprawled raw around. She liked better the old quarter, where she now was. It too had grown, but more in population than size or modernity—a brawling, polyglot, multiracial population, much of it transient, drifting in and out on the tides of space.

"Who holds St. Barbara's holds the planet." That saying was centuries obsolete, but the memory kept alive a certain respect. Though ice bull herds no longer threatened to stampede through the original exploration base; though the Troubles which left hostile bands marooned and desperate, turning marauder, had ended when the hand of the Terran Empire reached this far; though the early defensive works would be useless in such upheavals as threatened the present age, and had long since been demolished: still, one relic of them remained in Olga's Landing, at the middle of what had become a market square. Its guns had been taken away for scrap, its chambers echoed hollow, sunseeker vine clambered over the crumbling yellow stone of it, but St. Barbara's stood yet; and it was a little audacious for a hoyden to perch herself on top.

Diana often did. The neighborhood had stopped minding—after all, she was everybody's friend—and to strangers it meant nothing, except that human males were apt to shout and wave at the pretty girl. She grinned and waved back when she felt in the mood, but had learned to decline the invitations. Her aim was not always simply to enjoy the ever-shifting scenes. Sometimes she spied a chance to earn a credit or two, as when a newcomer seemed in want of a guide to the sights and amusements. Nonhumans were safe. Or an acquaintance— who in that case could be a man—might ask her to run some errand or ferret out some information. If he lacked money to pay her, he could provide a meal or a doss or whatever. At present she had no home of her own, unless you counted a ruinous temple where she kept hidden her meager possessions and, when nothing better was available, spread her sleeping bag.

Life spilled from narrow streets and surged between the walls enclosing the plaza. Pioneer buildings had run to brick, and never gone higher than three or four stories, under Imhotepan gravity. Faded, nearly featureless, they were nonetheless gaudy, for their doors stood open on shops, while booths huddled everywhere else against them. The wares were as multifarious as the sellers, anything from hinterland fruits and grains to ironware out of the smithies that made the air clangorous, from velvyl fabric and miniature computers of the inner Empire to jewels and skins and carvings off a hundred different worlds. A sleazy Terran vidplay demonstrated itself on a screen next to an exquisite dance recorded beneath the Seas of Yang and Yin, where the vaz-Siravo had been settled. A gun dealer offered primitive home-produced chemical rifles, stunners of military type, and—illegally—several blasters, doubtless found in wrecked spacecraft after the Merseian onslaught was beaten back. Foodstalls wafted forth hot, savory odors. Music thuttered, laughter and dance resounded from a couple of taverns. Motor vehicles were rare and small, but pushcarts swarmed. Occasionally a wagon forced its way through the crowd, drawn by a tame clopperhoof.

Folk were mainly human, but it was unlikely that many had seen Mother Terra. The planets where they were born and bred had marked them. Residents of Imhotep were necessarily muscular and never fat. Those whose families had lived here for generations, since Olga's Landing was a scientific base, and had thus melded into a type, tended to be dark-skinned and aquiline-featured. Men usually wore loose tunic and trousers, short hair, beards; women favored blouses, skirts, and braids; in this district, clothes might be threadbare but were raffishly bright. Members of the armed services on leave—a few from the local garrison, the majority from Daedalus—mingled with them, uniforms a stiff contrast no matter how bent on pleasure the person was. They were in good enough physical condition to walk fairly easily under a gravity thirty percent greater than Terra's, but crewpeople from civilian freighters frequently showed weariness and an exaggerated fear of falling.

A Navy man and a marine passed close by the tower. They were too intent on their talk to notice Diana, which was extraordinary. The harshness reached her: "—yeh, sure, they've grown it back for me." The spaceman waved his right arm. A short-sleeved undress shirt revealed it pallid and thin; regenerated tissue needs exercise to attain normal fitness. "But they said the budget doesn't allow repairing DNA throughout my body, after the radiation I took. I'll be dependent on biosupport the rest of my life, and I'll never dare father any kids."

"Merseian bastards," growled the marine. "I could damn near wish they had broken through and landed. My unit had a warm welcome ready for 'em, I can tell you."

"Be glad they didn't," said his companion. "Did you really want nukes tearing up our planets? Wounds and all, I'll thank Admiral Magnusson every day I've got left to me, for turning them back the way he did, with that skeleton force the pinchfists on Terra allowed us." Bitterly: "*He* wouldn't begrudge the cost of fixing up entire a man that fought under him."

They disappeared into the throng. Diana shivered a bit and looked around for something cheerier than such a reminder of last year's events.

Nonhumans were on hand in fair number. Most were Tigeries, come from the lowlands on various business, their orange-black-white pelts vivid around skimpy garments. Generally they wore air helmets, with pressure pumps strapped to their backs, but on some, oxygills rose out of the shoulders, behind the heads, like elegant ruffs. Diana cried greetings to those she recognized. Otherwise she spied a centauroid Donarrian; the shiny integuments of three Irumclagians; a couple of tailed, green-skinned Shalmuans; and—and—

"What the flippin' fury!" She got to her feet—they were bare, and the stone felt warm beneath them—and stood precariously balanced, peering.

Around the corner of a Winged Smoke house had come a giant. The Pyramid lay in that direction, but so did the spaceport, and he must have arrived there today, or word of him would have buzzed throughout the low-life parts of town. Thence he seemed to have walked all the kilometers, for no public conveyance on Imhotep could have accommodated him, and his manner was not that of officialdom. Although the babel racket dwindled at sight of him and people drew aside, he moved diffidently, almost apologetically. Tiredly, too, poor thing; his strength must be enormous, but it had been a long way to trudge in this gee-field.

"Well, *well*," said Diana to herself; and loudly, in both Anglic and Toborko, to any possible competition: "I saw him first!"

She didn't waste time on the interior stairs but, reckless, scrambled down the vines. Though the tower wasn't very tall, on Imhotep a drop from its battlements could be fatal. She reached the pavement running.

"Ah, ho, small one," bawled Hassan from the doorway of his inn, "if he be thirsty, steer him to the Sign of the Golden Cockbeetle. A decicredit to you for every liter he drinks!"

She laughed, reached a dense mass of bodies, began weaving and wriggling through. Inhabitants smiled and let her by. A drunk took her closeness wrong and tried to grab her. She gave his wrist a karate chop in passing. He yelled, but retreated when he saw how a Tigery glowered and dropped hand to knife. Kuzan had been a childhood playmate of Diana's. She was still her friend.

The stranger grew aware of the girl nearing him, halted, and watched in mild surprise. He was of the planet which humans had dubbed Woden, well within the Imperial sphere. It had long been a familiar of Technic civilization and was, indeed, incorporated in Greater Terra, its dwellers full citizens. Just the same, none had hitherto betrod Imhotep, and Diana knew of them only from books and database.

A centauroid himself, he stretched four and a half meters on his four cloven hoofs, including the mighty tail. The crown of his long-snouted, bony-eared head loomed two meters high. The brow ridges were massive, the mouth alarmingly fanged, but eyes were big, a soft brown. Two huge arms ended in four-fingered hands that seemed able to rip a steel plate in half. Dark-green scales armored his upper body from end to end, amber scutes his throat and belly. A serration of horny plates ran over his backward-bulging skull, down his spine to the tailtip. A pair of bags slung across his withers and a larger pair at his croup doubtless held traveling goods. Drawing close, Diana saw signs of a long life, scars, discolorations, wrinkles around the nostrils and rubbery lips, a pair of spectacles hung from his neck. They were for presbyopia, she guessed, and she had already noticed he was slightly lame in the off hind leg. Couldn't he afford corrective treatments?

Why, she herself was going to start putting money aside, one of these years, to pay for antisenescence. If she had to die at an age of less than a hundred, she wanted it to be violently.

Halting before him, she beamed, spread arms wide, and said, "Good day and welcome! Never before has our world been graced by any of your illustrious race. Yet even we, on our remote and lately embattled frontier, have heard the fame of Wodenites, from the days of Adzel the Wayfarer to this very hour. In what way may we serve you, great sir?"

His face was unreadable to her, but his body looked startled. "My, my," he murmured. "How elaborately you speak, child. Is that local custom? Please enlighten me. I do not wish to be discourteous through ignorance." He hesitated. "My intentions, I hope, shall always be of the best."

His vocal organs made Anglic a thunderous rumble, weirdly accented, but it was fluent and she could follow it. She had had practice, especially with Tigeries, who didn't sound like humans either.

For an instant, she bridled. "Sir, I'm no child. I'm nine—uh, that is, seventeen Terran years old. For the past three of those I've been on my own, highlands and lowlands both." Relaxing: "So I know my way around and I'd be happy to guide you, advise you, help you. I can show testimonials from persons of several species."

"*Hraa* . . . I fear I am in no position to, m-m, offer much compensation. I have been making my way—hand-to-mouth, is that your expression?—odd jobs, barter—at which I am not gifted— anything morally allowable, planet to planet, for longer than you have been in the universe, chi—young lady."

Diana shrugged. "We can talk about that. You're in luck. I'm not a professional tourist herder, chargin' a week's rent on the Emperor's favorite palace to take you around to every place where the prices are quasar-lofty and expectin' a fat tip at the end." She cocked her head. "You could've gone to the reception center near the Pyramid. It's got an office for xenosophonts. Why didn't you?"

"*Gruh,* I, I—to be frank, I lost my way. The streets twist about so. If you could lead me to the proper functionaries—"

Diana reached up to take him by the rugged elbow. "Wait a bit! Look, you're worn out, and you don't have a pokeful of money, and I can do better by you than the agency. All they really know is where to find you the least unsuitable lodgings. Why don't we go in where you can rest a while, and we'll talk, and if I only can steer you downtown, so be it." She paused before adding, slowly: "But you aren't here for any ordinary purpose, that's plain to see, and I do know most of what's not ordinary on Imhotep."

He boomed a chuckle. "You are a sprightly soul, no? Very well." He turned serious. "It may even be that my patron saint has answered my prayers by causing me to blunder as I did. M-m-m . . . my name is Francis Xavier Axor."

"Hm?" She was taken aback. "You're a Christian?"

"Jerusalem Catholic. I chose the baptismal name because its first bearer was also an explorer in strange places, such as I hoped to become."

And I. The heart jumped in Diana's breast. She had always sought out what visitors from the stars she could, because they were what they were—farers through the galaxy—O Tigery gods, grant that she too might someday range yonder! And, while she agilely survived in Old Town's dog-eat-dog economy, she had never driven a harder bargain with a nonhuman than she felt that being could afford, nor defrauded or defaulted.

Orders of magnitude more than she wanted any money of his, she wanted Axor's good will. He seemed like a darling anyway. And possibly, just barely possibly, he might open a path for her. . . .

Business was business, and Hassan's booze no worse than most in the quarter. "Follow me," she said. "I'm Diana Crowfeather."

He offered his hand, vast, hard, dry, warm. Wodenites were not theroids, but they weren't herpetoids either; they were endothermic, two-sexed, and viviparous. She had, however, learned that they bred only in season. It made celibate careers easier for them than for her species. Thus far she'd avoided entanglements, because that was what they could too readily become—entanglements—but it was getting more and more difficult.

"An honor to meet you," Axor said. "*Hraa,* is it not unusual for such a youthful female to operate independently? Perhaps not on Terra or its older colony planets, but here—Not that I wish to pry. Heavens, no."

"I'm kind of a special case," Diana replied.

He regarded her with care. Neither of her parents having been born on Imhotep, and both being tall, she was likewise. The gravity had made robust a frame that remained basically gracile; muscles rounded the curves of slim hips and long legs. Weight had not yet caused the small, firm bosom to sag. Her head was round, the face broad, with high cheekbones, tapering down to the chin; a straight nose flared at the nostrils, and the lips were full. Her eyes were large, gold-flecked hazel, beneath arching brows. Black hair, confined by a beaded headband, fell straight to the shoulders. A thin blouse and exiguous shorts showed most of her tawny-brown skin to the sun. Belted at her right side was a little purse for oddments, at her left a murderous Tigery knife.

"Well, but let's go," she laughed. Her voice was husky. "Aren't you thirsty? I am!"

The crowd yielded slowly before them, turbulent again, less interested in the newcomer now that he had been claimed than in its own checkered affairs.

Inside, the Sign of the Golden Cockbeetle amounted to a room broad and dim. Half a dozen men, outback miners to judge by their rough appearance, were drinking at a table with a couple of joygirls and a bemusedly watching Tigery. The latter sipped from a tube inserted through the chowlock of her air helmet. The whine of its pumps underlay voices. While oxygills were far better, not many could afford them or wanted the preliminary surgery, slight though that was. Diana didn't recognize the individual, but it was clear from her outfit that she belonged to another society than the one around Toborkozan. The group gave Axor a lengthy stare, then went back to their talk, dice, and booze.

The Wodenite ordered beer in appropriate quantity. His bio-chemistry was compatible with the human, barring minor matters that ration supplements took care of. Diana gave a silent cheer; her commission was going to be noticeably higher, percentagewise, than on distilled liquor. She took a stein for herself and savored the catnip coolness.

"Aaah!" breathed Axor in honest pleasure. "That quenches. God bless you for your guidance. Now if you can aid my quest—"

"What is it?"

"The story is long, my dear."

Diana leaned back in her chair; her companion must needs lie on the floor. She had learned, the hard way, how to rein in her inquisitiveness. "We've got all day, or as much more as you want." Within her there hammered: *Quest! What's he after, roamin' from star to star?*

"Perhaps I should begin by introducing myself as a person, however insignificant," Axor said. "Not that that part is interesting."

"It is to me," Diana assured him.

"Well—" The dragon countenance stared down into the outsize tankard. "To use Anglic names, I was born on the planet Woden, although my *haizark*—tribe? community? tuath?—my people are still comparatively primitive, nomads in the Morning Land, which is across the Sea of Truth from the Glimmering Realm to the west where the Terrans and the civilization that they brought are based. My country is mostly steppe, but in the Ascetic Hills erosion has laid bare certain Foredweller ruins. Those were long known to us, and often as a youngster did I regard them with awe. In the past generation, news of them has reached the cities. Watching and listening to the archaeologists who came, I grew utterly fascinated. A wish flowered in me to learn more, yes, to do such delving myself. I worked my way overseas to the Glimmering Realm in hopes of winning a merit scholarship. Such is common among the literate Wodenites. Mine happened to come from the university that the Galilean Order maintains in Port Campbell."

"Galilean Order—hm—aren't they, um, priests in the Jerusalem church? I've never met any."

Axor nodded in human wise. "They are the most scientifically minded organization within it. Very fitting that they should conduct studies of Foredweller remains. While under their tutelage, I was converted to the Faith. Indeed, I am ordained a Galilean." The slow voice quickened. "Father Jaspers introduced me to the great and holy thought that in those relics may lie an answer to the riddle of the Universal Incarnation."

Diana raised a palm. "Hold on, please. Foredwellers? Who're they?"

"They are variously known on the worlds as Ancients, Elders, Others—many names—The mysterious civilization that flourished in the galaxy—apparently through far more of it than this fraction of a single spiral arm which we have somewhat explored—vanishing millions of years ago, leaving scanty, glorious fragments of their works—" Dismay quavered in the deep tones. "You have not heard? Nothing like it exists anywhere in this planetary system? The indications seemed clear that here was a place to search."

"Wait, wait." Diana frowned into the shadows. "My education's been catch-as-catch-can, you realize, but—M-m, yes. Remnant walls and such. Rumors that the Chereionites built them once, whoever the Chereionites are or were. But I thought—um, um—yes, a spaceman from Aeneas told me about a lot of such sites on his planet. Except Aeneas is small, dry, thin-aired. He figured the Old Shen—that was his name for them—they must have originated on a planet of that type, and favored the same kind for colonization."

"Not necessarily. I venture to think that that is simply the kind where remnants are best preserved. The materials were as durable as the structures seem to have been beautiful. But everything in our cosmos is mortal. On airless globes, micrometeoroids would have worn them down. On planets with thick atmospheres, weather would do the same, while geological process wrought their own destructions. However, sometimes ruins have endured on terrestroid worlds, fossilized, so to speak. For example, a volcanic ashfall or a mudslide which later petrified has buried them. Something like this happened in the territory now covered by the Ascetic Hills of Woden. Since, the blanketing soil and rock have been gnawed away by the elements, revealing these wonders."

Axor sagged out of his excitement. "But you know of nothing anywhere in the Patrician System?" he finished dully.

Diana thought fast. "I didn't say that. Look, Imhotep is a superterrestrial planet, more than a third again the surface area of Daedalus—or Terra—not much less than that next to Woden, I'll bet. And even after centuries, it's not well mapped or anything. This was just a lonely scientific outpost till the Starkadian resettlement. Tigeries, explorin' their new lands—yes, they tell stories about things they've seen and can't account for—But I'd have to go and ask for details, and then we'd prob'ly have to engage a watership to ferry us, if some yarn sounded promisin'."

Axor had recovered his spirits. "Moreover, this system contains other planets, plus their larger moons," he said. "I came here first merely because Imhotep was the destination of the tramp freighter on which I could get passage. The colonized planet sunward, Daedalus?"

"Maybe. I haven't been on Daedalus since my mother died, when I was a sprat." Diana considered. Resolve thrilled along her nerves. She would not knowingly lead this sweet old seeker on a squiggle chase, but neither would she willingly let go of him—while hope remained that his search could carry her to the stars.

"As long as you are on Imhotep," she said, "that's the place to start, and I do know my way around Imhotep as well as anybody. Now for openers, can you explain what you're after and why you think you might find a clue here?"

She drained her stein and signalled for more. Hassan brought a bucket to recharge Axor's mug as well. Meanwhile the Wodenite, serene again, was telling her:

"As for the Foredwellers, their traces are more than an archaeological puzzle. Incredibly ancient as they are, those artifacts may give us knowledge of the Incarnation.

"For see you, young person, some three thousand standard years have passed since Our Lord Jesus Christ walked upon Terra and brought the offer of salvation to fallen man. Subsequently, upstart humankind has gone forth into the light-years; and with Technic civilization has traveled faith, to race after race after race.

"About such independently spacefaring beings as the Ymirites, one dares say nothing. They are too alien. It may be that they are not fallen and thus have no need of the Word. But painfully plain it is that every oxygen-breathing species ever encountered is in no state of grace, but prone to sin, error, and death.

"Now Our Lord was born once upon Terra, and charged those who came after with carrying the gospel over the planet. But what of other planets? Were they to wait for human missionaries? Or have some of them, at least, been granted the glory of their own Incarnations? It is not a matter on which most churches have ventured to dogmatize. Not only are the lives, the souls, so different from world to world, but here and there one nevertheless does find religions which look strangely familiar. Coincidence? Parallel development? Or a deeper mystery?"

He paused. Diana frowned, trying to understand. Questions like this were not the sort she was wont to ask. "Does it matter? I mean, can't you be as good a person regardless?"

"Knowledge of God always matters," said Axor gravely. "This is not necessary to individual salvation, no. But think what a difference in the teaching of the Word it would make, to know the truth—whatever the truth may be. If science can show that the gospel account of Christ is not myth but biography; and if it then finds that his ministry was, in empirical fact, universal—would not you, for example, my dear, would not you decide it was only reasonable to accept him as your Saviour?"

Uncomfortable, Diana tried to shift the subject. "So you think you may get a hint from the Foredweller works?"

"I cherish hopes, as did those scholars who conceived the thought before me. Consider the immense timeline, millions of years. Consider that the Builders must have been too widespread and numerous, too learned and powerful—yes, too wise, after their long, long history—to be destroyed by anything material. No, surely they abandoned their achievements, as we, growing up, put away childish things, and went on to a higher plane of existence. Yet surely, too, they nourished a benign desire to ease the path for those who came after. They would leave inscriptions, messages—time-blurred now, nearly gone; but perhaps the writers did not foresee how many ages would pass before travel began again between the stars. Still, what better could they bequeath us than their heritage of Ultimate Meaning?"

Diana had her large doubts. Likewise, obviously, did others, or

Axor wouldn't have had to bum his unpaid way across the Empire. She didn't have the heart to say that. "What have you actually found?" she asked.

"Not I alone, by no means I alone. For the most part, I have merely studied archaeological reports, and gone to see for myself. In a few instances, however—" The Wodenite drew breath. "I must not boast. What I deal with are the enigmatic remains of occasional records. Diagrams etched into a wall or a slab, worn away until virtually blank. Codings imprinted in molecules and crystals, evocable electronically but equally blurred and broken. Some, nobody can comprehend at all. Some do seem to be astronomical symbols—such as signs for pulsars, with signs for hydrogen atoms and for numbers to give periods and spatial relationships. One can estimate how those pulsars have slowed down and moved elsewhere, and thus try to identify them, and thence the sun toward which a record conceivably points. . . .

"On a barren globe five parsecs from here, amidst the tailings of a former mining operation, I found clues of this kind. They appeared to me to whisper of the sun Patricius."

Axor broke off, crossed himself, stared into remoteness.

After a while Diana made bold to speak again. "Well, your . . . your reverence, you needn't despair yet. What say we establish ourselves in town for a few days? You can rest up while I arrange conferences and transportation and so forth. You see, nothin' has turned up in the mountains; but Tigeries do tell about islands with what may be natural formations but might also be ruined walls, except that Imhotep never had any native sophonts. If that doesn't work out, I can inquire among spacefolk, get us passage offplanet, whatever you want. And it shouldn't cost you very heavily."

Axor smiled. The crocodilian expanse of his mouth drew a shriek from a joygirl. "A godsend indeed!" he roared.

"Oh, I'm no saint," Diana answered. He couldn't be so naive as to suppose she had immediately fallen in love with his cause— though it looked like being fun. "Why do I offer to do this? It's among the ways I scratch out my livin'. We got to agree on my daily wage; and I'll be collectin' my cumshaws on the side, that you don't have to know about. Mainly, I expect to enjoy myself." To mention her further dreams would be premature.

Axor put spectacles on nose to regard her the better. "You are a remarkable young being, donna Crowfeather," he said, a surprisingly courtly turn of phrase. "If I may ask, how does it happen you are this familiar with the planet?"

"I grew up here." Impulsively, perhaps because she was excited or perhaps because the beer had started to buzz faintly in her head, she added: "And my father was responsible for most of what you'll see."

"Really? I would be delighted to hear."

It was generally easy to confide in a chance-met xeno, as it was not with a fellow human. Furthermore, Axor's manner was reassuring; and no secrets were involved. The whole quarter knew her story, as did Tigeries across reaches of several thousand kilometers.

"Oh, my father's Dominic Flandry. You may have heard of him. He's become an Admiral of the Fleet, but forty-odd years ago he was a fresh-caught ensign assigned to the planet Starkad, in this same sector. Trouble with the Merseians was pilin' up and—Anyway, he discovered the planet was doomed. There were two sophont races on it, the land-dwellin' Tigeries and the underwater Seafolk; and there were five years to evacuate as many as possible before the sun went crazy. This was the only known planet that was enough like Starkad. It helped that Imhotep already had a scientific base and a few support industries, and that Daedalus was colonized and becomin' an important Naval outpost. Just the same, the resettlement's always been a wild scramble, always underfunded and undermanned, touch and go."

"The Terran Empire has many demands on its resources, starting with defense," said Axor. "Although one must deplore violence, I cannot but admire the gallantry with which Admiral Magnusson cast back the Merseian attack last year."

"The Imperial court and bureaucracy are pretty expensive too, I hear," Diana snapped. "Well, never mind. I don't pay taxes."

"I have, yes, I have encountered tales of Admiral Flandry's exploits," said Axor in haste. "But he cannot have spent much time on Imhotep, surely."

"Oh, no. He looked in once in a while, when he happened to be in the region. A natural curiosity. My mother and he—Well, I keep tellin' myself I shouldn't blame him. She never did."

Once Maria Crowfeather had admitted to her daughter that she got Dominic Flandry's child in hopes that that would lead to something permanent. It had not. After he found out on his next visit, he bade a charming, rueful goodbye. Maria got on with her own life.

"Your mother worked in the resettlement project?" Axor inquired tactfully.

Diana nodded. "A xenologist. She died in an accident, a sudden tidal bore on a strange coast, three standard years ago."

Maria Crowfeather had been born on the planet Atheia, in the autonomous community Dakotia. It had been among the many founded during the Breakup, when group after ethnic group left a Commonwealth that they felt was drowning them in sameness. The Dakota people had already been trying to revive a sense of identity in North America. Diana, though, kept only bits of memory, fugitive and wistful, about ancestral traditions. She had passed her life among Tigeries and Seafolk.

"Leaving you essentially orphaned," said Axor. "Why did nobody take care of you?"

"I ran away," Diana replied.

The man who had been living with Maria at the time of her death did not afterward reveal himself to be a bad sort. He turned out to be officious, which was worse. He had wanted to marry the girl's mother legally, and now he wanted to put the girl in the Navy brat school on Daedalus, and eventually see to it that she wed some nice officer. Meanwhile Tigeries were hunting through hills where wind soughed in waves across forests, and surf burst under three moons upon virgin islands.

"Did not the authorities object?" Axor wondered.

"They couldn't find me at first. Later they forgot."

Axor uttered a splintering noise that might be his equivalent of a laugh. "Very well, little sprite of all the world, let us see how you guide a poor bumbler. Make the arrangements, and leave me to my data and breviary until we are ready for departure. But can you give me an idea of what to expect?"

"I'll try, but I don't make any promises," Diana said. "Especially these days. You didn't arrive at the best time, sir."

Scales stirred above the brow ridges. "What do you mean, pray?" Grimness laid grip on her. She had ignored the news as much as possible. What could she do about it? Well, she had mentally listed various refuges, according to where she would be when the trouble exploded, if it was going to. But here she was committing herself to an expedition which could take her anyplace, and— "That ruckus with the Merseians last year was just a thing off in space," she said. "Since, I've kept hearin' rumors—ask your God to make them only rumors, will you?—Sir, we may be on the edge of a real war."

CHAPTER TWO

On Daedalus, the world without a horizon, a Tigery was still an uncommon sight, apt to draw everybody's attention. Targovi had made an exception of himself. The capital Aurea, its hinterland, communities the length of the Highroad River as far as the Phosphoric Ocean, no few of the settlements scattered elsewhere, had grown used to him. He would put his battered *Moonjumper* down at the spaceport, exchange japes with guards and officials, try to sell them something, then load his wares into an equally disreputable-looking van and be off. His stock in trade was Imhotepan, a jackdaw museum of the infinite diversity that is every planet's. Artifacts of his people he had, cutlery, tapestries, perfumes; things strange and delicate, made underwater by the Seafolk; exotic products of nature, skins, mineral gems, land pearls, flavorful wild foods—for the irony was that huge Imhotep had begotten life which Terrans, like Starkadians, could safely take nourishment from, whereas Terra-sized Daedalus had not.

For a number of years he had thus ranged, dickering, swapping, amusing himself and most whom he encountered, a generally amiable being whom—certain individuals discovered too late—it was exceedingly dangerous to affront. Even when tensions between Merseia and Terra snapped asunder, sporadic combats erupted throughout the marches, and at last Sector Admiral Magnusson took his forces to meet an oncoming armada of the Roidhunate, even then had Targovi plied his trade unhindered.

Thus he registered shock when he landed in routine fashion a twelvemonth later, and the junior port officer who gave him his admission certificate warned: "You had better stay in touch with us. Interplanetary traffic may be suddenly curtailed. You could find yourself unable to get off Daedalus for an indefinite time."

"*Eyada shkor!*" ripped from Targovi. His tendrils grew stiff. A hand dropped to the knife at his side. "What is this?"

"Possible emergency," said the human. "Understand, I am trying to be friendly. There ought to be a short grace period. If you then return here immediately, I can probably get you clearance to go home. Otherwise you could be stranded and unable to earn your keep, once your goods were sold and the proceeds spent."

"I . . . think . . . I would survive," Targovi murmured.

The officer peered across his desk. "You may be right," he said. "But *we* may not like the ways you would find. I would be sorry to see you jailed, or gunned down."

The Tigery looked predatory enough to arouse qualms. His resemblance to a man was merely in the roughest outlines. He stood as tall as an average one, but on disproportionately long and powerful legs whose feet were broad and clawed. Behind, a stubby tail twitched. The torso was thick, the arms and their four-fingered hands cabled with muscle. The round head bore a countenance flat and narrow-chinned, a single breathing slit in the nose, carnivore teeth agleam in the wide mouth. Beneath the fronded chemosensor tendrils, eyes were slanted and scarlet-hued. The large, movable ears were scalloped around the edges as if to suggest bat wings. Fur clothed him in silkiness that had now begun to bristle, black-striped orange except for a white triangle at the throat. His voice purred, hissed, sometimes growled or screeched, making its fluent Anglic an outlandish dialect.

He wore nothing at present but a breechclout, pocketed belt, knife, and amulet hung from his neck—these, and an oxygill. Its pleated pearly ruff lifted from his shoulders at the back of the head, framing the latter. Strange it might seem, to observe such a molecularly-convoluted intricacy upon such a creature, and to recollect what chemical subtleties went on within, oxygen captured and led into the bloodstream through capillary-fine tubes surgically installed. Yet it gave him the freedom to be barbaric, where he would else have been encumbered with a helmet and pump, or have perished. His kind had evolved under an air pressure more than nine times the Terran.

"I think your efforts might fail," he said low. Easing: "However, surely naught untoward will happen. You are kind to advise me, Dosabhai Patel. You wife may find some pleasant trinket in her mail. But what is this extremity you await?"

"I did not say we are bound to have one," replied the officer quickly.

"What could it be, does it come on us?"

"Too many wild rumors are flying about. Both naval and civil personnel are under orders not to add to them."

Targovi's chair had been designed for a human, but he was sufficiently supple to flow down into it. His eyelids drooped; he bridged his fingertips. "Ah, good friend, you realize I am bound to hear those rumors. Were it not best to arm me with truths whereby I may slay them? I am, of course, a simple, wandering trader, who knows no secrets. Yet I should have had some inkling if, say, a new Merseian attack seemed likely."

"Not that! Admiral Magnusson gave them a lesson they will remember for a while." Patel cleared his throat. "Understand, what happened was not a war."

Targovi did not overtly resent the patronizing lecture that followed, meant for a half-civilized xeno: "Bloody incidents are all too common. It is inevitable, when two great powers, bitter rivals, share an ill-defined and thinly peopled buffer zone which is, actually, an arena for them. This latest set of clashes began when negotiations over certain spheres of influence broke down and commanders in various locations grew, ah, trigger-happy. True, the Roidhunate did dispatch a task force to 'restore order.' Had it succeeded, the Merseians would undoubtedly have occupied the Patrician System, thereby making this entire sector almost indefensible and driving a salient deep into the Empire. We would have had to settle with them on highly disadvantageous terms. As you know, Admiral Magnusson beat them back, and diplomats on both sides are trying to mend things. . . . No, we are in no immediate danger from outside."

"From inside, then?" Targovi drawled. "Even we poor, uprooted vaz-Toborko—aye, even the vaz-Siravo beneath their seas—have learned a little about your great Empire. Rebellions and attempted rebellions have grown, regrettably, not infrequent, during the past half century. The present dynasty itself, did it not come to power by—?—"

"The glorious revolution was necessary," Patel declared. "Emperor Hans restored order and purged corruption."

"Ah, but his sons—"

Patel's fist struck the desktop. "Very well, you insolent barbarian! Daedalus, this whole system, the Empire itself were in grave peril last year. Admiral Magnusson rectified the situation, but it should never have arisen. The Imperial forces in these parts should have been far stronger. As matters stood, under a less brilliant commander, they would almost certainly have been smashed." He moistened his lips. "No question of disloyalty. No *lèse majesté*. But there is a widespread feeling on Daedalus, especially among Navy personnel, that Emperor Gerhart and his Policy Board have . . . not been well advised . . . that some of the counsel they heeded may actually have been treasonable in intent . . . that drastic reform has again become overdue. The Admiral has sent carefully reasoned recommendations to Terra. Meanwhile, dissatisfaction leads to restlessness. He may have to impose martial law, or—Enough. These matters are not for subjects like you and me to decide." Nonetheless eagerness lighted his features and shrilled in his voice. "You have had your warning, Targovi. Be off, but stay in touch; attend to your business and nothing else; and you will probably be all right."

The trader rose, spoke his courteous farewell, departed. In Terran-like gravity he rippled along, his padded feet silent across the floor.

Well-nigh the whole of Aurea was new, built to accommodate the burgeoning sector defense command that had been established on the planet, together with the civil bureaucracy and private enterprises that it drew. Architecture soared boldly in towers, sprawled in ponderous industrial plants. Vehicles beswarmed streets, elways, skies. Around the clock, the throb of traffic never ceased.

Hardly anything remained of the original town, demolished and engulfed. It had been small anyhow, for colonization was far-flung, enclaves in wilderness that could not be tamed but only, slowly, destroyed. Still, a bit from early days clung yet to a steep slope beneath the plateau. Targovi went there, to an inn he knew.

He mingled readily with the crowds. He might be the sole member of his race on Daedalus, but plenty of other xenosophonts were present. The vague borders of the Terran Empire held an estimated four million suns, of which perhaps a hundred thousand had some degree of contact with it. Out of that many, no few were bound to have learned from Technic civilization—if they had learned nothing else—the requirements for traveling between the stars. They included spacehands, Naval personnel, Imperial officials, besides those engaged on affairs of their own. Then too, colonization of Daedalus had not been exclusively human by any means. It made for a variegated scene, which Targovi enjoyed. His inmost wish was to get beyond this single planetary system, out into the freedom of the galaxy.

Descending, he followed a lane along a cliff. On his left were walls time-gnawed, unpretentious, reminiscent of those in the Old Town of Olga's Landing. On his right were a guard rail, empty air, and a tremendous view. The river glimmered silver, grandly curved, through hundreds of kilometers of its valley, sunset bound. That land lay in shades of dark, metallic green, save where softer tones showed that farmsteads or plantations had been wrested out of it. The northern mountains and the ice fields beyond them, the southward sweep of plains, faded out of sight, lost in sheer distance.

Closer by, the headwaters of the river rushed downward in cataracts. The mountainside was covered with native growth. Although air was cool at this altitude, Targovi caught a harsh pungency. Raindrops that were cars flitted to and fro through heaven. A spaceship lifted, her gravs driving her in silence, but the hull carving out muted thunder.

Ju Shao's inn perched ramshackle on the brink. Targovi entered the taproom. The owner bounded to greet him: a Cynthian by species, small, white-furred, bushy-tailed. "Welcome back!" she piped. "A sweet sight, you, after the klongs who've been infesting this place lately. What will you have?"

"Dinner, and a room for the night," Targovi answered. "Also—" His eyes flickered about. Besides himself, the customers thus far were just four humans in Navy uniform, seated around a table, talking over their liquor. "What mean you by 'klongs'?" he asked. "I thought you got folk here as well-behaved as is reasonable. Those who're not, the rest always cast out."

"Too many are akindle nowadays," Ju Shao grumbled. "Young, from Navy or Marine Corps. They yell about how the Imperium's abandoned us and how we need strong leadership—that sort of spew. They get drunk and noisy and start throwing things around. Then the patrol arrives, and I have to waste an hour recording a statement before I can clean up the mess." She reached high to pat his hand. "You're the right sort. You stay quiet till you need to kill, which you do without fuss. We can cook you a nice roast, real cowbeef. And I've gotten a packet of that stuff they grow on Imhotep—*ryushka*, is that the name?—if you'd like some."

"I thank you, but the Winged Smoke is only for when I can take my ease, out of any danger," Targovi said. "Bring me a bowl of tea while I talk with my . . . friends yonder. Afterward, aye, rare cowbeef will be good to taste again, the more so if you add your crinkletongue sauce, O mother of wonders."

He strolled to the occupied table. "Health and strength to you, Janice Combarelles," he said, translating the Toborko formality into Anglic.

The blond woman with the ringed planet of a lieutenant commander on her blue tunic looked up. "Why, Targovi!" she exclaimed. "Sit down! I didn't expect you back this soon, you scoundrel. You can't have escaped hearing how uneasy things have gotten, and that must be bad for a business like yours."

He accepted the invitation. "Well, but a merchant must needs keep aware of what is in the wind. I had hopes of finding you here," he said, truthfully if incompletely.

"Introductions first," Combarelles said to her companions. "This is Targovi. You may have noticed him before, roving about with his trade goods. We met when I was on a tour of duty in the Imhotep garrison. He helped vastly to relieve the dullness." Her corps was Intelligence, for which the big planet had slight demand. Starkadians of either species were not about to turn on the Empire that had saved them from extinction.

She named the others, men of her age. "We're out on the town, relaxing while we can," she explained. "Leaves may soon be hard to get."

Targovi lapped from the container that Ju Shao had brought him. "Forgive a foreigner," he requested. "The subtleties of politics lie far beyond his feeble grasp. What is it that you tauten yourselves against? Surely not the Merseians again."

"Yes and no," Combarelles replied. "They'll pounce on any weakness they think they see in us—"

"Same as we should do to them," muttered a man who had been drinking hard. "But the Empire's gone soft, bloated, ready to pay anything for one more lifetime's worth of peace, and to hell with the children and grandchildren. When are we going to get another Argolid dynasty?"

"Sh!" Combarelles cautioned. To Targovi: "He's right, though, after a fashion. His Majesty's badly served. We, out on the frontier, we've been made sacrificial goats to incompetence. If it weren't for Admiral Magnusson, we'd be dead. He's trying to set matters right, but—No, I shouldn't say more." She ignited a cigarette and smoked raggedly. "At that, the Merseians aren't infallible. I've found a terrible bitterness among them too."

"How could you do that?" Targovi asked innocently. "Merseia is far and far away."

Combarelles laughed. "Not all the Merseians are. Well, you see, actually I've been talking to prisoners. We took a few in the battle, and exchange hasn't yet been negotiated. My section has responsibility for them, and—No. I'd better not say any more except that we had a lot of luck, though that wouldn't have helped much if the admiral hadn't taken advantage of it. Tell us how things are on Imhotep. At least there we humans have been accomplishing something decent."

Targovi spun out anecdotes. They led in the direction of smuggling operations. "Oh, yes," Combarelles laughed, "we have the same problems."

"How could you, milady?" Targovi wondered. "I know no way to land unbeknownst, as guarded as this globe is, and they always inspect my humble cargoes."

"The trick is to set down openly, but in a port where inspectors don't go. Like Zacharia."

"Za—It seems I have heard the name, but—" In point of fact, he was quite familiar with it. He also knew things about the running of contraband which the authorities would have been glad to learn. Feigned ignorance was a way of leading conversation onward.

"A large island out in the Phosphoric Ocean. Autonomous since pioneer days. Secretive. If I were Admiral Magnusson, I'd set the treaty aside. He has the power to do it if he sees fit, and *I* would see fit." Combarelles shrugged. "Not that it matters if untaxed merchandise arrives once in a while and goes discreetly upriver. But . . . I've retrieved reports filed with Naval Traffic Control. I can't really believe that some of the vessels cleared to land on Zacharia were what they claimed to be, or else were simple smugglers. They looked too sleek for that."

"The admiral knows what he's doing," asserted a man stoutly.

"Y-yes. And what he's not doing. Those could be ships of his— No more! Say on, Targovi."

Targovi did. He told tales of his farings to the vaz-Siravo in their seas. On Starkad, his race and theirs had often been mortal enemies. Feelings lingered, not to mention abysses of difference. They tried to get along together these days, because they must, and usually they succeeded, more or less, but it could be difficult. This led to chat about the care and feeding of Merseians. . . .

Prisoners were not maltreated, if only because the opposition could retaliate. In particular, officers were housed as well as feasible. *Fodaich* Eidhafor the Bold, Vach Dathyr, highest among those plucked from ruined ships of the Roidhunate, got an entire house and staff of servants to himself, lent by a prosperous businessman who anticipated governmental favor for his civic-mindedness. It was guarded by electronics and a couple of live sentries. Lesser captives were held almost as lightly. Where could they flee to, on a planet where they would starve in the wilds and every soul in every settlement would instantly know them for what they were? The house was in a fashionable residential district a hundred kilometers north of Aurea. It stood alone on a knoll amidst flowerbeds, hedges, and bowers.

True night never fell on Daedalus. The city was distance-dwindled to a miniature mosaic of lights, sparse because it had no need to illuminate streets. Sunlight was a red-gold ring, broadest and most nearly bright to the west, where Patricius had lately set, fading and thinning toward the east, but at this hour complete. Otherwise the sky was a gray-blue in which nearly every star was lost.

Eidhafor awoke when a hand gently shook him by the shoulder. He sat up in bed. Windows filled the room with dusk. Beside him

stood a form shadowy but not human, not Merseian— "Hssh!" it
hissed. "Stay quiet." Fingers increased their pressure, not painfully,
but enough to suggest what strength lay behind them. "I mean you
no harm. Rather, I wish you well. If you do not cry out, then we shall
talk, only talk."

"Who are you?" Eidhafor rasped, likewise in Anglic. "What are
you? How did you get in?"

The stranger chuckled. Teeth flashed briefly white below the
ember gleam of eyes. "As to that last, *fodaich*, it was not difficult, the
more so when unawaited. A car that landed well away from here, a
hunter who used his tricks of stalking to get close, a pair of small
devices—surely the *fodaich* can imagine."

Eidhafor regained equilibrium. If murder had been intended, it
would have happened while he slept. "Under my oath to the Roidhun
and my honor within my Vach, I cannot talk freely to an unknown,"
he said.

"Understood," the stranger purred. "I will ask no secrets of you:
nothing but frankness, such as I suspect you have already indulged
in, and doubtless will again when you return home. It could well
prove in the interest of your cause."

"And what is your own interest?" Eidhafor flung.

"Softly, I beg you, softly. You will presently agree how unwise it
would be to rouse the household." The stranger let go his grip and
curled down to sit on the end of the bed. "No matter my name. We
shall concern ourselves with you for a while. Afterward I will depart
by the way I came, and you may go back to sleep."

Eidhafor squinted through the gloom. He had felt fur. And those
ears and tendrils—He had seen pictures in his briefings before the
fleet took off. "You are a Starkadian from Imhotep," he declared flatly.

"Mayhap." The eyes held steady. Could they see better in the
dark than human or Merseian eyes?

If so, they beheld a being roughly the size and shape of a big man.
Standing, Eidhafor would lean forward on tyrannosaurian legs,
counterbalanced by a heavy tail; but his hands and his visage were
humanoid, if you ignored countless details. External ears were
lacking. The skin was hairless, pale green, meshed by fine scales. He
was warmblooded, male, wedded to a female who had borne their
young alive. His species and the human had biochemistries so

closely similar that they desired the same kinds of worlds; and it might well be that the mind-sets were not so different, either.

"What could a Starkadian want of a Merseian?" he asked.

"It is true, there is a grievance," whispered back. "Had the Roidhunate had its way, all life of Starkad would long since be ashes. The Terrans rescued some of us. But that was a generation or more ago. Times change; gratitude is mortal; likewise is enmity, though apt to be longer-lived. If I am a Starkadian, then imagine that certain among us are reconsidering where our own best interests lie. Furthermore, Merseia almost took control of this system, thus of Imhotep. The next round may have another outcome. It would be well for us to gain understanding of you. If I am a Starkadian, then I have taken this opportunity to try for a little insight."

"A-a-ahhh," Eidhafor breathed.

Captain Jerrold Ronan was in charge of Naval Intelligence for the Patrician System. That was a more important and demanding job than it appeared to be or than his rank suggested. Subordinates had reason to believe that he stood high in the confidence of his superiors, including Admiral Magnusson.

Hence it would grossly have blown cover for Targovi, obscure itinerant chapman, to see him in person. Instead, the Tigery called from his van, away off in the outback. The message went through sealed circuits and an array of encoding programs.

At contact, by appointment: "Well?" snapped Ronan. "Be quick. Matters are close to the breaking point. I can't spare time for every hint-collector who imagines he's come across a sensational piece of revelation." He sighed. "Why did I ever give you direct access to me?"

The least of ripples went across Targovi's pelt, and underneath. His tone held smooth. "The noble captain is indeed overburdened, if he forgets the honor that his dignity requires he grant those who operate in his service. Let me remind him that he himself felt, years agone, an individual like this one could prove uniquely able to gather special kinds of clues."

The man's thin, freckled countenance drew into a scowl. "You and your damned pride! Close to insubordination—" He calmed. "All right. I'm harassed, and it probably has made me rude. You did pick up some useful leads in the past."

They had been leads to nothing enormous; nevertheless, they had been useful. Like humans, Merseians employed various agents not of their own species. A racial and cultural patchwork such as Daedalus, remote from the Imperial center, was vulnerable to subversion—and not just from Merseia; the Empire seethed with criminality, dissension, unbounded ambitions. To hold the sector, the Navy must be the police force of their main-base planet. Colonists tended to feel less constrained in the presence of an affable nonhuman trader than with somebody more readily imaginable as working undercover.

"I think this time I have truly significant news," Targovi said.

The screen image ran fingers through its red hair. "You've been on Daedalus a while?"

"Yes, sir. Going to and fro on my usual rounds, and some not so usual. Looking, listening, talking, snooping. Scarce need I tell the captain how much discontent is afoot, sense of betrayal, demands for amendment—especially in the Navy—although it may be that many persons spoke more freely before me than they would have before others. Sir, I cannot but feel that this sentiment is very largely being fomented. To a natural aggravation, which should but cause grumbling, come unfounded allegations, repeated until everyone takes their truth for given; inflammatory slogans; hostile japes—"

"That's merely your impression," Ronan interrupted. "And, no offense, you are not human. You are not even properly acquainted with Technic civilization. I hope you have something more definite to tell."

"I do, sir. First, scant doubt remains that spacecraft have been calling at Zacharia island, suspiciously often, for more than a year. I have garnered accounts of sightings by dwellers on the mainland and sailors who were at sea. They thought little about it. Yet when I compared data from the main traffic control bank, a most curious pattern emerged. Activity has been going on yonder, sir, and I misdoubt it is not harmless smuggling. Could it be Merseian?"

"No. Have a care. Remember, the Navy conducts secret operations. You will speak no more about this, not to anybody. Do you understand?"

Targovi glided past the question. "Sir, there is another eldritch thing, directly concerning the Merseians. I have word from green lips."

Ronan started. "What? How? Who with? How dared you?"

Targovi imitated a human smile. It made his teeth sheen sharp. "The captain must permit me my own small secrets. Did we not agree that any value I might have lies in my ability to work irregularly? Rest assured, no harm was done. Again, I have simply wormed out confidences which would not otherwise be forthcoming—although bits of memory and feeling that the Merseians let drop before their guards should have been heeded more closely than they were."

Ronan swallowed hard. "Say on."

"Those officers who know what actually happened are bewildered. Several are embittered. It is like the impression here that Daedalus was left neglected to face danger alone; but this impression has more reason behind it. Sir, the Merseian fleet was led with unprecedented stupidity. Its advance squadrons flew straight into the trap that Admiral Magnusson had set at Black Hole 1571—although the hazard should have been plain to any commander who knew aught of astrophysics or naval history. Then, instead of re-forming to mount a rescue operation, *Cyntath* Merwyn split his main strength north and south, creating two pincers which Terra's rear echelons broke one by one. It should never have happened."

"Aren't you glad it did?" Ronan asked dryly. "I daresay harsh things have been done to high-ranking people, back in the Roidhunate. It doesn't publicize its failures."

"Sir, this was a failure too grotesque. An experienced, senior officer admitted as much to me. His rage came nigh to making him vomit." Targovi paused. "And yet, captain, and yet . . . our fleet could have pursued the advantage gained further than it did. It could have inflicted far worse damage. Instead, it was content to let the bulk of the enemy armada retreat."

Ronan flushed. "Who are you to talk strategy? What do you know that Admiral Magnusson did not? Has it occurred to you that his first duty was not to risk our forces, but to save them?"

"Captain, I simply suggest—"

"You have said quite enough," Ronan bit off. "Do you care to submit a detailed report? No, don't answer that. It would be worthless. Or worse than worthless, in the present explosive situation." His image stiffened. "Agent Targovi, you will drop this line of inquiry. That is an order. Return to Imhotep. Do not, repeat not attempt any additional amateurish investigation of matters which do not concern you. If we should have an assignment for you later, you will be informed."

The Tigery was quiet for a space.

"May I ask why the captain is displeased?" he ventured.

"No. Official secrets."

"Aye, sir. If I have transgressed, I am . . . sorry."

Ronan relented a trifle. "I'll accept that you didn't know any better."

"Very good, sir. But—Well, about my *Moonjumper*, sir. Of course, everybody thinks I bought her, and my piloting instruction, out of my gains from storming a pirate stronghold on Imhotep. I can return now, with half my cargo unsold, claiming a family crisis. But would it not arouse wonder, should I fail to come back soon to Daedalus?"

"Are you that well known?" The man considered. "As you will. You do have a living to make." Part-time clandestines received a pittance for their efforts, though retirement benefits, when they could plausibly claim to be living off their savings, were fairly good. "But watch your actions. If you step over the bounds, you're dead."

"Understood, sir. Aught else? No, sir? Out." Targovi switched off.

By himself, he sank into thought. Rather, he went racing away on a dozen different trails of thought, the hunter's thrill along his nerves. Certain suspicions were strengthening.

He needed help, and was unsure where to seek it. Well, since he must go home anyway, he could begin there. If he probed deeper, he might die. Quite possibly. But if not—if he did a deed that they would notice on Terra itself—

CHAPTER THREE

At the Olga's Landing spaceport, he took his van from the hold of his ship. It was equally plebeian in appearance, a long and lumpy metal box, scratched and dented, meant for hauling stuff, with a control cab and a couple of passenger benches forward. Retractable wheels and pontoons seemed to be as much in case the gravs failed as for surface use.

Unlike the ship, the van had more capabilities than it showed. When Naval Intelligence had recruited and sketchily trained young Targovi, it provided him such equipment as he might conceivably need sometime. That was not usual for an agent whose anticipated job was simply to keep alert and report anything dubious he noticed in the course of his ordinary rounds. However, Targovi was a son of Dragoika, and she was chief among the Sisterhood that led the Tigeries of the Toborkozan region. Moreover, she was an old friend of Dominic Flandry. Though he had not visited the Patrician System for a decade and a half, he and she still exchanged occasional communications; and he had risen to Fleet Admiral, and gained the ear of the Emperor. One gave little extras to the restless son of Dragoika.

Targovi took off in a soft whirr. The mountains reared grandly around. Most were whitecapped; glaciers shimmered blue-green under the shrunken sun. Pioneers had melted the snow off Mt. Horn and emplaced thermonuclear fires underground to keep rock and air liveably warm. Now the ice bulls and the frost-loving plants they had grazed were gone. Woods fringed the city. Agriculture occupied lower reaches, as far down as sea level. But humans dared not breathe there, unless through a reduction helmet. At those pressures, the gases their lungs required became poisons.

It was otherwise for Targovi. After he had left the range behind and was humming east above its foothills, he pulled his oxygill out of its tiny sockets. Already it had been forcing him to inhale shallowly. He stowed it in its case with care, although the fabric was hard to damage, and proceeded to a wholly comfortable altitude. That was no lengthy descent, as steep as the density gradient is under Imhotepan gravity.

The continent rolled away beneath him, a single forest, infinite shadings of green and gold, silvered with rivers and lakes, mysterious as the Land of Trees Beyond where some aged people believed the spirits of the dead went. Overhead, the sky was deeply blue, fleeced with clouds, the great half-disc of the moon Zoser ghostly above the sea that presently hove in sight. A splendid world, he thought. Not Starkad, nothing could be, but why mourn for that which was forever lost? His generation had come to life here, not there. As yet they were few, often baffled or slain by a nature alien to them; but in time they would win to understanding, thence to mastery, and their descendants would dwell throughout the planet.

It was not sufficient for Targovi.

He located the Crystal River and followed its course till it emptied into Dawnside Bay. There, where a harbor could lie sheltered from tidal turbulence, the Kursovikians had built their new town. Other societies had settled elsewhere, seeking to carry on their particular ways, but the Kursoviki folk were largely seafarers.

They were also those who had always been in closest contact with the Terrans, whose mission headquarters stood on a ridge to the west. Low and softly tinted, the building looked subordinate to the gray stone mass on a hilltop that was the Castle of the Sisterhood. Targovi knew how much of an illusion that was.

Nonetheless, Toborkozan had struck roots and grown; it could survive without further help if need be. Houses—timber, often bearing carven totems on the roofs—were spread widely along cobbled streets. The waterships in port were nearly all wooden too, archaic windjammers because those had been what the wrights knew how to make; but most had gotten auxiliary engines, and some were hovercraft of fairly modern design. A ferrocrete field on the northern headland offered landing to aircars, as well as the gliders and propeller-driven wingboats which various Tigeries had constructed for themselves.

Targovi, privileged, set his vehicle down in the courtyard of the Castle and got out. Guards raised traditional halberds in salute. They carried firearms as well, for emigration had not extinguished every feud or kept fresh ones from arising, not to mention lawlessness, and it was better to watch over your own, yourself, than depend on the Terrans. Targovi learned that his mother was in her apartment and hastened thither.

Dragoika lived high in the Gaarnokh Tower. Gaarnokhs had not been among the species which could be introduced on Imhotep, but memory lingered of their horned mightiness. She was standing in a room floored with slate and walled with granite. Tapestries gentled it a trifle. Books and a single seashell goblet were from Starkad. The rest—bronze candelabrum, things of silver and glass, massive table, couches whose lines resembled a ship's—were crafted here. Carrying capacity between suns had been so limited; much worse decisions had had to be made than to abandon the works of an entire history. She was looking out an open ogive window, into the salt breeze and onward to surf on the reefs beyond the bay.

"Greeting, mother and chieftain," said Targovi.

Dragoika turned, purred, and came to take his hands in hers. Though the female mane that rippled down her back was grizzled, she moved lithely. The sumptuous female curves had become lean, but her breasts jutted proud. True, they weren't ornamental adipose tissue like human dugs, they were organs muscular and vascular, from which her infants had sucked not milk but blood. Targovi had seen Terran speculations that the need to maintain a high blood supply made her sex the more vigorous one, and that this accounted for its dominance in most Tigery cultures. His doubts about that did not in any important way diminish his respect for her.

"Welcome home, youngest son," she said. "How fared you?"

"Into a wind that stank of evil," he replied. "How fare the folk?"

"Well enough . . . thus far. But you are back sooner than is wont. It would not be for aye, this time?"

"It would not. It cannot. I tell you, death was in the wind I snuffed upon Daedalus. I must return."

Her tendrils drooped. "Ever will you go forth—someday, if you live, beyond any ken of mine. Overbold are you, my son."

"No more than you, mother, when you skippered a ship on the Zletovar Sea and the vaz-Siravo rose beweaponed from beneath."

"But you are male." Dragoika sighed. "The Terran example? Are you driven to do everything a female can do, as I've heard their females were once driven to match the males? I hoped for grandchildren from you."

"Why, you shall have them. Just find me a wife who's content if I'm often away."

"Or always away, like him who begot your friend Diana?" Dragoika's mood lightened. She did send a parting shot: "Long will it be ere many vaz-Toborko besides yourself are found on Daedalus, let alone worlds among the stars. How like you your celibacy?"

"Not much. It measures my feelings for you, mother, that I came here before seeking the waterfront minxes. However, if this is the price to pay—There is naught a fellow can get so far behind on, nor so quickly catch up on."

She whistled in merriment. "Well, then, scapegrace, come have a smoke and we'll talk." She surveyed him closely. "It was not filial piety brought you first to me. You've somewhat to ask."

"I do that," he admitted. Excitement pulsed within him. Dragoika got word from around this globe. If anyone could aid him onward, it was she.

The wind blew slow but powerful. It filled the upper square sails, lower fore-and-aft canvas, and jibs that drove *Firefish* southeast. Seas rushed, boomed, flung bitter spindrift off their crests; they shimmered green on their backs, dark purple in their troughs. Following the wake soared a flock of flying snakes.

Abruptly the lookout shouted. Sailors swarmed to the rail or into the rigging to see. Captain Latazhanda stayed more calm. She had received word on the ship's radio, and given directions.

The van lumbered down, extended pontoons, sought to lay alongside. Though Targovi maneuvered cautiously, he nearly suffered a capsizing. Waves under this gravity moved with real speed and force. His second pass succeeded. Leaning out an opened door, he made fast a towline tossed him and let his vehicle drop aft. He flew across on a gravity impeller.

Besides the crew, their passengers were on deck to meet him. He thrust aside awe at his first in-the-flesh sight of a Wodenite, and turned toward Diana Crowfeather. She sprang over the planks and into his arms.

"Targovi, you rascal, how wonderful!" she warbled. "What're you doin' here?" Anxiety smote. She stepped back, her hands still on his shoulders, and stared at him through the vitryl that snugged around her head. Aside from it and its pump, she was briefly clad. No matter the broad orbit, Imhotep's atmosphere has a greenhouse effect felt even at sea. "Is somethin' wrong?"

"Yea and nay," Targovi replied in his language, which she understood and the Wodenite presumably did not. "I would fain speak with you alone, little friend." He purred. "Fear not. I, the trader, have in mind to give you, in swap for this adventure of yours, a bigger and wilder one."

"Oh, but I've promised Axor—"

"He will be included. I count on you to persuade him. But let me be about my devoirs."

Saluting Latazhanda, he explained that he carried an urgent message. She and her crew were a rough lot, but had the manners not to inquire what it was. "I daresay you know whither we're bound," she remarked. "The Starboard and Larboard Islands, where this mad pair want to look at what may be ruins left by fay-folk of old." She rumbled a chuckle. "They're paying aplenty for the charter."

"Need is that I must take them from you. But I'll make your loss good, my lady. A fourth of the fare." Targovi winced as he spoke. The price would come out of his purse, and it was uncertain whether the Corps would ever honor that expense account.

"A fourth!" yowled Latazhanda. "Are you madder than they? I declined a lucrative cargo to make this trip. Three-fourths at least."

"Ah, but so enticing a puss as you cannot fail to attract the offers of ardent agents." Much consignment, brokerage, and other shoreside business was in male hands. "How I envy them. Your charms cause me to reward you with a third of the passage money you're forgoing."

Latazhanda gave him a long look. "I've heard of you, the chapman who goes beyond the sky. If you've time to take hospitality, your stories should be worth my accepting a mere two-thirds."

They haggled amicably and flirtatiously until they reached an agreement which included his spending the night in her cabin. She enjoyed variety, and he did not mind that part of the bargain at all.

What with additional introductions, and leisured preliminaries of acquaintanceship with F. X. Axor, the hour was near sunset when Targovi and Diana could be by themselves. That was in the crow's nest on the mainmast. He balanced against the surging and swaying as easily as any of his race, and it delighted her so much that she took a while to calm down and pay heed.

Wind swirled in shrouds, bore iodine odors. The ship creaked and whooshed. A low sun threw a bridge over the waters. Forsaking this quest for another would not be quite easy.

"My mother Dragoika told me about you and your comrade, of course," Targovi began. "You had called on her and she helped you arrange this transportation. My thanks to the gods, for you two must be their very sending."

"What do you want of us?" she asked.

"How would you like to go to Daedalus and roam about?"

"Oh, marvelous! I've only seen Aurea and its neighborhood—" Diana checked herself. "But I did promise Axor I'd be his guide, interpreter, assistant."

"Axor will come along. In fact, that is the whole idea."

"But don't you understand? He isn't travelin' for pleasure, nor for science, really. To him, this is a . . . a pilgrimage. We can't go 'til he's looked over the stones on those islands."

"They've lasted thousands of years—millions, if he is right. They can wait a bit longer. Tell him, what's true, this is a chance he had better seize. Soon none but Navy ships may be going between Patrician planets."

"What? Why?"

"And Javak the Fireplayer alone knows when the spacelanes will be open again. If Axor must be stranded, better on Daedalus than Imhotep. That air helmet of his seems to pain him."

"Yes, I think it does, though he never complains. It had to be made special for him. He's comfortable in Olga's Landin'."

"But what would there be for him to do? Whereas Daedalus may well be the world that has what he's seeking. Likelier, I should think. Have any such things ever been found on globes the size of Imhotep? Chances are, he's wasting his efforts. You, small person, are not, because you are having a glorious time simply traveling. However, you can have the same on Daedalus, and more. No need for a helmet. Plenty of handsome young men."

Diana sniffed and tossed her head as much as she could under these conditions. "I can take care of myself, thank you. Do you know of anything yonder that might be Foredweller remains?"

"In my traffickings I have seen curious sights, and heard tell of others. Once we're there, I will ask more widely and more closely, until I have a goal or three for you."

She gave him a hard stare. "Why do you want this?"

"Well, as a trader who smells trouble uptime, I need better information—"

She laughed. "Let's not play pretty games. Nobody can overhear us. You're no more a simple packman than I am. I've known for years. What you really are, it wouldn't've been polite to ask . . . 'til now."

He joined an acrid mirth to hers. "Hai, little friend of the universe, you are your father's daughter! . . . I suspected that you suspected. Certain remarks you made, looks you pierced me with, already ere your limbs lengthened—not what a child shows the son of her mother's associate when he's come back from an adventure and put her on his lap to tell her about it. . . . Aye, trusting you to keep silence, I admit to turning an honest credit now and then by keeping my senses open on behalf of your father's corps. Is that terrible?"

"Contrariwise," she replied enthusiastically. "The Navy staked you, didn't it? I never really believed what you said about the pirates."

"Well," he growled, miffed, "we can talk further another time. What matters this evening is that devils are loose. They know me too well on Daedalus. But who would be wary of an innocent old priest and his young girl companion, wandering about on a purely religious expedition?"

Diana tensed. "What'd we really be doin'?"

"Essentially, distracting attention from me. I have business I want to pursue, best not discussed here. You two will be conspicuous without posing a threat to anybody."

She scowled. "I can't just *use* him."

"You'll not." Targovi spread his hands. "Who dares say there are no Ancient relics along the Highroad River and—on islands beyond? Already millions of years ago, that must have been a good place to settle. I'll help you gather information about it."

She bit her lip. "You tempt me. But it isn't right."

"Think why I do this," he urged.

"Why?"

"Because everything I have seen, heard, discovered on Daedalus shouts a single thing. Admiral Magnusson plans to rebel. His forces will hail him Emperor, and he will lead them in an assault on Gerhart's."

Silence fell, save for wind, sea, and ship. Diana clutched the rail of the crow's nest, which was pitching violently, and stared horizon-ward. Finally she said low: "No big surprise. Olga's Landin', too, has been abuzz with rumors. People are mainly afraid of an Imperial counterattack. I've lined up several hidey-holes for myself. But prob'ly that's foolish. Why should anybody strike Imhotep? We'll simply wait the whole thing out."

"You care not about revolt and civil war?"

Diana shrugged. "What can I do about it? 'Twouldn't be the first time it's ever happened. From what I've heard, Olaf Magnusson would make a fine Emperor. He's strong, he's smart, and he can deal better with the Merseians."

"What makes you believe so?" Targovi asked slowly.

"Well, he . . . he's had to, for years, in this borderspace, hasn't he? When things finally blew up, it wasn't his fault. He met them and gave them a drubbin'. They respect strength. I've heard him blamed for not followin' up the victory and annihilatin' their fleet, but I think he was right. The Roidhun might not have been free to forgive that. Didn't you often advise me, always leave an enemy a line of retreat unless you fully intend to kill him? As is, we're back at peace, and the diplomats are workin' on a treaty."

"Ah, you are young. Myself, I have lost faith in the likelihood of water spontaneously running uphill, teakettles boiling if set on a cake of ice, and governments being wise or benevolent. Tell me, what do you know about Admiral Magnusson?"

"Why, why, what everybody knows."

"What is that? Spell it out for me. I am only a xeno."

Diana flushed. "Don't get sarcastic." Calming: "Well, if you insist. He was born on Kraken . . . m-m . . . forty-some Terra-years ago. It's a hard, harsh planet for humans. They grow tough, or they die. An independent lot; their spacefolk trade outside the Empire as well as inside, clear to Betelgeuse or Merseia itself. But they give us more'n their share of military recruits. Magnusson enlisted young, in the Marines. He distinguished himself in several nasty situations. Durin' the dust-up with Merseia at Syrax, he took command of the crippled ship he was aboard, after the officers were killed, and got her to safety. That made his superiors transfer him to the Navy proper and send him to the Foundry—the officer school in Sector Aldebaran. It has a fierce reputation."

"What did he do during the last succession crisis?"

"Which one? You mean the three-cornered fight for the throne that Hans Molitor won? Why, he—m-m, his age then—he must've been at the academy yet. But the accounts I've seen tell how he did well when a couple of later rebellions needed squelchin', plus in negotiatin' with the Merseians, so you can't say he hasn't been loyal. In fact, he's seldom visited Terra and never played office politics, they say, but he's risen fast regardless."

"It did no harm that he married a Nyanzan heiress."

"Oh, foof! You've got to have money to go far in the service, civil or military. I know that much. It doesn't mean he doesn't love her."

"That is the official biography. What have you learned about him as a person?"

"Oh, just the usual sort of thing you see on the news. No, I've also talked with some of the boys who serve under him. What they tell sounds all right to me. He does seem pretty humorless and strict, but he's always fair. The lowliest ranker who deserves a hearin' will get it. And he may be curt in everyday life, but when he unrolls his tongue—" Diana shivered. "I caught his speech last year, of course, after he'd saved us from the Merseians. I still get cold prickles, rememberin'."

"A hero, then," said Targovi down in his throat.

Diana's gaze sharpened. "What's wrong?"

"Best I say no more at this stage," he demurred. "I could be mistaken in my fears. But ask yourself what elements—criminal, mayhap—could be conspiring to take advantage of chaos. Ask yourself what harm I can work on any innocent party by helping uncover the truth, whatever the truth may prove to be."

"Um-m-m." She stared out beyond the sunset. "Persuadin' Axor—because I will not fool him, Targovi, though I could maybe shade the facts a trifle—m-m-m. . . . Yes, if I said Daedalus is a better huntin' ground for him, and we'd be wise to get there while we're sure we can, and you'll take us because you're sort of interested yourself—I think that would satisfy him. You see, he really does believe in goodness."

"Which you and I are not certain of. But we are certain of evil," said Targovi. His tone had gone steely. "You might also, Diana Crow-feather, consider the cost of a civil war launched by your hero. Destruction, death, maiming, pain, grief, billionfold. You are more compassionate than I am."

CHAPTER FOUR

The home of Admiral Sir Olaf Magnusson lay in the desirable tract a hundred kilometers north of Aurea. It was small, and the interior austere, for a man of wealth and power. But such was his desire, and any decisions he made, he enforced. The only luxuries, if they could be called that, were a gymnasium where he worked out for at least forty minutes in every fifteen hours, and an observation deck where he meditated when he felt the need. Naturally, his use of these was restricted to times when he was there, which had not been many of late.

He stood on the deck and let his gaze range afar—a tall man, thickly muscular, with wide, craggy features, heavy blond brows over sapphire-blue eyes, thinning sandy hair. The face was tanned and deeply lined; its left cheek bore the seam of a battle scar which he had never troubled to have removed and which had become a virtual trademark. What he saw was a vast sweep of land and sky. Close by, the land had been terraformed, planted in grass, roses, hollyhocks, Buddha's cup, livewell, oaks, maples, braidwoods, and more, the gardens of an empire brought together around human houses. Beyond was primeval Daedalus, trees and brush, leaves a somber, gleaming green, never a flower. Those were not birds that passed above, though their wings shone in the evening light as the wings of eagles would have. The sun, sinking west, had begun to lose its disc shape. Haze dimmed and reddened it enough for vision to perceive that, because the rays came through ever more air as it dropped below what should have been the horizon. Golden clouds floated above.

Olaf Magnusson did not really see this, unless with a half-aware fraction of his mind. Nor was he rapt in the contemplation of the All that his Neosufic religion enjoined. He had striven to be, but his thoughts kept drifting elsewhere, until at last he accepted their object as the aspect of the Divine which was set before him tonight.

Strength. Strength unafraid, unhesitant, serving a will which was neither cruel nor kind but which cleanly trod the road to its destiny. . . . He could not hold the vision before him for very long at a time. It was too superb for mankind. Into his awareness there kept jabbing mere facts, practicalities, things he must do, questions of how to do them—yes, crusades have logistic requirements too—

A footfall, a breath reached his hearing. He swung about, his big frame as sure-footed as a fencer's or a mountaineer's, both of which he was. His wife had come out. She halted, a meter away. "What's this?" he demanded. "Emergency?"

"No." He could barely hear her voice through the cold, whittering breeze, as soft as it was. "I'm sorry. I wouldn't have interrupted you, except that it's getting late and the children are hungry. I wondered if you would be having dinner with us."

His basso rasped. "For something like that, you break in on my devotions?"

"I'm sorry," she repeated. Yet she did not cringe, she stood before him in her own pride. And her sadness. "Ordinarily I wouldn't. But since you are going away for a long while at best, and God knows if you will ever come back—"

"What gives you that idea?"

Vida Lonwe-Magnusson smiled a bit. "You'd never have married an idiot, Olaf, no matter how much money she brought with her. Allow that I've gotten to know you over the years, in part, and I follow the news closely, and have studied history. What date have you set for the troops to spontaneously proclaim you Emperor? Tomorrow?"

Surprised despite himself, he gave her a long look. Unflinchingly, the brown eyes in the black face returned it. The slender body in the simple gown stood straight. They were excellent stock on Nyanza, their ancestors as ruthlessly selected by a hostile nature as his had been, although the oceanic planet had prospered afterward more than cold and heavy Kraken ever could. Among his thoughts when he was courting her had been that a crossbreeding should produce remarkable offspring.

Warmth touched him from within. "I wanted to spare you anxiety, Vida. Maybe what I actually did was cause you needlessly much. I never doubted your loyalty. But the fewer who knew, the better the odds. Premature disclosure would have been disastrous, as you can surely understand. Now everything is ready."

"And you are really going through with it?"

"You will be Empress, dear, Empress of the stars we never see on Daedalus."

She sighed. "I'd rather have you. . . . No, self-pity is the most despicable of all emotions. Let me only ask you, Olaf, here at the last moment, why you are doing this."

"To save the Empire."

"Truly? You've always had the name of a man stern but honorable. You gave your oath."

"It was the Imperium that broke faith, not we who fought and died while noblemen on Terra sipped their wine and profiteers practiced their corruptions."

"Is war the single way to reform? What will it do to the Empire? What of us, your people—your family—if you draw away our defenses? You kept this sector for Terra. Now you'll invite the Merseians to come back and take it."

Magnusson smiled, stepped forward, laid hands on her waist. "That you needn't worry about, Vida. You and the children will be perfectly safe. I'll explain in my proclamation, and details will go into the public data banks. But you need only think. This sector is my power base. Until we've occupied and organized significant real estate elsewhere, this is where our resources and reserves are. And the Patrician System is the keystone of it. Nearly every other set of planets in the vicinity is backward, impoverished, or totally useless to oxygen breathers. That's why the base is here, and the industries that support it. Gerhart's first thought will be to strike at Daedalus, cut me off from my wellspring. So of course I must leave enough strength behind to make that impossible, as well as to back my campaign. The Merseians will know better than to butt against it. I promise!"

"Well—" She shivered, stiffened, and challenged: "What else do you promise? Why should anybody go over to your cause, besides your devoted squadrons? Oh, I'm not saying you would be a bad ruler. But who can possibly be good enough to justify the price?"

"You have heard me talk, both at home and in public," he said. "I don't claim to be a superman or anything like that. Conceivably, a better candidate exists. But where? Who else will make the Imperium strong and virtuous again?"

His voice dropped, became vibrant: "And Vida, I will make up for lives lost, by orders of magnitude. For I will hammer out an end to this senseless, centuries-old conflict with the Roidhunate. The Merseians aren't monsters. They're aggressive, yes, but so were we humans in our heyday. They'll listen to men who are strong, as I've shown them I am, and who are reasonable, as I will show them I am. It has already happened, on a smaller scale. The galaxy has ample room for both our races.

"Will not a dream like that appeal to worlds gone weary?"

There was a stillness that lengthened. The sun began to spread itself out in a red-golden arc.

Vida laid her head against her man's breast. He closed his arms about her. "So be it," she whispered. "I'll hold the fort as best I can. You see, I often think it's foolish, but the fact won't go away that I love you, nor do I want it to."

"Good girl," he said into the fragrance of her hair. "Sure, let's enjoy a family dinner."

That would be a chance to re-inspire his sons.

CHAPTER FIVE

Moonjumper toiled out of Imhotep's gravity well, but once in clear space her gravs had the force to boost her across to Daedalus in less than fifty hours, at the present configuration of the planets. Within the potbellied hull, Targovi considerately maintained both weight and pressure at Terran standard, and wore his oxygill. Having put the ship on full automatic, he joined his passengers in the saloon. That was an elegant word for a dingy cabin into which Axor must coil himself while Diana perched on the table.

They had dimmed the lights and were looking in wonder at a viewscreen. It showed the receding globe, luminous white and blue-green; three ashy-silver moons; crystalline blackness aswarm with fire-gems that were stars; the radiant road of the Milky Way. "God will always be the supreme artist," rumbled the Wodenite, and crossed himself.

Targovi, who was a pagan if he was anything, fingered the charm suspended at his throat. It was a small turquoise hexagon with a gold inlay of an interlinked circle and triangle. "Supreme at surprises, too," he said. The longing surged in him. If this miserable tub of his had a hyperdrive, if he could outpace light and seek the infinite marvels yonder!

Yet a planet could keep presenting a person astonishments throughout his lifetime. The trick was to avoid any that were lethal. "It were wise to make sure you twain know what to expect when we arrive," he declared. "Daedalus has its uniquenesses. Diana, I would have to crawl over our friend to reach the cooler. Will you open it and serve us? You'll find meat, beer, cold tea, bread for yourself and for the Reverend if he wishes."

"*I* wish you'd remembered to stow some fruit," she complained mildly. "I do love frostberries, and promised F. X. a taste."

"There may be some in Aurea, imported." Targovi bounded to the table and curled up near the girl. He could do things like that in a low gee-field, and was so used to the gill that it was no nuisance. But he did need to keep active, lest his flesh go slack. He braced himself against what was going to hurt. "Let me not forget to supply you with money, unless Axor has more left him than I believe. You'll be buying all your food, as well as most other things. Food can get expensive on Daedalus, and you may be faring for many a day."

"Ah . . . I have heard, yes, I have heard that the native life is inedible by us," Axor said.

Diana, busy improvising a sandwich, nodded. "None is known that's poisonous, nor any disease we can catch," she told him, "but the flip side of this is that we get nothin' out of whatever we eat. Plant and animal kingdoms evolved there too, but not like yours or mine or Targovi's. Proteins with d-amino acids, for instance. Here." She handed him the sandwich. It was hefty, but vanished in his maw as a drop of water vanishes on a red-hot skillet. She whistled and set herself to carve him a piece of the roast—about half.

"Thus it was necessary to introduce Terran and similar plants, later animals?" he inquired.

"Aye," Targovi said, "the which wasn't easy. Plants need their microbes, their worms, a whole ecology ere they can flourish. And the native life wants not to be displaced. And it is adapted to the environment. Every patch of soil to be cultivated must first be sterilized down to bedrock—radiation or chemicals—and then the new organisms patiently nurtured. And meanwhile the old ones keep trying to reconquer it. Aquaculture is harder still."

"Why did the settlers make the effort?"

"It was cheaper than depending on synthetics. Also safer, in the long run. Industries can be shattered more readily than farms."

"You misapprehend, my son. I meant that I cannot see why humans chose to invade a planet like that in the first place."

"Oh, my, you are unworldly, aren't you, sweetheart?" Diana said while she fed him. "But you Wodenites never have been hell-bent to colonize like us. Is that because you don't breed so crazily? Anyhow, planets where humans can live without a lot of fancy gear aren't that common. Artificial miniworlds are fine . . . if you don't mind scanty elbow room, strict laws, dependency on outside resources, and vulnerability to attack. Else you take what you can get. By the time David Jones discovered Daedalus, the best places in known space were already claimed, and goin' into unknown space meant such a long haul that settlers would be cut off from their civilizations."

"'Civilizations,' plural," Targovi pointed out. "It wasn't only humans who arrived. Members of several races with more or less the same requirements came too. Some wanted simply to homestead, or to make a living by serving the homesteaders. But some had their special interests. Weird is the patchwork you'll find on Daedalus."

"Fascinating," said Axor. "I daresay that, as a political necessity, these communities enjoy basic local autonomy."

"Aye. Most won it in early days, negotiating with a weak planetary authority. Certain regions on Daedalus did have much potential. Islands especially; those were easiest to defend against the encroachments of native life. This happened in the Commonwealth era, you realize, when government was loose everywhere. After the Empire took over, the greatest of the baronies were rich enough to buy an Imperial pledge that they would be left alone as long as they paid their tribute and caused no trouble."

Diana passed out beverages and slathered mustard on bread for herself. "The Empire's always been fairly tolerant, hasn't it?" she remarked.

"It is becoming less so, I fear," the Tigery mumbled. "And as for what a 'new broom' might sweep away from us—"

"Then in spite of what you've said about Admiral Magnusson," the girl tossed back, "wouldn't he be off his orbit to try for the throne? I mean, he's got to operate out of Daedalus to start with, but if the dwellers don't like the idea and begin undercuttin' him—"

"They will meekly do whatever they are told, aside from black marketing and the like," Targovi said. "Likewise the fighting men. I'm sure many will be less than glad at being taken from home, back to war, this soon. But what will they dare do save shout hurrah with everybody else? Yours is a magnificent species in its fashion, little friend, but like every species it bears its special weaknesses."

He stroked his chin. His tendrils lay back flat, and a fang gleamed into view. "Furthermore," he murmured, "Magnusson, who is no simpleton, will have made his alliances with powerful factions on Daedalus. They will help keep order at his back, until he has overrun enough space elsewhere that Daedalus no longer matters. There are Paz de la Frontera . . . Lulach . . . Ghundrung . . . Zacharia— Zacharia—Aye, surely he has his understandings with persons in these and other places."

Axor looked distressed. "This conversation is taking a horrid turn," he said. "What can we do about it but tend our private affairs and pray to God for mercy upon helpless beings throughout the galaxy?"

"Well, we can get to Daedalus ere Javak looses his flames and we are forbidden to travel," Targovi said, not for the first time.

"Yes, yes, I understand, and you are very kind, aiding me on my quest." Axor gusted a sigh that nearly knocked Diana's beer bottle over. "We were speaking of happier matters. You were, *kh-h-h*, briefing me on Daedalus—the planet itself, pure from the hand of the Creator, before sinful sophonts arrived. I seem to recall mention of its being extraordinary in numerous ways."

"Well," said the human around a mouthful of sandwich, "it doesn't have a horizon."

Axor elevated his snaky neck. "I beg your pardon?"

"The parameters—pressure and temperature gradients, mainly— they're just right for light to get refracted around the curve of the globe. Theoretically, if you looked straight through a telescope, you'd see your own backside. Of course, in practice mountains and haze and so forth prevent. But the cycle of day and night—about a fifteen and a half hour rotation period, by the way, which is short for an inner planet anywhere—that's quite an experience."

"Dear me. Amazing."

"I have read of the same thing elsewhere," Targovi said, "but those worlds chance not to be habitable."

"In fact," Diana added, "I've heard how Terra itself'd be like that, *if* it kept the same air but was a few kilometers less in radius. How much less? Thirteen, is that the figure? Nothin' to speak of as far as gravity and such are concerned. Daedalus happens to fit those specs."

"Or else God made it thus, for some purpose that perhaps the Foredwellers came to know, and we ourselves may someday," Axor crooned. "Oh, wonderful!"

The word came as *Moonjumper* was in approach curve. The planet filled vision ahead. Its huge polar caps were blinding white. Between them the tropics, seventy degrees wide, and the subtropics shone azure on the seas, dun and deep green on land, beneath clouds which the rotation twisted into tight spirals. The single moon, Icarus, stood pockmarked behind.

Suddenly the outercom picked up a message on the official band and blared it forth. Against his will, after his vital recommendations for military and political reform had been ignored, Admiral Sir Olaf Magnusson had bowed to the unanimous appeal of his valiant legionaries, that he take leadership of the Terran Empire before it crumbled in chaos and fell victim to every consequent evil. He had imposed martial law. Civil space traffic was suspended, unless by special permit. Sensible persons would instantly see why: an average-sized vessel moving at interplanetary speeds carried the energy of a small- to medium-yield nuclear warhead.

As far as possible, citizens should carry on in their usual occupations, obedient to the authorities. Infractions would be severely punished. But there was nothing to fear, rather there was everything to await, a dawn of hope. In six hours the new Emperor would broadcast, explaining, reassuring, arousing his people. "Stand by. The Divine, in whatever form It manifests Itself to you, the Divine is with us."

"*Eyada shkor!*" Targovi breathed. "Once I read of an ancient tombstone on Terra. Upon it stood, 'I expected this, but not so soon.'"

"What'll we do?" Diana asked, webbed into a seat beside him in the cramped control cabin. "Turn back?"

"No. We are locked into Ground Control's pattern. Doubtless I could arrange release, but—it is natural for me to continue as programmed. The whole object of this game has been to get our feet on yon ball." Targovi brooded. Abruptly:

"See here. Were you not the child of Maria Crowfeather and Dominic Flandry, I might feel guilt at casting you adrift. As it is, I must work with what tools I have, and thank the gods that the steel is true. I meant to tell you more than I have done, as soon as we were at large, but now that must wait. Already have I told you too much for your safety, mayhap. However, it has been little more than my suspicions of what was about to strike, together with fears of what use certain folk might make of the uproar. Surely these thoughts have occurred to others. If you know naught further, you have naught further to conceal, and I do not think they will interrogate you too fiercely, the more so when Axor is clearly uninvolved in these matters. Stay calm, hold fast to your wits, make your own way, as you have ever done."

She half reached for him, withdrew her hand, and said only a little unsteadily, "What do you mean?"

"Why, I have reason to think it could be unhealthy for me to linger after we land," he replied. "Therefore I will not. Imagine that they suspect me of gunrunning, or allegiance to the Molitor dynasty, or intransigent mopery, or whatever. Aye, it's a shock that your companion has been in deep waters. You knew only that I offered you a ride to Daedalus in order that you and Axor might be my blind, for purposes you had no reason to suppose were fell. Do you hear me?"

Then they did clasp hands.

Daedalus had no weather control. A rainstorm was upon Aurea when *Moonjumper* descended. That would be helpful to Targovi, though he could surely have managed without.

A squad of Imperial marines waited to arrest the persons aboard. At the last minute, Targovi cut Ground Control off and, manually, set down on a vacant spot across the field. He went straight out the airlock and disappeared in the downpour. Efforts at chemotracking were soon nullified by the manifold smells in the old quarter. Known associates of his, such as the innkeeper Ju Shao, denied knowledge of his whereabouts. Too much else was going on for Security to pursue the matter in detail. A Tigery outlaw would be practically helpless and hopelessly conspicuous on Daedalus anyway, would he not?

Meanwhile the squad had surrounded his passengers and taken them off to detention. At first the marines were nervous, weapons ready. But they got no resistance. The pretty girl actually smiled at them, and the dragon gave them his blessing.

CHAPTER SIX

"The hour is upon us."

Tachwyr the Dark, Hand of the Vach Dathyr, stood silent for thirty pulsebeats after he had spoken, as if to let his words alloy themselves with the minds of his listeners. They were the members of the Grand Council over which he presided—the captains, under the Roidhun, of Merseia and its far-flung dominions.

Their faces filled the multiple screens of the communication set before him. He had had it brought out onto a towertop of his castle. At this tremendous moment he wanted to stand overlooking the lands of his Vach, while its ancient battle banners snapped above him in the wind. The sun Korych cast brilliance on forested mountainside, broad fields and clustered dwellings in the valley beneath, snowpeaks beyond. A fangryf winged on high, hunting. On a terrace below, his sons stood at attention, in ancestral armor, honoring their forebears and their posterity, the wholeness of the Race.

"That which we have worked for in secret has come to pass amidst trumpet calls," Tachwyr said. "Our patience reaps its reward. The word has reached me. Magnusson has risen. Already his ships are on their way to combat."

A hiss of joy went from every countenance. Gazes became full of an admiration that approached worship. He, Tachwyr the Dark, himself a commander of space squadrons until he succeeded to the Handship of the Dathyrs and ultimately got the lordship of Merseia—he, this gaunt and aging male in a plain black robe, had brought them to triumph.

He knew what the thought was, and raised a cautionary arm. "Not yet dare we exult," he said. "We have scarcely begun. Victory could elude us, as it eluded generation after generation before us. The great Brechdan Ironrede fashioned a scheme that would have ruined the Terrans utterly, and saw it crumble in his grasp. In his name, after the name of the Roidhun, shall we go forward."

"What precisely is the news?" asked Odhar the Curt.

"Scarcely more than I have said," Tachwyr answered. "The dispatch will enter your private databases, of course, and you can study it at leisure; but do not expect much detail across a gulf that is many parsecs wide and deep."

For an instant the wish twinged in him, for some interstellar equivalent of radio, instantaneous, rather than courier vessels and message torpedoes which might at the very best cover slightly over half a light-year per hour. If the pulsations of warped space that made them detectable across twice that distance could be modulated— and indeed they could, but only within detection range. The same quantum uncertainties that made it possible to evade the speed limitations of the relativistic state made it infeasible to establish relay stations. . . . Well, everybody labored under the same handicap. Much of Tachwyr's plan depended on using it against the enemy.

"Have instructions gone to our embassy on Terra?" inquired Alwis Longtail.

"Not yet," Tachwyr said. "First I want this group to consider my draft of the letter. You may well have suggestions, and in any event you should know just what the contents are."

"Is there any reason why those should be specific?"

"No, nothing has changed in that respect. We must trust Chwioch to fit his actions to whatever the situation happens to be." That faith was not misplaced. Chwioch might bear the sobriquet "the Dandy" from his youth, but even then he had been bailiff of Dhangodhan, and at present he could better be called "the Shrewd"—except that he preferred the Terrans underestimate him. He would find—no, create—a pretext for breaking off the negotiations toward a nonaggression pact which he had so skillfully been prolonging. That would send waves of dismay over nobles, rich commoners, and intellectuals throughout the Empire, which in turn would bring an outcry for a "new politics" pointed in a more comforting direction.

Meanwhile Chwioch would explain, on every occasion he could find or make, that in the absence of such a pact, incidents leading to armed clashes were inevitable. When a single capital ship carried weapons sufficient to devastate an entire planet, and when the Empire could not keep its own house in order, Merseia was obliged to secure the debatable regions. This might sometimes require hot pursuit, into space claimed by the Empire. Obviously the Roidhunate regretted every occurrence, and stood ready to renew efforts to establish a lasting peace as soon as the Terran government was able to join in.

But the Terran government was going to be preoccupied for a period that might run into years. . . .

"When shall we put the Navy on full alert?" asked Gwynafon of Brightwater.

"Perhaps never," Tachwyr said. "Definitely not soon, barring the unforeseeable contingency. After all, the Terran embassy here will be reporting what it observes. The commanders of chosen units are already prepared for action. Best we not be too impulsive as regards them, either. Let events develop a while."

The question had been ridiculous, especially since the entire strategy had been under repeated, intensive discussion. However, Gwynafon was new on the Council—and not very intelligent—and a nephew of the Roidhun—You used what materials the God put at your disposal.

Brief pain slashed through Tachwyr. Had Aycharaych been alive—The original plan was his, and he had taken a direct part in the early preparations. But Aycharaych died when the Dennitzans bombarded his planet. At least, he vanished; you could never be altogether sure of anything about the Chereionite. With him had passed away the central machinery of Merseia's Intelligence Service. The Roidhunate had been half blinded, hideously vulnerable, impotent to take any initiative, for a decade or worse, while a new structure was being forged. If Terra had struck meanwhile—

But that wasn't in the nature of an Empire old, sated, and corrupt. Instead, its politicians wondered aloud why their realm and the Roidhunate kept failing to reach agreement. Was there not an entire galaxy to share?

As if any responsible Merseian leader could turn his attention elsewhere, when such a power lurked at his back! Once upon a time humankind had borne the same universe-spanning ambitions that the Race did now. It might well come to cherish them again—if not on Terra, then on the daughter worlds. Or a different but allied species might, the Cynthians, or the Scothani for example. Even in its decadence, the Empire had the means to pose a mortal threat. It must be nullified before the Race could be fully free to seek that destiny the God had set. *We shall, ghost of Aycharaych, we shall. During those selfsame years of our misery, your scheme was coming to fruition. This is the day when victory begins.*

CHAPTER SEVEN

After the warships had glided from orbit, starward bound, the effective ruler of the Patrician System was Lieutenant General Cesare Gatto, Imperial Marine Corps. The civil governor and bureaucrats carried their routines on as best they were able, but this had never amounted to much. Since Daedalus became sector headquarters, the Navy had taken over most functions, from planetary police to mediator between communities. Gatto reigned as Magnusson's deputy, almost his viceroy.

It was thus somewhat of a surprise, as overworked as Gatto was, when he had the prisoner Diana Crowfeather brought to his office. Or perhaps not. A husband and father, he had never lost his taste for femininity. Besides, this was an unusual case, more so than he let on to his subordinates.

"Please be seated," he said as the door closed behind her. She took a chair and regarded him across the desk. He was a small, well-knit man with a high forehead above a furrowed, hooknosed face and pale blue eyes. His uniform tunic had the collar open and was devoid of the many decorations he had earned. A cigarette smoldered between his fingers.

His look in return was appreciative, baggy though the coverall was that had been issued her. "I'm afraid this past pair of weeks has been wearisome for you," he went on. "I hope the physical conditions, at least, were acceptable."

"It wasn't bad," she answered. "Except for the questionin' and, worse, the worry about my friends. Nobody would tell me a damn thing." Her tone defied more than it complained.

"Separate interrogations are standard procedure, donna. Rest assured, the Wodenite has suffered no harm. I hear he's spent most of his time screening books from the public database. Scholarly works and slushy novels."

"But what about Targovi?"

"The Imhotepan—I wish I knew. He's dropped from sight. Have you anything to add to your claim, and the Wodenite's, that you two cannot tell why he fled? Has some new thought occurred to you?"

"No, sir." Her chin jutted. "It might help if we had a better idea of why we were seized in the first place."

Gatto stared at his cigarette, puffed, raised his glance to hers, and said: "Very well, I'll be frank. You see, you and your companion have received clean bills of health. You yourself are known on Imhotep, of course, and a check by Security agents there verified the Wodenite's story of being on a religious tour, eccentric but harmless. Nobody can imagine how either of you could be conspirators, nor did interrogation indicate it. At worst, you persist in trying to find excuses for the Tigery. You could both have been released earlier, if the urgencies of preparing for Emperor Olaf's departure hadn't caused everything else to be postponed."

Diana bounced to her feet, radiant. "We can go? Terrific!"

"Sit back down," he said. "We're not quite done yet. Listen. I would probably never have known of your existence—I do have things to keep me busy—if it weren't for the special circumstances. Captain Jerrold Ronan is our head of Naval Intelligence. He personally ordered that the datafile of this, ah, Targovi be flagged. Therefore, when Targovi came back to Daedalus, the order to hold him for investigation was automatic. Ordinarily Captain Ronan's office would have disposed of the case as he saw fit. However, he has left with the Emperor, to handle similar duties during the campaign. Since the 'hold' order originated on such a high level, it was among those referred to me for review when I took charge here. Otherwise you'd doubtless have been released much sooner. As it was, nobody knew just what to do about you, and word took time to percolate up through channels, as frantic as the situation has been. I was struck by the report and decided to inquire further, personally. Something odd has been going on."

Diana's exuberance faded. "What? I'm as puzzled as you are. Oh, Targovi did drop hints about big game afoot, but nothin' definite."

"I know."

She flushed angrily. A narcoquiz was an undignified procedure, though they had had the decency to detail a couple of women officers to carry it out on her. "Be glad you turned out to know no more," Gatto said. "That would have called for a hypnoprobing, to extract everything. After all, we don't have the drugs or the equipment to process a Wodenite."

Diana gulped, mastered rage and anguish, became able to say: "Then you realize I'm aware Targovi was—*is* an undercover agent for Intelligence. Axor hasn't heard that, by the way. He'd only be sad about the, uh, duplicity. But why the flamin' hell did Targovi's own chief, uh, Ronan, want him checked out?"

"That is not in the database," Gatto replied. "Still, it seems obvious. Not everybody supports Emperor Olaf. Captain Ronan must have had reasons to suppose Targovi favored the Gerhart regime and was somehow in a position to make trouble. The fact that he eluded arrest and fled fairly well bears this idea out." He narrowed his eyes. "Your interrogation revealed that his action was not a complete surprise to you."

"Well, no Tigery ever took kindly to bein' caged. And I sympathize!"

"What is your attitude toward the succession crisis?"

Diana picked her words with care. "The quizzin' must've brought that up. But prob'ly not very clearly, because it's not very clear to me. Maybe Magnusson would do better by the Empire. I'm just a woods colt; I don't savvy politics." Her head and her voice lifted. "I *am* horrified at the prospect of civil war, and I'll be damned if I'll stand in a crowd shoutin' hooraw for anybody!"

Gatto smiled. "I like your outspokenness. Better curb it in public. . . . Well, you and Axor will be free to go as soon as I've issued the order. I'll also give you two a requisition on the first available passage back to Imhotep, though you may have to wait a while for that. Keep in touch with the provost's office, and you'll be notified."

She shook her head. "Thanks. But we came here to look for Foredweller remains, and I don't want to let Axor down."

"Ha, I suspect mainly you want an adventure. Have a care. Air traffic is strictly limited and controlled. Ground transportation is apt to be slow and precarious." His tone harshened. "If you are hoping to make contact with the renegade, out of some mistaken sense of loyalty to him, forget it. If it should happen, call the patrol immediately. Anything else will be treason, and punished accordingly."

Diana sighed. "I don't see how poor Targovi could manage that."

"No, the chances are that he is already dead. Else he would have been seen by now. I'm sorry, Donna Crowfeather. I realize you were fond of him. Bear in mind how he hoodwinked and used you."

She made a faint noise and started to rise. "Well, I'll be on my way."

"No, wait. I feel a certain responsibility. You're a young and attractive lady, unused to cosmopolitan environments. And much of Daedalus is becoming unruly. With most Navy personnel off to fight for his Majesty, the patrols are stretched thin. We have to concentrate on guarding vital areas. You propose to take off for the yonderlands. I think that would be most unwise."

Diana settled back. "Why? Don't the folk support your glorious leader?"

Gatto frowned. "I'm thinking about ordinary civil disorder and crime. Any counterrevolutionary activity will be smashed, promptly and totally."

"You really have given him your heart, haven't you?" she asked low.

He reddened and ignited a fresh cigarette. "Donna, I am an officer of the Imperial Navy. As such, I follow the orders of my superiors. But my allegiance is to the Empire itself, to the civilization that is ours. I do sincerely believe Sir Olaf will provide the kind of government we've been sorely in need of."

"Whether it's worth the price, you aren't sayin'."

"It is not my business to express political opinions." Gatto made a chopping gesture. "Enough." He smiled. "What I want to talk about a few minutes longer is you. I am concerned. Targovi's ship and planet-side vehicle are impounded. You and Axor will only be allowed to reclaim money and personal possessions from them. The inventory says that the cash isn't much. It can support the two of you for a while, but the Wodenite's food requirements are large, and any travel you undertake will soon exhaust the purse. Do give up your folly. I'll see to it that you both get safe, pleasant housing till you can return to Imhotep. And you might enjoy sightseeing with a, ah, a native guide, when I have some spare time."

"Thank you, sir. I've promises to keep, though. Don't worry about my safety, when I'm with Axor. Actually, he wouldn't swat a buzzbug, but people needn't know that, hm?"

Despite impatience to be off, she invested half an hour in being charming to the general.

CHAPTER EIGHT

The faces of war are two.

First there is its face of technology, organization, strategy, tactics, and, yes, philosophy. This confronted Admiral Sir Olaf Magnusson, the man who would be Emperor, and the higher officers serving him.

His fleet was not all gathered at Patricius. While he had summoned more of it there than was usual, more yet was perforce based throughout the sector—working out of much smaller stations than Daedalus and Icarus held—or on sentry-go through its spacelanes. Some commanders of these units, he knew, would rally to him when they got the news. Others, left to their own devices, would not. He must make sure of as many as possible.

Hence his primary force moved ahead of any dispatches to them, in a complex path which took it within communication distance of most squadrons. Arriving, he would make his proclamation and issue his orders to join him. Since in each instance he had overwhelming firepower at his beck, and since he *was* the sector commandant, he met no resistance. A number of the captains he summarily replaced, for over the years he had taken care to gather dossiers; but these he merely sent to cool their heels, in no disgrace. After thinking matters over, quite likely a fair percentage of them would give him their pledges.

Inevitably, couriers and message torps slipped by, bringing their accounts before he did. About half the units receiving these stayed where they were, waiting for him, if only because their leaders were unsure what else to do. The rest started off to join Gerhart. Not every ship got that far. Some underwent mutinies and turned back to Magnusson. Many men, women, and nonhumans adulated him.

The second face of war is different for every individual. Consider Ensign Helen Kittredge. We pick her name at random out of personnel data. These say little more about her than that she was twenty Terran years of age, born and raised amidst the starknesses of the planet Vixen, winning appointment to the Foundry, doing well as a cadet, newly commissioned and assigned to energy weapons control aboard the light battleship *Zeta Sagittarii*. That ship was in the detachment of Captain Fatima bint Suleiman, operating out of an asteroid belt in the lifeless system of a nameless sun. Bint Suleiman was among those who voluntarily sought out Magnusson. We may assume that Kittredge was of high heart and cheered the move. Besides idealism, she must have remembered that promotions were bound to become rapid.

Except for Patricius and a few other key stars, Magnusson made no effort to leave his sector defended. Instead he took the initiative, spearing straight on into the inner Empire. One might suppose that this invited the opposition to cut his lines of supply and communication. Actually, interstellar space is too incomprehensibly vast. Traffic need just move by slightly circuitous routes, varied from trip to trip, to be safe from detection and interception by any except the wildest unlikelihood.

Nor did Magnusson keep his fleet together for long. Grown large, it was still smaller by a seemingly appalling factor than the might which the Imperium could have massed against him. Nevertheless he divided it in five. Four, under trusted admirals, swung north and south and clockwise and counterclockwise, essentially running interference for him. The main part, himself in charge, drove directly toward Sector Aldebaran. *Zeta Sagittarii* was along, trailing his flagship, the super-dreadnaught *N. Aquilae*.

This likewise represented sound thinking. The fact was that the Imperium could not bring more than a fraction of its forces to bear. The rest must keep stations whatever happened, lest barbarians, bandits, and separate insurrections wreak such havoc that nothing would remain to rule over. There was also dread of what the Merseians might do. Furthermore, it is virtually impossible to compel battle in space. He who does not want to fight can run away. Beyond a light-year's distance, his hyperdrive vibrations are undetectable.

Hence Magnusson could apply great strength wherever he chose, at least in the outer sectors of the Empire. The regions around Sol, more populous and heavily guarded, he must avoid until he had organized sufficient power to invade them. He set about doing this.

It might appear he was overextending himself, and that if nothing else, the Gerhart faction could destroy him by attrition. He had reasons to expect that his advance would be too swift and decisive for that. However, he did go through the initial stages of his campaign in a straightforward manner.

Superficially, the procedure was simple. The five insurgent fleets went to planetary systems which were important because of location, population, industries, resources, or whatever the consideration might be. Each fleet swept aside any garrison vessels, which it always outnumbered and outgunned. Thereupon a world lay under threat of nuclear bombardment from on high. Even if it had ground defenses, the cost of using them looked prohibitive. Besides . . . well, did it matter that much who was Emperor? What had Gerhart done that beings, cities, continents should die for him? The martial law which Magnusson's people imposed scarcely touched civilians in their daily lives. They themselves promised glory and better times. Oftener than not, they were born on the planet in question, quietly recruited in advance.

Discipline was strict among the Olafists. Incorrect behavior brought punishment quick, condign, and public. This helped ingratiate them with local inhabitants. Moreover, they were apt to be young, friendly, eager, with stories to tell that put sparkle into dull provincial existences.

We can imagine Ensign Helen Kittredge on leave—let us say, on Ansa, which is like an idyll of Terra. Moonlight in a warm night shimmers across a lake; music sounds from a pavilion, but she and a young man of the planet have left its dance floor and wandered out along the water, under trees which breathe fragrance into the air. Earlier she lectured him earnestly on the new day that Emperor Olaf will bring, but now she has been swaying laughterful in his arms, and they sit down on soft turf, and perhaps she says yes, when the war is over she will take a long liberty here, but that time may be far off and meanwhile the night is theirs. . . .

Leaves were brief, because a fleet must go on to the next sun and the next. One may ask why the Gerhartists did not come in as soon as their foes had left and reclaim every conquest. The answer is multiplex. Such attempts would have been expensive, both to the Navy and to the worlds: for the Olafist detachments occupying them, though small, were busily enhancing defenses, and sure to fight while hope remained. Then too, the Imperium was in disarray, taken by surprise, its high command striving to make sense out of reports that came in late and garbled. Also, the idea was quite sensible that recapturing a few globes would be of scant use while Magnusson's wolf packs were on the prowl. Better to kill those first. Then the rebels left behind would have no choice but to surrender, especially if amnesty was offered their rank and file.

Therefore, slowly, often chaotically, the regular Navy marshalled what forces it could spare and went in search of combat.

The first major engagement occurred near a dim red dwarf star which had, then, merely a catalogue number, but which afterward was known to spacefarers as Battle Sun. Scoutcraft on both sides had been casting about, probing, peering, feeding into computers whatever scraps of data they could glean, dashing back to report. Gradually the pictures emerged, and the masters came to their decisions. They would fight.

Rear Admiral Richard Blenkiron, director of operations for Sector Aldebaran, personally led his armada. He was no coward. Terran-born, he was, besides, a man of considerable wit and charm. Unfortunately, he was not well suited to his position, being a political appointee serving out this assignment in preparation for something less martial and more lucrative. Nobody had foreseen war would reach these parts, as far inward as they lay.

Magnusson had anticipated that, and bypassed several occasions of combat. In two-dimensional terms, it can be said that he made an end run. If he could scatter the Aldebaranian fleet, hostiles at his back would hardly matter. They could be taken care of piecemeal. Meanwhile terror on Terra would be his ally. Therefore he too went looking for battle.

"Now hear this," intones the intercom system of *Zeta Sagittarii*.

A recording of Sir Olaf's message to his crews follows. He expects that all will do their duty, and win a victory never to be forgotten. Surely Ensign Kittredge joins in the customary cheers. Thereafter, coolly above a hammering heart, she takes her station.

Since both leaders wanted to meet, they advertised themselves on the way, traveling in dispersed formation to maximize the sphere of detectability. Upon making contact, they deployed according to their respective plans. The gap closed rapidly.

Interstellar war bears no more resemblance to interplanetary than the latter does to planetside combat. Shuttling in and out of quantum multi-space at thousands or even millions of times a second, a ship under hyperdrive is essentially untouchable by an ordinary weapon. A concentrated energy beam or material barrage just might happen to intercept often enough to do significant damage, but the odds against that are huge, and in any event a warcraft has her protections, armor plate, absorbers, computer-controlled negafields to repel incoming matter. Only when the drives of two vessels are in phase do they become solid, vulnerable, to each other.

It is not extraordinarily difficult to match phase. There is a limited range of jump frequencies that are feasible to use, for any given type of ship; and they are not infinitely divisible, but quantized. Of course, a standard evasive tactic is to keep shifting the frequency. This requires the enemy to predict the next one. In that, high-speed stochastic analysis is valuable though not infallible.

Since the object is to harm the adversary, phase-change evasion is merely one maneuver among many. Indeed, not uncommonly, by eerie tacit consent, ships turn off their hyperdrives and slug it out in the relativistic mode, at speeds far below that of light.

When near enough, Blenkiron used quasi-instantaneous modulated hyperwaves to call Magnusson and demand surrender. The reply he got was polite and cold. The exchange had been a formality throughout.

The fleets interpenetrated and began to fight. Rays and missiles flew. Nuclear detonations flowered in ghastly brief beauty. Where they connected, metal and flesh became incandescent gas. It whiffed away into space. Billions of years hence, some of it may minutely take part in the formation of new stars.

The old stars enclose everything in radiance. The Milky Way glows phantom-bright. Nebulae and sister galaxies glimmer mysterious. Glimpses go by, ships hurtling, graceful as dancers. None of this does Ensign Kittredge see. Her universe has shrunk to steel, meters, readouts, manual controls, brief commands from unseen lips. A reek of ozone is in the air. Once or twice the hull shudders to a distant burst.

N. Aquilae moved majestic at the center of Magnusson's command. Her planetoidal size, and the hundreds of live crewfolk as well as thousands of machines that this required, these were not basically for offensive purposes—although she did have the capability of laying waste a world. They were to provide such a host of defensive missiles, projectiles, rays, such a density of shielding fields, that the admiral and his staff would remain alive to make their assessments and give their orders.

Zeta Sagittarii was much less protected. She existed for the purpose of directly killing enemies.

The saying is ancient, that the first casualty of any battle is your own battle plan. Magnusson knew this and allowed for it. He had a general idea of what he hoped to do, but was flexible about it and permitted his captains broad discretion.

Blenkiron, on the other hand, could think of nothing but to hold his armada in standard configuration, as nearly as possible. That did maximize the mutual defense of his ships. When they had reduced the foe sufficiently, the formation was to open up, englobe the survivors, and deal death on them from every quarter. Such was the theory.

Magnusson had lured him to this exact place, and prepared it beforehand. Ships of his lay in orbit about Battle Sun, in normal state, dark, powerplants throttled down to life-support minimum— virtually undetectable. The fleet that flaunted itself looked inferior. Blenkiron's should have checked for hidden reserves, but found itself too busy; also, Battle Sun is surrounded by dust and gas, residue of a stillborn planetary system, which complicates surveyance. When Magnusson judged the moment ripe, he ordered the summons.

Abruptly his extra force went into hyperdrive—risky, that close to a stellar mass, but their engines were especially well tuned, so losses were light—and entered the fray. They did so from all directions, admittedly sparse but nonetheless pouring fire inward while Magnusson's main body drove straight through the opposed formation, loosing every demonic energy in its weapons.

Zeta Sagittarii has been part of this thrust. She takes a hit astern. It is, actually, a near miss, which does not vaporize her; but it wrecks the engine section and sends radiation and red-hot chunks of metal sleeting everywhere else. Or so we postulate. What we know is simply that she was lost.

Blenkiron panicked. He did not fall into gibbering idiocy, but he saw his fleet shattered and knew not what to do. The captain of the flagship, one Tetsuo Ogawa, became a hero by calmly "advising" him. By fits and starts, the Terrans broke off the engagement. For the most part they withdrew in good order. The majority escaped.

They were, however, in no condition to continue the fight. Magnusson had become free to lay his hand on all of Sector Aldebaran.

Zeta Sagittarii drifts off, sublight, a cold and twisted lump. In some intact compartments, capacitors maintain temperature and air renewal. It is not enough. Rescue craft, searching through the flotsam of battle, will not come within detection range of this hulk—as enormous as the least of reaches is between the stars—before their squadrons must proceed onward. Surviving crew will die of thirst, those who do not go in blood and vomit, of acute radiation poisoning.

We would like to imagine Ensign Kittredge is spared that. Suppose her turret split open under the blast. Exposed to the vacuum of space, she would lose consciousness within thirty seconds. A piece of metal shearing through her heart or her skull would be quicker still.

Admiral Sir Olaf Magnusson's victory became classic in the annals of warfare.

CHAPTER NINE

Diana's visitor surprised her. She had met Cynthians before, as ubiquitous as their species was, but not often, and never this person. For a moment she and he exchanged appraising looks. It was a male, she saw. If he had been wearing much more than a pouch and his silky white fur, she could not have been sure; the secondary sexual characteristics were few. Bipedal, though with arms nearly as long as his legs, he stood about ninety centimeters tall. Toes and the six fingers on either hand were almost equally prehensile. A bushy tail lifted up behind the round head and its pointed ears. Blunt-muzzled and long-whiskered, the face sported a natural blue-gray mask around luminous emerald-hued eyes. His voice was high-pitched, its Anglic clear though apt to come trilling and hissing through the pointed teeth.

"You are milady Crowfeather?" he said. "Permit self-introduction. I hight Shan U of Lulach. Is your Wodenite companion present?"

"No," she replied. "I don't know when he'll be back. What can I do for you?"

"Perhaps it is I who can do you a favor, milady. I have heard your partnership is in search of Ancient relics."

Diana decided this was understandable. She was merely one more human, but Axor inevitably generated gossip. "Well, yes. So far we've drawn a blank. The public database screened nothin' for us that looked the least bit promisin'. He went off today to talk with the local priest of his church, in case the padre had heard of anything.

I gather the parish takes in a big territory." She smiled wryly. "No doubt the two of them'll go on to every sort of theological shop talk."

"You cannot expect to find much information recorded about a planet when most of its land is wilderness that does not sustain colonists," declared Shan U. "Prospectors, timber cruisers, and other non-scientific explorers have scant incentive to go to the trouble of preparing scientific reports. The geographical separation of communities hinders the dissemination of locally available information." He arched his tail. "Ah, but it may be that I can put you in the way of some clues."

The heart sprang in Diana's breast. "You can? What? How?"

"Peace, I pray you. I am not, myself, qualified to be your guide. I am the captain of a riverboat. It will shortly be departing for Lulach. Now plying the great stream, year after year, one is bound to hear many a tale, and I recollect mentions, now and then, of impressive ruins glimpsed. Rumors about you and, especially, your companion having trickled as far as the waterfront, I thought I should come urge you to seek farther for informants."

"Oh? Where?"

"Why, along the river itself. Lulach alone holds many a merchant who has traveled widely over this planet, many a searcher for natural wealth who has adventured deep into the wildernesses. And beyond Lulach—Well, at any rate, I can convey you that far, and back again afterward if you discover zero there and decide not to range more widely. Would you like to inspect my vessel?"

"Where is it?"

"In the valley, at Paz de la Frontera, the head of navigation."

Diana's consideration was brief. If nothing else, she was sick of the cheap hotel where she and Axor had taken lodgings. At first she had enjoyed wandering around Aurea, seeing what there was to see and, as opportunity offered, asking about inexplicable structures. Now she had used those activities up, and had been sitting boredly in her room watching a teleplay. The latter end of this past couple of weeks had become wearisome.

In fact, she had begun regretting her refusal of Gatto's offer. Her immediate reason for that had been the fact that here she and Axor were on Daedalus; once they left it, they would probably not be able to return for a long time, if ever. Why not stay and investigate as originally planned? She was confident that the commandant would still be willing to arrange berths, if Daedalus turned out to be a blind alley—though while she waited for a ship, she might have trouble fending him off. The past several days had almost brought her to the point of thus swallowing her pride and making her appeal. What a waste of time, when there was that unfinished expedition on Imhotep to start all over again!

Her second reason for staying had, as Gatto guessed, been the desire, against every reasonable hope, to learn what had become of Targovi. As the initial exuberance of freedom damped down, she had more and more felt anger and grief on his behalf gnaw at her. Here was a chance to forget them for a while, and maybe even accomplish something.

"Sure," she caroled. "Just a minute."

Having recorded a message for Axor, she skinned out of her clothes and into brief shorts and skimpy blouse. The lowlands were hot in summer. To her belt she attached purse and knife. She kicked her bare feet into sandals. "Let's go, Joe."

Air traffic was under pettifogging emergency restrictions, but a train system, built in pioneer days, still ran, and a station lay near the hotel. As the car they had boarded whirred up off the ground and started downhill above the guide cable, Diana and Shan U settled into a seat. She took the window side and kept her gaze outward, upon the landscape. Unoffended, he stuffed a pipe with dried leaves that smelled like warm saddle leather when he lit them, and conversed.

"The Highroad River has always been a main artery of travel," he said in answer to a remark of hers. "It should become still more so in the present situation. Roads between the settlements along it range from wretched to nonexistent, and as for flight, why, now the very omnibuses are subject to endless, arbitrary inspections, delays, and other such nuisances. Boats remain free of this. Should you find that you do wish to go to Lulach, my *Waterblossom* is no speedster, I grant you, but the fare is modest, accommodations are comfortable, food is good, and the leisured pace will enable you to learn much about our planet en route—which is highly advisable if you would strike into its outback. You will also find yourselves in entertaining company. This trip it includes a live, traveling show."

"What?" asked Diana absently. She was watching the mountains fall away in ridges and steeps that became jungled hills. Clouds loomed ahead, brooding rain; lightning flickered in their depths. The wind of its speed shrilled faintly into the ancient car.

"Another Cynthian, albeit from Catawrayannis rather than the mother world. She brought her tricks, together with a performing beast, to earn her keep while she toured Daedalus, as she had been doing elsewhere. Such restless individuals are frequent in my race."

Wistfulness tugged at Diana. Maybe she could work up an act of her own and take it to the stars?

"Then, abruptly, space traffic, which had been well-nigh unrestricted, was well-nigh banned in and out of Daedalus," Shan U continued. "Poor Wo Lia found herself marooned in Aurea, while events held folk cemented to the newscasts, who might otherwise have come to see her performance. For a while she tried, but was near despair when I chanced to enter Ju Shao's inn, where she was staying."

Diana's attention revived. Ju Shao—hadn't she heard that name before? From Targovi? Memory was vague. "What's that?"

"*O-ai,* a place in the slum quarter, with a miscellaneous clientele, since it is both cheap and tolerant. I suggested to Wo Lia that she invest what remained of her funds in passage with me. People at our ports of call will doubtless be glad to see her show, and in Lulach, amidst her own species, she can find work of some kind to tide her over."

Diana hoped the skipper was not merely a glib salesbeing. Well, she'd inquire among his crew, and if the word was good—a riverboat trip should be all kinds of fun.

The train terminated at Central Station in Paz de la Frontera. That was some distance from the river. Diana started walking, under the guidance of Shan U, who skipped along with the gait of an arboreal. Meanwhile she looked around in wonderment.

The air was a steam bath, full of odors rank, smoky, sweet, indescribable. An overcast hung low, but as yet the rain was only an occasional heavy, spattering drop. For a space she threaded through a crowd between drab walls, but then suddenly she was out in the open. Bushes and thorny trees grew well apart across dusty ground. At a distance she spied farmland, food animals grazing on Terran grasses, grainfields a-ripple under a sullen wind. Closer at hand, on every side, were the clusters of habitation. Each group of houses, shops, public buildings had its distinctive style—here façades square and featureless, surrounding hidden courtyards; there domes and spires; yonder broad expanses of vitryl in metal frames; and on and on. None amounted to more than a few score units, most were less. Spaces between them varied from a roadway to some two hundred meters, but were always clearly that: boundaries, buffers. Traffic was sparse, mainly closed-up groundcars whose riders gave pedestrians wary glances. Children romped outside the settlements, always in distinct clutches. A band of men, in everyday subtropical garb but distinguished by scarlet brassards, tramped around a wooden stockade. Though they bore no firearms, simply knives and staves, they were plainly a kind of militia.

"Events, the upheaval, the uncertainty of everything, have made Paz tense," Shan U observed. "Riots have happened. I will be glad to depart."

Diana nodded. She knew the history of the area, in outline. It had been founded in early Imperial times as a colony of veterans who wished to stay on Daedalus with their families after discharge. Each household received help in establishing itself, especially in converting its grant of land to agricultural usefulness. The practice had continued to this day.

The trouble was, and worsened decade by decade, that the Empire recruited its defenders from an ever more motley set of human societies on Terra's daughter and granddaughter planets. Like tended to settle down with like, and not to get along very well with unlike. The situation might have been happier, given more openings to the outside; but Daedalus, afar in a frontier region, was relatively isolated. Rivalries festered. Nonhumans had long since abandoned any thought of living in Paz.

She remembered her mother quoting a quip of her father's: "The Terran Empire is a huge melting pot. However, what appears to be melting is the pot."

After passing through a couple of hamlets where life seemed to go on about as usual, the road entered one whose walls were mortared stone underneath tile roofs. Nobody else was in sight. Doors stood barred, windows curtained or shuttered. Silence closed in, save for muttering thunder and the *spat* of raindrops on pavement.

Shan U glanced around uneasily. "Best we make haste," he counselled. "This section has suffered an outbreak of lawlessness, and peaceable people have withdrawn till the Navy can send a patrol."

Four men came out of a lane and deployed across the way. They were dirty, unkempt, sour-smelling; beard stubble showed that two had not used any inhibitor for some time. One kept a pistol tucked under his belt, one flourished a club, one carried a knife, while a bola danced in the hands of the fourth.

"Well, well," said the first. "Well, well, *well*. Just stop where you are, if you please."

Shan U crouched, mewed, bottled his tail. Chill crawled along Diana's spine. "What do you want?" she demanded.

"Oh, nothing bad, nothing bad." They slouched and sidled forward. "Welcome to our fair com-mu-nity, little lady. How'd you like a good time?"

"Kindly let us by."

"Now, now, don't be in such a rush." The pistoleer stroked the butt of his weapon. His free thumb he jerked at the bola man, who grinned and sent a ball whistling through the air. "Easy, take it easy. Just a friendly warning. You make a rush to get away, and Chelo here, why, Chelo hasn't had any live target to practice on for days. That thing could break your ankle, lady. All we want to do is show you a real good time, and maybe have a little fun with the monkey-cat. Come along, now."

Diana lunged. Her knife flew forth. It was Tigery steel, the back heavy and rasp-surfaced, the edge sharp enough to cut a floating hair. Suddenly the shirtfront of the pistoleer gushed red. He howled. She pushed him against the clubber. They fell together. She stepped on the Adam's apple of the clubber, and heard it crack, in the course of attacking the knifeman. He slashed at her not unskillfully, but she parried, gave him the rasp across his face, and opened his fighting arm on the inside from elbow to wrist, after which he lost interest in anything but trying to stanch the blood. At this range the bola artist could not exercise his craft well. She severed the cord of a ball that snapped toward her, swayed back out of the way of the rest, and chased him several meters before letting him escape.

"C'mon," she said through the ululations at her feet, "let's get out of here 'fore the cops arrive."

"*Hee-yao!*" gasped Shan U as they made off. "I thought I knew about handling trouble, but you—"

"Oh, I don't go lookin' for fights," Diana said. "In fact, I hate them. I'd've tried to talk or bluff us past those klongs peacefully. But they weren't listenin'. Well, I grew up amongst Tigeries on Imhotep, and when they see danger clear before them, they don't shilly-shally."

Targovi, I learned from you. Pain smote her. *What has your fate been, dear brotherlin'?*

"Do you think the, the casualties will live?"

"I didn't try to do anything fatal, but there wasn't time for finickin', was there? Does it matter?"

Beneath the coolness she felt a dull but strengthening shock. She hadn't done anything like this before—not really—though Targovi had put her through lots of practice; and she had been around when a couple of Tigery brawls got bloody; and she had, herself, perforce been physically pretty emphatic three or four times when human males got the wrong idea and couldn't be persuaded out of it otherwise. *I'll prob'ly have the shakes for a while, once the adrenalin wears off. But not for long, I hope. I mustn't let what I've been through, what I've seen, prey on my mind. Nothin' was done here except justice. The war, now, the war is different, people killin' people they've got no grudge against and have never even met. Though some wars in history have been the lesser evil haven't they?*

I don't know, she thought in rising weariness. *I simply don't know. How good it'll be, floatin' quietly down the river with Axor, if that works out.*

She lost track of time and was a bit startled when they came to the waterfront. Warehouses bulked behind wharfs where a medley of craft lay tied and a hodgepodge of persons, human and nonhuman, bustled about. Machines scurried among them. Beyond, the stream flowed broad and brown. The opposite shore was dimmed by a thickening rain. Shan U registered a feline dislike of the wet, but Diana welcomed its warm sluicing. She felt cleansed.

They reached *Waterblossom*. The riverboat was easily a hundred meters long, though so wide that that was not immediately evident. Four loading towers and a couple of three-tiered deckhouses did not much clutter her. The low freeboard was garishly painted in stripes of red and gold; the topworks were white, brass-trimmed. Her captain had said she was made of Terran and Cynthian woods, which Daedalan organisms did not attack, and driven by an electric engine. Should he be unable to recharge its capacitors otherwise, he carried a steam generator which could burn nearly anything.

Half a dozen Cynthians and two humans were on deck, cheerily helping wheel a cage toward shelter from the rain. "*Ay-ah,* behold Wo Lia, the performer." Shan U pointed. "Come aboard and meet her. We can all have a nice cup of alefruit cider."

Diana frowned. She hated the idea of confining any creature. Still, yon beast didn't seem mistreated. More or less mansize, it hunkered on four limbs, black-furred, its head obscured by a heavy mane. She spied a short tail, and the forepaws had an odd, doubled-up look about them. Well, who could possibly know all the life forms, all the wonders of every kind, that filled the Imperial planets, let alone the galaxy and the universe? To fare forth—!

Shan U led her over the gangplank. She passed near the cage.

"Hs-s-s, little friend," went a whisper. Coming from low in the lungs, it sounded like an animal noise to anybody who did not know the Toborko language. "Stay calm. We will talk later. Make sure you and your camarado take passage on this boat."

Barely, Diana reined herself in. The humans doubtless noticed how she tensed before relaxing, but could put that down to the exotic surroundings. The Cynthians doubtless paid no heed to her shifts in stance or expression.

She forced herself to look afar, out again across the river. Underneath tangled strands of mane, the face in the cage was Targovi's.

CHAPTER TEN

Waterblossom set forth after the thunderstorm that had been brewing reached explosion point and then spent itself. Sweeping the length of the valley with that swiftness and violence which the rapid rotation of the planet engendered, it turned the air altogether clear. From her place in the bows, Diana looked westward across a thousand kilometers or more.

This was the first tranquil moment she had had in hours. The time had been frantic during which she made her way back to Aurea, located Axor, persuaded him—not easily, because her arguments were thin at best, and her excitement didn't reinforce them—to come along, got their baggage packed, returned through lightning-vivid cataracts of rain, settled into her tiny stateroom and improvised accommodations for the Wodenite down in the hold with the freight. Dinner had been served while the weather slacked off. Now the crew had cast loose and the boat was on her way.

Diana couldn't hear the engine, but its purr went as a subliminal quiver through her bare feet, and she did catch a faint gurgle from aft, the turbo drive at work. Speed was low, as ponderous and heavily laden as the hull was. At first traffic teemed, everything from rowboats to hydrofoils, but as Paz fell behind, the river rolled open, a brown stretch two kilometers wide from bank to forested bank, rippling around snags and sandbars, only a couple of barges and a timber raft under tow in the distance ahead. Quiet descended, and a measure of coolness. Flying creatures darted and skimmed, light amber on their wings.

Never before had Diana seen so far over the horizonless world. Ahead of her, the river and its valley went on. As that view grew ever more remote, they dwindled, shrank together, became at last a shining thread between burnished green darknesses; yet still she could see them. Whenever an opening appeared in the woods brooding on either side of her, she likewise looked across immensity. Left, the green lightened as forest gave way to prairie that eventually blurred off in haziness. Right, beyond foothills, she glimpsed toylike snow-peaks, the mountain range that warded off the glaciers of the Daedalan ice age.

The sinking sun kindled a sudden gleam far and far ahead. Why, that must be the ocean! Diana's pulse quickened. Vapors made the disc golden-red, softened its glare till she could gaze directly. It spread itself out until it was a great step pyramid—and out and out, stretching to become arcs of luminance curving north and south around what would have been worldedge on another planet.

There was no real night. Day slowly turned into a glimmering dusk, shadowless, starless apart from brilliant Imhotep and a few scattered points high overhead. She could easily have read by the light, though the range of vision contracted until everything beyond three or four kilometers—except Paz and Aurea behind her, a couple of villages before her, aglow—faded vaguely into dimness. Gradually sunshine became a complete ring. It was broadest and brightest in the direction of Patricius, a little wider than the disc by day. There it shone orange in hue, with a muted fierceness of white underneath. It narrowed and reddened as it swept away, until when it had closed itself opposite—some while after it had begun to form—it was a fiery streak. The sky near the ring went from pale blue sunside to purple darkside, shading toward violet at the zenith; below, the ring enclosed a darkness which was the planetary bulk.

Presently the moon Icarus rose in a confusion of silver which coalesced to a half shield as it climbed.

The forests ashore were full of shadow, but the river sheened like mercury on its murmurous course.

Diana did not reckon up how long she stood rapt, watching the hours unfold. When the deck shivered beneath hoofs, and a bone-deep basso rumbled forth, she came back to herself with a shock like falling off a cliff.

"Ah, a beautiful, incredible sight indeed," said Axor. "What an artist the Creator is. This experience might almost justify our making the journey we are on."

Misgiving pierced Diana. "Almost?"

"Why, I fear ours is a bootless expedition. I have been in the saloon, speaking with person after person, crew and passengers, including the two humans. None can attest to any objects that might be Foredweller remains. One did bespeak large ruins under the northern mountains, but another, who had actually been there, said they are remnants of a Terran mining operation, abandoned centuries ago when the ore gave out." A sigh boomed. "We should have stayed on Imhotep and completed our investigation as planned. Now we are confined on Daedalus for an indefinite time and . . . I am no longer young."

Guilt took her, however lightly, by the throat. "I'm sorry."

Axor lifted a hand. "Oh, no, no, dear friend. I do not blame you in the least. You urged upon me what seemed best to you in your—your impetuosity. Nor do I pity myself. That is the most despicable of emotions. I should not have let you rush me into taking this passage. My mistake, not yours. And we are seeing wonders along the way."

Diana braced herself. "We may even find what you're after," she said, as stoutly as possible. "These are just regular river travelers aboard with us, and, uh, one outworlder. In Lulach we'll find people who get around more on this planet." She hesitated. "A Zacharian, maybe. That island is mysterious. You've talked to me about how the Ancient relics on Aeneas have influenced the whole culture of the settlers. Could something like that be on Zacharia?"

"Well, we may hope." A bit of cheer lifted in Axor's tones. "'And now abideth faith, hope, and charity, these three; but the greatest of these is charity,'" he quoted. "Yet hope is no mean member of the triad."

Again she hated what she was doing to him, and wondered whether the need could ever justify it. She knew so little thus far. She had in fact, she realized, acted on faith—faith in Targovi—with hope for adventure and accomplishment, but damn small charity.

She squared her shoulders. Maybe some Daedalan place really did hold something for her old pilgrim.

Axor stretched luxuriously, an alarming sight if you didn't know him. "I was thinking, before going to bed, I would like a swim," he said. "Do you care to come along? I can easily catch up with the boat when we are finished, and carry you with me."

For a moment Diana was tempted. To frolic in yonder mightily sliding current—But she had no bathing suit, and didn't want to risk the men aboard seeing her nude. They appeared decent enough, in a rough-hewn fashion. However, after the incident in Paz, she'd rather not give anybody the wrong impression.

More important, she suddenly and sharply realized, here was her chance to talk to Targovi. "No, thanks," she said in a haste that drew a quizzical glance. "I'm tired and, uh, I want to watch this spectacle more. Go ahead. Have fun."

The Wodenite undulated over the rail. It was astonishing how gracefully he could move when he chose. He entered the water with scarcely a splash. Suffused light shimmered off his scales and spinal sierra. His tail drove him cleanly away.

Diana glanced aft. A Cynthian lookout perched atop the bridge, within which the pilot was occupied. Neither was paying her any attention, nor would they overhear low-voiced conversation. Everybody else had gone below; most of them were used to the magical ring, as she was not. She pattered over the planks.

Behind the after deckhouse, an awning had been stretched to shelter the cage which held Wo Lia's performing beast. It cast a degree of darkness over Targovi. She saw him as a shadowy figure rhythmically astir—exercises, to keep in condition while imprisoned. She hunkered down.

His catlike eyes knew her instantly. "Aaah, s-s-s, at last," he breathed, and crouched to face her. "How goes it, sprite?"

"Oh, I'm all right, but awful puzzled, and poor Axor's terribly discouraged," she blurted. "What's goin' on, anyway?"

He changed his language to Toborko, in a monotone which lost many nuances of that most musical tongue, but which would seem to a casual passerby as if the animal were crooning some weird song while the human, curious, listened.

"Well deserve you what explanation I can give, O valiant child, the more so when I shall belike call upon you to render services and take hazards such as neither of us can foresee. Vast are the stakes in this game, but the rules poorly known and capriciously changeable.

"You understand I have not been entirely a huckster but also an agent covert of Imperial Intelligence. My part was mainly to pass on to my superiors whatever I came across that seemed of possible interest, on this world near the Merseian marches and visited by beings of countless kinds. Yet did I help uncover one espionage undertaking, and found leads to others.

"Nevertheless, when I scented something truly enormous upon the wind, not only did my warnings go unheeded, I was forbidden to utter them or to continue in my search. More of that later, when we can talk freely and at length. Enough tonight that I have cause to believe Magnusson's revolt is not simply another uprising of angry men against bad masters. And from Zacharia the forbidden come breaths of still more strangeness than erstwhile.

"Aye, in Axor I saw a movable blind for myself. Attention will be upon him, but unlikely ever a suspicion. He can go in his harmlessness where most folk are banned, and I, I can perchance skulk behind. You, Diana Crowfeather, walk betwixt and between. What part you may play is, as yet, hidden in dawn-mists. I think you will play it well. You know my Tigery nature—sorry would I be to lose you, but sorry am I not for putting you at risk. Nor do I suppose you are ireful. You stand to win glory, with all that that may bring in its train. However this may be, clear it was that only through you could I recruit unwitting Axor.

"Ill was our luck, that the rebellion erupted just as we were approaching Daedalus. Else we could have landed and gone our ways, disappearing into the hinterlands by virtue of nobody thinking to keep watch over us. As was, knowing what standard procedures are, I foresaw that my reappearance at the time of crisis would automatically provoke precautionary detention if naught else. Whereupon the gigantic plot I have smelled would roll unhindered onward.

"Accordingly, I escaped. It seemed likely that you and Axor would be released after interrogation, for you did in fact know nothing. The question was how to keep myself free when the hue and cry was out for me, and how to rejoin you afterward.

"Therefore did I hide until after I felt sure the patrol would have visited Ju Shao's inn in Lowtown, and then sought it. She and I are friends of old, and I have in the past done her some favors when, hm, the Imperial authorities grew overly officious. You understand that an Intelligence agent has need of such connections. She tucked me away, kept me fed, and meanwhile conducted discreet inquiries.

"These soon turned up Wo Lia. She is actually an adventurer among the stars—aye, from Catawrayannis, albeit a return to her birthworld would be inadvisable—mainly a gambler, but not above occasional racketeering. The ship whereon she arrived had departed again; the interdict on civilian space travel left her stranded; uproar, and preoccupation with public events, gave her scant opportunity in Aurea. Hence she proved quite willing to take the role of itinerant showperson. In Lulach she can establish herself, one way or another, until the Empire calms down, one way or another. Ju Shao helped me disguise myself, and Wo Lia persuaded our good captain that, if he sought you out, he could belike sell a couple of tickets.

"Thus are we bound off. Needs must I remain in confinement till we reach Lulach. There will I slip free, and folk will feel sympathy for Wo Lia, whose performer escaped and may well starve to death in an inedible jungle. As for me, I have . . . business in Lulach."

"Can you trust her?" Diana whispered. "She might turn you in for the reward. I s'pose there is one."

"She, like Ju Shao, expects reward far more substantial, should our cause triumph. Why not? Funds ought to be abundantly available then, together with openings to the stars."

"But what *is* our cause? If you're on the side of Emperor Gerhart—why? To head off a civil war? But you can't; it's already begun. Mightn't Olaf Magnusson be the better man anyway? And what can we possibly do, stuck here on Daedalus, that'd make the slightest difference?"

She had, unthinkingly, used Anglic. "S-s-s-s!" Targovi warned. "Abide your time. Later we will talk." He settled back into a beast posture, as if falling asleep.

Diana sensed another presence. Turning her head, she saw that a human male had come on deck and was approaching. "Ah, hi," he called. "I thought I'd find you enjoying the view and the fresh air. But what's so interesting about the livestock?"

She rose and walked out from beneath the awning. "Oh, it's a kind new to me," she answered. "I don't know what planet it's from. Do you?"

"No. Wo Lia was evasive when I asked. Maybe export of that kind is illegal." The man beamed. He was young and rather good-looking. "Uh, care for a stroll around the deck? Such a lovely night. I'm still wide awake."

"Well, I am too, sort of." Diana joined him.

They paced. "We should get better acquainted," he said. "We'll be on this boat for a fairish while. I can show you around our ports of call, if you want, and Lulach when we get there. My pleasure."

She smiled. "Why, thank you." A flirtation should be fun, if she took care to keep it within limits. Besides, she might learn something useful.

CHAPTER ELEVEN

A dozen light-years off, the twin blue giant suns that were Alpha Crucis dominated heaven. Even observed in a viewscreen they left burning after-images, and it would have been dangerous to let an unprotected eye dwell upon them.

The immediate danger, though, was closer at hand, where the Merseian task force clashed with a Terran flotilla that had been unfortunate enough to intercept it. *Cyntath* Gadrol of the Vach Ynvory, called Cannonshield, commanding from the dreadnaught *Ardwyr,* had sprung his trap and set to work inflicting maximum destruction before the outnumbered Imperials should break off and flee. Where missiles burst, new stars bloomed in dreadful brief beauty. Where a rosy cloud swelled from one of them, rapidly fading away into blackness, a ship and her crew had died. The battle raged through a volume trillions of kilometers across.

Yet it was principally a holding action, cover for the squadron that slipped free and made for the real destination at utmost pseudovelocity. *Qanryf* Bryadan Arrowswift, Vach Hallen, watched a yellow light-point swell hour by hour, until at the end of five it out-shone Alpha Crucis and magnification revealed its disc. Despite his nickname, well-earned at home, Bryadan could stay quiet like that for a span like that: for he was on a hunt. Faint but marrow-thrilling, the energies driving the cruiser *Tryntaf* pulsed through him. Air from the ventilators, cold because his home was on an arctic shore of the Wilwidh Ocean, bore a likewise half-sensed exhilaration in reeks

218

of ozone and oil. Telltales flashed, meters quivered, displays danced through his cave of control machines. Their operators poised alert, speaking only when needful but then softly singing the words, as if in dreams of the triumph to come.

When his ship and her companions pierced the comet cloud, Bryadan tapped an intercom button. The face that sprang into the small screen was youthful, handsome, the green of the complexion slightly yellow because of partial Lafdiguan ancestry. It was also startled. "Foreseer!" exclaimed *Afal* Uroch of the Vach Rueth. He slapped hand to breast and tail to boots in salute. "At the captain's orders."

"In the name of his Supremacy the Roidhun," Bryadan responded with equal formality. "Are you prepared?"

"Yes, foreseer. The crew are ready and eager. Does the *qanryf* have some new word for us?"

"Yea and nay." Bryadan leaned forward. "I want to lay stress upon certain details in your orders. Yours will be the most precarious part of this entire operation. If you carry it off well, it will be the very heart-spring."

Uroch dared grin. "*Khraich*, they don't call me 'the Lucky' for nothing."

"With due heed to your honor," said Bryadan carefully, "I remind you that young, ambitious officers are apt to confuse courage and rashness. Your record of exploits has caused you to be chosen for your present assignment. Yet those same deeds required more dash than wisdom. Not that your judgment was ever unsound—in the particular circumstances you encountered. These will be different. We are to wield the surgeon's knife rather than the sword. In your case, it is especially important to uphold the distinction. Exactly what will happen, only the God knows. You may find yourself taken by surprise, in desperate straits, and tempted to unleash your entire firepower—since you are responsible for your crews, and thus for their wives and children. Or else you may see the enemy wide open to total destruction. In either instance, *afal,* you will resist the lure. Die if you must, together with those who have trusted you; or retreat unsuccessful if you must, taking years to live down the scorn of brother officers to whom you are forbidden to explain; but confine yourself to the precise goal given you."

A slight change of color and posture, a barely visible twitch of lips away from teeth, were all that Uroch revealed. "Yes, foreseer."

Bryadan made the gesture of affection, rare from a senior to a junior, and softened his tone. "I repeat, *afal,* my regard for your honor is of the highest. And so is my regard for your intelligence. Would I otherwise have approved you for this task? The God willing, and I believe He is, you will return with glory upon you. True, we cannot proclaim it in the universe—not yet—but your peers will know, and perhaps even your Roidhun."

Hurt in the face turned to stiffly controlled joy.

"I have this to add, and it is my real reason for addressing you now," Bryadan went on. "Before we lost contact with the main force, *Cyntath* Gadrol issued an announcement. Scoutships have reported Terran reinforcements approaching, but at such low strength that he can hold them, too, in play. We will have days, if necessary, to complete our task here, before the opposition can bring up sufficient power that we must withdraw. Therefore, *afal,* take your time. Explore the options before you choose. Remember that, useful though it be, our undertaking is only a fractional part of the great Unrevealed plan by which our superiors direct us. The destiny of the Race reaches ahead through millionfold years. Good hunting, *afal.*"

"And to you, foreseer," Uroch answered. As the screen blanked, exultation blazed from him.

The Merseians ran on hyperdrive as deeply into the gravity well of the Gorrazani sun as they dared. When they reverted to relativistic state, they assumed intrinsic velocities carefully arranged before-hand, aimed at the habitable planet of the system. They crossed the gap in less than three hours, under decelerations that would have made molecular films of living tissue if interior forcefields had not compensated.

The Gorrazanian home fleet got no chance to muster. Such units as were in orbit near the planet deployed and put up a gallant defense. Bryadan's command smashed it. Squadrons began to arrive from farther away. He broke them in detail. Meanwhile his broadcasters trampled local transmissions underfoot as they blared in the principal languages of the region:

"All folk heed, we wish you no harm. We are here expressly at the request of your rightful chieftains, the Liberation Council which wills an end to centuries of oppression. His Supremacy the Roidhun recognizes the Liberation Council as the legitimate government of the Gorrazanian Realm. Even so, we of Merseia have no desire to intervene in your affairs. Consider simply how remote our dominions are. It is the sheerest altruism for us to cross such stretches of space, under peril of attack by the aggressors of Imperial Terra, in answer to an appeal—not to give military aid, no, not for any warlike purpose, but to convey hospital supplies to the valiant armies of your Liberation Council. If we come armed, it is for self-defense. If we fight, it is because we were set upon, without the least provocation on our part. Note that we do not pursue the fleeing units of the lawless and discredited Folkmoot regime—"

Uroch wasn't listening. It was enough for him that the leaders of the Race had, in their wisdom, decreed certain actions be carried out here, and that a certain amount of blat must accompany the doing. Besides, he was busy.

As *Tryntaf* whipped in hyperbola close by the globe, his escadrille shot from her launch ports. It numbered a score, Fangryf-type gunboats, about midway between the Terran Comet and Conqueror classes—six-male craft, lean and deadly, equally at home in atmosphere and interplanetary space. They hit air at speeds that sent shudders through their hulls, made red flames around them, and left thunders trailing behind that rolled from horizon to horizon.

Braking, at the pilot console of his own vessel, Uroch saw land and sea sweep away beneath him: wrinkled mountains, multitudinously verdant plains, shining waters. Such buildings as he spied in magnifying screens were mostly low, rounded, widespread; few towers speared aloft, as they pridefully did on Merseia or Terra. It was in the nature of this species to expand underground— "in the bosom of the Mother," they often said. Despite scanty landmarks, he knew where he was going. He had been through exhaustive briefings.

What he did not know was what he would encounter along the way—Haa, yes, he did now! Warcraft flocked over the curve of the world to meet him.

"Evasive action," he said coolly into the outercom. "Close formation. Do not fire on them until ordered. Concentrate on defending yourselves." Underneath, his heart thuttered.

The Merseian group screamed about and headed northwest, at a mere kilometer of altitude. The Gorrazanians took a while to straighten out their formations and give chase. Bullets, missiles, energy beams raked ahead of them. The Merseian gunners, superbly computer-guided, shot down most of the material projectiles. Those that got through, and the rays, generally missed; those that struck, forcefields and armor generally absorbed. A member of the escadrille, flying rear guard, did fall—flash of light, tail of smoke, shattering burst on the ground. Uroch raised hand in homage. They would be remembered, yon brave males, if their comrades lived.

The sun dropped behind him. He flew through night, under stars and a small, hurtling moon. Occasional flickers aloft told of the battle in space. Metal throbbed around him. He heard the shrilling of cloven air. Information from orbit registered on his data displays: another opposition force was bound his way from the east.

But ahead, sheer, its heights coldly agleam with snow and glaciers, loomed a mountain range. Its contours were engraved on Uroch's brain well-nigh as fully as they were in his computer programs. This was why he had studied the planet unmercifully hard, the long way from Merseia: so that he could develop his contingency plans. The move that he found himself making was altogether in his style; and he had handpicked his follower pilots and made them learn nearly as much as he knew.

In a wild swoop, he lifted. Crags clawed after the belly of his craft. Ahead was a pass between two peaks, and on the far side an immense, many-branched canyon. Flesh could never have steered through, at the speeds wherewith he and his traveled. Robots could, barely. His living brain told them to do it.

Cliffs reared out of abyssal darknesses. Sonic shocks broke snowfields apart and sent them away in avalanches; clouds and plumes rose off them to glisten beneath the moon. Their rumbling drummed through the howl of outraged air.

No few of the Gorrazanian flyers were taken by such surprise that they crashed before they could pull clear. Shards and skulls went skittering down the heights. The rest of the defenders buzzed about in dismay. They had lost contact with the enemy.

As he emerged above a wintry lowland, Uroch fought temptation. He could bring his escadrille quickly around and take the pursuit from behind, catch them in their bewilderment, shatter and scatter a force that outnumbered his three or four to one. What a deed! They'd sing about it in ships and halls throughout the Roidhunate, for centuries to come.

He remembered his captain's words, set his jaw, and flew straight onward. The directive had been clear from the beginning. "*Except for the objective, you will inflict minimal damage. Wherever consonant with that objective and with maximum survival in your force, you will choose evasion over confrontation. If it appears that a major action is necessary to accomplishment of the purpose, you will withdraw as expeditiously as possible to your mother vessel, or to whatever other transport is most suitable.*"

Never had he been under orders more difficult to follow. He began to realize what it meant to be in the high command. Perhaps, flickered through him, that was another reason he had been chosen for this undertaking. Could they have him in mind for greater things? . . . *Dismiss that. Carry on your hunt.*

Inevitably, he had broad discretion. After a quick review of the data, he made his next decision and issued his instructions. The Merseians lifted spaceward.

He saw the planet in sapphire and silver splendor, the sun rising in dawn-hues over its brow; but his attention was aimed along a radius vector ahead, where two warships maneuvered about and lobbed lightnings at each other. However tenuous, the ionized gas that lingered for seconds after a nuclear detonation sufficed to hide his group from detection, when they orbited free-fall as he told them to. Thus he shook off the second ground-based flotilla that had been trying to intercept him.

The orbit soon bent his flyers back into atmosphere. With judicious nudges of thrust, they sought a hurricane which was traversing a southern ocean, and hid themselves in its violence. That required daring as well as skill; but people had reason to call Uroch "the Lucky."

As that luck would have it, the storm lumbered to the very shore he wanted. Otherwise he would have tried something else, maybe for several days. In the event, he could shout, "Haa-aa and away!" His warriors burst from the clouds and winds. They went like shooting stars above sere hills and a broad, green, canal-veined valley.

It was not well defended. The Gorrazanians had relied mainly on their space fleet. What planetary units they had were dispersed around the globe; a substantial portion was still at the antipodes, trying to find Uroch's raiders. Missiles and aircraft lifted in low numbers. The Merseians swatted them and came to rest, a-hover on their grav drives, above the target.

Aside from communication and detector masts, and a tower for local weather control, it revealed nothing special to the eye. Some domes snuggled into a landscape ruddy with ripening grain. Three sleepy villages clustered within a few kilometers: archaic earthen buildings, for the Gorrazanians are a conservative breed, no matter how many mercenary soldiers they export. A large modern structure, squarish and garish as their tastes called for, might have been a school or a museum or something of that kind.

Uroch didn't know. He had not even heard, officially, what it was that he was supposed to destroy. In the course of his studies en route he had deduced that it was probably a key command center—police, military, however you wanted to designate a corps trying to suppress revolutionary guerrillas. Without it, the Folkmoot would not be disastrously handicapped against the Liberation Council, but counterinsurgency operations would be set back.

It seemed a trivial reason for dispatching warships across hundreds of light-years and getting into a fight with the Terrans themselves. Uroch had schooled himself to refrain from wondering. The great lords of state had their plan. His duty was to execute his part thereof.

And . . . by the God, by all the pagan gods of the forefathers—he was about to!

"Goal attained," he said flatly into the outercom, while joy sang in his blood. "Fire by the numbers."

His flyer threw the first missile. It flashed in the sun, it smote, it blossomed as blue-white as Alpha Crucis. Dust, smoke, vapor rose in a column that swelled as it grew, reached the bottom of the stratosphere, smeared itself across heaven. Megaton after megaton followed. In the end there lay a monstrous crater, incandescent until its sides cooled to glass. The canals ran dark and poisoned. Everywhere around, the crops were afire.

"*Arrach,* let's go!" Uroch shouted.

How he and his males fought their way through vengeful metal swarms; how they won back to *Tryntaf*; how *Tryntaf* and her sisters returned to Gadrol's victorious fleet; how the Merseians, who had taken few losses, eluded Terran search and returned home without further combat—this is the stuff of epic. Yet behind it lay always a cool intelligence, whose painfully garnered knowledge and carefully crafted schemes made the heroism possible.

For Uroch, sufficient was that he came back to his wife, his sole wife thus far, and to the first son she had hitherto borne him, with a tale that would ring the lad on to achievements of his own, in those unbounded years that reached before the Race.

After the raid, night fell. A full moon rose above that which had been the villages. Light rippled bleak, shadows moved, under the hastening white shield. Wind rustled. It was cold, harsh with ash; the lethalness was not perceptible.

Big and shaggy, a Gorrazanian female sat beneath the remnant of a wall. In her four arms she rocked her dead child. In her rough voice she sang it a lullaby that it had always liked.

CHAPTER TWELVE

Miriam Abrams Flandry started home barely in time. Although news of civil war was recent, and nothing untoward had yet happened in the lanes between Sol and Niku, already apprehension pervaded the entire Empire. Word came in that, here and there, malcontents of many different sorts were proclaiming themselves adherents of would-be Emperor Olaf and making trouble or outright disaster for local authorities. Insurance rates had begun to skyrocket, which caused shipping firms to abandon route after route. It was natural to cancel service to the planet Ramnu, Niku IV, early on. There was no economic incentive to continue, after the quick announcement that the climate modification project was suspended for the duration of the emergency.

The woman had been on the surface, in the field, isolated among primitive autochthons. She just managed to catch the last liftoff for Maia. Of course, had she been stranded, Fleet Admiral Sir Dominic Flandry would have taken steps to get his wife back. He might well have unlimbered his speedster *Hooligan* and gone after her himself. But her survival meanwhile, on the grim world she loved, would have been doubtful.

As was, Maia III—Hermes—continued important enough that she could book passage from there directly to Terra. The vessel being a luxury liner which numbered noblefolk among her passengers, she had armed escort all the way, never mind how useful those ships might have been on the battlefront.

The xenologist kept to herself during the voyage, taking no part in its entertainments and intrigues. At meals she was minimally civil to her tablemates. It wasn't only that they and their games bored her. (Attractive and alone, she could have had a succession of bed partners; and after weeks among nonhumans, the physical sensation would have been welcome; but she would have had to *talk* with them, even *listen* to them. She'd rather wait for Dominic. The fact that he had probably not been waiting for her, in that sense, made no difference.) It was that she was full of grief and fear.

Grief for her dear Ramnuans, who had given her the name "Banner" that she still bore. She had come to see how the project was progressing, that would put an end to the planet's repeated civilizations-destroying glaciations, and how it was affecting the cultures she had studied for so long before her retirement. Shortly after she arrived, the order to shut down came in. Considering how bureaucracy operated, if Magnusson's insurrection were crushed immediately, which it obviously could not be, months must pass until work resumed. Ramnuans would perish by the additional thousands, or worse.

Fear for the Empire, Technic society and, yes, those other societies the Empire enclosed. Old and rotten it might be, its outworks crumbling less because strength had failed than because the will to be strong had. Nevertheless it was all that guarded the heritage of humanity and humanity's allies. Sometimes Flandry let his personal defenses drop in her presence and spoke of the Long Night that lay beyond the fall of the Empire.

And she had her kinfolk on Dayan to think about, and her natives on Ramnu, and friends strewn about among the stars, and—she and Dominic were not yet too old for a child or two. Not quite, he approaching seventy and she approaching fifty, given antisenescence plus the kind of DNA repair they could pay for. Besides, she had years ago deposited some ova in a biobank.

They had always been too busy, though, she and he; and now this wretched affair had begun.

He met her at debarkation, attired in a uniform that got them waved straight through inspection, and hurried her to the apartment they kept in Archopolis. There the champagne and caviar and such had to wait a while longer.

When they had feasted, the darkness would no longer be denied.

She asked what the truth was—not the news, but the truth. Reluctantly, he told her.

"The latest dispatches we've received make unpleasant reading. In just these weeks, Magnusson's driven a salient in nearly as far as Aldebaran. Of course, he isn't sitting on everything from there back to his Patrician base. And his blitzkrieg is bound to slow down while he consolidates those gains. But he needn't do much toward that end, you realize. He dominates the whole volume of space already. He can snap up any significant traffic that doesn't flow the way he wants, and lay waste any planet that won't give him whatever support he demands. None will refuse. Who can blame them?

"His forces have won every battle to date, except for a couple of draws. Most engagements have been fairly small; but seeing what harm a single capital ship can do, each victory has been a lopsidedly big addition to his score. He is a brilliant tactician, and his overall strategy is basically the same as what carried Hans Molitor to the throne." Flandry narrowed his gray eyes and stroked his mustache. "Or is it, entirely?" he murmured.

Banner regarded him across the table and spread her hands in an immemorial gesture. She was a lean, strong-featured woman, her own eyes luminous green, silver-streaked brown hair falling to her shoulders. "Do you suppose he can win?" she asked.

"He might." Flandry ignited a cigarette and inhaled deeply. "In view of the latest developments, his chances are starting to look pretty good. When I saw our darling Emperor Gerhart a week ago, he was in an absolute hissy fit." One reason the apartment was costly to rent was that it included state-of-the-art antibugging devices. Technicians personally loyal to Flandry made periodic inspections to be sure the system was still working.

Banner sighed. "Rhetorical question—or is it? Would it really be so awful if Magnusson took over? How did the present dynasty come to power, anyway, and how much is Gerhart really worth?"

"I keep telling you, darling scientist, you should take more interest in human history and politics," Flandry said. "Not but what it's understandable you don't. A filthy subject. I often wish I'd been born into some era like the Second Sugimoto, when everybody could cultivate his vine and fig tree, or his private arts or vices, without having to worry who'd come climbing over the wall next." He reached above the glasses and plates to stroke her cheek. "To be sure, then I'd never have met you."

Abruptly he got to his feet. The bathrobe flapped around his ankles as he strode to the transparency and stood raggedly smoking. Through a light rain and an early dusk, the city flashed hectic, as far as vision could fare. Within this room, the odor of roses and the lilt of a Mozart concerto receded toward infinity.

"I'm against revolutions," he said low. "No matter the alleged justification, it's never worth the short-range cost—lives and treasure beyond counting—or the long-range—ripping the fragile fabric of society. You know how in my younger days I did what I could to help put down a couple such attempts. If afterward I signed up with old Hans, why, the Wang dynasty had collapsed utterly, and he was the least bad of the contending warlords. At that, he turned out to be a tolerable Emperor, didn't he? Neither a figurehead nor a monster. What more dare we expect? And we may owe something to the memory of Edwin Cairncross, inasmuch as his try at usurpation was what got us reacquainted with each other, but surely you'll agree he was an undesirable sort."

She secured the sash of her kimono and went to join him. He laid an arm around her waist. His straight-lined countenance writhed into a smile. "Sorry about the oratory," he murmured. "I'll try to keep it properly caged henceforward."

She leaned close. "I never mind. It's nice to see you relax from your perpetual clowning." Her innate seriousness rose afresh. "But you haven't answered me. All right, the Empire was bumbling along fairly peacefully, and Magnusson's revolt is a disaster. Don't I know it myself? However—my parents always told me to look at every side of a question—would his success be a catastrophe? I mean, I've heard you say often enough that we no longer have any such thing as legitimate government. Maybe Magnusson would be better than Gerhart, who is rather a swine, isn't he?"

"Well, yes, he is," Flandry admitted, "although a shrewd swine. For a moderately important instance, you know he doesn't like me, but he's given to taking my advice, because he sees it's practical. And . . . Crown Prince Karl does have a high opinion of me, and is a thoroughly decent boy." He snickered. "If I'm still alive when he inherits the throne, I'll have to set about curing him of the latter."

She stared outward and upward. Stars were lost in the haze of light from the towers everywhere around, but— "Does it make that much difference who is Emperor? What can he, what can any person, any planet, do to change things?"

"Usually very little," Flandry agreed. This was by no means the first time they had been over the same ground. They were both aware and concerned, she less cynically than he. But some open wounds do not allow themselves to be left alone; and tonight they were feeling a freshly inflicted one. "The Policy Board, the provincial nobles, the bureaucrats and officers, the inertia of sheer size—Still, even a slight shift in course will touch billions of lives, and perhaps grind them out. And occasionally a pivotal event does happen. More and more, I wonder whether we may not be about to have that experience again."

"What do you mean?"

Flandry ran fingers through his sleek gray hair. "I'm not sure. Possibly nothing. Yet every intuition, every twitchy nerve I've developed in decades I misspent as an Intelligence agent when I might have gone fishing—my hunch screams to me that something peculiar is afoot." He pitched his cigarette expertly away, into an ashtaker, and swung about to face her, hands on her shoulders. "Listen, Banner. You've been in the yonderlands, you haven't followed the input as you would've with me if you'd stayed home. The Merseians have now hit us."

She gave him a stark smile. "Is that a surprise? Haven't they always taken what advantage they could, when the Empire's been in disarray? Nibbles here and there, no *casus belli* that might unite us against them—obviously, not in this case either, if the story hasn't been released."

"This case is oddly different," Flandry said. "There've been the predictable skirmishes in the marches, yes. No major thrust. But . . . they sent a task force, which passed straight through Imperial space—they sent a strike force to Gorrazan, on the far side of us."

"What?" She stiffened. "Why? It doesn't make sense."

"Oh, it does, it does, when you contemplate it from the proper, skewed angle." He spoke softly, as was his wont when discussing terrible things. "Yes, the Realm of Gorrazan is the pathetic souvenir of a botched attempt at empire, a few colonies and clients on a few second-rate worlds near the home sun. Yes, its government has been plagued by insurrectionists who proclaim a bright new ideology— God, how long has the universe endured the same old bright new ideologies?—and the rebels are known, to everybody except our journalists and academics, to have Merseian inspiration and help. Trouble at our backs. Certainly I'd instigate the identical thing behind Merseia if I could.

"But now—" He drew breath. "Word came in the other day. The Merseians sent a 'mercy mission.' They declare the need was so urgent they had to traverse our space, hoping we wouldn't notice, and we were wicked to pounce on them as they were in Sector Alpha Crucis approaching their destination. It was a shame that we compelled them to trounce what forces we could bring to bear. The diplomats will be discussing who's to blame, and who's to pay what reparations to whom, and the rest of that garbage, for years to come. Oh, yes, business as usual.

"But the fact is, the Merseians *could* have passed through unknown to us, if they'd wanted. They made their presence blatant when they neared our Alpha Crucis frontier. Our units had no choice but to attack and take losses. Meanwhile a Merseian detachment punched through to Gorrazan itself. It made rags of the home defense fleet. It could have blown up every governmental installation. The rebels could have taken over entirely. We'd either have intervened to prevent, and found ourselves bogged down in a nasty, lasting little war; or, likelier, we'd have done nothing, and in due course had a pro-Merseian power at our backs, small and weak but an almighty nuisance.

"Instead, the raiders contented themselves with taking out the Folkmoot's main command center. The government's badly hurt, but it can still fight. The Gorrazanian civil strife proceeds."

"What does that imply?" She guessed his answer.

"Why, when the news breaks, as it inevitably will, the powers that be in the Empire will fall into a rupturing controversy. Some will want to tie down strength in watchfulness, diametrically opposite to Magnusson's campaign, lest the situation explode in our rear end. Others will claim there's no danger in those parts, whether because the Liberation Council hasn't yet won or because the Liberation Council represents progress and this past incident proves how wrong we are to keep provoking the Roidhunate. The waste of energy, the confusion of purpose among us would be unbelievable if it didn't have so many precedents." Flandry shrugged. "Oh, the Merseians have studied us. They understand us better than we understand them. And . . . Magnusson has the kudos of having beaten them in battle, but he also promises that when he becomes Emperor, he'll negotiate a permanent peace with them."

"How do you read the sign?" she whispered.

"The entrails, do you mean?" His laugh turned into a groan. "I don't try. I know better. I only see that a most useful piece of psychological warfare has just been waged on Magnusson's account. Coincidence? Or an attempt to further the cause of sincerely desired peace? I can only nurse my suspicions. What can I, here on Terra, find out for sure? How can I?"

Again he laughed, but cheerfully, and hauled her to him. "So never mind, sweetheart! Let's enjoy ourselves while we may."

CHAPTER THIRTEEN

Being a mostly Cynthian town, Lulach looked smaller than it was. Buildings snuggled under trees, their roofs often decked with planted sod and their walls with flowering vines. Many houses were in the branches above—vegetation introduced from the mother world frequently grew enormous—where foliage hid them behind the play of sun and shadow. Streets were turf-covered, narrow and twisting, not many vehicles upon them and those compact. Wherever they could, dwellers went arboreally rather than on the ground.

A few large structures rose along the waterfront, among them a rambling timber inn. Diana and Axor established themselves there and set about exploring the area. Wo Lia took a room in the same place and got her performing animal put in its stable; local folk made considerable use of beasts for riding and hauling, though the farms to the north were mechanized.

Toward dawn, when fog off the river dusked the light night of Daedalus, she went out there, explaining to a sleepy kitchen helper whom she passed that she must see to the creature's well-being. The helper paid no particular attention to the cloth-wrapped bundle Wo Lia carried—for cleaning the cage, no doubt.

The stable was warm, murky, its air sweetened by a smell of horses and sharpened by a smell of changtus. Wo Lia groped her way to the cage and undid the catch on its door. Targovi bounded forth. "*Harrugh!*" he growled. "You took your time."

"I had to wait till you could get away unseen, didn't I?" she replied. "That cursed sun-ring makes life hard for entrepreneurs."

Targovi stretched and yawned mightily. "Ah, but this feels wonderful! Pray to your little gods that you never have to be locked up."

By his count, a pair of Terran weeks had passed since *Waterblossom* left Paz. He could scarcely have endured this confinement, had Wo Lia not let him out on a chain at every stop along the way, to dance and do tricks while she played a flute and collected coins. "What news have you heard?" he asked.

"Fresh word has lately come from the war front, borne by a courier boat to Aurea. Great excitement. Admiral Magnusson has offered to negotiate with Emperor Gerhart. He has his nerve, no?"

"Ai, he needn't fear immediate peace. It sounds good and helps smooth the way for his next onslaught. If ever the Imperium is ready to bargain in earnest, it will be too late for the Imperium, save that Magnusson might let Gerhart and his councillors retire to some obscure set of palaces and carouse themselves to death." Targovi crouched to unfold the bundle and examine its contents. "Any tale of the Merseians?"

"Of course. How could anybody on Daedalus not want the latest gossip about the neighbors? It's vague, though, except that a Navy spokesman insisted we have nothing to fear from them. A later commentary by several learned academics pointed out that, since the Merseians want a lasting peace as badly as all right-thinking Terrans do, they would probably rather see Magnusson on our throne, even though he did defeat them more than once in the past. So they will refrain from any actions that would look as if they were taking advantage of an opportunity he had created for them."

"Assuredly that is what learned academics would say." Targovi opened his purse and counted the money within. "This sum isn't quite what I remember."

"I had expenses," said Wo Lia blandly.

"Well, you weren't too generous to yourself, I see. The funds were bound to be lean regardless—and likewise, I fear, are those of my companions, by now." Much more important, anyway, was his combat knife. Targovi rose. "Best I be off. Fail not in the part that remains for you to play, for if you do, you will come to harm that may well prove fatal. On the other hand, success should bring excellent baksheesh."

"I know. If *you* fail, I will kindle a light for your ghost. *Wan jin rao.*"

Targovi slipped forth and vanished into the fog. Wo Lia waited a while before scurrying back and screaming for the landlady. Her priceless trained animal, the mainstay of her livelihood, was gone! She had cast about unavailingly, finding no trace. Had it escaped because the stablehands were careless? Had it been stolen? She demanded help in searching, the entire staff, the patrol, a posse of citizens. If the magnificent, irreplaceable creature was not found, she would have compensation. She would demand justice, she would file suit, she would not cease until she had her rightful due!

On the riverbank beyond the docks, screened by brush as well as murk, Targovi thankfully removed the mane from his head. Besides being messy and itchy, it had interfered with the oxygill it covered, making him chronically short of breath. A quick chemical rinse out of a bottle Wo Lia had provided, followed by a dip in the stream, got the black dye off his fur. He toweled himself fairly dry and put on the clothes his accomplice had brought him. Besides his breechcloth and belt, this included a loose robe with cowl that she had purchased in Aurea according to his specifications. While he was making no further attempt at disguise for the nonce, a full garment might come in handy at some later time.

The sun was again a disc, low above the river. Mist was breaking into thin white streamers, as warmth seeped into the valley. Though hunger gnawed in Targovi's guts, he decided he had better establish himself before seeking a foodstall. He padded back into town and through twilight still blue under the trees. Passersby gave him looks but sounded no alarm.

He had counted on that—bet his life on it, in fact. The public cry for him had not most likely been confined to the Aurea vicinity. Nobody would have imagined he'd be able to get this far undetected through habitation; and had he tried to make his way through the backwoods, he would have perished. Planet-wide bulletins would merely add to an already enormous perturbation.

Here in Lulach he continued just the trader from Imhotep whom folk had long known. He could have arrived on any of the numerous boats that came and went, day and night. Cynthians are inquisitive by nature, perhaps even more than humans; however, this was essentially a community of small businesses, therefore one which did not intrude on privacy.

Targovi knew he was yet on the "Wanted" list at patrol stations everywhere. Such interchange of information was automatic. Anybody who thought to inquire of the data bank at local headquarters would get a full description of him and his misdeeds, including the reward offered. He had spent a considerable while in his cage figuring out what to do about that.

The station house was a frame building in a grove of ocherous-glowing fruit trees. (A shame that no colonist could enjoy more than the sight. The flesh was not poisonous, but its flavor was almost nil and, eaten, it would make an inert mass in the stomach.) Since the founding of a major base on Daedalus, the Navy had taken over most police functions, except in areas such as Zacharia that retained autonomy. Few places required much in the way of law enforcement. A detail was apt to consist largely of personnel recruited in the district, who had served elsewhere but were now approaching retirement age. At need, they could summon swift help from outside.

Entering, Targovi found a Cynthian who sported a lieutenant's comets on a collar that was her principal outfit, chatting with a couple of elderly enlisted ratings. "Why, hail," she said in surprise. "What brings you here?"

"Something that calls for a confidential meeting, Rihu An," he replied.

She chirred her kind of laugh. "Do you have smuggled goods for sale, you rogue? The market has gotten brisk, too much so for my poor monies."

"No, this is more interesting."

She led him to the outer office, closed its door, and crouched expectant. "I lay on you a secret you must keep," he said. "Only in seeming am I a footloose peddler. The truth is that for long I have been a secret agent for Intelligence."

Her tail bottled. "What say you?"

He made a deprecating gesture. "Oh, I am no Flandry. I am among many who go about, alert, reporting whatever they learn, and sometimes helping in some or other petty operation. You know of us. You did not know I am of the fellowship. Urgency requires I reveal it to you."

Albeit relatively unsophisticated, Rihu An was capable. "Prove it."

"Certainly." He glided to the computer terminal. "*Ng-ng-r-r,* to avoid possible sleight-of-hand, would you care to take this yourself?" She sprang to the desktop. "Key for Central Database, please. Now key for Restricted—I'll turn my back while you put in your identification and certify you have a need to know. . . . Are you done? Very well, next comes this." He recited a string of numbers and letters.

Inwardly, his battle readiness heightened. He did not tense; that would have been dangerously self-limiting. Rather, he relaxed his body utterly, opening every sense to the fullest, until he caught the least whiffs of dust and smoke in the air, the least early-morning traffic murmurs from the town. This was his crucial moment.

The entire code for agents could have been changed. He was guessing that nobody had gone through that cumbersome process at an unscheduled time in the midst of crisis.

The announcement that he was a fugitive from arrest identified him simply as Targovi the merchant. One never blew a cover needlessly; in this case, it would have started people wondering whether other lowly individuals were agents too. Targovi was guessing that the warrant for him had only been entered in patrol databases, not in those of his service. The latter would be an inconvenient reminder to the corps of how divided against itself the Navy was; and it would probably not be of any help in laying him by the heels.

A wiser decision might well have been to go ahead and make the cross-correlation. Targovi was guessing that wisdom was in short supply these days. Magnusson's uprising must inevitably have generated limitless confusion. Moreover, it surely appalled many persons in the armed forces. On Daedalus they dared not protest; but they would drag their feet in carrying out orders, especially if those orders were less specific than might have been the case under normal circumstances.

If his assumptions proved wrong, Targovi would break out. If possible, he would avoid doing serious harm to Rihu An or her underlings, whom he knew and liked. He had friends hereabouts who would give him shelter while he hatched a new scheme.

As was, she turned wide eyes on him and breathed, "You, scruffy wanderer and tavern brawler, are in the guardians too? . . . Well, what do you require?"

Relief flooded through him. "I may say but little, other than that I keep my pelt as clean and well-groomed as yours. These are evil days."

"True," she said unhappily.

"We, you and I and all our kind, we cannot take sides against either of the rival Emperors, can we? What we serve is the Empire itself. What we obey is the orders we get from our superior officers."

"True," she said again. Her reluctance was plain to hear. Knowing her as he did, he had counted on it. She would not rebel against the rebellion—that would have been pointlessly self-destructive—but she would not be zealous either. Had the station commandant, Lieutenant Commander Miguel Gomez, been on duty, Targovi would have waited till he went off. Gomez was an honorable sort, but rather lavish in his admiration for Sir Olaf Magnusson. Luckily, commandants don't generally take night watches.

"Well, then," Targovi said, "my assignment concerns possible subversives and spies. Never mind whether they may be working for his Majesty Gerhart, or the Merseians, or whomever. I have my suspicions of one Wo Lia, who arrived lately on Shan U's *Waterblossom* from Paz. She is a scoundrelly character. Tracking her, I have gotten reason to think she may be more than that. Ere she can carry out whatever purpose has brought her—if it be something other than turning a few dishonest credits—I must follow her back trail, insofar as that is on record."

Rihu An waved at the terminal. "Serve yourself."

"M-m-m, this involves more than straightforward data retrieval. Consider how complex and unstable matters were at the tune of Sir Olaf's proclamation, which seems to be about when she landed on Daedalus. May I use your prime machine?"

Once more he prepared himself for trouble. The request was irregular. Rihu An might well insist on referring it to Gomez, who might well ask embarrassing questions. However, Targovi's confidence in chaos paid off afresh. She readily assented, took him to the inner office, and left him alone.

Ho-ho, ho-ho, he thought in Terran fashion, as he settled

down at the keyboard. His life had fairly well convinced him that every strength has its inherent weakness. Arrangements here were illustrative. If important data are available to anyone who has obtained the retrieval code, they are available from practically any terminal. The resolution of that difficulty is to make them accessible only through particular units, which can then be physically guarded— an extra layer of defense. Now he had wormed his way through. He could not only read out, he could write in.

Part of his clandestine training had, naturally, been in computer technics. He had studied further on his own. And, piloting a poorly automated spacecraft between planets, for years, he had gotten a great deal of practice at improvisation.

His short, powerful fingers danced across the board. Caution was necessary. An attempt to do too much would set off alarms, and he couldn't be sure what "too much" was. The information he fed into the database was strictly local and only slightly false. It admitted that he, Targovi, had been detained when he last landed at Aurea from Imhotep. That was understandable, with everything in uproar and most loyalties a matter of conjecture. Investigation had cleared him and his passengers. They were all harmless, if eccentric.

In his capacity of secret agent, he fed in his "finding" that Wo Lia was not up to any mischief that mattered politically—just in case somebody, as it might be Rihu An herself, took a peek. The fact of his being such an agent was to remain restricted information.

None of this cookery went to Central Database in Aurea. Programs there could too readily detect an intrusion. Targovi was satisfied to modify the records at Lulach and add a "Correction: Override" command. Why should a minor outpost like this maintain elaborate precautions in its system?

Whoever happened to inquire directly of Aurea would get quite a different story. If he thereupon compared what the terminals here had to tell, the well-known fat would be in the proverbial fire.

Targovi didn't expect that. In Aurea, if officialdom gave him any further thought whatsoever, he was presumed dead. In Lulach he had roused no dubiety. A civilian wanting to check up on him would almost certainly do so by retrieving the public record in this town. That would declare him to be just a merchant from Imhotep. If the civilian had access to patrol records—which, in the case against which Targovi was making provision, he might well have—they too would show nothing significantly different . . . in Lulach. It was most unlikely that such a person would call Aurea instead, or in addition. Why should he? Public hullabaloo about a Tigery outlaw would have died out and been to all intents and purposes forgotten. It was nearly impossible that the inquirer would go through the rigmarole involved in getting access to Intelligence data.

Granted, the possibility did exist that the person would prove to be that ultra-cautious. The probability of it was small but finite. If it came to pass, the remainder of Targovi's existence would doubtless be short and unpleasant. That didn't worry him. The risk gave an extra tang to his faring.

On his way out, he stooped low to whisper in Rihu An's ear: "I was wrong. We needn't concern ourselves with Wo Lia. She'll belike steal several of your citizens blind, but not in ways that will make them complain to you. I do, though, have others to trace. Remember, I am nobody but the trader whom everybody knows. It would be as well if you gave the station personnel the idea that all I wanted to do was make you a business proposition, which you very properly declined."

"That shall be," she answered as quietly. While he was engaged in the inner office, she had stayed alone in the outer, as if still conferring with him. In Intelligence work, the less you let people observe, the better.

"Abide in peace and repletion." Targovi departed. He had a second call to pay, but first he wanted breakfast.

CHAPTER FOURTEEN

From their island the Zacharians exported a variety of foods and high-quality manufactured goods to the rest of Daedalus. Keeping the business entirely in their own hands, they maintained dealerships in every important community. The local one occupied a building near the waterfront. Its artificial material, curved contours, and metallic hues marked it arrogantly out. Targovi must stand at a scanner and request admission before the door opened.

The woman who appeared was handsome in his sight, comely in that of most humans. Medium tall, full-hipped but slender and somewhat small-bosomed, she moved as lithely as he did. A brief white gown set off glowingly olive, flawless skin. The hair on her round head was light-brown, lustrous, falling springily to the wide shoulders. Her face was high of cheekbones, straight of nose, firm of chin, lips delicately sculptured, brows arched above gold-brown eyes whose largeness was not diminished by the epicanthic folds.

"Greeting, Minerva Zachary," he said.

She smiled. "Minerva has served her turn here and gone home." The voice was a musical contralto. "I am Pele. Who are you that knows her?"

"I beg your pardon, donna."

"Well, when members of our species often fail to tell us apart, I can hardly blame you." Zacharians were always as polite as occasion demanded—in their judgment.

Looking closer, Targovi began to see the differences. Fine lines in the countenance showed that Pele was distinctly older than Minerva; their kind aged slowly but were not immortal. She spoke with a faint accent suggesting that Anglic had not been the principal language in her home when she was a child; the islanders purposely kept several tongues in daily use. She didn't walk precisely like her predecessor; the islanders also made a point of practicing a variety of sports.

"Your name, please," she demanded rather than asked.

"Targovi—of Imhotep, as is obvious. I am a trader who has shuttled between my planet and this for years. On Daedalus I often proceed along the Highroad. They know me right well here."

Pele studied him. He could not have come to order any of her expensive wares. "I have no desire for trinkets."

"Could we speak in private? I am sure milady will be interested."

"Well—" She shrugged and led the way inside. The front of the building was the office; the rear, shut off, was the residence. Persons whom factors had entertained said those rooms—such of them as guests saw—were rather severely outfitted and decorated, though everything was of the best and, in its fashion, beautiful. The chamber which Targovi entered held conventional furniture, adjustable for comfort. Its commercial equipment was unobtrusive but first class, allowing a single individual to handle everything. The few pictures had been changed; Pele evidently preferred landscapes from alien planets to the more familiar scenes that Minerva chose. The musical background was now complex, atonal, impossible for the Tigery to appreciate. Did the esthetic tastes of a Zacharian alter as he or she passed through life?

"Be seated," Pele said. They took facing chairs on a richly textured blue carpet. "What is your errand?"

He knew little of her breed. His acquaintance with Minerva had been slight, instigated by her because she grew curious about him and not pursued for long. Otherwise he had only glimpsed Zacharians by chance, mostly in Aurea. They never seemed to leave their island in substantial numbers, unless they made interstellar trips out of their spaceport. Theirs was a society closed to outsiders. It made no production of secretiveness, exercised no censorship or anything like that. It simply didn't communicate much, nor admit any but a few selected visitors. None of those were journalists. People who returned talked freely enough of the uniqueness they had encountered; two or three of them had written books about the place. But nothing of its inwardness ever came through. It was as if each Zacharian face were a smiling mask.

Nevertheless Targovi could see that Pele wanted him to come to the point. "I approach you, donna, more on behalf of two friends than myself," he began. "Now I shall not insult you by claiming I have no personal concern in the matter. My situation is precarious. I landed at Aurea just as Sir Olaf Magnusson made his . . . declaration. Civilian space traffic is banned save by special permission, which has not been forthcoming for me thus far. Conveying passengers—the two I bespoke—rather than trade goods, I have naught to barter for the necessities of life, and scant money lingers in my purse."

The woman frowned. "This is no charitable organization, and it has no job openings."

Targovi imitated a human smile, keeping his lips closed because his carnivore's teeth could give the wrong signal. "I ask no favors, donna," he said ingratiatingly. "Already I am in your debt." He touched the oxygill that rose out of his robe. "Was not this, that keeps me breathing, produced on Zacharia?"

The flattery was wasted. "You paid for it, or somebody did. I have heard your species is physically strong. Try for a position as a dock-hand, day laborer, or the like. Most backwoods communities lack adequate machinery."

"No, hear me out, I pray you. Those whom I carried from Imhotep are unusual. I think they have something to offer which your people will find worthwhile. At least, the Wodenite does."

That caught her attention. "The Wodenite who arrived yesterday? I have seen him wandering about, and considered inviting him to come for a talk. And dinner, perhaps," Pele added in a flick of humor, "abundant though the servings must be."

"I can introduce him to you, milady. May I tell you the story?"

He gave her an account of Axor's quest, succinct because that should whet her appetite for details. "—In Olga's Landing he acquired a guide, a vagabond by the name of Diana Crowfeather—"

Pele raised her hand. "Wait. Is that the dark-haired ragamuffin girl who was strolling at his side?"

"Who else?" Targovi observed her grow thoughtful, and at the same time seem a bit amused. He continued: "Diana and I are old acquaintances. I decided to do her a kindness and provide passage to Daedalus, where I thought it likelier they would find relics such as they sought than on Imhotep. If naught else, here they would have access to records of whatever may have been discovered but never really publicized. Furthermore, Diana should enjoy this planet, more congenial and almost new to her. And, to be sure, Axor would pay me." Slipping fast by that bit of mendacity: "Unfortunately, as I said, the outbreak of hostilities left us stranded. In fact, we were arrested and interrogated.

"Upon release, Axor and Diana spent a while in Aurea searching for information about Ancient relics. What they learned made them decide to fare downstream. They might as well. I stayed behind, striving to wheedle a clearance for return to Imhotep. Nothing availed. Finally I took a boat to Lulach myself. It was an express, therefore it arrived nearly as soon." Considering the number of such craft and their short turnaround times, Targovi didn't anticipate anyone would attempt verification of his narrative.

"An intriguing story," Pele said, "but what significance has it to me?"

"Much, I trust, milady," he replied. "May I ask a question? Are there mysterious remnants on Zacharia?"

She gave him a close look. "No."

"Truly not?"

"We have occupied the island for centuries and modified every square centimeter of it. We would know."

Targovi sighed. "Then the clues that my comrades came upon are false. Ah, I hate the prospect of disappointing them. Their hopes were so high."

"It was always inevitable that all sorts of unfounded rumors would go about, concerning us. Why should I lie to you?" Pele stroked her jaw. "I have, myself, heard of huge, inexplicable walls and the like—but afar in the mainland jungles or glaciers. It may be nothing more than travelers' tales. Your associates should inquire further."

"That may be less than easy, donna; for their purses have grown lank too. What has occurred to me is this. You yourself know naught certain about Ancient relics, aside from their existence on some other planets. The subject has not interested you. However, during the centuries that Zacharians have dwelt on Daedalus, their explorers and factors must have ranged over the whole globe, as well as distant worlds. There must be ample records, and mayhap even individuals, to tell what is or is not real. It would save us—Axor—an effort that could prove hopelessly great."

"Do you wish me, then, to make a search of our database?" The woman pondered before continuing genially, "Well, I can. You have roused my curiosity."

"*Ng-ng,* milady is most generous," Targovi said, "but that is not truly what I had in mind. Could we come to Zacharia in person and pursue our inquiries? You know that printed words and pictures, valuable though they be, are not everything. There is no substitute for discourse, for the interplay of brains."

Pele sat straight. Her gaze sharpened. "Are you in search of free food and lodging?"

Targovi chuckled. "Plainly, yes, that is my chief motivation. Give me several standard days without pressure, perchance a week or two, and I can devise some means of keeping myself alive on Daedalus. I might even make trade arrangements with you Zacharians, or at any rate get your kind help in persuading the Navy to let me flit home. You have influence."

"I told you we are not a charitable organization."

"Nor am I a beggar, donna. My humble goods may prove worthless to you, but at the moment my stock in trade includes Axor himself. Think. He is likely the first Wodenite ever to betread Daedalus. Certainly none else have come here in living memory. Not only can he tell your savants much about his world and his folk—the sort of facts that do not get into dry dispatches—but he has roamed throughout the Empire. Not only is he a leading authority on the fascinating Ancients, he has experience of many and many contemporary societies. Let us admit that this entire sector is provincial, marginally touched by the currents of civilization. Axor will come like a breath of fresh air. I assure you, as a person he is delightful." Targovi interposed a few seconds of strategic silence. "And . . . the total situation in the galaxy has become totally fluid. Aught can happen, whether mortal danger or radiant opportunity. Axor is no political scientist or seeker of wealth and advantage. But he is widely traveled and he has thought deeply about the things he has witnessed—from his nonhuman, non-Cynthian, non-Merseian perspective. Who knows what clues toward action or precaution lie in what he has to tell? Dare you refuse yourselves the input he can give you?"

The quietness that fell again grew lengthy. At last Pele asked, "What does the girl want of us?"

"Why, simply the thrill of newness. Whatever you care to show her. She is young and adventurous . . . We three travel together, you understand."

Pele looked beyond him. "She *is* attractive," she murmured.

Targovi knew the reputation of Zacharian men. They practically never married outside their society; that meant exile. They did, though, spread their superior genes through the lesser breeds of humanity whenever they got the chance; and they had a way of creating frequent chances for themselves. Pele must be thinking she could put her brethren on the track of some fun.

To a degree, Targovi had taken this into his calculations. He didn't feel he was betraying Diana. She should be capable of reaching her own decisions and enforcing them. If not—well, she'd likely enjoy herself anyway, and bear no permanent scars.

Zacharian women were different, he recalled. They took occasional outsider lovers, whose later accounts of what had happened were awestruck and wistful. But they never became pregnant by such men. At most, if they thought someone was worthy, they would donate an ovum for *in vitro* fertilization. Their womb time they kept for their own kind.

Pele emerged from her reverie. "I'll call home and inquire," she said crisply. "I may well recommend a positive answer. You do make a plausible case for yourself. They'll send someone to investigate closer before they decide. He will want to talk with each of you. Where are you staying?"

"At the Inn of Tranquil Slumber. That is where my friends are, and I will take a room there too."

"You should find this house more hospitable when we summon you," Pele said. Conviviality provides openings for the probing of character. "At present I have my work to do. Good day."

Diana sped to meet him, over the cobblestones of the hostel

courtyard. "Oh, Targovi, old dear!" She hugged him till his firmly muscled ribs creaked. The fragrance of her hair and flesh filled his tendrils. "Welcome, welcome!"

"How have you two fared?" he asked.

She let him go and danced in the sunlight. "Wonderful," she caroled. "Listen. We went parleyin' around, and right away we heard about what's *got* to be Ancient ruins, with inscriptions, in the jungle south of Ghundrung."

"The Donarrian settlement? But that's far downstream, and then you'd have to outfit an expedition overland. Where's the money coming from?"

"Oh, we'll earn it. Axor already has an offer from a lumberin' company. He can snake a log through the woods cheaper'n any gravtrac can airlift it. And me, I've lived off odd jobs all my grown-up life. I won't have any trouble gettin' by. This is a live town." Diana sobered. "I'm sure we can find somethin' for you as well, if you want."

"But you'd take months, a year or more, to save what you will need!" Targovi exclaimed. "Meanwhile the war goes on."

She cocked her head and stared at him. "What's that got to do with us? I mean, sure, it's terrible, but we can't do anything about it. Can we?"

CHAPTER FIFTEEN

He drew a long breath. "Come aside with me and let us talk," he said.

Her jubilation died away as she sensed his uneasiness. "Of course." She tucked an arm beneath his and led him off. "I've found a trail out of town, through the woods, where nobody'll overhear us." Her smile was a trifle forlorn. "I want to learn what you've been up to anyway, and how you figure to stay out of jail, and, oh, everything."

"You shall, as much as is safe for you to know."

She bridled. "Now wait a minute! Either you trust me or you don't. I've let you rush me along this far, and conned Axor for you, because you didn't have a chance to explain. Or so you claimed. Not any more, fellow."

He raised his ears. "Ah, you are your father's child—and your mother's—eh, little friend? . . . Well, you leave me no choice. Not that I had much left me, after today. My thought was that you, being an honest young person, could best play the part I need played if you believed it was genuine."

"Hmf! You don't know me as well as you think." Diana frowned. "We might have to shade the truth for Axor. I'll hate that, but we might have to."

"Did I indeed underestimate your potential, all these years?" Targovi purred.

They said no more until they were well into the forest east of town. The trail ran along the river, a short way in from the high bank, so that water could be seen agleam beyond tree boles and canebrakes. Underneath canopies of darkling leaves, sun-flecked shadow was somewhat cooler than air out in the open, though still subtropical. It was full of unfamiliar odors, sweet, rank, spicy, or indescribable in Anglic or Toborko. Tiny, pale wings fluttered about. No songs resounded, but now and then curious whistles and glissandos went among the boughs above. The sense of ruthless fecundity was overwhelming. You understood what a war it had been, and was yet, to keep terrestroid life going on this—unusually Terra-like—world.

Diana remarked as much. "Makes you wonder how firm a grip we've got on any place, doesn't it?" she added. Her tone was hushed. "On our whole Empire, or civilization itself."

"The Merseians have long been trying to pry us loose from existence," Targovi snarled.

She gave him a troubled glance. "They can't be that bad. Can they? It's natural for a Tigery to think of them as purely evil. They'd've let your whole race, and the Seafolk's, die with Starkad. That plan of theirs depended on it. Only, well, it wasn't 'they,' not their tens of billions plottin' together, it was their government—a few key people in it, nobody else havin' any inklin'."

"Granted. I overspoke myself. Humans are too many, too widespread for extermination. But they can be diminished, scattered, conquered, rendered powerless. That is the Merseian aim."

"Why?" she wondered in hurt. "A whole galaxy, a whole universe, a technology that could make every last livin' bein' rich—why are we and they locked in this senseless feud?"

"Because both our sides have governments," Targovi said, calming down.

Presently: "Yet Terra's did rescue enough of my people that we have a chance to survive. I am not ungrateful, nor unaware of where Imhotep's best interest lies. I actually dream of serving Terra in a wider field than any one planet. What a grand game of play!"

"I'd sure like to get out there too." Diana shook herself. "S'pose we stop talkin' like world-weary eighteen-year-olds—"

"Sound counsel, coming from a seventeen-year-old."

She laughed before she went on: "All right, down to business. You're a secret agent of the Navy, no matter how low in grade. You're onto somethin' havin' to do with the fight for the throne. You need some kind of help from Axor and me. That's about the whole of what I know."

"I know not a great deal more myself," Targovi confessed. "What I have is a ghosting of hints, clues, incongruities. They whisper to me that naught which has been happening is what it pretends to be—that we are the victims of a gigantic hoax, like an ice bull which a hunter stampedes toward a cliff edge. But I have no proof. Who would listen to me, an outlaw?"

Diana squeezed his hand. The fur was velvety under her fingers. "I will."

"Thank you, small person who is no longer so small. Now, you too will find it hard to think ill of Admiral Sir Olaf Magnusson."

"What?" For an instant she was startled, until she remembered the Tigery touching on this matter before. "Oh, maybe he has let his ambition, his ego run away with him. But we did get a rotten deal out in this sector. He alone kept the Merseians from overrunin' us—"

"The crews of his ships had somewhat to do with it. Many died, many live crippled."

"Sure, sure. That doesn't change the fact that Sir Olaf provided the leadership that saved us. 'Twasn't the first time he'd done that sort of thing, either. And still he wants peace. A strong and honest man on the throne, a man who's dickered with the Merseians in the past and made them respect him—maybe he really can give us what nobody else can, a lastin' peace. Maybe that really is worth all the blood and sorrow that Gerhart's resistance is costin'."

"And mayhap not."

"Who can tell? *I* can't. The Empire's had succession crises before. It'll prob'ly have them again in the future. What can we ordinary people do except try to ride them out?"

"This crisis may be unique." Targovi marshalled his words before he proceeded:

"Let me give you the broad outlines first, details afterward. Terran personnel are not the only ones whom last year's clash left embittered. The Merseian captains were wholly inept. It wasn't like them in the least. Nor were the issues worth fighting over, save as a pretext for launching a total war against Terra, and everybody who has studied the matter knows Merseia isn't ready for that. Seemingly the eruption happened because their diplomats blundered, their lines of communication became tangled, and some hotheaded officers took more initiative than proper.

"But once conflict was rolling, the Merseians should have won. They did have superior strength in these parts. Altogether like them would have been to break our defense, take this sector over, then call for a cease-fire; and at the conference table, they would have held higher cards than Terra. They would have come out greatly advantaged.

"But they lost in space. Magnusson's outnumbered fleet cast them back with heavy casualties. We hear this was due to his brilliance. It was not. It was due to stupidity in the Merseian command.

"*Or was it?*"

They walked on mute for a spell, in the shadowy, steamy, twittering jungle.

"Later will I explain how I collected this information from the Merseians themselves," Targovi said at length. "Some was readily available, if anybody had directed that statements made by war prisoners should be recorded and collated. Nobody did. Strange, *ng-ng?* The gathering of more exact, higher-level data put me to a fair amount of trouble. You may find the story entertaining.

"Now I had also, in my rovings, picked up tales of things seen—spacecraft, especially, coming and going oftener than erstwhile—around Zacharia. This struck me as worthy of further investigation. No doubt the Zacharians have ever used their treaty-given privileges to carry on a bit of smuggling. Their industries need various raw materials and parts from elsewhere. In return, they have customers beyond the Patrician System. Why pay more taxes on the traffic than is unavoidable? The Zacharians never, m-m, overindulged in contraband. Rather, the slight measure of free trade benefited Daedalus in general. But of recent months, folk on the mainland or out at sea—on this horizonless planet—have marked added landings and takeoffs, ofttimes of ships that belong to no class they recognized. They thought little of it. I, who put their accounts together, thought much."

"You're worried about the Zacharians? Those cloned people? Why, how many of them ever set foot off their island?"

"Not cloned, precisely," he reminded. Having rarely been on this globe before, and then as a child, she had the ignorance which follows from lack of interaction. She had better get rid of it. "They reproduce in the common fashion. But they are genetically near-identical, apart from sex. A hermit society, theirs, despite its far-flung enterprises. Nobody really knows what goes on inside it, unless they be other Zacharians dwelling elsewhere in the Empire."

"Well, but, Targovi," Diana protested, "an individualist like you should be the last to think somebody's up to no good, just because they're different and value their privacy."

"In times of danger—and the winds were foul with danger, already then—you cannot afford to assume that anyone is trustworthy. Certainly not ere you've investigated them. A shame, from the moral viewpoint; but secret agents cannot afford morals, either."

"What'd you do?"

"What doctrine called for, my dear. Having found all this spoor, I reported to my superior. As it happens, he was at the top of Intelligence operations on Daedalus, Captain Jerrold Ronan. That was logical, when the Patrician System had never hitherto required surveillance of the truly intensive kind. What was *not* logical was Ronan's reaction. He forbade me to follow the trail any farther or bespeak it to anybody whatsoever, and ordered me straight back to Imhotep, despite the fact that this was an implausible move for a trader whose cargo was half unsold."

"And you didn't give up!" Diana cried. "You took it on yourself to keep on trackin'. Oh, you are a Tigery!"

"Well, it was irresistible," he said. "I had not flatly been barred from Daedalus, simply warned that I might be marooned—which was, itself, queer, for why should the sector command await any new emergency? In you and Axor, I found what seemed the perfect— stalking horses, is that your human phrase? Gently nudged this way or that on your innocent quest, you would draw attention off me. Never meant I to endanger you—"

"Though you didn't hesitate to take a chance with us." Diana caught his hand again. "Don't you mind. I don't. And who'd want to shoot at gentle old Axor? Killin' him would be a contract job anyway."

Fangs flashed as Targovi grinned. "What a waste, him a pacifist!" Soberly: "Well, the rebellion began—not a complete surprise to us— as we were approaching Daedalus. Needs must I pounce on my decision. We could return to Imhotep and abide there, safe and impotent, while events played themselves out. Or we could plunge forward and land. Did we do so, then belike a computer program had my meddlesome self listed for indefinite detention. I chose to risk that. If I decamped, you and Axor should not suffer worse than inconvenience.

"The rest of the story you know, until this day."

They walked on. The trail bent out of the woods, toward the verge of the riverbank. Long green blades rustled under a slow breeze. They resembled grass, but were not. A few boats traversed the water. The absence of aircraft overhead had begun to seem eerie. Patricius was declining toward mists that it turned sulfurous, that veiled the distant sea. Although this was summer, and Daedalus has an axis more tilted than Terra's, daylight is always brief; or else, if you reckon the sun-ring, it is never absent.

"Tell me about today," Diana said softly.

Targovi did. She clapped hands together in glee. "Hey, what a stunt, what a stunt!"

"Let us hope nobody looks too closely at the *mise-en-scène*." Targovi had acquired a good many-tag-ends of human languages other than Anglic. "I think your main part in the act will be to divert thoughts away from it."

She squinted westward. "You aim to get us to Zacharia, then?"

"Yes, and snoop about."

"What do you think you might find?"

Targovi shrugged with his tendrils. "It is a capital mistake to theorize in advance of the data. I have my suspicions, naturally. Clear does it seem, the Zacharians have close connection to Magnusson. For example, the lady Pele casually mentioned bringing in another person soon—which means by air, at a time when air traffic is restricted. Mayhap they've decided Magnusson will be the best Emperor, from their viewpoint. In any case, what support have they been giving him? Unmistakably, it's of importance. What hope they to gain? I doubt they nourish any mystique of the Terran Empire as an end in itself."

"Who does, any more?" Diana mumbled.

"Some of us deem its survival the lesser evil. But no matter that." Targovi paused. "Here is where I fall silent. Did I tell you my guess, you could well become tense, nervous, wary—and the Zacharians would see. They are not stupid. Ai, they are not stupid! For that matter, I seldom voice my thoughts to myself. They could be mistaken. I hope to arrive open-minded, no blinkers upon my senses."

"How about me?" Diana asked slowly.

"Relax and enjoy," he answered. "That will be your best service."

"And keep ready." She touched the haft of her Tigery knife.

"And, aye, prevent Axor from blurting out awkward information," Targovi said. "Can you?"

She deliberated. "M-m-m . . . well, he scarcely knows any more than you want him to. The main inconsistency, I think, is that you say you sold him passage to Daedalus—you bein' a huckster with an eye for any credits you could make—while he thinks you carried us out of benevolence. I'll slip him a hint that I paid you, from a bigger money stash than I'd admitted havin', for the sake of the trip. Not that anybody's likely to quiz him, but if they do, that should satisfy them. Otherwise . . . m-m-m . . . he did see you run from arrest in Aurea—Yes. Got it. You panicked because Tigeries can't stand long imprisonment. You were embarrassed to tell Pele Zachary that, because in fact the patrol soon caught you. Havin' been cleared anyhow and released, you followed us on an express boat the way you said." Laughter. "Yay, that should make you out to be the kind of half-civilized bumbler you want to seem!"

His gaze grew downright respectful. "You have it, I believe." Just the same, he felt compelled to add: "Remember, do not let yourself get caught up in this. Play calm, play safe. The last thing we want is an uproar."

"I understand," she said, "though I'll bet we get one regardless."

CHAPTER SIXTEEN

The aircar came from the *east*.

That meant, almost surely, from Aurea; and that in turn could mean trouble—fight, flight, outlawry proclaimed across the entire planet. Ordinarily Targovi would have felt no such forebodings. A number of vehicles still flew, some of them touching at Lulach, and they weren't all military. Not even a majority were. Civilian needs must still be served, if Daedalus was to continue providing Magnusson with the stuff of war.

But Pele went to meet this arrival.

At first Targovi knew no cause for apprehension. Rather, his blood flowed quick when she emerged from her building and strode off toward the airfield. He had grown weary of waiting. His stakeout had degenerated into routine, which never took long to bore him.

For a large part of each fair-weather rotation period he settled down under a shading kura tree beside a main street. There he eked out his dwindled exchequer by telling Toborko folk tales to whomever would stop, listen, and eventually toss him a coin or two. It was quite plausible that he would do this, and the fact that his position gave him a view of Zacharia House signified nothing, did it? At other times he wandered idly about; when nobody was looking, he might scramble onto untenanted boughs from whose leafage he could invisibly observe; he seldom left the place out of his sight, and then it was by prearrangement with Diana.

The girl passed her time in "a lot of pokin' around and people-watchin'," so it was no surprise that she occasionally lounged beneath the kura and followed the passing scene. Cynthians often paused to exchange banter with her. Several male human residents did likewise, and tried to get her to accompany them elsewhere. She accepted a few of their invitations, but just for times when Targovi would be on watch and—as they discovered—just to go sightseeing or canoeing or to a tavern for a little drinking and dancing.

She had persuaded Axor to postpone acceptance of the job he was offered, in hopes of something better. He took rambles or swims that covered a great many kilometers, and else usually sprawled in front of a terminal screening books from the public database. When Diana asked him if he wasn't lonely, he replied, "Why, no. You are kind to think of me. However, I always have God, and am making some splendid new friends. All of yesterday I visited with Montaigne." She didn't inquire who that was, not having hours in which to sit and hear him.

Since Targovi kept most of the vigils, it was only probable that Pele should set forth under his gaze. That was on an overcast afternoon, when odors of wilderness lay rank and dank in windless heat. Yet a tingle went through him. She had frequently emerged on errands that proved to be commonplace, or else to saddle a horse she kept at the inn and ride it away in the night, down game trails through the forest. He had been unable to track her then, and didn't believe it mattered. Today she walked fast, an eagerness in her gait that he thought he also glimpsed on her face; and the path she took among the trees wound toward the airfield.

Targovi had been yarning to half a dozen adult Cynthians and the young they had brought. He was becoming popular in that regard. "—And so," he said hastily, "the warrior Elgha and her companions heard from the wise female Dzhannit that they must make their way to the Door of the Evil Root. Ominous though that sounded, Dzhannit assured them that beyond it lay wisdom—not money, as Terrans might suppose, but knowledge of many new things. Long and hard would the road be, with more adventures upon it than can now be told." To a chorus of protests: "No, no. I must not keep you past your sleeptimes. Besides, it looks like rain, and better to stop here than in the middle of, say, a thrilling combat with the horrible, ravenous Irs monster. Tomorrow, my dears, I will resume."

As he bounded off at the speed which high-gravity muscles made possible, he wondered whether he would in fact ever finish the story. Well, if not, maybe someday one of those cubs, grown up, would hear it on Imhotep and remember him; or, a fonder hope, another Tigery would come to Lulach and get a request for it.

Pele had disappeared from view. That was desirable. She mustn't know she was being trailed. Targovi's tendrils picked the faint traces of her individual scent-complex out of the air. Yes, she was definitely bound for the field. He turned his pace into a soundless, casual-looking saunter that kept him in every shadow or behind every bole he could find. The intermingling of town and woods was a blessing to detectives.

It was also the reason why cars did not lower themselves at their destinations, but required a landing field like larger vehicles. That was a paved hectare on the outskirts, with a couple of hangars and a repair shop for whoever had need. A wire mesh fence surrounded it against stray wild animals. Periodic charges of poison kept the Daedalan jungle at bay. Everywhere yonder mass crowded murky beneath the low gray sky.

Pele Zachary waited at the gate. Hardly anyone else was in sight. The last part of the way here had been deserted. Nobody had reason to come nowadays, except to meet a specific flight. She must have gotten a call about this one. Targovi sidled into a thicket.

The teardrop shape of a car glinted downward. He bared his teeth. It was coming not from the west but the east!

It braked in racer style and dropped into a parking stall. A man got out, carrying a suitcase. He proceeded to the gate, where he and the woman kissed briefly before trading words. Side by side, they started toward the settlement.

When they had gone by Targovi, he stole after them through the brush that walled the street. The turf that made a tough surface for traffic was genetically engineered to kill any invading growth.

He required all his hunter's skill to move without rustle or crackle. It would have been easier at home. The dense Imhotepan atmosphere carried sound more loudly, but also let him hear better, providing added feedback. In Terran-like air he had often slipped small amplifiers into his ears. Those were in the secret compartments of *Moonjumper,* along with the rest of his specialized gear. He must make do with what nature had provided him.

That was not a gross handicap. He heard almost as well as a normal human; and his tendrils picked up vibrations too, which gave him useful cues. They whom he stalked were speaking Anglic. The accent was unique, but Targovi was accustomed to a variety of dialects. He caught most of what reached him and could deduce the rest. It was not the sort of conversation that called for whispers. Whoever accidentally overheard a part would make nothing special of it.

"I expected someone like Ares or Cernunnos," Pele was saying, "and sooner."

The man shrugged. He was her male counterpart, aside from being apparently younger. His height was greater by some ten centimeters, shoulders more broad, hips narrow, build generally muscular and masculine; but as athletic as she likewise was, the difference became less striking than it might have been. The same smooth olive complexion contrasted with brief white garments, the same brown hair clustered on a similarly brachycephalic head. His visage was distinctive, but almost entirely because of being a version of hers—larger, bonier, yet just as regular. When he spoke, his baritone had a harmoniousness of its own.

"They didn't delay consideration of your word on Zacharia," he said, "but inasmuch as I was in Aurea, they decided to have me stop on my way home and do the further investigating. If nothing else, I might have picked up some relevant information."

Targovi's pelt stood on end. The information could include those data he had been at such pains to suppress locally.

Well, if so, he'd be forewarned, and would hurry off to make what escape arrangements he was able for himself and his comrades. That was what justified the risk he took in this shadowing.

"Did you?" Pele asked.

Straining to hear, Targovi blundered. A withe whipped past him and smote a stand of cane. Leaves swished, stalks clacked. The man halted, as instantly alert as any Tigery. "What was that?" he barked.

Targovi was bound up the nearest tree. No human could have done it that fast. Besides his strength, he had agility, reaction time, and claws on his feet. Bark and vines alike he seized. A leathery-winged creature croaked alarm and fluttered out of the foliage.

"It was only—" The woman went unheard. The man left the path and thrust into the brush, peering about, a hand on the grip of the pistol belted at his waist. Zacharians had various legal privileges. . . . Targovi flattened himself on a branch.

"You are too nervous, Kukulkan," Pele said. "We always hear animals blundering around. They aren't edible, you see, and they don't devour crops, so they're hardly ever hunted."

The man satisfied himself. "No doubt you're right," he said. "I admit I am rather on edge."

"Why?"

He and she resumed walking. In a minute they would be beyond earshot. Targovi gauged his chances. He was no Cynthian, to try arboreal feats, but—He crouched and sprang. Soaring above the humans, he caught a limb ahead of them and did his best to blend with it.

This time they paid no heed to whatever they heard. "—may have to start Phase Two earlier than planned," Kukulkan Zachary said. "If only interstellar communications were faster! All they had to show me was a single message, though it came directly from Magnusson. In any event, we could find ourselves suddenly very busy."

"Hm." Pele tugged her chin. "Then you don't think we should invite those three outsiders?"

"That doesn't follow. I didn't mean we'll inevitably come under high pressure in the near future. If it does happen, we can dump them back on the mainland fast enough. They do sound interesting, and—who knows?—they might provide us with some extra cover."

Pele snickered. "I know what you'd like to cover."

Kukulkan grinned. "Those recordings you took of the girl are attractive. I was busy my entire time in Aurea."

"I've been busy but solitary too," Pele murmured.

He laughed in his turn and laid an arm about her waist. "Let's do something about that." They went on close together.

Targovi stayed behind. It was manifest that they would utter nothing more of any importance until well after they were safely inside their building. Also, they were entering habitation, and soon a Cynthian was bound to notice him aloft. That might cause gossip.

He returned to the ground and ambled lazily. Within him flickered fires. He had learned as much as he dared hope for. The Zacharians had no suspicions of him . . . thus far. They actually liked the idea of bringing his party to their island. What would come of that, only the gods knew, and maybe not they either. Javak the Fireplayer might once again take a hand in what would otherwise have been the working out of fate.

CHAPTER SEVENTEEN

Three hundred kilometers west of the mainland lifted Cliffness, the prow of Zacharia. Thence the island reached another two hundred, and from north to south eighty at its widest. Diana first saw it as the vehicle bearing her came into clear air. It still lay well ahead and below, but spread in its entirety by the strange perspectives of Daedalus. "O-o-oh-h," she breathed.

"A beautiful sight, true?" Kukulkan Zachary said. She barely noticed at first how his arm slipped around her waist, and later she didn't mind. "How glad I am that the seeing conditions were right for you."

Together with Axor and Targovi, they stood in an observation lounge. Since a good-sized craft was needed to carry the Wodenite in comfort, Kukulkan had gone all-out and summoned a first class passenger cruiser. It wasn't plying the global lanes anyway in wartime. Only ribs of metal crossed this section of the hull; the rest was vitryl, thick and strong but totally transparent. Apart from bulkheads fore and aft, you stood above the world in the middle of heaven.

Given the swift spin of Daedalus, Patricius did not much affect the doings of humans. This was a night flight because the hour chanced to be convenient. The sky ranged from deep violet-blue overhead, where a few stars glimmered, to berylline near the waters. Eastward towered clouds, their peaks and ridges frosted by the moon they hid, their lower steeps and canyons amethyst, their rains gleaming bronze and silver from the sun-ring. That lay around the rest of the Phosphoric Ocean, not as a boundary but as a shiningness unimaginably remote, within which the curve of the planet lost itself in its own vastness. There the sea gleamed like damascened steel; inwardly it shaded through turquoise to jet. Upon those darknesses swirled and sparked green fire, the light of tiny life that rode the surges.

Amidst all else, Zacharia was splendor and enigma. Most of it showed dimly verdant, the contours making intricate patterns, argent-threaded with rivers, lakes, and mists. Not far from the north coast a mountain range ran east to west, its snowpeaks now roseate, its flanks falling down into valleys which were mazes of blue-black. Light from dwellings sprinkled diamond dust across the island and several outlying cays. Movable motes betokened travelers in the air or down on the water.

The transport throbbed and the deck tilted subtly underfoot as it began descent toward the wonder.

Kukulkan slightly tightened his embrace while he steered Diana toward a sideboard. "Lacking a spaceship's acceleration compensators, we shall soon have to take seats for our landing," he said, his voice livelier than the words. "Let us enjoy a glass of champagne first—and many afterward."

"You're so, so, uh, kind," she stammered.

His exotic features lofted a smile. "Elementary courtesy, donna," he said, lips close to her ear; his breath stirred her hair. "Although in your case—" He let her go in a hand-gliding fashion and poured into both their goblets, with a glance toward Axor and Targovi. That was *pro forma,* when neither of them cared for the wine. But it was typical of him, Diana thought.

He could not have been more gracious back in Lulach. Nor, granted, could Pele Zachary have been, his—sibling?—but she was reserved and formal while Kukulkan had laid himself out.

Oh, yes, Diana knew full well when a man was undertaking to be charming. The question was whether he could manage it or not, and the answer depended on him, on how much thoughtfulness was behind the fine manners. For instance, no matter the skill with which he flattered her, she would have understood him entirely and scornfully if he had neglected her friends. Instead he gave them, if anything, more attention, and not just time but obvious concentration, real listening. Especially to Axor—Sure, he did have the responsibility of deciding whether to import such an odd pilgrim. However, he could have gone about it like some kind of personnel officer, brisk and overbearing. After all, it was the wanderers who were asking to be taken there, not the other way around.

Kukulkan had not. He'd arranged a lovely lunch at Pele's house and been marvelous to everybody. Diana had not yet sorted out her memories of the conversation. They were too dazzling. Kukulkan had been out, across the Empire, to world after world. . . . At the same time she was haunted by one remark. "Oh, yes, we need newness, we Zacharians, more than ever in this year of enclosure; we need it as we need food and air and light. I begin to believe that you can provide some, and so put us in your debt."

That was all. Talk had slipped elsewhere. She found herself yearning to know what he meant. Had she the right to abet spying on him, to violate his hospitality and trust? But she had given Targovi her promise, Targovi her brotherling, the son of Dragoika who had been like a mother to her after Maria her blood-mother died—and if he found no evidence of wrongdoing, what harm would she have done?

How could she say? How dared she say?

Kukulkan's glass clinked against hers. "Happy morrows," he toasted. She smiled back and tossed off a longer draught than was sophisticated. Tartness danced down her throat, bubbles tickled her nostrils. Presently she felt almost at ease—aware, without any belligerence, of the muscles beneath her skin and the Tigery knife at her belt. She hoped that whatever happened would indeed be happy; but whatever it turned out to be, surely an adventure awaited her.

Nacre Bay was a broad half-circle cut into the north coast. The Mencius Hills formed an inner arc, with a narrow flatland between them and the water. Through them flowed the Averroes River, glacier-fed by the Hellas Mountains farther south. Janua occupied the shore and the slopes behind.

It was not a town. Kukulkan had explained that Zacharia bore none. Most buildings stood by themselves, usually rather far apart. Aircars and telecommunications linked them as well as if they formed a village. However, it was most practical to have certain things close together—the small spaceport, a large airfield, a harbor for surface vessels, associated facilities—and in the course of time various industries and institutions had naturally located in the same area—which meant more homes and service enterprises—The region of relatively concentrated population got the name Janua. By ordinary standards it was dispersed enough, sprawling without official boundaries across more than two hundred square kilometers. As their pilot brought the cruiser down, Diana saw the same blend of forest and housing as at Lulach.

No, she realized, not the same at all. The hills were landscaped into terraces, ridgeways, contoured hollows, graceful sweeps of greensward. Gardens abounded. Trees grew orderly along roads or in bowers or groves. Some of the latter were quite large, but had clearly been planted and tended. They, like vegetation everywhere, were Terran, as near as she could judge. That was not very near, when she knew the life of the mother planet mostly from pictures, but Kukulkan had told her that the original settlers eradicated everything native and reshaped their new home according to their will.

Such houses as she glimpsed were unique in her experience. They seemed to be of stone or a stonelike synthetic, rectangular in plan, peak-roofed, fronted or surrounded by porticos, their colors subdued when not plain white. Even the large utilitarian structures down close to the shore followed that general style. She thought it was pretty—doubtless gorgeous when you got a close look—but already wondered if it might not prove monotonous. A frowning, rough-walled compound on the heights was well-nigh a relief to her eyes.

The spaceport was probably a standard model. She couldn't be certain, because she got only the most fleeting sight of it during approach. It was on the untenanted southern slope of the range, opposite the fortress-like place, as if to keep such inelegance from intruding on vision. The airfield, on the eastern rim of the bay, was screened by tall hedges below which ran flowerbeds.

They landed. Passengers unsnapped their harnesses and rose from their seats. "Welcome to Zacharia," said Kukulkan gravely, and offered Diana his arm. She didn't recognize the gesture. He chuckled and, his free hand taking hers, demonstrated what he had in mind. A delicious shiver went through her.

"Tomorrow we'll start showing you about," he said.

Axor cleared his throat, somewhat like a volcano. "We should not unduly impose on your generosity," he boomed. "If I may meet the appropriate persons and make use of the appropriate materials—"

"You shall, you shall," Kukulkan promised. "But first we must get you settled into your quarters, and let you rest after your journey."

The flight had been neither long nor taxing. Nevertheless Diana confessed a degree of weariness to herself. So incredibly much excitement!

Kukulkan escorted her into the terminal. A wall displayed a mural which puzzled her. It depicted a male and female human, nude, of the variant she had heard called "Mongoloid," emerging from clouds wherein drifted hints of stars, like a galaxy a-borning. "An ancestral creation myth," the man told her. "To us it symbolizes— Ah, but here is the greeting committee."

Almost the only folk present at this hour, they were four and, like the pilot, not as precisely similar in appearance as Kukulkan and Pele were, to that pair or to one another. While the gene pool in the population was fixed, homozygosity for every desired trait— including some that were not sex-linked—had proven to be a biological impossibility. Discrete combinations appeared in each generation; if you counted the slightest of the changes that were rung, they were manyfold. Yet the "family" resemblance overrode any minor variations in height, coloring, cast of features. Sex and age and the marks left by life were the principal differences between Zacharians. These were all older than the new arrivals, and, over and above the basic pridefulness of their breed, bore an air of distinction.

Their garb was what Diana would learn was formal: sandals on the feet, wreaths on the brows, the two men in tunics and the two women in flowing but unconstraining wraparound gowns, white with colored borders. Their names were foreign to her, Vishnu and Heimdal male, Kwan Yin and Isis female. The latter woman took the word, her gaze on Axor:

"Welcome. It is an honor and will be a pleasure to receive an outstanding scholar. I shall be your introducer to the Apollonium, since I am the one among us most familiar with the subject in which we hear you are interested. But my colleagues in general anticipate learning much from you."

"*Ochla*, I came to, to beg knowledge of you," the Wodenite faltered. "Although—no, I will not discuss religion more than is necessary, unless you desire, but the exchange of . . . ideas, information—" An earthquake quiver of avidity went through him from snout to tailtip. His dorsal plates moved like a saw, the light rippled off his scales.

Heimdal said to Targovi, on a note of polite skepticism: "Being in offplanet trade, I am willing to discuss possibilities with you. I cannot encourage optimism. The local market for Imhotepan curiosities was saturated long ago."

"We can at least talk," the Tigery replied, "and then mayhap I can, by your leave, look about this neighborhood. Something may occur to me, whereby we can both profit." Diana could sense the watchfulness beneath his affability.

"Come," Kukulkan murmured in her ear. "If you have no set purpose of your own among us, I'll be delighted to be your dragoman—provided I can fend off my envious brethren."

"Don't you have work to do?" she asked, anxious not to over-reach herself.

He shrugged and smiled. "My work is somewhat special, and at present I am, shall we say, on standby."

They went from the terminal. After the heat and damp of the valley, sea breezes were a benediction. A flatbed vehicle waited for Axor, in which Isis joined him; the rest got into a ground limo. Diana was aware of a boulevard flanked by trees and abstract sculpture, of windows aglow, of other cars but not many, of pedestrians and occasional horseback riders—handsome, physically perfect, eerily alike—The ride ended at a house which stood on what appeared to be a campus, to gauge by lawns, trees, and larger neighbor buildings.

The muted sunlight of night showed that the portico columns were fluted, their capitals running out in pleasing geometrical shapes. A frieze overhead depicted individuals of assorted sophont species, coming from right and left to a Zacharian who sat enthroned at the center. Diana couldn't make out whether the Zacharian was man or woman. Within, a mosaic anteroom gave on a spacious chamber with comfortable furniture, luxurious drapes, well-chosen pictures, laden bookshelves, archaic fireplace, everything meant for conversation.

"This is a hospice for visiting scholars," Kwan Yin explained. "Ordinarily they come from elsewhere on the island or the cays, to confer in person or to use specialized equipment. But we have lodged outsiders." Her courtesy remained intact as she added, "You will understand that it is beneath our dignity to be servants. Besides, we assume you will prefer some privacy. Therefore, this house is yours for the duration of your stay. We will conduct you through it and demonstrate the appliances. They are completely robotic, no menial work required. A selection of meals that we hope you will enjoy, when you are not dining with colleagues, is ready for heating. Supplements needed for Wodenite and Starkadian health are included. Should anything be lacking, you have only to call the service department of the Apollonium. Additional communicator codes are in the directory program. Please feel free to ask any questions and make any requests at any time."

A saying of her mother's, that Maria had said she got from Dominic Flandry, who had gotten it from somebody else, came back to Diana. "*This is Liberty Hall. You can spit on the mat and call the cat a bastard.*" She felt guilty, ungrateful, about the irreverence.

"We have modified two rooms as best we could for our xenosophont guests," Vishnu added. "I trust they will prove satisfactory."

The four finally left Diana alone in the boudoir assigned her. It was pleasant. The pictures on the walls were conventional scenes and historic portraits, but a hospice should stay neutral and the sight of the Hellas peaks from her south window was breathtaking. A bath adjoined. Closet and drawers held a variety of garments closer to her exact size than she could reasonably have expected. Also set forth were tobacco cigarettes, which she would not use; marijuana smokes, which she might; and a bottle of excellent whisky, which she immediately did.

Wallowing in a tubful of hot water, prior to a small supper and a long sleep, she found it unbelievable that Targovi should imagine evil of these people. Or at least, she forced herself to admit, she did not want to find it believable.

Heimdal would call on the Tigery and Isis on the Wodenite, for preliminary sightseeing and getting acquainted. Diana's guide would be Kukulkan. She gulped her brunch, marginally noticing that it was tasty, and had nothing but mumbles for her tablemates, before she returned to her room to dress for the occasion.

How? It was a problem new to her. While her mother lived, boys had begun shyly inviting her to picnics or dances or toboggan parties, that kind of thing; but they were her sort, from families stationed in an outpost where finery was rare. Since then she'd been encountering grown men and learning considerable wariness of them. Some were decent, of course, and she could have been safely married by now if she had wanted. The stars beckoned too brilliantly, though.

And for Kukulkan Zachary, the stars were reachable.

"Easy, lass, easy," she warned herself. Nevertheless her hand shook a bit while she combed luster back into her hair and secured it with a silver headband. After agonizing, she had chosen a white frock, knee-length, suitable for a broad leather belt; sturdy sandals, good to walk distances in; and a hooded blue cloak with a bronze-and-ruby snake brooch. Given such an outfit she could wear her knife as a very natural accessory. Not that she expected trouble. What she did need to do, in the middle of this overwhelmingness, was proclaim—to herself as much as anybody else—that she remained her own woman.

Kukulkan waited in the living room. He rose and bowed in Imperial court style. He himself wore everyday Terran-type shirt (saffron, open halfway down the chest), slacks (dark blue, form-hugging), and shoes (sturdy, scuffed, lots of hiking behind them). "Good day, milady," he greeted. "We're lucky. Magnificent weather, and nothing to hurry for."

"Good day," she replied, annoyed that her voice fluttered like her pulse. "You're so kind."

He took her hand. "My pleasure, I assure you. My joy." How white his teeth were, how luminous his slanty eyes.

"Well, I—I'm at your call, I reckon. Uh, what were you thinkin' of for today?"

"M-m, the afternoon is wearing on. We might start with a stroll up to Falconer's Park on the western headland. The name comes from a tremendous view. Later—well, the night will be clear again, and things stay open around the clock. Things like museums and art galleries, I mean. We don't have the ordinary sort of public entertainments or restaurants or anything like that. But automated food and drink services aren't bad, and eventually—well, if we happen to end at my home, I scramble a mean egg, and all we Zacharians keep choice wine cellars."

She laughed, more consciously than was her wont. "Thanks very much. Let's see what I can do before I collapse."

They left. A fresh breeze blew over the campus, smelling of grass lately mown. It soughed through silvery trembling of poplars, dark stoutness of chestnuts. A few persons were afoot among the ivied buildings. They wore ordinary clothes, and for the most part were getting along in years. But . . . scholars, scientists, lords and ladies of the arts, whose minds ranged beyond this heaven—?

"You've built yourselves a real paradise, haven't you?" Diana ventured.

The response surprised her. "There are those who would consider it a hell. This is ours, as water is for the fish and air for the bird. Each is forever denied the environment of the other."

"Humans can go into both," she said, mostly to show that she too had a brain. "You Zacharians get around on Daedalus, yes, throughout the Empire, don't you?" Smitten by realization, she hesitated before adding: "But we, the rest of us, we couldn't live here, could we? Even if you allowed us."

"We have special needs," he answered soberly. "We have never claimed to be . . . common humans. Foremost among our needs is the conserving of our heritage. Only here is it secure. Elsewhere our kind exists as individuals or nuclear families, all too susceptible to going wild."

"Uh, 'goin' wild'?"

"Outbreeding. Outmarrying, if you will. Losing themselves and their descendants in the ruck."

She stiffened. He saw and went on quickly. "Forgive me. That sounded more snobbish than I intended. It's a mere phrase in the local dialect. If you reflect upon our history you'll understand why we are determined to maintain our identity."

Interest quelled umbrage. Besides, he was intelligent and good-looking and they were bound along a stately street, downhill toward a bay whose minute plant life made the water shine iridescent. Persons they passed gave her glances—marvelling from children, knowing from adults, admiring and desiring from young men. Often the latter hailed Kukulkan and moved close in unmistakable hopes of an introduction. He gave them a signal which she guessed meant, "Scram. I saw her first." The compliment was as refreshing as the wind off the sea.

"Frankly, I'm ignorant of your past," she acknowledged. "I'm a waif, remember, who'd heard little more than the name of your people."

"Well, that can be remedied," said Kukulkan cordially, "though not in an hour, when our origins lie almost a thousand years back in time, on Terra itself."

"I know that, but hardly any more, not how or why it happened or anything. Tell me, please."

Pride throbbed through the solemnity of his tone. He was a superb speaker.

"As you wish. Travel beyond the Solar System was just beginning. Matthew Zachary saw what an unimaginably great challenge it cast at humankind, peril as well as promise, hardihood required for hope, adaptability essential but not at the cost of integrity. A geneticist, he set himself the goal of creating a race that could cope with the infinite strangeness it would find. Yes, machines were necessary; but they were not sufficient. *People* must go into the deeps too, if the whole human adventure were not to end in whimpering pointlessness. And go they would. It was in the nature of the species. Matthew Zachary wanted to provide them the best possible leaders."

Kukulkan waved his left hand, since Diana had his right arm. "No, not 'supermen,' not any such nonsense," he continued. "Why lose humanness in the course of giving biological organisms attributes which would always be superior in machines? He sought the optimum specimen—the all-purpose human, to use a colloquialism. What would be the marks of such a person? Some were obvious. A high, quick, wide-ranging intelligence; psychological stability; physical strength, coordination, organs and functions normal or better, resistance to disease, swift recuperation from any sickness or injury that did occur and was not irreversible—you can write the list yourself."

"I thought a lot of that had already been done," Diana said.

"Of course," Kukulkan agreed. "Genetic treatment was in process of eliminating heritable defects. To this day, they seldom recur, in spite of ongoing mutation and in spite of the fact that comparatively few prospective parents avail themselves of genetic services. Many can't, where they are. I daresay your conception was entirely random, 'natural.' But thanks to ancestors who did have the care, you are unlikely to come down with cancer or schizophrenia or countless other horrors that you may never even have heard named.

"Still, this does not mean that any zygote is as good as any other. The variations and combinations of the genes we accept as normal make such an enormous number that the universe won't last long enough to see every possibility realized. So we get the strong and the feeble, the wise and the foolish, *ad infinitum.* Besides, Zachary understood that that optimum human is unspecialized, is excellent at doing most things but not apt to be the absolute champion at any one of them.

"What is the optimum, except the type which can flourish under the widest possible range of conditions? Zachary acquired a female associate, Yukiko Nomura, who influenced his thinking. She may be responsible for the considerable proportion of Mongoloid traits in us. For example, the eyefold is useful in dry, cold, windy climes, and does no harm in others. By way of contrast, a black skin is ideal in the tropics of Terra under primitive conditions, or today on a planet like Nyanza; and it does not prevent its owner from settling in a different environment; but it does require more dietary iodine than a lighter complexion, and iodine shortages are not uncommon in nature. I could go on, but no matter now. And I admit that a number of the choices were arbitrary, perhaps on the basis of personal preference, when *some* choice had to be made.

"In the end, after years of labor and frequent failure, Zachary and Nomura put together the cell that became ancestral to us. It is not true what a derogatory legend says, that they supplied all the DNA. Their purpose was too grand for vanity. What they gave of their own was that small fraction they knew to be suitable. The rest they got elsewhere, and nearly everything underwent improvement before going into the ultimate cell.

"That cell they then caused to divide into two. For one X chromosome they substituted a Y, thus making the second cell male. They put both in an exogenetic apparatus and nurtured them to term. The infants they adopted, and raised to maturity and their destiny. Those were Izanami and Izanagi, mother and father of the new race.

"Ever afterward, we have guarded our heritage."

There was a long silence. Man and girl left the street for a road that swung out between trees and estates, toward the western promontory. Patricius declined, its light going tawny. The wind blew cooler, with a tang of salt.

"And you marry only amongst yourselves?" Diana asked finally.

"Yes. We must, or soon cease to be what we are. Permanent union with an outsider means excommunication. M-m—this is not boastfulness, it is realism—we do consider our genes a leaven, which we are glad to provide to deserving members of the general species. You are a rather extraordinary young lady, yourself."

Her face heated. "And not yet ready for motherhood, thanks!"

"Oh, I would never dream of distressing you."

She switched the subject back in a hurry. "Doesn't inbreedin' make for defective offspring?"

"Not when there are no defects in the parents. As for the inevitable mutations, tests for those are routine, early in pregnancy. You may find our noninvasive DNA-scanning technique interesting. The equipment for it is an export of ours, but protective restrictions on trade have kept it out of the inner Empire. No clinic on Imhotep has felt it could afford the cost."

Diana grimaced. "And any embryo that isn't 'perfect' you—terminate, is that the nice word?"

"As a matter of fact, seldom; only if the prospects for a satisfying life are nil. True, the mother usually elects to have the zygote removed. But it's brought to term externally . . . or in the womb of an ordinary Daedalan volunteer. We always find couples eager to adopt such a baby. Remember, it's not born with any serious handicap; as a rule, nothing undesirable is evident at all. It's still a superior human being. It is simply not a Zacharian."

"Well, that's better." Diana shook her head and sighed. "You're right, this is an almighty peculiar place. How'd it get started, anyway?"

Kukulkan scowled. "What the Founders did not foresee was the effect of an unpleasant characteristic of the species; and before you point this out yourself, I concede that Zacharians aren't free of it either. Perhaps, if we had had the upper hand, we would have developed into an oppressive master caste. As it was, we were a tiny minority, inevitably but annoyingly exclusive. Astarte Zachary, let us say, might be a loyal shipmate of Pierre Smith; she might take him for a lover; but never would she consider marrying him, or his brother, or anybody except a fellow Zacharian. The reasons were plain, and they were . . . humiliating. The ordinaries retaliated, more and more, with exclusionism of their own. Here and there, discrimination turned into outright persecution. 'Incest' was almost the least ugly of the words thrown at us. The collapse of the Polesotechnic League removed the last barrier against intolerance—not individual intolerance, which we could deal with, but institutionalized intolerance, discriminatory laws in society after society. Many among us found it easier to give up the struggle and merge into the commonality. The need for a homeland became ever more clear.

"Zacharia Island was the choice. At the time, settlement on Daedalus was young, small, embattled against nature. Our pioneers found this real estate unclaimed and saw the potential. They were workers and fighters. They took a leading role in defending against bandits, barbarians, eventually Merseians, during the Troubles. The price they demanded was a treaty of autonomy. When at last the Terran Empire extended its sway this far, the treaty was only slightly modified. Why should we not continue to govern ourselves as we wished? We caused no dissension, we paid our tribute, we made a substantial contribution to the regional economy. As you've seen, the rest of the Daedalans accept us on our traditional terms; and by now, elsewhere in the Empire, we are merely people who carry on some enterprises of business, exploration, or science. In short, having forsaken old dreams of leadership, we are just one more ethnic group within a domain of thousands."

"What sort of government do you have?" Diana asked.

Kukulkan's intensity yielded to a smile. "Hardly recognizable as such. Adults generally handle their private affairs and earn their livelihoods however they see fit. In case of difficulties, they have plenty of helpful friends. In case of serious disputes, those same friends act as arbitrators. What public business we have is in charge of a committee of respected elders. When it becomes more than routine, telecommunications bring all adults into the decision-making process. We are not too numerous for that. More important, consensus comes naturally to us."

Again, silence. The road climbed heights above the bay. There water shimmered quiet, but from up ahead Diana began to hear the crash of surf on rocks.

"What are you thinking, rare lady?" Kukulkan prompted.

"Oh, I—I don't know how to say it. You're bein' generous to me. I'd hate to sound, oh, ungracious."

"But?"

She let it out: "But isn't this life of yours awfully lonely? Everybody a copy of yourself, even your wife, even your kids—How do you stand it? It's not as if you were dullards. No! I think if I had to be by myself, for always, I'd want it to be on an empty planet, me and nobody else—no second and third me to keep feedin' back my thoughts, my feelin's, and, and everything."

"Fear not," he said quietly. "I expected your question and take no offense. A full answer is impossible. You must be a Zacharian before you can understand. But use that fine mind of yours and do a little logical imagining. We are not identical. Similar, yes, but not identical. Besides the genotypal variations, we have our different lives behind us, around us. That happens to multiple-birth children of ordinaries, too. They never tread out the same measure. Often they go widely separate ways. Recall that Pele is currently taking her turn as a factor, while her principal career is in industrial administration. Isis is a planetary archaeologist, Heimdal a merchant, Vishnu a xenologist, Kwan Yin a semantician . . . and thus it goes, as diverse as the cosmos itself.

"And we have our constant newness, our ever-changing inputs, here on our island. We are in touch with the outside universe. News comes in, books, dramas, music, arts, science, yes, fashions, amusements. Each individual perceives, evaluates, experiences this in his or her particular way, and then we compare, argue, try for a synthesis—Oh, we do not stagnate, Diana, we do not!"

In a corner of her consciousness she was unsure whether to be pleased or warned by so early a first-name familiarity from him. Mainly she struggled to define her response. "Just the same— somethin' you mentioned before, and your whole attitude toward us, your takin' in three raggedy castaways, when for centuries it's been a scarce privilege for any outsider to set foot here—Believe me, we appreciate your help and everything. But I can't keep from wonderin' if—what with the war cuttin' off that flow of information from the stars—if you aren't desperate already for anything fresh."

"You are wise beyond your years," he answered slowly. "'Desperate' is too strong a word. Father Axor is in fact very interesting, and his comrades come in the package. Deeper motivations—but only a Zacharian would understand. In your own right, Diana, you are more than welcome."

Still she saw around her a Luciferean isolation, and puzzled over how it had worked on the community, lifetime by lifetime. Targovi seemed abruptly less alien than this man at her side.

But then they reached land's end and stopped. He swept an arm across the sight. She gasped. Cliffs dropped down to skerries where breakers roared, white against blue, violet, green. The ocean went on beyond, without limit, finally dimming away in weather; at that distance, storm clouds were not rearing monsters but exquisitely sculptured miniatures. The bay sheened opalescent, the terrain rose in changeable play of golden light and blue-black shadow over its emerald richness. Westward, Patricius was beginning to reach out wings. Southward, vision was bounded by the Hellene snowpeaks, softly aflame.

When Kukulkan took her hand, it was natural to clutch his tightly. He smiled anew and pursued his thought: "Humankind needs your genes. They are valuable. It is your duty to pass them on."

CHAPTER EIGHTEEN

Admiral and self-proclaimed Emperor Sir Olaf Magnusson gave safe conduct to the ship from Terra, on condition that her crew surrender their arms and let his men take over. It was not that she posed any serious threat in herself, being an unescorted light cruiser stripped down and fine-tuned for speed. It was, perhaps, because the chief of the delegation she bore was Fleet Admiral Sir Dominic Flandry.

The trip was short from the rendezvous star to the sun of Sphinx, the planet on which Magnusson currently maintained his headquarters. That was a shrewd selection. Besides its location, strategic under present conditions, it was humanly habitable and the center of formidable industries occupying that entire system. It was not humanly inhabited; the name had been bestowed in a mood of despair at ever comprehending the natives. They simply paid the Empire its tribute and went about their inexplicable business. When Magnusson arrived, they were equally unemotional, offering him no resistance, providing him what he demanded, accepting his promises of eventual compensation, but volunteering nothing. This suited him well. He neither needed nor wanted another set of societies to fit into a governance still thinly spread and precariously established.

Those were relative terms. Throughout the space he controlled—by now a wedge driven into more than ten percent of the volume claimed by the Empire—life went on in most places with little change, except where curtailment of interstellar trade had repercussions. The same authorities carried out essentially the same tasks as before. The difference was that they reported, when they did, to his Naval commissioners rather than Gerhart's satraps. They saw to the filling of any requisitions. They gave no trouble; had they done so, they would soon have been overthrown by their subordinates, with the heartfelt cheers of populaces that might otherwise have suffered nuclear bombardment.

As yet, few had openly embraced the Olafist cause. The basic requirement laid on everybody was to refrain from resisting it. Should Gerhart's side prevail, you could explain that there had been no choice. Should Magnusson's, there would be ample time to switch loyalty.

Thus fared, in broad and oversimplified outline, the civilians. Some Navy officers took their oaths with antique seriousness, and led such personnel as would follow them into space or into the hills, to wage guerilla warfare on behalf of the Molitor dynasty. They were more than counterbalanced by those who swore allegiance to the new claimant. Seldom were the latter mere opportunists. Many bore old anger against a regime that they saw as having starved their service and squandered lives to no purpose. Others saw the revolution as a chance for public honesty, fairness, firmness—and even, by whatever means the leader selected, an end to the grindstone half-war with Merseia.

Thus Magnusson's grip on his conquests was secure enough as long as he suffered no major reversal. The moment it slackened, they would fall apart in his fingers. More closely knit, the inner Empire that Gerhart's faction held was less vulnerable. Yet once pierced, it could soon tear asunder: as interdependent nations, worlds, races hastened to yield before civil war destroyed their sacrosanct prosperity.

Hence Magnusson did not risk overextending himself. Instead, he directed his vanguard forces to make fast what they had captured and seek no further battle. Meanwhile he consolidated the guardianship of his rearward domains. This released squadron after squadron for frontline duty in his next great onslaught.

For their part, Gerhart's commanders were not anxious to fight again soon. They had taken a bad beating. Repairs and replacements were necessary, not least where morale was concerned. The total strength on their side remained hugely superior, but only a fraction was available for reinforcements, if the rest of the Empire was to be kept safe—especially against a surprise flank attack. Collecting the data, making the decisions, issuing the calls, obtaining the means, reorganizing the fleets and support corps, all this would take time.

So the conflict dwindled for the nonce into random skirmishes. Magnusson sent a message proposing negotiations. Rather to his surprise, an acceptance came back. Emperor Gerhart would dispatch several high-ranking officers and their aides to conduct exploratory talks. Almost on the heels of this word, Flandry followed.

"Why are you here?" Magnusson asked.

Flandry grinned. "Why, because his Majesty cherishes a statesmanlike wish for peace, reconciliation, and the return of his erring children to righteous ways and his forgiveness."

Magnusson glared. "Are you trying to make fun of me?"

They sat alone in what had been a room of the Imperial resident's house. It was small and plainly furnished, as befitted a person who had had little to do. A full-wall one-way transparency gave a view of surrounding native structures. They were like gigantic three-dimensional spiderwebs. Now that the orange sun was down, lights twinkled throughout them, changing color at every blink. Magnusson had dimmed interior illumination so his visitor might better see the spectacle. Unfiltered, the air was a bit cold, with a faint ferrous odor. Sometimes a deep hum penetrated the walls. And sometimes a cluster of sparks drifted across the sky, an atmospheric patrol or a space unit in high orbit, sign of power over foreignness.

Flandry reached in his tunic for a cigarette case. "No, I am quoting news commentaries I heard as I was preparing for departure. Unless the government buried all reports of your offer, which would have been hard to do, it must needs explain its response, whether positive or negative. I daresay your flacks use similar language."

Magnusson's big frame eased back into his chair. "Ah, yes. I was forgetting how sardonically superior you like to make yourself out to be. It's been years since we last met, and that was just in passing."

Flandry drew a cigarette from the silver box, tapped it on his thumbnail, ignited it and trickled smoke across his lean features. "You ask why I am here. I might ask you the same."

"Don't play your games with me," Magnusson snapped, "or I'll send you packing tomorrow. I invited you to talk privately because I had hopes the conversation would be meaningful."

"You don't expect that of the official discussions between my group and whatever staff members you appoint?"

"Certainly not. This was a charade from the beginning."

Flandry raised the glass of neat whisky at his elbow and sipped. "You initiated it," he said mildly.

"Yes. As a token of good will. You'd call it propaganda. But you must know I have to demonstrate the truth over and over—that I have no other aim than the safety and well-being of the Empire, which the corruption and incompetence of its rulers have been undermining for dangerously long." Magnusson, who had had no refreshment set out for himself, growled forth a laugh. "You're thinking I've started believing my own speeches. Well, I do. I always did. But I'll grant you, maybe I've been giving so many that I've gotten in the habit of orating."

He leaned forward. "I did expect that, at this stage, my proposal would be rebuffed," he said. "Apparently Gerhart decided to try sounding me out. Or, rather, his chief councillors did; he hasn't that much wit. Now it's hardly a secret that he—or, at any rate, the Policy Board—listens closely to whatever Dominic Flandry has to say. I suspect this mission was your idea. And you are leading it in person." His forefinger stabbed toward the man opposite. "Therefore my question really was, 'Why are *you* here?' Answer it!"

"That is," Flandry drawled, "on the basis of my presence you assume I have more in mind than a jejune debate?"

"You wouldn't waste your time on any such thing, you fox."

"Ah, you've found me out. Yes, I did urge that we accept your invitation, and believe me, I had to argue hard before I got agreement to such an exercise in futility. Not that the people with me unanimously know it is. Apart from a couple of leathery old combat commanders and one tough-minded old scholar, to keep the rest from going completely off into Cloud Cuckoo Land, they're career civil officials with excellent academic backgrounds. They believe in the power of sweet reason and moral suasion. I suggest that to meet with them you assign whatever officers of yours are in need of amusement."

"If I bother. You admit this has been an excuse to get you into play—which I'd already guessed. What do you intend?"

"Exactly what is happening."

Magnusson's heavy countenance stiffened. He clenched a fist on the arm of his chair. Behind him, the star-points in the spiderwebs blinked, changed, blinked, changed.

Flandry sat back, crossed shank over knee, inhaled and sipped. "Relax," he said. "You've nothing to fear from a solitary man, aging and unarmed, when a squad of guards must stand beyond that door. You spoke of us trying to sound you out. That means nothing around the conference table. What is anyone going to do—what can anyone do?—but bandy cliches? However, I've a notion that it may be possible for me to sound you out, as man to individual man." He made an appeasing gesture. "In return, I can tell you things, give you a sense of what the situation is on Terra and inside the Imperium, such as would be unwise to utter in the open."

"Why should I believe you?" Magnusson demanded hoarsely.

Again Flandry grinned. "Belief isn't compulsory. Still, my remarks are input, if you'll listen, and I think you'll find they accord with facts known to you. What is to keep you from lying to me? Nothing. Indeed, I take it for given that you will, or you'll refuse to respond, when words veer in inconvenient directions. Usually, though, you should have no reason not to be frank." His gray gaze caught Magnusson's and held on. "It's lonely where you are, isn't it, Sir Olaf?" he murmured. "Wouldn't you like to slack off for this little while and talk ordinary human talk? You see, that's all I'm after: getting to know you as a man."

"This is fantastic!"

"No, it's perfectly logical, if one uses a dash of imagination. You realize I'm not equipped to draw a psychomathematical profile of you, which could help us predict what you'll do next, on the basis of an evening's gab. I am not Aycharaych."

Magnusson started. "Him?"

"Ah," said Flandry genially, "you've heard of the late Aycharaych, perhaps had to do with him, since you've spent most of your time on the Merseia-ward frontier. A remarkable being, wasn't he? Shall we trade recollections of him?"

"Get to the point before I throw you out," Magnusson rasped.

"Well, you see, Sir Olaf, to us on Terra you're a rather mysterious figure. The output of your puffery artists we discount. We've retrieved all the hard data available on you, of course, and run them through every evaluation program in the catalogue, but scarcely anything has come out except your service record and a few incidentals. Understandable. No matter how much you distinguished yourself, it was in a Navy whose officers alone number in the tens of millions, operating among whole worlds numbering in the tens of thousands. Whatever additional information has appeared about you, in journalistic stories and such over the years, that's banked on planets to which you deny us access. As for your personality, your inner self, we grope in the dark."

Magnusson bridled. "And why should I bare my soul to you?"

"I'm not asking you to," Flandry said. "Tell me as much or as little, as truthful or false, as you like. What I am requesting is simply talk between us—that you and I set hostility aside tonight, relax, be only a couple of careerists yarning together. Why? Because then we on Terra will have a slightly better idea of what to prepare ourselves for. Not militarily but psychologically. You won't be a faceless monster, you'll be a human individual, however imperfectly we still see you. Fear clouds judgment, and worst when it's fear of the unknown.

"Wouldn't you like to make yourself clear to us? Then maybe a second round of negotiations could mean something. Suppose you're being defeated, the Imperium might well settle for less than the extermination of you and your honchos. Suppose you're winning, you might find us more ready to give you what you want, without further struggle." Flandry dropped his voice. "After all, Sir Olaf, you may be our next Emperor. It would be nice to know beforehand that you'll be a good one."

Magnusson raised his brows. "Do you seriously think an evening's natter can make that kind of difference?"

"Oh, no," Flandry said. "Especially when it's off the record. If I reach any conclusions, they'll be my own, and I wouldn't look for many folk at home to take my naked word. But I am not without influence. And every so often, a small change does make a big difference. And, mainly, what harm to either of us?"

Magnusson pondered. After a time: "Yes, what harm?"

Dinner was Spartan, as suited the master's taste. He took a single glass of wine with it, and afterward coffee. Flandry had two glasses, plus a liqueur from the resident's stock, sufficient to influence his palate and naught else. Nevertheless, that dining room witnessed speech more animated than ever before. In the main it was noncontroversial, reminiscent, verging on the friendly. Both men had had many odd experiences in their lives.

Flandry was practiced at keeping vigilance behind a mask of bonhomie. Magnusson was not; when he felt such a need, he clamped down a poker face. It appeared toward the end of things, after the orderly had cleared the table of everything except a coffeepot and associated ware. The hour was late. A window showed the spiderweb constellations thinning out as their lights died. Warm air rustled from a grille, for the nights here were cold. It wafted the smoke of Flandry's cigarettes in blue pennons. His brand of tobacco had an odor suggesting leaves on fire in a northern Terran autumn.

He finished his account of a contest on a neutral planet between him and a Merseian secret agent: "Before you object, I agree that poisoning him wasn't very nice. However, I trust I've made it clear that I could not let Gwanthyr go home alive if there was any way of preventing it. He was too able."

Magnusson scowled, then blanked his visage and said flatly, "You have the wrong attitude. You regard the Merseians as soulless."

"Well, yes. As I do everybody else, myself included."

Magnusson showed irritation. "Belay that infernal japing of yours! You know what I mean. You look on them as inevitable foes, natural enemies of humans, like a—a strain of disease bacteria." He paused. "If it weren't for your prejudice, I might seriously consider inviting you to join me. We could make a pretext for your wife to come out before you declared yourself. You claim your purpose is to hold off the Long Night—"

"As a prerequisite for continuing to enjoy life. Barbarism is dismal. The rule of self-righteous aliens is worse."

"I'm not sure but what that's another of your gibes, or your lies. No matter. Why can't you see that I'd bring an end to the decadence, give the Empire back strength and hope? I think what's blinkering you is your sick hatred of Merseians."

"You're wrong there," Flandry said low. "I don't hate them as a class. Far more humans have earned my malevolence, and the one being whose destruction became an end in itself for me didn't belong to either race." He could not totally suppress a wince, and hastened on: "In fact, I've been quite fond of a number of individual Merseians, mostly those I encountered in noncritical situations but sometimes those who crossed blades with me. They were honorable by their own standards, which in many respects are more admirable than those of most modern humans. I sincerely regretted having to do Gwanthyr in."

"But you can't see, you're constitutionally unable to see or even imagine that a real and lasting peace is possible between us and them."

Flandry shook his head. "It isn't, unless and until the civilization that dominates them goes under or changes its character completely. The Roidhun could make a personal appearance singing 'Jesus Loves Me' and I'd still want us to keep our warheads armed. You haven't had the chance to study them, interact with them, get to know them from the inside out, that I've had."

Magnusson lifted a fist. "I've fought them—done them in, as you so elegantly put it, by the tens of thousands to your measly dozen or two—since I enlisted in the Marines thirty years ago. And you have the gall to say I don't know them."

"That's different, Sir Olaf," Flandry replied placatingly. "You've met them as brave enemies, or as fellow officers, colleagues, when truces were being negotiated and in the intervals of so-called peace that followed. It's like being a player on one of two meteor ball teams. I am acquainted with the owners of the clubs."

"I don't deny hostility and aggressiveness on their part. Who does? I do say it's not been unprovoked—from the time of first contact, centuries ago, when the Terran rescue mission upset their whole order of things and found ways to get rich off their tragedy— and I do say they have their share of good will and common sense, also in high office—which are utterly lacking in today's Terran Imperium. It won't be quick or easy, no. But the two powers can hammer out an accommodation, a peace—an alliance, later on, for going out together through the galaxy."

Flandry patted a hand over the beginnings of a yawn. "Excuse me. I've been many hours awake now, and I must confess to having heard that speech before. We play the recordings you send our way, you know."

Magnusson smiled grimly. "Sorry. I did get carried away, but that's because of the supreme importance of this." He squared his blocky shoulders. "Don't think I'm naive. I do know Merseia from the inside. I've been there."

Flandry lounged back. "As a youngster? The data we have on you suggested you might have paid a couple of visits in the past."

Magnusson nodded. "Nothing treasonable about that. No conflicts were going on at the time. My birthworld, Kraken, has always traded freely, beyond the Terran sphere as well as within it."

"Yes, your people are an independent lot, aren't they? Do go on, please. This is precisely the sort of personal insight I've been trying for."

Magnusson went expressionless. "My father was a space captain who often took cargoes to and from the Roidhunate, sometimes to Merseia itself. That was before the Starkad incident caused relations to deteriorate entirely. Even afterward, he made a few trips, and took me along on a couple of them. I was in my early teens then— impressionable, you're thinking, and you're right, but I was also open to everything observation might show me. I got chummy with several young Merseians. No, this didn't convince me they're a race of angels. I enlisted, didn't I? And you know I did my duty. But when that duty involved getting together with Merseians in person, my senses and mind stayed open."

"It seems a pretty fragile foundation for a consequential political judgment."

"I studied too, investigated, collected opinions, thought and thought about everything."

"The Roidhunate is as complex as the Empire, as full of contradictions and paradoxes, if not more so," Flandry said in a level tone. "The Merseians aren't the sole species in it, and members of some others have been influential from time to time."

"True. Same as with us. What of it?"

"Why, we know still less about their xenos than we do about our own. That's caused us rude surprises in the past. For example, my longtime antagonist Aycharaych. I got the impression you also encountered him."

Magnusson shook his head. "No. Never."

"Really? You seem to recognize the name."

"Oh, yes, rumors get around. I'd be interested to hear whatever you can tell."

Flandry bit his lip. "The subject's painful to me." He dropped his cigarette down an ashtaker and straightened in his chair. "Sir Olaf, this has been a fascinating conversation and I thank you for it, but I am genuinely tired. Could I bid you goodnight? We can take matters up again at your convenience."

"A moment. Stay." Magnusson reflected. Decision came. He touched the call unit on his belt. A door slid aside and four marines trod through. They were Irumclagians, tall, slim, hard-skinned, their insect-like faces impassive.

"You are under arrest," Magnusson said crisply.

"I beg your pardon?" Flandry scarcely stirred, and his words came very soft. "This is a parley under truce."

"It was supposed to be," Magnusson said. "You've violated the terms by attempting espionage. I'm afraid you and your party must be interned."

"Would you care to explain?"

Magnusson snapped an order to the nonhumans. It was clear that they knew only the rudiments of Anglic. Three took positions beside and behind Flandry's chair. The fourth stayed at the door, blaster unholstered.

Magnusson rose to stand above the prisoner, legs widespread, fists on hips. He glowered downward. Wrath roughened his voice: "You know full well. I was more than half expecting it, but let you go ahead in hopes you'd prove to be honest. You didn't.

"For your information, I learned three days ago that the Terran spies specially sent to Merseia were detected and captured. I suspect they went at your instigation, but never mind; you certainly know what they were up to. The leading questions you fed me were part and parcel of the same operation. No wonder you came yourself. Nobody else would've had your devil's skill. If I hadn't been warned, I'd never have known—till the spies and you had returned home and compared notes. As it is, I now have one more proof that the God looks after His warriors."

Flandry met the fire-blue stare coolly and asked, "Won't our captivity be a giveaway?"

"No, I think not," Magnusson said, calming. "Nobody will expect those agents of yours to report back soon. Besides, the Merseians will start slipping the Terrans disinformation that seems to come from them. You can imagine the details better than I can. As for your mini-diplomatic corps here, won't the Imperium be happy when it does not return at once? When, instead, courier torps bring word that things look surprisingly hopeful?"

"The Navy isn't going to sit idle because of that," Flandry cautioned.

"Of course not. Preparations for the next phase of the war will go on. All my side has done is stop an attempt by your side that could have been disastrous if it had succeeded. Yes, I'm sure there are people back there whom you've confided your suspicions to; but what value have they without proof? After fighting recommences in earnest, who'll pay them any further attention?"

Magnusson sighed. "In a way, I'm sorry, Flandry," he said. "You're a genius, in your perverse fashion. This failure is no fault of yours. What a man you would have been in the right cause! I bear you no ill will and have no wish to mistreat you. But I dare not let you continue. You and your entourage will get comfortable quarters. When the throne is mine, I will . . . decide whether it may eventually be safe to release you."

He gave orders. Unresisting, Flandry rose to be led away. "My compliments, Sir Olaf," he murmured. "You are cleverer than I realized. Goodnight."

"Goodnight, Sir Dominic," replied the other.

CHAPTER NINETEEN

The climax was violent.

It began with delusive smoothness. "How I shall regret leaving this place," Axor mused at supper. "Though I will always thank God for the privilege of having encountered wonder here."

Targovi pricked up his ears. "Leaving?"

"Well, we cannot expect our hosts to maintain us forever—especially me, bearing in mind what my food must cost them. Working together with the lady Isis Zachary and her colleagues at the Apollonium in these past days, I have learned things of supreme value, and perhaps contributed some humble moiety in return, but now we seem to have exhausted our respective funds of information and the conclusions which discussion has led us to draw therefrom."

"Apollonium?" Targovi's question was absent-minded, practically a reflex. His thoughts were racing away.

Axor waved a tree-trunk arm around the room where he sprawled and the Tigery sat at table. He was really indicating the nighted campus beyond the hospice walls. "This center of learning, research, philosophy, arts. They do not call it a university because it has no teaching function. Being what they are, Zacharians require no schools except input to their homes, no teachers except their parents or, when they are mature, knowledgeable persons whom they can call when explanation is necessary."

"Oh, yes, yes. You've finished, you say?"

"Virtually. Dear friend," Axor trumpeted, "I cannot express my

287

gratitude for your part in bringing me to this haven. While they have never undertaken serious investigation of the Foredwellers, the Zacharians are insatiably curious about the entire cosmos. Their database contains every item ever reported or collected by such of their people as have gone to space. I retrieved scores of descriptions, pictures, studies of sites unknown to me. Comparison with the facts I already possessed began to open portals. Isis, Vishnu, and Kwan Yin were those who especially took fire and produced brilliant ideas. I would not venture to claim that we are on the way to deciphering the symbols, but we have identified regularities, recurrences, that look highly significant. Who knows where that may lead future scholarship? To the very revelation of Christ's universality, that will in time bring all sentient beings into his church?"

The crocodilian head lifted. "I should not lament my departure," the Wodenite finished. "Ahead of me, while this mortal frame lasts, lie pilgrimages to those planets about which I have learned, to the greater glory of God."

"Well, good," mumbled Targovi. "Know you when we must leave?"

"No, not yet. I daresay they will tell me at the next session. You might be thinking where we should ask them to deposit us on the mainland. They have promised to take us anyplace we like."

"Diana will be sad, I suppose. She's had a fine time. Where is she this eventide?"

Though Axor's visage was not particularly mobile, somehow trouble seemed to dim his brown eyes, and assuredly it registered in his basso profundo: "I cannot say. I have seldom seen her throughout our stay. She goes about in company with that man—what is his name?"

"Kukulkan, if she hasn't swapped escorts."

"Ah." Fingers that could have snapped steel bars twiddled with the spectacles hanging from the armored neck. "Targovi, I—this is most embarrassing, but I must speak—Well, I am not human, nor versed in human ways, but lately I . . . I have begun to fear for that maiden's virtue."

The Tigery choked back a yowl of laughter.

"You know her well," Axor continued. "Do you think, before it is too late—I pray it be not too late—you could advise her, as an, an elder brother?"

Opportunity! Targovi pounced. "I can try," he said. "Truth to tell, I too have fretted about her. I know humans well enough to understand what Kukulkan's intentions are. If we are bound away soon—what one Zacharian knows, they all seem to know—he'll press his suit."

"Oh, dear. And she so young, innocent, helpless." Axor crossed himself.

"I'll see if I can find them," Targovi proposed. "She may not thank me tonight, but afterward—" Despite an urgency which had become desperate, he must still hold down his merriment. Oh, aye, wouldn't Diana Crowfeather be overjoyed at having her business minded for her? His tail dithered. "Wish me luck."

Axor bowed his head and silently invoked a saint or two. Targovi shoved the rest of his meal aside and left.

The whole farce might have been unnecessary. He didn't know whether the hospice was bugged; lacking equipment hidden aboard *Moonjumper,* he had no way of finding out. Therefore he assumed it was, and furthermore that there was a stakeout—not a flesh-and-blood watcher, nothing that crude, but sensors in strategic locations. His going forth should, now, arouse no more misdoubts than his feckless wanderings about in the area appeared to have done.

At most, whoever sat monitoring might flash Kukulkan word that Targovi meant to deboost any seduction, and Kukulkan might thus do best to take the girl for a romantic ride over the mountains . . . if he had not already done so . . . The Zacharians did indeed stick together. No, more than that. They were almost a communal organism, like those Terran insectoids they had introduced to the island ecology—ants—though ants with individual intelligence far too high for Targovi's liking upon this night.

He went out the door. A breeze lulled cool, smelling of leaves and sea, ruffling his fur; he wore nothing but his breechcloth, belt, and knife. Lawns dreamed empty beneath a sky where clouds drifted, tinged argent by Icarus and bronze by the sun-ring. That band was blocked off in the south by the peaks, in places elsewhere by distant weather, but it and the moon gave ample light for humans to see by. He had been waiting for fog or rain to lend comparative darkness in which his vision would have the advantage.

Well, he could wait no longer.

Leaving the campus behind, he followed a street at a trot which should look reasonable under the circumstances, until it passed by a park. There he cut across. Trees roofed grass. He vanished into the gloom. At its farther edge he went on his belly and became a ripple of motion that could easily have been a trick of wind-blown cloud shadows.

From there on he was a Tigery hunter a-stalk, using every scrap of cover and every trick in the open, senses tuned to each least flicker, shuffling, whiff, quivering, clues and hints for which human languages lacked words. Often he froze for minutes while a man or a woman walked by, sometimes close enough to touch. Had dogs been about, he would perforce have left a number of the abominable creatures dead, but fortunately the Zacharians had better taste than to keep any. As was, he took more than an hour to approach his goal.

It stood high in the hills, on the fringe of settlement. A five-meter wall, thirty meters on a side, surrounded an area forbidden to visitors. When Heimdal was showing him about, Targovi had inquired what was within. "Defense," his guide answered. "You may not know it, but under the treaty we take responsibility for the defense of this island—not out into space, of course; that's the job of the Navy; but against whatever hostile force might break through or might come over the surface. We maintain our own installations. This one guards Janua."

Guards, aye. Flattened on the ground, Targovi felt a faint shudder. Something had passed beneath. Well, he had already eye-gauged that the spaceport—from which outsiders were also banned—lay just opposite, on the far side of the range. A connecting tunnel was logical.

His glance roved. Above the stony bulk of the wall, the Mencius ridge made a grayness beyond which glimmered the Hellene peaks. Sculptured slopes fell downward, multiply shadowed, frostily high-lighted. The Averroes River was brokenly visible, agleam. It plunged into the sheening of the bay. Phosphorescence traced runes over the ocean. Beneath him were soil, pebbles, prickly weeds, dew.

Attention went back to the fortress. No, he realized, it wasn't any such thing as St. Barbara's had been part of. It must be a command post for missiles, energy projectors, aircraft, and whatever else laired in the vicinity. He doubted there was much. Daedalus had long been under Imperial protection. Now it was under

Magnusson's, but that should make no immediate difference. Likewise, Targovi conjectured, security was lax. The Zacharians would have had no cause to be strict, not for centuries, and if requirements had changed overnight, organization and training could hardly have done the same.

Still, all it took was a single alarm, or afterward a single bullet or ray or flying torpedo. . . .

Hence he never considered the gate from which a road wound off. Instead, he slithered to a point well away, where he could stand in shadow and examine the wall. It sloped upward, as was desirable for solidity. The material was unfinished stone, perhaps originally to keep anyone from climbing on vacsoles—or was that notion too ridiculous? Erosion had blurred the roughness of the blocks but also pitted the mortar. A human could never have gone up, but a Tigery might, given strength and claws and eyesight adaptable to dim light. He found no indications of built-in warning systems. Why should they exist? Who, or what, would be so crazy as to attempt entry?

Being of the species he was, Targovi did not stop to wonder about his saneness. He had little more to go on than a hunter's hunch. What lay behind the wall, he could barely guess. What he could do after he found it was unknowable beforehand. He sorely missed the weapons and gear stowed in his ship. Yet he did not consider himself reckless. He went ahead with that which he had decided to do.

After long and close study, he had a way picked out. He crawled backward until he judged the distance sufficient for a running start. Lifting eyes, ears, and tendrils above the shrubs, he searched for possible watchers. None showed. Then better be quick, before any did! He sprang to his feet and charged.

Well-conditioned Tigeries under a single standard gravity can reach a sprint speed which outdoes their Terran namesake. Sheer momentum carried Targovi far up the barrier. Fingers and claws did the rest; he needed only an instant's purchase to thrust himself onward, too fast to lose his grip and fall. Over the top he went, fell, landed on pads that absorbed much of the shock, took the rest in rubbery muscles, and promptly dived for cover.

That was behind a hedge. It would do him scant good if someone had noticed. After a minute, having heard and smelled nothing, he hazarded a look. The grounds were deserted. His readiness flowed from fight-or-flight back to stealth.

A garden surrounded a fair-sized building. While not neglected, it showed signs of perfunctory care. That bore out Targovi's estimate, that this post had seen little use until quite recently, and was still weakly and slackly manned. Why not? What need had the Zacharians had for military skills since Daedalus came under the Pax Terrana? What reason had they, even now, to worry about intruders? Nonetheless Targovi continued cautious. His venture was wild at best.

First establish lines of retreat. A couple of big oaks offered those. A human could not leap from their upper boughs to the top of the wall, but a Tigery could. Avoiding paths, he eeled from hedge to bush. The building loomed ahead, darkling in the half-light of heaven. It too was old, weather-worn; it had the same peaked roof as those downhill but lacked their gracefulness, being an unrelieved block, though with ample windows and doors. Toward the rear, two of those windows glowed.

They were plain vitryl. Targovi slipped alongside and peered around an edge. Breath hissed between his fangs. The hair erected over his body. This was the total and stunning confirmation of his— fears?—expectations?—guesses?—The quarry he had been tracing stood terrible before him.

The windows gave on a room bare-walled and sparsely furnished, with a bath cubicle adjoining. Most of its space went to a computer. While engineering imposes basic similarity on all such machines, Targovi could see that this one had not been manufactured in the Terran Empire. Black-uniformed, blaster at belt and rifle grounded, on guard through the night watch, was a Merseian.

For a long spell, the Tigery stood moveless. Ring-gleam and cloud shadows, wind-sough in leaves, odors of green life, grittiness of masonry under his palms, seemed abruptly remote, things of dream, against the reality which confronted him. What to do?

The sensible thing was to withdraw unobserved, keep silence, let the Zacharians return him to the mainland, contact Naval Intelligence. . . .

Which would be the absolute in lunacy, he thought. What had happened when he just hinted that certain matters might rate investigation? And that was before Magnusson openly rebelled. How far today would a nonhuman outlaw get on his raw word?

The overwhelming majority of Daedalans and, yes, members of the armed forces desired the survival of the Empire. What else was there for them? But they'd need proof, evidence that nobody could hide or explain away.

"When we hunted the gaarnokh on Homeworld," Dragoika often said, "and he stood at bay, to spear him in the heart we must needs go in between his horns."

Targovi slipped along the wall to the next-nearest door. It was unlocked. Nobody came through the gate or up from the spaceport tunnel unless the leaders had complete confidence in him. Targovi entered a short hall which led to a corridor running the length of the building. Unlighted at this hour of rest, it reached dusky along rows of closed chambers—offices mainly, he assumed, long disused. Some must lately have been seeing activity, as must the weapon emplacements, wherever they were: but not much, because the Zacharians did not await any emergency. They *knew* Merseia wasn't going to attack the Patrician System.

Chiefly, Targovi decided, this strongpoint housed a few officers and their aides from the Roidhunate, observers, liaison agents, conveyors of whatever orders their superiors issued. Ships traveled to and fro, bringing replacements for those who went back to report. That traffic wouldn't be hard to keep secret. It was infrequent; its captains knew the right recognition codes; Planetary Defense Command would assign sentry vessels to orbits that never gave them a good look at such arrivals; and private landing facilities waited on the island.

The gatortails must have quarters under this roof. A smell of them reached Targovi as he neared. It was warm, like their blood, but neither Tigery-sweet nor human-sour—bitter. He bristled.

Partly by scent, partly by keeping track of direction and distance, he identified the door to his goal. It was closed. Unfortunate, that. He'd have to proceed without plan. But if he stood here hesitating his chances would rapidly worsen. Dawn drew nigh. Though most people's sleeptime might last later, many would soon be astir throughout Janua—must already be—and full sunlight upon wayfarers.

He thumbed the "open" plate and stepped aside. As the door slid back, the Merseian would look this way and wonder why nobody trod through. He'd likely come closer to see—Now Targovi heard click of boots on the floor, now the sound stopped but he caught a noise of breathing—not quickened, the guard didn't imagine an enemy at hand, he was probably puzzled, maybe thinking a collywobble had developed in these ancient circuits—

Targovi came around the jamb and sprang.

As he appeared, he saw what was needful, pivoted on his claws, and launched himself, in a single storm-swift movement. Driven by the muscles of his race, he struck faster than the Merseian could lift weapon. They tumbled down together. The rifle clattered aside. Targovi jammed his right forearm into a mouth that had barely started to gape in the green-skinned face. Only a stifled gurgle got around it.

He could have killed a human with a karate chop, but had not studied Merseian anatomy and dared not suppose it was that similar. His left hand darted to catch the opponent's right arm before the holstered blaster could be drawn. Strength strained against strength.

Meanwhile he hooked claws into the thick tail, which would else be a club smashing upon him or thumping a distress signal. The boots, which might have done likewise, he pinned between his calves.

The Merseian was powerful, less so than him but surging against his pressure, sure to break free somewhere. Targovi released the gun wrist. His own arm whipped around behind the neck of the foe. Low and blunt, unlike Axor's, the spinal ridge nevertheless bruised him—as his right arm shoved the head back over that fulcrum.

The Merseian clutched his blaster. Targovi heard a *crack*. The head flopped. The body shuddered, once, and lay still.

Whatever their variations, Merseian, Tigery, and human are vertebrates.

Targovi jumped off the corpse, snatched the rifle, crouched to cover the doorway. If the noise had roused someone, he'd have to try shooting his way free.

Minutes crawled by. Silence deepened. Light grew stronger in the windowpanes.

Targovi lowered the weapon. Nobody had heard. Or, if anybody did, it had been so briefly that the being sank back into sleep. After all, he had taken just seconds to kill the guard.

How much time remained before reveille, or whatever would reveal him? It was surely meager. Targovi got to work.

Having closed the door, he examined the computer. Aye, Merseian made, and he was ignorant of the Eriau language. Not entirely, though. Like most mentally alive persons in this frontier space, he had picked up assorted words and catchphrases. His daydream of operating among the stars had also led him to learn the alphabet. Moreover, Merseia had originally acquired modern technology from Terra; and logic and natural law are the same everywhere.

When they first arrived here, the gatortails must have brought this as their own mainframe computer. Not only would they be most familiar with it, they need not fear its being tampered with, whether directly or from afar. Besides making active use of it, they'd keep their database within. . . . Yes. Targovi believed he had figured out the elementary instruction he wanted.

He touched keys. "Microcopy everything."

The machine had rearranged molecules by the millions and deposited three discus-shaped containers on the drop shelf before Targovi finished the rest of his job. Yet what he did went swiftly. He stripped the tunic from the Merseian, who now resisted him with mere weight, and slashed it in places until he could tie it together as a package. The weapons would go in, as well as the data slabs and—He set things out of the way while his knife made the next cuts, and afterward fetched a towel from the bathroom. It wouldn't do to have his bundle drip blood.

Ready for travel, he opened the door a crack, peered, opened it wide, stepped through, closed it again. Quite possibly no one would be astir for another hour or two. Merseians tended to be early risers, but had no good reason to reset their circadian rhythms according to the short Daedalan period. In fact, they had good reason to refrain. The effort was lengthy and demanding; meanwhile they'd be at less than peak efficiency.

It was likewise possible that, whenever the rest of his mission got up, the sentry would not be immediately due for relief, and no other occasion would arise for them to pass this door.

Targovi couldn't count on any of that. Thus far his luck had been neither especially fair nor especially foul. Most of it he had made for himself. Had he come upon a different situation, he would have acted according to it as best he was able. Throughout, he had exploited surprise.

How much longer could he continue to do so? Not very!

He stole down corridor and hall. At the exit, he dropped to a belly-scraping all fours and crept, dragging his burden in his teeth. Up a tree—a flying leap to the outer wall and a bounce to the ground beyond—snake's way through brush till a dip of terrain concealed him—He rose and ran.

Zacharians stared at the carnivore form that sped inhumanly fast down their streets, a bundle under an arm. With his spare hand, he waved at them. They had gotten used to seeing the poor itinerant huckster around, his hopes of business gone, aimlessly adrift. If today he bounded along, why, he must be stretching his legs. He looked cheerful enough.

The sun-ring had contracted to a broad, incandescent arc in the east. The sky above was nearly white; a few clouds hung gilded. Westward the blue deepened. Dew sparkled on grass. Songbirds twittered. A red squirrel flamed along a bough. Here and there, savants passed from hall to ivy-covered hall. It would have been hard to imagine a scene more innocent.

When Targovi let himself into the hospice, he missed the scent of Diana. He went to her room and peeked in. The bed stood unused. For a second he stood irresolute. Should he try to find her? The loss of time could prove fatal. On the other hand, a third member of his party might tip the scales, and the gods knew that most weight now lay in the wrong pan. . . . And what of his sisterling herself? Ought he make her share his danger? Would she be safest staying behind? Maybe. The Zacharians might be satisfied with a straightforward interrogation and do her no harm. If she had been romping with the man Kukulkan, he should have the decency to use his influence on her behalf. . . . But maybe the Zacharians would work ghastliness upon her, in fear or in spite. Maybe none of them felt in any way honor-bound to an outsider lover.

Decision. Targovi couldn't hunt over Janua for her. But if she was where he thought was likely, it might not be too distant. He sought the infotrieve and keyed the area directory. Kukulkan's home address appeared on the screen. Houses lacked numbers, but streets had names, and coordinates on a grid indicated each location. Acacia Lane—yes—Targovi's disconsolate wanderings while Axor conferred and Diana flirted had had the purpose of learning the geography. Acacia Lane was south of here, not really out of the way when you were trying to escape.

He entered the Wodenite's room. Axor filled it, curled on a seat of mattresses. His breathing was like surf below the sea cliffs. Targovi slipped past the scaly body, bent over the muzzle, took hold of its nostrils. Those, he had discovered, were the most sensitive point. He tweaked them. Horny lids flipped back under craggy brow ridges. A row of teeth, meant for both ripping and crushing, gleamed into view. "*Ochla, hoo-oo, ksyan ngunggung,*" rolled between them. "What's this, eh, what, what?"

"Quick!" Targovi said. "Follow me. I've come on something unique. It won't last. You'll want to see it."

"Really. I was awake late, reading."

"Please. I beg you. You'll not regret it."

"Ah, well, if you insist." Hoofs banged, the floor creaked, Axor's tail scraped a wall. He followed Targovi out and across the greensward. Such people as were in sight gave them looks but continued on their own paths. The xenosophonts were no longer a novelty.

Where a pair of majestic trees shaded a bench, Targovi stopped. "This will be an unpleasant surprise," he warned. "Hold fast to your emotions. Reveal naught."

"What?" The Wodenite blinked. "But you said—"

"I lied. Here is the truth. Curl around. I want you to screen off what you're about to see."

Squatting, Targovi pulled his bundle from under the bench where he had left it and undid its knots. Three data slabs, two firearms of non-Technic make, and something wrapped in a wet red towel appeared. He unfolded the cloth. Axor failed to suppress a geyserish gasp. Beneath his gaze lay the severed head of a Merseian.

CHAPTER TWENTY

A few times in the past, Diana had felt she was being well and thoroughly kissed. Now she found her estimates had been off by an order of magnitude. Kukulkan's body pressed hard and supple. When she opened her eyes she saw his blurrily, but gold-brown, oblique, brilliant. The man-scent of him dizzied her. She felt his heartbeat against hers. She clung tight with her left arm and let her right fingers go ruffling through his hair.

His hand slid from her hip, upward, inside her half-opened blouse. It went under her brassiere. Sweetness exploded.

Wait! rang through. Dragoika's voice purred across the years: "Give yourself to the wind, but first be sure 'tis the wind of your wish." The loneliness of Maria Crowfeather—

Diana pulled back. She must exert force. "Hold on," she said with an unsteady laugh. "I need to come up for air."

"Oh, my beautiful!" His weight thrust her downward on the sofa where they sat.

She resisted. A gentle judo break, decisive since unawaited, freed her. She sprang from him and stood breathing hard, flushed and atremble but back in charge of herself.

"Easy, there," she said, smiling, because warmth still pulsed. She found occupation in pushing back her tousled locks. "Let's not get carried away."

He rose, too, himself apparently unoffended, though ardency throbbed in his tone: "Why not? What harm? What except love and joy?"

He refrained from advancing, so she stayed where she was, and wondered if she could really resist the handsomeness that confronted her. "Well, I—Oh, Kukulkan, it's been wonderful." And it had been, culminating in this night's flight above the Hellenes to a lake where they swam while the reflection of the sun-ring flashed everywhere around them, as if they swam in pure light; and ate pheasant and drank champagne ashore; and danced on a boat dock to music from the car's player, music and a dance she had never known before, a waltz by somebody named Strauss; and finally came back to his place, where one thing led to another. "I thank you, I do, I do. But soon I'll be gone."

"No, you won't. I'll see to that. You'll stay as long as you want. And I'll take you all over this planet, and eventually beyond, to the stars."

Did he mean it? Suppose he did!

She had no intention of remaining a virgin for life, or until any particular age. Pride, if nothing else, forbade becoming somebody's plaything or, for that matter, making a toy of a man. But she liked Kukulkan Zachary—more than liked him—and she must be a little special to him, or why would he have squired her around as he did? What an ingrate she was, not to trust him.

If only she'd had a reversible shot. She wanted neither a baby in the near future nor an abortion ever; but living hand-to-mouth on Imhotep, as often as not among the Tigeries, she just hadn't gotten around to the precaution. She *thought* this week was safe for her—

"I'd better go," she forced herself to say. "Let me think things over. Please don't rush me."

"At least let me kiss you goodbye until later," he replied in that melodious voice of his. "A few hours later, no more, I beg you."

She couldn't refuse him so small a favor, could she, in common courtesy?

He gathered her in. She responded. Resolution wobbled.

Whether or not it would have stood fast, she never knew. The front door, unlocked on the crimeless island, opened. Targovi came in. Behind him reared the dragon head of Axor.

Diana and Kukulkan recoiled apart. "What the flickerin' hell!" ripped from her. He snarled and tensed.

Targovi leveled the blaster he carried. "Don't," he said.

"Have you two jumped your orbits?" Diana yelled, and knew freezingly that they had not.

Kukulkan straightened. His features stiffened. "Drop that thing," he said as if giving a routine order to a servant. "Do you want the girl killed in a firelight?"

"Who is to start one?" Targovi retorted. He gestured at a window. Leafage turned young daylight to gold-spattered green. Like most local homes, this was tucked into its garden, well back from the street, screened by trees and hedges. It was obvious that the intruders had entered unseen.

Axor crowded in. He went to Diana, laid his enormous arms about her, drew her to his plated breast, as tenderly as her mother. "My dear, my dear, I am sorry," he boomed low. "Horror is upon us. Would that you could be spared."

For a minute she clung tight. It was as though strength and calm flowed out of him, into her. She stepped back. Her gaze winged around the scene and came to rest on Targovi. "Explain," she said.

His scarlet eyes smoldered back at her. "The spoor I followed proved true," he answered. "I followed it into the lair of the beast. Axor, show her what I brought back."

The Wodenite visibly shuddered. "Must I?"

"Yes. Don't diddle about. Every tailshake we wait, the odds mount against us."

While Axor took a package from a carrier bag and untied it, Targovi's words trotted remorseless: "The Zacharians are in collusion with the Merseians. This means they must be with Magnusson. The Merseians must be! You understand what this betokens."

"No," she protested, "please, no. Impossible. How could they keep the secret? Why would they do such a thing?"

Axor completed his task, and It stared sightlessly up at her.

"They are not like your folk," Targovi reminded. Struggling out of shock, she heard him dimly. "We must bring this evidence back."

"How?" challenged Kukulkan. Diana regarded him, which hurt like vitriol to do. He stood shaken but undaunted. "Would you steal a car and fly off? You might succeed in that, even committing another murder or two in the process. But missiles will come after you, rays, warcraft if necessary, to shoot you down. Meanwhile, whatever transmissions you attempt will be jammed—not that they'd be believed. A waterboat is merely ludicrous. Surrender, and I'll suggest clemency."

"You'll not be here." Targovi aimed the blaster. He had set it to narrow beam. Kukulkan never flinched.

"No!" shouted Diana and bellowed Axor together. She pursued with a spate of words: "D'you mean to silence him? What for? The alarm'll go out anyhow, when they find that poor headless body. Tie him up instead."

"You do it, then," the Tigery growled. "Be quick, but be thorough. Meanwhile, think whether you want to join us. Axor, stow the goods again."

"Into the bedroom," Diana directed. The irony smote her. "Oh, Kukulkan, this is awful! You didn't know anything about it, did you?"

Under the threat of Targovi's gun, he preceded her, turned, and said in steeliness: "I did. It would be idiotic of me to deny that. But I intended you no harm, lovely lass. On the contrary. You could have become a mother of kings."

She wiped away tears, drew her knife, slashed a sheet into bonds. "What do you want, you people? Why've you turned traitor?"

"We owe the Terran Empire nothing. It dragooned our forebears into itself. It has spurned our leadership, the vision that animated the Founders. It will only allow us to remain ourselves on this single patch of land, afar in its marches. Here we dwell like Plato's man in chains, seeing only shadows on the wall of our cave, shadows cast by the living universe. The Merseians have no cause to fear or shun us. Rather, they will welcome us as their intermediaries with the human commonality. They will grant us the same boundless freedom they desire for themselves."

"Are you s-s-certain about that? Lie down on the b-b-bed, on your stomach."

He obeyed. She began fastening his hands behind his back. Would he twist about, try to seize her for shield or hostage? She'd hate slashing him; but she stayed prepared. He lay passive, apart from speech: "What do *you* owe the Empire, Diana, this shellful of rotting flesh? Why should you die for it? You will, if you persist. You have nowhere to flee."

Instantly, almost involuntarily, she defied him. "We've got a whole big island where we can live off the farms and wildlife, plenty of hills and woods for cover. We'll survive."

"For hours; days, at most. In fear and wretchedness. Think. I offer you protection, amnesty. My kin will not be vindictive. They are above that. I offer you glory."

"He may intend it, or he may just want the use of you," Targovi said from the doorway. "In either case, sisterling, belike it's your safest trail. If we bind you, too, somebody will come erelong to see what's happened, and none should blame you."

"Naw." Diana secured Kukulkan's ankles. "I stay by my friends."

"A forlorn hope, we."

She hitched the strips to the bedframe, lest the prisoner roll himself off and out into the street. Straightening, she happened to spy an open closet. Hanging there were clothes for both man and woman.

Well, sure, she thought, Zacharians didn't marry. No point in it, for them. He had admitted as much, and mentioned children raised in interchangeable households, and she had wondered how lonesome he was in his heart and whether that was what drew him to her, and then they had gone on with their excursion. But, sure, Zacharians would have sex for other reasons than procreation. Interchangeable people? The idea was like a winter wind.

She stooped above the bonny face. He gave her a crooked smile. "Goodbye," she said to the alien.

Seeking Targovi: "All right, let's scramble out o' here."

"—*state secrets. Almost as dangerous are their persons, for they are armed and desperate. While capture alive is desirable for purposes of interrogation, killing them on sight is preferable to any risk of allowing them to continue their rampage—*"

Targovi heard the announcement out before he switched off the audio transceiver he had brought from the hospice. It was a natural thing to put in Axor's carrier, along with food, after they had voiced their decision to go on a long tramp through the hills, for the benefit of any electronic eavesdroppers. While the Wodenite recorded a message apologizing for thus cancelling his next appointment with Isis, explaining that he wished to savor the landscape and this was his last chance, his comrade had surreptitiously added a hiking outfit for Diana to the baggage.

Being a Tigery, Targovi skipped banalities like, "Well, now they know." He did murmur, "Interesting is how they phrase it, the scat about 'state secrets'. I should think most Zacharians will realize at once what this means. The rest should cooperate without questions."

"I s'pose the words're for the benefit of whatever outsiders may catch the broadcast," said Diana around a mouthful of sandwich. "F'r instance, on watercraft passin' within range. Not that they'd investigate for themselves."

The three rested in a hollow in the heights above Janua, well away from settlement. Its peacefulness was an ache in them. Birch stood around, leaves dancing to a breeze in the radiance of west-bound Patricius. Prostrate juniper grew among the white trunks, itself dark blue-green and fragrant. A spring bubbled from a mossy bank. Somewhere a mockingbird trilled.

"The Zacharians will be out like a swarm of *khrukai*—swordwings," Targovi said. "They'll use aircraft and high-gain sensors. We'll need all the woodcraft that is ours. And . . . we are not used to forest such as this."

Diana smote fist on ground. "Be damned if we'll die for naught, or skulk around useless till Magnusson's slaughtered his way to the throne!" Her head and voice drooped. "Only what can we do?"

Axor cleared his throat. "I can do this much, beloved ones," he said, almost matter-of-factly. "My size and lack of skill at conceal-ment will betray us even before my bodily need has exhausted the rations. Let me angle off and divert pursuit while you two seek the mountains." He lifted a hand against Diana's anguished cry. "No, no, it is the sole sensible plan. I came along because, much though I abhor violence, as a Christian should, yet there seemed to be a chance to end the war before it devours lives by the millions. Also, while I cannot believe the Merseians are creatures of Satan, they would deprive many billions of whatever self-determination is left. It is a worthy cause. Afterward, if you live, pray that we be forgiven for the harm we have done our opponents, and for the repose of their souls, as I will pray." His neck swayed upward from where he lay till light caught the crest of his head and made a crown of it. "Let me serve in the single way I am able. Lord, watch over my spirit, and the spirits of these my friends."

This time the girl could not stem tears. "Oh, Axor—!"

"Quiet, you two blitherers," Targovi grated. "What we want is less nobility and more thinking."

He jumped and paced, not man-style but as a Tigery does, weaving in and out among the trees and around the bushes. His right hand stroked the blade of his great knife over the palm of the left, again and again. Teeth gleamed when he muttered on the track of his thought.

"I led us hither because I dared not suppose my deed at the command post would go undetected enough longer for us to rustle transportation and reach the mainland. In that I was right. My hope was that the Zacharians would show such confusion at the news, being inexperienced in affairs like this, that we could double back and find means of escape—mayhap forcing the owner of a vehicle to cover for us. After all, they had not been well organized at the post. The hope was thin just the same, and now is not a wisp. I think their . . . oneness . . . makes them able to react to the unforeseen as coolly as an individual, not with the babble and cross purposes of an ordinary human herd taken by surprise. You heard the broadcast. Every car and boat will stay in a group of three or more, under guard. Every movement from the island will be stopped for inspection. This will prevail until we are captured or slain.

"Shall we yield? They might be content to shoot me, and the imprisonment of you two might not be cruel.

"You signal a no."

"My mother passed on an ancient sayin' to me," Diana told them. "Better to die on your feet than live on your knees."

"Ah, the young do not truly understand they *can* die," Axor sighed. "Yet if any possibility whatsoever is left us, what can we in conscience do other than try it?"

Still the Tigery prowled. "I am thinking, I am thinking—" Abruptly he halted. He drove the knife into a bole so that the metal sang. "Javak! Yes, it was on my horizon—a twisted path—But we must needs hurry, and not give the foe time to imagine we are crazy enough to take that way."

The south side of the Mencius range dropped a short distance before the land resumed its climb. This was unpeopled country, heavily wooded save where the canyon of the Averroes River slashed toward the sea, and on the higher flanks of the mountains. Kukulkan had told Diana it was a game and recreational preserve. The location of the spaceport here dated from troubled early days, when it might have become a target, minor though it was. Perhaps its isolation had been a factor in the conceiving of the Merseian plot.

Despite everything, the girl caught her breath at the sight. Clear, apart from a slight golden fleece of clouds, the sky was pale below, deepening to indigo at the zenith; but still night cast a dusk over the reaches around her. Heights to north and south walled in the world. Only at the ends of the vale did the sun-ring shine, casting rays that made the bottom a lake of amber. Where trees allowed glimpses, the hills above were purple-black, the snowcaps in the distance moltenly aglow. Air was cool on her brow. Quietness towered.

Wonder ended as Targovi pointed ahead.

Beyond the last concealment the forest afforded was a hundred-meter stretch, kept open though overgrown with brush and weeds. A link fence, to hold off animals, enclosed a ferrocrete field. Her pulse athrob but her senses and judgment preternaturally sharp, she gauged its dimensions as five hundred by three hundred meters. Service buildings clustered and a radionic mast spired at the farther end. Of the several landing docks, two were occupied. One craft she identified as interplanetary, a new and shapely version of *Moonjumper.* The other was naval—rather small as interstellar ships went, darkly gleaming, gun turret and launcher tubes sleeked into the leanness—akin to the Comet class, but not identical, not designed or wrought by humans—What ghost in her head blew a bugle call?

Huge and vague in the shadows, Axor whispered hoarsely, "We take the Zacharian vessel, of course."

"No, of course not," Targovi hissed. His eyes caught what light there was and burned like coals. "I was right in guessing the islanders are as militarily slovenly here as at the centrum, and have armed no watch. The thought of us hijacking a spaceship is too warlike to have occurred to them. But the Merseians are bound to have a guard aboard theirs. I know not whether that's a singleton or more, but belike whoever it is knows how to dispatch a seeker missile, or actually lift in chase." Decision. "However, we may well dupe them into supposing we are after the easier prey, and thus catch them off balance. The dim light will help—"

✿   ✿   ✿

When he burst from concealment, Axor carried Diana in the crook of an arm. She would otherwise have toiled far behind him and Targovi. The pounding of his gallop resounded through her. She leaned into his flexing hardness, cradled her rifle, peered after a mark.

It was an instant and it was a century across the clearing, until they reached the fence. Axor's free arm curved around to keep torn strands off her while he crashed through. Nevertheless, several drew blood. She barely noticed.

Men ran from the terminal, insectoidal at their distance, then suddenly near. She saw pistols in the hands of some. She heard a buzz, a thud. Axor grunted, lurched, went on. Diana opened fire. A figure tumbled and lay sprattling.

Targovi bounded alongside. The cargo carrier was straight ahead. He raised his arm, veered, and went for the Merseians'. Diana's vision swooped as Axor came around too. She glanced past his clifflike shoulder and saw the Zacharians in bewilderment. They numbered perhaps a dozen.

Targovi mounted the entry ramp of the dock. An airlock stood shut against him. He shielded his eyes with an arm and began to cut his way in with the blaster. Flame spurted blue-white, heat roiled, air seethed, sparks scorched his fur. A light ship like this relied on her forcefields and interceptors for protection in space. Nobody expected attack on the ground.

The Zacharians rallied and pelted toward him. They had courage aplenty, Diana thought in a breath. Axor went roaring and trampling to meet them. She threw a barrage. The men scattered and fled, except for one wounded and two shapeless.

Diana's trigger clicked on an empty magazine. Above her, Targovi's blaster sputtered out, its capacitors exhausted.

Axor thundered up the ramp. "Diana, get down!" he bawled. "Both of you, behind me!"

They scrambled to obey. He hammered his mass against the weakened lock. At the third impact it sagged aside.

Four Merseians waited. Their uniforms revealed them to be soldiers, unqualified to fly the craft they defended. Rather than shut the inner valve and risk it being wrecked too, they had prepared to give battle. Merseians would.

Axor charged. Beams and bullets converged on him. That could not check such momentum. Two died under his hoofs before he collapsed, shaking the hull. Targovi and Diana came right after. The Tigery threw his knife. A handgun rattled off a bulkhead. He and the Merseian went down together, embraced. His fangs found the green throat. Diana eluded a shot, got in close, and wielded her own blade.

Targovi picked himself up. "They'll've sent for help," he rasped out of dripping jaws. "Lubberly warriors though Zacharians be, I give us less than ten minutes. While I discover how to raise this thing, you close the portal." He whisked from sight.

The lock gave her no difficulty; the layout resembled that of *Moonjumper*. With the ship sealed, she made her way across a slippery deck to Axor. He lay breathing hard. Scorch marks were black over his scales. Redness oozed from wounds, not quite the same hue as hers, which was not quite the same as the Merseians', but it was all blood—water, iron, life. . . . "Oh, you're so hurt," she keened. "What can I do for you?"

He lifted his head. "Are you well, child?"

"Yes, nothin' hit me, but you, darlin', you—"

Lips drew back in a smile that others might have found frightening. "Not to fear. A little discomfort, yes, I might go so far as to say pain, but no serious injury. This carcass has many a pilgrimage ahead of it yet. Praises be to God and thanks to the more militant saints." The head sank. Wearily, soberly, he finished, "Now let me pray for the souls of the fallen."

A shiver went through Diana's feet. Targovi had awakened the engines.

Atmospheric warcraft zoomed over hills and mountains. He did not try keying in an order to shoot. Instead, he outclimbed them. Missiles whistled aloft. By then he had learned how to switch on the deflector field.

And after that he was in space. The planet rolled beneath him, enormous and lovely, burnished with oceans, emblazoned with continents, white-swirled with clouds. Once more he saw stars.

He could only take a moment to savor. Single-handing, he hadn't a meteorite's chance against attack by any Naval unit. "Diana," he said over the intercom, "come to the bridge, will you?" and devoted himself to piloting. He couldn't instruct the autosystem; the unfamiliar manual controls responded clumsily to him, and the navigational instruments were incomprehensible; he must eyeball and stagger his way. At least he'd managed to set a steady interior field of about a gee. Otherwise his comrades would be getting thrown around like chips in a casino.

Well, if he and they could walk from the landing, that was amply good—if they walked free.

The girl entered and took the copilot's seat. "I hope to bring us down at Aurea port," he told her. "No doubt the Zacharians will call frantically in, demanding the Navy blow us menaces out of the sky, and no doubt there are officers who will be happy to oblige. I lack skill to take us away on hyperdrive. You are the human aboard. What do you counsel?"

She considered, hand to smoke-smudged cheek—tangle-haired, sweaty, ragged, begrimed. Glancing at her, scenting her, knowing her, he wished he could be, for some hours, a male of her species.

"Can you set up a strong audiovisual transmission, that'll punch through interference on the standard band?" she asked.

He studied the console before him. "I think I can."

"Do." She closed her eyes and sagged in her harness.

But when he was ready, she came back to strength. To the computer-generated face in the screen she said: "I have a message for Commandant General Cesare Gatto. It's not crank, and it is top priority. If it don't get straight to him, courts-martial are goin' to blossom till you can't see the clover for 'em. The fact I'm in a space-craft you'll soon identify as Merseian should get you off your duffs. He'll want a recognition code, of course. Tell him Diana Crowfeather is bound home."

CHAPTER TWENTY-ONE

The database contained much that became priceless to the Navy in its operations against the revolt. Some continued valuable afterward, to Terran Intelligence, until the Merseians had completed necessary changes of plan and organization—an effort which, while it went on, kept them out of considerable mischief abroad. A part of the record dealt with Sir Olaf Magnusson. From previous experience and knowledge, Flandry reconstructed more of the story, conjecturally but with high probability.

A man stern and righteous lived under an Imperium effete and corrupt. Emperor Georgios meant well, but he was long a-dying, and meanwhile the favorites of the Crown Prince crowded into power. After Josip succeeded to the throne, malfeasance would scarcely trouble to mask itself, and official after official would routinely order atrocities committed on outlying worlds entrusted to them, that wealth might be wrung into their coffers. Erik Magnusson, space captain and trader of Kraken, forswore in his heart all allegiance to the Empire that had broken faith with him.

Somehow a Merseian or two, among those whom he occasionally met, sensed the unhappiness in him and passed word of it on to those who took interest in such matters. Upon his next visit to their mother planet, he received baronial treatment. In due course he met the great lord—not the Roidhun, who had more often been demigod than ruler, but the chief of the Grand Council, the day-by-day master of that whole vast realm, insofar as any single creature could ever be.

This was Brechdan Ironrede, the Hand of the Vach Ynvory, an impressive being whose soul was in many respects brother to the soul of Captain Magnusson. Well did he know what would appeal. There were humans by race who were Merseian subjects, just as there were Merseians by race who were Terran subjects—tiny minorities in either case, but significant on many levels. Those whom Brechdan summoned must have joined their voices to his. Why should Kraken pay tribute to an Imperium which enriched toadies, fettered commerce, and neglected defenses? The law of the Roidhun was strict but just. Under him, men could again be men. United, the two civilizations would linger no more in this handful of stars on a fringe of the galaxy; they would fare forth to possess the cosmos.

Erik Magnusson was converted. Perhaps Aycharaych, the telepath, confirmed it.

The man must have realized how slight the chance was that he could ever be of important service. He might or might not recruit a few others, he might or might not sometimes carry a message or an agent, but basically he was a reservist, a silent keeper of the flame. At home he could not even declare openly his love for Merseia.

But the time came when he gave Merseia his son.

The boy Olaf accompanied him there and remained. Nobody on Kraken suspected aught amiss when Erik returned without him. Olaf's mother was dead, his father had not remarried, his siblings had learned to refrain from pestering with questions. "I got him an apprentice's berth on a prospector ship. He'll learn more and better than in any of our schools."

The secret school he did enter was neither human or humane. High among its undertakings was to strengthen the strong and destroy the weak. Olaf survived. He learned science, history, combat, leadership, and tearlessness. Toward the end, Aycharaych took him in charge, Aycharaych the Chereionite, he of the crested eagle countenance and the subtle, probing intellect. Merseian masters had laid a foundation in the boy: knowledge, physique, purpose. Upon it Aycharaych now raised the psychosexual structure he wanted.

The Golden Face, the uttered wisdom, the Sleep and the Dreams and the words that whispered through them . . . carefully orchestrated pleasures of flesh, mind, spirit . . . dedication to a God unknowable—

Young Olaf Magnusson reappeared on Kraken after some years, taciturn about his adventures. He soon enlisted in the Imperial marines. From then on, he carried out his orders.

They were the directives of his superiors. Never was he a spy, a subversive, or anything but a bold, bright member of the Terran armed services—enlisted man, cadet on transfer, Navy officer. The commandment of the Merseians was to do his utmost, rise as fast and high as possible, and inwardly stand by for an opportunity that might well never come.

What action he saw at first was against barbarians, bandits, local rebels and recalcitrants, nothing to stir inner conflict. But when crisis erupted into combat at Syrax, he fought Merseians. What agony this cost him—and perhaps that was little, for he had been taught that death in battle is honorable, and an individual is only a cell in the bloodstream of the Race—was eased when a secret agent brought him praise and told him that henceforward he would be in the minds of the Roidhunate's mighty.

He had also called himself to the attention of the Empire's. His career plunged ahead like a comet toward its sun. If Merseia or its cat's paws made trouble, that was frequently in regions where he was stationed, and he distinguished himself. Knowing Eriau and two other major Merseian languages, he served on negotiating commissions, and gained still greater distinction. Beginning as an aide, he proffered such excellent suggestions that presently he was in charge; and under his direction, the Terrans got terms more advantageous to themselves than they had really hoped for. True, these were all *ad hoc* arrangements, concerning specific, spatially limited issues of secondary concern. Nonetheless Olaf Magnusson proved that he understood the Merseians and could get along with them. Manifestly, they did not hold his combat career against him; rather, they respected his ability and determination.

The Navy did likewise. Aloofness and austerity became advantageous traits in the reformist reign of Emperor Hans; they showed Magnusson to be no mere uniformed politician. He was a spit-and-polish disciplinarian, but always fair, and, given a deserving case, capable of compassion. Where he held office, morale rose high, also among civilians, especially after his broadcast speeches. Thus it became logical to make him responsible for the defense of an entire, strategically critical sector, bordering on the debatable spaces between Empire and Roidhunate.

Terra later had cause to give the High Command thanks for so wise a choice. What seemed like another quarrel between the powers, ugly but resolvable, abruptly escaped control. It flared into the worst emergency since Syrax. There was no rhyme or reason to that; but how often is there with governments? Once again a Merseian task force moved toward an undermanned Terran frontier "to restore order, assure the safety of the Race and its client species, and make possible the resumption of meaningful diplomatic discussions."

The meaning of those discussions would be obvious, when Merseia held a sizeable chunk ripped out of the Empire's most vulnerable side. The concessions demanded would not be such as to provoke full-scale war; but they would leave Terra sorely weakened. Time was lacking in which to send adequate reinforcements. Against the threat, Olaf Magnusson's fleet orbited alone.

"We will pay the price," the Merseian envoy had said in the hidden place. "You must it exact it ruthlessly. Spare us no blow that you can deal. Your duty is to become a hero."

The Imperials at Patricius met the foe and broke him. His shattered squadrons reeled back into the darkness whence they came. Merseian representatives called for an immediate reconvening of the high-level conference, and suddenly what they asked and offered was reasonable. Jubilation billowed through the Empire, yes, even on jaded Terra. Magnusson went there to receive a knighthood at the hands of the Emperor.

He returned to folk who adored him and felt cheated by their Imperium—almost as embittered as were many Merseians who had seen comrades die and ships lost because of unprecedented ineptitude. Sir Olaf began to speak out against the decadence of the state, of the entire body politic. He spoke both publicly and privately. Given his immense prestige and his remoteness from the center of things, no one ventured to quell him . . . until he proclaimed himself master of all, and his legions hailed him; and then it was too late.

"This is the day for which we have prepared throughout your lifetime," said the envoy in the hidden place.

"I am to reach the throne?" Magnusson asked, amazed in spite of having guessed what his engineered destiny was. "Why? To undermine

the Empire till it lies ready for conquest? I—do not like that thought. Nor do I really believe it's a possibility. Too many unforeseeables, too many whole worlds."

"Khraich, no. Victory shall be as quick and clean as we can make it. You are to come not as the executioner, but the savior."

"Hard to do."

"Explain why."

"Well—Hans Molitor had it easier. The Wang dynasty was extinct, aside from a few idiots who could raise no following. Everybody wished for a strong man and the peace he would impose. Hans was the ablest of the contending warlords. From the first, he had the most powerful forces behind him. Yet the struggle dragged on for bloody years. Gerhart may be unpopular, but he is a son of Hans, and people hope for better things from his son. I would not expect very much of the Navy, besides the units I lead, to support me, nor any large part of the populations. Most will see me as a disturber of their lives."

"You shall have our support. Abundant war material will flow to you through this sector, once you have achieved an initial success. Later, 'volunteers' will appear, in organized detachments drawn from subject species of ours. They need not be many or conspicuous; you can employ them with care, while affirming your loyalty to your own civilization. We will furnish proof of that, border incidents wherein your partisans show they continue ready to hold the foreign threat off.

"As soon as you seem clearly in the ascendant, you should find more and more Terrans—Navy officers included—embracing your cause. Your triumph should be total, and at relatively low cost. You will thereupon set about binding up the wounds of war, pardoning opponents but punishing evildoers, reforming, cleansing, strengthening, just as you promised. You should become the most widely beloved Emperor Terra has had since Pedro II."

"But what then? How does this serve the Race? You must be aware that the power of the Emperor is only absolute in theory. I couldn't decree submission to the Roidhun; I'd be dead within the hour."

"Assuredly. But you will call for a genuine peace, wherein both sides bargain honestly, and see to it that your side does so bargain. You will make appropriate appointments, first to the Policy Board and High Command, afterward elsewhere; the names will be furnished you. From time to time questions will arise, political, economic, social,

where you, the forceful and incorruptible Emperor, will make yourself arbiter. The list goes on. I will not weary you with it now. Your imagination can write much of it already.

"*Fear not, Olaf Magnusson. You should end your days old and honored. Your inheriting son should follow in your tracks. By then Merseian advisors will sit in his councils, and Merseian virtue be the ideal extolled by his intellectuals, and if certain edicts are nevertheless so distasteful as to cause revolts, Merseia will come to the help of the good Emperor. . . . Your grandsons will belong to the first generation of the new humanity.*"

CHAPTER TWENTY-TWO

Lieutenant General Cesare Gatto, Imperial Marine Corps, Commandant for the Patrician System, issued his orders immediately. An escadrille of corvettes left Daedalus orbit and accelerated downward. At the speed wherewith they hit atmosphere, it blazed and blasted about them, behind them.

They were too late by minutes, and buzzed back and forth over Zacharia like angry hornets. The interplanetary freighter which had been in port on the island had taken off. She could never have escaped pursuit, except by the means chosen. Rising several hundred kilometers, she nosed over and crash-dived. Under full thrust and no negafield protection, she became a shooting star. Afterward, Merseians would sing a ballad in praise of those comrades of theirs who had died such a death.

No Zacharians attempted flight. "Our people tried to stop them, but they were armed and resolved on immolation," their spokesman said over the eidophone. "We are staying together."

"You will destroy no evidence and make no resistance when his Majesty's troops land," Gatto snapped.

Tangaroa Zachary shrugged. His smile was as sorrowful a sight as the general had ever beheld. "No, we realize we are trapped, and will not make the situation worse for ourselves. You will find us cooperative. We are not conditioned to secrecy, thus hypnoprobing should be unnecessary; I suggest narcoquizzing a random sample of us."

"Behave yourselves, and I may put in a word on your behalf when the time comes for dealing out penalties. I may—provided you can explain to me what in God's name made you commit mass treason."

"We are that we are."

Gatto's broadcast ended a week of uncertainty and unease. Nobody but the most trusted members of his staff knew more than that he had let a Merseian vessel land at Aurea, and had had the crew hurried away in an opaque vehicle; that he had thereupon put the defense forces on alert against possible Merseian action; and that for reasons unspecified, a brigade occupied Zacharia and held it incommunicado. He needed the week to prepare forestalling measures, while his Intelligence agents feverishly studied three data slabs.

At the appropriate moment, various officers were surprised when placed under arrest. Their detention was precautionary; he could not be sure they would be able to instantly accept the truth about their idol Sir Olaf. Then Gatto went on the air.

From end to end of the system, that which he had to tell cut through the tension like a sword. Recoil came next, a lashing of outrage and alarm. Yet a curious quiet relief welled up underneath. How many folk had really wanted to undergo hazard and sacrifice for a change of overlords? Now, unless the Merseians took an ungloved hand in matters, the requirement upon them was just that they muddle through each day until the *status quo* could be restored.

By the hundreds, recordings of the announcement, together with copies and analyses of the proof, went off in message torpedoes and courier boats to the Imperial stars.

Gatto's image was not alone there. After his speech, the uptake had gone to a woman. She stood very straight against a plain red backdrop. A gray robe draped her slenderness. A white coif framed dark, fine features. Behind her stood two half-grown boys and a little girl. They wore the same headgear. On the planet Nyanza, it is the sign of mourning for the dead.

"Greeting," she said, low and tonelessly. "I am Vida Lonwe-Magnusson, wife of Admiral Sir Olaf. With me are the children we have had. Many of you sincerely believed in the rightfulness of his cause. You will understand how we four never thought to question it, any more than we question sunlight or springtime.

"Tonight we know that Olaf Magnusson's life has been one long betrayal. He would have delivered us into the power of our enemies—no, worse than enemies; those who would domesticate us to their service. I say to you, disown him, as we do here before you. Cast down him and his works, destroy them utterly, send the dust of them out upon the tides of endless space. Let us return to our true allegiance. No, the Empire is not perfect; but it is ours. *We* can better it.

"As for myself, when we have peace again I will go back to the world of my people, and bring my children with me. May all of you be as free. And may you be ready to forgive those who were mistaken. May those of you who are religious see fit to pray for the slain in this most abominable of wars. Perhaps a few of you will even find it in your hearts to pray for the soul of Olaf Magnusson.

"Thank you."

The task finished, she gathered her sons and her daughter to her, and they wept.

Winter night lay over the South Wilwidh Ocean. Waves ran black before a harrying wind, save where their white manes glimmered fugitively in what light there was. That came from above. The moon Neihevin seemed to fly through ragged clouds. So did a tiny, lurid patch, the nebula expanding from the ruin of Valenderay; and across more than a parsec, its radiation unfolded aurora in cold hues. Several speeding glints betokened satellites whose forcefields must still, after half a millennium, guard Merseia against the subatomic sleetstorm the supernova had cast forth. Hazy though it was, this luminance veiled most stars. Those that blinked in vision were far apart and forlorn.

Seas crashed, wind shrilled around the islet stronghold from which Tachwyr the Dark spoke with his Grand Council. The images somehow deepened his aloneness in the stony room where he sat.

"No, I have as yet no word of what went wrong," he told them. "Searching it out may require prolonged efforts, for the Terrans will put the best mask they can upon the facts. And it may hardly matter. Some blunder, accident, failure of judgment—that could well be what has undone us." Starkly: "The fact is that they have learned Magnusson was ours. Everywhere his partisans are deserting him. If they do not straightaway surrender to the nearest authorities, it is because they first want pardons. The enterprise itself has disintegrated."

"You say Magnusson *was* ours," Alwis Longtail murmured. "How do you know his fate? Might he be alive and bound hitherward?"

"That is conceivable," Tachwyr replied; "but I take for granted that the crew of his flagship mutinied too, when the news came upon them. We shall wish they killed him cleanly. He has deserved better than trial and execution on Terra—yes, better than dragging out a useless existence as a pensioner on Merseia."

"Likewise," said Odhar the Curt, "your statement that his followers are giving up must be an inference."

"True. Thus far I have only the most preliminary of reports. But think."

"I have. You are certainly correct."

"What can we do?" asked Gwynafon of Brightwater.

"We will not intervene," said Tachwyr to the dull member of the Council. "What initial gains we might make while the Terran Navy is trying to reorganize itself would be trivial, set next to the consequences. Much too readily could the militant faction among the humans, minority though it is, mobilize sentiment, seize control, and set about preparing the Empire for total confrontation with us.

"No, Merseia denies any complicity, blames whatever may have happened upon overzealous officers—on both sides, and calls for resumption of talks about a nonaggression pact. My lords, at this conference we should draft instructions to Ambassador Chwioch. I have already ordered the appropriate agencies to start planning what to feed the Imperial academies, religions, and news media."

"Then we might yet get two or three beasts out of this failed battue?" Alwis wondered.

"We must try," Odhar said. "Console yourselves with the thought that we invested little treasure or effort in the venture. Our net loss is minor."

"Except for hope," Tachwyr mumbled. He drew his robe close about him; the room felt chill. "I dreamed that I would live to behold—" He straightened. "By adversity, the God tempers the steel of the Race. Let us get on with our quest."

CHAPTER TWENTY-THREE

Imhotep spun toward northern autumn. Dwarfed Patricius burned mellower in skies gone pale. When full, the big moon Zoser rose early and set late; with its lesser companions Kanofer and Rahotep it made lambent the snowpeaks around Mt. Horn. Sometimes flakes dusted off them, aglitter, vanishing as they blew into the streets of Olga's Landing. Dead leaves scrittled underfoot. In Old Town crowds milled, music twanged, savory odors rose out of foodstalls and Winged Smoke houses; for this was the season when Tigery caravans brought wares up from the lowlands.

Fleet Admiral Sir Dominic Flandry had time to prowl about. Things had changed a good deal since last he was here, but memories lingered. One hour he went to the Terran cemetery and stood quiet before a headstone. Otherwise, mostly, he enjoyed being at liberty, while hirelings flitted in search of the persons he wanted.

After the loyalists—the Navy of Emperor Gerhart—reoccupied Sphinx and released him, he had set about learning just what had been going on. His connections got him more information than would ever become public. On that basis, he decided to send Banner a reassuring message but himself, before returning home, visit Daedalus. There he spent an especially interesting while on Zacharia. However, those individuals he most desired to see had gone back to Imhotep. Flandry followed, to learn that Diana Crowfeather and Father F. X. Axor were at sea on an archaeological expedition, while Targovi was off in the asteroid belt chaffering for precious metals.

Like everything else, the minerals industry was in a fluid state, and would remain thus until the aftermath of the recent unpleasantness had damped out. A smart operator could take advantage of that.

Having called on Dragoika in Toborkozan, Flandry engaged searchers. In Olga's Landing he took lodgings at the Pyramid and roved around the city.

Almost together, his detectives fetched his guests. Flandry bade them a cordial welcome over the eidophone, described the credit to their accounts in the bank, and arranged a date for meeting. Thereafter he commandeered an official dining room and gave personal attention to the menu and wine list.

From this high level, a full-wall transparency looked far over splendor. Westward the city ended at woods turned scarlet, russet, amber. Beyond the warm zone were boulders and crags, hardy native bush, thinly frozen rivulets and ponds, to the dropoff of the summit. Beyond the depths, within which blue shadows were rising, neighbor mountains waited for the sun. Their snows had come aglow; glaciers gleamed nebula-green.

In air, weight, warmth, the room was Terra. Recorded violins frolicked, fragrances drifted. It made the more plain what an enclave this was, and how much the more dear for that.

Flandry leaned back, let cigarette smoke trail, regarded his daughter through it. A charming lass, he thought. Granted, the outfit she had bought herself was scarcely in the latest Imperial court fashion—crimson minigown, leather sandals, bracelet and headband of massive silver set with raw turquoises, spotted gillycat pelt from right shoulder to left hip, where her Tigery knife rested—but it might well have ignited a new style there, and in any event the Imperial court was blessedly distant.

As he hoped, cocktails were bringing ease between him and her. But Targovi, to whom the drinking of ethanol was not a social custom and who had not started to inhale what was set before him, persisted in hunting down what he wanted to know. The Tigery had vanity enough to wear a beaded breechcloth and necklace of land pearls; a colloidal spray had made his fur shine. Still—"And so you, sir, you caught the same suspicions as I?" he inquired.

In the background Axor rested serene along the floor, listening with one bony ear while contemplating the sunset. He was clad merely in his scales and scutes, unless you counted the purse, rosary, and spectacles hung from his neck.

"Why, yes," Flandry said. "Magnusson's being a sleeper, as we call it in the trade—that possibility occurred to me, although an undertaking such as his would be the most audacious ever chronicled outside of cloak-and-blaster fiction. I thought of comparing his account of his early life with what various Merseians recalled. They could not all have been vowed to secrecy; and as for those who had been, a percentage would be susceptible. . . . Blatant inconsistencies would give me a strong clue. Unfortunately, Merseian counterintelligence nailed our agents before they could accomplish anything worthwhile. Fortunately, you had the same intuition, and this trio here in front of me carried out a coup more dramatic and decisive than I had dared fantasize."

"What's the latest news about the war?" Diana asked. "The truth, I mean, not that sugar puddin' on the screens."

Flandry's grin was wary. "I wouldn't dignify it with the name of war. Not as of weeks and weeks ago. Mainly, everything is in abeyance while Imperium and bureaucracy creak through the datawork. People who, in good faith, fought for Magnusson—they're too many to kill or imprison. Punishments will have to range from reprimands, through fines and reductions in rank, to cashiering. The scale and the chaos of making it all orderly defies imagination; beside it, the accretion disc of a black hole is as neat as a transistor. But it'll settle down eventually."

"Magnusson. Any word about him?"

Flandry frowned. "He died at the hands of his men. Do you really want to hear the details? I gather there are no plans to release them. Why risk rousing sympathy for him?"

"And I suppose," Targovi put in slowly, "the tale of how the conspiracy came to light, that will also stay secret?"

Flandry sighed. "Well, it wouldn't make the government look so terribly efficient, would it? Besides, my sources inform me that Merseia had indicated its release would make Merseia equally unhappy. It could jar the peace process . . . Not that you're forbidden to talk. The Empire is big, and you have no particular access to the media."

"What of the Zacharians?" came like surf from Axor. "Is mercy possible for those tormented souls?"

"Tormented, my foot!" cried Diana, and stamped hers. She checked herself, drank of her martini, and said, while a slight flush played across her cheekbones: "Not that I'm after genocide on them or any such thing. Javak, no! But what will happen? You got any notion, Dad?"

"Yes, I do," Flandry replied, glad to steer conversation into softer channels. "Not that a final decree has been issued; but I've been studying the situation, and . . . my word is not without leverage."

He likewise sipped, drew breath and smoke, before he continued: "They're unique. No other population, at least no other human population, could have kept a secret the way theirs did. Virtually every adult was privy to it. Let's eschew quibbles about what 'human' really means.

"Their children, of course, are innocent, had no idea of what was going on. Can we kill them? The Merseians might, to 'purge the Race.' Whatever its entropy level, the Empire has not yet sunk to that.

"Pardons, amnesties, and limited penalties are going to be the order of the day. They must, if we want to shore up this social structure of ours so it might last another century or two.

"I think the punishment of the Zacharians will be the loss of their country. They'll be forced to vacate—scatter—find new homes wherever they can. I'd not be surprised but what Merseia offers them a haven, and many of them accept. The rest—will have to make their way among the rest of us."

"And what will come of that?" Targovi mused.

Flandry spread his hands. "Who knows? We play the game move by move, and never see far ahead—the game of empire, of life, whatever you want to call it—and what the score will be when all the pieces at last go back into the box, who knows?"

He tossed off his drink, tossed away his cigarette, and stood up. "My friends," he said, "dinner awaits. Let us go in together and rejoice in what we have.

"But first—" his glance swooped about— "I'd like to give you three some extra reason for rejoicing. Diana, Targovi . . . are you really heart-bent on faring out yonder? I'm prepared to arrange that for you, however you choose. Trader, explorer, scientist, artist, or, God help you, Intelligence operative—I can see to it that you get the schooling and the means you'll need. I only ask that first you think hard about what you truly want."

The girl's and the Tigery's spirits fountained radiance.

"As for you, Father Axor," Flandry went on, "if you wish, I'll obtain adequate funding for your research. Shall I?"

"God bless you, whether you like it or not," the Wodenite replied, ocean-deep. "What you endow goes beyond space or time." He crossed his hands on his forelegs and smiled, as a being may who is winning salvation for himself and his beloved.

A TRAGEDY OF ERRORS

A TRAGEDY OF ERRORS

Once in ancient days, the then King of England told Sir Christopher Wren, whose name is yet remembered, that the new Cathedral of St. Paul which he had designed was "awful, pompous and artificial." Kings have seldom been noted for perspicacity.

Later ages wove a myth about Roan Tom. He became their archetype of those star rovers who fared forth while the Long Night prevailed. As such, he was made to fit the preconceptions and prejudices of whoever happened to mention him. To many scholars, he was a monster, a murderer and thief, bandit and vandal, skulking like some carrion animal through the ruins of the Terran Empire. Others called him a hero, a gallant and romantic leader of fresh young peoples destined to sweep out of time the remnants of a failed civilization and build something better.

He would have been equally surprised, and amused, by either legend.

"Look," one can imagine his ghost drawling, "we had to eat. For which purpose, it's sort o' helpful to keep your throat uncut, no? That was a spiny-tail period. Society'd fallen. And havin' so far to fall, it hit bottom almighty hard. The ee-conomic basis for things like buildin' spaceships wasn't there any more. That meant little trade between planets. Which meant trouble on most of 'em. You let such go on for a century or two, snowballin', and what've you got? A kettle o' short-lived dwarf nations, that's what—one-planet, one-continent, one-island nations; all of 'em one-lung for sure—where they haven't collapsed even further. No more information-collatin' services, so nobody can keep track o' what's happenin' amongst those millions o' suns. What few spaceships are left in workin' order are naturally the most valuable objects in sight. So they naturally get acquired by the toughest men around who, bein' what they are, are apt to use the ships for conquerin' or plunderin' . . . and complicate matters still worse.

"Well," and he pauses to stuff a pipe with Earthgrown tobacco, which is available in his particular Valhalla, "like everybody else, I just made the best o' things as I found 'em. Fought? Sure. Grew up fightin'. I was born on a spaceship. My dad was from Lochlann, but outlawed after a family feud went sour. He hadn't much choice but to turn pirate. One day I was in a landin' party which got bushwhacked. Next I heard, I'd been sold into slavery. Had to take it from there. Got some lucky breaks after a while and worked 'em hard. Didn't do too badly, by and large.

"Mind you, though, I never belonged to one o' those freaky cultures that'd taken to glorifyin' combat for its own sake. In fact, once I'd gotten some power on Kraken, I was a lot more int'rested in startin' trade again than in anything else. But neither did I mind the idea o' fightin', if we stood to gain by it, nor o' collectin' any loose piece o' property that wasn't too well defended. Also, willy-nilly, we were bound to get into brawls with other factions. Usually those happened a long ways from home. I saw to that. Better there than where I lived, no?

"We didn't always win, either. Sometimes we took a clobberin'. Like finally, what I'd reckon as about the worst time, I found myself skyhootin' away from Sassania, in a damaged ship, alone except for a couple o' wives. I shook pursuit in the Nebula. But when we came out on the other side, we were in a part o' space that wasn't known to us. Old Imperial territory still, o' course, but that could mean anything. And we needed repairs. Once my ship'd been self-fixin', as well as self-crewin', self-pilotin', self-navigatin,' aye-ya, even self-aware. But that computer was long gone, together with a lot of other gear. We had to find us a place with a smidgin of industrial capacity, or we were done for."

The image in the viewscreens flickered so badly that Tom donned armor and went out for a direct look at the system he had entered.

He liked being free in space anyway. He had more esthetic sense than he publicly admitted. The men of Kraken were quick to praise the beauty of a weapon or a woman, but would have considered it strange to spill time admiring a view rather than examining the scene for pitfalls and possibilities. In the hush and dreamlike liberty of weightlessness, Tom found an inner peace; and from this he turned outward, becoming one with the grandeur around him.

After he had flitted a kilometer from it, *Firedrake*'s lean hull did not cut off much vista. But reflections, where energy beams had scored through black camouflage coating to the steel beneath, hurt his eye. . . . He looked away from ship and sun alike. It was a bright sun, intrinsic luminosity of two Sols, though the color was ruddy, like a gold and copper alloy. At a distance of one and a half astronomical units, it showed a disc thirty-four minutes wide; and no magnification, only a darkened faceplate, was necessary to see the flares that jetted from it. Corona and zodiacal light made a bronze cloud. That was not a typical main sequence star, Tom thought, though nothing in his background had equipped him to identify what the strangeness consisted of.

Elsewhere glittered the remoter stars, multitudinous and many-colored in their high night. Tom's gaze circled among them. Yes, yonder was Capella. Old Earth lay on the far side, a couple of hundred light-years from here. But he wanted home, to Kraken: much less of a trip, ten parsecs or so. He could have picked out its sun with the naked eye, as a minor member of that jewel-swarm, had the Nebula not stood between. The thundercloud mass reared gloomy and awesome athwart a quarter of heaven. And it might as well be a solid wall, if his vessel didn't get fixed.

That brought Tom's attention back to the planet he was orbiting. It seemed enormous at this close remove, a thick crescent growing as the ship swung dayward, as if it were toppling upon him. The tints were green, blue, brown, but with an underlying red in the land areas that wasn't entirely due to the sunlight color. Clouds banded the

brightness of many seas; there was no true ocean. The southern polar
cap was extensive. Yet it couldn't be very deep, because its northern
counterpart had almost disappeared with summer, albeit the axial tilt
was a mere ten degrees. Atmosphere rimmed the horizon with
purple. A tiny disc was heaving into sight, the farther of the two small
moons.

Impressive, yes. Habitable, probably according to the spectroscope,
certainly according to the radio emissions on which he had homed.
(They'd broken off several light-years away, but by then no doubt
remained that this system was their origin, and this was the only
possible world within the system.) Nonetheless—puzzling. In a way,
daunting.

The planet was actually a midget. Its equatorial diameter was
6810 kilometers, its mass 0.15 Terra. Nothing that size ought to have
air and water enough for men.

But there were men there. Or had been. Feeble and distorted
though the broadcasts became, away off in space, Tom had caught
Anglic words spoken with human mouths.

He shrugged. One way to find out. Activating his impellers, he
flitted back. His boots struck hull and clung. He free-walked to the
forward manlock and so inboard.

The interior gee-field was operational. Weight thrust his armor
down onto his neck and shoulders. Yasmin heard him clatter and
came to help him unsuit. He waved her back. "Don't you see the frost
on me? I been in planet shadow. Your finger'd stick to the metal,
kid." Not wearing radio earplugs, she didn't hear him, but she got the
idea and stood aside. Gauntleted, he stripped down to coverall and
mukluks and lockered the space equipment. At the same time, he
admired her.

She was slight and dark, but prettier than he had realized at first.
That was an effect of personality, reasserting itself after what happened
in Anushirvan. The city had been not only the most beautiful and
civilized, but the gayest on all Sassania; and her father was Nadjaf
Kuli, the deputy governor. Now he was dead and his palace sacked,
and she had fled for her life with one of her Shah's defeated barbarian
allies. Yet she was getting back the ability to laugh. Good stock, Tom
thought; she'd bear him good sons.

"Did you see trace of humans?" she asked. He had believed her Anglic bore a charming accent—it was not native to her—until he discovered that she had been taught the classical language. Her gazelle eyes flickered from the telescope he carried in one fist on to his battered and weatherbeaten face.

"Trace, yes," he answered bluntly. "Stumps of a few towns. They'd been hit with nukes."

"Oh-h-h. . . ."

"Ease off, youngster." He rumpled the flowing hair. "I couldn't make out much, with nothin' better'n these lenses. We'd already agreed the planet was likely raided, that time the broadcasts quit. Don't mean they haven't rebuilt a fair amount. I'd guess they have. The level o', shall I say in two words, radio activity—" Tom paused. "You were supposed to smile at that," he said in a wounded tone.

"Well, may I smile at the second joke, instead?" she retorted impishly. They both chuckled. Her back grew straighter, in the drab one-piece garment that was all he had been able to give her, and somehow the strength of the curving nose dominated the tenderness of her mouth. "Please go on, my lord."

"Uh, you shouldn't call me that. They're free women on Kraken."

"So we were on Sassania. In fact, plural marriage—"

"I know, I know. Let's get on with business." Tom started down the corridor. Yasmin accompanied him, less gracefully than she had moved at home. The field was set for Kraken weight, which was 1.25 standard. But she'd develop the muscles for it before long.

He had gone through a wedding ceremony with her, once they were in space, at Dagny's insistence. "Who else will the poor child have for a protector but you, the rest of her life? Surely you won't turn her loose on any random planet. At the same time, she *is* aristocratic born. It'd humiliate her to become a plain concubine." .

"M-m-m . . . but the heirship problem—"

"I like her myself, what little I've seen of her; and the Kuli barons always had an honorable name. I don't think she'll raise boys who'll try to steal house rule from my sons."

As usual, Dagny was no doubt right.

Anxious to swap findings with her, Tom hurried. The passage reached empty and echoing; air from the ventilators blew loud and chilled him; the stylized murals of gods and sea beasts had changed from bold to pathetic—now that only three people crewed this ship. But they were lucky to be alive—would not have been so, save for the primitive loyalty of his personal guardsmen, who died in their tracks while he ran through the burning city in search of Dagny—when the Pretender's nonhuman mercenaries broke down the last defenses. He found his chief wife standing by the ship with a Mark IV thunderbolter, awaiting his return. She would not have left without him. Yasmin huddled at her feet. They managed to loose a few missiles as they lifted. But otherwise there was nothing to do but hope to fight another day. The damage that *Firedrake* sustained in running the enemy space fleet had made escape touch and go. The resulting absence of exterior force-fields and much interior homeostasis made the damage worse as they traveled. Either they found the wherewithal for repair here, or they stayed here.

Tom said to Yasmin while he strode: "We couldn't've picked up their radio so far out's we did, less'n they'd had quite a lot, both talk and radar. That means they had a pretty broad industrial base. You don't destroy that by scrubbin' cities. Too many crossroads machine shops and so forth; too much skill spread through the population. I'd be surprised if this planet's not on the way back up."

"But why haven't they rebuilt any cities?"

"Maybe they haven't gotten that far yet. Been less'n ten years, you know. Or, 'course, they might've got knocked clear down to savagery. I've seen places where it happened. We'll find out."

Walking beside the girl, Roan Tom did not look especially noteworthy, certainly not like the rover and trader chieftain whose name was already in the ballads of a dozen planets. He was of medium height, though so broad in shoulders and chest as to look stocky. From his father, he had the long head, wide face, high cheekbones, snub nose and beardlessness of the Lochlanna. But his mother, a freedwoman said to be of Hermetian stock, had given him dark-red hair, which was now thinning, and star-blue eyes. Only the right of those remained; a patch covered where the left had been. (Some day, somewhere, he'd find someone with the knowledge and facilities to grow him a new one!) He walked with the rolling gait of a Krakener, whose planet is mostly ocean, and bore the intertwining tattoos of his adopted people on most of his hide. A blaster and knife hung at his waist.

Dagny was in the detector shack. Viewscreens might be malfunctioning, along with a lot else, but such instruments as the radionic, spectroscopic, magnetic and sonic were not integrated with ship circuitry. They had kept their accuracy, and she was expert—not educated, but rule-of-thumb expert—in their use.

"Well, there," she said, looking around the console at which she sat. "What'd you see?"

Tom repeated in more detail what he had told Yasmin. Since Dagny spoke no Pelevah and only a little pidgin Anglic, while Yasmin had no Eylan, these two of his wives communicated with difficulty. Maybe that was why they got along so well. "And how 'bout you?" he finished.

"I caught a flash of radiocast. Seemed like two stations communicating from either end of a continental-size area."

"Still, somebody is able to chat a bit," Tom said. "Hopeful." He lounged against the doorframe. "Anyone spot us, d' you think?"

Dagny grinned. "What do you think?"

His lips responded. A positive answer would have had them in action at once, he to the bridge, she to the main fire control turret. They couldn't be sure they had not been noticed—by optical system, quickly brushing radar or maser, gadget responsive to the neutrino emission of their proton converter, several other possible ways—but it was unlikely.

"Any further indications?" Tom asked. "Atomic powerplants?"

"I don't know."

"How come?"

"I don't know what the readings mean that I get, particle flux, magnetic variations and the rest. This is such a confoundedly queer sun and planet. I've never seen anything like them. Have you?"

"No."

They regarded each other for a moment that grew very quiet. Dagny, Od's-daughter in the House of Brenning, was a big woman, a few years his senior. Her shoulder-length yellow mane was fading a bit, and her hazel eyes were burdened with those contact lenses that were the best help anyone on Kraken knew how to give. But her frame was still strong and erect, her hands still clever and murderously quick. It had been natural for an impoverished noble family to make alliance with an energetic young immigrant who had a goodly following and a spaceship. But in time, voyages together, childbirths and child-rearings, the marriage of convenience had become one of affection.

"Well . . . s'pose we better go on down," Tom said. "Sooner we get patched, sooner we can start back. And we'd better not be gone from home too long."

Dagny nodded. Yasmin saw the grimness that touched them and said, "What is wrong, my . . . my husband?"

Tom hadn't the heart to explain how turbulent matters were on Kraken also. She'd learn that soon enough, if they lived. He said merely, "There's some kind o' civilization goin' yet around here. But it may exist only as traces o' veneer. The signs are hard to figure. This is a rogue planet, you see."

"Rogue?" Yasmin was bemused. "But that is a loose planet—sunless—isn't it?"

"You mean a bandit planet. A rogue's one that don't fit in with its usual type, got a skewball orbit or composition or whatever. Like this'n."

"Oh. Yes, I know."

"What?" He caught her shoulder, not noticing how she winced at so hard a grip. "You've heard o' this system before?"

"No . . . please . . . no, my people never came to this side of the Nebula either, with what few ships we had. But I studied some astrophysics and planetography at Anushirvan University."

"Huh?" He let her go and gaped. "Science? Real, Imperial-era science, not engineerin' tricks?" She nodded breathlessly. "But I thought—you said—you'd studied classics."

"Is not scientific knowledge one of the classic arts? We had a very complete collection of tapes in the Royal Library." Forlornness came upon her. "Gone, now, into smoke."

"Never mind. Can you explain how come this globe is as it is?"

"Well, I . . . well, no. I don't believe I could. I would need more information. Mass, and chemical data, and—And even then, I would probably not be able. I am not one of the ancient experts."

"Hardly anybody is," Tom sighed. "All right. Let's get us a snack, and then to our stations for planetfall."

✧   ✧   ✧

Descent was tricky. Sensor-computer-autopilot linkups could no longer be trusted. Tom had to bring *Firedrake* in on manual controls. His few instruments were of limited use, when he couldn't get precise data by which to recalibrate them for local conditions. With no view-screens working properly, he had no magnification, infra-red and ultra-violet presentations, any of the conventional aids. He depended on an emergency periscope, on Dagny's radar readings called via intercom and on the trained reflexes of a lifetime.

Yasmin sat beside him. There was nothing she could do elsewhere, and he wanted to be able to assist her in her inexperience if they must bail out. The spacesuit and gravity impellers surrounded her with an awkward bulk that made the visage in the helmet look like a child's. Neither one of them had closed a faceplate. Her voice came small through the gathering throb of power: "Is it so difficult to land? I mean, I used to watch ships do it, and even if we are partly crippled— we could travel between the stars. What can an aircar do that we can't?"

"Hyperdrive's not the same thing as kinetic velocity, and most particular not the same as aerodynamic speed," Tom grunted. "To start with, I know the theory o' sublight physics."

"You do?" She was frankly astounded.

"Enough of it, anyhow. I can read and write, too." His hands played over the board. Vibration grew in the deck, the bulkheads, his bones. A thin shrilling was heard, the first cloven atmosphere. "A spaceship's a sort o' big and clumsy object, once out o' her native habitat," he said absently. "Got quite a moment of inertia, f'r instance. Means a sudden, hard wind can turn her top over tip and she don't right easy. When you got a lot o' sensitive machinery to do the work, that's no problem. But we don't." He buried his face in the periscope hood. Cloudiness swirled beneath. "Also," he said, "we got no screens and nobody at the guns. So we'd better be choosy about where we sit down. And . . . we don't have any way to scan an area in detail. Now do be quiet and let me steer."

Already in the upper air, he encountered severe turbulence. That was unexpected, on a planet which received less than 0.9 Terran . . . insolation, with a lower proportion of UV to boot. It wasn't that the atmosphere was peculiar. The spectroscope readout had said the mixture was ordinary oxy-nitro-CO_2, on the thin and dry side—sea-level pressure around 600 mm.—but quite breathable. Nor was the phenomenon due to excessive rotation; the period was twenty-five and a half hours. Of course, the inner moon, while small, was close in and must have considerable tidal effect—*Hoy!*

The outercom buzzed. Someone was calling. "Take that, Yasmin," Tom snapped. The ship wallowed. He felt it even through the cushioning internal gee-field, and the altitude meters were wavering crazily. Wind screamed louder. The clouds roiled near, coppery-headed blue-shadowed billows on the starboard horizon, deep purple below him. He had hoped that night and overcast would veil his arrival, but evidently a radar had fingered him. Or—"The knob marked A, you idiot! Turn it widdershins. I can't let go now!"

Yasmin caught her lower lip between her teeth and obeyed. The screen flickered to life. "Up the volume," Tom commanded. "Maybe Dagny can't watch, but she'd better hear. You on, Dagny?"

"Aye." Her tone was crisp from the intercom speaker. "I doubt if I'll understand many words, though. Hadn't you better start aloft and I leave the radar and take over fire control?"

"No, stand where you are. See what you can detect. We're not after a tussle, are we?" Tom glanced at the screen for the instant he dared. It was sidewise to him, putting him outside the pickup arc, but he could get a profile of the three-dimensional image.

The man who gazed out was so young that his beard was brownish fuzz. Braids hung from beneath a goggled fiber crash helmet. But his features were hard; his background appeared to be an aircraft cockpit; and his green tunic had the look of a uniform.

"Who are you?" he challenged. Seeing himself confronted by a girl, he let his jaw drop. "Who *are* you?"

"Might ask the same o' you," Tom answered for her. "We're from offplanet."

"Why did you not declare yourselves?" The Anglic was thickly accented but comprehensible, roughened with tension.

"We didn't know anybody was near. I reckon you had to try several bands before hittin' the one we were tuned to. Isn't a standard signal frequency any more." Tom spoke with careful casualness, while the ship bucked and groaned around him and lightning zigzagged in the clouds he approached. "Don't worry about us. We mean no harm."

"You trespass in the sky of Karol Weyer."

"Son, we never heard o' him. We don't even know what you call this planet."

The pilot gulped. "N-Nike," he said automatically. "The planet Nike. Karol Weyer is our Engineer, here in Hanno. Who are you?"

Dagny's voice said in Eylan, "I've spotted him on the scope, Tom. Coming in fast at eleven o'clock low.'"

"Let me see your face," the pilot demanded harshly. "Hide not by this woman."

"Can't stop to be polite," Tom said. "S'pose you let us land, and we'll talk to your Engineer. Or shall we take our business elsewhere?"

Yasmin's gauntlet closed convulsively on Tom's sleeve. "The look on him grows terrible," she whispered.

"Gods damn," Tom said, "we're friends!"

"What?" the pilot shouted.

"Friends, I tell you! We need help. Maybe you—"

"The screen went blank," Yasmin cried.

Tom risked yawing *Firedrake* till he could see in the direction Dagny had bespoken. The craft was in view. It was a one- or two-man job, a delta wing whose contrail betrayed the energy source as chemical rather than atomic or electric. However, instruments reported it as applying that power to a gravity drive. At this distance he couldn't make out if the boat had guns, but hardly doubted that. For a moment it glinted silvery against the darkling clouds, banked and vanished.

"Prob'ly hollerin' for orders," Tom said. "And maybe reinforcements. Chil'ren, I think we'd better hustle back spaceward and try our luck in some place more sociable than Hanno."

"Is there any?" Dagny wondered.

"Remains to be seen. Let's hope it's not our remains that'll be seen." Tom concentrated on the controls. Lame and weakened, the ship could not simply reverse. She had too much downward momentum and was too deep in Nike's gravity well. He must shift vectors slowly and nurse her up again.

After minutes, Dagny called through the racket and shudderings:

"Several of them—at least five—climbing faster than us, from all sides."

"I was afraid o' that," Tom said. "Yasmin, see if you can eavesdrop on the chit-chat between 'em."

"Should we not stay tuned for their call?" the Sassanian asked timidly.

"I doubt they aim to call. If ever anybody acted so scared and angry as to be past reason—No, hold 'er."

The screen had suddenly reawakened. This time the man who stared forth was middle-aged, leonine, bearded to the waist. His coat was trimmed with fur and, beneath the storm in his voice, pride rang. "I am the Engineer," he said. "You will land and be slaves."

"Huh?" Tom said. "Look, we was goin' away—"

"You declared yourselves friends!"

"Yes. We'd like to do business with you. But—"

"Land at once. Slave yourselves to me. Or my craft will open fire. They have tommics."

"Nukes, you mean?" Tom growled. Yasmin stifled a shriek. Karol Weyer observed and looked grimly pleased. Tom cursed without words.

The Nikean shook his head. Tom got a glimpse of that, and wasn't sure whether the gesture meant yes, no or maybe in this land. But the answer was plain: "Weapons that unleash the might which lurks in matter."

And our force-screen generator is on sick leave, Tom thought. *He may be lyin'. But I doubt it, because they do still use gravs here. We can't outrun a rocket, let alone an energy beam. Nor could Dagny, by herself, shoot down the lot in time to forestall 'em.*

"You win," he said. "Here we come."

"Leave your transceiver on," Weyer instructed. "When you are below the clouds, the fish will tell you where to go."

"Fish?" Tom choked. But the screen had emptied, save for the crackling and formlessnesses of static.

"D-d-dialect?" Yasmin suggested.

"Uh, yeh. Must mean somethin' like squadron leader. Good girl." Tom spared her a grin. The tears were starting forth.

"Slaves?" she wailed. "Oh, no, no."

"Course not, if I can help it," he said, *sotto voce* lest the hostiles be listening. "Rather die."

He did not speak exact truth. Having been a slave once, he didn't prefer death—assuming his owner was not unreasonable, and that some hope existed of getting his freedom back. But becoming property was apt to be worse for a woman than a man: much worse, when she was a daughter of Sassania's barons or Kraken's sea kings. As their husband, he was honor bound to save them if he could.

"We'll make a break," he said. "Lot o' wild country underneath. One reason I picked this area. But first we have to get down."

"What's gone by me?" Dagny called.

Tom explained in Eylan while he fought the ship. "But that doesn't make sense!" she said. "When they know nothing about us—"

"Well, they took a bad clobberin', ten years back. Can't expect 'em to act terribly sensible about strangers. And s'posin' this is a misunderstandin' . . . we have to stay alive while we straighten it out. Stand by for a rough jaunt."

The aircraft snarled into sight, but warily, keeping their distance in swoops and circles that drew fantastic trails of exhaust. For a moment Tom wondered if that didn't prove the locals were familiar with space-war techniques. Those buzzeroos seemed careful to stay beyond reach of a tractor or pressor beam that could have seized them. . . . But no. They were exposed to his guns and missiles, which had far greater range, and didn't know that these were unmanned.

Nevertheless, they were at least shrewd on this planet. From what Tom had let slip, and the battered condition of the vessel, Weyer had clearly guessed that the newcomers were weak. They could doubtless wipe out one or two aircraft before being hit, but could they handle half a dozen? That Weyer had taken the risk and scrambled this much of what must be a very small air fleet suggested implacable enmity. (Why? He couldn't be so stupid as to assume that everyone from offplanet was a foe. Could he?) What was worse, his assessment of the military situation was quite correct. In her present state, *Firedrake* could not take on so many opponents and survive.

She entered the clouds.

For a while Tom was blind. Thunder and darkness encompassed him. Metal toned. The instrument dials glowed like goblin eyes. Their needles spun; the ship lurched; Tom stabbed and pulled and twisted controls, sweat drenched his coverall and reeked in his nostrils.

Then he was through, into windy but uncluttered air. Fifteen kilometers beneath him lay that part of the north temperate zone he had so unfortunately chosen. The view was of a valley, cut into a checkerboard pattern that suggested large agricultural estates. A river wound through, shining silver in what first dawn-light reddened the eastern horizon. A few villages clustered along it, and traffic moved, barge trains and water ships. A swampy delta spread at the eastern end of a great bay.

That bay was as yet in the hour before sunrise, but glimmered with reflections. It had a narrow mouth, opening on a sea to the west. Lights twinkled on either side of the gate, and clustered quite thickly on the southern bayshore. Tom's glance went to the north. There he saw little trace of habitation. Instead, hills humped steeply toward a mountain which smoked. Forests covered them, but radar showed how rugged they were.

The outercom flashed with the image of the pilot who had first hailed him. Now that conditions were easier, Tom could have swiveled it around himself to let the scanner cover his own features. Yasmin could have done so for him at any time. But he refrained. Anonymity wasn't an ace in the hole—at most, a deuce or a trey—but he needed every card he had.

"You will bear east-northeast," the "fish" instructed. "About a hundred kilos upriver lies a cave. Descend there."

"Kilos?" Tom stalled. He had no intention of leaving the refuges below him for the open flatlands.

"Distances. Thousand-meters."

"But a cave? I mean, look, I want to be a good fellow and so forth, but how'm I goin' to spot a cave from the air?"

"Spot?" It was the Nikean's turn to be puzzled. However, he was no fool. "Oh, so, you mean espy. A cave is a stronghouse. You will know it by turrets, projectors, set down fields."

"Your Engineer's castle?"

"Think you we're so whetless we'd let you near the Great Cave? You might have a tommic boom aboard. No. Karol Weyer dwells by the bay gate. You go to the stronghouse guarding the Nereid River valley. Now change course, I said, or we fire."

Tom had used the talk-time to shed a good bit of altitude. "We can't," he said. "Not that fast. Have to get low first, before we dare shift."

"You go no lower, friend! Those are our folk down there."

"Be reasonable," Tom said. "A spaceship's worth your havin', I'm sure, even a damaged one like ours. Why blang us for somethin' we can't help?"

"Um-m-m . . . hold where you are."

"I can't. This is not like an aircraft. I've got to either rise or sink. Ask your bosses."

The pilot's face disappeared. "But—" Yasmin began.

"Shhh!" Tom winked his good eye at her.

He was gambling that they hadn't had spacecraft on Nike for a long time. Otherwise they wouldn't have taken such a licking a decade ago; and they'd have sent a ship after him, rather than those few miserable, probably handmade gravplanes. So if they didn't have anyone around who was qualified in the practical problems of handling that kind of vessel—

Not but what *Firedrake* wasn't giving him practical problems of his own. Wind boomed and shoved.

The pilot returned. "Go lower if you must,'"he said. "But follow my word, go above the northshore hills."

"Surely." *Right what I was hopin' for!* Tom switched to Eylan. "Dagny, get to the forward manlock."

"What do you say?" rapped the pilot.

"I'm issuin' orders to my crew," Tom said. "They don't speak Anglic."

"No! You'll not triple-talk me!"

Tom let out a sigh that was a production. "Unless they know what to do, we'll crash. Do you want live slaves and a whole space-ship, or no? Make up your mind, son."

"Um-m . . . well. At first ill-doing, we shoot."

Tom ignored him. "Listen, Dagny. You're not needed here any more. I can land on my altimeter and stuff. But I've got to set us down easy, and not get us hit by some overheated gunner. They must have what we need to make our repairs, but not to build a whole new ship, even s'posin' we knew how. So we can't risk defendin' ourselves, leastwise till we get away from the ship."

"She will be theirs," Dagny said, troubled. "And we will be hunted. Shouldn't we surrender peacefully and bargain with them?"

"What bargainin' power has a slave got? Whereas free, if nothin' else, I bet we're the only two on Nike that can run a spacecraft. Besides, we don't know what these fellows are like. They could be mighty cruel. No, you go stand by that manlock along with Yasmin. The minute we touch dirt, you two get out—fast and far."

"But Tom, you'll be on the bridge. What about you?"

"Somebody's got to make that landin'. I dunno how they'll react. But you girls won't have much time to escape yourselves. I'll come after you. If I haven't joined you soon, figure I won't, and do whatever comes natural. And look after Yasmin, huh?"

Silence dwelt for a moment amidst every inanimate noise. Until: "I understand. Tom, if we don't see each other again, it was good with you." Dagny uttered a shaken laugh. "Tell her to kiss you for both of us."

"Aye-ya." He couldn't, of course, with that suspicious countenance glowering out of the screen. But in what little Pelevah he had, he gave Yasmin her orders. She didn't protest, too stunned by events to grasp the implications.

Down and down. The tilted wilderness swooped at him.

"The steerin's quit on me!" Tom yelled in Anglic. "Yasmin, go fantangle the dreelsprail! Hurry!" She flung off her safety webbing and left the bridge, as fast as possible in her clumsy armor. "I've got to make an emergency landin'," Tom said to the Nikean officer.

Probably that caused them to hold their fire as he had hoped. He didn't know, nor wonder. He was too busy. The sonoprobe said firm solid below. The altimeter said a hundred meters, fifty, twenty-five, ten—Leaves surged around. Boughs and boles splintered. The farther trees closed in like a cage. Impact shook, drummed, went to silence. Tom cut the engines and gee-field. Native gravity, one-half standard, hit him with giddiness. He unharnessed himself. The deck was canted. He slipped, skidded, got up and pounded down the companionway.

The manlock valves opened at Dagny's control while *Firedrake* was still moving. The drop in air pressure hurt her eardrums. She glimpsed foliage against a sky red with dawn, gray with scattering stormclouds. The earthquake landing cast her to hands and knees. She rose, leaning against a bulkhead. Yasmin stumbled into sight. The faceplate stood open before the terrified young visage. "Chaos! Dog that thing!" Dagny cried. "We'll be at top speed." She was not understood. She grabbed the girl and snapped the plate shut herself. "You . . . know . . . fly?" she asked in her fragment of Anglic.

"Yes. I think so." Yasmin wet her lips. Her radio voice was unsteady in the other's earplugs. "I mean . . . Lord Tom explained how."

"No practice, though?" Dagny muttered in Eylan. "You're about to get some." In Anglic: "Follow I."

She leaned out of the lock. High overhead she descried the gleam of a wheeling delta wing. The forest roared with wind. A little clearing surrounded the ship where trees had been flattened. Beyond the shadowy tangle of their trunks and limbs, their neighbors made a wall of night.

"Go!" Dagny touched her impeller stud and launched herself. She soared up. Flight was tricky in these gusts. Curving about, she saw Yasmin's suit helplessly cartwheel. She returned, caught the Sassanian girl, laid one arm around her waist and used the other to operate her drive units for her in the style of an instructor. They moved off, slowly and awkwardly.

A scream split the air. Dagny glanced as far behind as she could. Two of the aircraft were stooping . . . One took a hoverstance above *Firedrake,* the other came after her and Yasmin. She saw the muzzle of an energy gun and slammed the two impeller sets into full forward speed. Alone, she might have dived under the trees. But Yasmin hadn't the skill, and two couldn't slip through those dense branches side by side. Tom had told her to look after Yasmin, and Dagny was his sworn woman.

She tried to summon before her the children they had had together, tall sons and daughters, the baby grandchildren, and Skerrygarth, their home that was the dowry she had brought him, towers steadfast above a surf that played white among the reefs—

Explosion smashed at her. Had she been looking directly aft, she would have been dazzled into momentary blindness. As it was, the spots before her eyes and the tolling in her ears lasted for minutes. A wave of heat pushed through her armor.

She yelled, clung somehow to Yasmin, and kept the two of them going. Fury spoke again and again. It dwindled with distance as they fled.

Finally it was gone. By that time the women had covered some twenty kilometers, more or less eastward. The sea-level horizon of Nike was only about six kilometers off; and this was not flat country. They were well into morning light and far beyond view of the spaceship. Dagny thought she could yet identify an aircraft or two, but maybe those sparks were something else.

Beneath her continued hills and ravines, thickly wooded, and rushing streams. The volcano bulked in the north; smoke plumed from a frost-rimmed crater. Southward the land rolled down to the quicksilver sheet of the bay. Its shore was marshy—an effect of the very considerable tides that the nearer moon raised—but a village of neat wooden houses stood there on piles. Sailboats that doubtless belonged to fishermen were putting out. They must exist in such numbers because of a power shortage rather than extreme backwardness; for Dagny saw a good-sized motorship as well, crossing the bay from the gate to the lower, more populous south side. Its hull was of planks and its wake suggested the engine was minimal. At the same time, its lines and the nearly smokeless stack indicated competent design.

Here the wind had gentled, and the clouds were dissipating fast. (Odd to have such small cells of weather, she thought in a detached logical part of herself. Another indication of an atmosphere disturbed by violent solar conditions?) They shone ruddy-tinted in a deep purple vault of sky. The sun stood bright orange above mists that lay on the Nereid River delta.

"Down we go, lass," Dagny said, "before we're noticed."

"What happened? Lord Tom, where is he?"

The sob scratched at Dagny's nerves. She snapped, biting back tears: "Use your brain, you little beast, if it's anything except blubber! He went first to the main fire-control turret. When he saw us attacked, he cut loose with the ship's weapons. I don't see how he could have gotten all those bastards, though. If they didn't missile him, they've anyhow bottled him up. On *our* account!"

She realized she'd spoken entirely in Eylan. Suppressing a growl, she took over the controls of both suits. With no need for haste, she could ease them past the branches that tried to catch them, down to the forest floor.

"Now," she said in Anglic. "Out." Yasmin gaped. Dagny set the example by starting to remove her own armor.

"Wh-why?"

"Find us. In . . . in . . . in-stru-ments. Smell metal, no? Could be. Not take chance. We got—got to—" Dagny's vocabulary failed her. She had wanted to explain that if they stayed with the suits, they ran the risk of detection from afar. And even if the Nikeans didn't have that much technology left, whatever speed and protection the equipment lent wasn't worth its conspicuousness.

She was almost grateful for every difficulty. It kept her mind—somewhat—off the overwhelming fact that Tom, her Roan Tom, was gone.

Or maybe not. Just maybe not. He might be a prisoner, and she might in time contrive to bargain for his release. No, she would not remember what she had seen done to prisoners, here and there in her wanderings, by vengeful captors!

Were that the case, though. . . . Her hand went first to the blaster at one coveralled hip, next to the broad-bladed knife; and there it lingered. If she devoted the rest of her days to the project, and if the gods were kind, she might eventually get his murderers into her clutch.

Yasmin shed the last armor. She hugged herself and shivered in a chill breeze. "But we haven't any radios except in our helmets," she said. "How can he contact us?"

Dagny framed a reply: "If he'd been able to follow us, he'd already be here, or at least have called. I left my squealer circuit on, for him to track us by. That was safe; its frequency varies continuously, according to synchronized governors in both our suits. But he hasn't arrived, and we daren't stay near this much metal and resonant electronic stuff." Somehow, by words and gestures, she conveyed the gist. Meanwhile she filled their pockets with rations and medications, arranged the weapons beneath their garments, checked footgear. Last she hid the armor under leaf mould and canebrake, and took precise note of landmarks.

Yasmin's head drooped until the snarled dark locks covered her face. "I am so tired," she whispered.

Think I'm not? My lips are numb with it. "Go!" Dagny snapped.

She had to show the city-bred girl how to conceal their trail through the woods.

After a couple of hours, unhounded, the air warming and brightening around them, both felt a little better. It was up-and-down walking, but without much underbrush to combat, for the ground was densely carpeted with a soft mossy growth. Here and there stood clumps of fronded gymnosperm plants. This native vegetation was presumably chlorophyll-bearing, though its greenness was pale and had a curious bluish overcast. Otherwise the country had been taken over by the more efficient, highly developed species that man commonly brought with him. Oaks cast sun-speckled shadows; birches danced and glistened; primroses bloomed in meadows, where grass had overwhelmed a pseudo-moss that apparently had a competitive advantage only in shade. A sweet summery smell was about, and Yasmin spoke of her homeland. Even Dagny, bred in salt winds and unrestful watery leagues, felt a stirring of ancient instinct.

She was used to denser atmosphere. Sounds—sough in leaves, whistle of birds, rilling of brooks they crossed, thud of her own feet— came as if muffled to her ears; and on a steep upgrade, her heart was apt to flutter. But oxygen shortage was more or less compensated for by a marvelous, almost floating low-gravity lightness.

A good many animals were to be seen. Again, terrestroid forms had crowded out most of the primitive native species. With a whole ecology open to them, they were now in the process of explosive evolution. A few big insect-like flyers, an occasional awkward amphibian, gave glimpses of the original biosphere. But thrushes, bulbuls, long-winged hawks rode the wind. Closer down swarmed butterflies and bees. A wild boar, tusked and rangy, caused Dagny to draw her blaster; but he went by, having perhaps learned to fear man. Splendid was the more distant sight of mustangs, carabao, an entire herd of antlered six-legged tanithars.

A measure of peace came upon Dagny, until at last she could say, "All right, we stop, eat, rest."

They sat under a broad-spreading hilltop cedar, that hid them from above while openness, halfway down the heights to the forest, afforded ample ground vision. They had made for the bay and were thus at a lower altitude. The waters sheened to south, ridges and mountains stood sharply outlined to north. In this clear air, the blueness of their distance was too slight to hide the basic ocherous tint of rocks and soil.

Dagny broke out a packet of dehydrate. She hesitated for a moment before adding water to the tray from a canteen she had filled en route. Yasmin, slumped exhausted against the tree trunk, asked, "What is the matter?" And, her eyes and mind wandering a little, she tried to smile. "See, yonder, apples. They are green but they can be dessert."

"No," Dagny said.

"What? Why not?"

"Heavy metal." Dagny scowled. How to explain? "Young planet. Dense. Lots heavy metals. Not good."

"Young? But—"

"Look around you," Dagny wanted to say. "That sun, putting out radiation like an early Type F—in amount—but the color and spectral distribution are late G or early K. I've never seen anything like it. The way it flares, I don't believe it's quite stabilized at its proper position on the main sequence yet. Because of anomalous chemical composition, I suppose. You get that with very young suns, my dear. They've condensed out of an interstellar medium made rich in metals by the thermonuclear furnaces of earlier star generations. Or so I've been told.

"I know for fact that planets with super-abundant heavy elements can be lethal to men. So much . . . oh, arsenic, selenium, radioactives. Slow poison in some areas, fast and horrible death in others. This water, that fruit, may have stuff to kill us."

But she lacked words or inclination. She said, "Iron. Makes red in rocks. No? Lots iron. Could be lots bad metal. Young planet. Lots air, no?"

She had, in truth, never heard of a dwarf world like this, getting such an amount of sunlight, that had hung onto a proper atmosphere. Evidently, she thought, there had not been time for the gas to leak into space. The primitive life forms were another proof of a low age.

☼   ☼   ☼

Beyond this, she didn't reason. She did not have the knowledge on which to base logic, nor did she have the scientific way of thinking. What little cosmology and cosmogony she had learned, for instance, was in the form of vague, probably distorted tradition— latter-day myth. And she was intelligent enough to recognize this.

Once, she imagined, any Imperial space officer had been educated in the details of astrophysics and planetology. And he would have seen, or read about, a far greater variety of suns than today's petty travels encompassed. So he would have known immediately what sort of system this was; or, if not, he would have known how to find out.

But that was centuries ago. The information might not actually be lost. It might even be moldering in the damp, uncatalogued library of her own Skerrygarth. Surely parts of it were taught in the universities of more civilized planets, though as a set of theoretical ideas, to be learned by rote without any need for genuine comprehension.

Practical spacefarers, like her and Tom, didn't learn it. They didn't get the chance. A rudiment of knowledge was handed down to them, largely by word of mouth, the minimum they needed for survival.

And speaking of survival—

She reached her decision. "Eat," she said. "Drink." She took the first sample. The water had a woodsy taste, nothing unfamiliar.

After all, humans did flourish here. Perhaps they were adapted to metal-rich soil. But the adaptation could scarcely be enormous. Had that been the case, terrestroid species would not be so abundant and dominant, after a mere thousand years or whatever on this planet.

Thus Nike was biochemically safe—at least, in this general region—at least, for a reasonable time. Perhaps, if outworlders stayed as long as one or two decades, they might suffer from cumulative poisoning. But she needn't worry that far ahead, when a hunt was on immediately and when Tom—

Grimly, she fueled her body. Afterward she stood watch while Yasmin caught a nap. What she thought about was her own affair.

When the Sassanian awoke, they held a lengthy conference. The order Dagny had to issue was not complicated:

"We're in enemy territory. But I don't believe it covers the whole planet, or even the whole area between this sea and the next one east. 'The Engineer of Hanno' is a typical feudal title. I've not heard before that 'engineer' changed meaning to the equivalent of 'duke' or 'king,' but it's easy to see how that could've happened, and I've met odder cases of wordshift. Well, our darling Engineer made it plain he regarded us as either the worst menace or the juiciest prey that'd come by in years. Maybe both. So he'd naturally call his full air power, or most of it, against us. Which amounted to half a dozen little craft, with gravmotors so weak they need wings! And look at those sailboats, and the absence of real cities, and the fact there's scarcely any radio in use . . . yes, they've fallen far on Nike. I'm sure that raid from space was only the latest blow. They must have a small half-educated class left, and some technicians of a sort; but the bulk of the people must've been poor and ignorant for many generations.

"And divided. I swear they must be divided. I've seen so many societies like this, I can practically identify them by smell. A crazy-quilt pattern of feudalisms and sovereignties, any higher authority a ghost. If as rich a planet as this one potentially is were united, it'd have made a far greater recovery by now, after the space attack, than it has done. Or it would have beaten the raiders off at least.

"So, if we have enemies here in Hanno, we probably have automatic friends somewhere else. And not dreadfully far away. At any rate, we're not likely to be pursued beyond the nearest border, nor extradited back here. In fact, the Engineer's rivals are apt to be quite alarmed when they learn he's clapped hands on a real space warship. They're apt to join forces to get it away from him. Which'll make you and me, my dear, much-sought-after advisors. We may or may not be able to get Tom back unhurt. I vow the gods a hundred Blue Giant seabeasts if we do! But we'll be free, even powerful.

"Or so I hope. We've nothing to go on but hope. And courage and wits and endurance. Have you those, Yasmin? Your life was too easy until now. But he asked me to care for you.

"You'll have to help. Our first and foremost job is to get out of Hanno. And I don't speak their damned language for diddly squat. You'll talk for both of us. Can you? We'll plan a story. Then, if and when you see there must be a false note in it, you'll have to cover— at once—with no ideas from me. Can you do that, Yasmin? You must!"

—But conference was perforce by single words, signs, sketches in the red dirt. It went slowly. And it was repeated, over and over, in every possible way, to make certain they understood each other.

In the end, however, Yasmin nodded. "Yes," she said, "I will try, as God gives me strength . . . and as you do." The voice was almost inaudible, and the eyes she turned on the bigger, older woman were dark with awe.

In midafternoon they reached a farm. Its irregular fields were enclosed by forest, through which a cart track ran to join a dirt road that, in turn, twisted over several kilometers until it entered the fisher village.

Dagny spent minutes peering from a thicket. Beside her, Yasmin tried to guess what evaluations the Krakener was making. *I should begin to learn these ways of staying alive,* the Sassanian thought. *More is involved than my own welfare. I don't want to remain a burden on my companions, an actual danger to them.*

And to think, not one year ago I took for granted the star rovers were ignorant, dirty, cruel, quarrelsome barbarians!

Yasmin had been taught about philosophic objectivity, but she was too young to practice it consistently. Her universe having been wrecked, herself cast adrift, she naturally seized upon the first thing that felt like a solid rock and began to make it her emotional foundation. And that thing happened to be Roan Tom and Dagny Od's-daughter.

Not that she had intellectual illusions. She knew very well that the Krakeners had come to help the Shah of Sassania because the Pretender was allied with enemies of theirs. And she knew that, if successful, they would exact good pay. She had heard her father grumble about it.

Nevertheless, the facts were: First, compatriots of hers, supposedly civilized, supposedly above the greed and short-sightedness that elsewhere had destroyed civilization . . . had proven themselves every bit as animalistic. Second, the star-rover garrison in Anushirvan turned out to be jolly, well-scrubbed, fairly well-behaved. Indeed, they were rather glamorous to a girl who had never been past her planet's moon. Third, they had stood by their oaths, died in their ships and at their guns, for her alien people. Fourth, two of them had saved her life, and offered her the best and most honorable way they could think of to last out her days. Fifth (or foremost?), Tom was now her husband.

She was not exactly infatuated with him. A middle-aged, battle-beaten, one-eyed buccaneer had never entered her adolescent dreams. But he was kind in his fashion, and a skillful lover, and . . . and perhaps she did care for him in a way beyond friendship . . . if he was alive—oh, let him be alive!

In any event, here was Dagny. She certainly felt grief like a sword in her. But she hid it, planned, guided, guarded. She had stood in the light of a hundred different suns, had warred, wandered, been wife and mother and living sidearm. She knew everything worth knowing (what did ancient texts count for?) except one language. And she was so brave that she trusted her life to what ability an awkward weakling of a refugee might possess.

Please don't let me fail her.

Thus Yasmin looked forth too and tried to make inferences from what she saw.

The house and outbuildings were frame, not large, well-built but well-weathered. Therefore they must have stood here for a good length of time. Therefore Imperial construction methods—alloy, prestressed concrete, synthetics, energy webs—had long been out of general use in these parts, probably everywhere on Nike. That primitiveness was emphasized by the agromech system. A couple of horses drew a haycutter. It also was wooden; even the revolving blades were simply edged with metal. From its creaking and bouncing, the machine had neither wheel bearings nor springs. A man drove it. Two half-grown boys, belike his sons, walked after. They used wooden-tined rakes to order the windrows. The people, like the animals, were of long slim deep-chested build, brown-haired and fair-complexioned. Their garments were coarsely woven smock and trousers.

No weapons showed, which suggested that the bay region was free of bandits and vendettas. Nevertheless Dagny did not approach. Instead, she led a cautious way back into the woods and thence toward the house, so that the buildings screened off view of the hayfield.

The Krakener woman scowled. "Why?" she muttered.

"Why what . . . my lady?"

"Why make—" Dagny's hands imitated whirling blades. "Here. Planet . . . canted? . . . little. No cold?"

"Oh. Do you mean, why do they bother making hay? Well, there must be times when their livestock can't pasture."

Dagny understood. Her nod was brusque. "Why that?"

"Um-m-m . . . oh, dear, let me think. Lord Tom explained to me what he—what you two had learned about this planet. Yes. Not much axial tilt. I suppose not an unusually eccentric orbit. So the seasons oughtn't to be very marked. And we are in a rather low latitude anyway, on a seacoast at that. It should never get too cold for grass. Too dry? No, this *is* midsummer time. And, well, they'd hardly export hay to other areas, would they?"

Dagny shrugged.

It is such a strange world, Yasmin thought. *All wrong. Too dense. That is, if it had a great many heavy metals, humans would never have settled here permanently. So what makes it dense should be a core of iron, nickel and things, squeezed into compact quantum states. The kind that terrestroid planets normally have. Yes, and the formation of a true core causes tectonic processes, vulcanism, the outgassing of a primitive atmosphere and water. Later we get chemical evolution, life, photosynthesis, free oxygen—*

*But Nike is too small for that! It's Mars type. We have a Mars type planet in our own system—*oh, lost and loved star that shines upon Sassania—*and it's got a bare wisp of unbreathable air. Professor Nasruddin explained to us. If a world is small, it has weak gravity. So the differential migration of elements down toward the center, that builds a distinct core, is too slow. So few gas molecules get unlocked from mineral combination by heat. . . . Nike isn't possible!*

(How suddenly, shockingly real came back to her the lecture hall, and the droning voice, young heads bent above notebooks, sunlight that streamed in through arched windows, and the buzz of bees, odor of roses, a glimpse of students strolling across a greensward that stretched between beautiful buildings.)

Dagny's fingers clamped about Yasmin's arm. "Heed! Fool!"

Yasmin started from her reverie. They were almost at the house. "Heavens! I'm sorry."

"Talk well." Dagny's voice was bleak with doubt of her.

Yasmin swallowed and stepped forth into the yard. She felt dizzy. The knocking of her heart came remote as death. Penned cows, pigs, fowl were like things in a dream. There was something infinitely horrible about the windmill that groaned behind the barn.

Neither shot nor shout met her. The door opened a crack, and the woman who peered out did so fearfully.

Why, she's nervous of us!

Relief passed through Yasmin in a wave of darkness. But an odd, alert calm followed. She perceived with utter clarity. Her thoughts went in three or four directions at once, all coherent. One chain directed her to smile, extend unclenched hands, and say: "Greeting to you, good lady." Another observed that the boards of the house were not nailed but pegged together. A third paid special heed to the windmill. It too was almost entirely of wood, with fabric sails. She saw that it pumped water into an elevated cistern, whence wooden pipes ran to the house and a couple of sheds. Attachments outside one of the latter indicated that there the water, when turned on, drove various machines, like the stone quern she could see.

No atomic or electric energy, then. Nor even solar or combustion power. And yet the knowledge of these things existed: if not complete, then sufficient to make aircraft possible, radio, occasional motorships, doubtless some groundcars. Why was it no longer applied by the common people? The appearance of this farm and of the fisher village as seen from a distance suggested moderate prosperity. The Engineer's rule could not be unduly harsh.

Well, the answer must be, Nike's economy had collapsed so far that hardly anyone could afford real power equipment.

But why not? Sunlight, wood, probably coal and petroleum were abundant. A simple generator, some batteries. . . . Such things took metal. A broken-down society might not have the resources to extract much. . . . Nonsense! Elements like iron, copper, lead, and uranium were surely simple to obtain, even after a thousand years of industrialization. Hadn't Dagny, who knew, said this was a young planet? Weren't young planets metal-rich?

Meanwhile the woman mumbled, "Day. You're from out-country?"

"Yes," Yasmin said. No use trying to conceal that. Quite apart from accent and garments (the Hannoan woman wore a broad-sleeved embroidered blouse and a skirt halfway to her ankles), they were not of the local racial type. But it was presumably not uniform over the whole planet. One could play on a peasantry's likely ignorance of anything beyond its own neighborhood.

"I am from Kraken," Yasmin said. "My friend is from Sassania." If no one on those comparatively cosmopolitan planets had heard of Nike, vice versa was certain. "We were flying on a mission when our aircraft crashed in the hills."

"That . . . was the flare . . . noises . . . this early-day?" the woman asked. Yasmin confirmed it. The woman drew breath and made a shaky sign in the air. "High 'Uns I thank! We feared, we, 'twas *them* come back."

Obvious who "they" were, and therefore impossible to inquire about them. A little hysterical with relief, the wife flung wide her door. "Enter you! Enter you! I call the men."

"No need, we thank you," Yasmin said quickly. The fewer who saw them and got a chance later to wonder and talk about them, the better. "Nor time. We must hurry. Do you know of our countries?"

"Well, er, far off." The woman was embarrassed. Yasmin noted that the room behind her was neat, had a look of primitive well-being—but how primitive! Two younger children stared half frightened from an inner doorway. "Yes, far, and I, poor farm-wife, well, hasn't so much as been to the Silva border—"

"That's the next country?" Yasmin pounced.

"Why . . . next cavedom, yes, 'tother side of the High Sawtooths east'ard. . . . Well, we're both under the Emp'ror, but they do say as the Prester of Silva's not happy with our good Engineer. . . . You! A-travel like men!"

"They have different customs in our part of the world," Yasmin said. "More like the Empire. Not your Empire. The real one, the Terran Empire, when women could do whatever a man might." That was a safe claim. Throughout its remnants, no one questioned anything wonderful asserted about the lost Imperium—except, perhaps, a few unpleasant scholars, who asked why it had fallen if it had been so great. "Yes, we're from far parts. My friend speaks little Anglic. They don't, in her country." That was why Dagny, clever Dagny, had said they should switch national origins. Krakener place names sounded more Anglic than Sassanian ones did, and Yasmin needed a ready-made supply.

"We have to get on with our mission as fast as possible," she said. "But we know nothing about these lands."

"Storm blow you off track?" the woman queried. As she relaxed, she became more intelligent. "Bad storm-time coming, we think. Lots rain already. Hope the hay's not ruined before it dries."

"Yes, that's what happened." *Thank you, madam, for inventing my explanation.* Yasmin could not resist probing further the riddle of Nike. "Do you really expect many storms?"

One child hustled after his father while they went in and took leather-covered chairs. The woman made a large to-do about coffee and cakes. Her name was Elanor, she said, and her husband was Petar Landa, a freeholder. One must not think them backwoods people. They were just a few hours from the town of Sea Gate, which lay nigh the Great Cave itself and was visited by ships from this entire coast. Yes, the Landa family went there often; they hadn't missed a Founders' Festival in ten years, except for the year after the friends came, when there had been none—

"You only needed a year to recover from something like that?" Yasmin exclaimed.

Dagny showed alarm, laying a hand on the Sassanian's and squeezing hard. Elanor Landa was surprised. "Well, Sea Gate wasn't hit. Not that important. Nearest place was . . . I forgot, all the old big cities went, they say, bombed after being looted, but seems to me I heard Terrania was nearest to Hanno. Far off, though, and no man I know was ever there, because 'twas under the Mayor of Bollen and he wasn't any camarado to us western cavedoms, they say—"

Yasmin saw her mistake. Unthinkingly, she had taken "year" to mean a standard, Terran year. It came the more natural to her because Sassania's wasn't very different. *Well*, thought the clarified brain within her, *we came here to get information that might help us escape. And surely, if we're to pretend to be Nikeans, we must know how the planet revolves.*

"I've forgotten," she said. "Exactly when was the attack?"

Elanor was not startled. Such imprecision was common in a largely illiterate people. Indeed, it was somewhat astonishing that she should say, "A little over five years back. Five and a quarter, abs'lut, come Petar's father's birthday. I remember, for we planned a feast, and then we heard the news. We had radio news then. Everyone was so scared. Later I saw one black ship roar over us, and waited for my death, but it just went on."

"I think we must use a different calendar from you in Kraken," Yasmin said. "And—being wealthier, you understand—not that Hanno *isn't*—but we did suffer worse. We lost records and—Well, let's see if Kraken and Sassania were attacked on the same day you heard about it. That was . . . let me think . . . dear me, now, how many days in a year?"

"What? Why, why, five hundred and ninety-one."

Yasmin allayed Elanor's surprise by laughing: "Of course. I was simply trying to recollect if an intercalary date came during the period since."

"A what?"

"You know. The year isn't an exact number of days long. So they have to put in an extra day or month or something, every once in a while." That was a reasonable bet.

It paid off, too. Elanor spoke of an extra day every eleventh Nikean year. Yasmin related how in Kraken they added a month— "What do you call the moons hereabouts? . . . I mean by a month, the time it takes for them both to get back to the same place in the sky. . . . We add an extra one every twentieth year." Her arithmetic was undoubtedly wrong, but who was going to check? The important point was that Nike circled its sun in 591 days of 25.5 hours each, as near as made no difference.

And hadn't much in the way of seasons, but did suffer from irregular, scarcely predictable episodes when the sun grew noticeably hotter or cooler.

And was poor in heavy metals. Given all the prior evidence, what Yasmin wormed from the chattersome Elanor was conclusive. Quite likely iron oxides accounted for the basic color. But they were too diffuse to be workable. Metals had never been mined on this globe; they were obtained electrochemically from the sea and from clays.

(Aluminum, beryllium, magnesium and the like; possibly a bit of heavy elements too, but only a bit. For the most part, iron, copper, silver, uranium, etc., had been imported from outsystem, in exchange for old-fashioned Terrestrial agroproducts that must have commanded good prices on less favored worlds. This would explain why, to the very present, Nike had such a pastoral character.)

The Empire fell. The starships came less and less often. Demoralization ruined the colonies in their turn; planets broke up politically; in the aftermath, most industry was destroyed, and the social resources were no longer there to build it afresh. Today, on Nike, heavy metals were gotten entirely through reclaiming scrap. Consequently they were too expensive for anything but military and the most vital civilian uses. Even the lighter elements came dear; some extractor plants remained, but not enough.

Elanor did not relate this directly. But she didn't need to. Trying to impress her distinguished guests, she made a parade of setting an aluminum coffeepot on the ceramic stove and mentioning the cost. (A foreigner could plausibly ask what that amounted to in real wages. It was considerable.) And, yes, Petar's grandmother had had a lot of ironware in her kitchen. When he inherited, Petar was offered enormous sums for his share. But he had it made into cutting-edge implements. He cared less about money than about good tools, Petar did. Also for his wife. See, ladies, see right here, I use a real steel knife.

"Gold," Dagny said, low and harsh in Yasmin's ear. "Animals, buy, ride."

The younger girl jerked to alertness. Tired, half lulled by Elanor's millwheel voice, she had drifted off into contemplation. Dagny said this was a young world. Nevertheless it was metal-poor. The paradox had an answer. This system could have formed in the galactic halo, where stars were few and the interstellar dust and gas were thin, little enriched. Yes, that must be the case. It had drifted into this spiral arm. . . . But wouldn't it, then, have an abnormal proper motion? Tom hadn't mentioned observing any such thing. Nor had he said there was anything peculiar about Nike's own orbit. Yet he had remarked on less striking facts. . . .

"Tell! Buy!"

Yasmin nodded frantically. "I understand. I understand." They carried a number of Sassanian gold coins. In an age when interstellar currency and credit had vanished, the metal had resumed its ancient economic function. The value varied from place to place, but was never low, and should be fabulous on Nike.

"Good lady," Yasmin said, "we are grateful for your kindness. But we have imposed too much. We should not take any of your men away from the hayfields when storms may be coming. If you will spare us two horses, we can make our own way to Vala and thence, of course, to your Engineer."

Like fun we will! We'll turn east. Maybe we'll ride horseback, maybe we'll take passage on a river boat—whatever looks safest—but we're bound for his enemy, the Prester of Silva!

"We'll pay for them," Yasmin said. "Our overlords provided us well with money. See." She extended a coin. "Will this buy two horses and their gear?"

Elanor gasped. She made a sign again, sat down and fanned herself. Her youngest child sensed his mother's agitation and whimpered.

"Is that gold?" she breathed. "Wait. Till Petar comes. He comes soon. We ask him."

That was logical. But suppose the man got suspicious.

Yasmin glanced back at Dagny. The Krakener made an imperceptible gesture. Beneath their coveralls were holstered energy weapons.

No! We can't slaughter a whole, helpless family!

I hope we won't need to.

I won't! Not for anything!

Tom reached the fire-control turret as two aircraft peeled off their squadron and dove.

The skyview was full of departing stormclouds, tinged bloody with dawn. Against them, his space-armored women looked tiny. Not so their hunters. Those devilfish shapes swelled at an appalling speed. Tom threw himself into a manual-operation seat and punched for Number Two blastcannon. A cross-hair screen lit for him with what that elevated weapon "saw." He twisted verniers. The auxiliary motors whirred. The vision spun giddily. There . . . the couple was separating . . . one to keep guard on him, its mate in a swoop after Dagny and Yasmin. Tom got the latter centered and pressed the discharge button.

The screen stepped down the searing brightness of the energy bolt. Through the open manlock crashed the thunderclap that followed. The Hannoan craft exploded into red-hot shards that rained down upon the trees.

"Gotcha!" Tom exulted. He fired two or three more times, raking toward the other boat where it hung on its negafield some fifty meters aloft. His hope was to scare it off and bluff its mates into holding their bombs—or whatever they had to drop on him. He didn't want to kill again. The first shot had looked necessary if the girls were to live. But why add to the grudge against him?

Not that he expected to last another five minutes.

No! Wait! Tom swiveled around to another set of controls. Why hadn't he thought of this at once?

The nearby pilot had needed a couple of seconds to recover from the shock of what happened to his companion. Now he was bound hastily back upward. He was too late. Tom focused a tractor beam on him. Its generator hummed with power. Ozone stung the nostrils; rewiring job needed, a distant aspect of Tom took note. Most of him was being a fisherman. He'd gotten his prey, and on a heavy line— the force locked onto the air-boat was meant to grab kilotons moving at cosmic velocities—but his catch was a man-eater. And he wanted to land it just so.

The vessel battled futilely to escape. Tom pushed it down near *Firedrake*'s hull, into the jumble of broken trees and canebrake that his own landing had made. Their branches probably damaged wings and fuselage, but their leaves, closing in above, hid any details of what was going on from the pilots overhead. Having jammed his capture against a fence of logs and brush, he held it there with a beam sufficiently narrow that the cockpit canopy wouldn't be pulled shut. Quickly, with a second tractor-pressor projection, he rearranged the tangle in the clearing, shifting trunks, snapping limbs and tossing them about, until he had a fairly good view through a narrow slot that wouldn't benefit observers in heaven. He trusted they were too poorly instrumented—or too agitated, or both—to see how useful the arrangement was for him, and would take the brief stirring they noticed as a natural result of a crash, heaped wood collapsing into a new configuration.

Thereafter he left the turret and made his way to the forward manlock. It was rather high off the ground; the access ladder had automatically extruded, plunging down into the foliage that fluttered shadowy around the base of the hull. Tom placed himself in the chamber, invisible from the sky, hardly noticeable from beneath, and studied his fish more closely.

Fish: yes, indeed. In two senses.

The pilot was that youthful squadron leader with whom he had spoken before. Tom tuned his helmet radio in on the frantic talk that went between the downed man, his companions and Karol Weyer in Sea Gate. He gathered they had no prehensile force-beams on Nike, and only vaguely inferred the existence of such things from their experience with "friends."

Friends? The raiders from space? Tom scowled.

But he couldn't stop to think beyond this moment. His notion had been to take a man and an aircraft—the latter probably the more highly valued—as hostages. They'd not nuke him now. But as for what followed, he must play his cards as he drew them. At worst, he'd gotten the girls free. Perhaps he could strike some kind of bargain, though it was hard to tell why any Nikean should feel bound to keep a promise made to an outworlder. At best. . . .

Hoy!

The canopy slid back. Tom got a look at the plane's interior. There was room for two in the cockpit, if one scrooched and aft of the seat was a rack of—something or other, he couldn't see what, but it didn't seem welded in place. His pulse leaped.

The pilot emerged, in a dive flattening himself at once behind a fallen tree. Weyer had said after several fruitless attempts to get a reply from Tom: "You in the ship! You killed one of ours. Another, and your whole ship goes. Do you seize me?" (That must mean "understand.") Next, to the flyboy: "Fish Aran, use own discretion."

So the young man, deciding he couldn't sit where he was forever, was trying to reach the woods. That took nerve. Tom laid his telescope to his good eye—his faceplate was open—and searched out details. Fiber helmet, as already noted; green tunic with cloth insignia, no metal; green trousers tucked into leather boots; a sidearm, but no indication of a portable communicator or, for that matter, a watch. Tom made sure his transmitter was off, trod a little further out in the lock chamber, and bawled from lungs that had often shouted against a gale at sea:

"Halt where you are! Or I'll chop the legs from under you!"

The pilot had been about to scuttle from his place. He froze. Slowly, he raised his gaze. Tom's armored shape was apparent to him, standing in the open lock, but not discernible by his mates. Likewise the blaster Tom aimed. The pilot's hand hovered at the butt of his own weapon.

"Slack off, son," the captain advised. "You wouldn't come near me with that pipgun—I said 'pip,' not even 'pop'—before I sizzled you. And I don't want to. C'mon and let's talk. That's right; on your feet; stroll over here and use this nice ladder."

The pilot obeyed, though his scramble across the log jam was hardly a stroll. As he started up, Tom said: "They'll see in a minute what you're doin', I s'pose, when you come above the foliage. . . . Belay, there, *I* can see you quite well already. . . . I want you to draw your gun, as if you'd decided to come aboard and reconnoiter 'stead o' headin' for the nearest beer hall. Better not try shootin' at me, though. My friends'd cut you down."

The Hannoan paused a moment, rigid with outrage, before he yielded. His face, approaching, showed pale and wet in the first light. He swung himself into the lock chamber. For an instant, he and Tom stood with guns almost in each other's bellies. The spaceman's gauntleted left hand struck like a viper, edge on, and the Nikean weapon clattered to the deck.

"You—you broke my wrist!" The pilot lurched back, clutching his arm and wheezing.

"I think not. I gauge these things pretty good if I do say so myself. And I do. March on ahead o' me, please." Tom conducted his prisoner into the passageway, gathering the fallen pistol en route. It was a slug-thrower, ingeniously constructed with a minimum of steel. Tom found the magazine release and pressed it one-handed. The clip held ten high-caliber bullets. But what the hoo-hah! The cartridge cases were wood, the slugs appeared to be some heavy ceramic, with a mere skirt of soft metal for the rifling in the barrel to get a grip on!

"No wonder you came along meek-like," Tom said. "You never could've dented me."

The prisoner looked behind him. Footfalls echoed emptily around his words. "I think you are alone," he said.

"Aye-ya. I told you my chums *could* wiff you . . . if they were present. In here." Tom indicated the fire control turret. "Sit yourself. Now, I'm goin' t'other side o' this room and shuck my armor, which is too hot and heavy for informal wear. Don't get ideas about plungin' across the deck at me. I can snatch my blaster and take aim quicker'n that."

The young man crouched in a chair and shuddered. His eyes moved like a trapped animal's, around and around the crowding machines. "What do you mean to do?" he rattled. "You can't get free. You're alone. Soon the Engineer's soldiers come, with 'tillery, and ring you."

"I know. We should be gone by then, however. Look here, uh, what's your name?"

An aristocrat's pride firmed the voice. "Yanos Aran, third son of Rober Aran, who's chief computerman to Engineer Weyer's self. I am a fish in the air force of Hanno—and you are a dirty friend!"

"Maybe so. Maybe not." Tom stripped fast, letting the pieces lie where they fell. He hated to abandon his suit, but it was too bulky and perhaps too detectable for his latest scheme.

"Why not? Didn't you business Evin Sato?"

"You mean that plane I gunned?"

"Yes. Evin Sato was my camarado."

"Well, I'm sorry about that, but wasn't he fixin' to shoot two o' my people? We came down frien—intendin' no harm, and you set on us like hungry eels. I don't want to hurt you, Yanos, lad. In fact, I hope betwixt us we can maybe settle this whole affair. But—" Tom's features assumed their grimmest look which had terrified stronger men than Aran— "you try any fumblydiddles and you'll find out things about friendship that your mother never told you."

The boy seemed to crumple. "I . . . yes, I slave me to you," he whispered.

He wouldn't stay crumpled long, Tom knew. He must be the scion of a typical knightly class. Let him recover from the dismay of the past half hour and the unbalancing effect of being surrounded by unknown power and he'd prove a dangerous pet. It was necessary to use him while he remained useable.

Wherefore Tom, having peeled down to coveralls, gave him his orders in a few words. A slight demurral fetched a brutal cuff on the cheek. "And if I shoot you with this blaster, short range low intensity," Tom added, "you won't have a neat hole drilled through your heart. You'll be cooked alive, medium rare, so you'll be some days about dying. Seize me?"

He didn't know if he'd really carry out his threat, come worst to worst. Probably not.

Having switched off the tractor beam, he brought Aran far down into the ship, to an emergency lock near the base. It was well hidden by leaves. The vague dawn-light aided concealment. They crept forth, and thence to the captured aircraft.

It had taken a beating, Tom saw. The wingtips were crumpled, the fuselage punctured. (The covering was mostly some fluorosynthetic. What a metal shortage they must have here!) But it ought to fly anyhow, after a fashion. Given a gravity drive, however weak, airfoils were mainly for auxiliary lift and control.

"In we go," Tom said. He squeezed his bulky form behind Aran's seat so that it concealed him. The blaster remained in his fist, ready to fire through the back.

But there was no trouble. Aran followed instructions. He called his squadron: "—Yes, you're right, I did 'cide I'd try looking at the ship. And no one! None aboard. 'Least, none I saw. Maybe robos fought us, or maybe the rest of the crew got away on foot, not seen. I found a switch, looked like a main powerline breaker, and opened it. Maybe now I can rise."

And he started the engine. The airboat climbed, wobbling on its damaged surfaces. A cheer sounded from the receiver. Tom wished he could see the face in the screen, but he dared not risk being scanned himself.

"You land, if Engineer Weyer approves," Aran directed. "Go aboard. Be careful. Me, best I take my craft back to base immediately."

Tom had figured that would be a natural move for a pilot on Nike, even a squadron leader. A plane was obviously precious. It couldn't get to the repair shop too fast.

He must now hope that Aran's expression and tone didn't give him away. The "fish" was no actor. But everyone was strung wire-taut. Nobody noticed how much more perturbed this fellow was. After a few further words had passed, Aran signed off and started west.

"Keep low," Tom said. "Like you can't get much altitude. Soon's you're out o' their sight here, swing north. Find us a good secret place to land. I think we got a bucketful to say to each other, no?"

One craft was bound eagerly down. The rest stayed at hover. They'd soon learn that the spaceship was, indeed, deserted. Hence they wouldn't suspect what had happened to Aran until he failed to report. However, that wasn't a long time. He, Roan Tom, had better get into a bolt-hole quick!

The volcano's northern side was altogether wild. On the lower flanks, erosion had created a rich lava soil and vegetation was dense. For some reason it was principally native Nikean, dominated by primitive but tree-sized "ferns." An antigrav flyer could push its way under their soft branches and come to rest beneath the overhang of a cliff, camouflaged against aerial search.

Tom climbed out of the cockpit and stretched to uncramp himself. The *abri* was rough stone at his back, the forest brooded shadowy before him. Flecks of copper sunlight on bluish-green fronds and the integuments of bumbling giant pseudo-insects made the scene look as if cast in metal. But water rilled nearby, and the smells of damp growth were organic enough.

"C'mon, son. Relax with me," Tom invited. "I won't eat you. 'Specially not if you've packed along a few sandwiches."

"Food? No." Yanos Aran spoke as stiffly as he moved.

"Well, then we'll have to make do with what iron rations I got in my pockets." Tom sighed. He flopped down on a chair-sized boulder, took out pipe and tobacco pouch, and consoled himself with smoke.

He needed consolation. He was a fugitive on an unknown planet. His ship had been taken, his wives were out of touch; an attempt to raise Dagny on the plane's transmitter, using a Krakener military band, had brought silence. She must already have discarded her telltale space armor.

"And all 'count of a stupid lingo mistake!" he groaned.

Aran sat down on another rock and regarded him with eyes in which alertness was replacing fear. "You say you are not truly our friend?"

"Not in your sense. Look, where I come from, the Anglic word 'friend' means . . . well, fellow you like, and who likes you. When I told your Engineer we were friends, I wanted him to understand we didn't aim him any harm, in fact we could do good business with him."

"Business!" Aran exploded.

"Whoops-la. Sorry. Said the wrong thing again, didn't I?"

"I think," Aran replied slowly, "what you have in mind is what we would call 'change.' You wanted to change goods and services with our people. And to you, a 'friend' is what we call a 'camarado.'"

"Reckon so. What're your definitions?"

"A friend is a space raider such as did business with our planet some five years agone. They destroyed the last great cities we had left from the Terran Empire days, and none knows how many million Nikeans they killed."

"Ah, now we're gettin' somewhere. Let's straighten out for me what did happen."

Aran's hostility had not departed, but it had diminished. He was intelligent and willing to cooperate within the limits of loyalty to his own folk. Information rushed out of him.

Nike did not appear to be unique, except in its planetology. Tom asked about that. Aran was surprised. Was his world so unusual per se?

He knew only vague traditions and a few fragmentary written accounts of other planetary systems. Nike was discovered and colonized five hundred-odd years ago—about a thousand standard years. It was always a backwater. Fundamentally agricultural because of its shortage of heavy metals, it had no dense population, no major libraries or schools. Thus, when the Empire fell apart, knowledge vanished more quickly and thoroughly here than most places. Nikean society disintegrated; what had been an Imperial sub-province became hundreds of evanescent kingdoms, fiefs and tribes.

The people were on their way back, Aran added defiantly. Order and a measure of prosperity had been restored in the advanced countries. As yet, they paid mere lip service to an "Emperor," but the concept of global government did now exist. Technology was improving. Ancient apparatus was being repaired and put back into service, or being reproduced on the basis of what diagrams and manuals could be found. Schemes had been broached for making interplanetary ships. Some dreamers had hoped that in time the Nikeans might end their centuries-long isolation themselves, by re-inventing the lost theory and practice of hyperdrive.

For that, of course, as for much else, the tinkering of technicians was insufficient. Basic scientific research must be done. But this was also slowly being started. Had not Aran remarked that his father was head computerman in the Engineer's court? He used a highly sophisticated machine which had survived to the present day and which two generations of modern workers had finally learned how to operate.

Its work at present was mainly in astronomy. While some elementary nucleonics had been preserved through the dark ages—being essential to the maintenance of what few atomic power plants remained—practically all information about the stars had vanished. Today's astronomers had learned that their sun (as distinguished from their planet) was not typical of its neighborhood. It was unpredictably variable, and not even its ground state could be fitted onto the main sequence diagram. No one had yet developed a satisfactory theory as to what made this sun abnormal, but the consensus was that it must be quite a young star.

One geologist had proposed checking this idea by establishing the age of the planet. Radioactive minerals should provide a clock. The attempt had failed, partly because of the near-nonexistence of isotopes with suitable half-lives and partly, Tom suspected, because of lousy laboratory technique. But passing references in old books did seem to confirm the idea held by latter-day theorists, that stars and planets condensed out of interstellar gas and dust. If so, Nike's sun could be very new, as cosmic time went, and not yet fully stabilized.

"Aye, I'd guess that myself," Tom nodded.

"Good! Important to be sure. You seize, can we make a mathematical model of our sun, then we can predict its variations. Right? And we will never predict our weather until then. Unforeseen storms are our greatest natural woe. Hanno's self, a southerly land, can get killing frosts any season."

"Well, don't take my authority, son. I'm no scientist. The Imperialists must've known for sure what kind o' star they had here. And a scholar of astronomy, from a planet where they still keep universities and such, should could tell you. But not me." Tom struck new fire to his pipe. "Uh, we'd better stay with less fun topics. Like those 'friends.'"

Aran's enthusiasm gave way to starkness. He could relate little. The raiders had not come in any large fleet, a dozen ships at most. But there was no effective opposition to them. They smashed defenses from space, landed, plundered, raped, tortured, burned, during a nightmare of weeks. After sacking a major city, they missiled it. They were human, their language another dialect of Anglic. Whether in sarcasm or hypocrisy or because of linguistic change, they described themselves to the Nikeans as "your friends, come to do business with you." Since "friend" and "business" had long dropped out of local speech, Tom saw the origin of their present meaning here.

"Do you know who they might have been?" Aran asked. His tone was thick with unshed tears.

"No. Not sure. Space's full o' their kind." Tom refrained from adding that he too wasn't above a bit of piracy on occasion. After all, he observed certain humane rules with respect to those whom he relieved of their portable goods. The really bestial types made his flesh crawl, and he'd exterminated several gangs of them with pleasure.

"Will they return, think you?"

"Well . . . prob'ly not. I'd reckon they destroyed your big population centers to make sure no one else'd be tempted to come here and start a base that might be used against 'em. They bein' too few to conquer a whole world, you see. 'Course, I wouldn't go startin' major industries and such again without husky space defenses."

"No chance. We hide instead," Aran said bitterly. "Most leaders dare allow naught that might draw other friends. Radio a bare minimum; no rebuilding of cities; yes, we crawl back to our dark age and cower."

"I take it you don't pers'nally agree with that policy."

Aran shrugged. "What matter my thoughts? I am but a third son. The chiefs of the planet have 'cided. They fought a war or two, forcing the rest to go with them in this. I myself bombed soldiers of

Silva, when its Prester was made stop building a big atomic power plant. Our neighbor cavedom! And we had to fight them, not the friends!"

Tom wasn't shocked. He'd seen human politics get more hashed than that. What pricked his ears up was the information that, right across the border, lived a baron who couldn't feel overly kindly toward Engineer Weyer.

"You can seize, now, why we feared you," Aran said.

"Aye-ya. A sad misunderstandin'. If you hadn't been so bloody impulsive, though—if you'd been willin' to talk—we'd've quick seen what the lingo problem was."

"No! You were the ones who refused talk. When the Engineer called on you to be slaves—"

"What the muck did he expect us to do after that?" Tom rumbled. "Wear his chains?"

"Chains? Why . . . wait—oh-oh!"

"Oh-oh, for sure," Tom said. "Another little shift o' meanin', huh? All right, what does 'slave' signify to you?"

It turned out that, on Nike, to be "enslaved" was nothing more than to be taken into custody: perhaps as a prisoner, perhaps merely for interrogation or protection. In Hanno, as in every advanced Nikean realm, slavery in Tom's sense of the word had been abolished a lifetime ago.

The two men stared at each other. "Events got away from both sides," Tom said. "After what'd happened when last spacemen came, you were too spooked to give us a chance. You reckoned you had to get us under guard right away. And we reacted to that. We've seen a lot o' cruelty and treachery. We couldn't trust ourselves to complete strangers, 'specially when they acted hostile. So . . . neither side gave the other time to think out the busi—the matter o' word shift. If there'd been a few minutes' pause in the action, I think I, at least, would've guessed the truth. I've seen lots o' similar cases. But I never had any such pause, till now."

He grinned and extended a broad, hard hand. "All's well that ends well, I'm told," he said. "Let's be camarados."

Aran ignored the gesture. The face he turned to the outworlder was only physically youthful. "We cannot," he said. "You wrecked a plane and stole another. Worse, you killed a man of ours."

"But—well, self-defense!"

"I might pardon you," Aran said. "I do not think the Engineer would or could. It is more than the damage you worked. More than the anger of the powerful Sato family, who like it not if a son of theirs dies unavenged because of a comic mix in s'mantics. It is the policy that he, Weyer's self, strove to bring."

"You mean . . . nothin' good can come from outer space . . . wall Nike off . . . treat anyone that comes as hostile . . . right?" Tom rubbed his chin and scowled sullenly.

Weyer was probably not too dogmatic, nor too tightly bound by the isolationist treaty, to change his mind in time. But Tom had scant time to spare. Every hour that passed, he and his womenfolk risked getting shot down by some hysteric. Also, a bunch of untrained Nikeans, pawing over his spaceship, could damage her beyond the capacity of this planet's industry to repair.

Also, he was needed back on Kraken soon, or his power there would crumble. And that would be a mortally dangerous situation for his other wives, children, grandchildren, old and good comrades. . . .

In short, there was scant value in coming to terms with Weyer eventually. He needed to reach agreement fast. And, after what had happened this day, he didn't see how he could.

Well, the first thing he must do was reunite his party. Together, they might accomplish something. If nothing else, they could seek refuge in the adjacent country, Silva. Though that was doubtless no very secure place for them, particularly if Weyer threatened another war.

"You should slave yourself," Aran urged. "Afterward you can talk."

"As a prisoner—a slave—I'd have precious little bargainin' leverage," Tom said. "Considerin' what that last batch o' spacers did, I can well imagine we bein' tortured till I cough up for free everything I've got to tell. S'posin' Weyer himself didn't want to treat me so inhospitable, he could break down anyhow under pressure from his court or his fellow bosses."

"It may be," Aran conceded, reluctantly, but too idealistic at his age to violate the code of his class and lie.

"Whereas if I can stay loose, I can try a little pressure o' my own.

I can maybe find somethin' to offer that's worth makin' a deal with me. That'd even appease the Sato clan, hm?" Tom fumed on his pipe. "I've got to contact my women. Right away. Can't risk their fallin' into Weyer's hands. If they do, he's got me! Know any way to raise a couple o' girls who don't have a radio and 're doin' their level best to disappear?"

Sunset rays turned the hilltop fiery. Farther down, the land was already blue with a dusk through which river, bay, and distant sea glimmered argent. Cloud banks towered in the east, blood-colored, dwarfing the Sawtooth Mountains that marked Hanno's frontier.

At the lowest altitude when this was visible—the highest to which a damaged, overloaded flyer could limp—the air was savagely cold. It wasn't too thin for breathing; the atmosphere's density gradient is less for small than for large planets. But it swept through the cracked canopy to sear Tom's nostrils and numb his fingers on the board. Above the drone of the combustion powerplant, he heard Yano Aran's teeth clatter. Stuffed behind the pilot chair, the boy might have tried to mug his captor. But he wasn't dressed for this temperature and was chilled half insensible. Tom's clothes were somewhat warmer. Besides, he felt he could take on any two Nikeans hand-to-hand.

The controls of the plane were simple to a man who'd used as wide a variety of machines as he. Trickiness came from the broken and twisted airfoil surfaces. And, of course, he must keep a watch for Weyer's boys. He didn't think they'd be aloft, nor that they would scramble and get here in the few minutes he needed. But you never knew. If one did show up maybe Tom could pot him with a lucky blast from the guns.

He swung through another carousel curve. That should be that. Now to skate away. He throttled the engine back. The negafield dropped correspondingly, and he went into a glide. But he was no longer emitting enough exhaust for a visible trail.

The tracks he had left were scribbled over half the sky. The sun painted them gold-orange against that deepening purple.

Abruptly, turbulence across the buckled delta wing gained mastery. The glide became a tailspin. Aran yelled.

"Hang on," Tom said. "I can ride 'er."

Crazily whirling, the dark land rushed at him. He stopped Aran's attempt to grab the stick with a karate chop and concentrated on his altimeter. At the last possible moment, allowing for the fact that he must coddle this wreck lest he tear her apart altogether, he pulled out of his tumble. A prop, jet or rocket would never have made it, but you could do special things with gravs if you had the knack in your fingers. Or whatever part of the anatomy it was.

Finally the plane whispered a few meters above the bay. Its riding lights were doused, and the air here was too warm for engine vapor to condense. Tom believed his passage had a fair chance of going unnoticed.

Hills shouldered black around the water. Here and there among them twinkled house lamps. One cluster bespoke a village on the shore. Tom's convoluted contrail was breaking up, but slowly. It glowed huge and mysterious, doubtless frightening peasants and worrying the military.

Aran stared at it likewise, as panic and misery left him. "I thought you wrote a message to your camarados," he said. "That's no writing."

"Couldn't use your alphabet, son, seein' I had to give 'em directions to a place with a local name. Could I, now? Even Kraken's letters look too much like yours. But these're Momotaroan phonograms. Dagny can read 'em. I hope none o' Weyer's folk'll even guess it is a note. Maybe they'll think I went out o' control tryin' to escape and, after staggerin' around a while, crashed. . . . Now, which way is this rendezvous?"

"Rendez—oh. The togethering I advised. Follow the north shore eastward a few more kilos. At the end of a headland stands Orgino's Cave."

"You absolutely sure nobody'll be there?"

"As sure as may be; and you have me for hostage. Orgino was a war chief of three hundred years agone. They said he was so wicked he must be in pact with the Wanderer, and to this day the commons think he walks the ruins of his cave. But it's a landmark. Let your camarados ask shrewdly, and they can find how to get there with none suspecting that for their wish."

The plane sneaked onward. Twilight was short in this thin air. Stars twinkled splendidly forth, around the coalsack of the Nebula.

The outer moon rose, gradually from the eastern cloudbanks, almost full but its disk tiny and corroded-bronze dark. An auroral glow flickered. This far south? Well, Nike had a fairly strong magnetic field—which, with the mean density, showed that it possessed the ferrous core it wasn't supposed to—but not so much that charged solar particles couldn't strike along its sharp curvature clear to the equator.

If they were highly energetic particles, anyhow. And they must be. Tom had identified enormous spots as well as flares on that ruddy sun disk. Which oughtn't to be there! Not even when output was rising. A young star, its outer layers cool and reddish because they were still contracting shouldn't have such intensity. Should it?

Regardless, Nike's sun did.

Well, Tom didn't pretend to know every kind of star. His travels had really not been so extensive, covering a single corner of the old Imperium, which itself had been insignificant compared to the whole galaxy. And his attention had naturally always been focused on more or less Sol-type stars. He didn't know what a very young or very old or very large or very small sun was like in detail.

Most certainly he didn't know what the effects of abnormal chemical composition might be. And the distribution of elements in this system was unlike that of any other Tom had ever heard about. Conditions on Nike bore out what spectroanalysis had indicated in space: impoverishment with respect to heavy elements. Since it had formed recently, the sun and its planets must therefore have wandered here from some different region. Its velocity didn't suggest that. However, Tom hadn't determined the galactic orbit with any precision. Besides, it might have been radically changed by a close encounter with another orb. Improbable as the deuce, yes, but then the whole crazy situation was very weird.

The headland loomed before him, and battlements against the Milky Way. Tom made a vertical landing in a courtyard. "All right." His voice sounded jarringly loud. "Now we got nothin' much to do but wait."

"What if they come not?" Aran asked.

"I'll give 'em a day or two," Tom said. "After that, we'll see." He didn't care to dwell on the possibility. His unsentimental soul was rather astonished to discover how big a part of it Dagny had become. And Yasmin was a good kid, he wished her well.

He left the crumbling flagstones for a walk around the walls. Pseudo-moss grew damp and slippery on the parapet. Once mail-clad spearmen had tramped their rounds here, and the same starlight sheened on their helmets as tonight, or as in the still more ancient, vanished glory of the Empire, or the League before it, or—And what of the nights yet to come? Tom shied from the thought and loaded his pipe.

Several hours later, the nearer moon rose from the hidden sea; its apparent path was retrograde and slow. Although at half phase, with an angular diameter of a full degree, it bridged the bay with mercury.

Rising at the half—local midnight, more or less—would the girls never show? He ought to get some sleep. His eyelids were sandy. Aran had long since gone to rest in the tumbledown keep. He must be secured, of course, before Tom dozed off . . . *No. I couldn't manage a snooze even if I tried. Where are you, Dagny?*

The cold wind lulled, the cold waves lapped, a winged creature fluttered and whistled. Tom sat down where a portcullis had been and stared into the woods beyond.

There came a noise. And another. Branches rustled. Hoofbeats clopped. Tom drew his blaster and slid into the shadow of a tower. Two riders on horseback emerged from the trees. For a moment they were unrecognizable, unreal. Then the moon's light struck Dagny's tawny mane. Tom shouted.

Dagny snatched her own gun forth. But when she saw who lumbered toward her, it fell into the rime-frosted grass.

Afterward, in what had been a feasting hall, with a flashlight from the aircraft to pick faces out of night, they conferred. "No, we had no trouble," Dagny said. "The farmers sold us those animals without any fuss."

"If you gave him a thirty-gram gold piece, on this planet, I reckon so," Tom said. "You could prob'ly've gotten his house thrown into the deal. He's bound to gossip about you, though."

"That can't be helped," Dagny said. "Our idea was to keep traveling east and hide in the woods when anyone happened by. But we'd no strong hope, especially with that wide cultivated valley to get across. Tom, dear, when I saw your sky writing, it was the second best moment of my life."

"What was the first?"

"You were involved there too," she said. "Rather often, in fact."

Yasmin stirred. She sat huddled on the floor, chilled, exhausted, wretched, though nonetheless drawing Aran's appreciative gaze. "Why do you grin at each other?" she wailed. "We're hunted!"

"Tell me more," Tom said.

"What can we *do?*"

"You can shut up, for the gods' sake, and keep out o' my way!" he snapped impatiently. She shrank from him and knuckled her eyes.

"Be gentle," Dagny said. "She's only a child."

"She'll be a dead child if we don't get out o' here," Tom retorted. "We got time before dawn to slip across the Silvan border in yon airboat. After that, we'll have to play 'er as she lies. But I been pumpin' my—shall I say, my friend, about politics and geography and such. I think with luck we got a chance o' staying free."

"What chance of getting our ship back, and repaired?" Dagny asked.

"Well, that don't look so good, but maybe somethin'll come down the slot for us. Meanwhile let's move."

They went back to the courtyard. The inner moon was so bright that no supplement was needed for the job on hand. This was to unload the extra fuel tanks, which were racked aft of the cockpit. The plane would lose cruising range, would indeed be unable to go past the eastern slope of the Sawtooths. But it would gain room for two passengers.

"You stay behind, natural," Tom told Aran. "You been a nice lad, and here's where I prove I never aimed at any hurt for you. Have a horse on me, get a boat from the village to Weyer's place, tell him what happened—and to tell him we want to be his camarados and change with him."

"I can say it." Aran shifted awkwardly from foot to foot. "I think no large use comes from my word."

"The prejudice against spacemen—"

"And the damage you worked. How shall you repay that? Since 'tis been 'cided there's no good in spacefaring, I expect your ship'll be stripped for its metal."

"Try, though," Tom urged.

"Should you leave now?" Aran wondered. "Weather looks twisty."

"Aye, we'd better. But thanks for frettin' 'bout it."

A storm, Tom thought, was the least of his problems. True, conditions did look fanged about the mountains. But he could sit down and wait them out, once over the border, which ought to remain in the bare fringes of the tempest. Who ever heard of weather moving very far west, on the western seacoast of a planet with rotation like this? What was urgent was to get beyond Weyer's pursuit.

Yasmin and Dagny fitted themselves into the rear fuselage as best they could, which wasn't very. Tom took the pilot's seat again. He waved good-bye to Yanos Aran and gunned the engine. Overburdened as well as battered, the plane lifted sluggishly and made no particular speed. But it flew, and could be out of Hanno before dawn. That sufficed.

Joy at reunion, vigilance against possible enemies, concentration on the difficult task of operating his cranky vessel drove weariness out of him. He paid scant attention to the beauties of the landscape sliding below, though they were considerable—mist-magical delta, broad sweep of valley, river's sinuous glow, all white under the moons. He must be one with the wind that blew across this sleeping land.

And blew.

Harder.

The plane bucked. The noise around it shrilled more and more clamorous. Though the cloud wall above the mountains must be a hundred kilometers distant, it was suddenly boiling zenithward with unbelievable speed.

It rolled over the peaks and hid them. Its murk swallowed the outer moon and reached tendrils forth for the inner one. Lightning blazed in its caverns. Then the first raindrops were hurled against the plane. Hail followed, and the snarl of a hurricane.

East wind! Couldn't be! Tom had no further chance to think. He was too busy staying alive.

As if across parsecs, he heard Yasmin's scream, Dagny's profane orders that she curb herself. Rain and hail made the cockpit a drum, himself a cockroach trapped between the skins. The wind was the tuba of marching legions. Sheathing ripped loose from wings and tail. Now and then he could see through the night, when lightning burned. The thunder was like bombs, one after the next, a line of them seeking him out. What followed was doomsday blackness.

His instrument panel went dark. His altitude control stick waggled loose in his hand. The airflaps must be gone, the vessel whirled leaf-fashion on the wind. Tom groped until his fingers closed on the grav-drive knobs. By modulating fields and thrust beams, he could keep a measure of command. Just a measure; the powerplant had everything it could do to lift this weight, without guiding it. But let him get sucked down to earth, that was the end!

He must land somehow, and survive the probably hard impact. How?

The river flashed lurid beneath him. He tried to follow its course. Something real, in this raving night—There was no more inner moon, there were no more stars.

The plane groaned, staggered, and tilted on its side. The starboard wing was torn off. Had the port one gone too, Tom might have operated the fuselage as a kind of gravity sled. But against forces as unbalanced as now fought him, he couldn't last more than a few seconds. Minutes, if he was lucky.

Must be back above the rivermouths, thought the tiny part of him that stood aside and watched the struggle of the rest. *Got to set down easy-like. And find some kind o' shelter. Yasmin wouldn't last out this night in the open.*

Harshly: *Will she last anyway? Is she anything but a dangerous drag on us? I can't abandon her. I swore her an oath, but I almost wish—*

The sky exploded anew with lightnings and showed him a wide vista of channels among forested, swampy islands. Trees tossed and roared in the wind, but the streams were too narrow for great waves to build up and—Hoy!

Suddenly, disastrously smitten, a barge train headed from Sea Gate to the upriver towns had broken apart. In the single blazing moment of vision that he had, Tom saw the tug itself reel toward safety on the northern side of the main channel. Its tow was scattered, some members sinking, some flung around, and one—yes, driven into a tributary creek, woods and waterplants closing behind it, screening it—

Tom made his decision.

He hoped for nothing more than a bellyflop in the drink, a scramble to escape from the plane and a swim to the barge. But lightning flamed again and again, enormous sheets of it that turned every raindrop and hailstone into brass. And once he was down near the surface of that natural canal, a wall of trees on either side, he got some relief. He was actually able to land on deck.

The barge had ended on a sandbar and lay solid and stable. Tom led his women from the plane. He and Dagny found some rope and lashed their remnant of a vehicle into place. The cargo appeared to be casks of petroleum. A hatch led below, to a cabin where a watchman might rest. Tom's flashlight picked out bunk, chair, a stump of candle.

"We're playin' a good hand," he said.

"For how long?" Dagny mumbled.

"Till the weather slacks off." Tom shrugged. "What comes after that, I'm too tired to care. I don't s'pose . . . gods, yes!" he whooped. "Here, on the shelf! A bottle—lemme sniff—aye-ya, booze! Got to be booze!" And he danced upon the deckboards till he cracked his pate on the low overhead.

Yasmin regarded him with a dull kind of wonder. "What are you so happy about?" she asked in Anglic. When he had explained, she slumped. "You can laugh . . . at that . . . tonight? Lord Tom, I did not know how alien you are to me."

Through hours the storm continued.

They sat crowded together, the three of them, in the uneasy candlelight, which threw huge misshapen shadows across the roughness of bulkheads. Rather Dagny sat on the chair, Tom on the foot of the bunk, while Yasmin lay. The wind-noise was muffled down here, but the slap of water on hull came loud. From time to time, thunder cannonaded, or the barge rocked and grated on the sandbar.

Wet, dirty, haggard, the party looked at each other. "We should try to sleep," Dagny said.

"Not while I got this bottle," Tom said. "You do what you like. Me, though, I think we'd better guzzle while we can. Prob'ly won't be long, you see."

"Probably not," Dagny agreed, and took another pull herself.

"What will we do?" Yasmin whispered.

Tom suppressed exasperation—she had done a good job in Petar Landa's house, if nowhere else—and said, "Come morning, we head into the swamps. I s'pose Weyer'll send his merry men lookin' for us, and whoever owns this hulk'll search after it, so we can't claim squatter's rights. Maybe we can live off the country, though, and eventually, one way or another, reach the border."

"Would it not be sanest . . . they do seem to be decent folk . . . should we not surrender to them and hope for mercy?"

"Go ahead, if you want," Tom said. "You may or may not get the mercy. But you'll for sure have no freedom. I'll stay my own man."

Yasmin tried to meet his hard gaze, and failed. "What has happened to us?" she pleaded.

He suspected that she meant, "What has become of the affection between you and me?" No doubt he should comfort her. But he didn't have the strength left to play father image. Trying to distract her a little, he said, with calculated misunderstanding of her question:

"Why, we hit a storm that blew us the exact wrong way. It wasn't s'posed to. But this's such a funny planet. I reckon, given a violent kind o' sun, you can get weather that whoops out o' the east, straight seaward. And, o' course, winds can move almighty fast when the air's thin. Maybe young Aran was tryin' to warn me. He spoke o' twisty weather. Maybe he meant exactly this, and I got fooled once more by his Nikean lingo. Or maybe he just meant what I believed he did, unreliable weather. He told me himself, their meteorology isn't worth sour owl spit, 'count o' they can't predict the solar output. Young star, you know. Have drink."

Yasmin shook her head. But abruptly she sat straight. "Have you something to write with?"

"Huh?" Tom gaped at her.

"I have an idea. It is worthless," she said humbly, "but since I cannot sleep, and do not wish to annoy my lord, I would like to pass the time."

"Oh. Sure." Tom found a paper and penstyl in a breast pocket of his coverall and gave them to her. She crossed her legs and began writing numbers in a neat foreign-looking script.

"What's going on?" Dagny said in Eylan.

Tom explained. The older woman frowned. "I don't like this, dear," she said. "Yasmin's been breaking down, closer and closer to hysteria, ever since we left those peasants. She's not prepared for a guerrilla existence. She's used up her last resources."

"You reckon she's quantum-jumpin' already?"

"I don't know. But I do think we should force her to take a drink, to put her to sleep."

"Hm." Tom glanced at the dark head, bent over some arithmetical calculations. "Could be. But no. Let her do what she chooses. She hasn't bubbled her lips yet, has she? And—we are the free people."

He went on with Dagny in a rather hopeless discussion of possibilities open to them. Once they were interrupted, when Yasmin asked if he had a trigonometric slide rule. No, he didn't. "I suppose I can approximate the function with a series," she said, and returned to her labors.

Has she really gone gollywobble? Tom wondered. *Or is she just soothin' herself with a hobby?*

Half an hour later, Yasmin spoke again. "I have the solution."

"To what?" Tom asked, a little muzzily after numerous gulps from the bottle. They distilled potent stuff in Hanno. "Our problem?"

"Oh, no, my lord. I couldn't—I mean, I am nobody. But I did study science, you remember, and . . . and I assumed that if you and Lady Dagny said this was a young system, you must be right, you have traveled so widely. But it isn't."

"No? What're you aimed at?"

"It doesn't matter, really. I'm being an awful picky little nuisance. But this *can't* be a young system. It has to be old."

Tom put the bottle down with a thud that overrode the storm-yammer outside. Dagny opened her mouth to ask what was happening. He shushed her. Out of the shadows across his scarred face, the single eye blazed blue. "Go on," he said, most quietly.

Yasmin faltered. She hadn't expected any such reaction. But, encouraged by him, she said with a waxing confidence:

"From the known average distance of the sun, and the length of the planet's year, anyone can calculate the sun's mass. It turns out to be almost precisely one Sol. That is, it has the mass of a G_2 star. But it has twice the luminosity, and more than half again the radius, and the reddish color of a late G or early K type. You thought those paradoxes were due to a strange composition. I don't really see how that could be. I mean, any star is something like 98 per cent hydrogen and helium. Variations in other elements can affect its development some, but surely not this much. Well, we know from Nikean biology that this system must be at least a few billion years old. So the star's instability cannot be due to extreme youth. Any solar mass must settle down on the main sequence far quicker than that. Otherwise we would have many, many more variables in the universe than we do.

"And besides, we can explain all the paradoxes so simply if we assume this system is old. Incredibly old, maybe almost as old as the galaxy itself."

"Belay!" Tom exclaimed, though not loudly. "How could this planet have this much atmosphere after so long a time? If any? Don't sunlight kick gases into space? And Nike hasn't got the gravity to nail molecules down for good. Half a standard Gee; and the potential is even poorer, the field strength dropping off as fast as it does."

"But my lord," Yasmin said, "an atmosphere comes from within a planet. At least, it does for the smaller planets, that can't keep their original hydrogen like the Jupiter types. On the smaller worlds, gas gets forced out of mineral compounds. Vulcanism and tectonism provide the heat for that, as well as radioactivity. But the major planetological forces originate in the core. And the core originates because the heavier elements, like iron, tend to migrate toward the center. We know Nike has some endowment of those. Perhaps more, even, than the average planet of its age.

"Earth-sized planets have strong gravity. The migration is quick. The core forms in their youth. But Mars-sized worlds . . . the process has to be slow, don't you think? So much iron combines first in surface rocks that they are red. Nike shows traces of this still today. The midget planets can't outgas more than a wisp until their old age, when a core finally has taken shape."

Tom shook his head in a stunned fashion. "I didn't know. I took for granted—I mean, well, every Mars-type globe I ever saw or heard of had very little air—I reckoned they'd lost most o' their gas long ago."

"There are no extremely ancient systems in the range that your travels have covered," Yasmin deduced. "Perhaps not in the whole Imperial territory. They aren't common in the spiral arms of the galaxy, after all. So people never had much occasion to think about what they must be like."

"Uh, what you been sayin', this theory . . . you learned it in school?"

"No. I didn't major in astronomy, just took some required basic courses. It simply appeared to me that some such idea is the only way to explain this system we're in." Yasmin spread her hands. "Maybe the professors at my university haven't heard of the idea either. The truth must have been known in Imperial times, but it could have been lost since, not having immediate practical value." Her smile was sad. "Who cares about pure science any more? What can you buy with it?

"Even the original colonists on Nike—Well, to them the fact must have been interesting, but not terribly important. They knew the planet was so old that it had lately gained an atmosphere and oxygen-liberating life. So old that its sun is on the verge of becoming a red giant. Already the hydrogen is exhausted at the core, the nuclear reactions are moving outward in a shell, the photosphere is expanding and cooling while the total energy output rises. But the sun won't be so huge that Nike is scorched for—oh, several million years. I suppose the colonists appreciated the irony here. But on the human time-scale, what difference did it make? No wonder their descendants have forgotten and think, like you, this has to be a young system."

Tom caught her hands between his own. "And . . . that's the reason . . . the real reason the sun's so rambunctious?" he asked hoarsely.

"Why, yes. Red giants are usually variable. This star is in a transition stage, I guess, and hasn't 'found' its period yet." Yasmin's smile turned warm. "If I have taken your mind off your troubles, I am glad. But why do you care about the aspect of this planet ten mega-years from now? I think best I do try to sleep, that I may help you a little tomorrow."

Tom gulped. "Kid," he said, "you don't know your own strength."

"What's she been talking about?" Dagny demanded.

Tom told her. They spent the rest of the night laying plans.

Now and then a mid-morning sunbeam struck copper through the fog. But otherwise a wet, dripping, smoking mystery enclosed the barge. Despite its chill, Tom was glad. He didn't care to be interrupted by a strafing attack.

To be sure, the air force might triangulate on the radio emission of his ruined plane and drop a bomb. However—

He sat in the cockpit, looked squarely into the screen, and said, "This is a parley. Agreed?"

"For the moment." Karol Weyer gave him a smoldering return stare. "I talked with Fish Aran."

"And he made it clear to you, didn't he, about the lingo scramble? How often your Anglic and mine use the same word different? Well, let's not keep on with the farce. If anybody thinks t'other's said somethin' bad, let's call a halt and thresh out what was intended. Aye?"

Weyer tugged his beard. His countenance lost none of its sternness. "You have yet to prove your good faith," he said. "After what harm you worked—"

"I'm ready to make that up to you. To your whole planet."

Weyer cocked a brow and waited.

"S'pose you give us what we need to fix our ship," Tom said. "Some of it might be kind of expensive—copper and silver and such, and handicrafted because you haven't got the dies and jigs—but we can make some gold payment. Then let us go. I, or a trusty captain o' mine, will be back in a few months . . . uh, a few thirty-day periods."

"With a host of friends to do business?"

"No. With camarados to 'change. Nike lived on trade under the Terran Empire. It can once more."

"How do I know you speak truth?"

"Well, you'll have to take somethin' on my word. But listen. Kind of a bad storm last night, no? Did a lot o' damage, I'll bet. How much less would've been done if you'd been able to predict it? I can make that possible." Tom paused before adding cynically, "You can share the information with all Nike, or keep it your national secret. Could be useful, if you feel like maybe the planet should have a really strong Emperor, name of Weyer, for instance."

☆   ☆   ☆

The Engineer leaned forward till his image seemed about to jump from the screen. "How is this?"

Tom related what Yasmin had told him. "No wonder your solar meteorologists never get anywhere," he finished. "They're usin' exactly the wrong mathematical model."

Weyer's eyes dwelt long upon Tom. "Are you giving this information away in hopes of my good will?" he said.

"No. As a free sample, to shake you loose from your notion that every chap who drops in from space is necessarily a hound o' hell. And likewise this. Camarado Weyer, your astronomers'll tell you my wife's idea makes sense. They'll be right glad to hear they've got an old star. But they'll need many years to work out the details by themselves. You know enough science to realize that, I'm sure. Now I can put you in touch with people that *already* know the details—that can come here, study the situation for a few weeks, and predict your weather like dice odds.

"That's my hole card. And you can only benefit by helpin' us leave. Don't think you can catch us and beat what we know out of us. First, we haven't got the information. Second, we'll die before we become slaves, in any meanin' o' the word. If it don't look like we can get killed fightin' the men you send to catch us, why, we'll turn our weapons on ourselves. Then all you've got is a spaceship that to you is nothin' but scrap metal."

Weyer drew a sharp breath. But he remained cautious. "This may be," he said. "Nonetheless, if I let you go, why should you bring learned people back to me?"

"Because it'll pay. I'm a trader and a warlord. The richer my markets, the stronger my allies, the better off I am." Tom punched a forefinger at the screen. "Get rid o' that conditioned reflex o' yours and think a bit instead. You haven't got much left that's worth anybody's lootin'. Why should I bother returnin' for that purpose? But your potential, that's somethin' else entirely. Given as simple a thing as reliable weather forecasts—you'll save, in a generation, more wealth than the 'friends' ever destroyed. And this's only one for instance o' what the outside universe can do for you. Man, you can't afford not to trust me!"

They argued, back and forth, for a long time. Weyer was intrigued but wary. Granted, Yasmin's revelation did provide evidence that Tom's folk were not utter savages like the last visitors from space. But the evidence wasn't conclusive. And even if it was, what guarantee existed that the strangers would bring the promised experts?

The wrangle ended as well as Tom had hoped, in an uneasy compromise. He and his wives would be brought to Sea Gate. They'd keep their sidearms. Though guarded, they were to be treated more or less as guests. Discussions would continue. If Weyer judged, upon better acquaintance, that they were indeed trustworthy, he would arrange for the ship's repair and release.

"But don't be long about makin' up your mind," Tom warned, "or it won't do us a lot o' good to come home."

"Perhaps," Weyer said, "you can depart early if you leave a hostage."

"You'll be all right?" Tom asked for the hundredth time.

"Indeed, my lord," Yasmin said. She was more cheerful than he, bidding him good-bye in the Engineer's castle. "I'm used to their ways by now, comfortable in this environment—honestly! And you know how much in demand an outworlder is."

"That could get dull. I won't be back too bloody soon, remember. What'll you do for fun?"

"Oh," she said demurely, "I plan to make arrangements with quite a number of men."

"Stop teasin' me." He hugged her close. "I'm goin' to miss you."

And so Roan Tom and Dagny Od's-daughter left Nike.

He fretted somewhat about Yasmin, while *Firedrake* made the long flight back to Kraken, and while he mended his fences there, and while he voyaged back with his scholars and merchants. Had she really been joking, at the very last? She'd for sure gotten almighty friendly with Yanos Aran, and quite a few other young bucks. Tom was not obsessively jealous, but he could not afford to become a laughingstock.

He needn't have worried. When he made his triumphant landing at Sea Gate, he found that Yasmin had been charming, plausible, devious and, in short, had convinced several feudal lords of Nike that it was to their advantage that the rightful Shah be restored to the throne of Sassania. They commanded enough men to do the job. If the Krakeners could furnish weapons, training, and transportation—

Half delighted, half stunned, Tom said, "So this time we had a lingo scramble without somethin' horrible happenin'? I don't believe it!"

"Happy endings do occur," she murmured, and came to him. "As now."

And everyone was satisfied except, maybe, some few who went to lay a wreath upon a certain grave.

In the case of the King and Sir Christopher, however, a compliment was intended. A later era would have used the words "awe-inspiring, stately, and ingeniously conceived."

THE NIGHT FACE

INTRODUCTION

———————— ✵ ————————

At first this was a novelette called "A Twelvemonth and a Day." I revised and expanded it for book publication, whereupon the then editor stuck it with the ridiculous title *Let the Spacemen Beware!* My thanks to Jim Baen, now in charge, for recognizing that readers have more intelligence than they were once given credit for having. In return, I admit that he's probably right in considering the original name too cumbersome; hence the new one.

Otherwise the tale is unchanged. It can stand alone without reference to anything else. However, you may be interested to know that it does fit into the same "future history" as the Polesotechnic League and the Terran Empire. Nicholas van Rijn, David Falkayn, Christopher Holm, Dominic Flandry, and quite a few more characters lived in its past. Now the Empire has fallen, the Long Night descended upon that tiny fraction of the galaxy which man once explored and colonized. Like Romano-Britons after the last legion had withdrawn, people out in the former marches of civilization do not even know what is happening at its former heart. They have the physical capability of going there and finding out, but are too busy surviving. They are also, all unawares, generating whole new societies of their own.

I do not, myself, believe that history will necessarily repeat itself to this extent. Nor do I deny that it might. Nobody knows. Equally uncertain, at the present state of our knowledge, is the validity of some assumptions about human genetics and psychobiology which I made for narrative purposes. Here is just a story which I hope you will enjoy.

—**Poul Anderson, 1978**

THE NIGHT FACE

✧ ∎ ✧

The *Quetzal* did not leave orbit and swing toward the planet until she got an all-clear from the boat which had gone ahead to make arrangements. Even then her approach was cautious, as was fitting in a region as little known as this. Miguel Tolteca expected he would have a couple of hours free to watch the scenery unfold.

He was not exactly a sybarite, but he liked to do things in style. First he dialed PRIVACY on his stateroom door, lest some friendly soul barge in to pass the time of day. Then he put Castellani's *Symphony No. 2 in D Minor* with Subsonics on the tapester, mixed himself a rum and conchoru, converted the bunk to a lounger, and sat back with his free hand on the controls of the exterior scanner. Its screen grew black and full of wintry unwinking stars. He searched in a clockwise direction until Gwydion swam into view, a tiny disc upon darkness, the clearest blue he had ever seen.

The door chimed. "Oa," called Tolteca through the comunit, irritated, "can you not read?"

"My mistake," said the voice of Raven. "I thought you were the chief of the expedition."

Tolteca swore, folded the lounger into a chair, and stepped across the little room. A slight, momentary change in weight informed him that the *Quetzal* had put on a spurt of extra acceleration. Doubtless to dodge some meteorite swarm, the engineer part of him thought.

391

They'd be more common here than around Nuevamerica, this being a newer system. . . . Otherwise the pseudogee field held firm. The spaceship was a precision instrument.

He opened the door. "Very well, Commandant." He pronounced the hereditary title with a curtness that approached insult. "What is so urgent?"

Raven stood still for an instant, observing him. Tolteca was a young man, middling tall, with wide, stiffly held shoulders. His face was thin and sharp, under brown hair drawn back into the short queue customary on his planet, and the eyes were levelly aimed. However much the United Republics of Nuevamerica made of their shiny new democracy, it meant something to stem from one of their old professional families. He wore the uniform of the Argo Astrographical Company, but that was only a simple, pleasing version of his people's everyday garb: blue tunic, gray culottes, white stockings, and no insignia.

Raven came in and closed the door. "By chance," he said, his tone mild again, "one of my men overheard some of yours dicing to settle who should debark first after you and the ship's captain."

"Well, that sounds harmless enough," said Tolteca sarcastically. "Do you expect us to observe any official pecking order?"

"No. What—um—puzzled me was, nobody mentioned my own detachment."

Tolteca raised his brows. "You wanted your men to sit in on the dice game?"

"According to what my soldier reported to me, there seems to be no doctrine for planetfall and afterward."

"Well," said Tolteca, "as a simple courtesy to our hosts, Captain Utiel and I—and you, if you wish—will go out first to greet them. There's to be quite a welcoming committee, we're told. But beyond that, good ylem, Commandant, what difference does it make who comes down the gangway in what order?"

Raven fell motionless again. It was the common habit of Lochlanna aristocrats. They didn't stiffen at critical instants. They rarely showed any physical rigidity; but their muscles seemed to go loose and their eyes glazed over with calculation. Tolteca sometimes thought that that alone made them so alien that the Namerican Revolution had always been inevitable.

Finally—thirty seconds later, but it seemed longer—Raven said, "I can see how this misunderstanding occurred, Sir Engineer. Your people have developed several unique institutions in the fifty years since gaining independence, and have forgotten some of our customs. Certainly the concept of exploration, even treaty-making, as a strictly private, commercial enterprise, is not Lochlanna. We have been making unconscious assumptions about each other. The fact that our two groups have kept so much apart on this voyage has helped maintain those errors. I offer apology."

It was not relevant, but Tolteca was driven to snap, "Why should you apologize to me? I'm doubtless also to blame."

Raven smiled. "But I am a Commandant of the Oakenshaw Ethnos."

As if that bland purr had attracted him, a cat stuck his head out of the Lochlanna's flowing surcoat sleeve. Zio was a Siamese tom, big, powerful, and possessed of a temper like mercury fulminate. His eyes were cold blue in the brown mask. "Mneowrr," he said remindingly. Raven scratched him under the chin. Zio tilted back his head and raced his motor.

Tolteca gulped down an angry retort. Let the fellow have his superiority complex. He struck a cigarette and smoked in short hard puffs. "Never mind that," he said. "What's the immediate problem?"

"You must correct the wrong impression among your men. My troop goes out first."

"What? If you think—"

"In combat order. The spacemen will stand by to lift ship if anything goes awry. When I signal, you and Captain Utiel may emerge and make your speeches. But not before."

For a space Tolteca could find no words. He could only stare.

Raven waited, impassive. He had the Lochlanna build, the result of many generations on a planet with one-fourth again the standard surface gravity. Though tall for one of his own race, he was barely of average Namerican height. Thick-boned and thick-muscled, he moved like his cat, a gait which had always appeared slippery and sneaking to Tolteca's folk. His head was typically long, with the expected disharmony of broad face, high cheekbones, hook nose, sallow skin which looked youthful because genetic drift had eliminated the beard. His hair, close cropped, was a cap of midnight, and his brows met above the narrow green eyes. His clothes were not precisely gaudy, but the republican simplicity of Nuevamerica found them barbaric—high-collared blouse, baggy blue trousers tucked into soft half boots, surcoat embroidered with twined snakes and flowers, a silver dragon brooch. Even aboard ship, Raven wore dagger and pistol.

"By all creation," whispered Tolteca at last. "Do you think we're on one of your stinking campaigns of conquest?"

"Routine precautions," said Raven.

"But, the first expedition here was welcomed like—like—Our own advance boat, the pilot, he was feted till he could hardly stagger back aboard!"

Raven shrugged, earning an indignant look from Zio. "They've had almost one standard year to think over what the first expedition told them. We're a long way from home in space, and even longer in time. It's been twelve hundred years since the breakup of the Commonwealth isolated them. The whole Empire rose and fell while they were alone on that one planet. Genetic and cultural evolution have done strange work in shorter periods."

Tolteca dragged on his cigarette and said roughly, "Judging by the data, those people think more like Namericans than you do."

"Indeed?"

"They have no armed forces. No police, even, in the usual sense; public service monitors is the best translation of their word. No—well, one thing we have to find out is the extent to which they do have a government. The first expedition had too much else to learn, to establish that clearly. But beyond doubt, they haven't got much."

"Is this good?"

"By my standards, yes. Read our Constitution."

"I have done so. A noble document for your planet." Raven paused, scowling. "If this Gwydion were remotely like any other lost colony I've ever heard of, there would be small reason for worry. Common sense alone, the knowledge that overwhelming power exists to avenge any treachery toward us, would stay them. But don't you see, when there is no evidence of internecine strife, even of crime—and yet they are obviously not simple children of nature—I can't guess what *their* common sense is like."

"I can," clipped Tolteca, "and if your bully boys swagger down the gangway first, aiming guns at people with flowers in their hands, I know what that common sense will think of us."

Raven's smile was oddly charming on that gash of a mouth. "Credit me with some tact. We will make a ceremony of it."

"Looking ridiculous at best—they don't wear uniforms on Gwydion—and transparent at worst—for they're no fools. Your suggestion is declined."

"But I assure you—"

"No, I said. Your men will debark individually, and unarmed."

Raven sighed. "As long as we are exchanging reading lists, Sir Engineer, may I recommend the articles of the expedition to you?"

"What are you hinting at now?"

"The *Quetzal*," said Raven patiently, "is bound for Gwydion to investigate certain possibilities and, if they look hopeful, to open negotiations with the folk. Admittedly you are in charge of that. But for obvious reasons of safety, Captain Utiel has the last word while we are in space. What you seem to have forgotten is that once we have made planetfall, a similar power becomes mine."

"Oa! If you think you can sabotage—"

"Not at all. Like Captain Utiel, I must answer for my actions at home, if you should make any complaint. However, no Lochlanna officer would assume my responsibility if he were not given corresponding authority."

Tolteca nodded, feeling sick. He remembered now. It hadn't hitherto seemed important. The Company's operations took men and valuable ships ever deeper into this galactic sector, places where humans had seldom or never been even at the height of the empire. The hazards were unpredictable, and an armed guard on every vessel was in itself a good idea. But then a few old women in culottes, on the Policy Board, decided that plain Namericans weren't good enough. The guard had to be soldiers born and bred. In these days of spreading peace, more and more Lochlanna units found themselves at loose ends and hired out to foreigners. They kept pretty much aloof, on ship and in camp, and so far it hadn't worked out badly. But the *Quetzal* . . .

"If nothing else," said Raven, "I have my own men to think of, and their families at home."

"But not the future of interstellar relations?"

"If those can be jeopardized so easily, they don't seem worth caring about. My orders stand. Please instruct your men accordingly."

Raven bowed. The cat slid from his nesting place, dug claws in the coat, and sprang up on the man's shoulder. Tolteca could have sworn that the animal sneered. The door closed behind them.

Tolteca stood immobile for a while. The music reached a crescendo, reminding him that he had wanted to enjoy approach. He glanced back at the screen. The ship's curving path had brought the sun Ynis into scanner view. Its radiance stopped down by the compensator circuits, it spread corona and great wings of zodiacal light like nacre across the stars. The prominences must also be spectacular, for it was an F_8 with a mass of about two Sols and a corresponding luminosity of almost fourteen. But at its distance, 3.7 Astronomical Units, only the disc of the photosphere could be seen, covering a bare ten minutes of arc. All in all, a most ordinary main sequence star. Tolteca twisted dials until he found Gwydion again.

The planet had gained apparent size, though he still saw it as little more than a chipped turquoise coin. The cloud bands and aurora should soon become visible. No continents, however. While the first expedition had reported Gwydion to be terrestroid in astonishing detail, it was about ten percent smaller and denser than Old Earth—to be expected of a younger world, formed when there were more heavy atoms in the universe—and thus possessed less total land area. What there was was divided into islands and archipelagos. Broad shallow oceans made the climate mild from pole to pole. Here came its moon, 1600 kilometers in diameter, 96,300 kilometers in orbital radius, swinging from behind the disc like a tiny hurried firefly.

Tolteca considered the backdrop of the scene with a sense of eeriness. This close, the Nebula's immense cloud of dust and gas showed only as a region where stars were fewer and paler than else-where. Even nearby Rho Ophiuchi was blurred. Sol, of course, was hidden from telescopes as well as from eyes, an insignificant yellow dwarf two hundred parsecs beyond that veil, which its light would never pierce. *I wonder what's happening there,* thought Tolteca. *It's long since we had any word from Old Earth.*

He recollected what Raven had ordered, and cursed.

✲ II ✲

The pasture where the *Quetzal* had been asked to settle her giant cylinder was about five kilometers south of the town called Instar.

From the gangway Tolteca had looked widely across rolling fields. Hedges divided them into meadows of intense blossom-flecked green; plow-lands where the first delicate shoots of grain went like a breath across brown furrows; orchards and copses and scattered outbuildings made toylike by distance. The River Camlot gleamed between trees which might almost have been poplars. Instar bestrode it, red tile roofs above flower gardens around which the houses were built.

Most roads across that landscape were paved, but narrow and leisurely winding. Sometimes, Tolteca felt sure, a detour had been made to preserve an ancient tree or the lovely upswelling of a hill. Eastward the ground flattened, sloping down to a dike that cut off his view of the sea. Westward it climbed, until forested hills rose abruptly on the horizon. Beyond them could be seen mountain peaks, some of which looked volcanic. The sun hung just above their snows. You didn't notice how small it was in the sky, for it radiated too brightly to look at and the total illumination was almost exactly one standard sol. Cumulus clouds loomed in the southwest, and a low cool wind ruffled the puddles left by a recent shower.

Tolteca leaned back on the seat of the open car. "This is more beautiful than the finest places on my own world," he said to Dawyd. "And yet Nuevamerica is considered extremely Earthlike."

"Thank you," replied the Gwydiona. "Though we can take little credit. The planet was here, with its intrinsic conditions, its native biochemistry and ecology, all eminently suited to human life. I understand that God wears a different face in most of the known cosmos."

"Uh—" Tolteca hesitated. The local language, as recorded by the first expedition and learned by the second before starting out, was not altogether easy for him. Like Lochlanna, it derived from Anglic, whereas the Namericans had always spoken Ispanyo. Had he quite understood that business with "God"? Somehow, it didn't sound conventionally religious. But then, the secular orientation of his own culture made him liable to misinterpret theological references.

"Yes," he said presently. "The variations in so-called terrestroid planets are not great from a percentage standpoint, but to human beings they make a tremendous difference. On one continent of my own world, for example, settlement was impossible until a certain common genus of plant had been eradicated. It was harmless most of the year, but the pollen it broadcast in spring happened to contain a substance akin to botulinus toxin."

Dawyd gave him a startled look. Tolteca wondered what he had said wrong. Had he misused some local word? Of course, he'd had to employ the Ispanyo name for the poison. . . . "Eradicate?" murmured Dawyd. "Do you mean destroyed? Entirely?" Catching himself, slipping back into his serene manner with what looked like practiced ease, he said, "Well, let us not discuss technicalities right away. It was doubtless one of the Night Faces." He took his hand from the steering rod long enough to trace a sign in the air.

Tolteca felt a trifle puzzled. The first expedition had emphasized in its reports that the Gwydiona were not superstitious, though they had a vast amount of ceremony and symbolism. To be sure, the first expedition had landed on a different island; but it had found the same culture everywhere that it visited. (And it had failed to understand why men occupied only the region between latitudes 25 and 70 degrees north, although many other spots looked equally pleasant. There had been so much else to learn.) When the *Quetzal*'s advance boat arrived, Instar had been suggested as the best landing site merely because it was one of the larger towns and possessed a college with an excellent reference library.

The ceremonies of welcome hadn't been overwhelming, either. The whole of Instar had turned out—men, women, and children with garlands, pipes, and lyres. There had been no few visitors from other areas; still the crowd wasn't as big as would have been the case on many planets. After the formal speeches, music was played in honor of the newcomers and a ballet was presented, a thing of masks and thin costumes whose meaning escaped Tolteca, but which made a stunning spectacle. And that was all. The assembly broke up in general cordiality—not the milling, backslapping, handshaking kind of reception that Namericans would have given, but neither the elaborate and guarded courtesy of Lochlann. Individuals had talked in a friendly way to individuals, given invitations to stay in private homes, asked eager questions about the outside universe. And at last most of them walked back to town. But each foreigner got a ride in a small, exquisite electric automobile.

Only a nominal guard of crewmen, and a larger detachment of Lochlanna, remained with the ship. No offense had been taken at Raven's wariness, but Tolteca still smoldered.

"Do you indeed wish to abide at my house?" asked Dawyd.

Tolteca inclined his head. "It would be an honor, Sir—" He stopped. "Forgive me, but I do not know what your title is."

"I belong to the Simnon family."

"No. I knew that. I mean your—not your name, but what you do."

"I am a physician, of that rite which heals by songs as well as medicines." (Tolteca wondered how much he was misunderstanding.) "I also have charge of a dike patrol and instruct youth at the college."

"Oh." Tolteca was disappointed. "I thought—You are not in the government then?"

"Why, yes. I said I am in the dike patrol. What else had you in mind? Instar employs no Year-King or—No, that cannot be what you meant. Evidently the meaning of the word 'government' has diverged in our language from yours. Let me think, please." Dawyd knitted his brows.

Tolteca watched him, as if to read what could not be said. The Gwydiona all had that basic similarity which results from a very small original group of settlers and no later immigration. The first expedition had reported a legend that their ancestors were no more than a man and two women, one blonde and one dark, survivors of an atomic blast lobbed at the colony by one of those fleets which went a-murdering during the Breakup. But admittedly the extant written records did not go that far back, to confirm or deny the story. Be the facts as they may, the human gene pool here was certainly limited. And yet—an unusual case—there had been no degeneracy: rather, a refinement. Early generations had followed a careful program of outbreeding. Now marriage was on a voluntary basis, but the bearers of observable hereditary defects—including low intelligence and nervous instability—were sterilized. The first expedition had said that such people submitted cheerfully to the operation, for the community honored them ever after as heroes.

Dawyd was a pure caucasoid, which alone proved how old his nation must be. He was tall, slender, still supple in middle age. His yellow hair, worn shoulder length, was grizzled, but the blue eyes required no contact lenses and the sun-tanned skin was firm. The face, clean-shaven, high of brow and strong of chin, bore a straight nose and gentle mouth. His garments were a knee-length green tunic and white cloak, golden fillet, leather sandals, a locket about his neck which was gold on one side and black on the other. A triskele was tattooed on his forehead, but gave no effect of savagery.

His language had not changed much from Anglic; the Lochlanna had learned it without difficulty. Doubtless printed books and sound recordings had tended to stabilize it, as they generally did. But whereas Lochlann barked, grunted, and snarled, thought Tolteca, Gwydion trilled and sang. He had never heard such voices before.

"Ah, yes," said Dawyd. "I believe I grasp your concept. Yes, my advice is often asked, even on worldwide questions. That is my pride and my humility."

"Excellent. Well, Sir Councillor, I—"

"But councillor is no—no calling. I said I was a physician."

"Wait a minute, please. You have not been formally chosen in any way to guide, advise, control?"

"No. Why should I be? A man's reputation, good or ill, spreads. Finally others may come from halfway around the world, to ask his opinion of some proposal. Bear in mind, far-friend," Dawyd added shrewdly. "Our whole population numbers a mere ten million, and we have both radio and aircraft, and travel a great deal between our islands."

"But then who is in charge of public affairs?"

"Oh, some communities employ a Year-King, or elect presidents to hold the chair at their local meetings, or appoint an engineer to handle routine. It depends on regional tradition. Here in Instar we lack such customs, save that we crown a Dancer each winter solstice, to bless the year."

"That isn't what I mean, Sir Physician. Suppose a—oh, a project, like building a new road, or a policy like, well, deciding whether to have regular relations with other planets—suppose this vague group of wise men you speak of, men who depend simply on a reputation for wisdom—suppose they decide a question, one way or another. What happens next?"

"Then, normally, it is done as they have decided. Of course, everyone hears about it beforehand. If the issue is important, there will be much public discussion. But naturally men lay more weight on the suggestions of those known to be wise than on what the foolish or the uninformed may say."

"So everyone agrees with the final decision?"

"Why not? The matter has been threshed out and the most logical answer arrived at. Oh, of course a few are always unconvinced or dissatisfied. But being human, and therefore rational, they accommodate themselves to the general will."

"And—uh—funding such an enterprise?"

"That depends on its nature. A strictly local project, like building a new road is carried out by the people of the community involved, with feasting and merriment each night. For larger and more specialized projects, money may be needed, and then its collection is a matter of local custom. We of Instar let the Dancer go about with a sack, and everyone contributes as much as is reasonable."

Tolteca gave up for the time being. He was further along than the anthropologists of the first expedition. Except, maybe, that he was mentally prepared for some such answer as he'd received, and could accept it immediately rather than wasting weeks trying to ferret out a secret that didn't exist. If you had a society with a simple economic structure (automation helped marvelously in that respect, provided that the material desires of the people remained modest) and if you had a homogeneous population of high average intelligence and low average nastiness, well, then perhaps the ideal anarchic state was possible.

And it must be remembered that anarchy, in this case, did not mean amorphousness. The total culture of Gwydion was as intricate as any that men had ever evolved. Which in turn was paradoxical, since advanced science and technology usually dissolved traditions and simplified interhuman relationships. However . . .

Tolteca asked cautiously, "What effect do you believe contact with other planets would have on your people? Planets where things are done in radically different ways?"

"I don't know," replied Dawyd, thoughtful. "We need more data, and a great deal more discussion, before even attempting to foresee the consequences. I do wonder if a gradual introduction of new modes may not prove better for you than any sudden change."

"For us?" Tolteca was startled.

"Remember, we have lived here a long time. We know the Aspects of God on Gwydion better than you. Just as we should be most careful about venturing to your home, so do I advise that you proceed circumspectly here."

Tolteca could not help saying, "It's strange that you never built spaceships. I gather that your people preserved, or reconstructed, all the basic scientific knowledge of their ancestors. As soon as you had a large enough population, enough economic surplus, you could have coupled a thermonuclear powerplant to a gravity beamer and a secondary-drive pulse generator, built a hull around the ensemble, and—"

"No!"

It was almost a shout. Tolteca jerked his head around to look at Dawyd. The Gwydiona had gone quite pale.

Color flowed back after a moment. He relaxed his grip on the steering rod. But his eyes were still stiffly focused ahead of him as he answered, "We do not use atomic power. Sun, water, wind, tides, and biological fuel cells, with electric accumulators for energy storage, are sufficient."

Then they were in the town. Dawyd guided the automobile through wide, straight avenues which seemed incongruous among the vine-covered houses and peaked red roofs, the parks and splashing fountains. There was only one large building to be seen, a massive structure of fused stone, rearing above chimneys with a jarring grimness. Just beyond a bridge which spanned the river in a graceful serpent shape, Dawyd halted. He had calmed down, and smiled at his guest. "My abode. Will you enter?"

As they stepped to the pavement, a tiny scarlet bird flew from the eaves, settled on Dawyd's forefinger, and warbled joy. He murmured to it, grinned half awkwardly at Tolteca, and led the way to his front door. It was screened from the street by a man-high bush with star-shaped leaves new for the spring season. The door had a lock which was massive but unused. Tolteca recalled again that Gwydion was apparently without crime, that its people had been hard put to understand the concept when the outworlders interviewed them. Having opened the door, Dawyd turned about and bowed very low.

"O guest of the house, who may be God, most welcome and beloved, enter. In the name of joy, and health, and understanding; beneath Ynis and She and the stars; fire, flood, fleet, and light be yours." He crossed himself, and reaching drew a cross on Tolteca's brow with his finger. The ritual was obviously ancient, and yet he did not gabble it, but spoke with vast seriousness.

As he entered, Tolteca noticed that the door was only faced with wood. Basically it was a slab of steel, set in walls that were—under the stucco—two meters thick and of reinforced concrete. The windows were broad; sunlight streamed through them to glow on polished wood flooring, but every window had steel shutters. The first Namerican expedition had reported it was a universal mode of building, but had not been able to find out why. From somewhat evasive answers to their questions, the anthropologists concluded it was a tradition handed down from wild early days, immediately after the colony was hellbombed; and so gentle a race did not like to talk about that period.

Tolteca forgot the matter when Dawyd knelt to light a candle before a niche. The shrine held a metal disc, half gold and half black with a bridge between, the Yang and Yin of immemorial antiquity. Yet it was flanked by books, both full-size and micro, that bore titles like *Diagnostic Application of Bioelectric Potentials*.

Dawyd got up. "Please be seated, friend of the house. My wife went into the Night." He hesitated. "She died, several years ago, and only one of my daughters is now unwedded. She danced for you this day, and thus is late coming home. When she arrives, we will take food."

Tolteca glanced at the chair to which his host had gestured. It was designed as rationally as any Namerican lounger, but made of bronze and tooled leather. He touched a fylfot recurring in the design. "I understand that you have no ornamentation which is not symbolic. That's very interesting; almost diametrically opposed to my culture. Just as an example, would you mind explaining this to me?"

"Certainly," Dawyd answered. "That is the Burning Wheel,

which is to say the sun, Ynis, and all suns in the universe. The Wheel also represents Time. Thermodynamic irreversibility, if you are a physicist," he added with a chuckle. "The interwoven vines are crisflowers, which bloom in the first haygathering season of our year and are therefore sacred to that Aspect of God called the Green Boy. Thus together they mean Time the Destroyer and Regenerator. The leather is from the wild areas, which belongs to the autumnal Huntress Aspect, and when she is linked with the Boy it reminds us of the Night Faces and, simultaneously, that the Day Faces are their other side. Bronze, being an alloy, man-made, says by forming the framework that man embodies the meaning and structure of the world. However, since bronze turns green on corrosion, it also signifies that every structure vanishes at last, but into new life—"

He stopped and laughed. "You don't want a sermon!" he exclaimed. "Look here, do sit down. Go ahead and smoke. We already know about that custom. We've found we can't do it ourselves—a bit of genetic drift; nicotine is too violent a poison for us but it doesn't bother me in the least if you do. Coffee grows well on this planet, would you like a cup, or would you rather try our beer or wine? Now that we are alone for a while, I have about ten to the fiftieth questions to ask!"

❊ III ❊

Raven spent much of the day prowling about Instar, observing and occasionally, querying. But in the evening he left the town and wandered along the road which followed the river toward the sea dikes. A pair of his men accompanied him, two paces behind, in the byrnies and conical helmets of battle gear. Rifles were slung on their shoulders. At their backs the western hills lifted black against a sky which blazed and smouldered with gold. The river was like running metal in that light, which saturated the air and soaked into each separate grass blade. Ahead, beyond a line of trees, the eastern sky had become imperially violet and the first stars trembled.

Raven moved unhurriedly. He had no fear of being caught in the dark, on a planet with an 83-hour rotation period. When he came to a wharf that jutted into the stream, he halted for a closer look. The wooden sheds on the bank were as solidly built as any residential house, and as handsome of outline. The double-ended fishing craft tied at the pier were graceful things, riotously decorated. They rocked a little as the water purled past them. A clean odor of their catches, and of tar and paint, drifted about.

"Ketch rigged," Raven observed. "They have small auxiliary engines, but I dare say those are used only when it is absolutely necessary."

"And otherwise they sail?" Kors, long and gaunt, spat between his front teeth. "Now why do such a fool thing, Commandant?"

"It's aesthetically more pleasing," said Raven.

"More work, though, sir," offered young Wildenvey. "I sailed a bit myself, during the Ans campaign. Just keeping those damn ropes untangled—"

Raven grinned. "Oh, I agree. Quite. But you see, as far as I can gather, from the first expedition's reports and from talking to people today, the Gwydiona don't think that way."

He continued, ruminatively, more to himself than anyone else, "They don't think like either party of visitors. Their attitude toward life is different. A Namerican is concerned only with getting his work done, regardless of whether it's something that really ought to be accomplished, and then with getting his recreation done—both with maximum bustle. A Lochlanna tries to make his work and his games approach some abstract ideal; and when he fails, he's apt to give up completely and jump over into brutishness.

"But they don't seem to make such distinctions here. They say, 'Man goes where God is,' and it seems to mean that work and play and art and private life and everything else aren't divided up; no distinction is made between them, it's all one harmonious whole. So they fish from sailboats with elaborately carved figureheads and painted designs, each element in the pattern having a dozen different symbolic overtones. And they take musicians along. And they claim that the total effect, food gathering plus pleasure plus artistic accomplishment plus I don't know what, is more efficiently achieved than if those things were in neat little compartments."

He shrugged and resumed his walk. "They may be right," he finished.

"I don't know why you're so worried about them, sir," said Kors. "They're as harmless a pack of loonies as I ever met. I swear they haven't any machine more powerful than a light tractor or a scoop shovel, and no weapon more dangerous than a bow and arrow."

"The first expedition said they don't even go hunting, except once in a while for food or to protect their crops," Raven nodded. He went on for a while, unspeaking. Only the scuff of boots, chuckling river, murmur in the leaves overhead and slowly rising thunders beyond the dike, stirred that silence. The young five-pointed leaves of a bush which grew everywhere around gave a faint green fragrance to the air. Then, far off and winding down the slopes, a bronze horn blew, calling antlered cattle home.

"That's what makes me afraid," said Raven.

Thereafter the men did not venture to break his wordlessness. Once or twice they passed a Gwydiona, who hailed them gravely, but they didn't stop. When they reached the dike, Raven led the way up a staircase to the top. The wall stretched for kilometers, set at intervals with towers. It was high and massive, but the long curve of it and the facing of undressed stone made it pleasing to behold. The river poured through a gap, across a pebbled beach, into a dredged channel and so to the crescent-shaped bay, whose waters tumbled and roared, molten in the sunset light. Raven drew his surcoat close about him; up here, above the wall's protection, the wind blew chill and wet and smelling of salt. There were many gray sea birds in the sky.

"Why did they build this?" wondered Kors.

"Close moon. Big tides. Storms make floods," said Wildenvey.

"They could have settled higher ground. They've room enough, for hellfire's sake. Ten million people on a whole planet!"

Raven gestured at the towers. "I inquired," he said. "Tidepower generators in those. Furnish most of the local electricity. Shut up."

He stood staring out to the eastern horizon, where night was growing. The waves ramped and the sea birds mewed. His eyes were bleak with thought. Finally he sat down, took a wooden flute from his sleeve, and began to play, absentmindedly, as something to do with his hands. The minor key grieved beneath the wind.

Kors' bark recalled him to the world. "Halt!"

"Be still, you oaf," said Raven. "It's her planet, not yours." But his palm rested casually on the butt of his pistol as he rose.

The girl came walking at an easy pace over the velvet-like pseudomoss which carpeted the diketop. She was some 23 or 24 standard years old, her slim shape dressed in a white tunic and wildly fluttering blue cloak. Her hair was looped in thick yellow braids, pulled back from her forehead to show a conventionalized bird tattoo. Beneath dark brows, her eyes were a blue that was almost indigo, set widely apart. The mouth and the heart-shaped face were solemn, but the nose tiptilted and faintly dusted with freckles. She led by the hand a boy of perhaps four, a little male version of herself, who had been skipping but who sobered when he saw the Lochlanna. Both were barefoot.

"At the crossroads of the elements, greeting," she said. Her husky voice sang the language, even more than most Gwydiona voices.

"Salute, peacemaker." Raven found it simpler to translate the formal phrases of his own world than hunt around in the local vocabulary.

"I came to dance for the sea," she told him, "but heard a music that called."

"Are you a shooting man?" asked the boy.

"Byord, hush!" The girl colored with embarrassment.

"Yes," laughed Raven, "you might call me a shooting man."

"But what do you shoot?" asked Byord. "Targets? Gol! Can I shoot a target?"

"Perhaps later," said Raven. "We have no targets with us at the moment."

"Mother, he says I can shoot a target! Pow! Pow! Pow!"

Raven lifted one brow. "I thought chemical weapons were unknown on Gwydion, milady," he said, as offhand as possible.

She answered with a hint of distress, "That other ship, which came in winter. The men aboard it also had—what did they name them—guns. They explained and demonstrated. Since then, probably every small boy on the planet has imagined—Well. No harm done, I'm sure." She smiled and ruffled Byord's hair.

"Ah—I hight Raven, a Commandant of the Oakenshaw Ethnos, Windhome Mountains, Lochlann."

"And you other souls?" asked the girl.

Raven waved them back. "Followers. Sons of yeomen on my father's estate."

She was puzzled that he excluded them from the conversation, but accepted it as an alien custom. "I am Elfavy," she said, accenting the first syllable. She flashed a grin. "My son Byord you already know! His surname is Varstan, mine is Simmon."

"What?—Oh, yes, I remember. Gwydiona wives retain their family name, sons take the father's, daughters the mother's. Am I correct? Your husband—"

She looked outward. "He drowned there, during a storm last fall," she answered quietly.

Raven did not say he was sorry, for his culture had its own attitudes toward death. He couldn't help wondering aloud, tactless, "But you said you danced for the sea."

"He is of the sea now, is he not?" She continued regarding the waves, where they swirled and shook foam loose from their crests. "How beautiful it is tonight."

Then, swinging back to him, altogether at ease. "I have just had a long talk with one of your party, a Miguel Tolteca. He is staying at my father's house, where Byord and I now live."

"Not precisely one of mine," said Raven, suppressing offendedness.

"Oh? Wait . . . yes, he did mention having some men along from a different planet."

"Lochlann," said Raven. "Our sun lies near theirs, both about 50 light-years hence in that direction." He pointed past the evening star to the Hercules region.

"Is your home like his Nuevamerica?"

"Hardly." For a moment Raven wanted to speak of Lochlann—of mountains which rose sheer into a red-sun sky, trees dwarfed and gnarled by incessant winds, moorlands, ice plains, oceans too dense and bitter with salt for a man to sink. He remembered a peasant's house, its roof held down by ropes lest a gale blow it away, and he remembered his father's castle gaunt above a glacier, hoofs ringing in the courtyard, and he remembered bandits and burned villages and dead men gaping around a smashed cannon.

But she would not understand. Would she?

"Why do you have so many shooting things?" exploded from Byord. "Are there bad animals around your farms?"

"No," said Raven. "Not many wild animals at all. The land is too poor for them."

"I have heard . . . that first expedition—" Elfavy grew troubled again. "They said something about men fighting other men."

"My profession," said Raven. She looked blankly at him. Wrong word then. "My calling," he said, though that wasn't right either.

"But killing *men!*" she cried.

"Bad men?" asked Byord, round-eyed.

"Hush," said his mother. "'Bad' means when something goes wrong, like the cynwyr swarming down and eating the grain. How can men go wrong?"

"They get sick," Byord said.

"Yes, and then your grandfather heals them."

"Imagine a situation where men often get so sick they want to hurt their own kind," said Raven.

"But horrible!" Elfavy traced a cross in the air. "What germ causes that?"

Raven sighed. If she couldn't even visualize homicidal mania, how explain to her that sane, honorable men found sane, honorable reasons for hunting each other?

He heard Kors mutter to Wildenvey, "What I said. Guts of sugar candy."

If that were only so, thought Raven, he could forget his own unease. But they were no weaklings on Gwydion. Not when they took open sailboats onto oceans whose weakest tides rose fifteen meters. Not when this girl could visibly push away her own shock, face him, and ask with friendly curiosity—as if he, Raven, should address questions to the sudden apparition of a sabertoothed weaselcat.

"Is that the reason why your people and the Namericans seem to talk so little to each other? I thought I noticed it in the town, but didn't know then who came from which group."

"Oh, they've done their share of fighting on Nuevamerica," said Raven dryly, "As when they expelled us. We had invaded their planet and divided it into fiefs, over a century ago. Their revolution was aided by the fact that Lochlann was simultaneously fighting the Grand Alliance—but still, it was well done of them."

"I cannot see why—Well, no matter. We will have time enough to discuss things. You are going into the hills with us, are you not?"

"Why, yes, if—What did you say? You too?"

Elfavy nodded. Her mouth quirked upward. "Don't be so aghast, far-friend. I will leave Byord with his aunt and uncle, even if they do spoil him terribly." She gave the boy a brief hug. "But the group does need a dancer, which is my calling."

"Dancer?" choked Kors.

"Not *the* Dancer. He is always a man."

"But—" Raven relaxed. He even smiled. "In what way does an expedition into the wilderness require a dancer?"

"To dance for it," said Elfavy. "What else?"

"Oh . . . nothing. Do you know precisely what this journey is for?"

"You have not heard? I listened while my father and Miguel talked it over."

"Yes, naturally I know. But possibly you have misunderstood something. That's easy to do, even for an intelligent person, when separate cultures meet. Why don't you explain it to me in your own words, so that I can correct you if need be?" Raven's ulterior motive was simply that he enjoyed her presence and wanted to keep her here a while longer.

"Thank you, that is a good idea," she said. "Well, then, planets where men can live without special equipment are rare and far between. The Nuevamericans, who are exploring this galactic sector, would like a base on Gwydion, to refuel their ships, make any necessary repairs, and rest their crews in greenwoods." She gave Kors and Wildenvey a surprised look, not knowing why they both laughed aloud. Raven himself would not have interrupted her naive recital for money.

She brushed the blown fair hair off her brow and resumed, "Of course, our people must decide whether they wish this or not. But meanwhile it can do no harm to look at possible sites for such a base, can it? Father proposed an uninhabited valley some days' march inland, beyond Mount Granis. To journey there afoot will be more pleasant than by air; much can be shown you and discussed en route; and we would still return before Bale time."

She frowned the faintest bit. "I am not certain it is wise to have a foreign base so near the Holy City. But that can always be argued later." Her laughter trilled forth. "Oh dear, I do ramble, don't I?" She caught Raven's arm, impulsively, and tucked her own under it. "But you have seen so many worlds, you can't imagine how we here have been looking forward to meeting you. The wonder of it! The stories you can tell us, the songs you can sing us!"

She dropped her free hand to Byord's shoulder. "Wait till this little chatterbird gets over his shyness with you, far-friend. If we could only harness his questions to a generator, we could illuminate the whole of Instar!"

"Awww," said the boy, wriggling free.

They began to walk along the diketop, almost aimlessly. The two soldiers followed. The rifles on their backs stood black against a cloud like roses. Elfavy's fingers slipped down from Raven's awkwardly held arm—men and women did not go together thus on Lochlann—and closed on the flute in his sleeve. "What is this?" she asked.

He drew it forth. It was a long piece of darvawood, carved and polished to bring out the grain. "I am not a very good player," he said. "A man of rank is expected to have some artistic skills. But I am only a younger son, which is why I wander about seeking work for my guns, and I have not had much musical instruction."

"The sounds I heard were—" Elfavy searched after a word. "They spoke to me," she said finally, "but not in a language I knew. Will you play that melody again?"

He set the flute to his lips and piped the notes, which were cold and sad. Elfavy shivered, catching her mantle to her and touching the gold-and-black locket at her throat. "There is more than music here," she said. "That song comes from the Night Faces. It is a song, is it not?"

"Yes. Very ancient. From Old Earth, they say, centuries before men had reached even their own sun's planets. We still sing it on Lochlann."

"Can you put it into Gwydiona for me?"

"Perhaps. Let me think." He walked for a while more, turning phrases in his head. A military officer must also be adept in the use of words, and the two languages were close kin. Finally he sounded a few bars, lowered the flute, and began.

> "The wind doth blow today my love,
> And a few small drops of rain.
> I never had but one true love,
> And she in her grave was lain.

> "I'll do as much for my true love
> As any young man may;
> I'll sit and mourn all at her grave
> For a twelvemonth and a day. . . .
>
> "The twelvemonth and a day being up,
> The dead began to speak:
> 'Oh who sits weeping on my grave
> And will not let me sleep?'"

He felt her grow stiff, and halted his voice. She said, through an unsteady mouth, so low he could scarce hear, "No. Please."

"Forgive me," he said in puzzlement, "if I have—" What?

"You couldn't know. I couldn't." She glanced after Byord. The boy had frisked back to the soldiers. "He was out of earshot. It doesn't matter, then, much."

"Can you tell me what is wrong?" he asked, hopeful of a clue to the source of his own doubts.

"No." She shook her head. "I don't know what. It just frightens me somehow. Horribly. How can you live with such a song?"

"On Lochlann we think it quite a beautiful little thing."

"But the dead don't speak. They are *dead!*"

"Of course. It was only a fantasy. Don't you have myths?"

"Not like that. The dead go into the Night, and the Night becomes the Day, is the Day. Like Ragan, who was caught in the Burning Wheel, and rose to heaven and was cast down again, and was wept over by the Mother—those are Aspects of God, they mean the rainy season that brings dry earth to life and they also mean dreams and the waking from dreams, and loss-remembrance-recreation, and the transformations of physical energy, and—Oh, don't you see, it's all one! It isn't two people separate, becoming nothing, desiring to be nothing, even. It mustn't be!"

Raven put away his flute. They walked on until Elfavy broke from him, danced a few steps, a slow and stately dance which suddenly became a leap. She ran back smiling and took his arm again.

"I'll forget it," she said. "Your home is very distant. This is Gwydion, and too near Bale time to be unhappy."

"What is this Bale time?"

"When we go to the Holy City," she said. "Once each year. Each Gwydiona year, that is, which I believe makes about five of Old Earth's. Everybody, all over the planet, goes to the Holy City maintained by his own district. It may be a dull wait for you people, unless you can join us. . . . Perhaps you can!" she exclaimed, and eagerness washed out the last terror.

"What happens?" Raven asked.

"God comes to us."

"Oh." He thought of dionysiac rites among various backward peoples and asked with great care, "Do you see God, or feel Vwi?" The last word was a pronoun; Gwydiona employed an extra gender, the universal.

"Oh, no," said Elfavy. "We are God."

※ **IV** ※

The dance ended in a final exultant jump, wings fluttering iridescent and the bird head turned skyward. The men who had been playing music for it put down their pipes and drums. The dancer's plumage swept the ground as she bowed. She vanished into a canebrake. The audience, seated and crosslegged, closed eyes for an unspeaking minute. Tolteca thought it a more gracious tribute than applause.

He looked around again as the ceremony broke up and men prepared for sleep. It didn't seem quite real to him, yet, that camp should be pitched, supper eaten, and the time come for rest, while the sun had not reached noon. That was because of the long day, of course. Gwydion was just past vernal equinox. But even at its mild and rainy midwinter, daylight lasted a couple of sleeps.

The effect hadn't been so noticeable at Instar. The town used an auroral generator to give soft outdoor illumination after dark, and went about its business. Thus it had only taken a couple of planetary rotations to organize this party. They marched for the hills at dawn. Already one leisurely day had passed on the trail, with two campings; and one night, where the moon needed little help from the travelers' glowbulbs; and now another forenoon. Sometime tomorrow—Gwydion tomorrow—they ought to reach the upland site which Dawyd had suggested for the spaceport.

Tolteca could feel the tiredness due rough kilometers in his muscles, but he wasn't sleepy yet. He stood up, glancing over the camp. Dawyd had selected a good spot, a meadow in the forest. The half-dozen Gwydiona men who accompanied him talked merrily as they banked the fire and spread out sleeping bags. One man, standing watch against possible carnivores, carried a longbow. Tolteca had seen what that weapon could do, when a hunter brought in an arcas for meat. Nonetheless he wondered why everyone had courteously refused those firearms the *Quetzal* brought as gifts.

The ten Namerican scientists and engineers who had come along were in more of a hurry to bed down. Tolteca chuckled, recalling their dismay when he announced that this trip would be on shank's mare. But Dawyd was right, there was no better way to learn an area. Raven had also joined the group, with two of his men. The Lochlanna seemed incapable of weariness, and their damned slithering politeness never failed them, but they were always a little apart from the rest.

Tolteca sauntered past the canebrake, following a side path. Though no one lived in these hills, the Gwydiona often went here for recreation, and small solar-powered robots maintained the trails. He had not quite dared hope he would meet Elfavy. But when she came around a flowering tree, the heart leaped in him.

"Aren't you tired?" he asked, lame-tongued, after she stopped and gave greeting.

"Not much," she answered. "I wanted to stroll for a while before sleep. Like you."

"Well, let's go into partnership."

She laughed. "An interesting concept. You have so many commercial enterprises on your planet, I hear. Is this another one? Hiring out to take walks for people who would rather sit at home?"

Tolteca bowed. "If you'll join me, I'll make a career of that."

She flushed and said quickly, "Come this way. If I remember this neighborhood from the last time I was here, it has a beautiful view not far off."

She had changed her costume for a plain tunic. Sunlight came through leaves to touch her lithe dancer's body; the hair, loosened, fell in waves down her back. Tolteca could not find the words he really wanted, nor could he share her easy silence.

"We don't do everything for money on Nuevamerica," he said, afraid of what she might think. "It's only, well, our particular way of organizing our economy."

"I know," she said. "To me it seems so . . . impersonal, lonely, each man fending for himself—but that may just be because I am not used to the idea."

"Our feeling is that the state should do as little as possible," he said, earnest with the ideals of his nation. "Otherwise it will get too much power, and that's the end of freedom. But then private enterprise must take over; and it must be kept competitive, or it will in turn develop into a tyranny." Perforce he used several words which Gwydiona lacked, such as the last. He had introduced them to her before, during conversations at Dawyd's house, when they had tried to comprehend each other's viewpoints.

"But why should the society, or the state as you call it, be opposed to the individual?" she asked. "I still don't grasp what the problem is, Miguel. We seem to do much as we please, all the time, here on Gwydion. Most of our enterprises are private, as you put it." *No*, he thought, *not as I put it. Your folk are only interested in making a living. The profit motive, in the economists' sense of the word, isn't there.* He forebore to interrupt. "But this unregulated activity seems to work for everyone's mutual benefit," she continued. "Money is only a convenience. Its possession does not give a man power over his fellows."

"You are universally reasonable," Tolteca said. "That isn't true of any other planet I know about. Nor do you need to curb violence. You hardly know what anger is. And hate—another word which isn't in your language. Hate is to be *always* angry with someone else." He saw shock on her face, and hurried to add, "Then we must contend with the lazy, the greedy, the unscrupulous—Do you know, I begin to wonder if we should carry out this project. It may be best that your planet have nothing to do with the others. You are too good; you could be too badly hurt."

She shook her head. "No, don't think that. Obviously we are different from you. Perhaps genetic drift has caused us to lose a trait or two otherwise common to mankind. But the difference isn't great, and it doesn't make us superior. Remember, you came to us. We never managed to build spaceships."

"Never chose to," he corrected her.

He recalled a remark of Raven's, one day in Instar. "It isn't natural for humans to be consistently gentle and rational. They've done tremendous things here for so small a population. They don't lack energy. But where does their excess energy go?" At the time, Tolteca had bristled. Only a professional killer would be frightened by total sanity, he thought. Now he began, unwilling, to see that Raven had asked a legitimate scientific question.

"There is much that we never chose to do," said Elfavy with a hint of wistfulness.

"I admit wondering why you don't at least colonize the uninhabited parts of Gwydion."

"We stabilized the population by general agreement, several centuries ago. More people would only destroy nature."

They emerged from the woods again. Another meadow sloped upward to a cliff edge. The grass was strewn with white flowers; the common bush of star-shaped leaves grew everywhere about, its buds swelling, the air heady from their odor. Beyond this spine of the hills lay a deep valley and then the mountains rose, clear and powerful against the sky.

Elfavy swept an arm in an arc. "Should we crowd out this?" she asked.

Tolteca thought of his own brawling unrestful folk, the forests they had already raped, and made no answer.

The girl stood a moment, frowning, on the clifftop. A west wind blew strongly, straining the tunic against her and tossing sunlit locks of hair. Tolteca caught himself staring so rudely that he forced his eyes away, across kilometers toward that gray volcanic cone named Mount Granis.

"No," said Elfavy with some reluctance, "I must not be smug. People did live here once. Just a few farmers and woodcutters, but they did maintain isolated homes. However, that is long past. Nowadays everyone lives in a town. And I don't believe we would reoccupy regions like this even if it were safe. It would be wrong. All life has a right to existence, does it not? Men shouldn't wear more of a Night Face than they must."

Tolteca found some difficulty in concentrating on her meaning, the sound was so pleasant. Night Face—oh, yes, part of the Gwydiona religion. (If "religion" was the right word. "Philosophy" might be better. "Way of life" might be still more accurate.) Since they believed everything to be a facet of that eternal and infinite Oneness which they called God, it followed that God was also death, ruin, sorrow. But they didn't say much, or seem to think much, about that side of reality. He remembered that their arts and literature, like their daily lives, were mostly sunny, cheerful, completely logical once you had mastered the complex symbolisms. Pain was gallantly endured. The suffering or death of someone beloved was mourned in a controlled manner which Raven admired, but Tolteca had trouble understanding .

"I don't believe your people could harm nature," he said. "You work with it, make yourselves part of it."

"That's the ideal." Elfavy snickered. "But I'm afraid practice has no more statistical correlation with preaching on Gwydion than anywhere else in the universe." She knelt and began to pluck the small white flowers. "I shall make a garland of jule for you," she said. "A sign of friendship, since the jule blooms when the growth season is being reborn. Now that's a nice harmonious thing for me to do, isn't it? And yet if you asked the plant, it might not agree!"

"Thank you," he said, overwhelmed.

"The Bird Maiden had a chaplet of jule," she said. By now he realized that the retelling of symbolic myths was a standard conversational gambit here, like a Lochlanna's inquiry after the health of your father. "That is why I wore a bird costume this time. It is her time of year, and today is the Day of the River Child. When the Bird Maiden met the River Child, he was lost and crying. She carried him home and gave him her crown." She glanced up. "It is a seasonal myth," she explained, "the end of the rains, lowland floods, then sunlight and the blossoming jule. Plus those moral lessons the elders are always quacking about, plus a hundred other possible interpretations. The entire tale is too complicated to tell on a warm day, even if the episode of the Riddling Tree is one of our best poems. But I always like to dance the story."

She fell silent, her hands busy in the grass. For lack of anything else, he pointed to one of the large budding bushes. "What's this called?" he asked.

"With the five-pointed leaves? Oh, baleflower. It grows every-where. You must have noticed the one in front of my father's house."

"Yes. It must have quite a lot of mythology."

Elfavy stopped. She glanced at him and away. For an instant the evening-blue eyes seemed almost blind. "No," she said.

"What? But I thought . . . I thought everything means something on Gwydion, as well as being something. Usually it has many different meanings—"

"This is only baleflower." Her voice grew thin. "Nothing else."

Tolteca pulled himself up short. Some taboo—no, surely not that, the Gwydiona were even freer from arbitrary prohibitions than his own people. But if she was sensitive about it, best not to pursue the subject.

The girl finished her work, jumped to her feet, and flung a wreath about his neck. "There!" she laughed. "Wait, hold still, it's caught on one ear. Ah, good."

He gestured at the second one she had made. "Aren't you going to put that on yourself?"

"Oh, no. A jule garland is always for someone else. This is for Raven."

"What?" Tolteca stiffened.

Again she flushed and looked past him toward the mountains. "I got to know him a little in Instar. I drove him around, showing him the sights. Or we walked."

Tolteca thought of the many times in those long moonlit nights when she had not been at home. He said, "I don't believe Raven is your sort," and heard his voice go ragged.

"I don't understand him," she whispered. "And yet in a way I do. Maybe. As I might understand a storm."

She started back toward camp. Tolteca must needs follow. He said bitterly, "I should think you, of everyone alive, would be immune to such cheap glamour. Soldier! Hereditary aristocrat!"

"Those things I don't comprehend," she said, her eyes still averted. "To kill people, or make them do your bidding, as if they were machines—But it isn't that way with him. Not really."

They went down the trail in stillness, boots thudding next to sandals. At last she murmured, "He lives with the Night Faces. All the time. I can't even bear to think of that, but he endures it."

Enjoys it, Tolteca wanted to growl. But he saw he had been back-biting, and held his peace.

❖ V ❖

They returned to find most of the party asleep, eyelids padded against the daylight. The sentry saluted them with a raised arrow. Elfavy continued to the edge of camp, where the three Lochlanna had spread their bedrolls. Kors snored, a gun in his hand; Wildenvey looked too young and helpless for his gory shipboard brags. Raven was still awake. He squatted on his heels and scowled at a sheaf of photographs.

As Elfavy approached, his grin sprang forth; even to Tolteca, he seemed quite honestly pleased. "Well, this is a happy chance," he called. "Will you join me? I have a pot of tea on the grill over the coals."

"No, thank you. I like that tea stuff of yours, but it would keep me from sleeping." Elfavy stood before him, looking down at the ground. The wreath dangled in her hand. "I only—"

"Never come between an Oakenshaw and his tea," said Raven. "Ah, there, Sir Engineer."

Elfavy's face burned. "I only wanted to see you for a moment," she faltered.

"And I you. Someone mentioned former habitation in this area, and I noticed traces on a ridge near here. Sol went there with a camera." Raven flowed erect and fanned out his self-developing films. "It was a thorp once, several houses and outbuildings. Not much left now."

"No. Long abandoned." The girl lifted her wreath and lowered it again.

Raven gave her a steady look. "Destroyed," he said.

"Oh? Oh, yes. I have heard this region was dangerous. The volcano—"

"No natural disaster," said Raven. "I know the signs. My men and I cleared away the brush with a flash pistol and dug in the ground. Those buildings had wooden roofs and rafters, which burned. We found two human skeletons, more or less complete. One had a skull split open, the other a corroded iron object between the ribs." He raised the pictures toward her eyes. "Do you see?"

"Oh." She stepped back. One hand crept to her mouth. "What—"

"Everyone tells me there is no record of men killing men on Gwydion," said Raven in a metallic voice. "It's not merely rare, it's unknown. And yet that thorp was attacked and burned once."

Elfavy gulped. Anger rushed into Tolteca, thick and hot. "Look here, Raven," he snapped, "you may be free to bully some poor Lochlanna peasant, but—"

"No," said Elfavy. "Please."

"Did every home up here suffer a like fate?" Raven flung the questions at her, not loudly but nonetheless like bullets. "Were the hills deserted because it was too hazardous to live in isolation?"

"I don't know." Elfavy's tone lifted with an unevenness it had not borne until now. "I . . . have seen ruins once in a while . . . nobody knows what happened." A sudden yell: "*Everything* isn't written in the histories, you know! Do you know every answer to every question about your own planet?"

"Of course not," said Raven. "But if this were my world, I'd at least know why all the buildings are constructed like fortresses."

"Like what?"

"You know what I mean."

"Why, you asked me that once before. . . . I told you," she stammered. "The strength of the house, the family—a symbol—"

"I heard the myth," said Raven. "I was also assured that no one has ever believed those myths to be literal truths, only poetic expressions. Your charming tale about Anren who made the stars has not prevented you from having an excellent grasp of astrophysics. So what are you guarding against? What are you afraid of?"

Elfavy crouched back. "Nothing." The words rattled from her. "If, if, if there were anything . . . wouldn't we have better weapons against it . . . than bows and spears? People get hurt—by accidents, by sickness and old age. They die, the Night has them—But nothing else! There can't be!"

She whirled about and fled.

Tolteca stepped toward Raven, who stood squinting after the girl. "Turn around," he said. "I'm going to beat the guts out of you."

Raven laughed, a vulpine bark. "How much combat karate do you know, trader's clerk?"

Tolteca dropped a hand to his gun. "We're in another culture," he said between his teeth. "A generation of scientific study won't be enough to map its thought processes. If you think you can go trampling freely on these people's feelings, no more aware of what you're doing than a bulldozer with a broken autopilot—"

They both felt the ground shiver. An instant afterward the sound reached them, booming down the sky.

The three Lochlanna were on their feet in a ring, weapons aimed outward, without seeming to have moved. Elsewhere the camp stumbled awake, men calling to each other through thunders.

Tolteca ran after Elfavy. The sun seemed remote and heatless, the explosions rattled his teeth together, he felt the earth's vibrations in his boots.

The noise died away, but echoes flew about for seconds longer. Dawyd joined Elfavy and threw his arms around her. A flock of birds soared up, screaming.

The physician's gaze turned westward. Black smoke boiled above the treetops. As Tolteca reached the Simnons, he saw Dawyd trace the sign against misfortune.

"What is it?" shouted the Namerican. "What happened?"

Dawyd looked his way. For a moment the old eyes were without recognition. Then he answered curtly, "Mount Granis."

"Oh." Tolteca slapped his forehead. The relief was such that he wanted to howl his laughter. Of course! A volcano cleared its throat, after a century or two of quiet. Why in the galaxy were the Gwydiona breaking camp?

"I never expected this," said Dawyd. "Though probably our seismology is less well developed than yours."

"Our man made some checks, and didn't think we would have any serious trouble if we built a spaceport here," said Tolteca. "That wasn't a real eruption, you know. Just a bit of lava and a good deal of smoke."

"And a west wind," said Dawyd. "Straight from Granis to us."

He paused before adding, almost absentmindedly, "The site I had in mind for your base is protected from this sort of thing. I checked the airflow patterns with the central meteorological computer at

Bettwis, and the fumes never will get there. It is a mere unlucky happenstance that we should be at this exact spot, this very moment. Now we must run, and may fear give speed to us."

"From a little smoke?" asked Tolteca incredulously.

Dawyd held his daughter close. "This is a young planetary system," he said. "Rich in heavy metals. That smoke and dust, when it arrives, will include enough such material to kill us."

By the time they got in motion, jogging south along a sparsely wooded ridge, the cloud had overshadowed them. Kors looked past a dim red ball of sun, estimating with an artilleryman's eye. His lantern jaw worked a moment, as if chewing sour cud, before he spoke.

"We can't go back the way we came, Commandant. That muck'll fall out all over these parts. We've got to keep headed this way and hope we can get out from under. Ask one of those yokels if he knows a decent trail."

"Must we have a trail?" puffed Wildenvey. "Let's cut right through the woods."

"Listen to the for-Harry's-sake heathdweller talk!" jeered Kors. "Porkface, I grew up in the Ernshaw. Have you ever tried to run through brush?"

"Save your breath, you two," advised Raven. He loped a little faster until he joined Dawyd and Elfavy at the head of the line. Grass whispered under his boots, now and then a hobnail rang on a stone and sparks showered. The sky was dull brown, streaked with black, the light from it like tarnished brass and casting no shadows. The only bright things in the world were an occasional fire-spit from Mount Granis, and Elfavy's flying hair.

Raven put the question to her. He spaced his words with his breathing, which he kept in rhythm with his feet. The girl replied in the same experienced manner. "In this direction, all paths converge on the Holy City. We ought to be safe there, if we can reach it soon enough."

"Before Bale time?" exclaimed Dawyd.

"Is it forbidden?" asked Raven, and wondered if he would use his guns to enter a refuge tabooed.

"No . . . no rule of conduct. . . . But nobody goes there outside Bale time!" Dawyd shook his head, bewildered. "It would be a meaningless act."

"Meaningless—to save our lives?" protested Raven.

"Unsymbolic," said Elfavy. "It would fit into no pattern." She lifted her face to the spreading darkness and cried, "But what sense would it make to breathe that dust? I want to see Byord again!"

"Yes. So. So be it." Dawyd shut his mouth and concentrated on making speed.

Raven's eyes, watching the uneven ground, touched the girl's quick feet and stayed there. Not until he tripped on a vine did he remember exactly where he was. Then he swore and forced himself to think of the situation. Without analytical apparatus, he had no way to confirm that volcanic ash was as dangerous as Dawyd claimed; but it seemed reasonable, on a planet like this. The first expedition had been warned about many vegetable species that were poisonous to man simply because they grew in soil loaded with heavy elements. It wouldn't take a lot of inhaled metallic material to destroy you: radioactives, arsenates, perhaps mercury liberated from its oxide by heat. A few gulps and you were done. Dying might take a while, prolonged by the medics' attempts to get a hopelessly big dose out of your body. Not that Raven intended to watch his own lungs and brain go rotten. His pistol could do him a final service. But Elfavy—

They stopped to rest at the head of a downward trail. One of the Gwydiona objected through a dried-out throat: "Not the Holy City! We'd destroy the entire meaning of Bale!"

"No, we wouldn't." Dawyd, who had been thinking as he trotted, answered with an authority that pulled their reddened eyes to him. "The eruption at the moment when we happened to be downwind was an accident so improbable it was senseless. Right? The Night Face called Chaos." Several men crossed themselves, but they nodded agreement. "If we redress the matter—restore the balance of events, of logical sequence—by entering the Focus of God (in our purely human *persona* at that, which makes our act a parable of man's conscious reasoning powers, his science)—what could be more significant?"

They mulled it over while the gloom thickened and Mount Granis boomed at their backs. One by one, they murmured assent. Tolteca whispered to Raven, in Ispanyo, "Oa, I do believe I see a new myth being born."

"Yes. They'll doubtless bring one of their quasi-gods into it, a few generations hence, while preserving an accurate historical account of what really happened!"

"But by all creation! Here they are, running from an unnecessarily horrible death, and they argue whether it would be artistic to shelter in this temple spot!"

"It makes more sense than you think," said Raven somberly. "I remember once when I was a boy, my very first campaign in fact. A civil war, the Bitter Water clan against my own Ethnos. We boxed a regiment of them in the Stawr Hills, expecting them to dig in. They wouldn't, because there were brave men's graves everywhere around, the Danoora who fell three hundred years ago. They came out prepared to be mowed down. When we grasped the situation, we let them go, gave them a day's head start. They reached their main body, which perhaps turned the course of the war. But that victory would have cost us too much."

Tolteca shook his head. "I don't understand you."

"You wouldn't."

"Any more than you would understand why men died to pull down the foreign castles on our planet."

"Well, maybe so."

Raven wondered how much lethal dust he was already breathing. Not enough to matter, yet, he decided. The air was still clean in his nostrils, he could still see far across hills and down forested slopes. The heavy particles and stones were not dangerous. It was the finely divided material, slowly settling over many hectares, which could kill men.

Like a mind-reader, Dawyd said to him, "The Holy City will be almost ideal for us. Airflow patterns protect it too from the ash, where it lies right under the Steeps of Kolumkill. The site was chosen with that in mind, even though our local volcanoes very rarely erupt. We shall have to wait there till the next rain, which may take a few days at this season. That will carry down the last airborne dust, leach from the soil what has fallen, wash the poison into the rivers and so into the sea, safely diluted. The City has ample food supplies, and I see no reason why we should not avail ourselves of them."

He rose. "But first we must get there," he finished. "Does everyone have his breath back?"

❊ VI ❊

The rest of the journey was little remembered. They went at a dogtrot, along well-kept trails, under cool leaves; they halted a few minutes at a time when it seemed indicated; but toward the end men lurched along in each other's arms. Three Namericans collapsed. Dawyd had poles chopped and raincoats spread to make litters for them. No one complained at the burden. Perhaps that was only because no energy was left to complain.

When he entered the Holy City, Raven himself scarcely saw it. He retained enough strength to spread a bedroll for Elfavy, who sprawled quietly down and passed out. He brought a cup of water for Dawyd, who lay on his back and stared with eyes emptied of awareness. He even washed the grime and sweat from himself before crawling into his own bag. But then darkness clubbed him.

When he awoke, it took a few seconds before he knew his own name, and a bit longer to fix his location. He rallied those drilled reflexes by which he could deny to himself that he was stiff and aching. Shadow from a wall covered him, but he looked straight up to the stars. Had he slept so long? The sky was utterly clear; men were indeed safe in this place. The constellations glittered in unfamiliar patterns. He could barely recognize the one they called The Plowman on Lochlann: its distortion made him feel cold and alone. The Nebula, dimming some parts of the sky and blotting out others, was somehow less alien.

He left his bag, hunkered in the dark and opened the packsack that had been his pillow with fingers too schooled to need light. Quickly he dressed. Dagger and pistol made a comforting drag on his flanks. He threw a wide-sleeved tunic over the drab route clothes, for it flaunted the crests of his family and nation, and he glided between men still unconscious, into the open.

The night was very quiet. He stood in a forum, if it could be so named. There was no paving in the Holy City, but thick pseudomoss lay cool and full of dew under his feet. On every side rose white marble buildings, long and low, fluted delicate columns upholding portico roofs where figures danced on friezes. Their doorless main entrances gaped wide atop mossy ramps, but the windows were mere slits. Colonnades and wings knitted them together in a labyrinthine unity. Behind the square that they defined stood a ring of towers, airily slender, with bronze cupolas that must show a soft green by daylight. The entire place was surrounded by an amphitheater, or whatever you wanted to call it: low moss-carpeted tiers enclosing the city like the sides of a chalice. Trees grew thickly on its top.

Down here on the bottom there were no trees; but many formal gardens—rather, a single, reticulated one, interwoven with the houses and the towers—held beds of Terran violets and thornless roses, native jule and sunbloom and baleflower and much else which Raven didn't recognize. Southward, above the rim of the chalice, those cliffs called the Steeps of Kolumkill shouldered against the stars.

He was able to see much detail, for the moon She was rising in the west. Its retrograde path would take it over the sky and through half a cycle of phases during half a night period. Already it was a white semicircle, a degree in angular diameter, filling the hollow with unreal light.

A fountain tinkled in the middle of the forum. Raven had cleaned himself there before he slept. He crossed to its little moss-grown bowl and drank until his mummy gullet felt alive again. The water gurgled back down a whimsical drainpipe, a grotesque fish face. Well, why shouldn't there be humor in the geometric center of sacredness? thought Raven. The people of Gwydion laughed more than most, not raucously like a Namerican or wolfishly like a Lochlanna, but a gentle mirth which found something comical in the grandest things. The water must come from some woodland spring, it had a wild taste.

He heard a noise and whirled about, one hand on his gun. Elfavy entered the moonlight. "Oh," he said stupidly. "Are you awake, milady?"

She chuckled. "No. I am sound asleep in my bed in Instar." Treading close: "I woke an hour or more ago, but didn't want to move. Not for a day, at least! Then I saw you here and—" Her voice trailed off.

Raven directed his heartbeat to slow down. It obeyed poorly. "Someone should keep watch," he said. "May as well be me."

"No need, far-friend. There are no dangers here."

"Wild animals?"

"Robots keep them off. Other robots maintain the grounds." She pointed to a little wheeled machine weeding a rosebed with delicate tendrils.

Raven grinned. "Ah, but who maintains the robots?"

"Silly! An automatic unit, of course. Every five years—local years, I mean, so it's about once in a generation—our engineers hold a midwinter ceremony where they inspect the facilities and bring in fresh supplies."

"I see. And otherwise no one ever comes here except at, uh, Bale time?"

She nodded. "No reason to. Shall we look around? Walking might get the cramp out of my legs." She made the suggestion with no trace of awe, as if offering to show him any local curiosum.

Their feet fell noiseless on the moss, and its springiness seemed to remove much of their exhaustion. The buildings looked like faerie work, there under the brutal mass of Kolumkill; but as he reached a doorway, Raven saw that their walls were heavy and strong as the rest of Gwydiona architecture. Within, light came from fluoros, recessed in the high ceiling; probably solar battery powered, Raven thought. The illumination was dim, but there was little to see anyhow: a gracious anteroom, archways opening on corridors.

"We mustn't go very deeply in," said the girl, "or we could get lost and blunder around for quite some time before finding our way out. Look." She pointed down a hall, toward an intersection whence five other passages radiated. "That is only the edge of the maze."

Raven touched a wall. It yielded to his fingers, the same rubbery gray substance that covered the floor. "What's this?" he asked. "A synthetic elastomer? Does it line the whole interior?"

"Yes," said Elfavy. Her tone grew indifferent. "There's nothing in here, really. Let's go up in one of the towers, then you can see the total pattern."

"A moment, if you grant." Raven opened one of the doors which marched along the nearest corridor. It was steel, as usual, though coated with the soft plastic, and had an inside bolt. The room beyond was ventilated through a slit-window. A toilet and water tap were the only furnishings, but a heap of stuffed bags filled one corner. "What's in those?" he inquired.

"Food, sealed in plastiskins," Elfavy answered. "An artificial food, which keeps indefinitely. I'm afraid you won't find it very exciting when we must live off it, but everything necessary for nutrition is included."

"You seem to live rather austerely at Bale time," said Raven. He watched her from the edge of an eye.

"It is no time to worry about material needs. Instead, you grab a sack of food and slit it open with your thumbnail when hungry, drink from a tap or fountain when thirsty, flop down anywhere when sleepy."

"I see. But what is the important thing you do, to which keeping alive is just incidental?"

"I told you." She left the room with a quick nervous stride. "We are God."

"But when I asked you what you meant by that, you said you couldn't explain."

"I can't." She evaded his glance. Her voice was not perfectly level. "Don't you see, it goes beyond language. Any language. Mankind employs several, you realize, besides speech. Mathematics is one, music another, painting another, choreography another, and so on. According to what you have told me, Gwydion seems to be the only planet where myth was also developed, deliberately and systematically, as still a different language—not by primitives who confused it with the concepts of science or common sense, but by people trained in semantics, who knew that each language describes one single facet of reality, and wanted myth to help them talk about something for which the others are inadequate. You can't believe, for instance, that mathematics and poetry are interchangeable!"

"No," said Raven.

She brushed back her tousled hair and went on, eager now. "Well, what happens at Bale time could only be described by a fusion of every language, including those no human being has yet imagined. And such super-language is impossible, because it would be self-contradictory."

"Do you mean that during Bale you perceive, or commune with, total reality?"

They came out into the open again. She hastened across the forum, through the barred shadow of a colonnade to the spires beyond. He had never seen anything so beautiful as the sight of her running in the moonlight. She stopped at a tower doorway, it cast a darkness over her and she said from the darkness, "That's merely another set of words, *liatha*. Not even a label. I wish you could be here yourself and know!"

They entered and started upward. A padded ramp wound around small rooms. The passage was wanly lit and stuffy. After a silence, Raven asked, "What was it you called me?"

"What?" He couldn't be sure in the gloom, but he thought her face was stained with quick color.

"*Liatha.* I don't know that word."

Her lashes fluttered down. "Nothing," she mumbled, "An expression."

"Ah, let me guess." He wanted to make a joke, to suggest that it meant oaf, barbarian, villain, swinedog, but remembered that Gwydiona had no such terms. Since she looked at him with enormous expectant eyes he must blunder, "Darling, beloved—"

She stopped, shrinking back against the wall in dismay. "You said you didn't know!"

The discipline of a lifetime kept him walking. When she rejoined him he made himself say, lightly, through a clamor, "You are most kind, peacemaker, but I don't need any further flattery than the fact that you have time to spare for me."

"There will be time enough for everything else," she whispered, "after you are gone."

The highest room, immediately under the cupola, was the only one which possessed a true window, rather than a slit. Moonlight cataracted past its bronze grille. The air was warm, but that light made Elfavy's hair seem to crackle with frost. She pointed out at the intricate interlocking of labyrinth, towers, and flowerbeds. "The hexagons inscribed in circles mean the laws of nature," she began in a subdued voice, "their regularity enclosed in some greater scheme. It is the sign of Owan the Sunsmith, who—" She stopped. Neither of them had been listening. They searched each other's faces under the fenced-off moon.

"Must you go?" she asked finally.

"I have made promises at home," he said.

"But after they are fulfilled?"

"I don't know." He considered the stranger sky. In the southern hemisphere, which was oriented more nearly toward the direction whence he had come, the constellations would be less changed. But no one lived in the southern hemisphere. "I've known people from one place, one culture, who tried to settle into another," he said. "It rarely works."

"It might. If there were willingness. A Gwydiona, for example, could be happy even on, well, on Lochlann."

"I wonder."

"Will you do something for me? Now?"

His pulses jumped. "If I can, milady."

"Sing me the rest of that song. The one you sang when we first met."

"What? Oh, yes, *The Unquiet Grave.* But you couldn't—"

"I would like to try again. Since you are fond of it. Please."

He hadn't brought his flute, but he sang low in the chilly light:

> "' 'Tis I, my love, sits on your grave
> And will not let you sleep;
> For I crave one kiss of your clay-cold lips
> And that is all I seek.'
>
> "'You crave one kiss of my clay-cold lips;
> But my breath smells earthy strong.
> If you have one kiss of my clay-cold lips
> Your time will not be long.'"

"No," said Elfavy. She gulped and hugged herself, seeking warmth. "I'm sorry."

He recalled again that there was no tragic art on Gwydion. None whatsoever. He wondered, what a *Lear* or an *Agamemnon* or an *Old Men At Centauri* might do to her. Or the real thing, even: Vard of Helldale, rebelling for a family honor he didn't believe in, defeated and slain by his own comrades; young Brand who broke his regimental oath, gave up friends and wealth and the mistress he loved more than the sun, to go live in a peasant's hut and tend his insane wife.

He wondered if he, himself, was healthy enough within the skull to live on Gwydion.

The girl rubbed her eyes. "Best we go down again," she said dully. "Others will soon be awake. They won't know what has become of us."

"We'll talk later," said Raven. "When we aren't so tired."

"Of course," she said.

✧ VII ✧

Rain came the following afternoon; first thunderheads banked over Kolumkill like blue-black granite, lightning livid in their caverns, then cataracts borne on a whooping east wind, finally a long slacking off when the Gwydiona romped nude on turf that glittered where sunbeams struck through the pillars of slowly falling water. Tolteca joined the ball game, as vigorous a one as he had ever played. Afterward they lounged about indoors, around a fire built on a hearth improvised from stones, and yarned. The men probed his recollections with an insatiable wish to learn more about the galaxy. They had tales to give in exchange, nothing of interhuman conflict— they seemed puzzled and troubled by that idea—but lusty enough, happenings of sea and forest and mountain.

"So we sat in that diving bell waiting to see if their grapple would find us before we ran out of air," Llyrdin said, "and I never played better chess in my life. It got right thick in there, too, before they snatched us up. They could have had the decency to be a few minutes longer about it, though. I had such a lovely end game planned out! But of course the board was upset as they hauled on the bell."

"And what might that symbolize?" Tolteca teased him.

Llyrdin shrugged. "I don't know. I'm not much of a thinker, myself. Maybe God likes a joke now and then. But if so, Vwi has a pawky sense of humor."

After the storm had passed, the party went on to the spaceport site. Tolteca put in a busy day and night investigating the area. It would serve admirably, he decided.

Though Bale time was drawing near and the Gwydiona were anxious to get home, Dawyd ordered a roundabout route. The rain had laid the volcanic dust, but more precipitation would be needed to purify the ground entirely. It would be foolish to retrace their path across that tainted soil. He aimed for a shoulder of the mountains which jutted out of the massif on the north, between the expedition and the coast. The pass across it rose above timberline, and travel was rugged. They stopped for some hours in the uppermost woods to rest before the final ascent. That was in the middle morning.

After he had eaten, Tolteca left camp to wash in a pool further down the stream which flowed nearby. Glacier-fed, the water numbed him, but after he had toweled himself he felt like a minor sun. He donned his clothes and wandered restlessly in search of a fall he could hear in the distance. A game trail led through the brush toward its foot. He was about to emerge there when he heard voices. Raven and Elfavy!

"Please," the girl said. Her tone trembled. "I beg you, be reasonable."

The distress in her shocked Tolteca. For a moment of rage he wanted to burst forth and have it out with Raven. He checked himself. Eavesdropping was ungentlemanly. Even if—or perhaps especially because—those two had been so much in each other's company since the first night in the Holy City. But if she was in some difficulty, he wanted to know about it so he could try to help her, and he didn't think she would tell him what the matter was if he put a direct question. There were cultural barriers, taboo or embarrassment, which only Raven was callous enough to hammer down.

Tolteca wet his lips. His palms grew sweaty and the pulse thuttered in his ears, nearly as loud as the stream that jumped over the bluff before him. *To Chaos with being a gentleman,* he decided violently, slipped behind a natural hedge and peered through the leaves.

The water foamed down into a dell filled with young trees. Their foliage made a shifting pattern of light and shadow under the deep upland sky. Rainbows danced in the water smoke, currents swirled about rocks covered with soft green growth, the stones on the riverbed seemed to ripple. Cool and damp, the air rang with the noise of the fall. High overhead wheeled a single bird of prey.

Raven stood on the bank, a statue in a black traveling cloak. The harsh face might have been cast in metal as he regarded the girl. She kept twisting her own gaze away from his, and her fingers wrestled with each other. Tiny droplets caught in her hair broke the sunlight into flaming shards, but that unbound mane was itself the brightest thing before Tolteca's eyes.

"I am being reasonable," Raven snapped. "When my nose is rubbed in something for the third time running, I don't ignore the smell."

"Third time? What do you mean? Why are you so angry today?"

Raven gave an elaborate sigh and ticked the points off on his fingers. "We've been over this ground before. First: your houses are built like fortresses. Yes, you tell me that's a symbol, but I have trouble believing that rational people like you would go to so much trouble and expense for something that was nothing but a symbol. Second: nobody lives alone any more, especially not in the wilderness. I can't forget that place where it was tried once. Those people were killed with weapons. Third: while we were looking over the port site, your father made a remark about caves in the cliff being easily made into Bale time shelters. When I asked him what he had in mind, he suddenly discovered he had an urgent matter to attend to elsewhere. When I asked a couple of the others, they grew almost as unhappy as you and mumbled something about taking insurance against unforeseeable accidents.

"What tore it for me was when I pressed Cardwyr for a real explanation, a few hours ago on the march. He'd been so frank with me in every other respect that I felt he'd continue that way. But instead, he came as near losing his temper as I've ever seen a Gwydiona do. I thought for a minute he was going to hit me. But he just stalked off telling me to improve my manners.

"Something is wrong here. Why don't you give us fair warning?"

Elfavy turned as if to depart. She blinked very fast, and a wetness glinted on her cheek. "I thought you . . . you invited me to go for a walk," she said. "But—"

He caught her by the arm. "Listen," he said more gently. "Please listen, I'm picking on you because, well, you've honored me with reason to think you won't lie or evade when something is really important to me. And this is. You've never seen violence, but I have. Much too often. I know what comes of it, and—I have to do what I can to keep it from you. Do you follow me? I have to."

She ceased pulling against him and stood shivering, her head bent so that the locks fell past her face and hid it. Raven studied her for a while. His mouth lost its hardness. "Sit down, my dear," he said at last.

Elfavy lowered herself to the ground as if strength had deserted her. He joined her and took one small hand in his. There went a stabbing through Tolteca.

"Are you forbidden to talk about this?" Raven asked, so low that the brawling of the fall nearly drowned the question.

She shook her head.

"Why won't you, then?"

"I—" Her fingers tightened around his palm, and she laid her other hand over it. He sat cat-passive while she gulped for breath. "I don't know. We don't—" Some seconds passed before she could get the words out. "We hardly ever talk about it. Or think about it. It's too dreadful."

There is such a thing as an unconscious taboo, Tolteca remembered through the tides in his brain, *laid by the self upon the self.*

"And it's not as if the bad things happen very often, now that . . . that we've learned how to take . . . precautions. Long ago it was worse—" She braced herself and looked squarely at him. "You live with greater hazards and horrors than ours, all the time, do you not?"

Raven smiled very slightly. "Ah-ah, there. I decline your counter-challenge. Let's stick to the main issue. Something occurs, or can occur, during Bale. That's plain to see. Your people must have wondered what, if they don't actually know."

"Yes. There have been ideas." Elfavy seemed to have recovered her nerve. She frowned at the earth for a space and then said almost coolly, "We are not much given on Gwydion to examining our own souls, as you from the stars seem to be. I suppose that is because we're simpler. Miguel said to me once that he would not have believed there could be an entire race so free of internal conflicts as us, until he came here." *She spoke my name!* "I don't know about that, but I do know that I've little skill in reading my own inmost thoughts. So I can't tell you with certainty why we so loathe to think about the danger at Bale time. However, might it not be that one hates to associate the most joyous moments of one's life with . . . with that other thing?"

"Might be," said Raven noncommittally.

She raised her head, tossing the tresses down her back, and went on. "Still Bale is when God comes, and God has Vwi Night Faces too. Not everyone returns from the Holy City."

"What happens to them?"

"There is a theory that the mountain ape is driven mad by the nearness of God and comes down into the lowlands, killing and destroying. That would account for the facts. Actually, I suppose if you forced every person on Gwydion to give you an opinion, as you forced me, most would say this idea must be the right one."

"Haven't you tried to check up on it? Why not leave somebody behind in the towns, waiting in ambush, to see?"

"No. Who would forego his trip to the Holy City, for any reason?"

"Hm. One might at least leave automatic cameras. But I can find out about that later. What's this mountain ape like?"

"An omnivore, which often catches game to eat. They travel in flocks."

"I should think a closed door and a barred window would serve against animals. And don't you keep guard robots at your sanctuaries?"

"Well, the idea is that the beast may be half intelligent. How could it be found on so many islands, if it did not sometimes cross the water on a log?"

"That could happen accidentally. Or the islands may be the remnants of an original continent. There must at least have been land bridges now and then, here and there, in the geological past."

"Well, perhaps," she said reluctantly. "But suppose the mountain ape is cunning enough to get by a guard robot. That needn't happen very often, you see, to cause trouble. Suppose it has gotten to the point of using tools that can break and pry. I don't believe that anyone has ever really investigated its habits. It usually stays far out in the wilderness. Only communities which lie near the edge of a great forest, like Instar, ever glimpse a wandering flock. Remember, we are only ten million people, scattered over a planet. It's too big for us to know everything."

She seemed entirely calm now. Her gaze went around the dell, up the tumbling river to the sky and the hunting bird. She smiled. "And it is right that the world be so," she said. "Would you want to live where there is no mystery and nothing unconquered?"

"No," Raven agreed. "I suppose that's why men went to the stars in the first place."

"And must keep looking ever further, as they suck the planets dry," Elfavy said with compassion tinged by the least hint of scorn. "We keep the frontiers that we already have."

"I like that attitude," Raven said. "But I don't see any sense in letting an active menace run loose. We'll look into this mountain ape business, and if that turns out to be the trouble, we'll soon find ways to deal with the brutes."

Elfavy's mouth fell open. She stared at him in a blind fashion. "No," she gasped, "you wouldn't exterminate them!"

"Um-m . . . that's right, you'd consider that immoral, wouldn't you? Very well, let the species live. But it can be eradicated in inhabited areas."

"What?" She yanked her hands from his.

"Now, wait a bit," Raven protested. "I know you don't have any nonsense here about the sacredness of life. You fish and hunt and butcher domestic animals, not for sport but quite cheerfully for economic reasons. What's the difference in this case?"

"The apes may be intelligent!"

"On a very low plane, maybe. I wouldn't let that bother me. But if you're so squeamish, I suppose they could simply be stunned and airlifted en masse to a distant plateau or some place. I'm sure they wouldn't much mind."

"Stop." She raised herself to a crouch. Through the close-fitting tunic, on the bare sun-gold arms and legs, Tolteca could see the tension that shook her. "Can you not understand? The Night Faces *must* be!"

"Brake back, there," Raven said. He reached for her. "I only suggested—"

"Let me alone!" She sprang to her feet and fled up the trail, almost brushing Tolteca but unaware of him in her weeping.

Raven swore, the word was less angry than hurt and bitter, and started to follow. *That's plenty,* Tolteca thought in a gust of temper, and stepped forth. "What's going on here?" he demanded.

Raven glided to a halt. "How long have you been listening?" he murmured in a tiger's voice.

"Long enough. I heard her ask you to let her be. So do it."

They confronted each other a little while. Shadow and sunlight speckled Raven's black shape. A breeze blew spray from the fall into Tolteca's face. He tasted it frigid on his lips, but a smell akin to blood was in his nostrils. *If he jumps me, I'll shoot. I will.*

Raven let out a deep breath. The heavy shoulders slumped noticeably. "I suppose that is best," he said, and turned around to stare at the river.

The swift end of the scene was like having a wall collapse on which Tolteca had been leaning. He knew with horror that his hand had been on his pistol butt, and snatched it away. *Ylem! What's happened to me?*

*What would have happened, if—*He needed his whole courage not to bolt.

Raven straightened. "Your chivalrous indignation does you credit," he said sarcastically, around the back of his head. "But I assure you I was only trying to keep her from getting murdered one fine festival night."

Still shaken, Tolteca grasped at the chance to smooth things over. "I know," he said. "But you have to respect the sensitivities of people. Different cultures have the damnedest geases."

"Uh-huh."

"Did you ever hear why trade with Orillion was abandoned, why nobody goes there any more? It seemed one of the most promising of the isolated worlds that we'd come upon. Honest, warmhearted people. So warmhearted that we couldn't possibly deal with them if we kept on refusing their offers of individual friendship . . . which involved homosexual relations. We couldn't even explain to them why it wouldn't do."

"Yes, I've heard of that case."

"You can't go bursting into the most important parts of people's lives like an artillery shell. Such compulsions have their roots in the very bottom of the unconscious mind. The people themselves can't think logically about them. Suppose I cast doubts on your father's honor. You'd probably kill me. But if you said something like that to me, I wouldn't get resentful to the point of homicide."

Raven faced him again, cocking one brow upward. "What are your touchy points, then?" he asked dryly.

"Eh? Why, well—family, I guess, even if that relationship isn't as strong as for a Lochlanna. My planet. Democratic government. Not that I mind discussing any of those things, arguing about them. I don't believe in fighting till there's a direct physical threat. And I can entertain the possibility that my notions are completely mistaken. Certainly there's nothing that can't be improved."

"The autonomous individual," Raven said. "I feel sorry for you."

He went on rapidly: "But there is something dangerous on Gwydion, especially at that so-called Bale season. I've learned that a certain animal, the mountain ape, is generally believed to be responsible. Do you have any information about the creature?"

"N-no. In most languages, 'ape' means a more or less anthropoid animal, fairly bright though without tools or a true speech. The type is common on terrestroid planets—parallel evolution."

"I know." Raven reached a decision. "Look here, you'll agree that action must be taken, for the safety of base personnel if nothing else. Later on we can worry about how to do it without offending local prejudices. But first we have to know what the practical problem is. Could the apes really be the destroyers? Elfavy was so irrational on the subject that I can't just take her word, or any Gwydiona's. I'll have to investigate for myself. You mentioned to me once that you've been on long hunting trips in the forests of several planets. And I suppose you are better than I at worming things out of people, especially when it involves their sore spots. So could you quietly find out what the spoor of the apes looks like, and so on? Then if we get a chance we can go off and have a look for ourselves. Agreed?"

❖ VIII ❖

There were no signs until the party was over the pass and down in the woods on the opposite slope. But then young Beodag, who was a forester by trade, spotted the traces and pointed them out to Tolteca and Raven. The trail was fairly clear, trampled grass and broken twigs, caerdu trees stripped of their succulent buds, holes where tubers or rodentoids had been snatched out of the ground. "Be careful," he warned. "They have been known to attack men. You really ought to take a larger party."

Raven slapped the holster of his pistol. "This will handle more than one flock of anything," he said. "Especially with a clip of explosive bullets in it."

"And, uh, more people might only alarm them," Tolteca said. "Besides, you couldn't help us. We've both had encounters before now with animals on the verge of intelligence, not to mention fully developed nonhuman races. We know what signs to watch for. I'm afraid you Gwydiona don't, as yet."

Beodag looked a trifle skeptical but didn't press the point. It was assumed here that any adult knew what he was doing. Dawyd and his men had only been told that it was desirable to investigate the mountain apes, since protection against their raids might be needed at the spaceport. Elfavy, retreated into an unhappy silence, had not given Tolteca the lie.

"Well," Beodag said, "luck attend you. But I doubt you will discover much. At least, I have never seen them carrying anything like tools. I've merely heard third- and fourth-hand stories, and you know how they can grow in the telling."

Raven nodded, turned on his heel, and headed into the forest. Tolteca hurried to catch up. The sound of the others was soon left behind, and the outworlders walked through a stillness broken only by rustlings and chirpings. The trees here grew tall, with sheer reddish trunks that broke into a dense roof of leaves high overhead. In that shade there was little underbrush, only a thick soft mould speckled with fungi. The air was warmer than usual at this altitude. It carried a pungent smell, reminding of thyme, sage, or savory.

"I wonder what makes that odor?" Tolteca said. He had his answer a few minutes later, when they crossed a meadow where lesser plants could grow. A thick stand of bushes had exploded into bloom, scarlet flowers surrounded by bee-like insects, filling the area with their scent. He stopped for a close inspection.

"You know," he said, "I think this must be a rather near relative of baleflower. Observe the leaf structure. Evidently this species blooms a little earlier in the year, though."

"M-m, yes." Raven stopped and rubbed his chin. The cold green eyes grew thoughtful. "It occurs to me that the true baleflower should be opening its buds very soon after we get back to Instar—which is to say, just about in time for the Bale festival, whatever that is.

In a culture like this, bearing in mind the like names, that's no coincidence. And yet they never seem to tell stories about the plant, the way they do about everything else in sight."

"I've noticed that," said Tolteca. "But we'd better not ask them bluntly why, not at least till we know more. When we return. I'm going to send our linguists into the ship's library to do an etymological and semantic study of that word *bale*."

"Good idea. While you're at it, dig up a bush sometime when nobody's looking and have it chemically analyzed."

"Very well," said Tolteca, though he winced at the implications.

"Meanwhile," said Raven, "we've another project. Let's go."

They re-entered the cathedral stillness of the forest. Their footfalls were muffled until their breathing seemed unnaturally loud. The trail of the ape band remained plain to see, prints in the ground, mutilated vegetation, excrement. "Pretty formidable animals, if they plow their way as openly as this," Raven remarked. "They're as sloppy as humans. I daresay they can move quietly when they hunt, however."

"Think we can get close enough to spy on them?" Tolteca asked.

"We can try. By all accounts, they have little shyness toward men. Certainly we can find some spot where they've stayed a few days and check the rubbish. You can tell if a bone was split with a rock, for instance, or if somebody has been chipping stone to shape."

"Suppose they do turn out to be what we're looking for? What then?"

"That depends. We can try to talk the Gwydiona out of their nonsensical attitude—"

"It isn't nonsense!" Tolteca protested indignantly. "Not in their own terms."

"It's always ridiculous to submit meekly to a threat," Raven said. "Stop being so tender with foolishness."

The memory rose in Tolteca of Elfavy's troubled face. "That's about enough out of you," he rapped. "This isn't your planet. It isn't even your expedition. Keep your place, sir."

They halted. A flush darkened Raven's high cheekbones. "Keep a leash on that tongue of yours," he retorted.

"We're not here to exploit them. You'll damned well respect their ethos or I'll see you in irons!"

"What the chaos do you know about an ethos, you cultureless moneysniffer?"

"I know better than to—to drive a woman to tears. You'll stop that too, hear me?"

"Ah, so," said Raven most softly. "That's the layout, eh?"

Tolteca braced himself for a fight. It came from an unawaited quarter. Suddenly the air was full of shapes.

They dropped from the trees, onto the ground, and threw themselves at the men. Raven sprang aside and pulled his gun loose. His first shot missed. There was no second. A hairy body climbed onto his back and another seized his arm. He went down in a welter of them.

Tolteca yelled and ran. An ape laid hold of his trouser leg. He smashed the other boot into the animal's muzzle. The hands let go. Two more leaped at him. He dodged their charge and pelted over the ground. Get his back against yonder bole, spray them with automatic fire—He whirled and raised his pistol.

An ape cast a stone it had been carrying. The missile smacked Tolteca's temple. Pain blinded him. He lurched, and then they were on him. Thick arms dragged him to earth. His nose was full of their hair and rank smell. Fangs snapped yellow, a centimeter before his face. He struck out wildly. His fist rebounded from ridged muscle. The drubbing and clawing became his whole universe. He whirled into a redness that rang.

When he came to himself, a minute or two afterward, he was pinioned by two of them. A third approached, unwinding a thin vine from its waist. His arms were lashed behind his back.

He shook his head, which throbbed and stabbed him and dripped blood down on his tunic, and looked around. Raven had been secured in the same manner. The apes squatted to stare, or bounced about chattering. They numbered a dozen or so, all males, somewhat over a meter tall, tailed, heavybodied, covered with greenish fur and tawny manes. The faces were blunt, and they had four-fingered hands with fairly well-developed thumbs. Several carried bones of leg or jaw from large herbivores.

"Oa," Tolteca groaned. "Are you—are—"

"Not too much damaged yet," Raven said tightly, through bruised lips. Somehow he found a harsh chuckle. "But my pride! *They* were tracking *us!*"

An ape picked up one of the dropped pistols, fingered it, and tossed it aside. Others removed the men's daggers from the sheaths, but soon discarded them likewise. Hard hands plucked and prodded at Tolteca, ripped his garments with their curious pluckings. It came to him with a gulp of horror that he might well die here.

He fought down panic and tested his bonds. Wrist was lashed to wrist by a strand too tough to break. Raven lay in a more relaxed position on his back, squirming a little as the apes played with him.

The largest howled a syllable. The gang stopped their noise and got briskly to their feet. Though short of leg and long of toe, they were true bipeds. The humans were hauled up with casual brutality and the procession started off deeper into the woods.

Only then, as the daze cleared fully from him, did Tolteca realize that the bones his captors carried were weapons, club and sharp-toothed knife. "Proto-intelligent—" he began. The ape beside him cuffed him in the mouth. Evidently silence was the rule on the trail.

He didn't stumble long through his nightmare. They came out into another meadow, where an insolently brilliant sun spilled light across grasses and blossoms. The males broke into a yell, which was answered by a similar number of females and young. Those came swarming from their camping place under a great boulder. For a moment the mob seethed with hands and fangs. Tolteca thought he would be pulled apart alive. A couple of the biggest males knocked their dependents aside and dragged the prisoners to the rock.

There they were hurled down. Tolteca saw that he had landed near a pile of gnawed bones and other offal. Carrion insects made a black cloud above it. "Raven," he choked, "they're going to eat us."

"What else?" said the Lochlanna.

"Oa, can't we make a break?"

"Yes, I think so. I've been very clumsily tied. So have you, but I can reach my knot. If you can distract 'em another minute or two—"

Two males approached with clubs raised. The rest of the flock squatted down, instantly quiet again, watching from bright sunken eyes. The silence hammered at Tolteca.

He rolled over, jumped to his feet, and ran. The nearest male uttered a noise that might have been a laugh and pounced to inter-cept. Tolteca zigzagged from him. Another shaggy form rose in his path. The whole gang began to scream. A club whistled toward

Tolteca's pate. He threw himself forward, down across the wielder's knees. The blow missed and the ape fell on top of him. He buried his head under the body, shield against other weapons. But his feet were seized and he was dragged forth. He saw two clubbers tower across the sky above him.

Suddenly Raven was there. The Lochlanna chopped with the edge of his hand, straight across the throat of one ape. The creature moaned and crumpled; blood ran from the mouth, bluish red. Raven had already turned on the other. His arms shot forth, he drove his thumbs under the brows and hooked out the eyeballs in a single motion. A third male rushed him, to meet a hideously disabling kick. Even at that instant, Tolteca was a little sickened.

Raven stooped and tugged at his bonds. The apes milled about several meters off, enraged but daunted. "All right, you're free," Raven panted. "You have a pocket knife, don't you? Let me have it."

Several rocks thudded within centimeters as he got moving. He unclasped the blade on the run and charged the nearest stone-throwing ape, a female. She struck awkwardly at him. He sidestepped. His slash was a calculated piece of savagery. She lurched back yammering. Raven returned to Tolteca, gave him the knife again, and picked up a thighbone. "They're out of rocks," he said. "Now we back away very slowly. We want to persuade them we aren't worth chasing."

For the first few minutes it went well. He knocked aside a couple of flung clubs. The males snarled, barked, and circled about, but did not venture to rush. When the humans reached the edge of the meadow, though, fury overcame fear. The leader whirled his weapon over his head and scuttled toward them. The rest followed.

"Back against this tree!" Raven commanded. He hefted his thighbone like a sword. When the leader's club came down, he parried the blow and riposted with a bang across the knuckles. The ape wailed and dropped the club. Raven drove the end of his own into the opened mouth. There was a crunch of splintering palate.

Tolteca also had his hands full. The knife was only good for close-in work, and two of the beasts had assailed him at once. A sharp jawbone ripped across his shoulder. He ignored it, clinched, and stabbed deep. Blood spurted over him. He pushed the wounded creature against the other, which went down under the impact, then rose and fled.

The surviving males retreated, growling and chattering. Raven stooped, seized their dying leader, and threw him at them. The body landed in the grass with a heavy thump. They edged back from it. "Let's go," Raven said.

They went, not too swiftly, stopping often to turn about in a threatening way. But there was no pursuit. Raven gusted an enormous sigh. "We're clear," he husked. "Animals don't fight to a finish like men. And . . . we've provided them food."

Tolteca's throat tightened. When they came back to the guns, which meant final safety, a cramp gripped him. He knelt down and vomited.

Raven seated himself to rest. "That's no shame on you," he said. "Reaction. You did pretty well for an amateur."

"It's not fear," Tolteca said. He shuddered with the coldness that ran through him, "It's what happened back there. What you did."

"Eh? I got us loose. That's bad?"

"Your . . . tactics. . . . Did you have to be so vicious?"

"I was simply being efficient, Miguel. Please don't think I enjoyed it."

"Oa, no. I'll give you that much. But—Oh, I don't know. What sort of a race do we belong to, anyway?" Tolteca covered his face.

After a while he recovered enough to say emptily, "This wouldn't have happened but for us. The Gwydiona give the apes a wide berth. There's room for all life on this planet. But we, we had to come blundering in."

Raven considered him for some time before asking, "Why do you think pain and death are so gruesome?"

"I'm not scared of them," Tolteca answered with a feeble flicker of resentment.

"I didn't say that. I was just thinking that down underneath, you don't feel they belong in life. I do. So do the Gwydiona." Raven climbed erect. "We'd better get back."

They limped toward the main trail. They had not quite reached it when Elfavy appeared with three bowmen and Kors.

She gasped and ran to meet them. Tolteca thought she might have been some wood nymph fleeing through the green arches. But though he looked much the gorier, it was Raven whom her hands seized. "What happened? Oh, I grew so worried—"

"We had trouble with the apes," Raven said. He urged her away from him, gently, with a rather sour smile. "Easy, there, milady. No great harm was done, but I'm a mess, and a bit too sore for embraces."

I wouldn't have done that, thought Tolteca desolately. Harsh-voiced, he related the incident.

Beodag whistled. "So they are on the verge of toolmaking! But I swear I've never observed that. I've never been attacked, either."

"And yet the bands you've met live a good deal closer to human settlement, don't they?" Raven asked.

Beodag nodded.

"That settles the matter," Raven declared. "Whatever the source of your trouble at Bale time, the mountain apes are not it."

"What? But if they have weapons—"

"*This* flock does. It must be far ahead of the others. Probably inbreeding of a mutation has made the local apes more intelligent than average. The others haven't even gotten to their stage, in spite of observing humans using implements, which I don't imagine these have ever done. And our friends here couldn't break into a house. A shinbone is no good as a crowbar. Besides, they lack the persistence. They could have overcome us, and should have after the harm we did, but gave up. Anyhow, why would they want to plunder a building? Human artifacts mean nothing to them. They threw aside not only our guns but our daggers. We can forget about them."

The Gwydiona men looked uneasy. Elfavy's eyes blurred. "Can't you forget that obsession for one day?" she pleaded. "It could have been such a beautiful day for you."

"All right," Raven said wearily. "I'll think about medicine and bandages and a pot of tea instead. Satisfied?"

"Yes," she said. Her smile was shaky. "For now I am satisfied."

✧ IX ✧

Festival dwelt in Instar. Tolteca was reminded of Carnival Week on Nuevamerica—not the commercialized feverishness of the cities, but masquerade and street dancing in the hinterlands, where folk still made their own pleasure. Oddly enough, for a people otherwise so ceremonious, the Gwydiona celebrated the time just before Bale by scrapping formality. Courtesy, honesty, nonviolence seemed too ingrained to lose. But men shouted and made horseplay, women dressed with a lavishness that would have been snickered at anytime else in the planet's long year, schools became playgrounds, each formerly simple meal was a banquet, and quite a few families broke out the wine and got humanly drunk. A wreath of jule, roses, and pungent margwy herb hung on every door; no hour of day or night lacked music.

And so it was over this whole world, thought Tolteca: in every town on every inhabited island, the year had turned green and the people were soon bound for their shrines.

He came striding down a gravel path. The sun stood at late morning and the boy Byord walked with a hand in his. Far and holy above western forests, the mountain peaks dreamed.

"What did you do then?" asked Byord, breathless.

"We stayed in the City and had fun till it rained," said Tolteca. "Then when it was safe, we proceeded to our goal, looked it over—a fine site indeed—and at last came back here."

He didn't want to relate, or remember, the ugly episode in the forest. "Exactly when did we get back?"

"Day before yesterday."

"Uh, yes, now I place it. Hard to keep track of time here, when nobody pays much attention to clocks and everything is so pleasant."

"The City—gol! What's it like?"

"Don't you know?"

"'Course not, 'cept they told my cousin a little about it in school. I wasn't born, last Bale. But I'm big enough already to go with my mother."

"The City is very beautiful," said Tolteca. He wondered how children as young as this fitted into a prolonged religious meditation, if that was what it was, and how they kept so well afterward the secret of what had happened.

Byord's mind sprang to another marvel. "Tell me 'bout planets, please. When I get big, I want to be a spaceman. Like you."

"Why not?" said Tolteca. Byord could get as good a scientific education here as anywhere in the known galaxy. By the time he was of an age to enroll, the astro academies on worlds like Nuevamerica would doubtless be eager to accept Gwydiona cadets. Gwydion itself would be more than a refueling stop, a decade hence. A people this gifted couldn't help themselves; they were certain to become curious about the universe (as if they weren't already so interested that only the intelligence of their questions made the number endurable)— and, yes, to influence it. The Empire had fallen, human society was once more in flux. What better ideal for the next civilization than Gwydion?

And why count myself out? thought Tolteca. *When we build our spaceports here—there'll soon be more than one—they'll require Namerican administrators, engineers, factors, liaison officers. Why shouldn't I become one, and live my life under Ynis and She?*

He glanced down at the tangled head beside him. He'd always shrunk from the idea of acquiring a ready-made family. But why not? Byord was a polite and talented boy who still remained very much a boy. It would be a pleasure to raise him. Even today's outing—undertaken frankly to ingratiate one Miguel Tolteca with Elfavy Simnon—had been a lot of fun.

When earlier, one of the Namerican spacemen had expressed a desire to settle here, Raven had warned him he'd go berserk in one standard year. But what did Raven know about it? The prediction was doubtless true for him. Lochlanna society, caste-ridden, haughty, ritualistic, and murderous, had nothing in common with Gwydion. *But Nuevamerica, now—Oh, I don't pretend I wouldn't miss the lights and tall buildings, theaters, bars, parties, excitement, once in a while. But what's to prevent me and my family from taking vacation trips there? As for our everyday lives, here are a calm, rational, but merry people with a really meaningful, implemented ideal of beauty, uncrowded in a nature which has never been trampled on. And not static, either. They have their scientific research, innovations in the arts, engineering projects. Look how they welcome the chance to have regular interstellar contact. How could I fail to fall in love with Gwydion?*

*Specifically, with—*Tolteca shut that thought off. He came from a civilization where all problems were practical problems. So let's not moon about, but rather take the indicated steps to get what we want. Raven had an inside track at the moment, but that needn't be too great a handicap, especially since Raven showed no signs of wanting to remain here. Since Byord was pestering him for yarns of other planets, Tolteca reminisced aloud, with some editing, and the rest of their walk passed quickly.

They entered the town. It seemed to have become queerly deserted in their absence. Where the dwellers had swarmed in the streets a few hours ago, they now were indoors. Here and there a man hurried from one place to another, carrying some burden, but that only emphasized the emptiness. However, though the air was quiet beneath the sun, one could hear an underlying murmur, voices behind walls.

Byord broke free of Tolteca's hand and skipped on the pavement. "We're going soon, we're going soon," he caroled.

"How do you know?" asked Tolteca. He had been told some while ago that there was no fixed date for Bale time.

Every freckle grinned. "I know, Adult Miguel! Aren't you comin' too?"

"I think I'd better stay and take care of your pets," said Tolteca. Byord maintained the usual small-boy zoo of bugs and amphibia.

"There's Granther! Hey, Granther!" Byord broke into a run. Dawyd, emerging from his house, braced himself. When the cyclone had struck him and been duly hugged, he pushed it toward the door.

"Go on inside, now," he said. "Your mother's making ready. She has to wash at least a few kilos of dirt off you, and pack your lunch, before we start."

"Thanks, Adult Miguel!" Byord whizzed through the entrance.

Dawyd chuckled. "I hope you aren't too exhausted," he said.

"Not at all," Tolteca answered. "I enjoyed it. We followed the river upstream to the House of the Philosophers. I never imagined a place devoted to abstract thinking would include picnic grounds and a carousel."

"Why not? Philosophers are human too, I'm told. It is refreshing for them to watch the children, romp with them . . . and perhaps a little respect for knowledge rubs off on the youngsters." Dawyd started down the street. "I have a job to do. Would you like to accompany me? You being a technical man, this may interest you."

Tolteca fell into step. "Are you leaving very soon, then?" he inquired.

"Yes. The signs have become clear, even to me. Older people are

not so sensitive; the young adults have been wild this whole morning."
Dawyd's eyes glittered. His lined brown face held less than its normal
serenity.

"It is about ten hours on foot by the direct path to the Holy City,"
he added after a moment. "Less, of course, for a man unencumbered
by children and the aged. If you should, yourself, feel the time upon
you, I do hope you will follow and join us there."

Tolteca drew a long breath, as if to smell the tokens. The air was
alive with the blooming of a hundred flowers, trees, bushes, vines;
nectar-gathering insects droned in the sunlight. "What are the
signs?" he asked. "No one has told me."

On other occasions, Dawyd, like the rest of his people, had grown
a little uneasy at questions about Bale, and changed the subject—which
was a simple task with so much to discuss, twelve hundred years of
separate history. Now the physician laughed aloud. "I *can't* tell you," he
said. "I know, that is all. How do buds know when to unfold?"

"But haven't you ever, in the rest of the year, made any scientific
study of—"

"Here we are." Dawyd halted at the fused stone building in the
center of town. It looked square and bleak above them. The portal
stood open and they entered, walking down cool shadowy halls.
Another man passed, holding a wrench. Dawyd waved at him. "A
technician," he explained, "making a final check on the central power
controls. Everything vital, or potentially dangerous, is stored here
during Bale. Motor vehicles in a garage at the end of yonder corridor,
for instance. My duty—Here we are."

He swung aside a door which gave on a huge and sunny room,
gaily painted walls lined with cribs and playpens. A mobile robot
stood by each, and a bright large machine murmured to itself in the
center of the floor. Dawyd walked around, observing. "This is a
routine and rather nominal inspection," he said. "The engineers have
already overhauled everything. As a physician, I have to certify that
the environment is sanitary and pleasant, but that has never been a
problem."

"What is it for?" Tolteca queried.

"Do you not know? Why, to care for infants, those too young to
accompany us to the Holy City. Byord is about as young as we ever
dare take them. The hospital wing of this building has robots to

nurse the sick and the very old during Bale time, but that's not under my supervision." Dawyd snapped his fingers. "What in the name of chaos was I going to tell you? Oh, yes. In case you have not already been warned. This entire building is locked up during Bale. Automatic shock beams are fired at anything—or anyone—that approaches within ten meters. Any moving object that gets through to the outside wall is destroyed by flame blasts. Stay away from here!"

Tolteca stood quiet, for the last words had been alarmingly rough.

Finally, he ventured, "Isn't that rather extreme?"

"Bale lasts about three Gwydiona days and nights," said Dawyd. He had fixed his stare on a pen and tossed the sentences over his shoulder. "That's more than ten standard days. Plus the time needed to walk to the Holy City and back. We don't take chances."

"But what is it you fear? What can happen?" Dawyd said, not entirely steadily, but so far upborne by his own euphoria that he could at last speak plainly, "It is not uncommon that some of those who go to the Holy City do not come back. On returning, the others sometimes find that in spite of locks and shutters, there has been destruction wrought in town. So we put our important machines and our helpless members here, with mechanical attendants, in a place which nothing can enter till the time locks open automatically."

"I've gathered something like that," Tolteca breathed. "But have you any idea what causes the trouble?"

"We are not certain. The mountain apes are often blamed, but the experience you related to me does seem to absolve them. Conceivably, I don't know; conceivably we are not the only intelligent race on Gwydion. There could be true aborigines, so alien that we failed to recognize any trace of their culture. Various legends about creatures that live underground or skulk in the deep forests may have some basis in fact. I don't know. And it is never a good idea to theorize in advance of the data."

"Didn't you, or your ancestors, ever attempt to get data?"

"Yes, many times. Cameras and other recording devices were planted again and again. But they were always evaded, or discovered and smashed." Dawyd broke off short and continued his inspection in silence. He moved a little jerkily.

They were leaving the fortress before Tolteca suggested

diffidently, "Perhaps we, from the ship, can observe what happens while you are gone."

Dawyd had calmed down again. "You are welcome to try," he said, "but I doubt you will have any success. You see, I don't expect the town will be entered. No such thing has happened for many years. Even in my own boyhood, a raid on a deserted community was a rare event. You must not believe this is a major problem for us. It was worse in the distant past, but nowadays it has so dwindled that there isn't even much incentive to study the problem."

Tolteca didn't think he would be unmotivated to look into the possibility of a native race on Gwydion. But he didn't wish to disturb his host further. He struck a cigarette as they walked on. The streets were now entirely bare save for Dawyd and himself. And yet the sun drenched them in light. It sharpened his feeling of eeriness.

"Actually, I'm afraid you will have a dull wait," said the older man. He was becoming more and more himself as the Namerican's questions receded in time. "Everybody gone, everything locked up, over the whole inhabited planet. Maybe you would like to fly down to the southern hemisphere and explore a little."

"I think we'll just stay put and correlate our findings," said Tolteca. "We have a lot. When you return—"

"We won't be worth much for a few days afterward," Dawyd warned him. "It isn't easy for mortal flesh, being God."

They reached his house. He stopped at the door, looking embarrassed. "I should invite you in, but—"

"I understand. Family rites." Tolteca smiled. "I'll stroll down to the park at town's end. You'll pass by there on your way, and I'll wave farewell."

"Thank you, far-friend."

The door closed. Tolteca stood a moment, inhaling deeply, before he ground the cigarette butt under his heel and walked off between shuttered walls.

✤ **X** ✤

The park was gay with flowers. A few of the expedition lounged under shade trees, also waiting to observe the departure. Tolteca saw

Raven, and clamped lips together. *I will not lose my temper.* He approached and gave greeting.

Raven answered with Lochlanna formality. The mercenary had put on full dress for the occasion, blouse, trousers, tooled leather boots, embroidered surcoat. He stood square, next to a baleflower bush as tall as himself. Its buds were opening in a riot of scarlet flowers. They smelled almost but not quite like the cousin species in the mountains, herbs, summer meadows, a phosphorus overtone, and something else that flitted half sensed below the surface of memory. The Siamese cat Zio nestled in Raven's arms; he stroked the beast with one hand and got a purr for answer.

Tolteca repeated Dawyd's warning about the fortress. Raven's dark head nodded. "I knew that. I'd do the same in their place."

"Yes, *you* would," said Tolteca. He remembered his resolution and added impersonally, "Such over-destructiveness doesn't seem characteristic of the Gwydiona, though."

"This isn't a characteristic season. Every five standard years, for about ten standard days, something happens to them. I'd feel easier if I knew what."

"My guess—" Tolteca paused. He hated to say it aloud. But finally: "A dionysiac religion."

"I can't swallow that," said Raven. "These people know about photosynthesis. They don't believe magical demonstrations make the earth fertile."

"They might employ such ceremonies anyhow, for some historical or psychological reason." Tolteca winced, thinking of Elfavy gasping drunken in the arms of man after man. But if he didn't say it himself, someone else would; and he was mature enough, he insisted, to accept a person on her own cultural terms. "Orgiastic."

"No," said Raven. "This is no more a dionysiac culture than yours or mine. Not at any time of year. Just put yourself in their place, and you'll see. That cool, reasonable, humorous mentality couldn't take a free-for-all seriously enough. Someone would be bound to start laughing and spoil the whole effect."

Tolteca looked at Raven with a sudden warmth for the man. "I believe you're right. I certainly want to believe it. But what do they do, then?" After a moment: "We have been more or less invited to join them, you realize. We could simply go watch."

"No. Best not. If you'll recall the terms in which that semi-invitation was couched, it was implicitly conditional on our feeling the same way as them—joining into the spirit of the festival, whatever that may mean. I don't think we could fake it. And by distracting them at such a time—more and more, I'm coming to think it's the focus of their whole culture—by doing that, we might lose their good will."

"M-m, yes, perhaps. . . . Wait! Perhaps we can join in. I mean, if it involves taking some drug. Probably a hallucinogen like mescaline, though something on the order of lysergic acid is possible too. Anyhow, couldn't Bale be founded on that? A lot of societies, you know, some of them fairly scientific, believe that their sacred drug reveals otherwise inaccessible truths."

Raven shook his head. "If that were so in this case," he answered, "they'd use the stuff oftener than once in five years. Nor would they be so vague about their religion. They'd either tell us plainly about the drug, or explain politely that we aren't initiates and it's none of our business what happens at the Holy City. Another argument against your idea is that they shun drugs so completely in their every-day life. They don't like the thought of anything antagonistic to the normal functioning of body and mind. Do you know, this past day is the first instance I've seen or heard or read of any Gwydiona even getting high on alcohol?"

"Well," barked Tolteca in exasperation, "suppose you tell me what they do!"

"I wish I could." Raven's disquieted gaze went to the baleflower. "Has the chemical analysis of this been finished?"

"Yes, just a few hours ago. Nothing special was found."

"Nothing whatsoever?"

"Oa, well, its perfume does contain an indole, among other compounds, probably to attract pollinating insects. But it's a quite harmless indole. If you breathed it at an extremely high concentration—several thousand times what you could possibly encounter in the open air—I suppose you might get a little dizzy. But you couldn't get a real jag on."

Raven scowled. "And yet this bush is named for the festival. And alone on the whole inhabited planet, has no mythology."

"Xinguez and I threshed that out, after he'd checked his linguistic references. Bear in mind that Gwydiona stems from a rather archaic dialect of Anglic, closely related to the ancestral English. That word *bale* can mean several things, depending on ultimate derivation. It can signify a bundle; a fire, especially a funeral pyre; an evil or sorrow; and, more remotely and with a different spelling, *Baal* is an ancient word for a god."

Tolteca tapped a fresh cigarette on his thumbnail and struck it with an uneven motion across the heel of his shoe. "You can imagine how the Gwydiona could intertwine such multiple meanings," he continued. "What elaborate symbolisms are potentially here. Those flowers have long petals, aimed upward; a bush in full bloom looks rather like a fire, I imagine. The Burning Bush of primitive religion. Hence, maybe, the name *bale*. But that could also mean 'God' and 'evil.' And it blooms just at Bale time. So because of all these coincidences, the bale-flower symbolizes the Night Faces, the destructive aspect of reality . . . probably the most cruel and violent phase thereof. Hence nobody talks about it. They shy away from creating the myths that are so obviously suggested. The Gwydiona don't deny that evil and sorrow exist, but neither do they go out of their way to contemplate the fact."

"I know," said Raven. "In that respect they're like Namericans." He failed to hide entirely the shade of contempt in the last word.

Tolteca heard, and flared. "In every other respect, too!" he snapped. "Including the fact that your bloody warlords are not going to carve up this planet!"

Raven looked directly at the engineer. So did Zio. It was disconcerting, for the cat's eyes were as cold and steady as the man's. "Are you quite certain," said Raven, "that these people are the same species as us?"

"Oa! If you think—your damned racism—just because they're too civilized to brew war like you." Tolteca advanced with fists cocked. *If Elfavy could only see!* it begged through the boiling within him. *If she could hear what this animal really thinks of her!*

"Oh, quite possibly interbreeding is still feasible," said Raven. "We'll find that out soon enough."

Tolteca's control broke. His fist leaped forward of itself.

Raven threw up an arm—Zio scampered to his shoulder—and blocked the blow. His hand slid down to seize Tolteca's own forearm, his other hand got the Namerican's biceps, his foot scythed behind the ankles. Tolteca went on his back, pinned. The cat squalled and clawed at him.

"That isn't necessary, Zio." Raven let go. Several of his men hurried up. He waved them away. "It was nothing," he called." I was only demonstrating a hold."

Kors looked dubious, but at that moment someone exclaimed, "Here they come!" and attention went to the road. Tolteca climbed back erect, too caught in a tide of anger, shame, and confusion to notice the parade much.

Not that there was a great deal to notice. The Instar folk walked with an easy, distance-devouring stride, in no particular order. They were lightly clad. Each carried the one lunch he would need on the way, some spare garments, and nothing else. But their chatter and laughter and singing were like a bird-flock, like sunlight on a wind-ruffled lake, and now and then one of the adults danced among the hurtling children. So they went past, a flurry of bright tunics, sunbrowned limbs, garlanded fair hair, into the hills and the Holy City.

But Elfavy broke from them. She ran to Raven, caught both the soldier's hands in her own, and cried, "Come with us! Can't you feel it, *liatha?*"

He watched her a long while, his features wooden, before he shook his head. "No. I'm sorry."

Tears blurred her eyes, and that wasn't the way of Gwydion either. "You can never be God, then?" Her head drooped, the yellow mane hid her face. Tolteca stood staring. What else could he do?

"If I might give you the power," said Elfavy. "I would give up my own." She sprang free, raised hands to the sun and shouted, "But it's impossible that you can't feel it! God is here already, everywhere. I see Vwi shining from you, Raven! You must come!"

He folded his hands together within the surcoat sleeves. "Will you stay here with me?" he asked.

"Always, always."

"Now, I mean. During Bale time."

"What? Oh—no, yes—you are joking?"

He said slowly, "I'm told the Night Faces are also revealed, some-times, under the Steeps of Kolumkill. That not everyone comes home every year."

Elfavy took a backward step from him. "God is more than good," she pleaded. "God is *real.*"

"Yes. As real as death."

"Great ylem!" exploded Tolteca. "What do you expect, man? Everybody who can walk goes there. Some must have incipient disease, or weak hearts, or old arteries. The strain—"

Raven ignored him. "Is it a secret what happens, Elfavy?" he asked.

Her muscles untensed. Her merriment trilled forth. "No. It's only that words are such poor lame things. As I told you that night in the sanctuary."

In him, the grimness waxed. "Well, words can describe a few items, at least. Tell me what you can. What do you do there, with your physical body? What would a camera record?"

The blood drained from her face. She stood unmoving. Eventually, out of silence that grew and grew around her: "No. I can't."

"Or you mustn't?" Raven grabbed her bare shoulders so hard that his fingers sank in. She didn't seem to feel it. "You mustn't talk about Bale, or you won't, or you can't?" he roared. "Which is it? Quick, now!"

Tolteca tried to stir, but his bones seemed locked together. The Instar people danced by, too lost in their joy to pay attention. The other Namericans looked indignant, but Wildenvey had casually drawn his gun and grinned in their eyes. Elfavy shuddered. "I can't tell!" she gasped.

Raven's expression congealed. "You don't know," he said. "Is that why?"

"Let me go!"

He released her. She stumbled against the bush. A moment she crouched, the breath sobbing in and out of her. Then instantly, like a curtain descending, she fell back into her happiness. Tears still caught sunlight on her cheeks, but she looked at the bruises on her skin, laughed at them, sprang forward and kissed Raven on his unmoving lips. "Then wait for me, *liatha!*" She whirled, skipped off, and was lost in the throng.

Raven stood without stirring, gazing after them as they dwindled up the road. Tolteca would not have believed human flesh could stay immobile so long.

At last the Namerican said, through an acrid taste in his mouth, "Well, are you satisfied?"

"In a way." Raven remained motionless. His words fell flat.

"Don't make too many assumptions," said Tolteca. "She's in an abnormal state. Wait till she comes back and is herself again, before you get your hopes up."

"What?" Raven turned his head, blinking wearily . He seemed to recognize Tolteca only after a few seconds. "Oh. But you're wrong. That's not an abnormal state."

"Huh?"

"Your planet has seasons too. Do you consider spring fever a disease? Is it unnatural to feel brisk on a clear fall day?"

"What are you hinting at?"

"Never mind." Raven lifted his shoulders and let them fall, an old man's gesture. "Come, Sir Engineer, we may as well go back to the ship."

"But—Oa!" Tolteca's finger stabbed at the Lochlanna. "Do you mean you've guessed—"

"Yes. I may be wrong, of course. Come." Raven picked up Zio and became very busy making the cat comfortable in his sleeve.

"What?"

Raven started to go.

Tolteca caught him by the arm. Raven spun about. Briefly, the Lochlanna's face was drawn into such a fury that the Namerican fell back. Raven clapped a hand to his dagger and whispered, "Don't ever do that again."

Tolteca braced his sinews. "What's your idea?" he demanded. "If Bale really is dangerous—"

Raven leashed himself. "I see your thought," he said in a calmer tone. "You want to go up there and stand by to protect her, don't you?"

"Yes. Suppose they do lie around in a comatose state. Some animal might sneak past the guard robots and—"

"No. You will stay down here. Everybody will. That's a direct order under my authority as military commander." Raven's severity ebbed. He wet his lips, as if trying to summon courage. "Don't you see," he added, "this has been going on for more than a thousand years. By now they have evolved—not developed, but blindly evolved—a system which minimizes the hazard. *Most* of them survive. The ancestors alone know what delicate balance you may upset by blundering in there."

After another pause: "I've been through this sort of thing before. Sent out men according to the best possible plan, and then sat and waited, knowing that if I made any further attempt to help them I'd only throw askew the statistics of their survival. It's even harder to deal with God, Who can wear any face." He started trudging. "You'll stay here and sweat it out, like the rest of us."

Tolteca stared after him. Thought trickled into his consciousness. *The chaos I will.*

�֍ **XI** ✶

Raven awoke more slowly than usual. He glanced at the clock. Death and plunder, had he been eleven hours asleep? Like a drugged man, too. He still felt tired. Perhaps that was because there had been evil dreams; he couldn't remember exactly what but they had left a scum of sadness in him. He swung his legs around and sat on the edge of the bunk, rested head in hands and tried to think. All he seemed able to do, though, was recall his father's castle, hawks nesting in the bell tower, himself about to ride forth on one of the horses they still used at home but pausing to look down the mountainside, fells and woods and the peasants' niggard fields, then everything hazed into blue hugeness. The wind had tasted of glaciers.

He pushed the orderly buzzer. Kors' big ugly nose came through the cabin door. "Tea," said Raven.

He scalded his mouth on it, but enough sluggishness departed him that he could will relaxation. His brain creaked into gear. It wasn't wise, after all, simply to wait close-mouthed till the Instar people came home. He'd been too abrupt with Tolteca; but the man annoyed him, and besides, his revelation had been too shattering. Now he felt able to discuss it. Not that he wanted to. What right had a storeful of greasy Namerican merchants to such a truth? But it was certain to be discovered sometime, by some later expedition. Maybe a decent secrecy could be maintained, if an aristocrat made the first explanation.

Tolteca isn't a bad sort, he made himself admit. *Half the trouble between us was simply due to his being somewhat in love with Elfavy. That's not likely to last, once he's been told. So he'll be able to look at things objectively and, I hope, find an honorable course of action.*

Elfavy. Her image blotted out the recollection of gaunt Lochlanna. There hadn't much been said or done, overtly, between him and her. Both had been too shy of the consequences. But now— *I don't know. I just don't know.*

He got up and dressed in plain workaday clothes. Zio pattered after him as he left his cabin and went down a short passageway to Tolteca's. He punched the doorchime, but got no answer. Well, try the saloon. . . . Captain Utiel sat there with a cigar and an old letter; he became aware of Raven by stages. "No, Commandant," he replied to the question, "I haven't seen Sir Engineer Tolteca for, oh, two or three hours. He was going out to observe high tide from the diketop, he said, and wouldn't be back for some time. Is it urgent?"

The news was like a hammerblow. Raven held himself motionless before saying, "Possibly. Did he have anyone with him? Or any instruments that you noticed?"

"No. Just a lunch and his sidearm."

Bitterness uncoiled in Raven. "Did you seriously believe he was making a technical survey?"

"Why—well, I didn't really think about it. . . . Well, he may simply have gone to admire the view. High tide is impressive, you know."

Raven glanced at his watch. "Won't be high tide for hours."

Utiel sat up straight. "What's the matter?"

Decision crystallized. "Listen carefully," said Raven. "I am going out too. Stand by to lift ship. Keep someone on the radio. If I don't return, or haven't sent instructions to the contrary, within—oh— thirty hours, go into orbit. In that event, and only in that event, one of my men will hand over to you a tape I've left in his care, with an explanation. Do you understand?"

Utiel rose. "I will not be treated in this fashion!" he protested.

"I didn't ask you that, Captain," said Raven. "I asked if you understood my orders."

Utiel grew rigid. "Yes, Commandant," he got out.

Raven went swiftly from the saloon. Once in the corridor, he ran.

Kors, on guard outside his cabin, gaped at him. "Fetch Wildenvey," said Raven, passed inside and shut the door. He clipped a tape to his personal recorder, dictated, released it, and sealed the container with wax and his family signet ring. Only then did he stop to snatch some bites from a food concentrate bar.

Wildenvey entered as he was slipping a midget transceiver into his pocket. Raven gave him the tape, with instructions, and added, "See if you can find Miguel Tolteca anywhere about. Roust the whole company to help. If you do, call me on the radio and I'll head back."

"Where you going, sir?" asked Kors.

"Into the hills. I am not to be followed."

Kors curled his lip and spat between two long yellow teeth. The gob clanged on the disposer chute. "Very good, sir. Let's go."

"You stay here and take care of my effects."

"Any obscene child of impropriety can do that, sir," said Kors, looking hurt.

Raven felt his own mouth drawn faintly upward. "As you will, then. But if ever you speak a word about this. I'll yank out your tongue with my bare fingers."

"Aye, sir." Kors opened a drawer and took out a couple of field belts, with supplies and extra ammunition in the pouches. Both men donned them.

Raven set Zio carefully on the bunk and stroked him under the chin. Zio purred. He tried to follow when they left. Raven pushed him back and closed the door in his face. Zio scolded him in absentia for several minutes.

Emerging from the spaceship, Raven saw that dusk was upon the land. The sky was deeply blue-black, early stars in the east, a last sunset cloud above the western mountains like a streak of clotting blood. He thought he could hear the sea bellow beyond the dike.

"We going far, Commandant?" asked Kors.

"Maybe as far as the Holy City."

"I'll break out a flitter, then."

"No, a vehicle would make matters worse than they already are. This'll be afoot. On the double."

"Holy muckballs!" Kors clipped a flashbeam to his belt and began jogging.

During the first hour they went through open fields. Here and there stood a barn or a shed, black under blackening heaven. They heard livestock low, and the whir of machinery tending empty farms. If no one ever came back, wondered Raven, how long would the robots continue their routines? How long would the cattle stay tame, the infants alive?

The road ended, the ground rose in waves, only a trail pierced the way among boles and brush. The Lochlanna halted for a breather. "You're chasing Tolteca, aren't you, Commandant?" asked Kors. "Shall I kill the son of a bitch when we catch him, or do you want to?"

"*If* we catch him," corrected Raven. "He has a long head start, even though we can travel a lot faster. No, don't shoot unless he resists arrest." He stopped a second, to underline what followed. "Don't shoot any Gwydiona. Under any circumstances whatsoever."

He fell silent, slumping against a tree in total muscular repose, trying to blank his mind. After ten minutes they resumed the march.

Trees and bushes walled either side of the trail, leaves made a low roof overhead. It was very dark; only the bobbing light of Kors' flash picked stones and dust into relief. Beyond the soft thud of their feet, they could hear rustlings, creakings, distant chirps and hoots and croaks, the cold tinkle of a brook. Once an animal screamed. The air cooled as they climbed, but it always remained mild, and it overflowed with odors. Raven thought he could distinguish the smells of earth and green growth, the damp smell of water when a rivulet crossed the trail, certain individual flower scents; but the rest was unfamiliar. Smell is the most evocative of the senses, and forgotten things seemed to move below Raven's awareness, but he couldn't identify them. Overriding all else was the clear brilliant odor of baleflower. In the past few hours, every bush had come to full bloom.

Seen by daylight, tomorrow, the land would look as if it burned.

Time faded. That was a trick you learned early, from the regimental bonzes who instructed noblemen's sons. You needed it, to survive the waiting and the waiting of war without your sanity cracking open. You turned off your conscious mind. Part of it might revive during pauses in the march. Surely it was hard to stop at the halfway point for a drink of water, a bit of field ration, and a rest, and not think about Elfavy. But the body had its own demands. The thing could be done, since it must.

The moon rose over Mount Granis. Passing an open patch of

ground and looking downslope, Raven saw the whole world turned to silver treetops. Then the forest gulped him again.

Some eight or nine hours after departure, Kors halted with an oath. His flashbeam picked out a thing that scuttled on spiderlike legs, a steel carapace and arms ending in sword blades.

"'S guts!" Raven heard a gun clank from a holster. The machine met the light with impersonal lens eyes, then slipped into the brush.

"Guard robot," said Raven. "Against carnivores. It won't attack humans. We're close now, so douse that flash and shut up."

He led the way, cat-cautious in darkness, thinking that Tolteca must indeed have beaten him here. Though probably not by very long. Maybe the situation could still be rescued. He topped the final steep climb and poised on the upper edge of the great amphitheater.

For a moment the moonlight blinded him. She hung gibbous over the Steeps, turning them bone color and drowning the stars. Then piece by piece Raven made out detail: mossy tiers curving downward to the floor, the ring of towers enclosing the square of the labyrinth, even the central fountain and its thin mercury-like jet. Even the gardens full of baleflower, though they looked black against all that slender white. He heard a mumble down in the forum, but couldn't see what went on. With great care he padded forward into the open.

"Hee-ee," said a man who sat on an upper terrace. "That's hollow, Bale-friend."

Raven stopped dead. Kors said something raw at his back. Slowly, Raven turned to face the man. It was Llyrdin, who had played chess in a diving bell and gone exploring for a spaceport in the mountains. Now he sat hugging his knees and grinning. There was blood on his mouth.

"It is, you know," he said. "Hollow. Hollow is God. I hail hollow, hollow hallow hullo."

Raven looked into the man's eyes, but the moonlight was so reflected from them that they stared blank. "Where did the blood come from?" he asked most quietly.

"She was empty," said Llyrdin. "Empty and so small. It wasn't good for her to grow up and be hollow. Was it? That much more nothing?" He rubbed his chin, regarded the wet fingers, and said plaintively, "The machines took her away. That wasn't fair. She was only a year and a half hollow."

Raven started down into the chalice.

"She came up about to my waist," said the voice behind him. "I think once, very long ago, before the hollow, I taught her to laugh. I even gave her a name once, and the name was Wormwood." Raven heard him begin to weep.

Kors took out his pistol, unsnapped the holster from his belt and clamped it on as a rifle stock. "Easy there," said Raven, not looking back but recognizing the noise. "You won't need that."

"The muck I won't," said Kors.

"We aren't going to fire on any Gwydiona. And I doubt if Tolteca will give trouble . . . now."

XII

They reached level sward and passed beneath a tower. Raven remembered it was the one he had climbed before. A child stood in the uppermost window, battering herself against the grille and uttering no sound.

Raven went through a colonnade. Just beyond, at the edge of the forum, some fifty Instar people were gathered, mostly men. Their clothes were torn, and even in the moonlight, across meters of distance, Raven could see unshaven chins.

Miguel Tolteca confronted them. "But Llyrdin killed that little girl!" the Namerican shouted. "He killed her with his hands and ran away wiping his mouth. And the robots took the body away. And you do nothing but stare!"

Beodag the forester trod forth. Awe blazed on his face. "Under She," he called, his voice rising and falling, with something of the remote quality of a voice heard through fever. "And She is the cold reflector of Ynis, and Ynis Burning Bush, though we taste the river. If the river gives light, O look how my shadow dances!"

"As Gonban danced for his mother," said the one next to him. "Which is joy, since man comes from darkness when he is born."

"Night Faces are Day Faces are God!"

"Dance, God!"

"Howl for God, Vwi burns!"

An old man turned to a young girl, knelt before her and said, "Give me your blessing, Mother." She touched his head with an infinite tenderness.

"But have you gone crazy?" wailed Tolteca.

It snarled in the crowd of them. Those who had begun to dance stopped. A man with tangled graying hair advanced on Tolteca, who made a whimpering sound and retreated. Raven recognized Dawyd.

"What do you mean?" asked Dawyd. His tone was metal.

"I mean . . . I want to say . . . I don't understand—"

"No," said Dawyd. "What do you *mean*? What is your significance? Why are you here?"

"T-t-to help—"

They began circling about, closing off Tolteca's retreat. He fumbled after his sidearm, but blindly, as if knowing how few he could shoot before they dragged him down.

"You wear the worst of the Night Faces," Dawyd groaned. "For it is no face at all. It is Chaos. Emptiness. Meaninglessness."

"Hollow," whispered the crowd. "Hollow, hollow, hollow."

Raven squared his shoulders. "Stick close and keep your mouth shut," he ordered Kors. He stepped from the colonnade shadows, into open moonlight, and approached the mob.

Someone on its fringe was first to see him: a big man, who turned with a bear's growl and shambled to meet the newcomers. Raven halted and let the Gwydiona walk into him. A crook-fingered hand swiped at his eyes. He evaded it, gave a judo twist, and sent the man spinning across the forum.

"He dances!" cried Raven from full lungs. "Dance with him!" He snatched a woman and whirled her away. She spun top fashion, trying to keep her balance. "Dance on the bridge from Yin to Yang!"

They didn't—quite. They stood quieter than it seemed possible men could stand. Tolteca's mouth fell open. His face was a moonlit lake of sweat. "Raven," he choked, "oa, ylem, Raven—"

"Shut up," muttered the Lochlanna. He edged next to the Namerican. "Stick by me. No sudden movements, and not a word."

Dawyd cringed. "I know you," he said. "You are my soul. And eaten with forever darkness and ever and no, no, no."

Raven raked his memory. He had heard so many myths, there

must be one he could use . . . Yes, maybe. . . . His tones rolled out to fill the space within the labyrinth.

"Hearken to me. There was a time when the Sunsmith ran in the shape of a harbuck with silver horns. A hunter saw him and pursued him. They fled up a mountainside which was all begrown with crisflower, and wherever the harbuck's hoofs touched earth the crisflower bloomed, but wherever the hunter ran it withered. And at last they came to the top of the mountain, whence a river of fire flowed down a sheer cliff. The chasm beyond was cold, and so misty that the hunter could not see if it had another side. But the harbuck sprang out over the abyss, and sparks showered where his hoofs struck—"

He held himself as still as they, but his eyes flickered back and forth, and he saw in the moonlight how they began to ease. The tiniest thawing stirred within him. He was not sure he had grasped the complex symbolism of the myth he retold in any degree. Certainly he understood its meaning only vaguely. But it was the right story. It could be interpreted to fit this situation, and thus turn his escape into a dance, which would lead men back into those rites that had evolved out of uncounted man-slayings.

Still talking, he backed off, step by infinitesimal step, as if survival possessed its own calculus. Kors drifted beside him, screening Tolteca's shivers from their eyes.

But they followed. And others began to come from the buildings, and from the towers after they had passed through the colonnade again. When Raven put his feet on the first upward tier, a thousand faces must have been turned to him. None said a word, but he could hear them breathing, a sound like the sea beyond Instar's dike.

And now the myth was ended. He climbed another step, and another, always meeting their upturned eyes. It seemed to him that She had grown more full since he descended into this vale. But it couldn't have taken that long. Could it?

Tolteca grasped his hand. The Namerican's fingers were like ice. Kors' voice would have been inaudible a meter away. "Can we keep on retreating, sir, or d'you think those geeks will rush us?"

"I wish I knew," Raven answered. Even then, he was angered at the word Kors used.

Dawyd spread his arms. "Dance the Sunsmith home!" he shouted.

The knowledge of victory went through Raven like a knife. Nothing but discipline kept him erect in his relief. He saw the crowd swirl outward, forming a series of interlocked rings, and he hissed to Kors, "We've made it, if we're careful. But we mustn't do anything to break their mood. We have to continue backing up, slowly, waiting a while between every step, as they dance. If we disappear into the woods during the last measure, I think they'll be satisfied."

"What's happening?" The words grated in Tolteca's throat.

"Quiet, I told you!" Raven felt the man stagger against him. Well, he thought, it had been a vicious shock, especially for someone with no real training in death. Talk might keep Tolteca from collapse, and the dancers below—absorbed as children in the stately figure they were treading—wouldn't be aware that the symbols above them whispered together.

"All right." Raven felt the rhythm of the dance indicate a backward step for him. He guided Tolteca with a hand to the elbow. "You came here with some idiotic notion of protecting Elfavy. What then?"

"I, I, I went down to . . . the plaza . . . They were—mumbling. It didn't make sense, it was ghastly—"

"Not so loud!"

"I saw Dawyd. Tried to talk to him. They all, all got more and more excited. Llyrdin's little daughter yelled and ran from me. He chased her and killed her. The cleaning robots s-s-simply carried off the body. They began . . . closing in on me—"

"I see. Now, steady. Another backward step. Halt." Raven froze in his tracks, for many heads turned his way. At this distance under the moon, they lacked faces. When their attention had drifted back to the dance, Raven breathed.

"It must be a mutation," he said. "Mutation and genetic drift, acting on a small initial population. Maybe, even if it sounds like a myth, that story of theirs is true, that they're descended from one man and two women. Anyhow, their metabolism changed. They're violently allergic to tobacco, for instance. This other change probably isn't much greater than that, in glandular terms. They may well still be interfertile with us, biologically speaking. Though culturally . . . no, I don't believe they are the same species. Not any more."

"Baleflower?" asked Tolteca. His tone was thin and shaky, like a hurt child's.

"Yes. You told me it emits an indole when it blooms. Not one that particularly affects the normal human biochemistry; but theirs isn't normal, and the stuff is chemically related to the substances associated with schizophrenia. *They* are susceptible. Every Gwydiona springtime, they go insane."

The soundless dance below jarred into a quicker staccato beat. Raven used the chance to climb several tiers in a hurry.

"It's a wonder they survived the first few generations," he said when he must stop again. "Somehow, they did, and began the slow painful adaptation. Naturally, they don't remember the insane episodes. They don't dare. Would you? That's the underlying reason why they've never made a scientific investigation of Bale, or taken the preventive measures that look so obvious to us. Instead, they built a religion and a way of life around it. But only in the first flush of the season, when they still have rationality but feel the exuberance of madness in their blood—only then are they even able to admit to themselves that they don't consciously know what happens. The rest of the time, they cover the truth with meaningless words about an ultimate reality.

"So their culture wasn't planned. It was worked out blindly, by trial and error, through centuries. And at last it reached a point where they do little damage to themselves in their lunacy.

"Remember, their psychology isn't truly human. You and I are mixtures, good, bad, and indifferent qualities; our conflicts we always have with us. But the Gwydiona seem to concentrate all their personal troubles into these few days. That's why there used to be so much destruction, before they stumbled into a routine that can cope with this phenomenon. That, I think, is why they're so utterly sane, so *good*, for most of the year. That's why they've never colonized the rest of the planet. They don't know the reason—population control is a transparent rationalization—but I know why: no baleflower. They're so well adapted that they can't do without it. I wonder what would happen to a Gwydiona deprived of his periodic dementia. I suspect it would be rather horrible.

"Their material organization protects them: strong buildings, no isolated homes, no firearms, no atomic energy, everything that might be harmed or harmful locked away for the duration of hell. This Holy City, and I suppose every one on the planet, is built like a warren, full of places to run and dodge and hide and lock yourself away when someone runs amok. The walls are padded, the ground is soft, it's hard to hurt yourself.

"But of course, the main bulwark is psychological. Myths, symbols, rites, so much a part of their lives that even in their madness they remember. Probably they remember more than in their sanity: things they dare not recall when conscious, the wild and tragic symbols, the Night Faces that aren't talked about. Slowly, over the generations and centuries, they've groped their way to a system which keeps their world somewhat orderly, somewhat meaningful, while the bale-flower blooms. Which actually channels the mania, so that very few people get hurt any more; so they act out their hates and fears, dance them out, living their own myths . . . instead of clawing each other in the physical flesh."

The dance was losing pattern. It wouldn't end after all, Raven thought, but merely dissolve into aimlessness. Well, that would serve, if he could vanish and be forgotten.

He said to Tolteca, "You had to come bursting into their dream universe and unbalance it. You killed that little girl."

"Oa, name of mercy." The engineer covered his face.

Raven sighed. "Forget it. Partly my fault. I should have told you at once what I surmised."

They were halfway up the terraces when someone broke through the dancers and came bounding toward them. Two, Raven saw, his heart gone hollow. The moonlight cascaded over their blonde hair, turning it to frost.

"Stop," called Elfavy, low and with laughter. "Stop, Ragan."

He wondered what sort of destiny the accidental likeness of his name to that of a myth would prove to be.

She paused a few steps below him. Byord clutched her hand, looking about from bright soulless eyes. Elfavy brushed a lock off her forehead, a gesture Raven remembered. "Here is the River Child, Ragan," she called. "And you are the rain. And I am the Mother, and darkness is in me."

Beyond her shoulder, he saw that others had heard. They were ceasing to dance, one by one, and staring up.

"Welcome, then," said Raven. "Go back to your home in the meadows, River Child. Take him home, Bird Maiden."

Byord's small face opened. He screamed.

"*Don't eat me, mother!*"

Elfavy bent down and embraced him. "No," she crooned, "oh, no, no, no. You shall come to me. Don't you recall it? I was in the ground, and rain fell on me and it was dark where I was. Come with me, River Child."

Byord shrieked and tried to break free. She dragged him on toward Raven. From the crowd below, a deep voice lifted, "And the earth drank the rain, and the rain was the earth, and the Mother was the Child and carried Ynis in her arms."

"Jingleballs!" muttered Kors. His scarecrow form slouched forward, to stand between his Commandant and those below. "That tears it."

"I'm afraid so," said Raven.

Dawyd sprang onto the lowest tier. His tone rang like a trumpet: "They came from the sky and violated the Mother! Can you hear the leaves weep?"

"Now what?" Tolteca glared at them, where they surged shadowed on the moon-gray turf. "What do they mean? It's a nightmare, it doesn't make sense!"

"Every nightmare makes sense," Raven answered. "The homicidal urge is awake and looking for something to destroy. And it has just figured out what, too."

"The ship, huh?" Kors hefted his gun.

"Yes," said Raven. "Rainfall is a fertilization symbol. So what kind of symbol do you think a spaceship landing on your home soil and discharging its crew is? What would you do to a man who attacked your mother?"

"I hate to shoot those poor unarmed bastards," said Kors, "but—"

Raven snarled like an animal: "If you do, I'll kill you myself!"

He regained control and drew out his miniradio. "I told Utiel to lift ship thirty hours after I'd gone, but that won't be soon enough. I'll warn him now. There mustn't be any vessel there for them to assault. Then we'll see if we can save our own hides."

Elfavy reached him. She flung Byord at his feet, where the boy sobbed in his terror, not having sufficient mythic training to give pattern to that which stirred within him. Elfavy fixed her gaze wide upon Raven. "I know you," she gasped. "You sat on my grave once, and I couldn't sleep."

He thumbed the radio switch and put the box to his lips. Her fingernails gashed his hand, which opened in sheer reflex. She snatched the box and flung it from her, further than he would have believed a woman could throw. "No!" she shrilled. "Don't leave the darkness in me, Ragan! You woke me once!"

Kors started forward. "I'll get it," he said. Elfavy pulled his knife from its sheath as he passed and thrust it between his ribs. He sank on all fours, astonished in the moonlight.

Down below, a berserk howl broke loose as they saw what had happened. Dawyd shuffled to the radio, picked it up, gaped at it, tossed it back into the mob. They swallowed it as a whirlpool might.

Raven stooped down by Kors, cradling the helmeted head in his arms. The soldier bubbled blood. "Get started, Commandant. I'll hold 'em." He reached for his gun and took an unsteady aim.

"No." Raven snatched it from him. "We came to them."

"Horse apples," said Kors, and died.

Raven straightened. He handed Tolteca the gun and the dagger withdrawn from the body. A moment he hesitated, then added his own weapons. "On your way," he said. "You have to reach the ship before they do."

"You go!" Tolteca screamed. "I'll stay—"

"I'm trained in unarmed combat," said Raven. "I can hold them a good deal longer than you, clerk."

He stood thinking. Elfavy knelt beside him. She clasped his hand. Byord trembled at her feet.

"You might bear in mind next time," said Raven, "that a Lochlanna has obligations."

He gave Tolteca a shove. The Namerican drew a breath and ran.

"O the harbuck at the cliff's edge!" called Dawyd joyously. "The arrows of the sun are in him!" He went after Tolteca like a streak. Raven pulled loose from Elfavy, intercepted her father, and stiff-armed him. Dawyd rolled down the green steps, into the band of men that yelped. They tore him apart.

Raven went back to Elfavy. She still knelt, holding her son. He had never seen anything so gentle as her smile. "We're next," he said. "But you've time to get away. Run. Lock yourself in a tower room."

Her hair swirled about her shoulders with the gesture of negation. "Sing me the rest."

"You can save Byord too," he begged.

"It's such a beautiful song," said Elfavy.

Raven watched the people of Instar feasting. He hadn't much voice left, but he did his lame best.

> "—'Tis down in yonder garden green,
> Love, where we used to walk,
> The fairest flower that e'er was seen
> Is withered to a stalk.

> "'The stalk is withered dry, my love;
> So will our hearts decay.
> So make yourself content, my love,
> Till God calls you away.'"

"Thank you, Ragan," said Elfavy.

"Will you go now?" he asked.

"I?" she said. "How could I? We are the Three."

He sat down beside her, and she leaned against him. His free hand stroked the boy's damp hair.

Presently the crowd uncoiled itself and lumbered up the steps. Raven arose. He moved away from Elfavy, who remained where she was. If he could hold their attention for half an hour or so—and with luck, he should be able to last that long—they might well forget about her. Then she would survive the night.

And not remember.

THE SHARING OF FLESH

THE SHARING OF FLESH

Moru understood about guns. At least the tall strangers had demonstrated to their guides what the things that each of them carried at his hip could do in a flash and a flameburst. But he did not realize that the small objects they often moved about in their hands, while talking in their own language, were audiovisual transmitters. Probably, he thought they were fetishes.

Thus, when he killed Donli Sairn, he did so in full view of Donli's wife.

That was happenstance. Except for prearranged times at morning and evening of the planet's twenty-eight-hour day, the biologist, like his fellows, sent only to his computer. But because they had not been married long and were helplessly happy, Evalyth received his 'casts whenever she could get away from her own duties.

The coincidence that she was tuned in at that one moment was not great. There was little for her to do. As Militech of the expedition— she being from a half barbaric part of Kraken where the sexes had equal opportunities to learn arts of combat suitable to primitive environments—she had overseen the building of a compound; and she kept the routines of guarding it under a close eye. However, the inhabitants of Lokon were as cooperative with the visitors from heaven as mutual mysteriousness allowed. Every instinct and experience assured Evalyth Sairn that their reticence masked nothing except awe, with perhaps a wistful hope of friendship. Captain Jonafer agreed. Her position having thus become rather a sinecure, she was trying to learn enough about Donli's work to be a useful assistant after he returned from the lowlands.

Also, a medical test had lately confirmed that she was pregnant. She wouldn't tell him, she decided, not yet, over all those hundreds of kilometers, but rather when they lay again together. Meanwhile, the knowledge that they had begun a new life made him a lodestar to her.

On the afternoon of his death she entered the biolab whistling. Outside, sunlight struck fierce and brass-colored on dusty ground, on prefab shacks huddled about the boat which had brought everyone and everything down from the orbit where *New Dawn* circled, on the parked flitters and gravsleds that took men around the big island that was the only habitable land on this globe, on the men and the women themselves. Beyond the stockade, plumy treetops, a glimpse of mud-brick buildings, a murmur of voices and mutter of footfalls, a drift of bitter woodsmoke, showed that a town of several thousand people sprawled between here and Lake Zelo.

The bio-lab occupied more than half the structure where the Sairns lived. Comforts were few, when ships from a handful of cultures struggling back to civilization ranged across the ruins of empire. For Evalyth, though, it sufficed that this was their home. She was used to austerity anyway. One thing that had first attracted her to Donli, meeting him on Kraken, was the cheerfulness with which he, a man from Atheia, which was supposed to have retained or regained almost as many amenities as Old Earth knew in its glory, had accepted life in her gaunt grim country.

The gravity field here was 0.77 standard, less than two-thirds of what she had grown in. Her gait was easy through the clutter of apparatus and specimens. She was a big young woman, good-looking in the body, a shade too strong in the features for most men's taste outside her own folk. She had their blondness and, on legs and forearms, their intricate tattoos; the blaster at her waist had come down through many generations. Otherwise she had abandoned Krakener costume for the plain coveralls of the expedition.

How cool and dim the shack was! She sighed with pleasure, sat down, and activated the receiver. As the image formed, three-dimensional in the air, and Donli's voice spoke, her heart sprang a little.

"—appears to be descended from a clover."

The image was of plants with green trilobate leaves, scattered low among the reddish native pseudo-grasses. It swelled as Donli brought the transmitter near so that the computer might record details for later analysis. Evalyth frowned, trying to recall what . . . Oh, yes. Clover was another of those life forms that man had brought with him from Old Earth, to more planets than anyone now remembered, before the Long Night fell. Often they were virtually unrecognizable; over thousands of years, evolution had fitted them to alien conditions, or mutation and genetic drift had acted on small initial populations in a nearly random fashion. No one on Kraken had known that pines and gulls and rhizobacteria were altered immigrants, until Donli's crew arrived and identified them. Not that he, or anybody from this part of the galaxy, had yet made it back to the mother world. But the Atheian data banks were packed with information, and so was Donli's dear curly head—

And there was his hand, huge in the field of view, gathering specimens. She wanted to kiss it. *Patience, patience,* the officer part of her reminded the bride. *We're here to work. We've discovered one more lost colony, the most wretched one so far, sunken back to utter primitivism. Our duty is to advise the Board whether a civilizing mission is worthwhile, or whether the slender resources that the Allied Planets can spare had better be used elsewhere, leaving these people in their misery for another two or three hundred years. To make an honest report, we must study them, their cultures, their world. That's why I'm in the barbarian highlands and he's down in the jungle among out-and-out savages.*

Please finish soon, darling.

She heard Donli speak in the lowland dialect. It was a debased form of Lokonese, which in turn was remotely descended from Anglic. The expedition's linguists had unraveled the language in a few intensive weeks. Then all personnel took a brain-feed in it. Nonetheless, she admired how quickly her man had become fluent in the woods-runners' version, after mere days of conversation with them.

"Are we not coming to the place, Moru? You said the thing was close by our camp."

"We are nearly arrived, man-from-the-clouds."

A tiny alarm struck within Evalyth. What was going on? Donli hadn't left his companions to strike off alone with a native, had he? Rogar of Lokon had warned them to beware of treachery in those parts. But, to be sure, only yesterday the guides had rescued Haimie Fiell when he tumbled into a swift-running river . . . at some risk to themselves . . .

The view bobbed as the transmitter swung in Donli's grasp. It made Evalyth a bit dizzy. From time to time, she got glimpses of the broader setting. Forest crowded about a game trail, rust-colored leafage, brown trunks and branches, shadows beyond, the occasional harsh call of something unseen. She could practically feel the heat and dank weight of the atmosphere, smell the unpleasant pungencies. This world—which no longer had a name, except World, because the dwellers upon it had forgotten what the stars really were—was ill suited to colonization. The life it had spawned was often poisonous, always nutritionally deficient. With the help of species they had brought along, men survived marginally. The original settlers doubtless meant to improve matters. But then the breakdown came—evidence was that their single town had been missiled out of existence, a majority of the people with it—and resources were lacking to rebuild; the miracle was that anything human remained except bones.

"Now here, man-from-the-clouds."

The swaying scene grew steady. Silence hummed from jungle to cabin. "I do not see anything," Donli said at length.

"Follow me. I show."

Donli put his transmitter in the fork of a tree. It scanned him and Moru while they moved across a meadow. The guide looked childish beside the space traveler, barely up to his shoulder; an old child, though, near-naked body seamed with scars and lame in the right foot from some injury of the past, face wizened in a great black bush of hair and beard. He, who could not hunt but could only fish and trap to support his family, was even more impoverished than his fellows. He must have been happy indeed when the flitter landed near their village and the strangers offered fabulous trade goods for a week or two of being shown around the countryside. Donli had projected the image of Mora's straw hut for Evalyth—the pitiful few possessions, the woman already worn out with toil, the surviving sons who, at ages said to be about seven or eight, which would equal twelve or thirteen standard years, were shriveled gnomes.

Rogar seemed to declare—the Lokonese tongue was by no means perfectly understood yet—that the low-landers would be less poor if they weren't such a vicious lot, tribe forever at war with tribe. *But really,* Evalyth thought, *what possible menace can they be?*

Moru's gear consisted of a loinstrap, a cord around his body for preparing snares, an obsidian knife, and a knapsack so woven and greased that it could hold liquids at need. The other men of his group, being able to pursue game and to win a share of booty by taking part in battles, were noticeably better off. They didn't look much different in person, however. Without room for expansion, the island populace must be highly inbred.

The dwarfish man squatted, parting a shrub with his hands. "Here," he grunted, and stood up again.

Evalyth knew well the eagerness that kindled in Donli. Nevertheless he turned around, smiled straight into the transmitter, and said in Atheian: "Maybe you're watching, dearest. If so, I'd like to share this with you. It may be a bird's nest."

She remembered vaguely that the existence of birds would be an ecologically significant datum. What mattered was what he had just said to her. "Oh, yes, oh, yes!" she wanted to cry. But his group had only two receivers with them, and he wasn't carrying either.

She saw him kneel in the long, ill-colored vegetation. She saw him reach with the gentleness she also knew, into the shrub, easing its branches aside.

She saw Moru leap upon his back. The savage wrapped legs about Donli's middle. His left hand seized Donli's hair and pulled the head back. The knife flew back in his right.

Blood spurted from beneath Donli's jaw. He couldn't shout, not with his throat gaping open; he could only bubble and croak while Moru haggled the wound wider. He reached blindly for his gun. Moru dropped the knife and caught his arms; they rolled over in that embrace, Donli threshed and flopped in the spouting of his own blood. Moru hung on. The brush trembled around them and hid them, until Moru rose red and dripping, painted, panting, and Evalyth screamed into the transmitter beside her, into the universe, and she kept on screaming and fought them when they tried to take her away from the scene in the meadow where Moru went about his butcher's work, until something stung her with coolness and she toppled into the bottom of the universe whose stars had all gone out forever.

Haimie Fiell said through white lips: "No, of course we didn't know till you alerted us. He and that—creature—were several kilometers from our camp. *Why* didn't you let us go after him right away?"

"Because of what we'd seen on the transmission," Captain Jonafer replied. "Sairn was irretrievably dead. You could've been ambushed, arrows in the back or something, pushing down those narrow trails. Best stay where you were, guarding each other, till we got a vehicle to you."

Fiell looked past the big gray-haired man, out the door of the command hut, to the stockade and the unpitying noon sky. "But what that little monster was doing meanwhile—" Abruptly he closed his mouth.

With equal haste, Jonafer said: "The other guides ran away, you have told me, as soon as they sensed you were angry. I've just had a report from Kallaman. His team flitted to the village. It's deserted. The whole tribe's pulled up stakes. Afraid of our revenge, evidently. Though it's no large chore to move, when you can carry your household goods on your back and weave a new house in a day."

Evalyth leaned forward. "Stop evading me," she said. "What did Moru do with Donli that you might have prevented if you'd arrived in time?"

Fiell continued to look past her. Sweat gleamed in droplets on his forehead. "Nothing, really," he mumbled. "Nothing that mattered . . . once the murder itself had been committed."

"I meant to ask you what kind of services you want for him, Lieutenant Sairn," Jonafer said to her. "Should the ashes be buried here, or scattered in space after we leave, or brought home?"

Evalyth turned her gaze full upon him. "I never authorized that he be cremated, Captain," she said slowly.

"No, but—Well, be realistic. You were first under anesthesia, then heavy sedation, while we recovered the body. Time had passed. We've no facilities for, um, cosmetic repair, nor any extra refrigeration space, and in this heat—"

Since she had been let out of sickbay, there had been a kind of numbness in Evalyth. She could not entirely comprehend the fact that Donli was gone. It seemed as if at any instant yonder doorway would fill with him, sunlight across his shoulders, and he would call to her, laughing, and console her for a meaningless nightmare she had had. That was the effect of the psycho-drugs, she knew and damned the kindliness of the medic.

She felt almost glad to feel a slow rising anger. It meant the drugs were wearing off. By evening she would be able to weep.

"Captain," she said, "I saw him killed. I've seen deaths before, some of them quite messy. We do not mask the truth on Kraken. You've cheated me of my right to lay my man out and close his eyes. You will not cheat me of my right to obtain justice. I demand to know exactly what happened."

Jonafer's fists knotted on his desktop. "I can hardly stand to tell you."

"But you shall, Captain."

"All right! All right!" Jonafer shouted. The words leaped out like bullets. "We saw the thing transmitted. He stripped Donli, hung him up by the heels from a tree, bled him into that knapsack. He cut off the genitals and threw them in with the blood. He opened the body and took heart, lungs, liver, kidneys, thyroid, prostate, pancreas, and loaded them up too, and ran off into the woods. Do you wonder why we didn't let you see what was left?"

"The Lokonese warned us against the jungle dwellers," Fiell said dully. "We should have listened. But they seemed like pathetic dwarfs. And they did rescue me from the river. When Donli asked about the birds—described them, you know, and asked if anything like that was known—Moru said yes, but they were rare and shy; our gang would scare them off; but if one man would come along with him, he could find a nest and they might see the bird. A house he called it, but Donli thought he meant a nest. Or so he told us. It'd been a talk with Moru when they happened to be a ways offside, in sight but out of earshot. Maybe that should have alerted us, maybe we should have asked the other tribesmen. But we did not see any reason to—I mean, Donli was bigger, stronger, armed with a blaster. What savage would dare attack him? And anyway, they *had* been friendly, downright frolicsome after they got over their initial fear of us, and they'd shown as much eagerness for further contact as anybody here in Lokon has, and—" His voice trailed off.

"Did he steal tools or weapons?" Evalyth asked.

"No," Jonafer said. "I have everything your husband was carrying, ready to give you."

Fiell said: "I don't think it was an act of hatred. Moru must have had some superstitious reason."

Jonafer nodded. "We can't judge him by our standards."

"By whose, then?" Evalyth retorted. Supertranquilizer or no, she was surprised at the evenness of her own tone. "I'm from Kraken, remember. I'll not let Donli's child be born and grow up knowing he was murdered and no one tried to do justice for him."

"You can't take revenge on an entire tribe," Jonafer said.

"I don't mean to. But, Captain, the personnel of this expedition are from several different planets, each with its characteristic societies. The articles specifically state that the essential mores of every member shall be respected. I want to be relieved of my regular duties until I have arrested the killer of my husband and done justice upon him."

Jonafer bent his head. "I have to grant that," he said low.

Evalyth rose. "Thank you, gentlemen," she said. "If you will excuse me, I'll commence my investigation at once."

—While she was still a machine, before the drugs wore off.

In the drier, cooler uplands, agriculture had remained possible after the colony otherwise lost civilization. Fields and orchards, painstakingly cultivated with neolithic tools, supported a scattering of villages and the capital town Lokon.

Its people bore a family resemblance to the forest dwellers. Few settlers indeed could have survived to become the ancestors of this world's humanity. But the highlanders were better nourished, bigger, straighter. They wore gaily dyed tunics and sandals. The well-to-do added jewelry of gold and silver. Hair was braided, chins kept shaven. Folk walked boldly, without the savages' constant fear of ambush, and talked merrily.

To be sure, this was only strictly true of the free. While *New Dawn*'s anthropologists had scarcely begun to unravel the ins and outs of the culture, it had been obvious from the first that Lokon kept a large slave class. Some were sleek household servants. More toiled meek and naked in the fields, the quarries, the mines, under the lash of overseers and the guard of soldiers whose spearheads and swords were of ancient Imperial metal. But none of the space travelers was unduly shocked. They had seen worse elsewhere. Historical data banks described places in olden time called Athens, India, America.

Evalyth strode down twisted, dusty streets, between the gaudily painted walls of cubical, windowless adobe houses. Commoners going about their tasks made respectful salutes. Although no one feared any longer that the strangers meant harm, she did tower above the tallest man, her hair was colored like metal and her eyes like the sky, she bore lightning at her waist and none knew what other godlike powers.

Today soldiers and noblemen also genuflected, while slaves went on their faces. Where she appeared, the chatter and clatter of everyday life vanished; the business of the market plaza halted when she passed the booths; children ceased their games and fled; she moved in silence akin to the silence in her soul. Under the sun and the snow-cone of Mount Burus, horror brooded. For by now Lokon knew that a man from the stars had been slain by a lowland brute; and what would come of that?

Word must have gone ahead to Rogar, though, since he awaited her in his house by Lake Zelo next to the Sacred Place. He was not king or council president or high priest, but he was something of all three, and it was he who dealt most with the strangers.

His dwelling was the usual kind, larger than average but dwarfed by the adjacent walls. Those enclosed a huge compound, filled with buildings, where none of the outworlders had been admitted. Guards in scarlet robes and grotesquely carved wooden helmets stood always at its gates. Today their number was doubled, and others flanked Rogar's door. The lake shone like polished steel at their backs. The trees along the shore looked equally rigid.

Rogar's major-domo, a fat elderly slave, prostrated himself in the entrance as Evalyth neared. "If the heaven-born will deign to follow this unworthy one, *Kiev* Rogar is within—" The guards dipped their spears to her. Their eyes were wide and frightened.

Like the other houses, this turned inward. Rogar sat on a dais in a room opening on a courtyard. It seemed doubly cool and dim by contrast with the glare outside. She could scarcely discern the frescos on the walls or the patterns on the carpet; they were crude art anyway.

Her attention focused on Rogar. He did not rise, that not being a sign of respect here. Instead, he bowed his grizzled head above folded hands. The major-domo offered her a bench, and Rogar's chief wife set a bombilla of herb tea by her before vanishing.

"Be greeted, *Kiev*," Evalyth said formally.

"Be greeted, heaven-born." Alone now, shadowed from the cruel sun, they observed a ritual period of silence.

Then: "This is terrible what has happened, heaven-born," Rogar said. "Perhaps you do not know that my white robe and bare feet signify mourning as for one of my own blood."

"That is well done," Evalyth said. "We shall remember."

The man's dignity faltered. "You understand that none of us had anything to do with the evil, do you not? The savages are our enemies too. They are vermin. Our ancestors caught some and made them slaves, but they are good for nothing else. I warned your friends not to go down among those we have not tamed."

"Their wish was to do so," Evalyth replied. "Now my wish is to get revenge for my man." She didn't know if this language included a word for justice. No matter. Because of the drugs, which heightened the logical faculties while they muffled the emotions, she was speaking Lokonese quite well enough for her purposes.

"We can get soldiers and help you kill as many as you choose," Rogar offered.

"Not needful. With this weapon at my side I alone can destroy more than your army might. I want your counsel and help in a different matter. How can I find him who slew my man?"

Rogar frowned. "The savages can vanish into trackless jungles, heaven-born."

"Can they vanish from other savages, though?"

"Ah! Shrewdly thought, heaven-born. Those tribes are endlessly at each other's throats. If we can make contact with one, its hunters will soon learn for you where the killer's people have taken themselves." His scowl deepened. "But he must have gone from them, to hide until you have departed our land. A single man might be impossible to find. Lowlanders are good at hiding, of necessity."

"What do you mean by necessity?"

Rogar showed surprise at her failure to grasp what was obvious to him. "Why, consider a man out hunting," he said. "He cannot go with companions after every kind of game, or the noise and scent would frighten it away. So he is often alone in the jungle. Someone from another tribe may well set upon him. A man stalked and killed is just as useful as one slain in open war."

"Why this incessant fighting?"

Rogar's look of bafflement grew stronger. "How else shall they get human flesh?"

"But they do not live on that!"

"No, surely not, except as needed. But that need comes many times as you know. Their wars are their chief way of taking men; booty is good too, but not the main reason to fight. He who slays, owns the corpse, and naturally divides it solely among his close kin. Not everyone is lucky in battle. Therefore these who did not chance to kill in a war may well go hunting on their own, two or three of them together hoping to find a single man from a different tribe. And that is why a lowlander is good at hiding."

Evalyth did not move or speak. Rogar drew a long breath and continued trying to explain: "Heaven-born, when I heard the evil news, I spoke long with men from your company. They told me what they had seen from afar by the wonderful means you command. Thus it is clear to me what happened. This guide—what is his name? Yes, Moru—he is a cripple. He had no hope of killing himself a man except by treachery. When he saw that chance, he took it."

He ventured a smile. "That would never happen in the highlands," he declared. "We do not fight wars, save when we are attacked, nor do we hunt our fellowmen as if they were animals. Like yours, ours is a civilized race." His lips drew back from startlingly white teeth. "But, heaven-born, your man was slain. I propose we take vengeance, not simply on the killer if we catch him, but on his tribe, which we can certainly find as you suggested. That will teach all the savages to beware of their betters. Afterward we can share the flesh, half to your people, half to mine."

Evalyth could only know an intellectual astonishment. Yet she had the feeling somehow of having walked off a cliff. She stared through the shadows, into the grave old face, and after a long time she heard herself whisper: "You . . . also . . . here . . . eat men?"

"Slaves," Rogar said. "No more than required. One of them will do for four boys."

Her hand dropped to her gun. Rogar sprang up in alarm. "Heaven-born," he exclaimed, "I told you we are civilized. Never fear attack from any of us! We—we—"

She rose too, high above him. Did he read judgment in her gaze? Was the terror that snatched him on behalf of his whole people? He cowered from her, sweating and shuddering. "Heaven-born, let me show you, let me take you into the Sacred Place, even if you are no initiate . . . for surely you are akin to the gods, surely the gods will not be offended—Come, let me show you how it is, let me prove we have no will and no *need* to be your enemies—"

There was the gate that Rogar opened for her in that massive wall. There were the shocked countenances of the guards and loud promises of many sacrifices to appease the Powers. There was the stone pavement beyond, hot and hollowly resounding underfoot. There were the idols grinning around a central temple. There was the house of the acolytes who did the work and who shrank in fear when they saw their master conduct a foreigner in. There were the slave barracks.

"See, heaven-born, they are well treated, are they not? We do have to crush their hands and feet when we choose them as children for this service. Think how dangerous it would be otherwise, hundreds of boys and young men in here. But we treat them kindly unless they misbehave. Are they not fat? Their own Holy Food is especially honorable, bodies of men of all degree who have died in their full strength. We teach them that they will live on in those for whom they are slain. Most are content with that; believe me, heaven-born. Ask them yourself . . . though remember, they grow dull-witted, with nothing to do year after year. We slay them quickly, cleanly, at the beginning of each summer—no more than we must for that year's crop of boys entering into manhood, one slave for four boys, no more than that. And it is a most beautiful rite, with days of feasting and merry-making afterward. Do you understand now, heaven-born? You have nothing to fear from us. We are not savages, warring and raiding and skulking to get our man-flesh. We are civilized—not godlike in your fashion, no, I dare not claim that, do not be angry— but civilized—surely worthy of your friendship, are we not? Are we not, heaven-born?"

✿   ✿   ✿

Chena Barnard, who headed the cultural anthropology team, told her computer to scan its data bank. Like the others, it was a portable, its memory housed in *New Dawn*. At the moment the spaceship was above the opposite hemisphere, and perceptible time passed while beams went back and forth along the strung-out relay units.

Chena leaned back and studied Evalyth across her desk. The Krakener girl sat so quietly. It seemed unnatural, despite the drugs in her bloodstream retaining some power. To be sure, Evalyth was of aristocratic descent in a warlike society. Furthermore, hereditary psychological as well as physiological differences might exist on the different worlds. Not much was known about that, apart from extreme cases like Gwydion—or this planet? Regardless, Chena thought, it would be better if Evalyth gave way to simple shock and grief.

"Are you quite certain of your facts, dear?" the anthropologist asked as gently as possible. "I mean, while this island alone is habitable, it's large, the topography is rugged, communications are primitive, my group has already identified scores of distinct cultures."

"I questioned Rogar for more than an hour," Evalyth replied in the same flat voice, looking out of the same flat eyes as before. "I know interrogation techniques, and he was badly rattled. He talked.

"The Lokonese themselves are not as backward as their technology. They've lived for centuries with savages threatening their border-lands. It's made them develop a good intelligence network. Rogar described its functioning to me in detail. It can't help but keep them reasonably well informed about everything that goes on. And, while tribal customs do vary tremendously, the cannibalism is universal. That is why none of the Lokonese thought to mention it to us. They took for granted that we had our own ways of providing human meat."

"People have, m-m-m, latitude in those methods?"

"Oh, yes. Here they breed slaves for the purpose. But most lowlanders have too skimpy an economy for that. Some of them use war and murder. Among others, they settled it within the tribe by annual combats. Or—Who cares? The fact is that, everywhere in this country, in whatever fashion it may be, the boys undergo a puberty rite that involves eating an adult male."

Chena bit her lip. "What in the name of chaos might have started it? Computer! Have you scanned?"

"Yes," said the machine voice out of the case on her desk. "Data on cannibalism in man are comparatively sparse, because it is a rarity. On all planets hitherto known to us it is banned and has been throughout their history, although it is sometimes considered forgivable as an emergency measure when no alternative means of preserving life is available. Very limited forms of what might be called ceremonial cannibalism have occurred, as for example the drinking of minute amounts of each other's blood in pledging oath brotherhood among the Falkens of Lochlann—"

"Never mind that," Chena said. A tautness in her throat thickened her tone. "Only here, it seems, have they degenerated so far that—Or is it degeneracy? Reversion, perhaps? What about Old Earth?"

"Information is fragmentary. Aside from what was lost during the Long Night, knowledge is under the handicap that the last primitive societies there vanished before interstellar travel began. But certain data collected by ancient historians and scientists remain.

"Cannibalism was an occasional part of human sacrifice. As a rule, victims were left uneaten. But in a minority of regions, the bodies, or selected portions of them, were consumed, either by a special class, or by the community as a whole. Generally this was regarded as theophagy. Thus, the Aztecs of Mexico offered thousands of individuals annually to their gods. The requirement of doing this forced them to provoke wars and rebellions, which in turn made it easy for the eventual European conqueror to get native allies. The majority of prisoners were simply slaughtered, their hearts given directly to the idols. But in at least one cult the body was divided among the worshippers.

"Cannibalism could be a form of magic, too. By eating a person, one supposedly acquired his virtues. This was the principal motive of the cannibals of Africa and Polynesia. Contemporary observers did report that the meals were relished, but that is easy to understand, especially in protein-poor areas.

"The sole recorded instance of systematic nonceremonial cannibalism was among the Carib Indians of America. They ate man because they preferred man. They were especially fond of babies and used to capture women from other tribes for breeding stock. Male children of these slaves were generally gelded to make them docile and tender. In large part because of strong aversion to such practices, the Europeans exterminated the Caribs to the last man."

The report stopped. Chena grimaced. "I can sympathize with the Europeans," she said.

Evalyth might once have raised her brows; but her face stayed as wooden as her speech. "Aren't you supposed to be an objective scientist?"

"Yes. Yes. Still, there is such a thing as value judgment. And they did kill Donli."

"Not they. One of them. I shall find him."

"He's nothing but a creature of his culture, dear, sick with his whole race." Chena drew a breath, struggling for calm. "Obviously, the sickness has become a behavioral basic," she said. "I daresay it originated in Lokon. Cultural radiation is practically always from the more to the less advanced peoples. And on a single island, after centuries, no tribe has escaped the infection. The Lokonese later elaborated and rationalized the practice. The savages left its cruelty naked. But highlander or lowlander, their way of life is founded on that particular human sacrifice."

"Can they be taught differently?" Evalyth asked without real interest.

"Yes. In time. In theory. But—well, I do know enough about what happened on Old Earth, and elsewhere, when advanced societies undertook to reform primitive ones. The entire structure was destroyed. It had to be.

"Think of the result, if we told these people to desist from their puberty rite. They wouldn't listen. They couldn't. They *must* have grandchildren. They *know* a boy won't become a man unless he has eaten part of a man. We'd have to conquer them, kill most, make sullen prisoners of the rest. And when the next crop of boys did in fact mature without the magic food . . . what then? Can you imagine the demoralization, the sense of utter inferiority, the loss of that tradition which is the core of every personal identity? It might be kinder to bomb this island sterile."

Chena shook her head. "No," she said harshly, "the single decent way for us to proceed would be gradually. We could send missionaries.

By their precept and example, we could start the natives phasing out their custom after two or three generations . . . and we can't afford such an effort. Not for a long time to come. Not with so many other worlds in the galaxy, so much worthier of what little help we can give. I am going to recommend this planet be left alone."

Evalyth considered her for a moment before asking: "Isn't that partly because of your own reaction?"

"Yes," Chena admitted. "I cannot overcome my disgust. And I, as you pointed out, am supposed to be professionally broad-minded. So even if the Board tried to recruit missionaries, I doubt if they'd succeed." She hesitated. "You yourself, Evalyth—"

The Krakener rose. "My emotions don't matter," she said. "My duty does. Thank you for your help." She turned on her heel and went with military strides out of the cabin.

The chemical barriers were crumbling. Evalyth stood for a moment before the little building that had been hers and Donli's, afraid to enter. The sun was low, so that the compound was filling with shadows. A thing leathery-winged and serpentine cruised silently overhead. From outside the stockade drifted sounds of feet, foreign voices, the whine of a wooden flute. The air was cooling. She shivered. Their home would be too hollow.

Someone approached. She recognized the person glimpse-wise, Alsabeta Mondain from Nuevamerica. Listening to her well-meant foolish condolences would be worse than going inside. Evalyth took the last three steps and slid the door shut behind her.

Donli will not be here again. Eternally.

But the cabin proved not to be empty to him. Rather, it was too full. That chair where he used to sit, reading that worn volume of poetry which she could not understand and teased him about, that table across which he had toasted her and tossed kisses, that closet where his clothes hung, that scuffed pair of slippers, that bed—it screamed of him. Evalyth went fast into the laboratory section and drew the curtain that separated it from the living quarters. Rings rattled along the rod. The noise was monstrous in twilight.

She closed her eyes and fists and stood breathing hard. *I will not go soft*, she declared. *You always said you loved me for my strength— among numerous other desirable features, you'd add with your slow grin, but I remember that yet—and I don't aim to let slip anything that you loved.*

I've got to get busy, she told Donli's child. *The expedition command is pretty sure to act on Chena's urging and haul mass for home. We've not many days to avenge your father.*

Her eyes snapped open. *What am I doing,* she thought, bewildered, *talking to a dead man and an embryo?*

She turned on the overhead fluoro and went to the computer. It was made no differently from the other portables. Donli had used it. But she could not look away from the unique scratches and bumps on that square case, as she could not escape his microscope, chemanalyzers, chromosome tracer, biological specimens . . . She seated herself. A drink would have been very welcome, except that she needed clarity. "Activate!" she ordered.

The On light glowed yellow. Evalyth tugged her chin, searching for words. "The objective," she said at length, "is to trace a lowlander who has consumed several kilos of flesh and blood from one of this party, and afterward vanished into the jungle. The killing took place about sixty hours ago. How can he be found?"

The least hum answered her. She imagined the links; to the master in the ferry, up past the sky to the nearest orbiting relay unit, to the next, to the next, around the bloated belly of the planet, by ogre sun and inhuman stars, until the pulses reached the mother ship; then down to an unliving brain that routed the question to the appropriate data bank; then to the scanners, whose resonating energies flew from molecule to distorted molecule, identifying more bits of information than it made sense to number, data garnered from hundreds or thousands of entire worlds, data preserved through the wreck of Empire and the dark ages that followed, data going back to an Old Earth that perhaps no longer existed. She shied from the thought and wished herself back on dear stern Kraken. *We will go there,* she promised Donli's child. *You will dwell apart from these too many machines and grow up as the gods meant you should.*

"Query," said the artificial voice. "Of what origin was the victim of this assault?"

Evalyth had to wet her lips before she could reply: "Atheian. He was Donli Sairn, your master."

"In that event, the possibility of tracking the desired local inhabitant may exist. The odds will now be computed. In the interim, do you wish to know the basis of the possibility?"

"Y-yes."

"Native Atheian biochemistry developed in a manner quite parallel to Earth's," said the voice, "and the early colonists had no difficulty in introducing terrestrial species. Thus they enjoyed a friendly environment, where population soon grew sufficiently large to obviate the danger of racial change through mutation and/or genetic drift. In addition, no selection pressure tended to force change. Hence the modern Atheian human is little different from his ancestors of Earth, on which account his physiology and biochemistry are known in detail.

"This has been essentially the case on most colonized planets for which records are available. Where different breeds of men have arisen, it has generally been because the original settlers were highly selected groups. Randomness, and evolutionary adaptation to new conditions, have seldom produced radical changes in bio-type. For example, the robustness of the average Krakener is a response to comparatively high gravity; his size aids him in resisting cold, his fair complexion is helpful beneath a sun poor in ultraviolet. But his ancestors were people who already had the natural endowments for such a world. His deviations from their norm are not extreme. They do not preclude his living on more Earth-like planets or interbreeding with the inhabitants of these.

"Occasionally, however, larger variations have occurred. They appear to be due to a small original population or to unterrestroid conditions or both. The population may have been small because the planet could not support more, or have become small as the result of hostile action when the Empire fell. In the former case, genetic accidents had a chance to be significant; in the latter, radiation produced a high rate of mutant births among survivors. The variations are less apt to be in gross anatomy than in subtle endocrine and enzymatic qualities, which affect the physiology and psychology. Well known cases include the reaction of the Gwydiona to nicotine and certain indoles, and the requirement of the Ifrians for trace amounts of lead. Sometimes the inhabitants of two planets are actually intersterile because of their differences.

"While this world has hitherto received the sketchiest of

examinations—" Evalyth was yanked out of a reverie into which the lecture had led her "—certain facts are clear. Few terrestrial species have flourished; no doubt others were introduced originally, but died off after the technology to maintain them was lost. Man has thus been forced to depend on autochthonous life for the major part of his food. This life is deficient in various elements of human nutrition. For example, the only Vitamin C appears to be in immigrant plants; Sairn observed that the people consume large amounts of grass and leaves from those species, and that fluoroscopic pictures indicate this practice has measurably modified the digestive tract. No one would supply skin, blood, sputum, or similar samples, not even from corpses." *Afraid of magic,* Evalyth thought drearily, *yes, they're back to that too.* "But intensive analysis of the usual meat animals shows these to be under-supplied with three essential amino acids, and human adaptation to this must have involved considerable change on the cellular and sub-cellular levels. The probable type and extent of such change are computable.

"The calculations are now complete." As the computer resumed, Evalyth gripped the arms of her chair and could not breathe. "While the answer is subject to fair probability of success. In effect, Atheian flesh is alien here. It can be metabolized, but the body of the local consumer will excrete certain compounds, and these will import a characteristic odor to skin and breath as well as to urine and feces. The chance is good that it will be detectable by neo-Freeholder technique at distances of several kilometers, after sixty or seventy hours. But since the molecules in question are steadily being degraded and dissipated, speed of action is recommended."

I am going to find Donli's murderer. Darkness roared around Evalyth.

"Shall the organisms be ordered for you and given the appropriate search program?" asked the voice. "They can be on hand in an estimated three hours."

"Yes," she stammered. "Oh, please—Have you any other . . . other . . . advice?"

"The man ought not to be killed out of hand, but brought here for examination, if for no other reason than in order that the scientific ends of the expedition may be served."

That's a machine talking, Evalyth cried. *It's designed to help research. Nothing more. But it was his.* And its answer was so altogether Donli that she could no longer hold back her tears.

The single big moon rose nearly full, shortly after sundown. It drowned most stars; the jungle beneath was cobbled with silver and dappled with black; the snow-cone of Mount Burus floated unreal at the unseen edge of the world. Wind slid around Evalyth where she crouched on her gravsled; it was full of wet acrid odors, and felt cold though it was not, and chuckled at her back. Somewhere something screeched, every few minutes, and something else cawed reply.

She scowled at her position indicators, aglow on the control panel. Curses and chaos, Moru had to be in this area! He could not have escaped from the valley on foot in the time available, and her search pattern had practically covered it. If she ran out of bugs before she found him, must she assume he was dead? They ought to be able to find his body regardless, ought they not? Unless it was buried deep. Here. She brought the sled over to hover, took the next phial off the rack and stood up to open it.

The bugs came out many and tiny, like smoke in the moonlight. Another failure?

No! Wait! Were not those motes dancing back together, into a streak barely visible under the moon, and vanishing downward? Heart thuttering, she turned to the indicator. Its neurodetector antenna was not aimlessly wobbling, but pointed straight west-northwest, declination thirty-two degrees below horizontal. Only a concentration of the bugs could make it behave like that. And only the particular mixture of molecules to which the bugs had been presensitized, in several parts per million or better, would make them converge on the source.

"Ya-a-ah!" She couldn't help the one hawk-yell. But thereafter she bit her lips shut—blood trickled unnoticed down her chin—and drove the sled in silence.

The distance was a mere few kilometers. She came to a halt above an opening in the forest. Pools of scummy water gleamed in its rank growth. The trees made a solid-seeming wall around. Evalyth clapped her night goggles down off her helmet and over her eyes. A lean-to became visible. It was hastily woven from vines and withes, huddled against a part of the largest trees to let their branches hide it from the sky. The bugs were entering.

Evalyth lowered her sled to a meter off the ground and got to her feet again. A stun pistol slid from its sheath into her right hand. Her left rested on the blaster.

Moru's two sons groped from the shelter. The bugs whirled around them, a mist that blurred their outlines. *Of course,* Evalyth realized, nonetheless shocked into a higher hatred. *I should have known they did the actual devouring.* More than ever did they resemble gnomes—skinny limbs, big heads, the pot bellies of undernourishment. Krakener boys of their age would have twice their bulk and be noticeably on the way to becoming men. These nude bodies belonged to children, except that they had the grotesqueness of eld.

The parents followed them, ignored by the entranced bugs. The mother wailed. Evalyth identified a few words. "What is the matter, what are those things—oh, help—" But her gaze was locked upon Moru.

Limping out of the hutch, stooped to clear its entrance, he made her think of some huge beetle crawling from an offal heap. But she would know that bushy head though her brain were coming apart. He carried a stone blade, surely the one that had hacked up Donli. *I will take it away from him, and the hand with it,* Evalyth wept. *I will keep him alive while I dismantle him with these my own hands, and in between times he can watch me flay his repulsive spawn.*

The wife's scream broke through. She had seen the metal thing, and the giant that stood on its platform, with skull and eyes shimmering beneath the moon.

"I have come for you who killed my man," Evalyth said.

The mother screamed anew and cast herself before the boys. The father tried to run around in front of her, but his lame foot twisted under him, and he fell into a pool. As he struggled out of its muck, Evalyth shot the woman. No sound was heard; she folded and lay moveless. "Run!" Moru shouted. He tried to charge the sled. Evalyth twisted a control stick. Her vehicle whipped in a circle, heading off the boys. She shot them from above, where Moru couldn't quite reach her.

He knelt beside the nearest, took the body in his arms and looked upward. The moonlight poured relentlessly across him. "What can you now do to me?" he called.

She stunned him too, landed, got off and quickly hog-tied the four of them. Loading them aboard, she found them lighter than she had expected.

Sweat had sprung forth upon her, until her coverall stuck dripping to her skin. She began to shake, as if with fever. Her ears buzzed. "I would have destroyed you," she said. Her voice sounded remote and unfamiliar. A still more distant part wondered why she bothered speaking to the unconscious, in her own tongue at that. "I wish you hadn't acted the way you did. That made me remember what the computer said, about Donli's friends needing you for study.

"You're too good a chance, I suppose. After your doings, we have the right under Allied rules to make prisoners of you, and none of his friends are likely to get maudlin about your feelings.

"Oh, they won't be inhuman. A few cell samples, a lot of tests, anesthesia where necessary, nothing harmful, nothing but a clinical examination as thorough as facilities allow.

"No doubt you'll be better fed than at any time before, and no doubt the medics will find some pathologies they can cure for you. In the end, Moru, they'll release your wife and children."

She stared into his horrible face.

"I am pleased," she said, "that to you, who won't comprehend what is going on, it will be a bad experience. And when they are finished, Moru, I will insist on having you, at least, back. They can't deny me that. Why, your tribe itself has, in effect, cast you out. Right? My colleagues won't let me do more than kill you, I'm afraid, but on this I will insist."

She gunned the engine and started toward Lokon, as fast as possible, to arrive while she felt able to be satisfied with that much.

And the days without him and the days without him.

The nights were welcome. If she had not worked herself quite to exhaustion, she could take a pill. He rarely returned in her dreams. But she had to get through each day and would not drown him in drugs.

Luckily, there was a good deal of work involved in preparing to depart, when the expedition was short-handed and on short notice. Gear must be dismantled, packed, ferried to the ship, and stowed. *New Dawn* herself must be readied, numerous systems recommissioned and tested. Her militechnic training qualified Evalyth to double as mechanic, boat jockey, or loading gang boss. In addition, she kept up the routines of defense in the compound.

Captain Jonafer objected mildly to this. "Why bother, Lieutenant? The locals are scared blue of us. They've heard what you did—and this coming and going through the sky, robots and heavy machinery in action, floodlights after dark—I'm having trouble persuading them not to abandon their town!"

"Let them," she snapped. "Who cares?"

"We did not come here to ruin them, Lieutenant."

"No. In my judgment, though, Captain, they'll be glad to ruin us if we present the least opportunity. Imagine what special virtues *your* body must have."

Jonafer sighed and gave in. But when she refused to receive Rogar the next time she was planetside, he ordered her to do so and to be civil.

The *Kiev* entered the biolab section—she would not have him in her living quarters—with a gift held in both hands, a sword of Imperial metal. She shrugged; no doubt a museum would be pleased to get the thing. "Lay it on the floor," she told him.

Because she occupied the single chair, he stood. He looked little and old in his robe. "I came," he whispered, "to say how we of Lokon rejoice that the heaven-born has won her revenge."

"Is winning it," she corrected.

He could not meet her eyes. She stared moodily at his faded hair. "Since the heaven-born could . . . easily . . . find those she wished . . . she knows the truth in the hearts of us of Lokon, that we never intended harm to her folk."

That didn't seem to call for an answer.

His fingers twisted together. "Then why do you forsake us?" he went on. "When first you came, when we had come to know you and you spoke our speech, you said you would stay for many moons, and after you would come others to teach and trade. Our hearts rejoiced. It was not alone the goods you might someday let us buy, nor that your wisemen talked of ways to end hunger, sickness, danger, and sorrow. No, our jubilation and thankfulness were most for the wonders you opened. Suddenly the world was made great, that had been so narrow. And now you are going away. I have asked, when I dared, and those of your men who will speak to me say none will return. How have we offended you, and how may it be made right, heaven-born?"

"You can stop treating your fellow men like animals," Evalyth got past her teeth.

"I have gathered . . . somewhat . . . that you from the stars say it is wrong what happens in the Sacred Place. But we only do it once in our lifetimes, heaven-born, and because we must!"

"You have no need."

Rogar went on his hands and knees before her. "Perhaps the heaven-born are thus," he pleaded, "but we are merely men. If our sons do not get the manhood, they will never beget children of their own, and the last of us will die alone in a world of death, with none to crack his skull and let the soul out—" He dared glance up at her. What he saw made him whimper and crawl backwards into the sun-glare.

Later Chena Darnard sought Evalyth. They had a drink and talked around the subject for a while, until the anthropologist plunged in: "You were pretty hard on the sachem, weren't you?"

"How'd you—Oh." The Krakener remembered that the interview had been taped, as was done whenever possible for later study. "What was I supposed to do, kiss his maneating mouth?"

"No." Chena winced. "I suppose not."

"Your signature heads the list, on the official recommendation that we quit this planet."

"Yes. But—now I don't know. I was repelled. I am. However— I've been observing the medical team working on those prisoners of yours. Have you?"

"No."

"You should. The way they cringe and shriek and reach to each other when they're strapped down in the lab and cling together afterward in their cell."

"They aren't suffering any pain or mutilation, are they?"

"Of course not. But can they believe it when their captors say they won't? They can't be tranquilized while under study, you know, if the results are to be valid. Their fear of the absolutely unknown— Well, Evalyth, I had to stop observing. I couldn't take any more." Chena gave the other a long stare. "You might, though."

Evalyth shook her head. "I don't gloat. I'll shoot the murderer because my family honor demands it. The rest can go free, even the boys. Even in spite of what they ate." She poured herself a stiff draught and tossed it off in a gulp. The liquor burned on the way down.

"I wish you wouldn't," Chena said. "Donli wouldn't have liked it. He had a proverb that he claimed was very ancient—he was from my city, don't forget, and I have known . . . I did know him longer than you, dear. I heard him say, twice or thrice, *Do I not destroy my enemies if I make them my friends?*"

"Think of a venomous insect," Evalyth replied. "You don't make friends with it. You put it under your heel."

"But a man does what he does because of what he is, what his society has made him." Chena's voice grew urgent; she leaned forward to grip Evalyth's hand, which did not respond. "What is one man, one lifetime, against all who live around him and all who have gone before? Cannibalism wouldn't be found everywhere over this island, in every one of these otherwise altogether different groupings, if it weren't the most deeply rooted cultural imperative this race has got."

Evalyth grinned around a rising anger. "And what kind of race are they to acquire it? And how about according me the privilege of operating on my own cultural imperatives? I'm bound home, to raise Donli's child away from your gutless civilization. He will not grow up disgraced because his mother was too weak to exact justice for his father. Now if you will excuse me, I have to get up early and take another boatload to the ship and get it inboard."

That task required a while. Evalyth came back toward sunset of the next day. She felt a little more tired than usual, a little more peaceful. The raw edge of what had happened was healing over. The thought crossed her mind, abstract but not shocking, not disloyal: *I'm young. One year another man will come. I won't love you the less, darling.*

Dust scuffed under her boots. The compound was half stripped already, a corresponding number of personnel berthed in the ship. The evening reached quiet beneath a yellowing sky. Only a few of the expedition stirred among the machines and remaining cabins. Lokon lay as hushed as it had lately become. She welcomed the thud of her footfalls on the steps into Jonafer's office.

He sat waiting for her, big and unmoving behind his desk. "Assignment completed without incident," she reported.

"Sit down," he said.

She obeyed. The silence grew. At last he said, out of a still face: "The clinical team has finished with the prisoners."

Somehow it was a shock. Evalyth groped for words. "Isn't that too soon? I mean, well, we don't have a lot of equipment, and just a couple of men who can see the advanced stuff, and then without Donli for an expert on Earth biology—Wouldn't a good study, down to the chromosomal level if not further—something that the physical anthropologists could use—wouldn't it take longer?"

"That's correct," Jonafer said. "Nothing of major importance was found. Perhaps something would have been, if Uden's team had any inkling of what to look for. Given that, they could have made hypotheses and tested them in a whole-organism context and come to some understanding of their subjects as functioning beings. You're right, Donli Sairn had the kind of professional intuition that might have guided them. Lacking that, and with no particular clues, and no cooperation from those ignorant, terrified savages, they had to grope and probe almost at random. They did establish a few digestive peculiarities—nothing that couldn't have been predicted on the basis of ambient ecology."

"Then why have they stopped? We won't be leaving for another week at the earliest."

"They did so on my orders, after Uden had shown me what was going on and said he'd quit regardless of what I wanted."

"What—? Oh." Scorn lifted Evalyth's head. "You mean the psychological torture."

"Yes. I saw that scrawny woman secured to a table. Her head, her body were covered with leads to the meters that clustered around her and clicked and hummed and flickered. She didn't see me; her eyes were blind with fear. I suppose she imagined her soul was being pumped out. Or maybe the process was worse for being something she couldn't put a name to. I saw her kids in a cell, holding hands. Nothing else left for them to hold onto, in their total universe. They're just at puberty; what'll this do to their psychosexual development? I saw their father lying drugged beside them, after he'd tried to batter his way straight through the wall. Uden and his helpers told me how they'd tried to make friends and failed. Because naturally the prisoners know they're in the power of those who hate them with a hate that goes beyond the grave."

Jonafer paused. "There are decent limits to everything, Lieutenant," he ended, "including science and punishment. Especially when, after all, the chance of discovering anything else is unusual is slight. I ordered the investigation terminated. The boys and their mother will be flown to their home area and released tomorrow."

"Why not today?" Evalyth asked, foreseeing his reply.

"I hoped," Jonafer said, "that you'd agree to let the man go with them."

"No."

"In the name of God—"

"Your God." Evalyth looked away from him. "I won't enjoy it, Captain. I'm beginning to wish I didn't have to. But it's not as if Donli's been killed in an honest war or feud—or—he was slaughtered like a pig. That's the evil in cannibalism; it makes a man nothing but another meat animal. I won't bring him back, but I will somehow even things, by making the cannibal nothing but a dangerous animal that needs shooting."

"I see." Jonafer too stared long out of the window. In the sunset light his face became a mask of brass. "Well," he said finally, coldly, "under the Charter of the Alliance and the articles of this expedition, you leave me no choice. But we will not have any ghoulish ceremonies, and you will not deputize what you have done. The prisoner will be brought to your place privately after dark. You will dispose of him at once and assist in cremating the remains."

Evalyth's palms grew wet. *I never killed a helpless man before!*

But he *did,* it answered. "Understood, Captain," she said.

"Very good, Lieutenant. You may go up and join the mess for dinner if you wish. No announcements to anyone. The business will be scheduled for—" Jonafer glanced at his watch, set to local rotation "—2600 hours."

Evalyth swallowed around a clump of dryness. "Isn't that rather late?"

"On purpose," he told her. "I want the camp asleep." His glance struck hers. "And want you to have time to reconsider."

"No!" She sprang erect and went for the door.

His voice pursued her. "Donli would have asked you for that."

Night came in and filled the room. Evalyth didn't rise to turn on the light. It was as if this chair, which had been Donli's favorite, wouldn't let her go.

Finally she remembered the psychodrugs. She had a few tablets left. One of them would make the execution easy to perform. No doubt Jonafer would direct that Moru be tranquilized—now, at last—before they brought him here. So why should she not give herself calmness?

It wouldn't be right.

Why not?

I don't know. I don't understand anything any longer.

Who does? Moru alone. He knows why he murdered and butchered a man who trusted him. Evalyth found herself smiling wearily into the darkness. *He had superstition for his sure guide. He's actually seen his children display the first signs of maturity. That ought to console him a little.*

Odd, that the glandular upheaval of adolescence should have commenced under frightful stress. One would have expected a delay instead. True, the captives had been getting a balanced diet for a chance, and medicine had probably eliminated various chronic low-level infections. Nonetheless the fact was odd. Besides, normal children under normal conditions would not develop the outward signs beyond mistaking in this short a time. Donli would have puzzled over the matter. She could almost see him, frowning, rubbing his forehead, grinning one-sidedly with the pleasure of a problem.

"I'd like to have a go at this myself," she heard him telling Uden over a beer and a smoke. "Might turn up an angle."

"How?" the medic would have replied. "You're a general biologist. No reflection on you, but detailed human physiology is out of your line."

"Um-m-m . . . yes and no. My main job is studying species of terrestrial origin and how they've adapted to new planets. By a remarkable coincidence, man is included among them."

But Donli was gone, and no one else was competent to do his work—to be any part of him, but she fled from that thought and from the thought of what she must presently do. She held her mind tightly to the realization that none of Uden's team had tried to apply Donli's knowledge. As Jonafer remarked, a living Donli might well have suggested an idea, unorthodox and insightful, that would have led to the discovery of whatever was there to be discovered, if anything was. Uden and his assistants were routineers. They hadn't even thought to make Donli's computer ransack its data banks for possibly relevant information. Why should they, when they saw their problem as strictly medical? And, to be sure, they were not cruel. The anguish they were inflicting had made them avoid whatever might lead to ideas demanding further research. Donli would have approached the entire business differently from the outset.

Suddenly the gloom thickened. Evalyth fought for breath. Too hot and silent here; too long a wait; she must do something or her will would desert her and she would be unable to squeeze the trigger.

She stumbled to her feet and into the lab. The fluoro blinded her for a moment when she turned it on. She went to his computer and said: "Activate!"

Nothing responded but the indicator light. The windows were totally black. Clouds outside shut off moon and stars.

"What—" The sound was a curious croak. But that brought a releasing gall: *Take hold of yourself, you blubbering idiot, or you're not fit to mother the child you're carrying.* She could then ask her question. "What explanations in terms of biology can be devised for the behavior of the people on this planet?"

"Matters of that nature are presumably best explained in terms of psychology and cultural anthropology," said the voice.

"M-m-maybe," Evalyth said. "And maybe not." She marshalled a few thoughts and stood them firm amidst the others roiling in her skull. "The inhabitants could be degenerate somehow, not really human." *I want Moru to be.* "Scan every fact recorded about them, including the detailed clinical observations made on four of them in the past several days. Compare with basic terrestrial data. Give me whatever hypotheses—anything that does not flatly contradict established facts. We've used up the reasonable ideas already."

The machine hummed. Evalyth closed her eyes and clung to the edge of the desk. *Donli, please help me.*

At the other end of forever, the voice came to her:

"The sole behavioral element which appears to be not easily explicable by postulates concerning environment and accidental historical developments, is the cannibalistic puberty rite. According to the anthropological computer, this might well have originated as a form of human sacrifice. But that computer notes certain illogicalities in the idea, as follows.

"On Old Earth, sacrificial religion was normally associated with agricultural societies, which were more vitally dependent on continued fertility and good weather than hunters. Even for them, the offering of humans proved disadvantageous in the long run, as the Aztec example most clearly demonstrates. Lokon has rationalized the practice to a degree, making it a part of the slavery system and thus minimizing its impact on the generality. But for the lowlanders it is a powerful evil, a source of perpetual danger, a diversion of effort and resources that are badly needed for survival. It is not plausible that the custom, if ever imitated from Lokon, should persist among every one of those tribes. Nevertheless it does. Therefore it must have some value and the problem is to find what.

"The method of obtaining victims varies widely, but the requirement always appears to be the same. According to the Lokonese, one adult male body is necessary and sufficient for the maturation of four boys. The killer of Donli Sairn was unable to carry off the entire corpse. What he did take of it is suggestive.

"Hence a dipteroid phenomenon may have appeared in man on this planet. Such a thing is unknown among higher animals elsewhere, but is conceivable. A modification of the Y chromosome would produce it. The test for that that modification, and thus the test of the hypothesis, is easily made."

The voice stopped. Evalyth heard the blood slugging in her veins. "What are you talking about?"

"The phenomenon is found among lower animals on several worlds," the computer told her.

"It is uncommon and so is not widely known. The name derives from the Diptera, a type of dung fly on Old Earth."

Lightning flickered. "Dung fly—good, yes!"

The machine went on to explain.

Jonafer came along with Moru. The savage's hands were tied

behind his back, and the spaceman loomed enormous over him. Despite that and the bruises he had inflicted on himself, he hobbled along steadily. The clouds were breaking and the moon shone ice-white. Where Evalyth waited, outside her door, she saw the compound reach bare to the saw-topped stockade and a crane stand above like a gibbet. The air was growing cold—the planet spinning toward an autumn—and a small wind had arisen to whimper behind the dust devils that stirred across the earth. Jonafer's footfalls rang loud.

He noticed her and stopped. Moru did likewise. "What did they learn?" she asked.

The captain nodded. "Uden got right to work when you called," he said. "The test is more complicated than your computer suggested—but then, it's for Donli's kind of skill, not Uden's. He'd never have thought of it unassisted. Yes, the notion is true."

"How?"

Moru stood waiting while the language he did not understand went to and fro around him.

"I'm no medic." Jonafer kept his tone altogether colorless. "But from what Uden told me, the chromosome defect means that the male gonads here can't mature spontaneously. They need an extra supply of hormones—he mentioned testosterone and androsterone, I forget what else—to start off the series of changes which bring on puberty. Lacking that, you'll get eunuchism. Uden thinks the surviving population was tiny after the colony was bombed out, and so poor that it resorted to cannibalism for bare survival, the first generation or two. Under those circumstances, a mutation that would otherwise have eliminated itself got established and spread to every descendant."

Evalyth nodded. "I see."

"You understand what this means, I suppose," Jonafer said. "There'll be no problem to ending the practice. We'll simply tell them we have a new and better Holy Food, and prove it with a few pills. Terrestrial-type meat animals can be reintroduced later and supply what's necessary. In the end, no doubt our geneticists can repair that faulty Y chromosome."

He could not stay contained any longer. His mouth opened, a gash across his half-seen face, and he rasped: "I should praise you for saving a whole people. I can't. Get your business over with, will you?"

Evalyth trod forward to stand before Moru. He shivered but met her eyes. Astonished, she said: "You haven't drugged him."

"No," Jonafer said. "I wouldn't help you." He spat.

"Well, I'm glad." She addressed Moru in his own language: "You killed my man. Is it right that I should kill you?"

"It is right," he answered, almost as levelly as she. "I thank you that my woman and my sons are to go free." He was quiet for a second or two. "I have heard that your folk can preserve food for years without it rotting. I would be glad if you kept my body to give to your sons."

"Mine will not need it," Evalyth said. "Nor will the sons of your sons."

Anxiety tinged his words: "Do you know why I slew your man? He was kind to me, and like a god. But I am lame. I saw no other way to get what my sons must have; and they must have it soon, or it would be too late and they could never become men."

"He taught me," Evalyth said, "how much it is to be a man."

She turned to Jonafer, who stood tense and puzzled. "I had my revenge," she said in Donli's tongue.

"What?" His question was a reflexive noise.

"After I learned about the dipteroid phenomenon," she said. "All that was necessary was for me to keep silent. Moru, his children, his entire race would go on being prey for centuries, maybe forever. I sat for half an hour, I think, having my revenge."

"And then?" Jonafer asked.

"I was satisfied and could start thinking about justice," Evalyth said.

She drew a knife. Moru straightened his back. She stepped behind him and cut his bonds. "Go home," she said. "Remember him."

STARFOG

STARFOG

"From another universe. Where space is a shining cloud, two hundred light-years across, roiled by the red stars that number in the many thousands, and where the brighter suns are troubled and cast forth great flames. Your spaces are dark and lonely."

Daven Laure stopped the recording and asked for an official translation. A part of *Jaccavrie*'s computer scanned the molecules of a plugged-in memory cylinder, identified the passage, and flashed the Serievan text onto a reader screen. Another part continued the multitudinous tasks of planetary approach. Still other parts waited for the man's bidding, whatever he might want next. A Ranger of the Commonalty traveled in a very special ship.

And even so, every year, a certain number did not come home from their missions.

Laure nodded to himself. Yes, he'd understood the woman's voice correctly. Or, at least, he interpreted her sentences approximately the same way as did the semanticist who had interviewed her and her fellows. And this particular statement was as difficult, as ambiguous as any which they had made. Therefore: (a) Probably the linguistic computer on Serieve had done a good job of unraveling their basic language. (b) It had accurately encoded its findings—vocabulary, grammar, tentative reconstruction of the underlying worldview—in the cylinders which a courier had brought to Sector HQ. (c) The reencoding, into his own neurones, which Laure underwent on his way here, had taken well. He had a working knowledge of the tongue which—among how many others?—was spoken on Kirkasant.

"Wherever that may be," he muttered.

The ship weighed his words for a nanosecond or two, decided no answer was called for, and made none.

Restless, Laure got to his feet and prowled from the study cabin, down a corridor to the bridge. It was so called largely by courtesy. *Jaccavrie* navigated, piloted, landed, lifted, maintained, and, if need be, repaired and fought for herself. But the projectors here offered a full outside view. At the moment, the bulkheads seemed cramped and barren. Laure ordered the simulacrum activated.

The bridge vanished from his eyes. Had it not been for the G-field underfoot, he might have imagined himself floating in space. A crystal night enclosed him, unwinking stars scattered like jewels, the frosty glitter of the Milky Way. Large and near, its radiance stopped down to preserve his retinas, burned the yellow sun of Serieve. The planet itself was a growing crescent, blue banded with white, rimmed by a violet sky. A moon stood opposite, a worn golden coin.

But Laure's gaze strayed beyond, toward the deeps and then, as if in search of comfort, the other way, toward Old Earth. There was no comfort, though. They still named her Home, but she lay in the spiral arm behind this one, and Laure had never seen her. He had never met anyone who had. None of his ancestors had, for longer than their family chronicles ran. Home was a half-remembered myth; reality was here, these stars on the fringes of this civilization.

Serieve lay near the edge of the known. Kirkasant lay somewhere beyond.

"Surely not outside of spacetime," Laure said.

"If you've begun thinking aloud, you'd like to discuss it," *Jaccavrie* said.

He had followed custom in telling the ship to use a female voice and, when practical, idiomatic language. The computer had soon learned precisely what pattern suited him best. That was not identical with what he liked best; such could have got disturbing on a long cruise. He found himself more engaged, inwardly, with the husky contralto that had spoken in strong rhythms out of the recorder than he was with the mezzo-soprano that now reached his ears.

"Well . . . maybe so," he said. "But you already know everything in the material we have aboard."

"You need to set your thoughts in order. You've spent most of our transit time acquiring the language."

"All right, then, let's run barefoot through the obvious." Laure paced a turn around the invisible deck. He felt its hardness, he sensed the almost subliminal beat of driving energies, he caught a piny whiff of air as the ventilators shifted to another part of their odor-temperature-ionization cycle; but still the stars blazed about him, and their silence seemed to enter his bones. Abruptly, harshly, he said: "Turn that show off."

The ship obeyed. "Would you like a planetary scene?" she asked. "You haven't yet looked at those tapes from the elf castles on Jair that you bought—"

"Not now." Laure flung himself into a chair web and regarded the prosaic metal, instruments, manual override controls that surrounded him. "This will do."

"Are you feeling well? Why not go in the diagnoser and let me check you out? We've time before we arrive."

The tone was anxious. Laure didn't believe that emotion was put on. He refrained from anthropomorphizing his computer, just as he did those nonhuman sophonts he encountered. At the same time, he didn't go along with the school of thought which claimed that human-sensibility terms were absolutely meaningless in such connections. An alien brain, or a cybernetic one like *Jaccavrie*'s, could think; it was aware; it had conation. Therefore it had analogies to his.

Quite a few Rangers were eremitic types, sane enough but basically schizoid. That was their way of standing the gaff. It was normal for them to think of their ships as elaborate tools. Daven Laure, who was young and outgoing, naturally thought of his as a friend.

"No, I'm all right," he said. "A bit nervous, nothing else. This could turn out to be the biggest thing I . . . you and I have tackled yet. Maybe one of the biggest anyone has, at least on this frontier. I'd've been glad to have an older man or two along." He shrugged. "None available. Our service should increase its personnel, even if it means raising dues. We're spread much too thin across—how many stars?"

"The last report in my files estimated ten million planets with a significant number of Commonalty members on them. As for how many more there may be with which these have reasonably regular contact—"

"Oh, for everything's sake, come off it!" Laure actually laughed, and wondered if the ship had planned things that way. But, regardless, he could begin to talk of this as a problem rather than a mystery.

"Let me recapitulate," he said, "and you tell me if I'm misinterpreting matters. A ship comes to Serieve, allegedly from far away. It's like nothing anybody has ever seen, unless in historical works. (They haven't got the references on Serieve to check that out, so we're bringing some from HQ.) Hyperdrive, gravity control, electronics, yes, but everything crude, archaic, bare-bones. Fission instead of fusion power, for example . . . and human piloting!

"That is, the crew seem to be human. We have no record of their anthropometric type, but they don't look as odd as people do after several generations on some planets I could name. And the linguistic computer, once they get the idea that it's there to decipher their language and start cooperating with it, says their speech appears to have remote affinities with a few that we know, like ancient Anglic. Preliminary semantic analysis suggests their abstractions and constructs aren't quite like ours, but do fall well inside the human psych range. All in all, then, you'd assume they're explorers from distant parts."

"Except for the primitive ship," *Jaccavrie* chimed in. "One wouldn't expect such technological backwardness in any group which had maintained any contact, however tenuous, with the general mass of the different human civilizations. Nor would such a slow, under-equipped vessel pass through them without stopping, to fetch up in this border region."

"Right. So . . . if it isn't a fake . . . their gear bears out a part of their story. Kirkasant is an exceedingly old colony . . . yonder." Laure pointed toward unseen stars. "Well out in the Dragon's Head sector, where we're barely beginning to explore. Somehow, somebody got that far, and in the earliest days of interstellar travel. They settled down on a planet and lost the trick of making spaceships. Only lately have they regained it."

"And come back, looking for the companionship of their own kind." Laure had a brief, irrational vision of *Jaccavrie* nodding. Her tone was so thoughtful. She would be a big, calm, dark-haired woman, handsome in middle age though getting somewhat plump . . . "What the crew themselves have said, as communication got established, seems to bear out this idea. Beneath a great many confused mythological motifs, I also get the impression of an epic voyage, by a defeated people who ran as far as they could."

"But Kirkasant!" Laure protested. "The whole situation they describe. It's impossible."

"Might not that Vandange be mistaken? I mean, we know so little. The Kirkasanters keep talking about a weird home environment. Ours appears to have stunned and bewildered them. They simply groped on through space till they happened to find Serieve. Thus might their own theory, that somehow they blundered in from an altogether different continuum, might it not conceivably be right?"

"Hm-m-m. I guess you didn't see Vandange's accompanying letter. No, you haven't, it wouldn't've been plugged into your memory. Anyway, he claims his assistants examined that ship down to the bolt heads. And they found nothing, no mechanism, no peculiarity, whose function and behavior weren't obvious. He really gets indignant. Says the notion of interspace-time transference is mathematically absurd. I don't have quite his faith in mathematics, myself, but I must admit he has one common-sense point. If a ship could somehow flip from one entire cosmos to another . . . why, in five thousand years of interstellar travel, haven't we gotten some record of it happening?"

"Perhaps the ships to which it occurs never come back."

"Perhaps. Or perhaps the whole argument is due to misunderstanding. We don't have any good grasp of the Kirkasanter language. Or maybe it's a hoax. That's Vandange's opinion. He claims there's no such region as they say they come from. Not anywhere. Neither astronomers nor explorers have ever found anything like a . . . a space like a shining fog, crowded with stars—"

"But why should these wayfarers tell a falsehood?" *Jaccavrie* sounded honestly puzzled.

"I don't know. Nobody does. That's why the Serievan government decided it'd better ask for a Ranger."

Laure jumped up and started pacing again. He was a tall young man, with the characteristic beardlessness, fair hair and complexion, slightly slanted blue eyes of the Fireland mountaineers on New Vixen. But since he had trained at Starborough, which is on Aladir not far from Irontower City, he affected a fashionably simple gray tunic and blue hose. The silver comet of his calling blazoned his left breast.

"I don't know," he repeated. There rose in him a consciousness of that immensity which crouched beyond this hull. "Maybe they are telling the sober truth. We don't dare not know."

When a mere few million people have an entire habitable world to themselves, they do not often build high. That comes later, along with formal wilderness preservation, disapproval of fecundity, and inducements to emigrate. Pioneer towns tend to be low and rambling. (Or so it is in that civilization wherein the Commonalty operates. We know that other branches of humanity have their distinctive ways, and hear rumors of yet stranger ones. But so vast is the galaxy—these two or three spiral arms, a part of which our race has to date thinly occupied—so vast, that we cannot even keep track of our own culture, let alone anyone else's.)

Pelogard, however, was founded on an island off the Branzan mainland, above Serieve's arctic circle: which comes down to almost 56°. Furthermore, it was an industrial center. Hence most of its buildings were tall and crowded. Laure, standing by the outer wall of Ozer Vandange's office and looking forth across the little city, asked why this location had been chosen.

"You don't know?" responded the physicist. His inflection was a touch too elaborately incredulous.

"I'm afraid not," Laure confessed. "Think how many systems my service has to cover, and how many individual places within each system. If we tried to remember each, we'd never be anywhere but under the neuroinductors."

Vandange, seated small and bald and prim behind a large desk, pursed his lips. "Yes, yes," he said. "Nevertheless, I should not think an *experienced* Ranger would dash off to a planet without temporarily mastering a few basic facts about it."

Laure flushed. An experienced Ranger would have put this conceited old dustbrain in his place. But he himself was too aware of youth and awkwardness. He managed to say quietly, "Sir, my ship has complete information. She needed only scan it and tell me no precautions were required here. You have a beautiful globe and I can understand why you're proud of it. But please understand that to me it has to be a way station. My job is with those people from Kirkasant, and I'm anxious to meet them."

"You shall, you shall," said Vandange, somewhat mollified. "I merely thought a conference with you would be advisable first. As for your question, we need a city here primarily because upswelling ocean currents make the arctic waters mineral-rich. Extractor plants pay off better than they would farther south."

Despite himself, Laure was interested. "You're getting your minerals from the sea already? At so early a stage of settlement?"

"This sun and its planets are poor in heavy metals. Most local systems are. Not surprising. We aren't far, here, from the northern verge of the spiral arm. Beyond is the halo—thin gas, little dust, ancient globular clusters very widely scattered. The interstellar medium from which stars form has not been greatly enriched by earlier generations."

Laure suppressed his resentment at being lectured like a child. Maybe it was just Vandange's habit. He cast another glance through the wall. The office was high in one of the buildings. He looked across soaring blocks of metal, concrete, glass, and plastic, interlinked with trafficways and freight cables, down to the waterfront. There bulked the extractor plants, warehouses, and sky-docks. Cargo craft moved ponderously in and out. Not many passenger vessels flitted between. Pelogard must be largely automated.

The season stood at late spring. The sun cast brightness across a gray ocean that a wind rumpled. Immense flocks of seabirds dipped and wheeled. Or were they birds? They had wings, anyhow, steely blue against a wan sky. Perhaps they cried or sang, into the wind skirl and wave rush; but Laure couldn't hear it in this enclosed place.

"That's one reason I can't accept their yarn," Vandange declared.

"Eh?" Laure came out of his reverie with a start.

Vandange pressed a button to opaque the wall. "Sit down. Let's get to business."

Laure eased himself into a lounger opposite the desk. "Why am I conferring with you?" he counterattacked. "Whoever was principally working with the Kirkasanters had to be a semanticist. In short, Paeri Ferand. He consulted specialists on your university faculty, in anthropology, history, and so forth. But I should think your own role as a physicist was marginal. Yet you're the one taking up my time. Why?"

"Oh, you can see Ferand and the others as much as you choose," Vandange said. "You won't get more from them than repetitions of what the Kirkasanters have already told. How could you? What else have they got to go on? If nothing else, an underpopulated world like ours can't maintain staffs of experts to ferret out the meaning of every datum, every inconsistency, every outright lie. I had hoped, when our government notified your section, headquarters, the Rangers would have sent a real team, instead of—" He curbed himself. "Of course, they have many other claims on their attention. They would not see at once how important this is."

"Well," Laure said in his annoyance, "if you're suspicious, if you think the strangers need further investigation, why bother with my office? It's just an overworked little outpost. Send them on to a heart world, like Sarnac, where the facilities and people really can be had."

"It was urged," Vandange said. "I, and a few others who felt as I do, fought the proposal bitterly. In the end, as a compromise, the government decided to dump the whole problem in the lap of the Rangers. Who turn out to be, in effect, you. Now I must persuade you to be properly cautious. Don't you see, if those . . . beings . . . have some hostile intent, the very worst move would be to send them on— let them spy out our civilization—let them, perhaps, commit nuclear sabotage on a vital center, and then vanish back into space." His voice grew shrill. "That's why we've kept them here so long, on one excuse after the next, here on our home planet. We feel responsible to the rest of mankind!"

"But what—" Laure shook his head. He felt a sense of unreality. "Sir, the League, the troubles, the Empire, its fall, the Long Night . . . every such thing—behind us. In space and time alike. The people of the Commonalty don't get into wars."

"Are you quite certain?"

"What makes *you* so certain of any menace in—one antiquated ship? Crewed by a score of men and women. Who came here openly and peacefully. Who, by every report, have been struggling to get past the language and culture barriers and communicate with you in detail—what in cosmos' name makes you worry about them?"

"The fact that they are liars."

Vandange sat awhile, gnawing his thumb, before he opened a

box, took out a cigar and puffed it into lighting. He didn't offer Laure one. That might be for fear of poisoning his visitor with whatever local weed he was smoking. Scattered around for many generations on widely differing planets, populations did develop some odd distributions of allergy and immunity. But Laure suspected plain rudeness.

"I thought my letter made it clear," Vandange said. "They insist they are from another continuum. One with impossible properties, including visibility from ours. Conveniently on the far side of the Dragon's Head, so that we don't see it here. Oh, yes," he added quickly, "I've heard the arguments. That the whole thing is a misunderstanding due to our not having an adequate command of their language. That they're really trying to say they came from— well, the commonest rationalization is a dense star cluster. But it won't work, you know. It won't work at all."

"Why not?" Laure asked.

"Come, now. Come, now. You must have learned some astronomy as part of your training. You must know that some things simply do not occur in the galaxy."

"Uh—"

"They showed us what they alleged were lens-and-film photographs taken from, ah, inside their home universe." Vandange bore down heavily on the sarcasm. "You saw copies, didn't you? Well, now, where in the real universe do you find that kind of nebulosity— so thick and extensive that a ship can actually lose its bearings, wander around lost, using up its film among other supplies, until it chances to emerge in clear space? For that matter, assuming there were such a region, how could anyone capable of building a hyperdrive be so stupid as to go beyond sight of his beacon stars?"

"Uh . . . I thought of a cluster, heavily hazed, somewhat like the young clusters of the Pleiades type."

"So did many Serievans," Vandange snorted. "Please use your head. Not even Pleiadic clusters contain that much gas and dust. Besides, the verbal description of the Kirkasanters sounds like a globular cluster, insofar as it sounds like anything. But not much. The ancient red suns are there, crowded together, true. But they speak of far too many younger ones.

"And of far too much heavy metal at home. Which their ship

demonstrates. Their use of alloying elements like aluminum and beryllium is incredibly parsimonious. On the other hand, electrical conductors are gold and silver, the power plant is shielded not with lead but with inert-coated osmium, and it burns plutonium which the Kirkasanters assert was mined!

"They were astonished that Serieve is such a light-metal planet. Or claimed they were astonished. I don't know about that. I do know that this whole region is dominated by light elements. That its interstellar spaces are relatively free of dust and gas, the Dragon's Head being the only exception and it merely in transit through our skies. That all this is even more true of the globular clusters, which formed in an ultratenuous medium, mostly before the galaxy had condensed to its present shape—which, in fact, practically don't occur in the main body of the galaxy, but are off in the surrounding halo!"

Vandange stopped for breath and triumph.

"Well." Laure shifted uneasily in his seat and wished *Jaccavrie* weren't ten thousand kilometers away at the only spaceport. "You have a point. There are contradictions, aren't there? I'll bear what you said in mind when I, uh, interview the strangers themselves."

"And you will, I trust, be wary of them," Vandange said.

"Oh, yes. Something queer does seem to be going on."

In outward appearance, the Kirkasanters were not startling. They didn't resemble any of the human breeds that had developed locally, but they varied less from the norm than some. The fifteen men and five women were tall, robust, broad in chest and shoulders, slim in waist. Their skins were dark coppery reddish, their hair blue-black and wavy; males had some beard and mustache which they wore neatly trimmed. Skulls were dolichocephalic, faces disharmonically wide, noses straight and thin, lips full. The total effect was handsome. Their eyes were their most arresting feature, large, long-lashed, luminous in shades of gray, or green, or yellow.

Since they had refused—with an adamant politeness they well knew how to assume—to let cell samples be taken for chromosome analysis, Vandange had muttered to Laure about nonhumans in surgical disguise. But that the Ranger classed as the fantasy of a provincial who'd doubtless never met a live xeno. You couldn't fake so many details, not and keep a viable organism. Unless, to be sure, happenstance had duplicated most of those details for you in the course of evolution . . .

Ridiculous, Laure thought. *Coincidence isn't that energetic.*

He walked from Pelogard with Demring Lodden, captain of the *Makt,* and Demring's daughter, navigator Graydal. The town was soon behind them. They found a trail that wound up into steeply rising hills, among low, gnarly trees which had begun to put forth leaves that were fronded and colored like old silver. The sun was sinking, the air noisy and full of salt odors. Neither Kirkasanter appeared to mind the chill.

"You know your way here well," Laure said clumsily.

"We should," Demring answered, "for we have been held on this sole island, with naught to do but ramble it when the *reyad* takes us."

"*Reyad?*" Laure asked.

"The need to . . . search," Graydal said. "To track beasts, or find what is new, or be alone in wild places. Our folk were hunters until not so long ago. We bear their blood."

Demring wasn't to be diverted from his grudge. "Why are we thus confined?" he growled. "Each time we sought an answer, we got an evasion. Fear of disease, need for us to learn what to expect—Ha, by now I'm half minded to draw my gun, force my way to our ship, and depart for aye!"

He was erect, grizzled, deeply graven of countenance and bleak of gaze. Like his men, he wore soft boots, a knee-length gown of some fine-scaled leather, a cowled cloak, a dagger and an energy pistol at his belt. On his forehead sparkled a diamond that betokened authority.

"Well, but, Master," Graydal said, "here today we deal with no village witchfinders. Daven Laure is a king's man, with power to act, knowledge and courage to act rightly. Has he not gone off alone with us because you said you felt stifled and spied on in the town? Let us talk as freefolk with him."

Her smile, her words in the husky voice that Laure remembered from his recordings, were gentle. He felt pretty sure, though, that as much steel underlay her as her father, and possibly whetted sharper. She almost matched his height, her gait was tigerish, she was herself weaponed and diademmed. Unlike Laure's close cut or Demring's short bob, her hair passed through a platinum ring and blew free at full length. Her clothes were little more than footgear, fringed shorts, and thin blouse. However attractive, the sight did not suggest seductive feminity to the Ranger—when she wasn't feeling the cold that struck through his garments. Besides, he had already learned that the sexes were mixed aboard the *Makt* for no other reason than that women were better at certain jobs than men. Every female was accompanied by an older male relative. The Kirkasanters were not an uncheerful folk, on the whole, but some of their ideals looked austere.

Nonetheless, Graydal had lovely strong features, and her eyes, under the level brows, shone amber.

"Maybe the local government was overcautious," Laure said, "but don't forget, this is a frontier settlement. Not many light-years hence, in that part of the sky you came from, begins the unknown. It's true the stars are comparatively thin in these parts—average distance between them about four parsecs—but still, their number is too great for us to do more than feel our way slowly forward. Especially when, in the nature of the case, planets like Serieve must devote most of their effort to developing themselves. So, when one is ignorant, one does best to be careful."

He flattered himself that was a well-composed conciliatory speech. It wasn't as oratorical as one of theirs, but they had lung capacity for a thinner atmosphere than this. He was disappointed when Demring said scornfully, "*Our* ancestors were not so timid."

"Or else their pursuers were not," Graydal laughed.

The captain looked offended. Laure hastily asked: "Have you no knowledge of what happened?"

"No," said the girl, turned pensive. "Not in truth. Legends, found in many forms across all Kirkasant, tell of battle, and a shipful of people who fled far until at last they found haven. A few fragmentary records—but those are vague, save the Baorn Codex; and it is little more than a compendium of technical information which the Wisemen of Skribent preserved. Even in that case"—she smiled again— "the meaning of most passages was generally obscure until after our modern scientists had invented the thing described for themselves."

"Do you know what records remain in Homeland?" Demring asked hopefully.

Laure sighed and shook his head. "No. Perhaps none, by now. Doubtless, in time, an expedition will go from us to Earth. But after five thousand trouble-filled years—And your ancestors may not have started from there. They may have belonged to one of the first colonies."

In a dim way, he could reconstruct the story. There had been a fight. The reasons—personal, familial, national, ideological, economic, whatever they were—had dropped into the bottom of the millennia between then and now. (A commentary on the importance of any such reasons.) But someone had so badly wanted the destruction of someone else that one ship, or one fleet, hounded another almost a quarter way around the galaxy.

Or maybe not, in a literal sense. It would have been hard to do. Crude as they were, those early vessels could have made the trip, if frequent stops were allowed for repair and resupply and refilling of the nuclear converters. But to this day, a craft under hyperdrive could only be detected within approximately a light-year's radius by the instantaneous "wake" of space-pulses. If she lay doggo for a while, she was usually unfindable in the sheer stupendousness of any somewhat larger volume. That the hunter should never, in the course of many months, either have overhauled his quarry or lost the scent altogether, seemed conceivable but implausible.

Maybe pursuit had not been for the whole distance. Maybe the refugees had indeed escaped after a while, but—in blind panic, or rage against the foe, or desire to practice undisturbed a brand of utopianism, or whatever the motive was—they had continued as far as they possibly could, and hidden themselves as thoroughly as nature allowed.

In any case, they had ended in a strange part of creation: so strange that numerous men on Serieve did not admit it existed. By then, their ship must have been badly in need of a complete overhaul, amounting virtually to a rebuilding. They settled down to construct the necessary industrial base. (Think, for example, how much plant you must have before you make your first transistor.) They did not have the accumulated experience of later generations to prove how impossible this was.

Of course they failed. A few score—a few hundred at absolute maximum, if the ship had been rigged with suspended-animation lockers—could not preserve a full-fledged civilization while coping with a planet for which man was never meant. And they had to content themselves with that planet. Once into the Cloud Universe, even if their vessel could still wheeze along for a while, they were no longer able to move freely about, picking and choosing.

Kirkasant was probably the best of a bad lot. And Laure thought it was rather a miracle that man had survived there. So small a genetic pool, so hostile an environment . . . but the latter might well have saved him from the effects of the former. Natural selection must have been harsh. And, seemingly, the radiation background was high, which led to a corresponding mutation rate. Women bore from puberty to menopause, and buried most of their babies. Men struggled to keep them alive. Often death harvested adults, too, entire families. But those who were fit tended to survive. And the planet did have an unfilled ecological niche: the one reserved for intelligence. Evolution galloped. Population exploded. In one or two millennia, man was at home on Kirkasant. In five, he crowded it and went looking for new planets.

Because culture had never totally died. The first generation might be unable to build machine tools, but could mine and forge metals. The next generation might be too busy to keep public schools, but had enough hard practical respect for learning that it supported a literate class. Succeeding generations, wandering into new lands, founding new nations and societies, might war with each other, but all drew from a common tradition and looked to one goal: reunion with the stars.

Once the scientific method had been created afresh, Laure thought, progress must have been more rapid than on Earth. For the natural philosophers knew certain things were possible, even if they didn't know how, and this was half the battle. They must have got some hints, however oracular, from the remnants of ancient texts. They actually had the corroded hulk of the ancestral ship for their studying. Given this much, it was not too surprising that they leaped in a single lifetime from the first moon rockets to the first hyperdrive craft—and did so on a basis of wildly distorted physical theory, and embarked with such naïvete that they couldn't find their way home again!

All very logical. Unheard of, outrageously improbable, but in this big a galaxy the strangest things are bound to happen now and again. The Kirkasanters could be absolutely honest in their story.

If they were.

"Let the past tend the past," Graydal said impatiently. "We've tomorrow to hunt in."

"Yes," Laure said, "but I do need to know a few things. It's not clear to me how you found us. I mean, you crossed a thousand light-years or more of wilderness. How did you come on a speck like Serieve?"

"We were asked that before," Demring said, "but then we could not well explain, few words being held in common. Now you show a good command of the Hobrokan tongue, and for our part, albeit none of these villagers will take the responsibility of putting one of us under your educator machine . . . in talking with technical folk, we've gained various technical words of yours."

He was silent awhile, collecting phrases. The three people continued up the trail. It was wide enough for them to walk abreast, somewhat muddy with rain and melted snow. The sun was so far down that the woods walled it off; twilight smoked from the ground and from either side, though the sky was still pale. The wind was dying but the chill deepening. Somewhere behind those dun trunks and ashy-metallic leaves, a voice went "K-kr-r-r-*ruk*!" and, above and ahead, the sound of a river became audible.

Demring said with care: "See you, when we could not find our way back to Kirkasant's sun, and at last had come out in an altogether different cosmos, we thought our ancestors might have originated there. Certain traditional songs hinted as much, speaking of space as dark for instance; and surely darkness encompassed us now, and immense loneliness between the stars. Well, but in which direction might Homeland lie? Casting about with telescopes, we spied afar a black cloud, and thought, if the ancestors had been in flight from enemies, they might well have gone through such, hoping to break their trail."

"The Dragon's Head Nebula," Laure nodded.

Graydal's wide shoulders lifted and fell. "At least it gave us something to steer by," she said.

Laure stole a moment's admiration of her profile. "You had

courage," he said. "Quite aside from everything else, how did you know this civilization had not stayed hostile to you?"

"How did we know it ever was in the first place?" she chuckled. "Myself, insofar as I believe the myths have any truth, I suspect our ancestors were thieves or bandits, or—"

"Daughter!" Demring hurried on, in a scandalized voice: "When we had fared thus far, we found the darkness was dust and gas such as pervade the universe at home. There was simply an absence of stars to make them shine. Emerging on the far side, we tuned our neutrino detectors. Our reasoning was that a highly developed civilization would use a great many nuclear power plants. Their neutrino flux should be detectable above the natural noise level—in this comparatively empty cosmos—across several score light-years or better, and we could home on it."

First they sound like barbarian bards, Laure thought, *and then like radionicians. No wonder a dogmatist like Vandange can't put credence in them.*

Can I?

"We soon began to despair," Graydal said. "We were nigh to the limit—"

"No matter," Demring interrupted.

She looked steadily first at one man, then the other, and said, "I dare trust Daven Laure." To the Ranger: "Belike no secret anyhow, since men on Serieve must have examined our ship with knowledgeable eyes. We were nigh to our limit of travel without refueling and refurbishing. We were about to seek for a planet not too unlike Kirkasant where—But then, as if by Valfar's Wings, came the traces we sought, and we followed them here.

"And here were humans!

"Only of late has our gladness faded as we begin to see how they temporize and keep us half prisoner. Wholly prisoner, maybe, should we try to depart. Why will they not rely on us?"

"I tried to explain that when we talked yesterday," Laure said. "Some important men don't see how you could be telling the truth."

She caught his hand in a brief, impulsive grasp. Her own was warm, slender, and hard. "But you are different?"

"Yes." He felt helpless and alone. "They've, well, they've called for me. Put the entire problem in the hands of my organization.

And my fellows have so much else to do that, well, I'm given broad discretion."

Demring regarded him shrewdly. "You are a young man," he said. "Do not let your powers paralyze you."

"No. I will do what I can for you. It may be little."

The trail rounded a thicket and they saw a rustic bridge across the river, which ran seaward in foam and clangor. Halfway over, the party stopped, leaned on the rail and looked down. The water was thickly shadowed between its banks, and the woods were becoming a solid black mass athwart a dusking sky. The air smelled wet.

"You realize," Laure said, "it won't be easy to retrace your route. You improvised your navigational coordinates. They can be transformed into ours on this side of the Dragon's Head, I suppose. But once beyond the nebula, I'll be off my own charts, except for what few listed objects are visible from either side. No one from this civilization has been there, you see, what with millions of suns closer to our settlements. And the star sights you took can't have been too accurate."

"You are not going to take us to Homeland, then," Demring said tonelessly.

"Don't you understand? Homeland, Earth, it's so far away that I myself don't know what it's like anymore!"

"But you must have a nearby capital, a more developed world than this. Why do you not guide us thither, that we may talk with folk wiser than these wretched Serievans?"

"Well . . . uh . . . Oh, many reasons. I'll be honest, caution is one of them. Also, the Commonalty does not have anything like a capital, or—But yes, I could guide you to the heart of civilization. Any of numerous civilizations in this galactic arm." Laure took a breath and slogged on. "My decision, though, under the circumstances, is that first I'd better see your world Kirkasant. After that . . . well, certainly, if everything is all right, we'll establish regular contacts, and invite your people to visit ours, and—Don't you like the plan? Don't you want to go home?"

"How shall we, ever?" Graydal asked low.

Laure cast her a surprised glance. She stared ahead of her and down, into the river. A fish—some kind of swimming creature—

leaped. Its scales caught what light remained in a gleam that was faint but startling against those murky waters. She didn't seem to notice, though she cocked her head instinctively toward the splash that followed.

"Have you not listened?" she said. "Did you not hear us? How long we searched in the fog, through that forest of suns, until at last we left our whole small bright universe and came into this great one that has so much blackness in it—and thrice we plunged back into our own space, and groped about, and came forth without having found trace of any star we knew—" Her voice lifted the least bit. "We are lost, I tell you, eternally lost. Take us to your home, Daven Laure, that we may try to make ours there."

He wanted to stroke her hands, which had clenched into fists on the bridge rail. But he made himself say only: "Our science and resources are more than yours. Maybe we can find a way where you cannot. At any rate, I'm duty bound to learn as much as I can, before I make report and recommendation to my superiors."

"I do not think you are kind, forcing my crew to return and look again on what has gone from them," Demring said stiffly. "But I have scant choice save to agree." He straightened. "Come, best we start back toward Pelogard. Night will soon be upon us."

"Oh, no rush," Laure said, anxious to change the subject. "An arctic zone, at this time of year—We'll have no trouble."

"Maybe you will not," Graydal said. "But Kirkasant after sunset is not like here."

They were on their way down when dusk became night, a light night where only a few stars gleamed and Laure walked easily through a clear gloaming. Graydal and Demring must needs use their energy guns at minimum intensity for flashcasters. And even so, they often stumbled.

Makt was three times the size of *Jaccavrie*, a gleaming torpedo shape whose curve was broken by boat housings and weapon turrets. The Ranger vessel looked like a gig attending her. In actuality, *Jaccavrie* could have outrun, outmaneuvered, or outfought the Kirkasanter with ludicrous ease. Laure didn't emphasize that fact. His charges were touchy enough already. He had suggested hiring a modern carrier for them, and met a glacial negative. This craft was their property and bore the honor of the confederated clans that had built her. She was not to be abandoned.

Modernizing her would have taken more time than increased speed would save. Besides, while Laure was personally convinced of the good intentions of Demring's people, he had no right to present them with up-to-date technology until he had proof they wouldn't misuse it.

One could not accurately say that he resigned himself to accompanying them in his ship at the plodding pace of theirs. The weeks of travel gave him a chance to get acquainted with them and their culture. And that was not only his duty but his pleasure. Especially, he found, when Graydal was involved.

Some time passed before he could invite her to dinner *à deux*. He arranged it with what he felt sure was adroitness. Two persons, undisturbed, talking socially, could exchange information of the subtle kind that didn't come across in committee. Thus he proposed a series of private meetings with the officers of *Makt*. He began with the captain, naturally; but after a while came the navigator's turn.

Jaccavrie phased in with the other vessel, laid alongside and made air-lock connections in a motion too smooth to feel. Graydal came aboard and the ships parted company again. Laure greeted her according to the way of Kirkasant, with a handshake. The clasp lasted a moment. "Welcome," he said.

"Peace between us." Her smile offset her formalism. She was in uniform—another obsolete aspect of her society—but it shimmered gold and molded itself to her.

"Won't you come to the saloon for a drink before we eat?"

"I shouldn't. Not in space."

"No hazard," said the computer in an amused tone. "I operate everything anyway."

Graydal had tensed and clapped hand to gun at the voice. She had relaxed and tried to laugh. "I'm sorry. I am not used to . . . you." She almost bounded on her way down the corridor with Laure. He had set the interior weight at one standard G. The Kirkasanters maintained theirs fourteen percent higher, to match the pull of their home world.

Though she had inspected this ship several times already, Graydal looked wide-eyed around her. The saloon was small but sybaritic. "You do yourself proud," she said amidst the draperies, music, perfumes, and animations.

He guided her to a couch. "You don't sound quite approving," he said.

"Well—"

"There's no virtue in suffering hardships."

"But there is in the ability to endure them," She sat too straight for the form-fitter cells to make her comfortable.

"Think I can't?"

Embarrassed, she turned her gaze from him, toward the viewscreen, on which flowed a color composition. Her lips tightened. "Why have you turned off the exterior scene?"

"You don't seem to like it, I've noticed." He sat down beside her. "What will you have? We're fairly well stocked."

"Turn it on."

"What?"

"The outside view." Her nostrils dilated. "It shall not best me."

He spread his hands. The ship saw his rueful gesture and obliged. Space leaped into the screen, star-strewn except where the storm-cloud mass of the dark nebula reared ahead. He heard Graydal suck in a breath and said quickly, "Uh, since you aren't familiar with our beverages, I suggest daiquiris. They're tart, a little sweet—"

Her nod was jerky. Her eyes seemed locked to the screen. He leaned close, catching the slight warm odor of her, not quite identical with the odor of other women he had known, though the difference was too subtle for him to name. "Why does that sight bother you?" he asked.

"The strangeness. The aloneness. It is so absolutely alien to home. I feel forsaken and—" She filled her lungs, forced detachment on herself, and said in an analytical manner: "Possibly we are disturbed by a black sky because we have virtually none of what you call night vision." A touch of trouble returned. "What else have we lost?"

"Night vision isn't needed on Kirkasant, you tell me," Laure consoled her. "And evolution there worked fast. But you must have gained as well as atrophied. I know you have more physical strength, for instance, than your ancestors could've had." A tray with two glasses extended from the side. "Ah, here are the drinks."

She sniffed at hers. "It smells pleasant," she said. "But are you sure there isn't something I might be allergic to?"

"I doubt that. You didn't react to anything you tried on Serieve, did you?"

"No, except for finding it overly bland."

"Don't worry," he grinned. "Before we left, your father took care to present me with one of your salt-shakers. It'll be on the dinner table."

Jaccavrie had analyzed the contents. Besides sodium and potassium chloride—noticeably less abundant on Kirkasant than on the average planet, but not scare enough to cause real trouble—the mixture included a number of other salts. The proportion of rare earths and especially arsenic was surprising. An ordinary human who ingested the latter element at that rate would lose quite a few years of life expectancy. Doubtless the first refugee generations had, too, when something else didn't get them first. But by now their descendants were so well adapted that food didn't taste right without a bit of arsenic trioxide.

"We wouldn't have to be cautious—we'd know in advance what you can and cannot take—if you'd permit a chromosome analysis," Laure hinted. "The laboratory aboard this ship can do it."

Her cheeks turned more than ever coppery. She scowled. "We refused before," she said.

"May I ask why?"

"It . . . violates integrity. Humans are not to be probed into."

He had encountered that attitude before, in several guises. To the Kirkasanter—at least, to the Hobrokan clansman; the planet had other cultures—the body was a citadel for the ego, which by right should be inviolable. The feeling, so basic that few were aware of having it, had led to the formation of reserved, often rather cold personalities. It had handicapped if not stopped the progress of medicine. On the plus side, it had made for dignity and self-reliance; and it had caused this civilization to be spared professional gossips, confessional literature, and psychoanalysis.

"I don't agree," Laure said. "Nothing more is involved than scientific information. What's personal about a DNA map?"

"Well . . . maybe. I shall think on the matter." Graydal made an obvious effort to get away from the topic. She sipped her drink, smiled, and said, "Mm-m-m, this *is* a noble flavor."

"Hoped you'd like it. I do. We have a custom in the Commonalty—" He touched glasses with her.

"Charming. Now we, when good friends are together, drink half what's in our cups and then exchange them."

"May I?"

She blushed again, but with pleasure. "Certainly. You honor me."

"No, the honor is mine." Laure went on, quite sincere: "What your people have done is tremendous. What an addition to the race you'll be!"

Her mouth drooped. "If ever my folk may be found."

"Surely—"

"Do you think we did not try?" She tossed off another gulp of her cocktail. Evidently it went fast to her unaccustomed head. "We did not fare forth blindly. Understand that *Makt* is not the first ship to leave Kirkasant's sun. But the prior ones went to nearby stars, stars that can be seen from home. They are many. We had not realized how many more are in the Cloud Universe, hidden from eyes and instruments, a few light-years farther on. We, our ship, we intended to take the next step. Only the next step. Barely beyond that shell of suns we could see from Kirkasant's system. We could find our way home again without trouble. Of course we could! We need but steer by those suns that were already charted on the edge of instrumental perception. Once we were in their neighborhood, our familiar part of space would be visible."

She faced him, gripping his arm painfully hard, speaking in a desperate voice. "What we had not known, what no one had known, was the imprecision of that charting. The absolute magnitudes, therefore the distances and relative positions of those verge-visible stars . . . had not been determined as well as the astronomers believed. Too much haze, too much shine, too much variability. Do you understand? And so, suddenly, our tables were worthless. We thought we could identify some suns. But we were wrong. Flitting toward them, we must have bypassed the volume of space we sought . . . and gone on and on, more hopelessly lost each day, each endless day—

"What makes you think you can find our home?"

Laure, who had heard the details before, had spent the time admiring her and weighing his reply. He sipped his own drink, letting the sourness glide over his palate and the alcohol slightly, soothingly burn him, before he said: "I can try. I do have instruments your people have not yet invented. Inertial devices, for example, that work under hyperdrive as well as at true velocity. Don't give up hope." He paused. "I grant you, we might fail. Then what will you do?"

The blunt question, which would have driven many women of his world to tears, made her rally. She lifted her head and said—haughtiness rang through the words: "Why, we will make the best of things, and I do not think we will do badly."

Well, he thought, *she's descended from nothing but survivor types. Her nature is to face trouble and whip it.*

"I'm sure you will succeed magnificently," he said. "You'll need time to grow used to our ways, and you may never feel quite easy in them, but—"

"What are your marriages like?" she asked.

"Uh?" Laure fitted his jaw back into place.

She was not drunk, he decided. A bit of drink, together with these surroundings, the lilting music, odors and pheromones in the air, had simply lowered her inhibitions. The huntress in her was set free, and at once attacked whatever had been most deeply perturbing her. The basic reticence remained. She looked straight at him, but she was fiery-faced, as she said:

"We ought to have had an equal number of men and women along on *Makt.* Had we known what was to happen, we would have done so. But now ten men shall have to find wives among foreigners. Do you think they will have much difficulty?"

"Uh, why no. I shouldn't think they will," he floundered. "They're obviously superior types, and then, being exotic—glamorous . . ."

"I speak not of amatory pleasure. But . . . what I overheard on Serieve, a time or two . . . did I miscomprehend? Are there truly women among you who do not bear children?"

"On the older planets, yes, that's not uncommon. Population control—"

"We shall have to stay on Serieve, then, or worlds like it." She sighed. "I had hoped we might go to the pivot of your civilization, where your real work is done and our children might become great."

Laure considered her. After a moment, he understood. Adapting to the uncountably many aliennesses of Kirkasant had been a long and cruel process. No blood line survived which did not do more than make up its own heavy losses. The will to reproduce was a requirement of existence. It, too, became an instinct.

He remembered that, while Kirkasant was not a very fertile planet, and today its population strained its resources, no one had considered reducing the birthrate. When someone on Serieve had asked why, Demring's folk had reacted strongly. The idea struck them as obscene. They didn't care for the notion of genetic modification or exogenetic growth either. And yet they were quite reasonable and noncompulsive about most other aspects of their culture.

Culture, Laure thought. *Yes. That's mutable. But you don't change your instincts; they're built into your chromosomes. Her people must have children.*

"Well," he said, "you can find women who want large families on the central planets, too. If anything, they'll be eager to marry your friends. They have a problem finding men who feel as they do, you see."

Graydal dazzled him with a smile and held out her glass. "Exchange?" she proposed.

"Hoy, you're way ahead of me." He evened the liquid levels, "Now."

They looked at each other throughout the little ceremony. He nerved himself to ask, "As for you women, do you necessarily have to marry within your ship?"

"No," she said. "It would depend on . . . whether any of your folk . . . might come to care for one of us."

"That I can guarantee!"

"I would like a man who travels," she murmured, "if I and the children could come along."

"Quite easy to arrange," Laure said.

She said in haste: "But we are buying grief, are we not? You told me perhaps you can find our planet for us."

"Yes. I hope, though, if we succeed, that won't be the last I see of you."

"Truly it won't."

They finished their drinks and went to dinner. *Jaccavrie* was also an excellent cook. And the choice of wines was considerable. What was said and laughed at over the table had no relevance to anyone but Laure and Graydal.

Except that, at the end, with immense and tender seriousness, she said: "If you want a cell sample from me . . . for analysis . . . you may have it."

He reached across the table and took her hand. "I wouldn't want you to do anything you might regret later," he said.

She shook her head. The tawny eyes never left him. Her voice was slow, faintly slurred, but bespoke complete awareness of what she was saying. "I have come to know you. For you to do this thing will be no violation."

Laure explained eagerly: "The process is simple and painless, as far as you're concerned. We can go right down to the lab. The computer operates everything. It'll give you an anesthetic spray and remove a small sample of flesh, so small that tomorrow you won't be sure where the spot was. Of course, the analysis will take a long while. We don't have all possible equipment aboard. And the computer does have to devote most of her—most of its attention to piloting and interior work. But at the end, we'll be able to tell you—"

"Hush." Her smile was sleepy. "No matter. If you wish this, that's enough. I ask only one thing."

"What?"

"Do not let a machine use the knife, or the needle, or whatever it is. I want you to do that yourself."

". . . Yes. Yonder is our home sky." The physicist Hirn Oran's son spoke slow and hushed. Cosmic interference seethed across his radio voice, nigh drowning it in Laure's and Graydal's earplugs.

"No," the Ranger said. "Not off there. We're already in it."

"What?" Silvery against rock, the two space-armored figures turned to stare at him. He could not see their expressions behind the faceplates, but he could imagine how astonishment flickered above awe.

He paused, arranging words in his mind. The star noise in his receivers was like surf and fire. The landscape overwhelmed him.

Here was no simple airless planet. No planet is ever really simple, and this one had a stranger history than most. Eons ago it was apparently a subjovian, with a cloudy hydrohelium and methane atmosphere and an immense shell of ice and frozen gases around the core; for it orbited its sun at a distance of almost a billion and a half kilometers, and though that primary was bright, at this remove it could be little more than a spark.

Until stellar evolution—hastened, Laure believed, by an abnormal infall of cosmic material—took the star off the main sequence. It swelled, surface cooling to red but total output growing so monstrous that the inner planets were consumed. On the farther ones, like this, atmosphere fled into space. Ice melted; the world-ocean boiled; each time the pulsations of the sun reached a maximum, more vapor escaped. Now nothing remained except a ball of metal and rock, hardly larger than a terrestrial-type globe. As the pressure of the top layers were removed, frightful tectonic forces must have been liberated. Mountains—the younger ones with crags like sharp teeth, the older ones worn by meteorite and thermal erosion—rose from a cratered plain of gloomy stone. Currently at a minimum, but nonetheless immense, a full seven degrees across, blue core surrounded and dimmed by the tenuous ruddy atmosphere, the sun smoldered aloft.

Its furnace light was not the sole illumination. Another star was passing sufficiently near at the time that it showed a perceptible disk . . . in a stopped-down viewscreen, because no human eye could directly confront that electric cerulean intensity. The outsider was a B_8 newborn out of dust and gas, blazing with an intrinsic radiance of a hundred Sols.

Neither one helped in the shadows cast by the pinnacled upthrust which Laure's party was investigating. Flashcasters were necessary.

But more was to see overhead, astride the dark. Stars in thousands powdered the sky, brilliant with proximity. And they were the mere fringes of the cluster. It was rising as the planet turned, partly backgrounding and partly following the sun. Laure had never met a sight to compare. For the most part, the individuals he could pick out in that enormous spheroidal cloud of light were themselves red: long-lived dwarfs, dying giants like the one that brooded over him. But many glistened exuberant golden, emerald, sapphire. Some could not be older than the blue which wandered past and added its own harsh hue to this land. All those stars were studded through a soft glow that pervaded the entire cluster, a nacreous luminosity into which they faded and vanished, the fog wherein his companions had lost their home but which was a shining beauty to behold.

"You live in a wonder," Laure said.

Graydal moved toward him. She had had no logical reason to come down out of *Makt*'s orbit with him and Hirn. The idea was simply to break out certain large ground-based instruments that *Jaccavrie* carried, for study of their goal before traveling on. Any third party could assist. But she had laid her claim first, and none of her shipmates argued. They knew how often she and Laure were in each other's company.

"Wait until you reach our world," she said low. "Space is eldritch and dangerous. But once on Kirkasant—we will watch the sun go down in the Rainbow Desert; suddenly, in that thin air, night has come, our shimmering star-crowded night, and the auroras dance and whisper above the stark hills. We will see great flying flocks rise from dawn mists over the salt marshes, hear their wings thunder and their voices flute. We will stand on the battlements of Ey, under the banners of those very knights who long ago rid the land of the firearms, and watch the folk dance welcome to a new year—"

"If the navigator pleases," said Hirn, his voice sharpened by an unadmitted dauntedness, "we will save our dreams for later and attend now to the means of realizing them. At present, we are supposed to choose a good level site for the observing apparatus. But, ah, Ranger Laure, may I ask what you meant by saying we are already back in the Cloud Universe?"

Laure was not as annoyed to have Graydal interrupted as he might normally have been. She'd spoken of Kirkasant so often that he felt he had almost been there himself. Doubtless it had its glories, but by his standards it was a grim, dry, storm-scoured planet where he would not care to stay for long at a time. Of course, to her it was beloved home; and he wouldn't mind making occasional visits if— No, chaos take it, there was work on hand!

Part of his job was to make explanations. He said: "In your sense of the term, Physicist Hirn, the Cloud Universe does not exist."

The reply was curt through the static. "I disputed that point on Serieve already, with Vandange and others. And I resented their implication that we of *Makt* were either liars or incompetent observers."

"You're neither," Laure said quickly. "But communications had a double barrier on Serieve. First, an imperfect command of your language. Only on the way here, spending most of my time in contact with your crew, have I myself begun to feel a real mastery of Hobrokan. The second barrier, though, was in some ways more serious: Vandange's stubborn preconceptions, and your own."

"I was willing to be convinced."

"But you never got a convincing argument. Vandange was so dogmatically certain that what you reported having seen was impossible, that he didn't take a serious look at your report to see if it might have an orthodox explanation after all. You naturally got angry at this and cut the discussions off short. For your part, you had what you had always been taught was a perfectly good theory, which your experiences had confirmed. You weren't going to change your whole concept of physics just because the unlovable Ozer Vandange scoffed at it."

"But we were mistaken," Graydal said. "You've intimated as much, Daven, but never made your meaning clear."

"I wanted to see the actual phenomenon for myself, first," Laure said. "We have a proverb—so old that it's reputed to have originated on Earth— 'It is a capital mistake to theorize in advance of the data.' But I couldn't help speculating, and what I see shows my speculations were along the right lines."

"Well?" Hirn challenged.

"Let's start with looking at the situation from your viewpoint," Laure suggested. "Your people spent millennia on Kirkasant. You lost every hint, except a few ambiguous traditions, that things might be different elsewhere. To you, it was natural that the night sky should be like a gently shining mist, and stars should crowd thickly around. When you developed the scientific method again, not many generations back, perforce you studied the universe you knew. Ordinary physics and chemistry, even atomistics and quantum theory, gave you no special problems. But you measured the distances of the visible stars as light-months—at most, a few light-years—after which they vanished in the foggy background. You measured the concentration of that fog, that dust and fluorescing gas. And you had no reason to suppose the interstellar medium was not equally dense everywhere. Nor had you any hint of receding galaxies.

"So your version of relativity made space sharply curved by the mass packed together throughout it. The entire universe was two or three hundred light-years across. Stars condensed and evolved—you could witness every stage of that—but in a chaotic fashion, with no particular overall structure. It's a wonder to me that you went on to gravitics and hyperdrive. I wish I were scientist enough to appreciate how different some of the laws and constants must be in your physics. But you did plow ahead. I guess the fact you knew these things were possible was important to your success. Your scientists would keep fudging and finagling, in defiance of theoretical niceties, until they made something work."

"Um-m-m . . . as a matter of fact, yes," Hirn said in a slightly abashed tone. Graydal snickered.

"Well, then *Makt* lost her way, and emerged into the outer universe, which was totally strange," Laure said. "You had to account somehow for what you saw. Like any scientists, you stayed with accepted ideas as long as feasible—a perfectly correct principle which my people call the razor of Occam. I imagine that the notion of contiguous space-times with varying properties looks quite logical if you're used to thinking of a universe with an extremely small radius. You may have been puzzled as to how you managed to get out of one 'bubble' and into the next, but I daresay you cobbled together a tentative explanation."

"I did," Hirn said. "If we postulate a multidimensional—"

"Never mind," Laure said. "That's no longer needful. We can account for the facts much more simply."

"How? I have been pondering it. I think I can grasp the idea of a universe billions of light-years across, in which the stars form galaxies. But our home space—"

"Is a dense star cluster. And as such, it has no definite boundaries. That's what I meant by saying we are already in it. In the thin verge, at least." Laure pointed to the diffuse, jeweled magnificence that was rising higher above these wastes, in the wake of the red and blue suns. "Yonder's the main body, and Kirkasant is somewhere there.

But this system here is associated. I've checked proper motions and I know."

"I could have accepted some such picture while on Serieve," Hirn said. "But Vandange was so insistent that a star cluster like this cannot be." Laure visualized the sneer behind his faceplate. "I thought that he, belonging to the master civilization, would know whereof he spoke."

"He does. He's merely rather unimaginative," Laure said. "You see, what we have here is a globular cluster. That's a group made up of stars close together in a roughly spherical volume of space. I'd guess you have a quarter million, packed into a couple of hundred light-years' diameter.

"But globular clusters haven't been known like this one. The ones we do know lie mostly well off the galactic plane. The space within them is much clearer than in the spiral arms, almost a perfect vacuum. The individual members are red. Any normal stars of greater than minimal mass have gone off the main sequence long ago. The survivors are metal-poor. That's another sign of extreme age. Heavy elements are formed in stellar cores, you know, and spewed back into space. So it's the younger suns, coalescing out of the enriched interstellar medium, that contain a lot of metal. All in all, everything points to the globular clusters being relics of an embryo stage in the galaxy's life.

"Yours, however—! Dust and gas so thick that not even a giant can be seen across many parsecs. Plenty of mainsequence stars, including blues which cannot be more than a few million years old, they burn out so fast. Spectra, not to mention planets your explorers visited, showing atomic abundances far skewed toward the high end of the periodic table. A background radiation too powerful for a man like me to dare take up permanent residence in your country.

"Such a cluster shouldn't be!"

"But it is," Graydal said.

Laure made bold to squeeze her hand, though little of that could pass through the gauntlets. "I'm glad," he answered.

"How do you explain the phenomenon?" Hirn asked.

"Oh, that's obvious . . . now that I've seen the thing and gathered some information on its path," Laure said. "An improbable situation, maybe unique, but not impossible. This cluster happens to have an extremely eccentric orbit around the galactic center of mass. Once or twice a gigayear, it passes through the vast thick clouds that surround that region. By gravitation, it sweeps up immense quantities of stuff. Meanwhile, I suppose, perturbation causes some of its senior members to drift off. You might say it's periodically rejuvenated.

"At present, it's on its way out again. Hasn't quite left our spiral arm. It passed near the galactic midpoint just a short while back, cosmically speaking; I'd estimate less than fifty million years. The infall is still turbulent, still condensing out into new stars like that blue giant shining on us. Your home sun and its planets must be a product of an earlier sweep. But there've been twenty or thirty such since the galaxy formed, and each one of them was responsible for several generations of giant stars. So Kirkasant has a lot more heavy elements than the normal planet, even though it's not much younger than Earth. Do you follow me?"

"Hm-m-m . . . perhaps. I shall have to think." Hirn walked off, across the great tilted block on which the party stood, to its edge, where he stopped and looked down into the shadows below. They were deep and knife sharp. The mingled light of red and blue suns, stars, starfog played eerie across the stone land. Laure grew aware of what strangeness and what silence—under the hiss in his ears—pressed in on him.

Graydal must have felt the same, for she edged close until their armors clinked together. He would have liked to see her face. She said: "Do you truly believe we can enter that realm and conquer it?"

"I don't know," he said, slow and blunt. "The sheer number of stars may beat us."

"A large enough fleet could search them, one by one."

"If it could navigate. We have yet to find out whether that's possible."

"Suppose. Did you guess a quarter million suns in the cluster? Not all are like ours. Not even a majority. On the other coin side, with visibility as low as it is, space must be searched back and forth, light-year by light-year. We of *Makt* could die of eld before a single vessel chanced on Kirkasant."

"I'm afraid that's true."

"Yet an adequate number of ships, dividing the task, could find our home in a year or two."

"That would be unattainably expensive, Graydal."

He thought he sensed her stiffening. "I've come on this before," she said coldly, withdrawing from his touch. "In your Commonalty they count the cost and the profit first. Honor, adventure, simple charity must run a poor second."

"Be reasonable," he said. "Cost represents labor, skill, and resources. The gigantic fleet that would go looking for Kirkasant must be diverted from other jobs. Other people would suffer need as a result. Some might suffer sharply."

"Do you mean a civilization as big, as productive as yours could not spare that much effort for a while without risking disaster?"

She's quick on the uptake, Laure thought. *Knowing what machine technology can do on her single impoverished world, she can well guess what it's capable of with millions of planets to draw on. But how can I make her realize that matters aren't that simple?"*

"Please, Graydal," he said. "Won't you believe I'm working for you? I've come this far, and I'll go as much farther as need be, if something doesn't kill us."

He heard her gulp. "Yes. I offer apology. *You* are different."

"Not really. I'm a typical Commonalty member. Later, maybe, I can show you how our civilization works, and what an odd problem in political economy we've got if Kirkasant is to be rediscovered. But first we have to establish that locating it is physically possible. We have to make long-term observations from here, and then enter those mists, and—One trouble at a time, I beg you!"

She laughed gently. "Indeed, my friend. And you will find a way." The mirth faded. It had never been strong. "Won't you?" The reflection of clouded stars glistened on her faceplate like tears.

Blindness was not dark. It shone.

Standing on the bridge, amidst the view of space, Laure saw nimbus and thunderheads. They piled in cliffs, they eddied and streamed, their color was a sheen of all colors overlying white— mother-of-pearl—but here and there they darkened with shadows and grottoes; here and there they glowed dull red as they reflected a nearby sun. For the stars were scattered about in their myriads, dominantly ruby and ember, some yellow or candent, green or blue. The nearest were clear to the eye, a few showing tiny disks, but the majority were fuzzy glows rather than lightpoints. Such shimmers grew dim with distance until the mist engulfed them entirely and nothing remained but mist.

A crackling noise beat out of that roiling formlessness, like flames. Energies pulsed through his marrow. He remembered the old, old myth of the Yawning Gap, where fire and ice arose and out of them the Nine Worlds, which were doomed in the end to return to fire and ice; and he shivered.

"Illusion," said *Jaccavrie*'s voice out of immensity.

"What?" Laure started. It was as if a mother goddess had spoken.

She chuckled. Whether deity or machine, she had the great strength of ordinariness in her. "You're rather transparent to an observer who knows you well," she said. "I could practically read your mind."

Laure swallowed. "The sight, well, a big, marvelous, dangerous thing, maybe unique in the galaxy. Yes, I admit I'm impressed."

"We have much to learn here."

"Have you been doing so?"

"At a near-capacity rate, since we entered the denser part of the cluster." *Jaccavrie* shifted to primness. "If you'd been less immersed in discussions with the Kirkasanter navigation officer, you might have got running reports from me."

"Destruction!" Laure swore. "I was studying her notes from their trip outbound, trying to get some idea of what configuration to look for, once we've learned how to make allowances for what this material does to starlight—Never mind. We'll have our conference right now, just as you requested. What'd you mean by 'an illusion'?"

"The view outside," answered the computer. "The concentration of mass is not really as many atoms per cubic centimeter as would be found in a vaporous planetary atmosphere. It is only that, across light-years, their absorption and reflection effects are cumulative. The gas and dust do, indeed, swirl, but not with anything like the velocity we think we perceive. That is due to our being under hyperdrive. Even at the very low pseudo-speed at which we are feeling our way, we pass swiftly through varying densities. Space itself is not actually shining; excited atoms are fluorescing. Nor does space roar at you. What you hear is the sound of radiation counters and other instruments which I've activated. There are no real, tangible currents working on our hull, making it quiver. But when we make quantum micro-jumps across strong interstellar magnetic fields, and those fields vary according to an extraordinarily complex pattern, we're bound to interact noticeably with them.

"Admittedly the stars are far thicker than appears. My instruments can detect none beyond a few parsecs. But what data I've gathered of late leads me to suspect the estimate of a quarter million total is conservative. To be sure, most are dwarfs—"

"Come off that!" Laure barked. "I don't need you to explain what I knew the minute I saw this place."

"You need to be drawn out of your fantasizing," *Jaccavrie* said. "Though you recognize your daydreams for what they are, you can't afford them. Not now."

Laure tensed. He wanted to order the view turned off, but checked himself, wondered if the robot followed that chain of his impulses too, and said in a harshened voice: "When you go academic on me like that, it means you're postponing news you don't want to give me. We have troubles."

"We can soon have them, at any rate," *Jaccavrie* said. "My advice is to turn back at once."

"We can't navigate," Laure deduced. Though it was not unexpected, he nonetheless felt smitten.

"No. That is, I'm having difficulties already, and conditions ahead of us are demonstrably worse."

"What's the matter?"

"Optical methods are quite unsuitable. We knew that from the experience of the Kirkasanters. But nothing else works, either. You recall, you and I discussed the possibility of identifying supergiant stars through the clouds and using them for beacons. Though their light be diffused and absorbed, they should produce other effects— they should be powerful neutrino sources, for instance—that we could use."

"Don't they?"

"Oh, yes. But the effects are soon smothered. Too much else is going on. Too many neutrinos from too many different sources, to name one thing. Too many magnetic effects. The stars are so close together, you see; and so many of them are double, triple, quadruple, hence revolving rapidly and twisting the force lines; and irradiation keeps a goodly fraction of the interstellar medium in the plasma state. Thus we get electromagnetic action of every sort; plus synchrotron and betatron radiation, plus nuclear collision, plus—"

"Spare me the complete list," Laure broke in. "Just say the noise level is too high for your instruments."

"And for any instruments that I can extrapolate as buildable," *Jaccavrie* replied. "The precision their filters would require seems greater than the laws of atomistics would allow."

"What about your inertial system? Bollixed up, too?"

"It's beginning to be. That's why I asked you to come take a good look at what's around us and what we're headed into, while you listen to my report." The robot was not built to know fear, but Laure wondered if she didn't spring back to pedantry as a refuge: "Inertial navigation would work here at kinetic velocities. But we can't traverse parsecs except by hyperdrive. Inertial and gravitational mass being identical, too rapid a change of gravitational potential will tend to cause uncontrollable precession and nutation. We can compensate for that in normal parts of space. But not here. With so many stars so closely packed, moving among each other on paths too complex for me to calculate, the variation rate is becoming too much."

"In short," Laure said slowly, "if we go deeper into this stuff, we'll be flying blind."

"Yes. Just as *Makt* did."

"We can get out into clear space time, can't we? You can follow a more or less straight line till we emerge."

"True. I don't like the hazards. The cosmic ray background is increasing considerably."

"You have screen fields."

"But I'm considering the implications. Those particles have to originate somewhere. Magnetic acceleration will only account for a fraction of their intensity. Hence the rate of nova production in this cluster, and of super-novae in the recent past, must be enormous. This in turn indicates vast numbers of lesser bodies—neutron stars, rogue planets, large meteoroids, thick dust banks—things that might be undetectable before we blunder into them."

Laure smiled at her unseen scanner. "If anything goes wrong, you'll react fast," he said. "You always do."

"I can't guarantee we won't run into trouble I can't deal with."

"Can you estimate the odds on that for me?"

Jaccavrie was silent. The air sputtered and sibilated. Laure found his vision drowning in the starfog. He needed a minute to realize he had not been answered. "Well?" he said.

"The parameters are too uncertain." Overtones had departed from her voice. "I can merely say that the probability of disaster is high in comparison to the value for travel through normal regions of the galaxy."

"Oh, for chaos' sake!" Laure's laugh was uneasy. "That figure is almost too small to measure. We knew before we entered this nebula that we'd be taking a risk. Now what about coherent radiation from natural sources?"

"My judgment is that the risk is out of proportion to the gain," *Jaccavrie* said. "At best, this is a place for scientific study. You've other work to do. Your basic—and dangerous—fantasy is that you can satisfy the emotional cravings of a few semibarbarians."

Anger sprang up in Laure. He gave it cold shape: "My order was that you report on coherent radiation."

Never before had he pulled the rank of his humanness on her.

She said like dead metal: "I have detected some in the visible and short infrared, where certain types of star excite pseudoquasar processes in the surrounding gas. It is dissipated as fast as any other light."

"The radio bands are clear?"

"Yes, of that type of wave, although—"

"Enough. We'll proceed as before, toward the center of the cluster. Cut this view and connect me with *Makt*."

The hazy suns vanished. Laure was alone in a metal compartment. He took a seat and glowered at the outercom screen before him. What had gotten into *Jaccavrie*, anyway? She'd been making her disapproval of this quest more and more obvious over the last few days. She wanted him to turn around, report to HQ, and leave the Kirkasanters there for whatever they might be able to make of themselves in a lifetime's exile. Well . . . her judgments were always conditioned by the fact that she was a Ranger vessel, built for Ranger work. But couldn't she see that his duty, as well as his desire, was to help Graydal's people?

The screen flickered. The two ships were so differently designed that it was hard for them to stay in phase for any considerable time, and thus hard to receive the modulation imposed on spacepulses. After a while the image steadied to show a face. "I'll switch you to Captain Demring," the communications officer said at once. In his folk, such lack of ceremony was as revealing of strain as haggardness and dark-rimmed eyes.

The image wavered again and became the Old Man's. He was in his cabin, which had direct audiovisual connections, and the background struck Laure anew with outlandishness. What history had brought forth the artistic conventions of that bright-colored, angular-figured tapestry? What song was being sung on the player, in what language, and on what scale? What was the symbolism behind the silver mask on the door?

Worn but indomitable, Demring looked forth and said, "Peace between us. What occasions this call?"

"You should know what I've learned," Laure said. "Uh, can we make this a three-way with your navigator?"

"Why?" The question was machine steady.

"Well, that is, her duties—"

"She is to help carry out decisions," Demring said. "She does not make them. At maximum, she can offer advice in discussion." He waited before adding, with a thrust: "And you have been having a great deal of discussion already with my daughter, Ranger Laure."

"No . . . I mean, yes, but—" The younger man rallied. He did have psych training to call upon, although its use had not yet become reflexive in him. "Captain," he said, "Graydal has been helping me understand your ethos. Our two cultures have to see what each other's basics are if they're to cooperate, and that process begins right here, among these ships. Graydal can make things clearer to me, and I believe grasps my intent better, than anyone else of your crew."

"Why is that?" Demring demanded.

Laure suppressed pique at his arrogance—he was her father— and attempted a smile. "Well, sir, we've gotten acquainted to a degree, she and I. We can drop formality and just be friends."

"That is not necessarily desirable," Demring said.

Laure recollected that, throughout the human species, sexual customs are among the most variable. And the most emotionally charged. He put himself inside Demring's prejudices and said with what he hoped was the right slight note of indignation: "I assure you nothing improper has occurred."

"No, no." The Kirkasanter made a brusque, chopping gesture. "I trust her. And you, I am sure. Yet I must warn that close ties between members of radically different societies can prove disastrous to everyone involved."

Laure might have sympathized as he thought, *He's afraid to let down his mask—is that why their art uses the motif so much?—but underneath, he is a father worrying about his little girl.* He felt too harassed. First his computer, now this! He said coolly, "I don't believe our cultures are that alien. They're both rational-technological, which is a tremendous similarity to begin with. But haven't we got off the subject? I wanted you to hear the findings this ship has made."

Demring relaxed. The unhuman universe he could cope with. "Proceed at will, Ranger."

When he had heard Laure out, though, he scowled, tugged his beard, and said without trying to hide distress: "Thus we have no chance of finding Kirkasant by ourselves."

"Evidently not," Laure said. "I'd hoped that one of my modern locator systems would work in this cluster. If so, we could have zigzagged rapidly between the stars, mapping them, and had a fair likelihood of finding the group you know within months. But as matters stand, we can't establish an accurate enough grid, and we have nothing to tie any such grid to. Once a given star disappears in the fog, we can't find it again. Not even by straight-line backtracking, because we don't have the navigational feedback to keep on a truly straight line."

"Lost." Demring stared down at his hands, clenched on the desk before him. When he looked up again, the bronze face was rigid with pain. "I was afraid of this," he said. "It is why I was reluctant to come back at all. I feared the effect of disappointment on my crew. By now you must know one major respect in which we differ from you. To us, home, kinfolk, ancestral graves are not mere pleasures. They are an important part of our identities. We are prepared to explore and colonize, but not to be totally cut off." He straightened in his seat and turned the confession into a strategic datum by finishing dry-voiced:

"Therefore, the sooner we leave this degree of familiarity behind us and accept with physical renunciation the truth of what has happened to us—the sooner we get out of this cluster—the better for us."

"No," Laure said. "I've given a lot of thought to your situation. There *are* ways to navigate here."

Demring did not show surprise. He, too, must have dwelt on contingencies and possibilities. Laure sketched them nevertheless:

"Starting from outside the cluster, we can establish a grid of artificial beacons. I'd guess fifty thousand, in orbit around selected stars, would do. If each has its distinctive identifying signal, a spaceship can locate herself and lay a course. I can imagine several ways to make them. You want them to emit something that isn't swamped by natural noise. Hyperdrive drones, shuttling automatically back and forth, would be detectable in a light-year's radius. Coherent radio broadcasters on the right bands should be detectable at the same distance or better. Since the stars hereabouts are only light-weeks or light-months apart, an electromagnetic network wouldn't take long to complete its linkups. No doubt a real engineer, turned loose on the problem, would find better answers than these."

"I know," Demring said. "We on *Makt* have discussed the matter and reached similar conclusions. The basic obstacle is the work involved, first in producing that number of beacons, then—more significantly—in planting them. Many man-years, much shipping, must go to that task, if it is to be accomplished in a reasonable time."

"Yes."

"I like to think," said Demring, "that the clans of Hobrok would not haggle over who was to pay the cost. But I have talked with men on Serieve. I have taken heed of what Graydal does and does not relay of her conversations with you. Yours is a mercantile civilization."

"Not exactly," Laure said. "I've tried to explain—"

"Don't bother. We shall have the rest of our lives to learn about your Commonalty. Shall we turn about, now, and end this expedition?"

Laure winced at the scorn but shook his head. "No, best we continue. We can make extraordinary findings here. Things that'll attract scientists. And with a lot of ships buzzing around—"

Demring's smile had no humor. "Spare me, Ranger. There will never be that many scientists come avisiting. And they will never plant beacons throughout the cluster. Why should they? The chance of one of their vessels stumbling on Kirkasant is negligible. They will be after unusual stars and planets, information on magnetic fields and plasmas and whatever else is readily studied. Not even the anthropologists will have any strong impetus to search out our world. They have many others to work on, equally strange to them, far more accessible."

"I have my own obligations," Laure said. "It was a long trip here. Having made it, I should recoup some of the cost to my organization by gathering as much data as I can before turning home."

"No matter the cost to my people?" Demring said slowly. "That they see their own sky around them, but nonetheless are exiles—for weeks longer?"

Laure lost his patience. "Withdraw if you like, Captain," he snapped. "I've no authority to stop you. But I'm going on. To the middle of the cluster, in fact."

Demring retorted in a cold flare: "Do you hope to find something that will make you personally rich, or only personally famous?" He reined himself in at once. "This is no place for impulsive acts. Your vessel is undoubtedly superior to mine. I am not certain, either, that *Makt*'s navigational equipment is equal to finding that advanced base where we must refuel her. If you continue, I am bound in simple prudence to accompany you, unless the risks you take become gross. But I urge that we confer again."

"Any time, Captain." Laure cut his circuit.

He sat then, for a while, fuming. The culture barrier couldn't be that high. Could it? Surely the Kirkasanters were neither so stupid nor so perverse as not to see what he was trying to do for them. Or were they? Or was it his fault? He'd concentrated more on learning about them than on teaching them about him. Still, Graydal, at least, should know him by now.

The ship sensed an incoming call and turned Laure's screen back on. And there she was. Gladness lifted in him until he saw her expression.

She said without greeting, winter in the golden gaze: "We officers have just been given a playback of your conversation with my father. What is your" (outphasing occurred, making the image into turbulence, filling the voice with staticlike ugliness, but he thought he recognized) "intention?" The screen blanked.

"Maintain contact," Laure told *Jaccavrie.*

"Not easy in these gravitic fields," the ship said.

Laure jumped to his feet, cracked fist in palm, and shouted, "Is everything trying to brew trouble for me? Bring her back or so help me, I'll scrap you!"

He got a picture again, though it was blurred and watery and the voice was streaked with buzzes and whines, as if he called to Graydal across light-years of swallowing starfog. She said—was it a little more kindly?— "We're puzzled. I was deputed to inquire further, since I am most . . . familiar . . . with you. If our two craft can't find Kirkasant by themselves, why are we going on?"

Laure understood her so well, after the watches when they talked, dined, drank, played music, laughed together, that he saw the misery behind her armor. For her people—for herself—this journey among mists was crueler than it would have been for him had he originated here. He belonged to a civilization of travelers; to him, no one planet could be the land of lost content. But in them would always stand a certain ridge purple against sunset, marsh at dawn, ice cloud walking over wind-gnawed desert crags, ancient castle, wingbeat in heaven . . . and always, always, the dear bright nights that no other place in man's universe knew.

They were a warrior folk. They would not settle down to be pitied; they would forge something powerful for themselves in their exile. But he was not helping them forget their uprootedness.

Thus he almost gave her his true reason. He halted in time and, instead, explained in more detail what he had told Captain Demring. His ship represented a considerable investment, to be amortized over her service life. Likewise, with his training, did he. The time he had spent coming hither was, therefore, equivalent to a large sum of money. And to date, he had nothing to show for that expense except confirmation of a fairly obvious guess about the nature of Kirkasant's surroundings.

He had broad discretion—while he was in service. But he could be discharged. He would be, if his career, taken as a whole, didn't seem to be returning a profit. In this particular case, the profit would consist of detailed information about a unique environment. You could prorate that in such terms as: scientific knowledge, with its potentialities for technological progress; space-faring experience; public relations—

Graydal regarded him in a kind of horror. "You cannot mean . . . we go on . . . merely to further your private ends," she whispered. Interference gibed at them both.

"No!" Laure protested. "Look, only look, I want to help you. But you, too, have to justify yourselves economically. You're the reason I came so far in the first place. If you're to work with the Commonalty, and it's to help you make a fresh start, you have to show that that's worth the Commonalty's while. Here's where we start proving it. By going on. Eventually, by bringing them in a bookful of knowledge they didn't have before."

Her gaze upon him calmed but remained aloof. "Do you think that is right?"

"It's the way things are, anyhow," he said. "Sometimes I wonder if my attempts to explain my people to you haven't glided right off your brain."

"You have made it clear that they think of nothing but their own good," she said thinly.

"If so, I've failed to make anything clear." Laure slumped in his chair web. Some days hit a man with one club after the next. He forced himself to sit erect again and say:

"We have a different ideal from you. Or no, that's not correct. We have the same set of ideals. The emphases are different. You believe the individual ought to be free and ought to help his fellowman. We do, too. But you make the service basic, you give it priority. We have the opposite way. You give a man, or a woman, duties to the clan and the country from birth. But you protect his individuality by frowning on slavishness and on anyone who doesn't keep a strictly private side to his life. We give a person freedom, within a loose framework of common-sense prohibitions. And then we protect his social aspect by frowning on greed, selfishness, callousness."

"I know," she said. "You have—"

"But maybe you haven't thought how we *must* do it that way," he pleaded. "Civilization's gotten too big out there for anything but freedom to work. The Commonalty isn't a government. How would you govern ten million planets? It's a private, voluntary, mutual-benefit society, open to anyone anywhere who meets the modest standards. It maintains certain services for its members, like my own space rescue work. The services are widespread and efficient enough that local planetary governments also like to hire them. But I don't speak for my civilization. Nobody does. You've made a friend of me. But how do you make friends with ten million times a billion individuals?"

"You've told me before," she said.

And it didn't register. Not really. Too new an idea for you, I suppose, Laure thought. He ignored her remark and went on:

"In the same way, we can't have a planned interstellar economy. Planning breaks down under the sheer mass of detail when it's attempted for a single continent. History is full of cases. So we rely on the market, which operates as automatically as gravitation. Also as efficiently, as impersonally, and sometimes as ruthlessly—but we didn't make this universe. We only live in it."

He reached out his hands, as if to touch her through the distance and the distortion. "Can't you see? I'm not able to help your plight. Nobody is. No individual quadrillionaire, no foundation, no government, no consortium could pay the cost of finding your home for you. It's not a matter of lacking charity. It's a matter of lacking resources for that magnitude of effort. The resources are divided among too many people, each of whom has his own obligations to meet first.

"Certainly, if each would contribute a pittance, you could buy your fleet. But the tax mechanism for collecting that pittance doesn't exist and can't be made to exist. As for free-will donations—how do we get your message across to an entire civilization, that big, that diverse, that busy with its own affairs?—which include cases of need far more urgent than yours.

"Graydal, we're not greedy where I come from. We're helpless."

She studied him at length. He wondered, but could not see through the ripplings, what emotions passed across her face. Finally she spoke, not altogether ungently, though helmeted again in the reserve of her kindred, and he could not hear anything of it through the buzzings except: ". . . proceed, since we must. For a while, anyhow. Good watch, Ranger."

The screen blanked. This time he couldn't make the ship repair the connection for him.

At the heart of the great cluster, where the nebula was so thick as to be a nearly featureless glow, pearl-hued and shot with rainbows, the stars were themselves so close that thousands could be seen. The spaceships crept forward like frigates on unknown seas of ancient Earth. For here was more than fog; here were shoals, reefs, and riptides. Energies travailed in the plasma. Drifts of dust, loose planets, burnt-out suns lay in menace behind the denser clouds. Twice *Makt* would have met catastrophe had not *Jaccavrie* sensed the danger with keener instruments and cried a warning to sheer off.

After Demring's subsequent urgings had failed, Graydal came aboard in person to beg Laure that he turn homeward. That she should surrender her pride to such an extent bespoke how worn down she and her folk were. "What are we gaining worth the risk?" she asked shakenly.

"We're proving that this is a treasure house of absolutely unique phenomena," he answered. He was also hollowed, partly from the long travel and the now constant tension, partly from the half estrangement between him and her. He tried to put enthusiasm in his voice. "Once we've reported, expeditions are certain to be organized. I'll bet the foundations of two or three whole new sciences will get laid here."

"I know. Everything astronomical in abundance, close together and interacting." Her shoulders drooped. "But our task isn't research. We can go back now, we could have gone back already, and carried enough details with us. Why do we not?"

"I want to investigate several planets yet, on the ground, in different systems," he told her. "Then we'll call a halt."

"What do they matter to you?"

"Well, local stellar spectra are freakish. I want to know if the element abundances in solid bodies correspond."

She stared at him. "I do not understand you," she said. "I thought I did, but I was wrong. You have no compassion. You led us, you lured us so far in that we can't escape without your ship for a guide.

You don't care how tired and tormented we are. You can't, or won't, understand why we are anxious to live."

"I am myself," he tried to grin. "I enjoy the process."

The dark head shook. "I said you won't understand. We do not fear death for ourselves. But most of us have not yet had children. We do fear death for our bloodlines. We *need* to find a home, forgetting Kirkasant, and begin our families. You, though, you keep us on this barren search—why? For your own glory?"

He should have explained then. But the strain and weariness in him snapped: "You accepted my leadership. That makes me responsible for you, and I can't be responsible if I don't have command. You can endure another couple of weeks. That's all it'll take."

And she should have answered that she knew his motives were good and wished simply to hear his reasons. But being the descendant of hunters and soldiers, she clicked heels together and flung back at him: "Very well, Ranger. I shall convey your word to my captain."

She left, and did not again board *Jaccavrie*.

Later, after a sleepless "night," Laure said, "Put me through to *Makt*'s navigator."

"I wouldn't advise that," said the woman-voice of his ship.

"Why not?"

"I presume you want to make amends. Do you know how she— or her father, or her young male shipmates that must be attracted to her—how they will react? They are alien to you, and under intense strain."

"They're human!"

Engines pulsed. Ventilators whispered. "Well?" said Laure.

"I'm not designed to compute about emotions, except on an elementary level," *Jaccavrie* said. "But please recollect the diversity of mankind. On Reith, for example, ordinary peaceful men can fall into literally murderous rages. It happens so often that violence under those circumstances is not a crime in their law. A Talatto will be patient and cheerful in adversity, up to a certain point: after which he quits striving, contemplates his God, and waits to die. You can think of other cultures. And they are within the ambience of the Commonalty. How foreign might not the Kirkasanters be?"

"Um-m-m—"

"I suggest you obtrude your presence on them as little as possible. That makes for the smallest probability of provoking some unforeseeable outburst. Once our task is completed, once we are bound home, the stress will be removed, and you can safely behave toward them as you like."

"Well . . . you may be right." Laure stared dull-eyed at a bulkhead. "I don't know. I just don't know."

Before long, he was too busy to fret much. *Jaccavrie* went at his direction, finding planetary systems that belonged to various stellar types. In each, he landed on an airless body, took analytical readings and mineral samples, and gave the larger worlds a cursory inspection from a distance.

He did not find life. Not anywhere. He had expected that. In fact, he was confirming his whole guess about the inmost part of the cluster.

Here gravitation had concentrated dust and gas till the rate of star production became unbelievable. Each time the cluster passed through the clouds around galactic center and took on a new load of material, there must have been a spate of supernovae, several per century for a million years or more. He could not visualize what fury had raged; he scarcely dared put his estimate in numbers. Probably radiation had sterilized every abode of life for fifty light-years around. (Kirkasant must, therefore, lie farther out—which fitted in with what he had been told, that the interstellar medium was much denser in this core region than in the neighborhood of the vanished world.)

Nuclei had been cooked in stellar interiors, not the two, three, four star-generations which have preceded the majority of the normal galaxy—here, a typical atom might well have gone through a dozen successive supernova explosions. Transformation built on transformation. Hydrogen and helium remained the commonest elements, but only because of overwhelming initial abundance. Otherwise the lighter substances had mostly become rare. Planets were like nothing ever known before. Giant ones did not have thick shells of frozen water, nor did smaller ones have extensive silicate crusts. Carbon, oxygen, nitrogen, sodium, aluminum, calcium were all but lost among . . . iron, gold, mercury, tungsten, bismuth, uranium and transuranics—On some little spheres Laure dared not land. They radiated too fiercely. A heavily armored robot might someday set foot on them, but never a living organism.

The crew of *Makt* didn't offer to help him. Irrational in his hurt, he didn't ask them. *Jaccavrie* could carry on any essential communication with their captain and navigator. He toiled until he dropped, woke, fueled his body, and went back to work. Between stars, he made detailed analyses of his samples. That was tricky enough to keep his mind off Graydal. Minerals like these could have formed nowhere but in this witchy realm.

Finally the ships took orbit around a planet that had atmosphere. "Do you indeed wish to make entry there?" the computer asked. "I would not recommend it."

"You never recommend anything I want to do," Laure grunted. "I know air adds an extra factor to reckon with. But I want to get some idea of element distribution at the surface of objects like that." He rubbed bloodshot eyes. "It'll be the last. Then we go home."

"As you wish." Did the artificial voice actually sigh? "But after this long time in space, you'll have to batten things down for an aerodynamic landing."

"No, I won't. I'm taking the sled as usual. You'll stay put."

"You are being reckless. This isn't an airless globe where I can orbit right above the mountaintops and see everything that might happen to you. Why, if I haven't misgauged, the ionosphere is so charged that the sled radio can't reach me."

"Nothing's likely to go wrong," Laure said. "But should it, you can't be spared. The Kirkasanters need you to conduct them safely out."

"I—"

"You heard your orders." Laure proceeded to discuss certain basic precautions. Not that he felt they were necessary. His objective looked peaceful—dry, sterile, a stone spinning around a star.

Nevertheless, when he departed the main hatch and gunned his gravity sled to kill velocity, the view caught at his breath.

Around him reached the shining fog. Stars and stars were caught in it, illuminating caverns and tendrils, aureoled with many-colored fluorescences. Even as he looked, one such point, steely blue, multiplied its brilliance until the intensity hurt his eyes. Another nova. Every stage of stellar evolution was so richly represented that it was as if time itself had been compressed—cosmos, what an astrophysical laboratory!

(For unmanned instruments, as a general rule. Human flesh couldn't stand many months in a stretch of the cosmic radiation that sleeted through these spaces, the synchrotron and betatron and Cerenkov quanta that boiled from particles hurled in the gas across the intertwining magnetism of atoms and suns. Laure kept glancing at the cumulative exposure meter on his left wrist.)

The solar disk was large and lurid orange. Despite thermostating in the sled, Laure felt its heat strike at him through the bubble and his own armor. A stepdown viewer revealed immense prominences licking flame-tongues across the sky, and a heartstoppingly beautiful corona. A Type K shouldn't be that spectacular, but there were no normal stars in sight—not with this element distribution and infall.

Once the planet he was approaching had been farther out. But friction with the nebula, over gigayears, was causing it to spiral inward. Surface temperature wasn't yet excessive, about 50° C., because the atmosphere was thin, mainly noble gases. The entire world hadn't sufficient water to fill a decent lake. It rolled before him as a gloom little relieved by the reddish blots of gigantic dust storms. Refracted light made its air a fiery ring.

His sled struck that atmosphere, and for a while he was busy amidst thunder and shudder, helping the autopilot bring the small craft down. In the end, he hovered above a jumbled plain. Mountains bulked bare on the near horizon. The rock was black and brown and darkly gleaming. The sun stood high in a deep purple heaven. He checked with an induction probe, confirmed that the ground was solid—in fact, incredibly hard—and landed.

When he stepped out, weight caught at him. The planet had less diameter than the least of those on which men live, but was so dense that gravity stood at 1.22 standard G. An unexpectedly strong wind shoved at him. Though thin, the air was moving fast. He heard it wail through his helmet. From afar came a rumble, and a quiver entered his boots and bones. Landslide? Earthquake? Unseen volcano? He didn't know what was or was not possible here. Nor, he suspected, did the most expert planetologist. Worlds like this had not hitherto been trodden.

Radiation from the ground was higher than he liked. Better do his job quickly. He lugged forth apparatus. A power drill for samples—he set it up and let it work while he assembled a pyroanalyzer and fed it a rock picked off the chaotic terrain. Crumbled between alloy jaws, flash heated to vapor, the mineral gave up its fundamental composition to the optical and mass spectrographs. Laure studied the printout and nodded in satisfaction. The presence of atmosphere hadn't changed matters. This place was loaded with heavy metals and radioactives. He'd need a picture of molecular and crystalline structures before being certain that they were as easily extractable as he'd found them to be on the other planets; but he had no reason to doubt it.

Well, he thought, aware of hunger and aching feet, *let's relax awhile in the cab, catch a meal and a nap, then go check a few other spots, just to make sure they're equally promising; and then—*

The sky exploded.

He was on his belly, faceplate buried in arms against the flash, before his conscious mind knew what had happened. Rangers learn about nuclear weapons. When, after a minute, no shock wave had hit him, no sound other than a rising wind, he dared sit up and look.

The sky had turned white. The sun was no longer like an orange lantern but molten brass. He couldn't squint anywhere near it. Radiance crowded upon him, heat mounted even as he climbed erect. *Nova,* he thought in his rocking reality, and caught Graydal to him for the moment he was to become a wisp of gas.

But he remained alive, alone, on a plain that now shimmered with light and mirage. The wind screamed louder still. He felt how it pushed him, and how the mass of the planet pulled, and how his mouth was dry and his muscles tautened for a leap. The brilliance pained his eyes, but was not unendurable behind a self-adapting faceplate and did not seem to be growing greater. The infrared brought forth sweat on his skin, but he was not being baked.

Steadiness came. Something almighty strange was happening. It hadn't killed him yet, though. As a check, with no hope of making contact, he tuned his radio. Static brawled in his earplugs.

His heart thudded. He couldn't tell whether he was afraid or exhilarated. He was, after all, quite a young man. But the coolness of his training came upon him. He didn't stop feeling. Wildness churned beneath self-control. But he did methodically begin to collect his equipment, and to reason while he acted.

Not a nova burst. Main sequence stars don't go nova. They don't vary in seconds, either . . . but then, every star around here is abnormal. Perhaps, if I'd checked the spectrum of this one, I'd have seen indications that it was about to move into another phase of a jagged output cycle. Or perhaps I wouldn't have known what the indications meant. Who's studied astrophysics in circumstances like these?

What had occurred might be akin to the Wolf-Rayet phenomenon, he thought. The stars around him did not evolve along ordinary lines. They had strange compositions to start with. And then matter kept falling into them, changing that composition, increasing their masses. That must produce instability. Each spectrum he had taken in this heart of the cluster showed enormous turbulence in the surface layers. So did the spots, flares, prominences, coronas he had seen. Well, the turbulence evidently went deeper than the photospheres. Actual stellar cores and their nuclear furnaces might be affected. Probably every local sun was a violent variable.

Even in the less dense regions, stars must have peculiar careers. The sun of Kirkasant had apparently been stable for five thousand years—or several million, more likely, since the planet had well-developed native life. But who could swear it would stay thus? Destruction! The place had to be found, had to, so that the people could be evacuated if need arose. You can't let little children fry—

Laure checked his radiation meter. The needle climbed ominously fast up the dial. Yonder sun was spitting X rays, in appreciable quantity, and the planet had no ozone layer to block them. He'd be dead if he didn't get to shelter—for choice, his ship and her force-screens—before the ions arrived. Despite its density, the globe had no magnetic field to speak of, either, to ward them off. Probably the core was made of stuff like osmium and uranium. Such a weird blend might well be solid rather than molten. *I don't know about that. I do know I'd better get my tail out of here.*

The wind yelled. It began driving ferrous dust against him, borne from somewhere else. He saw the particles scud in darkling whirls and heard them click on his helmet. Doggedly, he finished loading his gear. When at last he entered the sled cab and shut the air lock, his vehicle was trembling under the blast and the sun was reddened and dimmed by haze.

He started the motor and lifted. No sense in resisting the wind. He was quite happy to be blown toward the night side. Meanwhile he'd gain altitude, then get above the storm, collect orbital velocity and—

He never knew what happened. The sled was supposedly able to ride out more vicious blows than any this world could produce. But who could foretell what this world was capable of? The atmosphere, being thin, developed high velocities. Perhaps the sudden increased irradiation had triggered paroxysm in a cyclone cell. Perhaps the dust, which was conductive, transferred energy into such a vortex at a greater rate than one might believe. Laure wasn't concerned about meteorological theory.

He was concerned with staying alive, when an instant blindness clamped down upon him with a shriek that nigh tore the top off his skull, and he was whirled like a leaf and cast against a mountainside.

The event was too fast for awareness, for anything but reaction. His autopilot and he must somehow have got some control. The crash ruined the sled, ripped open its belly, scattered its cargo, but did not crumple the cab section. Shock harness kept the man from serious injury. He was momentarily unconscious, but came back with no worse than an aching body and blood in his mouth.

Wind hooted. Dust went hissing and scouring. The sun was a dim red disk, though from time to time a beam of pure fire struck through the storm and blazed off metallic cliffsides.

Laure fumbled with his harness and stumbled out. Half seen, the slope on which he stood caught at his feet with cragginess. He had to take cover. The beta particles would arrive at any moment, the protons, within hours, and they bore his death.

He was dismayed to learn the stowed equipment was gone. He dared not search for it. Instead, he made his clumsy way into the murk.

He found no cave—not in this waterless land—but by peering and calculating (odd how calm you can grow when your life depends on your brain) he discovered in what direction his chances were best, and was rewarded. A one-time landslide had piled great slabs of rock on each other. Among them was a passage into which he could crawl.

Then nothing to do but lie in that narrow space and wait.

Light seeped around a bend, with the noise of the storm. He could judge thereby how matters went outside. Periodically he crept to the entrance of his dolmen and monitored the radiation level. Before long it had reached such a count that—space armor, expert therapy, and all—an hour's exposure would kill him.

He must wait.

Jaccavrie knew the approximate area where he intended to set down. She'd come looking as soon as possible. Flitting low, using her detectors, she'd find the wrecked sled. More than that she could not do unaided. But he could emerge and call her. Whether or not they actually saw each other in this mountainscape, he could emit a radio signal for her to home on. She'd hover, snatch him with a forcebeam, and reel him in.

But . . . this depended on calm weather. *Jaccavrie* could overmaster any wind. But the dust would blind both her and him. And deafen and mute them; it was conductive, radio could not get through. Laure proved that to his own satisfaction by experimenting with the mini-radar built into his armor.

So everything seemed to depend on which came first, the end of the gale or the end of Laure's powerpack. His air renewer drew on it. About thirty hours' worth of charge remained before he choked on his own breath. If only he'd been able to grab a spare accumulator or two, or better still, a hand-cranked recharger! They might have rolled no more than ten meters off. But he had decided not to search the area. And by now, he couldn't go back. Not through the radiation.

He sighed, drank a bit from his water nipple, ate a bit through his chow lock, wished for a glass of beer and a comfortable bed, and went to sleep.

When he awoke, the wind had dropped from a full to a half gale; but the dust drift was so heavy as to conceal the glorious starfog night that had fallen. It screened off some of the radiation, too, though not enough to do him any good. He puzzled over why the body of the planet wasn't helping more. Finally he decided that ions, hitting the upper air along the terminator, produced secondaries and cascades which descended everywhere.

The day-side bombardment must really have got fierce!

Twenty hours left. He opened the life-support box he had taken off his shoulder rack, pulled out the sanitary unit, and attached it. Men don't die romantically, like characters on a stage. Their bodies are too stubborn.

So are their minds. He should have been putting his thoughts in order, but he kept being disturbed by recollections of his parents, of Graydal, of a funny little tavern he'd once visited, of a gaucherie he'd rather forget, of some money owing to him, of Graydal—He ate again, and drowsed again, and the wind filled the air outside with dust, and time closed in like a hand.

Ten hours left. No more?

Five. Already?

What a stupid way to end. Fear fluttered at the edge of his perception. He beat it. The wind yammered. How long can a dust storm continue, anyhow? Where'd it come from? Daylight again, outside his refuge, colored like blood and brass. The charged particles and X rays were so thick that some diffused in to him. He shifted cramped muscles, and drank the stench of his unwashed skin, and regretted everything he had wanted and failed to do.

A shadow cast on the cornering rock. A rustle and slither conducted to his ears. A form, bulky and awkward as his own, crawling around the tunnel bend. Numb, shattered, he switched on his radio. The air was fairly clear in here and he heard her voice through the static: ". . . you are, you are alive! Oh, Valfar's Wings upbear us, you live!"

He held her while she sobbed, and he wept, too. "You shouldn't have," he stammered. "I never meant for you to risk yourself—"

"We dared not wait," she said when they were calmer. "We saw, from space, that the storm was enormous. It would go on in this area for days. And we didn't know how long you had to live. We only knew you were in trouble, or you'd have been back with us. We came down. I almost had to fight my father, but I won and came. The hazard wasn't so great for me. Really, no, believe me. She protected me till we found your sled. Then I did have to go out afoot with a metal detector to find you. Because you were obviously sheltered somewhere, and so you could only be detected at closer range than she can come. But the danger wasn't that great, Daven. I can stand much more radiation than you. I'm still well inside my tolerance, won't even need any drugs. Now I'll shoot off this flare, and she'll see, and come so close that we can make a dash—You are all right, aren't you? You swear it?"

"Oh, yes," he said slowly. "I'm fine. Better off than ever in my life." Absurdly, he had to have the answer, however footling all questions were against the fact that she had come after him and was here and they were both alive. "We? Who's your companion?"

She laughed and clinked her faceplate against his. "*Jaccavrie,* of course. Who else? You didn't think your womenfolk were about to leave you alone, did you?"

The ships began their trek homeward. They moved without haste. Best to be cautious until they had emerged from the nebula, seen where they were, and aimed themselves at the Dragon's Head.

"My people and I are pleased at your safety," said Demring's image in the outercom screen. He spoke under the obligation to be courteous, and could not refrain from adding: "We also approve your decision not to investigate that planet further."

"For the first, thanks," Laure answered. "As for the second—" He shrugged. "No real need. I was curious about the effects of an atmosphere, but my computer has just run off a probability analysis of the data I already have, which proves that no more are necessary for my purposes."

"May one inquire what your purposes are?"

"I'd like to discuss that first with your navigator. In private."

The green gaze studied Laure before Demring said, unsmiling: "You have the right of command. And by our customs, she having been instrumental in saving your life, a special relationship exists. But again I counsel forethought."

Laure paid no attention to that last sentence. His pulse was beating too gladly. He switched off as soon as possible and ordered the best dinner his ship could provide.

"Are you certain you want to make your announcement through her?" the voice asked him. "And to her in this manner?"

"I am. I think I've earned the pleasure. Now I'm off to make myself presentable for the occasion. Carry on." Laure went whistling down the corridor.

But when Graydal boarded, he took both her hands and they looked long in silence at each other. She had strewn jewels in her tresses, turning them to a starred midnight. Her clothes were civilian, a deep blue that offset coppery skin, amber eyes, and suppleness. And did he catch the least woodsy fragrance of perfume?

"Welcome," was all he could say at last.

"I am so happy," she answered.

They went to the saloon and sat down on the couch together. Daiquiris were ready for them. They touched glasses. "Good voyage," he made the old toast, "and merry landing."

"For me, yes." Her smile faded. "And I hope for the rest. How I hope."

"Don't you think they can get along in the outside worlds?"

"Yes, undoubtedly." The incredible lashes fluttered. "But they will never be as fortunate as . . . as I think I may be."

"You have good prospects yourself?" The blood roared in his temples.

"I am not quite sure," she replied shyly.

He had intended to spin out his surprise at length, but suddenly he couldn't let her stay troubled, not to any degree. He cleared his throat and said, "I have news."

She tilted her head and waited with that relaxed alertness he liked to see. He wondered how foolish the grin was on his face. Attempting to recover dignity, he embarked on a roundabout introduction.

"You wondered why I insisted on exploring the cluster center, and in such detail. Probably I ought to have explained myself from the beginning. But I was afraid of raising false hopes. I'd no guarantee that things would turn out to be the way I'd guessed. Failure, I thought, would be too horrible for you, if you knew what success would mean. But I was working on your behalf, nothing else.

"You see, because my civilization is founded on individualism, it makes property rights quite basic. In particular, if there aren't any inhabitants or something like that, discoverers can claim ownership within extremely broad limits.

"Well, we . . . you . . . our expedition has met the requirements of discovery as far as those planets are concerned. We've been there, we've proven what they're like, we've located them as well as might be without beacons—"

He saw how she struggled not to be too sanguine. "That isn't a true location," she said. "I can't imagine how we will ever lead anybody back to precisely those stars."

"Nor can I," he said. "And it doesn't matter. Because, well, we took an adequate sample. We can be sure now that practically every star in the cluster heart has planets that are made of heavy elements. So it isn't necessary, for their exploitation, to go to any particular system. In addition, we've learned about hazards and so forth, gotten information that'll be essential to other people. And therefore"—he chuckled—"I guess we can't file a claim on your entire Cloud Universe. But any court will award you . . . us . . . a fair share. Not specific planets, since they can't be found right away. Instead, a share of everything. Your crew will draw royalties on the richest mines in the galaxy. On millions of them."

She responded with thoughtfulness rather than enthusiasm. "Indeed? We did wonder, on *Makt,* if you might not be hoping to find abundant metals. But we decided that couldn't be. For why would anyone come here for them? Can they not be had more easily, closer to home?"

Slightly dashed, he said, "No. Especially when most worlds in this frontier are comparatively metal-poor. They do have some veins of ore, yes. And the colonists can extract anything from the oceans, as on Serieve. But there's a natural limit to such a process. In time, carried out on the scale that'd be required when population has grown . . . it's be releasing so much heat that planetary temperature would be affected."

"That sounds farfetched."

"No. A simple calculation will prove it. According to historical records, Earth herself ran into the problem, and not terribly long after the industrial era began. However, quite aside from remote prospects, people will want to mine these cluster worlds immediately. True, it's a long haul, and operations will have to be totally automated. But the heavy elements that are rare elsewhere are so abundant here as to more than make up for those extra costs." He smiled. "I'm afraid you can't escape your fate. You're going to be . . . not wealthy. To call you 'wealthy' would be like calling a supernova 'luminous.'

You'll command more resources than many whole civilizations have done."

Her look upon him remained grave. "You did this for us? You should not have. What use would riches be to us if we lost you?"

He remembered that he couldn't have expected her to carol about this. In her culture, money was not unwelcome, but neither was it an important goal. So what she had just said meant less than if a girl of the Commonalty had spoken. Nevertheless, joy kindled in him. She sensed that, laid her hand across his, and murmured, "But your thought was noble."

He couldn't restrain himself any longer. He laughed aloud. "Noble?" he cried. "I'd call it clever. Fiendishly clever. Don't you see? I've given you Kirkasant back!"

She gasped.

He jumped up and paced exuberant before her. "You could wait a few years till your cash reserves grow astronomical and buy as big a fleet as you want to search the cluster. But it isn't needful. When word gets out, the miners will come swarming. They'll plant beacons, they'll have to. The grid will be functioning within one year, I'll bet. As soon as you can navigate, identify where you are and where you've been, you can't help finding your home—in weeks!"

She joined him, then, casting herself into his arms, laughing and weeping. He had known of emotional depth in her, beneath the schooled reserve. But never before now had he found as much warmth as was hers.

Long, long afterward, air locks linked and she bade him good night. "Until tomorrow," she said.

"Many tomorrows, I hope."

"And I hope. I promise."

He watched the way she had gone until the locks closed again and the ships parted company. A little drunkenly, not with alcohol, he returned to the saloon for a nightcap.

"Turn off that color thing," he said. "Give me an outside view."

The ship obeyed. In the screen appeared stars, and the cloud from which stars were being born. "Her sky," Laure said. He flopped on to the couch and admired.

"I might as well start getting used to it," he said. "I expect I'll spend a lot of vacation time, at least, on Kirkasant."

"Daven," said *Jaccavrie*.

She was not in the habit of addressing him thus, and so gently. He started. "Yes?"

"I have been—" Silence hummed for a second. "I have been wondering how to tell you. Any phrasing, any inflection, could strike you as something I computed to produce an effect. I am only a machine."

Though unease prickled him, he leaned forward to touch a bulkhead. It trembled a little with her engine energy. "And I, old girl," he said. "Or else you also are an organism. We're both people."

"Thank you," said the ship, almost too low to be heard.

Laure braced himself. "What did you have to tell me?"

She forgot about keeping her voice humanized. The words clipped forth: "I finished the chromosome analysis some time ago. Thereafter I tried to discourage certain tendencies I noticed in you. But now I have no way to avoid giving you the plain truth. They are not human on that planet."

"What?" he yelled. The glass slipped from his hand and splashed red wine across the deck. "You're crazy! Records, traditions, artifacts, appearance, behavior—"

The ship's voice came striding across his. "Yes, they are human descended. But their ancestors had to make an enormous adaptation. The loss of night vision is merely indicative. The fact that they can, for example, ingest heavy metals like arsenic unharmed might be interpreted as simple immunity. But you will recall that they find unarsenated food tasteless. Did that never suggest to you that they have developed a metabolic requirement for the element? And you should have drawn a conclusion from their high tolerance for ionizing radiation. It cannot be due to their having stronger proteins, can it? No, it must be because they have evolved a capacity for extremely rapid and error-free repair of chemical damage from that source. This in turn is another measure of how different their enzyme system is from yours.

"Now the enzymes, of course, are governed by the DNA of the cells, which is the molecule of heredity—"

"Stop," Laure said. His speech was as flat as hers. "I see what you're at. You are about to report that your chromosome study proved the matter. My kind of people and hers can't reproduce with each other."

"Correct," *Jaccavrie* said.

Laure shook himself, as if he were cold. He continued to look at the glowing fog. "You can't call them nonhuman on that account."

"A question of semantics. Hardly an important one. Except for the fact that Kirkasanters apparently are under an instinctual compulsion to have children."

"I know," Laure said.

And after a time: "Good thing, really. They're a high-class breed. We could use a lot of them."

"Your own genes are above average," *Jaccavrie* said.

"Maybe. What of it?"

Her voice turned alive again. "I'd like to have grandchildren," she said wistfully.

Laure laughed. "All right," he said. "No doubt one day you will." The laughter was somewhat of a victory.

CHRONOLOGY OF TECHNIC CIVILIZATION

✧COMPILED BY SANDRA MIESEL✧

The Technic Civilization series sweeps across five millennia and hundreds of light-years of space to chronicle three cycles of history shaping both human and non-human life in our corner of the universe. It begins in the twenty-first century, with recovery from a violent period of global unrest known as the Chaos. New space technologies ease Earth's demand for resources and energy permitting exploration of the Solar system.

ca. 2055 "The Saturn Game" (*Analog Science Fiction*, hereafter *ASF*, February, 1981)

22ⁿᵈ C The discovery of hyperdrive makes interstellar travel feasible early in the twenty-second century. The Breakup sends humans off to colonize the stars, often to preserve cultural identity or to try a social experiment. A loose government called the Solar Commonwealth is established. Hermes is colonized.

2150 "Wings of Victory" (*ASF*, April, 1972)
The Grand Survey from Earth discovers alien races on Yithri, Merseia, and many other planets.

23ʳᵈ C The Polesetechnic League is founded as a mutual protection association of space-faring merchants. Colonization of Aeneas and Altai.

24th C	"The Problem of Pain" (*Fantasy and Science Fiction*, February, 1973)
2376	Nicholas van Rijn born poor on Earth. Colonization of Vixen.
2400	Council of Hiawatha, a futile attempt to reform the League. Colonization of Dennitza.
2406	David Falkayn born noble on Hermes, a breakaway human grand duchy.
2416	"Margin of Profit" (*ASF*, September, 1956) [van Rijn] "How to Be Ethnic in One Easy Lesson" (in *Future Quest*, ed. Roger Elwood, Avon Books, 1974)

✿ ✿ ✿

2423	"The Three-Cornered Wheel" (*ASF*, April, 1963) [Falkayn]

✿ ✿ ✿

stories overlap

2420s	"A Sun Invisible" (*ASF*, April, 1966) [Falkayn] "The Season of Forgiveness" (*Boy's Life*, December, 1973) [set on same planet as "The Three-Cornered Wheel"]

The Man Who Counts (Ace Books, 1978 as *War of the Wing-Men*, Ace Books, 1958 from "The Man Who Counts," *ASF*, February-April,1958) [van Rijn]

"Esau" (as "Birthright," *ASF* February, 1970) [van Rijn]

"Hiding Place" (*ASF*, March, 1961) [van Rijn]

✿ ✿ ✿

stories overlap

2430s	"Territory" (*ASF*, June, 1963) [van Rijn] "The Trouble Twisters" (as "Trader Team," *ASF*, July-August, 1965) [Falkayn]

"Day of Burning" (as "Supernova," *ASF* January, 1967) [Falkayn]
Falkayn saves civilization on Merseia, mankind's future foe.

"The Master Key" (*ASF* August, 1964) [van Rijn]

Satan's World (Doubleday, 1969 from *ASF*, May-August, 1968) [van Rijn and Falkayn]

"A Little Knowledge" (*ASF*, August, 1971)

The League has become a set of ruthless cartels.

✳ ✳ ✳

2446	"Lodestar" (in *Astounding: The John W. Campbell Memorial Anthology.* ed. Harry Harrison. Random House, 1973) [van Rijn and Falkayn] Rivalries and greed are tearing the League apart. Falkayn marries van Rijn's favorite granddaughter.
2456	*Mirkheim* (Putnam Books, 1977) [van Rijn and Falkayn] The Babur War involving Hermes gravely wounds the League. Dark days loom.
late 25th C	Falkayn founds a joint human-Ythrian colony on Avalon ruled by the Domain of Ythri. [same planet—renamed—as "The Problem of Pain."]
26th C	"Wingless" (as "Wingless on Avalon," *Boy's Life*, July, 1973) [Falkayn's grandson] "Rescue on Avalon" (in *Children of Infinity* ed. Roger Elwood. Franklin Watts, 1973) Colonization of Nyanza.
2550	Dissolution of the Polesotechnic League.
27th C	The Time of Troubles brings down the Commonwealth. Earth is sacked twice and left prey to barbarian slave raiders.
ca. 2700	"The Star Plunderer" (*Planet Stories*, hereafter *PS*, September, 1952) Manuel Argos proclaims the Terran Empire with citizenship open to all intelligent species. The Principate phase of the Imperium ultimately brings peace to 100,000 inhabited worlds within a sphere of stars 400 light-years in diameter.
28th C	Colonization of Unan Besar. "Sargasso of Lost Starships" (*PS*, January, 1952) The Empire annexes old colony on Ansa by force.

29th C *The People of the Wind* (New American Library
from *ASF*, February—April, 1973)
The Empire's war on another civilized imperium
starts its slide towards decadence. A descendant of
Falkayn and an ancestor of Flandry cross paths.

30th C The Covenant of Alfzar, an attempt at détente
between Terra and Merseia, fails to achieve peace.

3000 Dominic Flandry born on Earth, illegitimate son of a
an opera diva and an aristocratic space captain.

3019 *Ensign Flandry* (Chilton, 1966 from shorter version
in *Amazing,* hereafter *AMZ*, October, 1966)
Flandry's first collision with the Merseians.

3021 *A Circus of Hells* (New American Library, 1970,
incorporates "The White King's War," *Galaxy*,
hereafter *Gal*, October, 1969.)
Flandry is a Lieutenant (j.g.).

3022 Degenerate Emperor Josip succeeds weak old
Emperor Georgios.

3025 *The Rebel Worlds* (New American Library, 1969)
A military revolt on the frontier world of Aeneas
almost starts an age of Barracks Emperors. Flandry
is a Lt. Commander, then promoted to Commander.

3027 "Outpost of Empire" (*Gal*, December, 1967)
[not Flandry]
The misgoverned Empire continues
fraying at its borders.

3028 *The Day of Their Return* (New American Library,
1973) [Aycharaych but not Flandry]
Aftermath of the rebellion on Aeneas.

3032 "Tiger by the Tail" (*PS*, January, 1951) [Flandry]
Flandry is a Captain and averts a barbarian invasion.

3033 "Honorable Enemies" (*Future Combined
with Science Fiction Stories*,
May, 1951) [Flandry]
Captain Flandry's first brush with
enemy agent Aycharaych.

3035	"The Game of Glory" (*Venture*, March, 1958) [Flandry] Set on Nyanza, Flandry has been knighted.
3037	"A Message in Secret" (as *Mayday Orbit*, Ace Books, 1961 from shorter version, "A Message in Secret," *Fantastic*, December, 1959) [Flandry] Set on Altai.
3038	"The Plague of Masters" (as *Earthman, Go Home!*, Ace Books, 1961 from "A Plague of Masters," *Fantastic*, December, 1960—January, 1961) [Flandry] Set on Unan Besar.
3040	"Hunters of the Sky Cave" (as *We Claim These Stars!*, Ace Books, 1959 from shorter version, "A Handful of Stars," *Amz*, June, 1959) [Flandry and Aycharaych] Set on Vixen.
3041	Interregnum: Josip dies. After three years of civil war, Hans Molitor will rule as sole emperor.
3042	"The Warriors from Nowhere" (as "The Ambassadors of Flesh," *PS*, Summer, 1954) Snapshot of disorders in the war-torn Empire.
3047	*A Knight of Ghosts and Shadows* (New American Library, 1975 from *If* September/October—November/December, 1974) [Flandry] Set on Dennitza. Flandry meets his illegitimate son and has a final tragic confrontation with Aycharaych.
3054	Emperor Hans dies and is succeeded by his sons, first Dietrich, then Gerhart.
3061	*A Stone in Heaven* (Ace Books, 1979) [Flandry] Admiral Flandry pairs off with the daughter of his first mentor from *Ensign Flandry*.
3064	*The Game of Empire* (Baen Books, 1985) [Flandry] Flandry is a Fleet Admiral, meets his illegitimate daughter Diana.
early 4th millennium	The Terran Empire becomes more rigid and tyrannical in its Dominate phase. The Empire and Merseia wear each other out.

mid 4ᵗʰ
millennium   The Long Night follows the Fall of the Terran Empire.
                 War, piracy, economic collapse, and isolation
                 devastate countless worlds.

3600   "A Tragedy of Errors" (*Gal*, February, 1968)
                 Further fragmentation among surviving human worlds.

3900   "The Night Face" (Ace Books, 1978 as *Let the
                 Spacemen Beware!*, Ace Books, 1963 from shorter
                 version "A Twelvemonth and a Day," *Fantastic
                 Universe*, January, 1960)
                 Biological and psychological divergence among
                 Surviving humans.

4000   "The Sharing of Flesh" (*Gal*, December, 1968)
                 Human explorers heal genetic defects and
                 uplift savagery.

7100   "Starfog" (*ASF*, August. 1967)
                 Revived civilization is expanding. A New Vixen man
                 from the libertarian Commonalty meets descendants
                 of the rebels from Aeneas.

*Although Technic Civilization is extinct, another—and perhaps
better—turn on the Wheel of Time has begun for our galaxy. The
Commonalty must inevitably decline just as the League and Empire
did before it. But the Wheel will go on turning as long as there are
thinking minds to wonder at the stars.*

❦ ❦ ❦

Poul Anderson was consulted about this chart
but any errors are my own.